T...
HEIG...
ZERVOS

and

AVALANCHE
EXPRESS

Colin Forbes writes a novel every year. For the past twenty-seven years he has earned his living solely as a full-time writer.

He visits all the locations which will appear in a new novel. Forbes says, 'It is essential for me to see for myself where the book will take place. Only in this way can I conjure up the unique atmosphere of the chosen locales.'

He has explored most of Western Europe, the East and West coasts of America, and has made excursions to Africa and Asia. Each new book appears on all major bestseller lists. He is translated into thirty languages.

Surveys have shown that his readership is divided equally between men and women.

COLIN FORBES

'Has no equal'
SUNDAY MIRROR

THE
HEIGHTS OF
ZERVOS

and

AVALANCHE
EXPRESS

COLIN FORBES

PAN BOOKS

The Heights of Zervos first published 1970 by William Collins.
Revised edition first published 1972 by Pan Books
Avalanche Express first published 1977 by William Collins.
First published by Pan Books 1977

This omnibus edition published 2004 by Pan Books
an imprint of Pan Macmillan Ltd
Pan Macmillan, 20 New Wharf Road, London N1 9RR
Basingstoke and Oxford
Associated companies throughout the world
www.panmacmillan.com

ISBN 0330 34267 2

A CIP catalogue record for this book is available from
the British Library.

Typeset by SetSystems, Saffron Walden, Essex.
Printed and bound in Great Britain by
Mackays of Chatham plc, Chatham, Kent

THE HEIGHTS OF ZERVOS

Author's Note

I wish to record my thanks to Mr Michael Willis of the Imperial War Museum for his invaluable technical assistance.

)

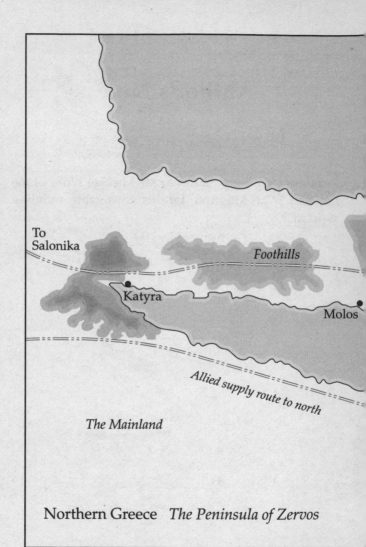

To
Salonika

Foothills

Katyra

Molos

Allied supply route to north

The Mainland

Northern Greece *The Peninsula of Zervos*

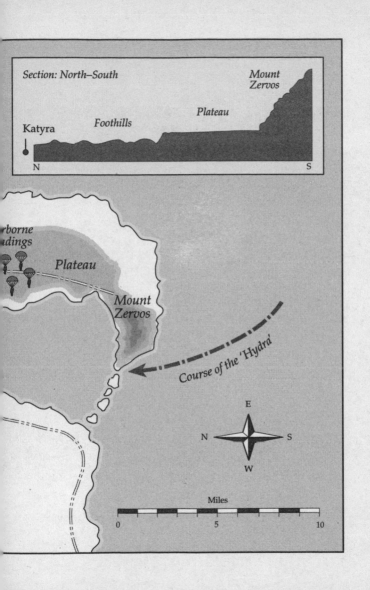

Section: North–South

Mount
Zervos

Plateau

Foothills

Katyra

N   S

rborne
dings

Plateau

Mount
Zervos

Course of the 'Hydra'

E

N   S

W

Miles

0   5   10

Chapter One

Thursday, April 3, 1941

Less than ten minutes to zero, to detonation point, Macomber, lying on his stomach along the top of the oil tanker wagon, listened to the German patrol closing in round the Bucharest railyard. His escape route was blocked, his body chilled to the bone by the snow which drifted down through the night, and the frightening barks of the Alsatian dogs assaulted his ears, a sound punctuated by orders rapped out in German. 'Watch the wire . . . At the first sign of movement open fire . . . Gunther, take the signal-box – you can see what's happening from up there . . .'

It was the third night of April and Rumania was still gripped by winter, still showed no inkling of spring on the way, still lay numbed under the icy wind which flowed from the east, from the Russian steppes and Siberia beyond. The insidious cold of 2 AM was penetrating Macomber's leather coat as he remained sprawled over the curve of the tanker, not daring to flex even a gloved finger as a German soldier walked beside the track below, and the crunch of boots breaking the crusted snow came up to the trapped Scot like the sound of twigs snapping.

The sub-zero temperature, the realization that arms, legs, feet were gradually losing all feeling, the trudge of marching troops below the wagon – these were the least of his worries when he remembered what was supporting his precariously poised body. He was lying on top of several thousand gallons of refined aviation spirit, petrol already bound for the Luftwaffe even though the Wehrmacht had occupied Rumania only recently, and a ten-kilogram composite demolition charge was attached under the belly of this huge tanker. The time fuse he had set was ticking down to zero, synchronized with other charges spaced out along the petrol train. And now the patrol had arrived and was checking for an intruder, searching for a saboteur – although perhaps sabotage had not yet entered their minds as they systematically surrounded the petrol train.

The snow, damp and paralysingly cold, was building up over his exposed neck, forming an icy collar where his woollen scarf parted company with his bare skin, but he remained perfectly motionless, thankful that his head at least was protected by the soft hat squashed over his brow. There's too damned much of me for this concealment game, he was thinking. Over six feet tall, over fourteen stone in weight, there was far too much of him, but he dismissed the thought as he stared at the illuminated hands of his watch, a watch strapped to the inside of his wrist as a precaution against the phosphorescent face betraying his position. Eight minutes to zero. Eight minutes before the charges detonated – and the tankers detonated seconds later – turning the railyard into a flaming furnace, a furnace which would cremate Ian Macomber. And there was yet a further hazard which made it impossible for him to protect himself against the elements which were slowly embalming him with a covering of freezing snow – as though to prepare his body for the imminent cremation. Ice had formed over the metal surface of the cylindrical tanker, ice which would send him slithering down into the path of the searching patrol if he altered his position by so much as a centimetre. So he lay still as a dead man while he watched a field-grey figure pass under a lamp close to the wire, mount the steps to the signal-box and enter the stilt-legged structure which over-looked the petrol train.

The lamp was hooded against direct observation from aircraft flying overhead, as were all the lamps inside the yard – hooded to avoid giving guidance to Allied planes which might appear on their way to bomb the vital oil-fields at Ploesti. Not that Macomber was expecting an RAF raid – the chronic shortage of bombers, the lack even of a machine which could fly the distance, guaranteed the Germans the safety of their newly acquired oil reserves – which made the sabotaging of oil for Germany vital. More footsteps crunched in the snow and then stopped immediately below where Macomber lay. His muscles tensed involuntarily and then relaxed. The metal ladder attached to the tanker's side ended a few inches beyond his head where the final rung rested close to the huge cap concealing him. Was someone coming up the ladder to investigate? His brain was still wrestling with this contingency when it received a further shock: something metallic clanged against a wheel. The demolition charge was hidden behind the front wheel. Christ, they'd found it!

'Get under the wagon – cross to the other site and wait there!' The voice spoke in German, a language Macomber understood and spoke fluently. An NCO issuing an order to a soldier – so there were two of them standing not fifteen feet below him. The voice continued, harsh and keyed up by the sub-zero temperature. 'If he runs for it, he'll run for the wire. I'm posting men the whole length of the train . . .' So they knew someone was inside the railyard. Macomber blinked as a snow flurry percolated under his hat and clouded his eyes; fearful lest the snow should begin to freeze his eyelids, he blinked several times while he waited for the soldier to crawl under the tanker. He would, of course, find the demolition charge. At least there was little sign of activity from the signal-box where he could see two shadowed figures under a blue light behind the windows – Gunther was checking with the signalman presumably. Feet crunched through the snow again, were swallowed up quickly as the NCO continued his march to post more men along the train – men who would inevitably close the door to escape. Not that he had a chance in hell of covering the hundred yards which would take him to the hole in the wire where he had cut his way through, and the wirecutters in his pocket were now so much dead weight; with the place so well covered he could never hope to cut a fresh hole before they spotted him. He heard a fresh sound from below, the rasp of metal against the tanker as the soldier began clambering under the wagon. A clumsy Jerry, this one. Perhaps a stupid one, too, but not stupid enough to miss seeing the charge . . .

More scrabbling noises, hurrying noises from under the tanker. The German didn't like passing over the track in case the train started moving. An illogical fear since the wagons would never be moved during the search, but Macomber understood the reaction and had experienced it himself. Wondering whether he would ever be able to stir again, Macomber lay motionless and waited for the noises to stop suddenly, which would warn him that the charge had been found. And then he would wait again, but only briefly before the soldier's shout announced his lethal discovery. The scrabbling sounds ceased and Macomber held his breath, waiting for the shout, but he heard only a wheezing cough and a shuffle of frozen feet. The damned fool had missed seeing it, thank God. He was now standing on the other side of the tanker, the side nearest the signal-box – which put him between Macomber and the wire. The Scot checked his watch. Five minutes to zero.

The uncanny silence of winter's darkness descended on the railyard once more. The dogs had been taken farther up the line, the sound of feet crunching through the snow had ceased, and the wind was dropping. The stage was set, the Wehrmacht were in position, and now it only remained for Macomber's nerve to break, for him to be apprehended when he climbed down the small ladder and ended his career by the tracks of a desolate junction few people had ever heard of. As the snow fell more slowly the silence was so complete he heard in the distance coals going down the iron hopper in the eastern railyard. The silence was broken by the sound of a window opening in the signal-box, opening with a fracturing crack as ice on the ledge shattered. Gunther leaned out of the window and stared directly at the snow-shrouded hump on top of the last petrol wagon.

Macomber stared back at Gunther's silhouette, moving only his eyes to take in this new source of danger. He was boxed in: observed from a distance and trapped by the soldier below. His eyes swivelled back to his watch. Four minutes to zero and still no way out, not even the ghost of a diversion he could take advantage of. It was his swansong as a British saboteur, the end of his dangerous passage down through the Balkans, a trail not only blazed by the series of devastating explosions which had destroyed vast quantities of strategic war materials – but also a trail which the German Abwehr Intelligence service had followed, often only one step behind him. He weighed up his chances.

With a great deal of luck the Luger in his coat pocket would eliminate the soldier below the wagon, but then there was the German in the signal-box who had apparently noticed nothing amiss, who had left the window while he talked to the signalman again; there was the wire fence he could never hope to climb; and there was the line of Wehrmacht troops posted along the train with instructions to watch that wire, to shoot on sight. His mind raced, estimating possibilities, and his watch raced faster. Three minutes and thirty seconds to go. He had calculated the odds and decided they were loaded impossibly against him. The sound of the car starting up so startled him he almost lost his balance; he hadn't even realized it was there, but now the driver switched on a light inside the vehicle and he saw it parked close to the signal-box on the far side of the wire. A Mercedes. The driver was having trouble firing the motor. A chance in a thousand – but the repeating rattle of the car's engine struggling to fire revived his hopes enormously, stirring the blood inside his half-congealed body as he worked out how to exploit this heaven-sent diversion.

Between the misfires of the numbed engine he heard feet clumping below the wagon as the unseen soldier stamped the ground to bring back the circulation into his frozen system, then the wheezing cough again. The feet began tramping through the snow, moving away from the wagon and over the empty neighbouring track, and Macomber guessed that he was improvising his own sentry-go to neutralize the appalling cold. The open window in the signal-box was still unoccupied as the marching German moved farther away; if only that bloody engine would start, would begin shifting the Mercedes – because stationary the car was useless.

His nerves prickled with desperate impatience as the driver tried again and again to wake up the dead motor, and Macomber's prayers were with the driver as he went on struggling to spark life from the sullen engine. The motor caught, ticked over unenthusiastically, died again. God, he'd really thought it was going. He gritted his teeth to prevent them chattering with the cold, stared at the empty window in the signal-box, watched the marching German cross a second track close to the lamp. Another laboured spasm when the car seemed to be going, another false start which faded away – and Macomber suddenly realized that the wheezing German was growing curious about the car because he was marching towards the wire now. Then the engine caught, ticked over, continued ticking as the Scot moved for the first time in ten minutes, breaking the stiffened rigidity of his posture to reach inside his coat pocket and haul out the Luger.

He aimed the Luger, fired once. The car was moving slowly, and he had aimed at the rear window – away from the driver who must remain in control of his vehicle, who must be panicked if the plan was to have any chance of working. The bullet shattered the rear window and its report echoed in the darkness as a voice roared out across the railyard in German. 'He's in that car ... on the other side of the wire ... Don't let him get away!' The darkness, the falling snow, distorted the direction from which the voice came, but Macomber's bellowed command carried a long distance. Someone opened fire, a burst from a machine-pistol which sprayed the rear of the accelerating Mercedes. A fusillade of shots crackled in the darkness and men ran forward, leaving the train. A German, finding the wire barring his way, shouted a warning, retreated behind the signal-box, threw a grenade, then another. The explosions were bright flashes, muffled assaults on the eardrums, the men were pouring through the hole in the shattered wire, a muddle of field-grey figures rushing past the hooded lamp as men already beyond the wire fired long bursts at the retreating vehicle. The Mercedes was still moving, turning a sharp corner and accelerating afresh when the patrol left behind the wire and vanished into the night.

Macomber wasted no time on the ladder. Levering himself over the side farthest away from the signal-box, he fell heavily in the snow, cushioning his fall by rolling away from the wagon. The shock of the impact was still with him as he forced himself to his feet, glanced quickly in both directions and scrambled under the tanker between its wheels. He emerged from underneath gripping the Luger, and his gaze was fixed on the point of maximum danger – the signal-box. Gunther had taken up position was leaning out of the window with his rifle, unaffected by the headlong rush away from the railyard. There's always one who uses his head, Macomber thought grimly as the German leaned out farther, raised his rifle and took swift aim at the blurred shadow moving away from the last petrol wagon. Macomber jerked the Luger high, hoped the damned barrel wasn't blocked with ice from his fall, steadied the gun and fired. The sound of his shot was drowned in the rattle of firearms beyond the wire as the German flopped over the window ledge, lost his rifle and hung in mid-air, face downwards. Macomber ran towards the wire, ran awkwardly because his legs were still stiff and unwieldy from the long wait, and as he ran he hoped to God the signalman wasn't the courageous type who raised alarms, but from a brief glance at the window he saw no sign of him – he was crouched on the floor between his levers.

He slowed down to pass through the tangle of wire and then began running in earnest, running to the left – away from the signal-box and away from the road where the Mercedes had driven off. Behind him, some distance up the yard, dogs were barking excitedly; the other section of the patrol had gone to the front of the train to start a systematic search. He ran slowly but steadily, his eyes growing accustomed to the unlit darkness as he threaded his way between man-high piles of wooden sleepers, ran with his Luger held well forward so he could aim it quickly in case of emergency, but this fringe area of the railyard was deserted and he reached the parked Volkswagen safely. Now to start his own engine. At the sixth attempt the car fired and he paused only to haul off the German army blanket he had draped over bonnet and radiator, stuffing it on the passenger seat before driving away across the snow. The blanket had frozen into a natural canopy and it retained its strange shape as he left the field and drove onto a road which would take him the long way back into Bucharest. Remembering what he had deposited under the petrol train, he pressed his foot down as soon as he reached the road, building up speed dangerously as the wheels whipped over the ice-coated surface. His watch registered thirty seconds beyond zero.

He swore in German, the language he had accustomed himself to speak always, to think in, even to dream in as part of his German cover. Surely all the bloody time fuses couldn't be defective? Or had he gone through all this for nothing? He shivered uncontrollably as he accelerated to even greater speed, gripping the wheel tightly to overcome the tremor. Reaction? Probably. Beyond his headlight beams the flat countryside was a mystery, a realm of darkness which might have contained anything, but from frequent reconnaissance in daylight hours he knew there were only bleak, endless fields stretching away to the Danube. A paling fence rushed towards him, disappeared as he lost speed and started to take a bend, then the skid began. He reacted instinctively, guiding rather than forcing the steering, following the spin while the headlights swept a crazy arc over the snowbound landscape. When he pulled up, by some miracle still on the road, the Volkswagen had swung through one hundred and eighty degrees, so he faced the way he had come at the moment of detonation.

The first sound was a dull boom, like the firing of a sixteen-inch naval gun, followed by a series of repeating booms which thundered out across the plain. A tremendous flash illuminated the snow with a searing light, then the flash died and was succeeded by an appalling roar, a deafening, blasting sound as the petrol went up, wagon after wagon in such swift succession that the night seemed to break apart, to open up with volcanic force, to burst and boil with fire. During all his sabotage missions Macomber had never seen anything like it – the moonless night was suddenly lit with a vast orange conflagration which showed the huddled rooftops of Bucharest to his left, rooftops white with snow and then palely coloured by the glow of the seething fire enveloping the railyard from end to end. He was turning the car when the smoke came, a billowing cloud of blackness which temporarily smothered the orange glow and rolled towards the city. Reversing cautiously, he edged the rear of the Volkswagen into the paling fence, which cracked like glass in its frozen state, pitching an intact section into the field beyond. He changed gear, turned a cautious semi-circle, straightened up, accelerated and headed for Bucharest.

The sabotaging of the petrol train was Macomber's last assignment in the Balkans, since the taking over of Rumania by the Wehrmacht would soon make any further explosive excursions well-nigh impossible, and while he drove into the outer suburbs of Bucharest his attention was concentrated on the hazards which lay ahead – the hazard of escaping from Rumania, of crossing German-occupied Bulgaria and entering neutral Turkey where he could catch a boat for Greece. The Greek mainland – where Allied troops had recently landed to meet the threat of German invasion – meant safety, but reaching the haven was quite a different matter. He could only hope to pass through the intervening control points by preserving his impersonation of a German up to the last moment, but it was the Abwehr he feared most. It was the Abwehr who had sent men into the Balkans to end the wave of sabotage and Macomber knew the Abwehr were closing in on him, might even be within twenty-four hours of discovering his true identity. So it was back to his flat to pick up the already packed bag, then on the road again, south for Bulgaria and Istanbul beyond.

Lord, he was tired! Macomber rubbed the back of his hand over his eyes as he drove slowly through the deserted streets – driving at speed inside a built-up area might attract attention. The old stone buildings, five storeys tall, were in darkness, except where here and there a high window showed a light – some family woken by the unnerving explosions which had broken over the city – but the lights were going out again as he drove along a devious route which avoided the main highway, feeling the tension rising as he drew closer to the flat. Returning late at night it was always like this – because you never knew who might be waiting for you on the darkened staircase. Reversing the Volkswagen into the garage which had once served as a stable, he parked it facing the double doors, ready for a speedy departure in case of emergency; then, lighting one of

13

the foul-tasting German cigars he had come to like, he began the five-minute walk to the apartment block.

As he walked steadily through the crusted snow he found his thoughts wandering back over the years to when he had walked through other cities without fear. Through New York as a boy when they had lived there with his American mother, and later, as a youth, through the streets of Edinburgh when his father, a Scot, had decided he should be educated in his home country. He thrust the memories out of his mind quickly, reminding himself that sentiment blunted the edge of alertness. He was nearly there. It would have been more convenient to rent a garage opposite where he lived, but the stopping of a car in the small hours could signal his arrival to anyone who might be waiting for him.

At the entrance to the narrow street, hardly wider than an alley, he dropped the cigar in the snow where it sputtered and extinguished itself. No point in illuminating your approach. He had deliberately chosen this apartment block because its entrance led off from a side street, which made it more difficult for anyone following to be sure which doorway you vanished inside. As he walked along the twisting, canyon-like street, his head bowed with fatigue, he automatically noted the footprints in the snow which preceded him, but people in this district worked a late shift in the factories and so far the footprints did not disturb him. Providing the doorstep to his own entrance was virgin snow – no one in the apartment block worked at night. The footprints went on past his entrance and the doorstep was hidden beneath unspoilt snow. Now for the worst part, the trip up the staircase. Inside his coat pocket his right hand gripped the Luger he had reloaded in the garage; he used his left hand to insert the key gently, turn it quietly and push the door open until it was backed against the wall. Stepping inside, he shut the door with equal care. Then he listened before switching on his pocket torch and aiming it up the staircase. Dry steps. The oppressive silence of three in the morning which always hinted at menace in the shadows.

He went up slowly, pausing at each landing to swivel his torch up the next flight, looking for the shadow which shouldn't be there. When he arrived on the fifth floor outside his own door he paused again, in no hurry to unlock it. A sixth flight led up to the caretaker's cramped quarters in the roof and a brief swing of his torch showed dry steps to where the staircase turned up the last flight. In any case Josef was away in Constanta. Taking out his key, he was about to insert it when he changed his mind. He should never have come back here; this was pushing his luck a shade too far. It must have been the sapping fatigue, the temptation of a few hours in bed which had made him take this needless risk. The place where you stayed was always the most dangerous – they'd taken Forester in his Budapest flat. I'll damned well hold out a few hours longer, let sleep wait until I'm well clear of the city. He had the torch still in his hand when a hard, pipe-like object was rammed into the small of his back and a voice spoke in German.

'Be very careful, Herr Wolff. This is a gun, so why die so early in life? Put on the landing light, please, but do not turn round.'

Macomber's hand, which should have been gripping the Luger, now gripped the torch – another sign of the dreadful weariness which had made him overlook his normal precautions. He raised the hand still holding the torch, wondered briefly whether he could utilize the weapon, whether he could swing round and wield the torch as a club, and dismissed the idea as soon as it entered his head. The man on the landing knew exactly what he was doing, had the gun muzzle pressed firmly into his back, so firmly he would have plenty of time to squeeze the trigger and blow his victim's spine in half at the first hint of a wrong movement. Macomber fumbled for the switch, pressed it down. Light from the low-powered bulb percolated dismally across the landing.

'We will go inside,' the voice continued, a mature experienced voice. 'Use your key to open the door – and be careful!'

Thirty seconds later the pistol in the German's hand was aimed at a point a fraction above Macomber's stomach as he backed through the doorway into his small bedroom. As requested, he pressed down the switch and only the far bedside light came on. 'What is

THE HEIGHTS OF ZERVOS

the matter with the overhead light?' the German demanded.

'It's defective – the same switch operates both lights.'

The German, having flashed his own torch into each room, had chosen this one because it was the smallest. Macomber continued backing inside the room where the space for manoeuvre was precisely nil, which presumably was why the German had preferred it, and the watchful look on his adversary's face produced the same reaction in the Scot as the steadiness of the pistol: this was a man who wouldn't be taken by surprise, who wouldn't make a single mistake, a man who would squeeze the trigger instantly if he considered such drastic action necessary. Thin-faced, a shorter man than Macomber, he was in his early forties and he wore a similar leather coat and a similar soft hat. Behind rimless glasses his eyes were unblinking as he gestured for the Scot to sit at the far side of the bed.

'If we're going to talk in here may I take off my coat,' Macomber began, 'and then you can start telling me what the hell this is all about.'

The thin German nodded and issued no further warning about being careful; he simply held his pistol levelled and watched the slow careful movements of taking off the coat. Macomber had noted the rubber overshoes peeping out of his visitor's own coat pocket, which explained his mode of entry – he must have used a skeleton key to open the street door, must then have taken off his overshoes and stepped over the doorstep without disturbing the snow. A man who thought of everything – or almost everything. The Scot hung his coat on a hook at the end of the huge wardrobe which was the other main item of furniture in the room, taking up so much space with the double bed that he had to squeeze his way round in the morning when dressing. He hung the coat carefully to conceal the instability of the wardrobe, the fact that it wobbled easily on its rotting plinth, and he hung the coat with one pocket outwards, the pocket containing the Luger. When he turned round the German reacted instantly. 'You have a gun inside your jacket – take it out very carefully and drop it on the bed, Herr Wolff.'

Macomber used his fingertips to extract the second Luger by the butt, keeping his index finger well away from the trigger as he eased the weapon out of the shoulder holster and let it fall on the bed. The shock had gone, his brain was working again, and at least this manoeuvre had succeeded – by drawing the German's attention to the second gun he had distracted his attention from the coat. The German used his left hand to pick up the Luger and slip it into his pocket. 'Now sit on your side of the bed, Herr Wolff. Incidentally, your German is quite flawless. I congratulate you. My name is Dietrich. Of the Abwehr, of course.'

'Then why the devil do you want to see me?'

Dietrich said nothing while he closed and locked the bedroom door to guard against the arrival of an associate of Macomber's. The precaution taken, the Abwehr man leaned against the door as he began his interrogation.

'It has been a long time to this moment, Herr Wolff – I will call you that until you decide to tell me your real name.'

'My real name?' Macomber stared at Dietrich as though he must be mad. 'I am Hermann Wolff . . .'

'It has been a long time since January 1940,' the Abwehr man continued as though he hadn't heard the Scot. 'A long way, too, from Budapest to this apartment. I almost caught up with you once in Györ, but I made the mistake of letting my assistant come for you. What happened to him? We never saw him again.'

'As a citizen of the Reich . . .'

'You demand to be taken to police headquarters?' Dietrich was amused and smiled unpleasantly. 'Do you really think you would enjoy that experience – particularly if I take you to Gestapo headquarters instead?'

'I shall complain direct to Berlin – I know people there,' Macomber growled. 'I am a German businessman sent here by my firm in Munich and I have correspondence with me to prove this . . .'

'I'm sure you have,' Dietrich replied sarcastically. 'I'm also sure that it would stand up to superficial examination – until we checked back with your so-called employers. You nearly had me killed tonight, Herr Wolff – and by my own people. I was inside that Mercedes the Wehrmacht opened fire on and I had to drive like a maniac to stay alive, so I decided it might be interesting to come straight here – in case you escaped. I have been following you for some time but I lost you this evening on your way to the railyard.'

'I still haven't the least idea what the hell you're talking about,' Macomber told him coolly. He re-crossed his legs and put his hands together in his lap where Dietrich could see them, and at the same time he hooked his right foot round the electric cord attached to the table-lamp plug. Dietrich smiled without humour.

'I was at the railyard tonight, Wolff – when the shooting started. Now do you understand?'

'Which railyard? What am I supposed to understand about this rubbish?'

'That there is no way out, that you have come to the end of the line. That railyard was the end of the line for you – literally.'

'I don't understand one damned thing,' Macomber rasped, 'but if you open the drawer in that other bedside table over there you may grasp what a bloody fool you're making of yourself.' Then the Scot waited.

It was a chance, no more, and Macomber knew that within a few minutes he would be dead or free. He scratched at his knee as though it tickled and this covered the slight movement of his leg testing the cord. The cable felt to be looped firmly round his ankle, but he could only test it by feel; if he dropped his eyes for even a second Dietrich would guess that something was wrong. Macomber waited, saying not a word while the Abwehr man wondered about the closed drawer.

Everything depended on whether Macomber's offhand tone of voice, his arrogant manner, had half-convinced the German there might be something important in the bedside table. The Scot's expression had changed during the past minute, had become a mixture of boredom and contempt, as though the pistol had no existence, as though he thought the Abwehr man an idiot and had proof of the fact – inside the closed drawer.

The bait was tempting. The little table was close enough for Dietrich to lean forward, to reach out with one hand and open it, to see what was there. And he still had Macomber safely on the far side of the bed, his hands pacifically clasped in his lap, unable to come anywhere near the Abwehr man without standing up and running down the narrow space between wardrobe and bed – with Dietrich holding his pistol.

'What is in this drawer?' the Abwehr man asked waspishly.

Macomber said nothing and the battle of nerves continued as the Scot used the only weapon available – silence. The German watched him a few moments longer and then he nodded again, as much as to say very well, we will have a look at this great revelation. He stood up from the door, took a step towards the table, his pistol aimed point-blank at Macomber's chest, but his prisoner was looking at the door with a bored expression. Dietrich used his left hand to reach down for the handle, the hand closest to Macomber, who had foreseen his dilemma. With his gun in his right hand while the other reached for the drawer it was physically impossible for him to keep the pistol muzzle trained on the Scot. Macomber was sitting with his hands limply at rest when the telephone beyond the locked door began to ring.

'Who will that be at this hour?' Dietrich demanded.

Macomber shrugged his shoulders, made no reply. The Abwehr man was becoming rattled – the Scot's refusal to speak was getting on his nerves and the muffled ringing of the phone irritated him. And he wanted to see what was inside the drawer before he found out who was calling Wolff, so everything became urgent. He grabbed at the handle, jerked open the drawer, saw a leather-bound book which might have been a diary, and while he stared at the book he wasn't watching the Scot. Still sitting on the bed, Macomber gave his right foot a tremendous jerk. The plug came out of the wall socket, the room went dark, the table lamp fell onto the bed. Macomber lay sprawled on the floor, waiting for the first shot. But the German didn't fire, which showed extraordinary self-control and quick thinking – a shot would reveal his position. To avoid his boots making a sound, Macomber swivelled on his knees, felt up to the coat, scooped the Luger out of the pocket, then pressed his shoulder against the wardrobe and waited for endless seconds. Had he heard the quietest of noises, a swift slither? He was certain the Abwehr man had changed position, that he had moved along the wall and was now standing with his back to the locked door, facing the other end of the unstable wardrobe. Still on his knees, Macomber heaved massively. The wardrobe toppled, left him, over a hundredweight of solid wood moving through an angle of ninety degrees. It struck something brutally and Macomber heard a muffled cry which cut off suddenly as the wardrobe completed its turn and landed on its side. He used his left hand to locate the coat still attached to the hook, fumbled inside the other pocket and pulled out the torch. The beam showed Dietrich lying under the great weight, the upper half of his body turned to one side, crumpled and motionless, although he still wore his glasses. The left side of his head was oddly misshapen where the wardrobe had crushed his skull.

The phone bell had stopped ringing in the outer room but from its limited duration and the lateness of the hour Macomber guessed who had called him. He had difficulty easing open the door past Dietrich's sprawled body and then he went across the living-room and opened the front door. No sound from below. Locking the door, he went back into the bedroom, turned off the light switch, rescued the table lamp, fixed in the plug and then switched on again. The identity cards were inside the dead man's wallet which he levered from his breast pocket. Two of them, and Dietrich was who he claimed to be. One card – the card tucked away inside a secret pocket – identified him as a high-ranking officer of the Abwehr, but it was the other card which interested Macomber. *Dr Richard Dietrich, archaeologist.* He had heard of this practice

– the carrying of a civilian card for use when the Abwehr wished to conceal its true identity. Amid the shambles of the room, with the body lying under the wardrobe he couldn't move without help, Macomber sat on the edge of the bed and lit a cigar while he studied the card for several minutes. Then he went back to the living-room and called a number, puffing at his cigar while he waited for the operator to put him through. Baxter answered sleepily, became alert within a few seconds. 'Hermann here . . .' Macomber began.

'I tried to call you a few minutes ago.'

'I know. Get over to Marie's – she's had some news from Munich.'

He slammed down the receiver, hoping the line wasn't tapped, but they had spoken in German and 'Marie's' identified no address; only the mention of Munich warned Baxter that a grave emergency had arisen. While he waited, Macomber sat calmly smoking because there was nothing more to do; the flat held not a single piece of incriminating evidence and the only papers concerned the fictitious Wolff, papers prepared by the ingenious Baxter. Ten minutes after their brief call had ended, the Englishman who was posing as a Spanish mineralogist with Fascist sympathies arrived and he listened without speaking while Macomber explained what had happened, then looked at the two cards the Scot gave him. 'Roy, I want to use that card to take me out of Europe – the civilian version. Can you fix it up for me damned fast – you've still got some of my pictures, haven't you?'

'Should be able to.' Baxter, a wiry, sallow-faced individual in his late thirties stared up from his chair in the living-room. 'You really think you can get away with it – using the card of a man you've just killed? I'd say you were carrying it a bit far this time. The risk is colossal.'

Baxter studied the huge Scot who stood smoking his cigar without replying immediately. An impressive figure, Mac, he was thinking, but the last man he would personally have chosen to lead a sabotage team: he was too prominent, stood out too much in a crowd. It was characteristic of Macomber that he should have turned this seeming disadvantage into a major asset, always taking up an aggressive role when he was in the company of Germans, which in itself made his impersonation so much more convincing in Nazi-occupied Europe. The brutal thrust was absent from his personality now as, for a brief period only, he was able to be himself, to let the natural, dry-humoured smile show at the corners of his mouth. But to impersonate a senior officer of the Abwehr! The idea alone made Baxter want to shudder. Macomber smiled easily as he spoke.

'Look, Roy, as a cover Hermann Wolff is blown sky-high – the presence of Dietrich in there proves that. So I need a fresh identity. Audacity always pays – it's paid me all the way down through the Balkans and it will get me safely home to Greece.'

'Sometimes, Mac, I think you like the big bluff. You play it that way because it suits your temperament as much as for any other reason . . .'

'I play it that way because it works. And I need that card fixed during the next few hours, so you're going to have to break all records. As soon as you've gone I'm clearing out of Bucharest and I'd like you to deliver the card to me in Giurgiu. I'll wait at that inn where we once spent a weekend. Can you manage it by noon? Today.'

'I might manage it.' Which was Baxter's way of saying he would be in Giurgiu by noon. 'There's the description to change as well as the photo, but the new quick-drying inks should help. I might even fix up the other one too,' he grinned quickly, 'just in case you want to go the whole hog.' He gestured towards the bedroom. 'Leaving the late Herr Dietrich in there?'

'No, he's got to disappear for several days, but if you'll help me shift that wardrobe I'll cope with the rest. And this, by the way, is your last job. Get that card to me and then make your own way home.' Macomber paused, a gleam of humour in his brown eyes. 'That is, unless you'd sooner come out with me?'

'Thanks, but no thanks. The sort of tricks you go in for would leave me a nervous wreck before we were half-way to the Turkish border.' Baxter grinned wryly. 'If it's all the same to you I'll creep out all by myself.' He looked towards the bedroom again. 'You really think it's wise trying to move him? The city is stiff with German army trucks swarming out to the railyard. Seems someone left a few bombs lying around the place earlier tonight.'

'Then I'll avoid the trucks. But if I'm using Herr

26

Dietrich's card he has to disappear for a while. So long as they don't find him his local people won't know for sure what's happened – don't forget the Abwehr operate on their own a good deal.'

'Better you than me.' Baxter stood up, hoping he wasn't showing too great an eagerness to get away from the flat. 'What do I do with the store of demolition charges? Smash the time fuses and leave them there?'

'Don't bother.' Macomber checked his watch and moved impatiently. 'The Germans have a few more of them, so it's pointless and takes time. Now, I've got to get that body out of here.'

'I'll help you to shift that evidence if you like . . .'

'Just help me to shift the wardrobe and then push off. I'd sooner deal with this on my own.' A typical reaction, Baxter thought, and he marvelled at the Scot's steady nerves. Forester, Dyce, Lemaitre – all the rest of the sabotage team were dead and Mac was the sole survivor, possibly because of his habit of working alone. And he can have it, he told himself as he followed Macomber inside the bedroom.

Macomber felt a little more relaxed as he drove the Volkswagen through the still-dark streets of Bucharest, a reaction which would have astounded the less phlegmatic Baxter. Down side roads which led to the main highway the Scot had already seen several army trucks trundling through the snow and for a short distance he must travel along that highway himself. The army blanket, thawed out by the heat of the car on his journey from the railyard, was thrown over the back seat, but it still assumed an odd shape – it had proved impossible to disguise completely the hump of Dietrich's body underneath. So relaxation was perhaps not a correct descripion of the Scot's present frame of mind. Even so he was relieved, relieved to have accomplished the mind-numbing trip he had made down the apartment block's fire-escape with the Abwehr man looped over his shoulder. The iron treads of the fire-escape had been coated with ice, he had heard a window open in the darkness during his grim journey down the staircase, and there had been no cover to hide his progress across the walled yard to the back street where he had parked his Volkswagen. But for Macomber the worst phase of this problem was over – providing he could avoid those army trucks.

He drove very slowly as he approached the exit to the main highway, then pulled up with his engine still ticking over. He waited half a minute and when nothing passed the exit he drove out and turned left, north towards the railway, the direction which would take him into open country most quickly. He drove steadily at a medium speed and his headlights showed up sombre buildings, their iron balconies laced with snow; later a desolate square, the trees naked and frosted with a bowed statue in the centre; later still shabby tenements forming a continuous wall of poverty. Lord, he'd be glad to leave this place. He was close to the outskirts when the emergency began.

Driving at a sober speed along the empty highway, although the fog of fatigue was settling on his weary mind, he still watched the road keenly as he glanced at his watch. 4.15 AM. A little over two hours ago he had been lying on top of that petrol wagon with the sounds of the dogs in his ears. He turned a bend, saw an army truck emerging from a side street ahead, and then he was driving behind it as the vehicle rattled forward over the uneven road. Headlights glared in his rear mirror, roared up behind him, only slowing when he thought he was going to be run down by the second army truck. He was boxed in by the Wehrmacht.

There was no side turning he could take now except the turning a mile ahead he intended using, so he had to put up with the unwelcome escort as they drove on into the countryside. He glanced back quickly, saw the truck behind within twenty feet of the Volkswagen, and when he looked back again where the road curved he saw a stream of headlights coming up. He had slotted himself inside a whole convoy of German trucks. Clenching the cigar more tightly, he concentrated on holding the same speed as the vehicle ahead, his eyes fixed on the red light, the closed canvas covers, while in his rear mirror the oncoming headlights behind remained a constant glare. Even leaving this damned convoy was going to be tricky. He timed it carefully, drawing nearer to the vehicle in front as the vital side turning approached, and he was on the verge of signalling when he saw the pole barricading the side road, the German military policeman behind it. They

29

had blocked it off to prevent civilian traffic entering this route. He drove past his escape exit without a glance while he searched for a solution, tried to foresee the next move. A mile farther on the road forked; the left fork leading to the railyard, the right one across the plain. But logically they would have blocked this off, too, so he would be forced to continue with the convoy until it reached the railyard he had half-destroyed, an area which must be swarming with troops. Perhaps, after all, Baxter had had a point.

As they drove on through the night the fatigue grew worse, encouraged by the monotonous rumble of the truck engines, increased by the necessity to go on staring at the red light ahead, and when the German vehicle's canvas covers parted briefly his headlights picked up the silhouette of a helmet: the trucks were packed with German troops. Wiping sweat away from his forehead, Macomber began to conduct the only possible manoeuvre which might extricate him from the trap, gradually reducing speed so that the truck in front moved farther away. But there was a limit to the loss of speed the driver behind would tolerate, and Macomber was gambling on the lack of enthusiasm for his job which might be expected in the middle of the night. He drove on until there was a gap of twenty yards between the Volkswagen and the truck ahead and then held it at that distance, expecting at any moment a furious burst of hooting from his rear. He had decided to try and use a very minor road turning off to the right, a road which was a dead end, leading over the fields and across the railway to a large farm, but he wanted to conceal the fact that he had turned off up this dangerous dead end. If the driver behind reported the presence of the lone Volkswagen when he reached the railyard they mustn't know where to look for him. The next bend was the crucial point and it needed split-second timing.

A copse of trees flashed into the lights of the vehicle in front and then vanished as the truck turned the corner. Macomber glanced in the mirror, saw the headlights locked onto him, suddenly speeded up. The car raced forward over the wheel-gutted snow, left well behind the truck in his rear as he accelerated, praying he wouldn't go into another skid. As he reduced speed to go round the curve his lights shone on the trees, then he was momentarily out of sight of the truck behind. The wooden gate was set back from the road and he almost missed it, but he saw it just in time, swung his wheel, crashed through the obstacle, turned behind a stone wall and felt the Volkswagen wobble from side to side as it passed over iron-hard ruts. Leaving the engine running, he switched off the lights and waited.

He was chewing at his cigar-end when a glow of lights appeared beyond the wall, silhouetting the naked tree-trunks like a natural palisade. The truck's engine was losing speed as the driver saw the bend, and too much loss of speed enormously increased the danger of his seeing the smashed gate, the tracks left by the Volkswagen in the snow when it plunged into the field. Macomber sat motionless while the truck lost even more speed and lumbered ponderously round the bend, then it sounded as though it were stopping. He had been spotted – the smashed gate, the tyre tracks had been seen! He grabbed the door handle, ready for a futile flight into the wasteland, knowing that the truck had only to follow him once the headlights picked up the fugitive, doubtful whether his legs had the strength to carry him far, when the engine ticked over more strongly and the truck rumbled past the gateway towards the railyard.

He left the car at once, stumbled his way over the ruts in the darkness, found a buttress which he used to haul himself up to where he could see over the wall and back along the road. Between the pole-shapes of the trees he observed the headlights moving towards him, saw a gap between the fourth and fifth set of lights. There would be orders about maintaining an even distance in convoy but there was always a laggard – if only he would continue to lag behind! Macomber ran back towards the Volkswagen, sprawling headlong in the snow when his foot caught in a rut, clambering swiftly to his feet again and reaching the car as the first set of headlights lit the top of the wall. The second vehicle followed closely, then the third and the fourth. Now! The Volkswagen rocked unsteadily as he drove towards the gateway and when he arrived at the exit the road was clear. Turning out of the field, he pressed his foot down and sped after the retreating rear light of the truck in the distance.

The turning onto the farm track came sooner than he

expected and he swung the wheel automatically, glancing back the way he had come. No headlights behind: the fifth truck had not yet arrived at the bend. Within a hundred yards the track dropped into a bowl and his own lights were hidden from the main road. As he drove along the track, his headlight beams showing up clumps of frosted grass on either side, he concentrated on the immediate problem – the disposal of Dietrich. In summer, with the grasses grown tall, he could have dumped him in a dozen places, but with the ground frozen to the consistency of iron, the grasses ankle-high and the fields a white sheet against which the body would show up clearly, any unlucky chance might disclose the evidence in daylight. He would have to do better than that.

Five minutes later he was driving up a slope as he approached the bridge which crossed the railway; even in the daytime it was a lonely spot but at this hour there was an atmosphere of eerie desolation about the place and spiked reeds caught in the headlights reminded him he was driving across marshland. He slowed down to take a dangerous turn beyond the bridge and heard the clanking of goods wagons moving up from the south. On the spur of the moment he pulled up, left the engine running and got out to look over the bridge. A hooded lamp a short distance away shone down on a steam engine which passed under him hauling a train of empty coal trucks bound for the eastern section of the railyard, a section unaffected by the explosions. The trucks were on their way to the coal hopper where they would be filled and sent on their long journey to Germany. Macomber felt a sudden lightening of the dreadful fatigue which was steadily wearing him out, making even thought difficult. There could be a ready-made solution to his problem twenty feet below him.

Long weeks of observation had made the Scot an expert on the workings of that railyard, and he knew the coal would be loaded into the trucks as soon as the train arrived. The first trucks were already passing under him as he gauged their speed and the moment when the centre of a truck was exactly below where he stood. Without further calculation he switched off the car lights, opened the rear door and wrestled out the blanketed bundle. Hoisting the German on his shoulders, a major effort in itself, he staggered to the parapet and waited, gauging the right moment afresh, knowing he couldn't afford to misjudge his timing by so much as a second. He waited until one truck was centred under the bridge and flopped the bundle across the wall; as the rear of the truck rolled out of sight he heaved and held his breath. The body dropped, landed in the centre of the next coal truck, vanished under the bridge. Dr Richard Dietrich, archaeologist, was on his way home to Germany.

Chapter Two

Saturday, April 5

Dietrich.

The name on the identity card immediately caught the attention of the Turkish passport control officer. *Dr Richard Dietrich, German national, born Flensburg. Profession: archaeologist. Age: thirty-two.* Officer Sarajoglu buttoned up his collar against the cold and studied the card thoughtfully as though he found it suspect. Behind him in the harbour of the Golden Horn a tugboat siren shrieked non-stop, a piercing sound which the raw, early morning wind from the Black Sea carried clear across Istanbul. Sarajoglu, a man sensitive to atmospheres, was unable to define the feeling of suspense which hung over the waterfront. At half past six on a morning when winter still gripped the straits, the worst always seemed likely to happen.

'You are travelling on business?' the Turk inquired.

'I am leaving Turkey.' Dietrich took a small cigar out of his mouth and flicked ash which fell on the counter separating them. He was a very large man, dressed in a belted leather coat and a dark, soft hat. His reply had been arrogant in manner and wording, implying that since he was leaving the country his activities were of no concern to this bureaucrat. Sarajoglu concealed his annoyance but proceeded to make a gesture of independence, conveying that although German troops had recently marched into Rumania and Bulgaria, his country was still neutral territory: using a gloved finger, he poked the German's ash off the counter. It fell off the edge and landed on Dietrich's highly polished boot. Sarajoglu, who had watched the fall of the ash, looked up and stared at the German. No reaction. Dietrich had clasped his hands behind his back and was staring through a frost-coated window at the harbour.

He was a man whose sheer physical presence was formidable – a man over six feet tall who must weigh at least fourteen stone, Sarajoglu estimated. Even so, the head seemed a little large for the body, a squarish head with a short nose, the mouth wide and firm-lipped, the jaw-line suggesting great energy and enormous determination. But it was the eyes which the Turk found most arresting, large brown eyes which moved slowly and deliberately as though assessing everything. He might be on the list of known German agents, Sarajoglu was thinking. Without much hope, he held onto the card and asked Dietrich to wait a moment.

'I have to catch that boat, the *Hydra*,' Dietrich informed him roughly, 'so hurry it up,' he rumbled as the Turk moved away into a small room behind the counter. Pretending not to have heard, Sarajoglu closed the door, opened a filing cabinet, took out the confidential list of German agents and ran his eye down it. No, his memory had not deceived him: Dietrich was not on the list. He turned to a youth who was typing at a desk close to the wall.

'The *Hydra* – she hasn't changed her sailing schedule so far as you know?'

'No, she's sailing at 7.30 AM and making the normal ferry run – Istanbul to Zervos. Why, sir?'

'Nothing really. But there are three Germans aboard the vessel already and now I've got a fourth outside. It's just unusual – Germans travelling to Greece at this stage of the war.'

'Greece isn't at war with Germany – only with Italy.'

'Yes, and that's a curious situation.' Sarajoglu bit the edge of the identity card between his teeth and failed to notice that some of the ink had flaked off. 'Curious,' he repeated. 'The Greeks have been fighting Germany's ally, Italy, for over six months but the Germans still remain neutral. I heard yesterday that British forces are landing in Greece – one of our captains saw their transports in the Piraeus. They must anticipate a German attack.'

'They probably hope to prevent one.' The typist peered through the window towards the counter beyond. 'Is that him – the big brute out there?'

Ah, so you don't like the look of him either, Sarajoglu thought. He stared through the window where he could see the German standing passive and immobile, and this total lack of nervousness impressed him. When a passenger's papers were taken away even the innocent ones displayed a certain perturbation, as though they feared an inadvertent mistake in their documentation. Dietrich, however, stood so still that he might have been carved from wood except for the curl of cigar smoke rising towards the roof of the shed. 'Yes,' Sarajoglu replied, 'that is Dr Richard Dietrich. He is thirty-two years old – so why is he not in the German army, I wonder?'

'Better ask him.' As the typist resumed work Sarajoglu's lips tightened. He flicked the cutting edge of the card sharply across the youth's ear, noted with satisfaction that he had flinched, then went outside to the counter. The German was standing in exactly the same position as when he had left him, hands behind his back, staring out at the harbour, his manner outwardly unruffled by this deliberate delay. Sarajoglu felt even more irked as he laid the card on the counter and spoke with exaggerated courtesy. 'You may go now, Dr Dietrich. A pleasant trip.'

The German picked up the card without haste, put it away inside his wallet, his eyes on Sarajoglu all the time. He stood with that typically German stance, his legs splayed well apart, his body like a human tree-trunk. The Turk began to feel uncomfortable: there had been precise instructions from above as to how to deal with German tourists – don't offend them and treat them with every courtesy so there can be no cause for complaint from Berlin. He felt relieved when Dietrich turned away, nodding curtly to the porter who hastily picked up the single bag and followed him out of the shed and up the ice-sheathed gangway. Inside his cabin Dietrich was feeling in his pocket for the tip when the porter, still nervous of his German passenger, clumsily knocked over the water carafe. Dietrich shook his head brusquely as the porter stooped to pick up the remnants, told him he'd done enough damage already and handed over the modest tip, a sum which normally would have provoked a sarcastic response. But as the German went on staring at him, clearly inviting his immediate departure, the porter thought better of it and left the cabin with a polite mumble.

As soon as the porter had gone, Macomber locked the door, picked up the two largest pieces of broken carafe and deposited them in the wastepaper basket. God, it was a relief to be inside neutral Turkey, to be on board, to be alone in his cabin. And within thirty hours he would be able to revert to his real identity, to be known once more as Ian Macomber, to talk in English all day long if he wished. He went over to the washbasin and looked in the mirror above it, gazing into the glass like a man seeing the result when surgical bandages have been removed.

For the first time since he had left the flat in Bucharest his features relaxed, the crinkles of humour appeared at the corners of his mouth, and even though still wearing the German hat and leather coat the Teutonic image was gone. It was going to be irksome – keeping up his German impersonation until he landed safely on Greek soil – but it was necessary. He was travelling with German papers and the Greek captain might not appreciate his sudden conversion to another nationality. So for one more day and one more night he must go on playing the part of Dr Richard Dietrich, German archaeologist. The knock on the door startled him, reminded him of the extreme fatigue he was labouring under – and also that the danger might not be past yet. He unlocked the door, his hand clutching the Luger inside his coat pocket, opened it cautiously. It was the chief steward and he showed surprise when Macomber addressed him in fluent Greek.

'What do you want?'

'You speak our language – it is most unusual for a German . . .'

'I said what do you want?'

'Is everything to your satisfaction, sir? Good. If you need something you have only to call me . . .' The voluble steward chattered on while Macomber stared at him bleakly, then he said something which again startled the Scot. 'I'm sure you'll be interested to know we have three of your fellow-countrymen also on board . . .'

For a muddled moment Macomber thought he was referring to three Englishmen, then he recovered his tired wits. 'Are they together?' he inquired in a bored tone which concealed his anxiety about the reply.

'No, sir, they are all travelling separately.' The steward paused and there was a malicious gleam in his quick-moving eyes. 'There are also two British passengers.'

'You find that amusing?'

'No, sir.' The steward replied hastily, taken aback by the grimness of this overbearing German. He tried to correct his blunder. 'I shall be in the dining-room where breakfast is being prepared, so if you require anything . . .'

'Then I shall ask you! And take this – I want a comfortable trip, so do your duty.' Macomber had handed the flabbergasted man a generous tip before turning his back and closing the cabin door, but it had suddenly occurred to him that the steward could be a valuable source of information and he had already decided to question him further about the other passengers. But not now – it would arouse too much interest. Alone again, Macomber stripped off the hat and coat and doused himself in ice-cold water. Three Germans aboard, he was thinking as he dried himself slowly; perhaps it wasn't all over yet. When he had reached Istanbul he had avoided going anywhere near the British Legation – because the Legation was the very place the Abwehr might be watching for his arrival. It was too late to arrest him but it certainly wasn't too late to have him killed. Not that he feared the Abwehr's revenge – they had a far more powerful motive for ensuring that he never reached Allied territory alive, and they were perfectly capable of putting an assassin aboard the *Hydra*, an assassin not necessarily of German nationality. It's what I'm carrying in my head they'd like to destroy, he reminded himself. Information gathered over months of patient observation in the Balkans – data about assembly points, storage depots, the routes along which supplies were being sent to the Reich . . .

He finished drying himself, glanced at the inviting bunk and looked away quickly. Lord, it had been a swine of a trip from Bucharest. Four hours' sleep in forty-eight, his reflexes shot to hell, but he'd better check this damned ship – and forget any ideas about sleep until he was actually on Greek soil. He put on the leather coat and the hat, tested the action of his Luger, glanced in the mirror. He was back in business again. The arrogant, uncompromising image of Dr Richard Dietrich stared back at him. Replacing the gun inside his coat, he left the cabin to carry out his inspection of the 5,000-ton Greek ferry.

The bitter wind raked his face as soon as he reached the deck, a wind unpleasant enough, he soon found, to keep the handful of fellow-passengers below decks. Half an hour later, his tour of the vessel completed, he stood near the stern where he could keep an eye on the gangway for late arrivals. It was just possible that the Abwehr might send someone on board at the last moment. Standing by the rail, Macomber seemed impervious to the weather as he quietly smoked his cigar. The lifeboat covers were still crusted with last night's snowfall, the masthead rigging still encased with glassy ice, but the battered yellow funnel was dripping moisture as the ship began to get up steam.

To all outward appearances Macomber had wandered round the vessel with the idle curiosity of the newly arrived passenger who is interested in his temporary home, but now as he smoked his cigar he was cataloguing his discoveries in his mind.

From the chief steward he had learned that the *Hydra* carried a crew of six, that the captain's name was Nopagos, and that he had plied this regular passage between Istanbul and Zervos for the past fourteen years. Macomber stirred at the rail as the chief steward reappeared at his elbow, chattering amiably.

'Looks as though we've got our full complement of passengers aboard, sir.'

Macomber nodded, wondering whether he had overdone the tip: the steward was becoming his shadow. He checked his watch. 'There's still time for last-minute arrivals.' Again he was subtly probing for information.

'Doubt that, sir. I was talking to the ticket office manager a few minutes ago on the phone – he sold seven tickets for this trip, so it looks as though that's the lot.'

Macomber nodded again and the steward, sensing that he was no longer in a talkative mood, excused himself. Left alone once more, the Scot continued his mental inventory. Two British civilians he hadn't yet seen, one man in his late twenties while his companion was probably a few years beyond thirty. Which was interesting, since both men were of military age. One Greek civilian who lived on Zervos and apparently had something to do with the monastic order which owned the ferry – again a man of military age, but Macomber presumed that his slight limp had kept him out of the Greek Army. And, finally, the three Germans. He had seen two of them briefly, both civilians in their early forties who had the appearance of businessmen, but the third, a man called Schnell, had apparently come aboard very early in the morning and locked himself away in his cabin. 'With his cabin trunk,' as the voluble steward had explained earlier. On this point the Scot had detected an uncertain note in the steward's voice and he had asked a question.

'You find that odd – that he should keep a trunk in his cabin?'

'Well, sir, it takes up a lot of space and I offered to have it put in the hold when he came aboard. After all, we shall be docking at Zervos in twenty-four hours. He was quite abrupt with me, the way some . . .' He had paused and Macomber, knowing he had been about to say 'the way some Germans are', had smiled grimly to himself. But the steward had changed his wording in time. '. . . the way some people are when they arrive early. He insisted it stayed with him in the cabin so he must be carrying something valuable.'

Something valuable? Macomber frowned as he recalled the steward's words – it was this cabin trunk and its unknown contents which occupied his thoughts as he gazed out over the muddle of decrepit-looking tramps and coasters which congested the Golden Horn harbour. He heard a sound behind him and remained staring out across the water, one large boot resting on the lower rail. Was it likely that an attempt would be made to assassinate him at this late hour – a few minutes before putting to sea? Out of the corner of his eye he watched the Greek approaching, heard the faint slur of his limping step.

The man's name was Grapos and even with that slight limp Macomber thought he would be an asset to any army: of only medium height there was, nevertheless, a suggestion of tremendous physical strength in those broad shoulders and that powerful chest which swelled the coloured shirt. Not a prosperous individual, Macomber decided: his grey jacket and trousers were of poor quality, the red tie round his neck was faded and his boots were shabby. The steward had told him of an unexpected facility Grapos possessed – the monks had taught him to speak English. The Greek was very close now, stopping almost behind the Scot, and his eyes were shrewd and alert.

'Always it seems so long before the boat sails,' he began. 'You have been to Zervos before?'

'Once.' Macomber replied in Greek and turned his head away to study the harbour. Grapos might have been surprised had he known how much Macomber had registered in that brief glance. The Greek's face was strong-featured, the jawline formidable, and the long straggle of dark moustache which curved round the corners of his wide mouth gave him the look of a bandit or guerrilla. He was one of the most villainous-looking characters Macomber had encountered since entering the Balkans. But the point which had alerted

the Scot was the fact that Grapos had spoken to him in
Greek. Which could only mean that he had eaves-
dropped while Macomber was conversing in that
language with the steward, unless that talkative individual had informed Grapos that they had a Greek-
speaking German aboard.

'There is bad weather on the way,' Grapos remarked
and looked upwards.

'Why do you say that?' Macomber's tone was brus-
que and unencouraging, but the Greek seemed not to
notice.

'Because of the birds.' Grapes lifted a hand and
pointed to where a cloud of seagulls wheeled and
floated in erratic circles high above the white-coated
domes and minarets onshore.

'Don't you always get birds over a harbour?'
Macomber sounded bored with the company which
had thrust itself upon him, but now he was observing
the large, hairy-backed hands which gripped the rail as
though they might pull a section loose bodily.

'Yes, but not so many, and they are uneasy – you
can tell by the way they fly. I have seen them fly like
that over Zervos before the great storms. This will be a
bad voyage,' he went on cheerfully. 'We shall run into
a storm before we land at Katyra. Let us hope it does
not strike us off Cape Zervos. You see,' he continued
with relish, 'the entrance to the gulf is very narrow and
the cape has been the graveyard of a hundred ships or
more . . .' He broke off, grinning savagely as he dis-

played a row of perfect white teeth. 'But, of course, you know – you have been there before.'

Macomber said nothing as he hunched his broad shoulders and threw the smoked cigar butt into the water. Two ships away along the wharf another vessel was preparing to leave, her white funnel belching out clouds of murky smoke which the wind dispersed in chaotic trails. Behind him he heard footsteps retreating, one of them out of step. Grapos had taken the hint and was on his way to find someone else who would listen to his chatter. Extracting a Zeiss Monokular glass, a single-lens field-glass, from his pocket, Macomber focused it on the other vessel getting up a head of steam. The Rumanian flag whipped in the wind from her masthead and she was, he knew, the *Rupescu*. Her decks were strangely deserted for a ship on the point of departure and at the head of the gangplank two seamen stood as though on guard. It was quite clear that shortly she would follow the *Hydra* across the Sea of Marmara and into the Dardanelles, which he found interesting.

From the steward he had learned that the *Rupescu*, a fast motor vessel, was twelve hours out of the Bulgarian port of Varna and the situation could be a little tricky since she was bound for the Aegean. German troops now controlled Bulgaria so technically the Allies might regard the *Rupescu* as an enemy vessel, a prize to be sought out by the Royal Navy. Certainly the British Legation at Istanbul would already have wirelessed

Egypt of her presence in the straits, but Macomber doubted whether she would be seized – the British Government had broken off diplomatic relations with Rumania but had not yet declared war on that unhappy country. Satisfied with what he had seen – nothing out of the ordinary – Macomber put away his glass and then stiffened as a shabbily dressed man dashed up the gangway. Under his arm he carried a batch of newspapers and he flourished one in the Scot's face when he came along the desk. Macomber bought a copy, glancing at the banner headline before he went below. *German Army Poised To Attack?*

The engines were throbbing steadily as he made his way along a narrow companionway and walked calmly into the saloon, a small cramped room with panelled walls which was already reeking of acrid cigar smoke. Pulling out his copy of the *Frankfurter Zeitung*, Macomber sank heavily into an ancient arm-chair in a corner which allowed him to see the whole room while he pretended to read. Hahnemann, a thin-faced German in his early forties and dressed like a travelling salesman in a cheap suit, sat in the diagonally opposite corner smoking one of the cigars responsible for the bad air. In another corner, a heavily built German of medium height, his clothes well-cut and dark, sat reading some typed sheets and also smoking a cigar. That would be Volber. The fourth corner was occupied by a small bar where a man in white uniform was polishing a glass. Thank God, Macomber was thinking, those two don't exactly look like sociable types. I could do without useless conversation in German at the moment. The thought had hardly passed through his head when two men opened the doors and stood hesitating as though not sure whether to come in. Their first words warned Macomber. They were British.

'Go on in, for God's sake,' Prentice said impatiently to Ford, who was standing in the doorway. 'Don't just stand gawping. We've paid our fares just like the rest of these johnnies.'

Ford's face was expressionless as he carefully made his way through the smoke to a table close to the bar. As they settled behind a low table the steward took Macomber's order and a minute later placed a glass of beer in front of him. Ford kept his voice low as he made the remark. 'That chap who's just got his beer looks like another bleedin' Jerry.'

'I think they all are,' Prentice murmured nonchalantly. 'This is a funny, funny war at times.' Unlike Ford, who sat stiffly and kept an eye on the other three men without appearing to do so, Prentice was outwardly the soul of relaxation. When the steward arrived for their order he deliberately raised his voice so the whole room could hear. 'A beer and a glass of *ouzo*, laddie.'

'Beg, please?' The steward looked at a loss. Prentice leaned round him and stabbed a finger in the direction of Macomber's table, his voice louder still. 'One *ouzo* and a beer – beer – like that chap over there ordered.'

The other two Germans glanced in his direction and then looked away, but the Scot, who had lowered his paper, stared hard across the room with an unpleasantly inquiring expression.

'Tough-looking basket, that big one,' Ford remarked, keeping his own voice quiet. 'If I met him in Libya I'd let him have two in the pump. Yes, two – just to be sure.'

The drinks were served and Ford sipped at his palely coloured beer cautiously, then grimaced. 'They've got the washing-up water mixed in with the beer.' He eyed Prentice's glass with even more distaste. 'You're not really drinking that, are you?' But his question was purely rhetorical – Prentice would drink anything, smoke anything, eat anything. Some of the dishes he'd consumed during their brief stay in Turkey had astounded and appalled the conservative Ford. Prentice pushed the glass of yellowish liquid towards him.

'Go on, it tastes just like whisky.' He watched with amusement while his companion took a gulp and then almost dropped the glass, looking round suddenly to make sure his experience hadn't been observed. Macomber was still watching him over his paper.

'Lovely!' Ford choked. 'A delicate mixture of nail varnish and turpentine. If that's the Greek national drink no wonder the Romans licked them. It still seems odd travelling with a bunch of Jerries for company.' He looked round the saloon as he heard a distant rattle. The gangway being hauled up probably. In one corner the thin-faced German was absorbed in a book while the man crouched over some typed sheets made notes with a pencil. They might have been aboard a normal peacetime boat and the war seemed a long way from Istanbul.

'It really is damned funny,' Prentice began, his lean, humorous face serious for a change. 'Here we are on a Greek ferry just leaving for Zervos – in the middle of a life-and-death war with Adolf Hitler's Reich – and because the Greeks are fighting the Italians but not the Germans, we can travel with three Jerries we mustn't even bump into if we meet them in the corridor. I must remember this trip when I write me memoirs, Ford.'

'Yes, sir,' said Ford automatically, and received a sharp dig in the ribs for his pains. He understood the hint and swore inwardly. He'd be glad when this ferry trip was over and they could get back to normal service life, to being Lieutenant Prentice and Staff-Sergeant Ford. Before they had boarded the *Hydra* Prentice had given him a stern lecture in their Istanbul hotel bedroom and he had tripped up already.

'Ford,' Prentice had begun, 'for the purposes of this sea trip back to Greece and while we're on board the ferry, I want you to forget I'm a lieutenant and, what's more important still, forget that you're a staff-sergeant. We're sporting civvies, but if you keep on calling me "sir" it's a dead giveaway. There may even be a German tourist on that broken-down old Greek ferry.' Prentice hadn't really believed that this would happen

51

but he was dramatizing the situation to try and make Ford forget his years of professional training for a few hours.

'I'll watch it, sir,' Ford had replied and had then watched Prentice throw his trilby on the bed with a despairing cry.

'Ford!' he had bellowed. 'You've just done it again! Look, I know we're at the fag-end of our trip with the military mission to carry out liaison with the Turks in case Jerry attacks them, but we really have got to watch it . . .'

The trouble really had been the Turks themselves. Anxious to keep out of the war if they could – and who could blame them for that? – they had invited the British to send a military mission to discuss possible defence measures if the worst happened. But to avoid provoking the attack they feared, or rather, to avoid giving Berlin an excuse for launching that attack, they had insisted that the mission should travel in civilian clothes. A Signal Corps man, Prentice had found plenty to discuss with his Turkish opposite numbers in the way of a plan for setting up communications, and Staff-Sergeant Ford, ex-Royal Artillery, was now one of that rare breed, an ammunition examiner, an expert on explosives, both British and foreign. In this role he had also finished his work late when he had been taken to see a Turkish dam it was proposed to blow up in the event of a German invasion. So both of them had returned to Istanbul to find the plane with the military mission aboard had already left for Athens.

'When's the next one?' Prentice had light-heartedly asked the chap at the Legation.

'There isn't one,' the Legation official had informed him coldly. 'You'll have to catch a boat out of here. The very first available boat,' he had added. 'I've already looked it up for you – it's a ship called the *Hydra*. Sailing for Greece tomorrow morning. Just after dawn,' he had concluded with a twinge of waspish humour which Prentice, who hated rising early, had not fully appreciated.

Later, Prentice had discovered that normally there was a regular service operating between Istanbul and Athens, but the Turks had just cancelled this because of rumours of German troop movements along their northern borders. So, that left the ferry to the peninsula of Zervos, which was in northern Greece, much closer to Salonika than Athens, but at least it would land them on Greek soil. The Legation, of course, had been in the devil of a hurry to see the last of them. Prentice had a shrewd idea that the Ambassador was having kittens at the thought of British soldiers disguised as civilians wandering the streets of Istanbul. As he expressed it quietly to Ford in the saloon of the *Hydra* while he swallowed the *ouzo* in two gulps: 'I really think if there'd been a boat leaving for Russia they'd have pushed us on that.'

'Maybe. I still think it's queer there should be three Jerries all on the same trip on this leaky old tub,' Ford persisted. He could hear the rattle of a chain somewhere. They'd be off any minute now.

Prentice grinned. 'They may be embassy staff transferred from Istanbul to their place in Salonika.' He studied Ford, noted again the stocky build, the neatly cut black hair and the alert eyes which watched the room constantly. Always wanting to have a go, was Ford. An aggressive, controlled chap who carried an air of competence and energetic ability. As for Prentice, he never went out of his way to have a go, but if the necessity arose he was more than able to cope with his leisured, laconic manner. The difference was that for Ford, the army was a way of life, whereas for Prentice it was a necessary but time-wasting interval which kept him from his advertising job in the West End of London.

'But if they're embassy staff,' Ford went on obstinately, his hands cupped to hide his mouth, 'why are they travelling separately? They don't know each other, that's obvious enough.'

Prentice felt the ship moving away from the quayside and checked his watch. 7.30 AM. Ford had a point there, he was thinking. And if they were embassy staff going to Salonika why the devil hadn't they taken the train from Istanbul along that line through Macedonia? By all accounts it was a nightmare trip, stopping at every little out-of-the-way village and taking anything up to a couple of days, but at least it would have got them there direct. So why were they in such a rush to reach Greece by the earliest possible hour? Why, Prentice kept asking himself? Why?

*

Field-Marshal von List stood up from behind the desk at his GHQ in southern Bulgaria and walked to the window, still holding the meteorological report. Beside the desk his staff officer, Colonel Wilhelm Genke, waited patiently. The field-marshal was worried and from long experience Genke knew that this was not the moment to speak. The clock on the desk registered 7.30 AM.

His face seasoned and grim, List gazed out at the view, and this didn't please him either because it was a reminder of the piece of paper he held in his hands. It was an hour after dawn and beyond the stone houses of the village he could make out where the mountains rose to meet the clouds which hung low over Bulgaria, clouds which promised more snow on the way. Which the Met report also promised. He could vaguely see the snow from where he stood – great drifts of it piled up on the lower slopes under the cloud ceiling. His voice was harsh when he spoke.

'It's foul, unspeakably foul weather. They could be wrong, I suppose. They're wrong half the time, these so-called weather experts. Look at what happened in Norway.'

Genke coughed, timing his intervention carefully. 'Spring is late all over Europe, sir. There is still deep snow across the Russian steppes and no sign of a thaw . . .'

'Don't let's talk about Russia yet. We have to settle this business first.' List turned round, a tinge of sarcasm in his voice. 'Berlin, of course, is quite confident.'

'Berlin is always confident when other people have to do the work, sir. But you have exceptionally powerful forces under your command.'

On that point, at least, the field-marshal agreed. The Twelfth Army comprised two motorized, three mountain Alpenkorps and light infantry divisions, three regiments of the Liebstandarte Adolf Hitler Division – and five Panzer divisions, the spearhead of the coming onslaught on Greece and Yugoslavia. A force of enormous strength and great mobility – theoretically powerful enough to overwhelm everything which stood in their path. But there was deep snow on the Greek mountains, deep snow on Olympus and Zervos. Could the machines overcome the hazards of this damnably prolonged winter? The question was never far from his mind – and zero hour was almost here.

Gazing out of the window, he thought that Bulgaria was the most Godforsaken spot he had encountered in his life, and even as he watched, white flakes drifted down outside the window, several clinging to the glass and beginning to build up opaque areas. Would spring never come? Yes, zero hour was very close indeed. Beyond the window he heard a familiar sound – the grind and clatter of tank tracks moving over cobbled streets. The supporting Panzers were rolling towards the border and would be in position before nightfall. The timetable had been set in motion and the operation was under way. Now no power on earth except Berlin could stop it. And within hours even Berlin would have forfeited that prerogative. From outside the house came the sound of a vehicle stopping, its engine still left running. Genke shuffled his feet.

'The car has arrived, sir.'

List buttoned up his coat to the neck, put the peaked cap on his head and started for the door. But on the way he paused to glance at the wall map which an orderly would take down as soon as they had left, a map of the southern Balkans and eastern Mediterranean zones. Then Genke opened the door and Field-Marshal von List strode out with his assistant following. Genke had noted that pause to glance at the map and he knew which area had attracted List's attention. He had looked first at Istanbul, then his eye had followed the sea route through the Dardanelles and across the Aegean where it had finally alighted on a certain peninsula.

Zervos.

'The *Rupescu*?' The Senior Naval Intelligence Officer at Alexandria looked up at his assistant, Lieutenant-Commander Browne. 'Is that the Rumanian ship the Legation people at Istanbul sent the message about?'

'Yes, sir. It left the Bulgarian port of Varna yesterday and arrived at the Golden Horn a few hours ago. There's some mystery as to her ultimate destination.'

'What mystery?'

'It's a bit vague, sir. Apparently she's bound for Beirut but it's her first trip out of the Black Sea for months and I suppose the Legation's bothered because the Germans control Rumania now.'

'I see. That's rather delicate – we still haven't declared war on Rumania. You're suggesting we keep an eye on her? To make sure she is heading for the Lebanon?'

Browne looked out of the window where a white jetty sparkled in the early morning sunshine, its arm enclosing a basin of brilliant blue water where warships lay at anchor. A transport bound for Greece was just beyond the jetty wall, sailing north-west and leaving behind a clear wake of white on the blue. 'It's the only vessel in the area which has the remotest connexion with the Axis powers – and so far we have no idea what she's carrying.'

'Probably collecting rather than carrying – trying to pick up a cargo before war is eventually declared and we can pounce on her. We're very stretched, you know that, Browne.'

'I was thinking of the *Daring*, sir. She's patrolling off the Turkish coast and could intercept the *Rupescu* soon after dark. I'm not thinking of boarding her – but it might be interesting to get her reaction when a British destroyer comes in close.'

'Send Willoughby a message, then. And radio another one to Istanbul. We've had two requests already from those querulous diplomats.' The senior officer looked at the wall clock. 7.30 AM. Yes, it would be after nightfall before Willoughby arrived.

Chapter Three

Saturday, 10 pm

The tension had slowly risen aboard the *Hydra*, a tension which seemed reproduced by the steady beat of her throbbing engines as she left the Dardanelles and proceeded far out into the open Aegean. By nightfall she was midway between the Turkish and Greek coasts, steaming through seas which were beginning to curdle. The tension rose from small, meaningless incidents. The meeting at a doorway between Prentice and the squat, dark-haired German, Volber, when the latter had started to push his way through first and had then changed his mind offering prior entry to Prentice. The episode at dinner when a cork came out of a bottle like a pistol shot and for several seconds the company had frozen. The careful way in which passengers of different nationalities turned to go in another direction when they saw someone coming towards them.

'It's not frightfully funny any more,' Prentice had remarked over dinner irritably. 'Look at the way they're sitting – like pallbearers at a funeral.'

'They'd have more fun at a funeral – afterwards, anyway,' Ford had pointed out. 'It's almost as though they're waiting for something to happen.' All the others

occupied a table to themselves. Macomber, Hahnemann, Volber and Grapos – all sitting in splendid
isolation with empty tables between them while each
ate and drank as though he were the only person in the
room, taking care to make no sound except for the
occasional clink of cutlery. Even the captain, Nopagos,
who came in later, was unable to help. He had
explained this briefly to Prentice in his careful English
while visiting each table in turn before taking a table of
his own.

'It is difficult, Mr Prentice – British and Germans on
board, you understand.'

'Frightened there'll be a rumpus?' Prentice had
inquired genially.

'Rum . . . pus?'

'A battle, a fight.' Prentice had play-acted with his
fists, glad of the chance to pull someone's leg, then had
relented when he saw the Greek's doleful expression.
'Don't worry, we'll be good. But I bet you'll be damned
glad to drop this lot off at Katyra in the morning.'

'The safe arrival in port is always the happy time,'
Nopagos replied ambiguously and went away to his
solitary table.

When dinner was over one passenger, Macomber,
lingered in the room long after the others had left,
smoking his cigar and drinking coffee from the pot the
steward had provided after clearing his table. Like the
saloon, the dining-room was panelled and small gold
curtains were still drawn back from the porthole windows. Occasionally, he glanced out of the nearest

window which gave him a view across the moonlit sea to the north-east, a sea which had now ceased to tremble with small waves and was already developing massive undulations which heaved towards the vessel with foam-topped crests. The dining-room was beginning to sway ponderously and the Scot shifted his feet wider apart to counter the movement as the woodwork creaked ominously, the horizon beyond the porthole dipping out of sight and then clambering into view again. The fourth German, Schnell, had still not appeared, and Macomber had mentioned this to the steward when he had brought the extra pot of coffee. 'Perhaps he's dead,' he had said with rough humour, 'he could be for all we've seen of him.'

'He had dinner served in his cabin,' the steward had remarked, 'and he wanted a Thermos of coffee made up for the night. Probably he doesn't sleep well at sea.'

'He won't if he drinks a whole Thermos of this,' Macomber had replied. The coffee was Turkish and the prospect of consuming it in such quantities suggested a steel-plated stomach and an inability to sleep at all.

'We get passengers like that occasionally,' the steward had prattled on. 'They just don't seem to like mixing with strangers. This man is like that – he was in the toilet when the dinner was taken in, as though he didn't even wish to see the steward. He's Austrian, I think,' he had added.

'Indeed? Why do you say that?'

'His big cabin trunk has labels on it from the Hotel Sacher in Vienna. The steward thinks he spends a lot of time sitting by his porthole gazing out to sea – there was a pair of field-glasses opened by the table next to his wrist-watch. Call me if you want anything else, sir.' Left alone by himself Macomber had drunk two cups of the strong-tasting liquid while he thought about the invisible Herr Schnell. It was ten o'clock when he walked out of the deserted dining-room to take a final tour of the vessel, and at this hour the *Hydra* had the feel of a ghost ship, one of those phantom vessels which drift round the seaways of the world and are only seen as a mirage in the night. There was no one about as he descended a creaking staircase and began to walk along the empty companionway on the deck containing the passenger cabins. He had chosen this staircase deliberately and his rubber-soled boots made no sound as he paused by the first cabin which the Austrian occupied. Cabin One was silent but there were narrow streaks of light in the louvred upper half of the closed door. He made no attempt to see through the louvres – he had tested that possibility with his own cabin door earlier in the evening – but clearly the mysterious Schnell was still secreted inside his own quarters. He might not be awake, Macomber was thinking as he stood quite still, since a man who spends hours inside one small room is likely to get drowsy and fall asleep with the lights still on.

The next cabin was the wireless-room. Here, instead of pausing, Macomber walked past slowly, seeing through the half-open door the Greek wireless operator reading a newspaper as one hand reached out for a sandwich. So far everything seemed normal, perfectly normal, but the Scot could not rid himself of a feeling of growing unease. The next cabin was in darkness. Volber's. The German who looked like the owner of a small business – or a member of the Gestapo. Often the two types could easily be confused. Cabin Three still had the lights on and from behind the closed door came the faint sounds of dance music. Herr Hahnemann was tuned in to Radio Deutschland, perhaps feeling a little homesick aboard this swaying ferry in the middle of the Aegean. There were lights in the next cabin, too, the temporary home of the two Britishers. Macomber paused outside and then walked steadily on as the mumble of voices died suddenly. When a cabin door opened behind him he was careful not to turn round. An interesting thought had struck him: was Volber really asleep inside that darkened cabin or was he somewhere else, having deliberately given the impression that he had gone down for the night? Silently he passed his own darkened cabin and began to mount the staircase at the other end of the companionway. The vessel was steaming steadily westward and as he opened the door at the top he faced the stern, consciously bracing himself and squaring his shoulders as the moan of the wind took on a higher note, rasping his face with its icy blast. Macomber had experienced the wind from the plains of Hungary, a wind which swept straight in from the depths of faraway Siberia, but as he slammed the door shut he thought he had never felt a more penetrating chill.

The deck was deserted. No sign of Volber. But the boat was still there, the vessel he had seen through the porthole from his dining-room table. She was moving along a course parallel to the *Hydra*'s, ploughing through the rising seas perhaps three kilometres to starboard. The deck was lifting sufficiently for him to hold onto the rail as he made his way to the stern, his face muscles drawn tight and not from the bitter wind which froze his skin. Taking out his Monokular glass, which was small enough to conceal inside the palm of one hand, he looked back along the deck. Lifeboats, the snow melted and gone during the day, swung slowly on their davits, reproducing the movement of the sea. A thin trail of smoke floated from the *Hydra*'s funnel, was caught up by the wind and thrown into a spiral. There was no sign of life anywhere. He aimed his glass, saw the other ship as a blur which merged in one long glow-worm of light, focused, brought the lights forward as separate portholes, noted the white funnel and the unidentifiable flag which whipped from the mast-head. For perhaps a minute he stood motionless, one part of his mind on the lens, the other part alert for the slightest sound which might warn him that he was no longer alone on that empty deck, a sound which might warn him of the attempt on his life he had feared ever since coming aboard. Then he closed the glass, pocketed it and checked his watch once more. 10.10 PM. Yes, it was the *Rupescu*, the vessel which had got up steam as soon as the *Hydra* had made preparations to leave the Golden Horn. Shoulders hunched against the wind, he made his way back along the unstable deck and went down into the warmth which met him as soon as he opened the door. Inside his own cabin he took off his hat and coat, lit a fresh cigar, put the Luger within easy reach and settled down to wait. Assassins often preferred to operate at night.

'It was the big German,' Ford said as he closed the cabin door and re-locked it. 'I caught him on the staircase at the far end – he still had his coat and hat on and he was going up on deck. I don't like it.'

'Don't like what?' Prentice withdrew his hand from where it had rested near the pillow which concealed his Webley ·455 revolver and began studying the patience cards spread out over his bunk.

'The feel of this old tub – those Jerries being aboard and not talking to each other. They come from the same country and they haven't said a blasted word to each other from what I've seen.'

'Perhaps they're English in disguise – that would explain the non-fraternization.' He picked up a card, placed it over another. 'Not been formally introduced, you see.'

Ford lit the last of his army issue cigarettes, the ones he could only smoke when they were alone, and started thudding a heel against the woodwork as he sat down on his bunk. Prentice looked up and stared pointedly at the thudding heel until Ford stopped the noise, then went back to his game. 'You could always get some kip,' he suggested hopefully.

'Couldn't sleep a wink,' the staff-sergeant told him emphatically. 'Not with those Jerries aboard creeping all over the shop when it's long past their bedtime.' He got up and went over to the porthole, pulling the curtain aside with a jerk. 'That ship's still there, too. Wonder why it's keeping so close to us?'

Prentice slammed down a card and lit a Turkish cigarette quickly while he watched the sergeant who continued staring out of the porthole in his shirt-sleeves. 'Ford, there are things called sea-lanes. Ships are liable to follow them. If you've ever crossed the Channel you'll see quite a few ships not far from each other the whole way across. I really think that Turkish food must have done you a power of harm – you're not normally as jittery as this.'

Ford turned away from the porthole, closing the curtain again. 'And I'm not normally travelling on a boat with a load of Jerries for company. There's something strange going on – I can feel it.'

'Three Jerries . . .' Prentice started to point out.

'Four! There's that other one the captain mentioned to us earlier in the day – the one that never comes out of his cabin at the end of the companionway.'

'All right, four! But hardly a load of Jerries – you make it sound as though there's a division of them aboard. What can four of them do aboard a Greek ferry in the middle of the Aegean which – when I last heard of it – is controlled by the Royal Navy? If you go on like this, Ford,' he continued with a mischievous grin, 'you'll end up in sick bay with some MO asking you what scared you in your cradle! Now, how do you expect me to get this game out if you persist in banging your foot and peering through portholes as though you anticipated a whole German army arriving at any moment?'

'Sorry. It's probably that last meal we had in Istanbul. What was that dish again?'

'Fried octrangel,' said Prentice absent-mindedly as he turned his attention to the cards. 'It's a baby octopus. A great delicacy.' He didn't look up to see Ford's face, but a few minutes later he became aware again of the restless sergeant's movements and glanced up to see him putting on his coat over his jacket.

'Feel like a breath of fresh air,' Ford explained. 'Don't mind, do you?'

'Yes, I think I do.' The lieutenant spoke sharply. 'Going out on your own isn't really a very good idea.'

Ford's eyes gleamed as he dropped the coat onto his bunk. 'You don't much like it either, then?'

'I just don't think it's too clever for us to separate at this time of night. There!' He dropped a card on a small pile. 'You see, it's coming out.' Prentice smiled grimly to himself as he went on playing: Ford had smoked him out there. No, he wasn't entirely happy about the situation aboard this ferry, but he saw no point in alarming the staff-sergeant at this stage. Prentice was a man who, despite his outwardly extrovert air, preferred to keep his fears to himself. Those Germans who were worrying Ford could, of course, be spies, and if they were they had chosen the right place to come – the strategically important peninsula of Zervos. As he played out his game Prentice was thinking of a military conference he had attended in Athens just before departing for Turkey, a conference he had attended because a question of communications had been involved. He could hear Colonel Wilson's clipped voice speaking now as he automatically placed a fresh card.

'It's the very devil,' Wilson had said, 'getting permission to sent some of our chaps to Mount Zervos. The official in the Greek War Ministry who's responsible says Zervos is seventy miles from the Bulgarian frontier and in any case the peninsula comes under the command of the Greek army in Macedonia. He just won't have us there.'

'Not even to send a small unit to set up an observation post?' Prentice had ventured. 'From what I gather the monastery under the summit looks clear across the gulf to the coast road taking our supplies up to the Alkiamon Line.'

'You gather correctly,' Wilson had told him crisply. 'But the monastery seems to be the stumbling-block. Apparently for many years the whole peninsula has been a monastic sanctuary and you need a government permit even to land there. They won't grant one of those to a woman – the only women allowed in the area are the wives and relatives of fishermen who live there . . .' He had paused, his expression icy until the ripple of laughter had died. Perhaps he had sounded unnecessarily indignant on that score. 'The guts of the thing is that this Greek official practically suggests we'd be violating something sacred by sending in a few troops . . .'

'You believe him?' Prentice had interjected quietly, never backward in speaking up when his interest was aroused. There had been an awkward pause before Wilson had answered that one. Only a tiny fraction of the Greek population was believed to hold secret Nazi sympathies, but it was feared that one or two of these undesirable gentry might occupy key positions inside the Greek government.

'We can only take his word,' Wilson had replied eventually. 'But the thing that sends shivers up the spines of our planning staff is the idea of German troops capturing that monastery. It's perched nearly three thousand feet up at the southern tip of the peninsula and has a clear view across to that vital coast road. And that's not all. There's some freak in the weather up there which means the summit of Mount Zervos is nearly always cloud-free – so you get an uninterrupted view of that road even when visibility's nil a few miles away. A Jerry observation post stuck up there would put us in a proper pickle.'

Afterwards, a Royal Artillery major had further enlightened Prentice: beyond the head of the gulf a range of hills formed a natural defence line, but if the Wehrmacht attacked and were able to emplace heavy guns on the lower slopes they could bring down an annihilating fire on the coast road from behind these hill crests – *providing they had an observation post on Mount Zervos which could guide the fall of the bombardment*. The major ended up by saying that if the Germans ever did get the Allies in such a position it would be little short of a massacre.*

Prentice dropped another card in place and sighed as the *Hydra* tilted again, a slow, deliberate roll as though revolving on an axis. While in Turkey he'd almost forgotten that conference, never believing for one instant that he would ever set eyes on Zervos, and here he was less than eight hours' sailing time from that benighted peninsula. And why the hell did ships always have to leave almost at dawn and arrive somewhere else at that Godforsaken hour? Finishing the game, he started shuffling the cards, uncertain whether to play again. Then he stopped shuffling. Ford was again standing by the porthole, the curtain drawn back, and there was something in his manner which caught Prentice's attention. 'What's up?' he asked.

'It's this ship – she's coming in damned close, whatever you say about sea-lanes.'

Prentice stood up quickly and went over to the porthole. The unknown vessel was now sailing on a parallel course less than a quarter of a mile from the

* Later in the war the same threat materialized at Monte Cassino where a German observation post reported to the gunners every movement of Allied troops.

Hydra's hull and even as he watched the gap seemed to be narrowing. 'She is damned close,' he agreed, and felt a faint prickling of the short hairs at the back of his neck. He watched for a little while longer to be sure the ship wasn't simply passing them, then took a decision. 'I think we'd better pay our friend, Captain Nopagos, a little visit . . .' He broke off in mid-sentence. 'What was that?'

'Sounded like someone falling over in the passage – I think he hit our door . . .'

'Better see – and watch it!' Prentice dropped the pack of cards on his bunk, sat down and idly let his hand rest on the bunk close to the pillow which hid the Webley. He looked half-asleep as he watched Ford, who had now reached the locked door. Ford hesitated, listened for a moment, then heard a groan and a shuffling sound. He unlocked the door, opening it cautiously.

The Greek steward who looked after the cabins was lying face down in the companionway, his body wriggling as a slight moan escaped him. Ford looked both ways along the passage and saw that it was deserted. The *Hydra* was moving in a heavy swell, rocking slowly as the sea lifted and lowered it. He bent down quickly and noted that the man's hands were underneath him as though clasped to his stomach. There was no sign of injury so far as he could see – the poor devil must have been taken sick while walking down the companionway. He looked back inside the cabin and called out to Prentice.

'It's the steward. I think he's had an attack or something. I'd better go along and find someone . . .'

'Hold it a minute!' Prentice's nerves were on edge and his mind raced as he took in the implications of this unexpected incident. Ford going off to seek help would mean they were separated, a situation which could be dangerous. There was something queer going on, very queer indeed. 'No, don't do that,' he told Ford quickly. 'Can we get him in here? Let's have a look at him first.' He stepped into the companionway to give Ford a hand, stooping down to hoist the steward by the shoulders while the sergeant took the legs. They were standing in this position, still in the companionway with their hands encumbered, when the cabin door next to them was thrown open and Hahnemann came out. At waist-height he held a German machine-pistol, the weapon aimed at Ford's chest as he spoke in English.

'Put the Greek down and lift your hands. Be careful! If I shoot, the Greek dies, too.'

They put the steward down gently and as he reached the floor his hands and feet began to scrabble about in a more life-like fashion. His face turned and Prentice saw that he was scared stiff, his complexion whiter than the jacket he wore. With Ford, he raised his hands, turning slowly as he stood up so that he could look down the passage where he caught a glimpse through the half-closed door of the wireless-room. The radio operator still sat in front of his seat but now his hands were tied behind the back of his neck and then the view closed off as Volber came out holding a Luger pistol.

'Look at the wall!' snapped Hahnemann. 'And keep still.'

They faced the wall and Prentice felt Volber's quick hands pat his clothes and explore his body for hidden weapons. The shock of the hold-up was going now and Prentice's mind coldly searched for a way of upsetting the enemy who had decided to continue the war on neutral territory. The Greek steward was standing up and faced the wall when Hahnemann gave the order. The German issued his instructions in a crisp, controlled manner which warned Prentice that any counter-action would have to be swift, unexpected and totally effective.

'And now you go inside the cabin. Quickly!'

Prentice obeyed the order without hesitation. In fact, he went inside so quickly that Hahnemann was caught off-balance as the lieutenant tore through the open doorway, hooked his right heel behind the panel and slammed it in the German's face. His instinct was to dive for the revolver under the pillow, but knowing he hadn't the time, he jumped close to the wall as the door was thrown open again. Hahnemann jumped into the room, literally leapt through the doorway, turning as he saw Prentice a fraction of a second too late. The lieutenant grasped the machine-pistol by the barrel and swung the muzzle viciously to one side, still holding on, then jerked it backwards beyond the German who

COLIN FORBES

had expected him to pull it away from him. The muzzle
was still aimed futilely at the outer wall. Continuing
the rearward jerk, Prentice felt the weapon come free
and in the same second felt his feet slip under him. He
went over on the back of his head, still gripping the
weapon as clouds of dizziness addled his brain and he
saw only shadows through a mist. He was still struggling through the mists, seeing them clear gradually,
when something hard and heavy hit him in the side.
Hahnemann had just kicked him. When he recovered a
grip on himself the German was standing over him
with the machine-pistol aimed at the centre of his chest.
In the doorway Ford stood grimly silent with Volber's
Luger pointed at his stomach.

'Get up!' said Hahnemann savagely, backing away
as Prentice, wondering why the hell he was still alive,
clambered painfully to his feet. That hadn't been too
clever. The back of his head felt to be split in two and
an iron hammer was banging down the split. He gulped
in several breaths of air, trying to hear what Hahnemann was saying. 'Over by the wall. Quick!' Tottering
a little, Prentice went over to the outer wall and leant
against it where Ford joined him a moment later.
Volber went out of the cabin, closing the door behind
him. It had all happened so swiftly that he was still
wondering what the hell they hoped to achieve, was
still suffering from a partial sense of shock. Alongside
him Ford stared at the German with an intent look,
waiting for him to make just one small mistake. The
trouble was he didn't look like a man who repeated his

mistakes – letting Prentice break loose had put him in a state of total alertness, and although he was guarding two men on his own he stood back far enough to give his gun a good field of fire. One brief burst would kill both of them: Ford, as a weapons and explosives expert, was under no illusions on this point.

'Why are you aboard this ship, Lieutenant Prentice?' demanded Hahnemann.

Prentice glanced at the table where Volber had left the papers and paybook he had extracted from their pockets while searching them for weapons. Hahnemann must have looked at these while he was coming up out of the mists. He wasn't in any hurry to reply – time was a factor the German clearly valued, as though he were following a carefully worked out timetable, and Prentice had detected a note of anxiety behind the question, so his reply was deliberately non-informative. 'To travel from Istanbul to Zervos,' he said. For a horrible second he thought he had made a fatal mistake. Hahnemann's finger tightened on the trigger and Prentice braced himself for the lacerating burst of bullets, but the German regained control and smiled unpleasantly.

'That I understood! Now, Lieutenant Prentice, before I shoot Sergeant Ford in the stomach I will ask the question again. Why are you travelling on this particular ship on this particular night? You understand? Good.'

Prentice found he was sweating badly on the palms of his hands and under his armpits. He hadn't the least idea of what Hahnemann was talking about but he doubted whether he could convince the German of this. His brain reeled as he sought desperately for words which might half-satisfy their interrogator, and with a tremendous effort he managed a ghastly smile in an endeavour to lower the temperature before it was too late. 'I take it you're in the German army?' For the first time Hahnemann showed a trace of uncertainty and Prentice followed up his tiny advantage quickly. 'Then you'll know that according to the Geneva Convention all we have to give you is name, rank and number. You've got those there on that table already.'

It was a hair-line gamble, switching the conversation to this topic, but Prentice was counting on the German's training to make him pause, to cool his anger, to gain control again. To his great relief he saw the machine-pistol muzzle swing to a point between himself and Ford where it could fire in either direction. The German had, at least temporarily, recovered his balance. Prentice had now assessed Hahnemann as a highly trained individual who normally kept an ice-cold grip on his emotions, but who also, occasionally, in a state of fury, lost that grip and went berserk. They had just witnessed such an occasion when their lives had trembled on the brink.

'What were you doing in Turkey?' Hahnemann asked suddenly.

'Trying to get a berth home to Athens.' Prentice's quick tongue rattled on. 'And the civilian clothes were loaned to us by the Turks. Our ship struck a mine off the Turkish coast two days ago and we were dragged out of the sea more dead than alive. We were the only survivors – and don't ask me the name of the ship or how many she was carrying because you wouldn't answer that either if I were holding the gun. And don't ask me why the Turks didn't intern us because I don't know – except that they seemed damned glad to get rid of us at the earliest possible moment. They'd have put us on the normal Istanbul–Athens service, but that was cancelled at the last minute so we were hustled aboard this ferry. The first available ship out, they said – and this was it.'

It had been a long speech and he hoped to God that it had satisfied Hahnemann on the one question which seemed to bother him – why were they aboard the *Hydra*? There was a hint of respect in the German's eyes now and Prentice decided to press a point home, forgetting that it's always a mistake to overdo a good thing.

'So we're your prisoners-of-war at the moment,' Prentice continued, 'but don't forget that the Royal Navy controls the Aegean. If there's a British destroyer in the area you may find me holding that gun within a few hours, so let's drop the threats.'

'There is a British destroyer near here?' The gun muzzle was aimed straight at Prentice's chest and the note of cold fury had come back into the German's voice. 'You know this?' The words were an accusation and Hahnemann's jaw muscles were rigid with tension, a tension which instantly communicated itself to the two men with their backs to the wall. The tip of the gun muzzle quivered, the outward sign of the nervous vibration bottled up inside the man holding the weapon. Christ! Prentice was thinking, we're a nervous twitch away from a fusillade. Where the devil did I go wrong? He spoke carefully but quickly, his eyes fixed on Hahnemann's as he struggled to gauge the effect of his words while he was talking. 'I'm not thinking of any particular destroyer – I'm in the army, not the navy – you know that. But these seas are constantly patrolled so it's just a matter of luck – yours or ours.' He shut up, hoping for the best, determined not to overdo it a second time. His shirt was clinging to his wet back and he daren't look at Ford in case Hahnemann thought he was passing a signal. It was becoming a nightmare and he had a grisly feeling they might not live through it.

'Turn round and lie on the floor – stretch out your hands to the fullest extent.'

The unexpected order threw Prentice off balance; it was impossible to keep up with this German through his swift changes of mood, but at least there weren't going to be any more of those trigger-loaded questions. He was on his knees when he grasped the meaning of the order, saw out of the corner of his eye the vicious arc of the machine-pistol butt descending on poor Ford's head, and as the sergeant slumped unconscious over the floor he swung round to swear at the German. The muzzle was aimed point-blank at his chest. Prentice was obeying the fresh order to look at the wall when a ton-weight landed on his tender scalp. A brilliant burst of light flashed before his eyes and then vanished in the flood of darkness which overwhelmed him.

The rifle muzzle was pressed into Macomber's face when he opened the cabin door in response to the urgent knocking, and the threat was accompanied by an apology in German. 'You must remain in your cabin until further orders, Herr Dietrich. I am sorry . . .'

'Whose orders?' Macomber stood with his hand behind his back, his manner harsh and unimpressed by the sight of the weapon. For a moment it seemed as though he would push Volber out of the way by walking straight into him. The German had paused, uncertain how to handle this aggressive reaction, but Hahnemann, who stood close behind with a machine-pistol in his hands, was not taken aback.

'By order of the Wehrmacht!'

Macomber stared past Volber, ignoring the squat man as he gazed bleakly at Hahnemann. Again it seemed as though he would push the rifle barrel aside and Hahnemann instinctively raised his own weapon. 'That is not enough,' Macomber rumbled Teutonically. 'The officer's name, if you please.' He might have been a colonel addressing a subordinate.

'Lieutenant Hahnemann, Alpenkorps.' The German had replied automatically and had felt the reflex of snapping his heels to attention, but he desisted just in time. Now he was furious with his own reply, but there was something about the passenger which he found intimidating, an air of authority which was disturbing. 'You will stay in your cabin,' he barked. 'Do you understand? Anyone found outside their cabin without permission will be shot!' Immediately he had spoken he had doubts, and the steely look in Macomber's eye was anything but reassuring. Who the hell could he be? 'Lieutenant Hahnemann?' Macomber repeated slowly, and there was an uncomfortable, mocking note in his voice. 'I think I can remember that for later!'

Hahnemann persisted, but more quietly. 'Please give my sergeant the key of your cabin so it can be locked from the outside.'

Macomber gazed thoughtfully at Hahnemann a moment longer, then turning on his heel so that the cabin door hid part of his body, he slipped the Luger back inside his coat pocket and re-entered the cabin, ignoring the request for the key. Volber he could have dealt with, but the lieutenant's machine-pistol was quite another matter. With a muttered expression of annoyance Hahnemann walked forward, extracted the key himself and locked the door on the outside. The Scot straightened up from the newspaper spread over the table, his expression grim. This was even worse than he had imagined: they were taking over the whole ship.

His initial reaction on opening the door was that the assassins had come for him. This fleeting impression had been succeeded by the revelation that they were not interested in him at all, that a major Wehrmacht operation was under way, a stroke as audacious as the Norwegian campaign.* He stood listening, his head cocked to one side. Yes, he was right – the *Hydra*'s engines were slowing. For the mid-sea rendezvous, of course. They must have taken control of the engine-room at an earlier stage and by now they would command the bridge. An efficient operation planned with the usual meticulous care and attention to detail – including the bringing aboard of Herr Schnell and his outsize cabin trunk containing the weapons. Retrieving his smoking cigar from the ash-tray, he switched off the light and used his torch to find his way across the cabin to the porthole.

The *Hydra*'s engines had almost stopped and the *Rupescu* was so close that a collision seemed likely. Standing by the porthole without any attempt at concealment, his cigar glowing for anyone who cared to see it, he watched the transfer of the German troops from the Rumanian vessel to the Greek ferry. The soldiers, wearing life-jackets, were coping with a heavy swell – had they arrived later or had the weather worsened earlier the operation might have proved impossible. German luck again, Macomber thought bitterly – like the luck of the marvellous weather over France in 1940. You can't get far without luck, he was thinking as he watched a boatload of troops being

* Norway was seized by apparently innocent merchant ships full of German troops which sailed up the Norwegian coast within gun range of the unsuspecting Royal Navy.

lowered to the sea. There must have been almost twenty men aboard and he was praying for an accident as the craft almost capsized when the waves heaved up to meet it, but at the last moment someone released the ropes and the boat followed the natural curvature of the sea. The uniformed troops wore soft, large-peaked caps and were heavily laden with equipment. Alpenkorps. A unit of the élite mountain troops who had conquered Norway, men trained to fight in appalling terrain such as the peninsula of Zervos.

He remained standing there for some time, his body now fully accustomed to the sway of the ship under his widespread feet, and during that time he counted the transfer of over two hundred men to the Greek ferry. More than enough to take Zervos, providing they received heavy reinforcements in the near future. After all, unless the Allies had put their own troops ashore on the peninsula the only people who stood in their way were a handful of monks at the monastery and a few fishermen at Katyra. Even when the transfer had been completed, when a boat containing, so far as Macomber could make out, the crew of the *Rupescu*, had accomplished the narrow crossing, he still waited at the porthole as the *Hydra*'s engines began to throb with power.

The ferry had resumed its interrupted voyage, was moving away and leaving the Rumanian vessel behind like an empty carcass, when Macomber opened the porthole and thrust his head out into the elements. The rising force of the knife-edged wind chilled his face as he watched the *Rupescu* slowly settling in the growing turbulence of the sea. They had switched off all the lights before they left her but by the light of the moon he saw her bows awash, the curling waves submerging her decks, the water-logged wallow of the doomed vessel. The sea-cocks had been opened, of course. He was still leaning out of the porthole when her superstructure disappeared under the billowing waves, leaving for a brief moment only the white funnel thrust up like some strange lighthouse in mid-Aegean. Then that, too, sank and there was no trace left that the *Rupescu* had ever existed.

Macomber withdrew his head, rammed the porthole shut, switched on the cabin light and began slapping his hands across his body to warm up. Sitting down on the bunk, he resisted the fatal temptation to sprawl his legs along it, and lit a fresh cigar. Still no chance to sleep, and it looked as though it might be a long while yet before he dared close his eyes. The period of standing by the porthole had tired his limbs horribly but his growing fury and the night sea air had made him steadily more alert, and now as he smoked the anger helped him to think. All his eager anticipations of returning to a haven of peace had temporarily left him, had left him at the first sight of those uniforms he knew so well. He had to do something to upset the timetable, the careful plan they would be working to, because they were bad improvisers and when things went wrong they reacted badly. His main hope was to persist in his impersonation, to throw them off-balance at the outset, to gain the freedom to move around the ship freely. He stood up to fight down the sleepiness he felt again, shoved the hat on his head, the hat which made him look even more Germanic, and glanced in the washbasin mirror. No need to assume an expression of grimness: that was already only too evident. You're *Dietrich*, he said softly, so from now on forget a chap called Macomber ever existed. And they'll have to maintain radio silence so they can't check anything. It's the first encounter that matters. You're Dietrich, Dr Richard Dietrich. He sat down again in the chair, impatient for the first confrontation, and when they came for him it was close to midnight.

Chapter Four

Saturday, Midnight

With his machine-pistol cradled under his arm, Lieutenant Hahnemann, now dressed in Alpenkorps uniform, unlocked the door, turned the handle and kicked it open with his foot. Dietrich was sitting at the little table, still wearing his coat and hat with his legs stretched out before him and crossed at the ankles. He was smoking a fresh cigar and the rude entry had no effect on him, caused no change in his relaxed stance; rather it seemed as though he went out of his way to demonstrate his bored unconcern. Dietrich folded his arms. He was regarding Hahnemann as he might have regarded a piece of badly cooked meat, then he transferred his attention to the tall, beak-nosed man who walked briskly in behind the lieutenant. A striking-looking German in his early forties, he held himself very erect as his cold blue eyes studied the seated passenger, and under his civilian coat, which he wore open at the front, Dietrich saw the boots and uniform of the Alpenkorps.

'This is Colonel Burckhardt,' Hahnemann informed him harshly. He paused as though expecting some reaction. 'People normally stand in the colonel's presence,' he went on bleakly.

'Tell this man to go away so we can talk.' Dietrich addressed the suggestion to Burckhardt who was looking down at him with interest. The passenger hadn't moved since he had entered the cabin.

'You can talk with both of us,' Burckhardt began tersely. 'Unless you have a very good reason for wishing to speak to me alone.' Like Hahnemann earlier, Burckhardt was wondering why he had reacted in a way he had hardly intended. And yet . . .

'What I have to say is not for junior officers.' Dietrich's brief mood of amiability was vanishing rapidly and he looked at the colonel grimly. 'I should have thought you hadn't a great deal of time to waste, so shall we get on with it?'

Burckhardt's expression showed no reaction, but inwardly he felt a trifle off-balance – he had been going to say almost precisely the same thing and now this aggressive-looking brute had forestalled him. He had the odd feeling that he was losing ground so he spoke decisively to the lieutenant. 'Hahnemann, you have duties to attend to. Leave me with this man until I call you.'

'He may be armed,' Hahnemann protested.

'Of course I am armed,' Dietrich replied swiftly, anticipating Burckhardt's next question. A lesser man than Colonel Heinz Burckhardt might have felt annoyance, but the colonel had risen to command an élite arm of the Wehrmacht and he had a grudging appreciation of an independent attitude. 'I am going to take out a Luger pistol,' Dietrich explained, staring at

Hahnemann as though he doubted his ability to grasp plain German, 'so kindly keep a hold on yourself – and your weapon.' Producing the pistol from his coat pocket, he laid it on the table. 'It is fully loaded, incidentally – I never bluff when I have to use a weapon, which, fortunately, is a rare occasion.' The sight of the regulation pistol, a minor point, subtly reinforced Burckhardt's growing interest in the huge German passenger. For a moment Hahnemann hesitated whether to pick up the gun, but Dietrich's attention was so clearly concentrated on the colonel, was so obviously no longer aware of his presence, that he felt at a loss and glanced at Burckhardt for instructions.

'Leave us,' the colonel told him brusquely. 'I shall be on the bridge in a few minutes.'

Dietrich waited until the cabin door had closed and then stood up slowly. The action startled Burckhardt, who was six feet tall; he had realized that Dietrich also was a tall man but now he was able to see that the German civilian stood two to three inches above him. Rarely impressed by another man's physique, Burckhardt found himself a little overawed by the formidable figure who stood before him with his shoulders hunched and his hands clasped behind his broad back. Dietrich waited a moment, then put a hand inside his coat, extracted something and dropped it on the table. 'My papers, Colonel Burckhardt.'

With a mounting sense of irritation Burckhardt looked at the card carefully, glancing up to find Dietrich watching him without any particular expression.

'You're an archaeologist, I see, Dr Dietrich?' He couldn't keep the flatness out of his voice: he had suspected that this passenger was someone important from Berlin; it was the only explanation for his arrogant manner.

'Look at them carefully,' Dietrich urged him gruffly. 'See anything unusual about them?'

'No!' Burckhardt replied after a second perusal and there was a snap in his voice now.

'Good!' Dietrich lifted his shoulders and towered over the colonel as he went on with withering sarcasm. 'I was travelling aboard a Greek ferry which might at any time have been stopped and searched by a British destroyer. Under those conditions would you really expect me to present them with papers showing I am a senior officer of the Abwehr?'

Burckhardt stood quite still and his heart sank. Here was the explanation for Dietrich's overbearing attitude since he had entered the cabin. God, the Abwehr! That damned Intelligence organization of the incredibly influential Admiral Canaris. They never told anyone what they were going to do – not until they had done it. And they never told anyone where they were going until they had been there and arrived back in Berlin. They were responsible to no one except the wily old admiral who had started his career with naval Intelligence, and who was now answerable only to the Führer himself. The Abwehr was disliked – feared might be a better word – by all the regular Intelligence services because it lived a life of its own, but even more because of its legendary record of coups. In some uncanny way the admiral managed to be right every time in his forecast of enemy intentions. Oh yes, Burckhardt had heard of the Abwehr, but this was the first time he had met one of them. That is, assuming Dietrich was who he claimed to be ... He looked up suspiciously as something else landed on the table.

'Now you can see what I would have dropped through the nearest porthole if we had been stopped – along with the Luger, of course.'

Dietrich's tone was ironic, close to sneering, and Burckhardt caught the tone and felt the blood rush to his head, so for a short time while he examined the second card Baxter had doctored and handed over in Giurgiu, his normally ice-cold judgement deserted him. Dietrich walked across the cabin to look out through the porthole, still talking over his shoulder.

'You will require absolute proof of my identity, so you had better send a wireless message to Berlin. I can give you the signal code.'

'Not while we are at sea,' Burckhardt rapped out. 'We must preserve radio silence at all costs.'

'I had assumed that,' Dietrich retorted brusquely. 'I meant after you had gone ashore. You have dealt with the two Englanders, I hope?'

'Yes, Hahnemann dealt with the whole operation most efficiently. They are only a lieutenant and a sergeant travelling home from Turkey.'

'You knew then beforehand that these two men were being put on board?'

Burckhardt paused, staring at the back of the Abwehr man who continued gazing out to sea. There was something in the way the question had been phrased which disturbed him, which made him delay his departure for the bridge. Had there been some awful slip-up somewhere? 'Knew?' he repeated warily.

'Yes, "knew", I said. Did you know?' Dietrich had swung round and was talking with his cigar in his mouth, his legs splayed as he continued to dominate the conversation.

'No,' the colonel admitted reluctantly. 'I was worried when I first heard about them but they are of very junior rank . . .'

'Are you certain of that? Papers can be easily forged or doctored – including army pay-books. These two men could be far more important for all we know.' He paused to give his insidious suggestion maximum impact. 'They could be on board because some hint of your operation has reached the Allies. You may be lucky they never reached the wireless-room.' He leaned forward grimly. 'I take it they did not reach the wireless-room?'

'Of course not! That was part of Hahnemann's job . . .'

'Any idea which arm of the service they're attached to?'

Burckhardt felt himself go very cold. Until this unnerving interview he had assumed that the two Englanders were only on board by chance, but now the Abwehr man was raising diabolical possibilities. 'Ford, the staff-sergeant, is an ammunition examiner,' he said slowly.

Had Dietrich detected the note of reluctance in his voice? He pressed the colonel for further information instantly. 'And the other man, the so-called lieutenant – Prentice?'

'He is with the Signals Corps.'

'Ah! So undoubtedly an expert wireless operator . . .' Dietrich shrugged his shoulders, his devastating point made. He puffed at his cigar for several seconds and then said something equally disturbing. 'Since we know they have been in Turkey for several weeks it seems an even stranger coincidence that they should choose this particular trip for returning to Greece. Don't you agree?'

'Several weeks? You know this? Is this why you are on board?' Burckhardt took a step towards Dietrich who regarded him without replying. 'They were supposed to have been saved from a ship which sank off the Turkish coast a few days ago . . .'

'What ship?' Dietrich pounced on the statement. 'Is this the story they have told you?'

'Yes, when Lieutenant Hahnemann was questioning them . . .'

'He has Intelligence training, this Hahnemann?' The ironic note was back in Dietrich's voice.

'No, but he is clever and he said their story rang true. The lieutenant – Prentice – told him this . . .'

'I have seen this British lieutenant,' the Abwehr man replied slowly and deliberately, 'and I would say he not only has his wits about him – he is also capable of making up a convincing story on the spur of the moment. I don't like the way the situation is developing, Colonel Burckhardt. You should have the two Englanders questioned again.'

Burckhardt's expression was remote. Under other circumstances, without the enormous responsibility of the expedition resting on his shoulders, he might have thought differently, and he had no way of knowing that he was confronted by a master of the art of psychological aggression. Without realizing it, he had been subjected to a kaleidoscope of changing impressions and anxieties from the moment he had entered the cabin, and during this ordeal he had subconsciously accepted the Abwehr man's credentials at face value. In fact, the subject of the identity of Dietrich had subtly been turned into questioning the identity of the British prisoners. He was also becoming a little worried about his own position. Had this devil been put aboard the *Hydra* to check up on the operation because it involved a naval phase – the seizure of the *Hydra* and its subsequent voyage to their objective! 'I'll get Hahnemann to have another word with the prisoners,' he said crisply.

'This Prentice, he speaks German, then?' Dietrich was staring through the porthole again as he asked the question.

'Not so far as I know – but Hahnemann speaks excellent English. I must leave for the bridge now.' He was talking again to Dietrich's back as the Abwehr man used his hand to smear a hole in the steamed-up glass. The temperature was probably at least thirty degrees higher inside the cabin than on the high seas.

'Did Hahnemann find out anything else when he was interrogating the prisoners?' Dietrich went on peering intently through the porthole and something in his attitude made the colonel wait a few seconds longer.

'I believe there was some mention of a British destroyer being in the area, but I'm convinced he was bluffing.'

'Bluffing!' Dietrich straightened up, swung round abruptly. 'First you talk about it being a coincidence that those men are aboard and now you hope he was bluffing! I'm afraid a very serious situation has arisen – a strange vessel is coming in fast from the north-east and unless I'm very much mistaken it is a British destroyer.'

Burckhardt turned to go quickly, and when Dietrich was left to his own devices he had, by default, been granted the privilege to roam round the vessel as freely as he wished.

Burckhardt was leaving the cabin when he very nearly collided with Hahnemann who was rushing down the companionway. Halting abruptly, the soldier saluted and spoke breathlessly. 'There's an emergency, sir. Lieutenant Schnell would like to see you on the bridge – it's very urgent . . .'

'I know!' Burckhardt was already pushing past him, heading for the staircase. Hard-faced young men of the Alpenkorps, fully uniformed, pressed themselves against the companionway wall with their rifles at their sides to let him pass. One man hastily extinguished a cigarette under his boot. The doorways to the three cabins recently occupied by the German passengers were open and inside more men of the Alpenkorps sat on the floors and leaned against the walls, their faces tense as they watched their colonel pass. The grapevine had worked already, reporting the rumour that a British destroyer was approaching fast. The whole atmosphere of the Greek ferry had changed, had become more akin to that of a troopship. Dodging round kit piled in the passage, Burckhardt made a mental note to get that shifted and then leapt up the staircase. Pushing open the door at the top he received a blast of cold wind and a douche of icy spray full in the face. Without even bothering to wipe himself he glanced quickly along the deserted, wave-washed deck. All the troops were under strict instructions to remain below decks and he was satisfied with the outward appearance of normality. Strange how the sea seemed far worse up here than down below. The thought flashed through his mind as he went into the wheelhouse.

Inside the enclosed area everything was quiet and there was a feeling of disciplined control, but under the silence Burckhardt sensed an atmosphere of nerves tautly strained as the *Hydra* ploughed on through mounting seas. Lieutenant Schnell of the German Navy, wearing inconspicuous dark trousers and a dark woollen sweater, was holdng the wheel while the ferry's captain, Nopagos, stood a few feet away with a signalling lamp in his hands. Behind him, crouched on his knees out of sight, an Alpenkorps soldier held a machine-pistol trained on the captain's back.

'Over there. To starboard.' It was the helmsman who had spoken, nodding his head towards the north east. Schnell was a typical German naval officer, round-faced, his dark hair neatly trimmed, a man of thirty with watchful eyes and a steady manner. Taking in the situation at a glance, Burckhardt accepted a pair of field-glasses from another soldier whose uniform was covered with a civilian raincoat. To starboard a slim grey silhouette was bearing down on the *Hydra*, a silhouette with lights at her masthead. Burckhardt focused the glasses on the ship and his lips tightened. Yes, it was a British destroyer sailing on an oblique course which would take her across the bows of the ferry within a mile or two. He handed back the glasses and moved into the shadows in case other glasses were aimed in his direction from that distant bridge. They wouldn't be able to pick out individuals yet, but within a few minutes they'd pick up all the detail they wanted if the destroyer maintained its present course. He spoke quickly to Schnell. 'What is Nopagos doing with that signalling lamp in his hands?'

'He will have to use it in a minute . . .'

'I don't like that.'

'We have no alternative.' Schnell had half-turned

round to stare at the oncoming warship. 'She is bound to signal us, so tell the Greek I understand the use of signals at sea.'

Burckhardt thought quickly. It was a damnable situation: the very existence of the expedition now depended on the signal-lamp in the hands of a Greek whose ship had just been shanghaied from under him. He saw the knuckles of Schnell's hands whiten under the overhead light as he gripped the wheel and steadily kept to his course. Still crouched on the floor, the Alpenkorps soldier with the machine-pistol moved gently with the sway of the ship, his face drawn with tension as he watched Burckhardt and then transferred his gaze to Nopagos' back. Burckhardt maintained his outward appearance of calm confidence, his hands thrust into his coat pockets, although inwardly his nerves were screwed up to fever pitch. He began speaking to Nopagos in his careful, Teutonic-sounding Greek.

'The British destroyer may start signalling. If that happens you only use your lamp when I give the order. I want you to understand this clearly – the man at the wheel is a German naval officer thoroughly conversant with signalling procedures. He will be watching. If you make any attempt to send a distress signal, we shall know. If there is an emergency we shall engage the British destroyer and we shall undoubtedly be sunk. I hope you realize that it is unlikely anyone will be saved in seas like this...' Without putting it in so many words he managed to convey that Nopagos' crew were hostages. He had just finished speaking when the moonlit wake of the oncoming destroyer became clearly visible. A few seconds later the door to the bridge opened and Dietrich came inside. Burckhardt swung round and turned away again when he saw who it was. Completely unruffled by his reception, the Abwehr man walked across to join the colonel after glancing at the approaching destroyer.

'It's probably just a routine check,' he remarked, 'but let's hope they are not expecting a signal from their friends locked up below.'

A nerve jumped by the side of Burckhardt's neck underneath his collar. Dietrich had hardly arrived before voicing the most alarming suggestion at this critical moment. He had just quietened his mind after the Abwehr man's remark when the door burst open again and Hahnemann strode onto the bridge with a furious expression. He had hesitated to stop Dietrich following Burckhardt up to the bridge but now felt he should keep an eye on him. Burckhardt turned on him instantly. 'Hide that gun you bloody fool – they may be watching the bridge. And while you're here – had either of those British soldiers any means of signalling in their possession?'

'No signalling lamp,' Hahnemann reassured him quickly. 'They definitely had no signalling equipment of any kind. The lieutenant, Prentice, had a revolver under his pillow. But nothing to send a message with.'

Burckhardt glanced at Dietrich with an expression-less face, but the Abwehr man was still studying

Hahnemann, who glared back at him defiantly. 'And no torch?' Dietrich queried in a deceptively mild tone. 'Not even a pocket torch?'

Hahnemann looked confused. He started to answer Dietrich, then his face stiffened and he addressed Burckhardt. 'One of them had a torch, yes, sir. It was inside the pocket of his coat hanging up behind the door.'

Dietrich caught Burckhardt's glance and he lifted his eyebrows in an expression of foreboding, then frowned at Schnell who had turned to say something. 'Here it comes, sir. They've started.' Across the swelling Aegean where the waves were growing higher a light began to wink on and off from the destroyer. Schnell had half-turned to starboard, his eyes fixed on the flashing lamp which went on with its brief explosions. On the bridge no one moved or spoke as all eyes were fixed hypnotically on the signalling light and Burckhardt could feel the stillness of men suspended in a state of horrible anticipation. So much depended on the next few minutes but Burckhardt had no intention of surrendering, whatever happened. He had had some experience of the devastating fire a British destroyer could lay down; in Norway he had seen a German troop transport reduced to a burning hulk by only a few salvoes. What those four-inch guns might do to the hull of the *Hydra* was something he preferred not to contemplate. The lamp stopped flashing and Schnell spoke.

'We are asked to identify ourselves.'

Burckhardt stood up a little straighter and gave Nopagos his instructions in Greek. 'Signal that we are the Greek ship *Hydra*. Nothing more. And remember that Lieutenant Schnell is a naval officer.'

The tension on the bridge was becoming almost unbearable, like a physical affliction. Nopagos wiped his lips and glanced behind to where the Alpenkorps man gazed straight at him, the muzzle of the machine-pistol aimed at the small of his back. Burckhardt nodded confidently without speaking, as much as to say get on with it. The captain adjusted his cap and started to flash the lamp while Schnell watched him coldly, his hands still on the wheel. To the colonel it seemed to take an age to send the short message. Was marine signalling really so complicated? Was Nopagos managing to trick Schnell while he inserted a desperate SOS among the jumble of flashes? A dozen appalling possibilities ran through his mind but he could do nothing but wait, hoping that his threat had struck home to the Greek. The lamp stopped flashing. Nopagos mopped the back of his neck with a coloured handkerchief as Schnell addressed Burckhardt over his shoulder.

'He has identified us simply as the *Hydra*, ownership Greek. Nothing more.'

With a supreme effort Burckhardt resisted the impulse to let his shoulders relax; both the Alpenkorps soldiers kept glancing towards him for reassurance. German soldiers, Burckhardt had noticed before, were never entirely happy at sea – the existence of the British Navy probably had something to do with their lack of enthusiasm for water-borne expeditions. He watched the destroyer still moving on her oblique course. Would her captain be satisfied with that signal? Just a routine check, Dietrich had suggested. But a moment later he had raised the unnerving suggestion that the two British soldiers might have been put on board deliberately – that the destroyer out there was expecting another flashing signal from a porthole confirming that all was well aboard the *Hydra*. Blast the Abwehr!

'They're signalling again!' Schnell spoke quietly, his eyes on the distant flashing light which was now less than a quarter of a mile away. Burckhardt stood quite still, resisting the impulse to pace up and down the bridge: it was vital at this moment to preserve an absolute outward calm. He felt that his feet had been glued to the deck for hours and God knew there were enough signs of tension on the bridge already. The signal-lamp in Nopagos' hands wobbled slightly – if he had to carry on answering these bloody questions much longer he was going to crack. The soldier crouched behind the Greek captain was sweating profusely, his forehead gleaming from the light over the bridge. Hahnemann was lightly tapping a nervous fingernail on the butt of his machine-pistol and Burckhardt wanted to roar at him for God's sake stop it! Schnell, a highly experienced naval officer, was still holding the wheel tightly. All these little details Burckhardt took in automatically while the lamp on the British destroyer blandly went on flashing its message. Only Dietrich seemed undisturbed, almost at ease as he stared at the ceiling with the unlit cigar motionless in the centre of his mouth. He dropped his eyes and caught the colonel watching him.

'There is a Greek called Grapos aboard,' Dietrich commented. 'I think he could be dangerous if he isn't watched carefully.'

'I dealt with him myself,' said Hahnemann in a flat tone. 'He was sleeping in the saloon – he had no cabin – and I was able to knock him out before he knew I was there. He's tied up in one of the holds.' The endless strain of waiting had neutralized his natural dislike of the Abwehr man and he looked at Dietrich without resentment.

'I do have this ship under control,' Burckhardt added icily.

'Perhaps it might be better if I went below,' Dietrich said almost amiably. He glanced to his left and saw that Hahnemann was leaving the bridge as a cloud of spray broke over the bows of the *Hydra*. When the lieutenant had gone there was a loaded silence as the light from the destroyer continued flashing, the ferry's engines went on throbbing heavily, and the sea heaved endlessly under them. After the winking light had stopped, Schnell cleared his throat twice before speaking. 'They wish us to report where we're from, our ultimate destination and the time of arrival.'

Without hesitation Burckhardt rapped out more instructions in Greek. 'Tell them we're bound from Istanbul, that our destination is Katyra, Zervos, and our estimated time of arrival 05.30 hours.' Nopagos blinked, glanced again at the sweating soldier behind him, took a firmer grip on the lamp and began signalling. The gun muzzles of the destroyer could be clearly seen in the moonlight as the vessel remorselessly continued on course without altering direction by as much as a single degree. Burckhardt found it unnerving – why was all this interest being shown in an ancient Greek ferry which spent its life plying between Istanbul and the remote peninsula of Zervos? He kept a tight grip on himself as Dietrich's rumbling voice spoke again behind his back. 'I'm wondering now whether this signalling isn't a smoke-screen put out until they get close to us. If they were expecting their own private signal from the prisoners below the course they are maintaining would make sense – they would keep on that course until they fired the first shot across our bows. Ten minutes should tell us the worst.' And having fired this last shot across the colonel's bows he quietly left the bridge and went out on deck.

Tight-lipped, Burckhardt heard him go, relieved that at long last the Abwehr man was leaving the bridge. But secretly Burckhardt agreed that Dietrich's estimate was just about right. In the next ten minutes they should know the worst.

Chapter Five

Sunday, April 6

As he struggled in the darkness with the ropes which bound his wrists, Prentice was bathed in sweat from his exertions. He lay in his bunk sprawled on his side, his ankles also tightly bound together while a further length of rope joined his wrists to his ankles, a rope drawn up so tautly that his knees were permanently bent. The fact that they had thought of turning out the cabin lights didn't help him either; it meant he had to work blindly by feel and this made ten times more difficult a task which already seemed insuperable. And because his hands were tied behind his back he had soon given up the attempt to fiddle with the knots he couldn't see, and a little later, when it struck him that they had probably used Alpenkorps climbing rope, he gave up his efforts to break the cords by stretching his wrists against them – a rope which could support a man dangling from a cliff face was hardly likely to weaken under the mere pressure of two straining wrists. So it seemed hopeless: a rope which couldn't be broken and which couldn't be untied. There was, however, one other alternative. Prentice was thin-boned and he had unusually slim wrists, so now he was concentrating all his strength on compressing his hands into the smallest possible area and then trying to pull them upwards through the loops which imprisoned him. His success to date had fallen rather short of the milder achievements of Houdini and for a few minutes he stopped struggling while he rested.

He was turned on his left side, facing inwards to the cabin, and while he rested he contented himself with straining to see the time by the light of the phosphorescent numerals of his watch on the table. Almost 12.10 AM so far as he could make out. In that case the guard would be looking in on them shortly – he checked the cabin every quarter-hour. With typical Teutonic punctuality he had, so far, arrived at precisely the quarter-hour. He lay listening for the sound of footsteps and heard only the distant murmur of voices. Twisting his head round, he called out in a loud whisper, 'All right, Ford?'

The sergeant, similarly bound in the next bunk, was just recovering from the pounding headache which had assailed him when he regained consciousness after the blow from Hahnemann's machine-pistol. From the sound of Prentice's voice he guessed that the lieutenant had enjoyed a less painful return to the land of the living, something which didn't entirely surprise him when he recalled Prentice's speedy recovery from a hangover after a night of Turkish hospitality. He wet his lips before replying. 'Fine and dandy, sir. We'll have to sue the *Hydra*'s owners for damages when we arrive back.'

Prentice grinned in the darkness. 'We might just do that, laddie. Now, the guard'll be looking in any minute, so pretend you're still out cold.'

'Got it, sir.' The faint hammering inside his brain was sending waves of dizziness through Ford, a sensation which wasn't improved by the Aegean waves outside which regularly lifted the ship and tilted the cabin with an unpleasant rolling motion. Combined with his dizziness, Ford had the feeling that he was turning over and over and over. It cost him a certain effort to make his inquiry. 'Making any progress, sir?'

'A bit,' Prentice lied cheerfully, 'but not enough yet. I think they used steel hawser cable to truss us up.' He checked his watch again. Nearly a quarter past twelve. Was the guard going to be late this time? The curtains were closed over the porthole so the cabin was in almost total darkness except for the light seeping in from the door which was not quite closed. He found that slightly ajar door tantalizing – for all the use the unlocked door was to Prentice at the moment it might have been locked and bolted on the outside. But it did give him warning of the guard's approach as he proceeded with his unvarying patrol. After he had entered the cabin to make his quick check on the prisoners he continued his slow tread along the companionway and Prentice, who had exceptional hearing, found previously that he was able to follow the tramp of the retreating boots and their progress up the distant staircase which ended with the thud of a door closing. So his sentry-go also took in the open deck aloft, God help him. But for Prentice this made sense – the German commander, knowing there was little risk of an emergency while they were on board, was conserving his manpower, letting his troops rest as best they could before morning. Prentice lifted his head, then called out quickly, 'Here he comes!'

The Alpenkorps guard reached the door and reacted with his normal caution, switching on the light and entering the cabin with his rifle levelled. He stood there for a moment, watching the two inert bodies, then peered round the cabin to make sure that it was empty. As he left he switched off the light and closed the door firmly. Lying on his bunk, Prentice used a little army language worthlessly – now he couldn't hear the basket marching away and, more to the point, he wouldn't be able to hear him coming back again. Gritting his teeth, he renewed the struggle to free himself, pushing down his left hand to hold the rope taut while he compressed his right hand and pulled upwards, wriggling a wrist which was now moist with sweat. The moisture might help, might eventually make it a little easier to slip his wrist upwards out of that biting rope. To give himself extra leverage he pressed his bound feet against the side of the bunk, breathing heavily as he strained desperately at the rope. Five minutes later he lay limp and exhausted by his exertions, taking in great breaths of muggy air as he summoned up his strength for a renewed onslaught. The cabin seemed to be tilting more steeply now and the woodwork was groaning as though the timbers might give under the enormous pressure of the sea. The effort to free himself had been so great that his head was beginning to ache badly and he felt that he had a steel band drawn round his temples. A light flashed briefly and he bit his lips. God, this is no time to black-out. A second later he lay still as a dead man, his heart pounding with excitement. That flash of light hadn't been his eyes playing him tricks. The light had flashed from the companionway as someone opened and closed the door soundlessly. *Someone had come inside the cabin!*

Fear. Uncertainty. Growing alarm. The emotions darted across his fatigued brain as he continued to lie quite still, straining his ears, trying to accustom his eyes to the darkness quickly. The trouble was that damned sentry lighting up the cabin had taken away his night sight for a few minutes and he wished he hadn't watched him through half-closed eyes. Had Ford also realized what had happened – that some unknown person had crept inside their cabin with uncanny silence? He had no idea. His ears had still provided no evidence that there was someone else present but instinctively Prentice knew that they were no longer alone. He found the stillness unnerving, the creaking of the ship ominous, and the thought that someone who moved like a ghost was approaching him terrifying. His mind was strained, his nerves strung up to fever pitch with their recent experiences, and now a nightmare idea flooded over him – someone had been sent in to kill them quietly. A knife in the chest, then a swift despatch overboard into the Aegean. Feverishly his imagination worked it out: the German commander might not want his unit to know about an episode like this, or perhaps there was an SS section aboard. Lying helpless in the darkness, his nerves close to breaking-point, he foresaw the next step – the hand coming out of the darkness to feel over his chest, finding the right place, the upheld hand striking downwards with one savage thrust. Keep a grip on yourself, for Christ's sake, Prentice . . . His heart jumped, his throat went dry, he felt he was choking – now he could see something, a shadow which had interposed itself between the bunk and the phosphorescent hands of his watch on the table. The intruder was feet away, standing beside his bunk, looking down at him. He tried to call out, but croaked instead, a sound like a bullfrog. A hand touched his cheek and he jerked involuntarily.

'Keep quiet! Listen!'

Prentice was stunned, lay absolutely still with sheer shock. The voice had spoken in English with a distinct Scots burr. He swallowed quickly and kept his voice down to little more than a whisper.

'Who is it?'

The voice ignored the question, speaking in an urgent Morse-code fashion. 'Keep still! I have a knife . . . I'll cut the ropes on your hands . . . a British destroyer is close . . .' Prentice felt cold steel between his wrists, stiffening the rope as the knife began to saw the fibres apart. '. . . at the back of the ship is a raft . . . use the knife to cut it free . . . when the raft is on the sea and you are away from the ship . . .' The knife sawed steadily, one of the ropes snapped. '. . . you send up a distress light . . . they're on the raft . . .' Another rope snapped as Prentice pulled his hands away from each other to increase the tension on the remaining rope. He spoke quickly.

'I ought to know who you are – I may be able to help you later . . .'

'Shut up!' The knife was sawing more slowly now and Prentice realized that the man who was freeing him was taking care the knife didn't jab into him as the last rope snapped. The voice went on speaking. 'The distress light will be seen . . . by the destroyer . . . but Burckhardt won't dare shoot at you since that will warn the destroyer something's wrong . . .' Prentice felt the last rope part, freeing his hands, then heard the measured tramp of an Alpenkorps guard approaching along the companionway, the boots clumping dully on the wood.

He froze, his feet still tied. It wasn't time, not nearly time, for the guard to check on them. The intruder had entered the cabin soon after the guard had left – deliberately so. Prentice had already grasped that. So had the guard changed his routine? He was going to enter the cabin and catch him with his hands free – and catch this unknown helper in the act. The guard's tread was closer now, was slowing down prior to switching on the light and coming inside. Another thought struck Prentice and he felt a shiver run through his body since he could hear the guard coming the door must be slightly open. Yes, it was! A thin line of light showed round the door frame. The intruder hadn't closed the door properly and the swaying of the ship had opened it wider. Lying quite still in the darkness, Prentice realized that they were finished. The guard had closed the door last time, so when he noticed that it was open, and even if he hadn't intended coming in this time ... He wondered what the feelings of the unknown Scot were who was waiting with them in the unlit cabin without making a sound. He still had the knife – would he use it on one of his own men? Would he even get the chance? That partly opened door would alert the guard and he'd come inside prepared for anything. Lying back on the bunk, he turned himself sideways and hid his hands, hoping they would still look to be roped up. Another huge wave caught the vessel, thudding against the hull with such force that he felt it was coming through. A second later he heard a further thud outside in the companionway and a muttered oath in German. The wave had caught the guard off-balance. Bathed in sweat, his heart pounding solidly, he waited and listened. For a moment there was a drawn-out silence, followed by a metallic click. The guard cocking his weapon? Prentice had a fierce impulse to call out a warning, but he kept his mouth closed, then heard the tread of the guard's footsteps again just beyond the cabin door. He had turned his head sideways now, his eyes almost closed as he watched the entrance for the first shaft of light which would tell him the door was being opened. Then he heard more footsteps coming along the companionway, brisk footsteps which hurried. He could imagine the scene clearly – the guard noticing the door which should have been closed, his beckoning to a comrade who was hurrying along the passage to join him. Then the two of them would burst inside the cabin and it would be all over. The hurrying footsteps stopped outside the door and voices were raised in German. Prentice knew a little German, but not enough to speak it, and they were talking too rapidly for him to grasp what they were saying. Perhaps the new arrival was the sentry who normally checked their cabin? His mind was still grappling with possibilities when he heard feet hurrying away along the passage, followed by the deliberate tread of the sentry's footsteps as he also proceeded into the distance and up the staircase. A door thudded shut. Both men had gone.

'You must cut the ropes on your feet yourself...' The voice of the unknown man spoke quickly again. 'There's a coat and cap on the floor ... you turn left when you leave the cabin ... hurry!'

The knife had already been placed on Prentice's leg and he was working on the ropes round his ankles when light flooded briefly into the cabin and then the door closed again. Prentice looked up quickly but he was too late – he saw no more than the departure of a shadow as the intruder disappeared. While he was sawing at the ropes the ship began to roll more violently, the angle of the cabin's tilt increasing steadily.

They were moving into dirty weather. Behind him he heard a creak inside Ford's bunk and the sergeant's voice was a careful whisper. 'Who the devil was that?'

'God knows, but the Scots accent was unmistakable. He must be a stowaway.' Prentice was free now and he nearly stumbled full length as the vessel rose abruptly while he was feeling his way across the darkened cabin. He'd have to risk a light – there had been a fierce urgency in the intruder's final words and in less than fifteen minutes the sentry would be back. And this time he would come inside their cabin. Switching on the light, he noted that the door was firmly closed, then ran across to Ford's bunk. He used his knife to cut the ropes as he talked. 'We've got to get on that raft and away from this ship pdq. Then we can loose off a signal to that destroyer . . .' Ford was rubbing the circulation back into his wrists when Prentice tried on the coat which had been dropped on the floor. An Alpenkorps greatcoat, it was a little too long and fitted loosely across the shoulders, but he thought it might serve. The soft, large-peaked cap was also ill-fitting but he settled it on his head as the sergeant looked at him.

'You're the spitting image of a Jerry,' Ford informed him. 'And your face fits, too.'

'Thanks very much . . .' Prentice was moving towards the door, the knife concealed inside his pocket. 'I'll walk on the left – you keep to my right. That way I'll try and cover you if any cabin doors are open.' Switching off the light, he paused while he listened with his ear pressed to the inner side of the door. He thought he understood now the restless wakefulness of those murmuring voices he had heard earlier – if the Alpenkorps men below decks knew of the destroyer's presence that would be more than enough to spoil their beauty sleep. It also meant that they were likely to be alert, which would make their walk along that companionway a hundred times more dangerous. He whispered to Ford quickly. 'Here we go. If anyone calls out to us we just keep moving as though we haven't heard. Now!' Opening the door quietly, he peered out. The passage was deserted in both directions. He walked straight out, closed the door behind them, and began walking down the companionway with Ford at his side.

The first cabin door was half-open and before he had reached it he heard voices speaking in German. He walked at a steady pace, not too quickly, not too slowly, staring ahead as they drew level with the doorway. Out of the corner of his eye he had a glimpse of a smoke-filled cabin, a blur of uniformed bodies, and then they had passed it. Maintaining the same pace, Prentice kept his eyes fixed on the distant staircase where a pile of army packs lay huddled near the lowest tread. The next cabin door was also open, wide open. Smoke drifted into the companionway as the vessel heeled violently and Ford had to grab at the rail to save his balance. Prentice briefly slowed his pace while the sergeant caught up. That had been lucky – if it had happened opposite the open cabin door, Ford, dressed in British civilian clothes, would have been completely exposed to view. Prentice's mind was coldly alert as they came close to the doorway. From inside he could hear more animation, the sound of raucous laughter as a voice ended in a shout. Someone telling a story, he guessed. One Alpenkorps soldier, his fair hair cut to a stubble, lounged inside with his shoulder resting on the door frame and his back turned towards the companionway. Prentice kept walking forward and as he began to walk past the doorway another burst of laughter echoed inside the cabin. An NCO stood in the middle of the room, half-turned away from the doorway, waving his hands as he pantomimed something. An energetic attempt to keep up morale, Prentice was thinking, something to take the minds of the men off that destroyer outside in the night. But he thought the laughter was a little forced and short-lived. The main thing was it concentrated attention inside the cabin as they walked past it. Only one more cabin to pass, and the door was closed.

Then they were walking past the door and within a few paces of the staircase. At the foot of the steps Ford glanced down, saw inside a German army pack which had its flap drawn back. With his interest in explosives he paused involuntarily as he saw the demolition charge and the timing mechanisms. By his side Prentice sensed the pause and grasped his arm, urging him upwards without a word. The lieutenant was mounting the steps when the bows of the *Hydra* plunged downwards, elevating the staircase in his face so suddenly that he nearly fell over backwards, tightening his grip on the rail just in time. Half-way up, he looked quickly back along the companionway as he continued climbing. It was still deserted.

When he pushed open the door at the top it was almost torn from his grasp by the force of the wind. He waited until Ford was safely on deck, then used both hands to close it without a slamming noise. With the howl of the wind and the heavy slap of heaving water it seemed a needless precaution, but the thud of a door closing is a special sound and that guard might be somewhere on deck. The water-washed deck gleamed in the moonlight and beyond the funnel to port a burst of spray exploded near the rail. With Ford motionless at his side Prentice scanned the deck which seemed to be deserted. A moment later a gust of wind whipped the ill-fitting Alpenkorps cap from his head and blew it into the sea. He had lost the most distinctive part of his disguise. He looked to starboard and was staggered to see how close the destroyer was steaming, frowning when he saw the signal lamp flashing. Was she calling on the *Hydra* to heave-to? With a very slight turn of his head he looked towards the stern and saw the raft waiting for them, its canvas cover drawn back, and by the light of the moon he could see the rescue loops hanging from its sides and bobbing with the *Hydra*'s motion.

The raft had been covered with the canvas when he had last seen it and he hadn't recognized what the cover concealed. If it really carried distress lights they might just make it, might attract the destroyer's attention and be picked up. Not that he was too enthusiastic about the prospect of being aboard that tiny craft in seas like these. The whole surface of the Aegean was heaving up in a series of mountainous crests which raced towards the ferry with an insidious gliding movement as though intent on overwhelming it. He was about to make his way towards the raft, waiting for a moment when the ferry was pulling itself out of one of the great rolling dips, when he caught a brief twitch of a shadow to starboard beyond the funnel. The shadow of a huge man wearing a soft hat and standing close to a swaying lifeboat. Putting a warning hand on Ford's sleeve, Prentice kept perfectly still. It was the big German who had come aboard as a passenger at Istanbul. From the way he was standing he appeared to be talking to someone who was out of sight under the wall of the bridge. Go away, Prentice prayed. Get lost! The German began to move, to turn in his direction.

'Italian mines have been sown in the Gulf of Zervos.' This latest signal from the destroyer should have reassured Burckhardt but it sent a chill through him.

It should have reassured him because the destroyer's commander had sent the captain of the *Hydra* a friendly warning; but instead he was appalled. The passage from the narrow entrance to Katyra, at the head of the gulf, was a distance of twenty miles, and the prospect of sailing twenty miles at night through mine-strewn waters was not an experience he contemplated with great enthusiasm. Mechanically, he ordered Nopagos to signal a message of thanks to the destroyer while inwardly he cursed his allies. In the interests of security the Italian High Command had been given no warning of the Zervos operation, but it was the most fiendish luck that on this night of all nights they should suddenly decide to sow mines from the air in the vital gulf. This, he told himself grimly, is going to be a voyage to remember.

'Go down and have the British prisoners escorted to my cabin.'

He gave the instruction to the soldier not preoccupied with guarding Nopagos, his eyes still on the warship as the soldier left the bridge. There might be something in what that damnably arrogant Abwehr man had hinted at . . . His thought broke off as Nopagos completed signalling and stood waiting with a resigned look on his face as the destroyer sent a short series of flashes in reply. Yes, Burckhardt decided, it was a good idea to have the British prisoners questioned again, but this time he would let his second-in-command, Major Eberhay, undertake the interrogation. Like Lieutenant Hahnemann, Eberhay also spoke English.

'They wish us *bon voyage*!' Schnell was unable to keep the relief and exultation out of his voice.

Burckhardt could hardly believe it, but the feeling of salvation which flooded over him did not affect his judgement. He issued the warning swiftly to Schnell. 'Be sure to maintain exactly the same course and speed – it may be a trick to test our reaction.' He switched to speaking in Greek. 'Captain Nopagos, kindly stay exactly where you are until I give you further orders.' From the destroyer they would easily be able to see the *Hydra*'s bridge, Burckhardt was thinking as he remained in the shadows, and if the British commander were shrewd his glasses would at this moment be focused on the ferry's bridge. He watched the destroyer's course without too much hope and inside his coat pocket his hands were clenched tight. Had they really got away with it?

'She's still on course.' It was Schnell who had spoken and the note of anxiety had crept back into his voice. With an expressionless face Burckhardt continued to stare at the warship as more steam emerged from her funnel and she began to change course for the north-west. Incredibly, they had got away with it. Speaking a word of congratulation to Schnell, he left the bridge and went down the staircase in time to meet Major Eberhay who was at the foot of the steps. Behind him strolled Dietrich and behind the Abwehr man Hahne-mann was running along the companionway towards them. Several Alpenkorps soldiers were moving away in the opposite direction. 'What's the matter?' he asked Eberhay.

'The British prisoners have escaped . . .'

'They were tied up!'

'We are searching now,' Eberhay explained crisply, his manner quite unruffled. 'Put two more men on the bridge,' he told Hahnemann, who issued an order, summoning two soldiers from the nearby cabin and then going up the staircase as they followed him. 'And I have met Herr Dietrich,' he went on as Burckhardt appeared to be on the verge of saying something, 'we have been discussing the British destroyer . . .'

'It's turning away . . .' Burckhardt began.

'You are sure?' Dietrich interjected.

Eberhay stared up curiously at the Abwehr man as Burckhardt stood on the bottom stair and glared at Dietrich with a look of thunder. More troops were filing out of the cabins under the orders of Sergeant Volber who was instructing several to search the engine-room, to mount a double guard on the wireless operator's quarters, but not to go out on the open deck yet. Volber would take a small section to the deck himself.

Dietrich was facing the colonel bleakly, not at all disconcerted by Burckhardt's attitude. 'I heard of a similar case,' he told them. 'One of our merchant ships off Norway raised the Argentinian flag as a British destroyer approached. The warship turned away as you say this one is doing now. But it made a complete circle and came up unexpectedly on the stern of the ship and boarded her before the sea-cocks could be opened. So the danger may only be starting.' Burckhardt stood quite still on the step, his feeling of relief ebbing away; he remembered the incident this damned Abwehr man had just recalled. Dietrich turned to Eberhay without waiting for a reply. 'So, if you don't mind, I'll come on deck with you and see what that ship is doing.'

Burckhardt said nothing as he walked past them,

heading for his cabin while Dietrich followed the major up the staircase, turning up his coat collar when they reached the deck. A guard stationed permanently outside the door stood to attention as Eberhay went briskly to the bridge. Inside he noted that Hahnemann had stationed two more soldiers in the rear away from the light and stared with keen interest at the destroyer as Dietrich joined him.

'It will be an hour before we know whether they've really gone,' Dietrich commented as he looked at Eberhay. The contrast between the two men was startling. Whereas Dietrich was easily the largest man aboard the *Hydra*, Eberhay was small and lightly built, his face lean and alert as a fox's and his manner almost dandified. In his early thirties, he wore over his uniform a civilian raincoat belted close to his slim waist. The name sounded Hungarian in origin, Dietrich reflected, and there was certainly Balkan blood in his veins. Which probably accounted for the air of intelligence and sophistication which radiated from him.

'The escape of the prisoners is unfortunate,' Eberhay remarked, offering his cigarette case, 'but we shall soon find them.' Dietrich shook his head, noting that the contents were Turkish as he extracted his own case and took out a cigar. Eberhay lit the cigar for him as he stooped low to reach the match. 'I'm going on deck now to supervise the search.'

'It is the manner of their escape which is more than unfortunate – it could be catastrophic,' the Abwehr man observed.

THE HEIGHTS OF ZERVOS

Eberhay glanced sharply up at him and then, without replying, made his way onto the open deck followed by Dietrich. As they arrived in the open the *Hydra* plunged its bows into a massive wave and a torrent of spray drenched them. Dodging close to the starboard side of the funnel, Eberhay mopped his face with a silk handkerchief. Dietrich had also moved and now he was standing by a swaying lifeboat where he caught the full blast of the icy wind. He had to pull his hat down tight over his large head and on another man the compressed hat might have looked absurd, but on this man, Eberhay reflected, it only emphasized an air of physical menace which seemed to emanate from him.

'Your name suggests a Balkan heritage,' Dietrich rumbled, switching unexpectedly to an entirely different topic.

'My grandfather moved from Budapest to Munich last century,' Eberhay replied stiffly and a little uncomfortably. 'The family has been entirely German since then.' Something about Dietrich suggested to the sensitive Eberhay a whiff of the Gestapo, and he was reminding himself to mention this to Burckhardt when he saw two Alpenkorps soldiers slip past on the port side, their bodies crouched low as they made their way towards the stern. Dietrich had turned and was also looking towards the stern as though something had caught his attention, then he turned away again, and a moment later they heard one of the Alpenkorps call out.

Eberhay ran forward, saw two men standing near
the raft as the Alpenkorps soldiers charged along the
deck and within seconds a furious struggle had begun.
Prentice found himself thrown back against the rail,
temporarily winded. A clenched fist scraped his jaw as
he jerked his head aside and lifted one knee. The soldier
twisted to avoid the thrust, lost his balance and Prentice
crashed down on top of him, his right hand reaching
for the man's throat. But the German foresaw the attack
again and buried his head in his chest to ward off the
hand, trying to grab blindly for the lieutenant's hair.
They fought ineffectually for a short time and then
Prentice tore himself loose from the soldier's grasp and
jumped up as though fleeing. The German came to his feet
confidently, ran forward and received Prentice's aimed
shoe on the point of his kneecap. He was doubling up
as his opponent crashed into him and rammed him
against the rail. Prentice had used the natural tilt of the
vessel to port to give him added momentum and now
the German was half-spreadeagled over the side as the
vessel went on dropping to port, lifting the German
over the rail. Scooping his arm under the German's
crooked legs he hoisted and the soldier went over the
side head first into the heaving sea. Eberhay had seen
the danger and had run forward with his pistol held by
the barrel to club Prentice. He himself had earlier given
the order that under no circumstances must there be
shots fired which might alert the destroyer which now
presented its stern to the *Hydra*. Eberhay was close to

the lieutenant when he slipped on a wet patch and sprawled headlong on the deck. In front of the funnel he saw running men as he lifted his head. 'Volber!' he shouted and then dropped his head just in time to escape Prentice's aimed shoe. Volber and two other men were struggling with Prentice while Ford still fought on the deck with the other Alpenkorps soldier as Eberhay looked quickly over the side. The seething waves had swallowed up the man who had gone overboard and there was no sign of him amid the churning crests.

In less than a minute both Prentice and Ford had been overpowered and were being taken along the deck with their arms pinioned behind them. Eberhay had warned Volber that they were wanted for questioning and that they must be looked after carefully, a necessary precaution after one of their comrades had been thrown overboard. Accidents could happen so easily and he didn't want Prentice tripped and thrown down the full length of the staircase. When he turned round, Dietrich was supporting his balance with a hand against a ventilator while he stared at the raft as though it might be alive.

'They almost got away,' were his first words.

'But they didn't . . .' Eberhay was unsure how to reply. The remark infuriated him since Dietrich seemed completely unconcerned that one of their men had just drowned.

'Three more minutes and they'd have been over the

side,' the Abwehr man growled. He glared at Eberhay as though it were all his fault. 'And you wouldn't have dared open fire for fear you warned that destroyer.'

Eberhay rubbed his bruised hands with his silk handkerchief, almost lost balance again as the deck started to rise, then leant against the ventilator. The trend of Dietrich's remarks greatly disturbed him: he had heard that the Abwehr's chief, Canaris, had such a contempt for soldiers that he refused to allow any man who wore a military decoration to enter his office. It looked very much as though his aide shared his chief's views of the Wehrmacht. It had been a most unfortunate incident and the only officer present had been Eberhay himself. He tried flattery. 'You took a risk yourself coming out into the open like that.'

'So far as I could see they had no guns. I am not interested in displays of courage, Major Eberhay,' he went on bitingly. 'My usefulness to the Reich lies in staying alive as long as I can. Considering what has happened I must have a word with Colonel Burckhardt immediately.' He looked across the Aegean in a westerly direction. 'There are certain things which must be cleared up before we reach the entrance to the Gulf of Zervos. Have you ever made this trip before? No? It will be an experience for you – going into the gulf through that narrow entrance on such a night will be like entering the gates of hell.'

Chapter Six

Sunday, AM

At 2.50 AM the *Hydra* was steaming into the eye of the storm as seas of unimaginable violence began to take hold of her. The hull shuddered under the impact of the seventy-mile-an-hour wind, the bows of the vessel climbed a rolling wall of water, a Niagara of spray burst in the air and was flung against the window of the bridge with hammering force, blinding their view for several seconds. To stay upright, Burckhardt gripped the rail tightly as he watched the mighty waves swarming in endless succession towards the ship from Cape Zervos, waves which seethed and heaved with a dizzying motion, advancing relentlessly as though bent on the ship's destruction. Close to the colonel stood his shadow, Dietrich, his hat jammed low over his head and an unlit cigar between his lips. A few feet in front of Burckhardt the wheel was held by Schnell, standing with his legs apart and braced, the strain showing in his stooped shoulders, while to his right Nopagos, his face lined and drawn, held onto the rail as he gazed fixedly ahead. Turning, he spoke quickly to Burckhardt, his manner so harsh that for a moment it seemed the Greek had once more resumed command of his own ship.

COLIN FORBES

'We must wait till morning – if you continue you will wreck us on the rocks.'

'For the sake of your crew you must see that does not happen.'

Burckhardt answered decisively but his outwardly determined attitude did not reflect his thoughts. The view from the bridge was quite terrifying; although the moon was fading there was still sufficient light to see what lay before them as a series of menacing shadows, and to the north-east the cliffs of the peninsula soared up into the night towards the three-thousand-foot summit of Mount Zervos. As the *Hydra* straddled the crest of another giant roller Burckhardt was able briefly to see the entrance to the gulf, a gap between the shadows so frighteningly narrow that from a distance it seemed as though the hull of the ship might well scrape both sides of the bottleneck. The bows plunged downwards into a fresh trough, the view was lost, and Burckhardt comforted himself with the thought that distance across water at night was doubly deceptive. So when they came closer the entrance must widen, even comfortably so, if that was a word which could be used under such turbulent conditions. Schnell, who didn't understand a word of Greek, asked the colonel what Nopagos had said.

'He wants us to wait until morning. I have said no.'

Dietrich noted that Schnell made no reply to this and he suspected that the German naval officer secretly agreed with Nopagos, who was acting as pilot. But

Burckhardt would continue on course, he was sure of this, and his assumption was correct. The colonel was in an impossible dilemma: he was compelled to maintain the pre-arranged timetable, to land the expedition at Katyra by dawn. Under no circumstances could there be any possibility of turning back or waiting – his key force had a vital role to play in a far more gigantic operation and play it they must, whatever happened. Or perish in the attempt. And as Burckhardt stared from the bridge it seemed highly likely that they might indeed perish – his staff and the two hundred Alpenkorps troops huddled below decks.

The men on the bridge wore life-jackets – a precaution which Nopagos had insisted on – and the troops below were also similarly protected. But to Dietrich, as he surveyed the way ahead, the precaution seemed futile. If they struck the cliffs the *Hydra* would be pounded to pieces and no one could hope to survive in the boiling waters which surrounded them. As the vessel climbed again, breasting a further crest, he saw with appalling clarity – even through the foam-flecked window of the bridge – the mouth of the gulf, a rock-bound narrows which would require skilful seamanship in the calmest of seas in broad daylight, but at three in the morning, at the height of an Aegean storm, Schnell was going to have to take the ship on a course which most Greek sailors would have pronounced suicidal. And the weather was definitely deteriorating.

Eberhay stood a few feet away to the Abwehr man's left, and he stood so quietly and inconspicuously, almost like a wraith, that once Dietrich had looked to see if he were still there. He was watching the grim spectacle with interest and it might have been assumed he was nerveless, but in that earlier glance Dietrich had noticed a gleam of sweat across the small man's forehead. He made his remark to the major, knowing that Burckhardt was bound to hear him. 'If the vessel founders we mustn't forget that Greek tied up in the hold.'

'The guard has his instructions,' Eberhay replied. 'In the event of an emergency he will bring Grapos on deck. I gave the order myself.'

Burckhardt pretended not to have heard the exchange but the muscles across his stomach tightened a shade and he cursed the Abwehr man silently. 'If the vessel founders . . .' '. . . in the event of an emergency.' The phrases pointed up dramatically the desperate course of action he was committed to and he found the reminders unpleasant. Despite the hardening experiences of war Burckhardt was now frightened as he realized that the storm was growing worse. The deck rocked under his feet, the engines throbbed with the agonized vibration of machinery strained to the limit, and the howl of the gale was rising to a shriek. If they weren't careful the ferry was going to slip out of control. He could feel the tension reacting across his shoulder-blades from standing erect in one position, but he remained standing like a statue, determined to give an example of fortitude, compelling himself to watch the rise and fall of the sea which was going up and down like a lift. Yes, conditions were much worse, dangerously so. Beyond the bridge the world was a series of shifting shadows, shallow mountain peaks of sea which were now soaring and surging high above the *Hydra*'s masthead as the ship sank into another trough. It was weird and nerve-shattering – to see the waves jostling all around and high above them, dark, sliding slopes of water which might overwhelm them at any moment. He had a horrible feeling that exactly this could happen – the sea closing over them as the ferry capsized and plunged down to the floor of the Aegean. Then, once more, the ship seemed to gather itself to mount wearily and falteringly yet another glassy slope as it dragged itself up out of the depths. At the very moment when he least wanted it, he heard Dietrich speaking again.

'Nopagos could be right – we may end up as a wreck on the rocks.'

'That is a chance we must take. Personally, I am confident that Schnell will take us through.' Burckhardt paused, struggling to control his sudden rage. He had purposely left out that remark of Nopagos' when relaying what the Greek had said to Schnell, and it infuriated him that Dietrich should have repeated it for all to hear. But in spite of the immense pressure, the almost unbearable responsibility resting on his shoulders, Burckhardt's brain was still working and he had registered something he hadn't previously known.

'You understand Greek, then?' he asked abruptly.

'Perfectly. I speak it fluently – rather more fluently than yourself, incidentally.' Dietrich's tone of voice became scathing, a tone of voice which prickled the colonel's raw nerves. 'Why the devil do you think they chose me for this trip – one of the first qualifications, surely, is a mastery of Greek?'

'Any other languages?' It was just something to say and Burckhardt wasn't in the least interested in the reply.

'Yes, French. I don't anticipate being able to employ that particular talent on this voyage.' He spoke banteringly and his brief outburst seemed forgotten. This was another aspect of the Abwehr man's character which Burckhardt found so disconcerting: his moods changed with astonishing swiftness and kept you off-balance. He stiffened as Nopagos turned and spoke urgently, his eyes pleading.

'There is still time to change your mind – but you must decide now.'

'We are entering the gulf at the earliest possible moment. It is your duty to see that we make safe passage. For the sake of your crew, if for no other reason.'

Nopagos' manner altered. He stood up very straight and stared directly at the German with an authoritative expression. 'In that case we must change course. There is a dangerous cross-current from the east we must allow for if we are not to pile up on the rocks to the west. Tell your wheelsman . . .'

Burckhardt relayed the instructions automatically in

German, instructions which he didn't understand completely and which he mistrusted. Nopagos had given the incredible order that they must steer straight for the cliffs of Zervos and the strangeness of the order raised an entirely fresh spectre in Burckhardt's already anxiety-laden mind. Quietly, he tried to resolve the fear before it was too late. Nopagos was undoubtedly a Greek patriot – his whole attitude had confirmed this to Burckhardt hours earlier – so to what lengths might he go to prevent the *Hydra* and its cargo of Alpenkorps troops ever reaching Katyra? Would he deliberately wreck his own vessel on those fearsome cliffs? He had a crew of his own countrymen aboard but would this prevent him from taking action which could only end in the death of every man aboard? Like Dietrich, Burckhardt was secretly under no illusion as to the chances of survival if the ship went down. If anything, they were less than they might have been ten minutes ago. It all depended on the inscrutable mind of one middle-aged Greek.

'There *is* a cross-current.' It was Dietrich who had spoken and now Burckhardt could feel the first signs of the ship heeling from starboard to port. The *Hydra*, its overstrained engines thumping heavily, began to move chaotically in the churning seas, like a gyroscope out of control. Sick with dread, Burckhardt watched Schnell struggling with the wheel to keep the vessel on the nightmarish course Nopagos had dictated, a course which seemed to have no direction at all as the ferry wallowed amid the inferno of near-tidal high waves rolling in all directions as the cross-current grew stronger. Soon the ship was being driven two ways – forward by the labouring engines and sideways by the powerful current from the east. Then for several minutes they suffered the illusion that they were making no progress – until the illusion was shattered in a particularly terrifying manner. Burckhardt had been under the impression that great bursts of spray in the near-distance were the product of huge waves colliding with each other and disintegrating, but as the spray settled briefly he saw an immense shadow rising in the night and knew that he was staring at the almost vertical rock face of the towering cliffs which barred their way. The surf was exploding at the base of the cliffs as the waves destroyed themselves against the barrier. Horror-struck, he heard Dietrich's voice close to his ear, a low rumble like a knell of doom. 'I estimate we are six hundred metres from them . . .' The *Hydra* reached the crest of a wave and now they were near enough to see huge billows shattering against the awful monolith of rock, sending up blurred spray which rose a good hundred feet above the gyrating crests of the Aegean far below. Burckhardt felt a constriction of the throat as he gazed with fascination at the spectacle – the rock face rearing upwards, the spurs at its base momentarily exposed as the sea receded, the lift of the *Hydra*'s bows, so close now that with their next fall it seemed they must ram down on that immovable rock base. And from the heaving bridge they could hear a new, sinister sound – the boom of the sea as it drove against the massive bastion of the headland. For the first time Burckhardt felt compelled to speak, to voice a navigational question. He had to lift his voice so that Schnell, still crouched over the wheel, could hear him above the shrieking wind and the steady roar of sea breaking against the cliff face.

'What's gone wrong? We're nearly on top of Cape Zervos!'

Schnell made no reply, didn't even turn round as Burckhardt took a step forward, grabbing Nopagos tightly by the arm as he spoke harshly in Greek, trying to trap the man into an admission by the suddenness of his approach. 'We're too close, aren't we? You've done it deliberately . . .'

Nopagos stood perfectly still, his body frozen rigid under the German's grip. As he turned to gaze directly at the colonel, Hahnemann arrived on the bridge, slamming the door shut behind him and then waiting. Nopagos spoke with dignity. 'You think I would destroy my own men? Because you are a soldier you think you are the only one with responsibilities?' He looked down at the gloved hand which held his forearm. 'You are hurting me, Colonel. This is no moment to panic. You must leave it to Schnell – or hand over the wheel to me.' Burckhardt relaxed his grip, let go, his eyes still on the Greek's face. No hint of triumph, no suggestion of treachery in those steady eyes; only a touch of resignation. Burckhardt was unmoved by the suggestion that his nerve was going – it was immaterial to him at this moment what Nopagos thought so long as he got the truth out of the man. And he believed him. The tilt of the deck almost threw him clear across the bridge as the *Hydra* heeled over again, but the soldier who was guarding Nopagos saved him. Holding firmly onto the rail Burckhardt listened while Hahnemann reported that all was well below but more than half the unit was sea-sick. As Hahnemann spoke Burckhardt was waiting for the first grind and shudder as the ferry struck. The lieutenant completed his report, saluted, and left the bridge. He closed the door as water surged over the port side, enveloping him when the wave broke against the bridge, and for a moment Burckhardt thought he had gone, but when the flood subsided Hahnemann was still clinging to the rail and he took advantage of the respite to dash below.

The not unexpected news he had brought depressed Burckhardt: within three hours the unit had to go ashore and the landing might be opposed. For such an operation the troops should be in the peak of condition and already half their energy must have drained away under the impact of their experiences so far – and the voyage was not yet accomplished. In fact, the worst probably lay ahead. Suppressing a sigh, he turned to face the cliffs and saw only spray. A second later every man on the bridge was petrified and their expressions of hypnotized fear were etched on Burckhardt's mind – a long drawn-out grinding noise was heard and the ship shuddered. *She had struck!* The message flashed through his brain and then the engines, which had missed a beat, started up reluctantly and he knew that it was this which had caused the diabolical sound and tremor. He caught Dietrich's eye and the Abwehr man nodded, as much as to say, yes, this is gruelling. Burckhardt turned to look ahead as the vessel climbed, the spray faded and the entrance to the gulf appeared again. Within minutes their position had changed radically and they were now lying close to the narrows and well clear of the Zervos cliffs. But within a matter of only a few more minutes an even graver crisis faced them.

The enormously powerful cross-current which had carried them clear of the cliffs now threatened to carry the *Hydra* to a new and equally total destruction. From the bridge Burckhardt could now see why Nopagos had advised the apparently suicidal course of steaming directly for the notorious cape – it was an attempt to take them close enough to the narrows to pass through the bottleneck before the cross-current swept them sideways beyond it. The Greek mainland to the west lay several miles away, but from its distant coast a chain of rocks stretched out across the gulf entrance, a chain which ended close enough to the cliffs of the Zervos peninsula to compress the entrance dangerously narrow. And the only navigable channel, Schnell had explained earlier, lay through the bottleneck, guarded by the last rock in the chain. Burckhardt was staring grimly at that rock as the ferry ploughed its way forward towards the entrance, half its engine-power neutralized by the insidious sideslip motion of the cross-current which, only a few minutes before their saviour, was fast becoming their most deadly enemy.

In size the rock was more like a small island, a pointed island which rose straight out of the sea to its peak, a saw-toothed giant against which a warship might well destroy itself at the first impact, whereas the ferry they were aboard was a little more fragile than a steel-plated cruiser. Mountainous waves were surging half-way up the rock's face and the bursting spray smothered its peak. It had the appearance of waiting for them.

'It is fortunate that we did not plan to scale the so-called cliff path,' Eberhay commented. He had said the first thing which came into his head to break the tension permeating the bridge like a disease. 'I hardly imagine it would have been a great success,' he went on lightly. 'There might have been some difficulty in disembarking the troops at the base of the cliff.'

'I don't believe there is a path,' Burckhardt replied. When the operation had been planned one of the experts had mentioned this path which he said climbed the apparently sheer face in a series of zigzag walks leading eventually to the summit close to the monastery. Superficially, it had seemed an attractive idea – Burckhardt could have taken his main objective soon after landing instead of going to the head of the gulf and then marching twenty miles back down the peninsula. From the monastery he could have sent out patrols

to the north to occupy the peninsula from the heights –
the operation would, in fact, have taken place in
precisely the reverse direction from the one now contemplated. The operation had been revised to its present form when the planners had realized that the Greek
ferry reached the cape in the early hours of the morning; the prospect of scaling the cliffs at night had been
considered impracticable and the ferry had to complete
its run to preserve the appearance of normality up to
the last moment.

'Yes, there is a track,' Dietrich informed the colonel.
'It links up the anchorite dwellings built into the cliff
face. The anchorites are hermit monks who spend all
their lives in isolation from their fellows – hence the
extraordinary places they live in.' He chuckled throat-
ily. 'I have always thought it must be similar to solitary
confinement during a lifetime in prison.'

'How do you know this?' Burckhardt was twisted
round one hand still gripping the rail as the bridge
swayed alarmingly.

'Because I paid a visit to Zervos five years ago.'
Dietrich regarded the colonel ironically. 'Which is
simply another of my qualifications for being here. I
travelled all over the peninsula.'

'You went to the monastery?' Burckhardt put the
question casually but the information interested him
intensely. He had only one man, among the two
hundred aboard who knew Zervos personally – Lieutenant Hahnemann – and he had worried over this ever

since the expedition had been planned. Perhaps, after all, the Abwehr officer was going to prove extremely useful during the dangerous hours ahead.

'Yes, I visited the monastery. Why?'

'I simply wondered how widespread your travels had been. I understand there is no landing place along the peninsula coast between the cape and Katyra at the head of the gulf.'

'There is Molos – twenty kilometres south of Katyra.'

'Yes, I know. It is a small fishing village – but has it access to the interior?'

'It depends what you call access.' Dietrich was still holding the cigar unlit in his mouth and he didn't bother to remove it to reply to the colonel. 'There is a footpath which goes up into the mountains but often it is washed away during the winter.'

'I see.' Burckhardt replied as though this were news, but he had heard this at the planning stage and it confirmed that Dietrich did know the geography of the peninsula. 'There is a road south from Katyra, of course?'

'You know perfectly well there is, or I presume you would not be on board this ship. It is little more than a track and winds its way among the hills. You should have brought mules with you,' he told Burckhardt bluntly.

'We considered them – but it was hardly practicable to transfer animals from the *Rupescu* to this ferry.' Satisfied with Dietrich's replies he turned away, but the Abwehr man had the last word.

'All this is assuming that we ever penetrate that gulf. You see what is happening, don't you?'

Burckhardt, who had let his attention slip for the shortest period of time, looked ahead and stiffened. During the very brief interval while he had conversed with Dietrich, the *Hydra*, caught up in the main force of the cross-current, had been swept three-quarters of the way across the entrance and now he heard a fresh sound, a sound more muted than the breaking of the sea against the cape but no less sinister – the dull boom of the swaying Aegean against the base of the saw-tooth. They were very close to the narrows – close enough to see that there the water was quieter, although still it heaved and bubbled like a tidal race, but they were equally close to the saw-tooth. He looked away to starboard where the big rollers were rounding Cape Zervos and hurtling towards the ferry, a piling-up of the sea which had more than once shaken the vessel as though she were a toy ship. It was these mountainous rollers which posed Burckhardt's second nightmare. If a big one came just at the wrong moment as they were passing the saw-tooth ... He noticed Schnell again turning his head to look to port, and Schnell's frequent glances in that direction worried him. The naval officer was clearly aware that they were engaged in a lethal race – to pass through the narrows before they piled-up against the rock. There was no longer anything they could do except to hope. Everything seemed to conspire to screw up their tense nerves to an unbearable pitch – the engines were beating foggily as though on the verge of breaking down altogether; the vessel's movements were becoming laboured and had a discouraging, waterlogged feel; the cross-current seemed to be carrying them sideways faster than the bows of the ship moved forward. He heard Eberhay clear his throat and the sound alerted him, made him look again to port. They were about to enter the narrows but the saw-tooth was less than thirty metres from the hull. A wave broke on the rock's side and spray reached the apexed summit. Out of the corner of his eye Burckhardt caught a slight movement – Nopagos was staring in the opposite direction towards the cape as though transfixed.

Following his gaze, the colonel clenched his teeth and felt coldness like an affliction chill his spine. Another roller was coming, a roller more mountainous than any Burckhardt had seen. There must have been some accumulation of the waters, even an overtaking and merging of three giant waves to form the foam-crested colossus bearing down on them like an upheaval from the deep. All heads were turned in that direction now, even Schnell's before he dragged his gaze to for'ard by some supreme effort of will. The crest of the monster was well above funnel height. Hands gripped the rails tightly, bodies stood rigid with fright. Even Burckhardt took several steps back as Dietrich moved aside for him to brace his back against the rear wall. With the wood pressed against his shoulder-blades he stared incredulously at the appalling spectacle. The wave seemed to be climbing higher and higher, swallowing up more of the sea to swell itself to mammoth proportions. We'll be overwhelmed, Burckhardt thought, we'll never emerge from this: we'll plunge down to the floor of the gulf like a submarine out of control. God, had there been some frightful underwater upheaval, some shift in the earth's surface on the Aegean floor? The wave was within ten metres now. Half the wave's height would be clear over them . . . His hands locked on the rail, felt the greasy sweat inside his gloves, and then the *Hydra* tried to climb, to carry itself up the side of the monstrous wave – and instead was swept sideways. Lifted like a paper boat, it seemed no longer to move forward at all as the screw churned frantically inside the pounding sea. Eberhay lost his grip and was hurled bodily across the bridge where he collided with the Alpenkorps soldier. Bracing himself afresh, determined not to follow Eberhay, the colonel looked to port again. For a moment he saw nothing except the wave travelling westward, a shifting wobble of sea which shimmered his vision, then a window appeared in the water and his jaw muscles tautened. Just beyond the ship, it appeared, the saw-tooth was rushing towards them like the wall of a building toppling over on the port deck. He waited for the shuddering crash of hull disintegrating against immovable rock, the sinking sensation as the *Hydra* foundered.

Spray blinded the view. Unexpectedly he realized that the ferry was listing to starboard, was over the crest. Ahead lay the smoother water where the gulf

COLIN FORBES

was protected from the fury of the storm by the wall of
the cape. He looked back through the window at the
rear of the bridge in time to see the saw-tooth submerging under the surge of the sea, the spray bursting high
above the summit as the whole rock was temporarily
drowned under the immense fall of water. Then the
rock began to reappear as water drained down its sides
and Burckhardt's mind functioned again. *The rock was
behind them*. They had moved inside the Gulf of Zervos.

Three minutes later he was about to leave the bridge,
his mind concentrated on the peril of the Italian sea-
mines, when Hahnemann reported that the unit's wireless set had been sabotaged.

'The Gestapo? Dietrich a member of the Gestapo? What
the devil put that crazy idea into your head, Eberhay?'

Burckhardt stared grimly across the table at his
second-in-command. It was a suggestion he could have
done without at this stage of the operation as the *Hydra*
proceeded steadily up the gulf through the darkness.
All its lights were ablaze to preserve the appearance of
normality and from the bridge a powerful searchlight
was beamed ahead as Schnell and Nopagos strained
their eyes for the first sight of the dreaded mines. Inside
the colonel's cabin Eberhay crossed his slim legs and
smiled faintly. The two men were alone and it had
seemed an ideal moment to voice his doubts. 'It is just
a feeling I had,' he explained, 'when I was talking to
him on deck some time ago.'

'Just a feeling!' Burckhardt was more annoyed than ever. 'No evidence – just a feeling. And why should Berlin secretly put a Gestapo official on board this ship?' His voice became more biting. 'You have a theory on that, I'm sure.'

'Yes, I have.' The little major, accustomed to the colonel's moods, was unruffled. 'Since there appears to be a traitor on board it could be someone the Gestapo has previously suspected. We know someone helped the Englanders to escape, and if the unit has been infiltrated this would account for Dietrich's presence – he is trying to locate the spy. Naturally, if he is Gestapo, he doesn't take us into his complete confidence. They never do. And the sabotage of the wireless set proves that someone is trying to hinder the expedition . . .'

'I agree,' Dietrich spoke the words from the door he had opened silently and Burckhardt's manner became icier as the Abwehr man came inside and joined them at the table after carefully closing the door. The sentry outside the cabin should have stopped him, of course, and the colonel reminded himself to deal with that later. But it was an interesting example of how the Abwehr man's powerful personality was dominating almost everyone on board. A short while earlier Burckhardt had overheard an Alpenkorps soldier explaining to his cabin mates that the Abwehr officer had been sent personally by the Führer to watch over the operation, a suggestion which had not endeared him to the huge German who now sat at one end of the table holding his cigar while he spoke.

'Major Eberhay is, of course, correct. Someone aboard this Greek ferry is trying to prevent you from ever reaching your objective. And he has the freedom of action to sabotage your wireless set. That I personally find most inconvenient – I wished to send a message to Berlin via your GHQ in Bulgaria at the earliest possible moment. When would you have been able to break radio silence?'

'Not while we are on board,' Burckhardt replied evasively. 'But you may still be able to send your message later.'

Dietrich looked relieved, nodding as he lit his cigar. 'That is certain?'

'I cannot be sure yet when that will be.' He paused, conscious of a feeling that he was being too close-mouthed with this Abwehr officer. For all he knew he could be Admiral Canaris' right-hand man. 'We have a second wireless set in perfect condition,' he said briskly. 'Military signals will, of course, have priority, but you will be able to communicate with Bulgaria at a certain time after we have gone ashore.'

'The other set is permanently out of action?'

'Possibly not. Someone smashed the tuning coil but the wireless op may be able to repair it in time.'

'It had been left unguarded?'

'No, not originally. But the man who was guarding it became sick and went to the lavatory. He was there for some time and because of his condition he didn't check the set immediately when he returned.'

'How can you smash up a tuning coil?'

Eberhay, who had seen the damaged set, explained this. 'Anything heavy would do the job – a pistol butt, or a rifle's – anything. It could be done in less than a minute.'

'Why did Schnell keep to his cabin during the early part of the voyage?' asked Dietrich. The sudden switch in topic surprised both German officers and again it was Eberhay who replied. 'He made the same trip aboard the *Hydra* a fortnight ago to study the vessel and its route. Although he was disguised on that earlier trip we wanted to eliminate any risk that one of the crew might recognize him this time.'

'And he carried the weapons for use in taking over the vessel inside that cabin trunk which caused so much comment?'

'Yes!' It was Burckhardt who answered now, disliking the final qualification in Dietrich's question. 'Both wireless sets, incidentally, are now under heavy guard. And the seizure of this vessel went exactly according to plan.'

'I agree that that part of the operation was well organized,' Dietrich said blandly with the underlying implication that the later stages had been little better than a dog's breakfast. Withdrawing suddenly from the conversation, he sat back in his chair and regarded both men through his cigar smoke. The German officers had taken off their outer civilian coats and wore field-grey Alpenkorps uniform: a tunic buttoned up to the neck, trousers ankle-wrapped with puttees, and heavily nailed boots. The footgear, Dietrich thought, was an

improvement on the normal Wehrmacht jackboot he so
disliked. Round his waist each man wore a wide leather
belt with a hip holster slung on the left side and the
Luger pistol set butt forward. He remained motionless
while someone hammered urgently on the outside of
the door and a moment later the knocking was
repeated. Burckhardt called out for them to come in
and Lieutenant Hahnemann appeared.

'What is it?' Burckhardt asked quietly.

'One of the ten-kilogram demolition charges is missing and a time fuse.'

Dietrich came to life suddenly, was standing up as
he fired the question, his great body overshadowing
Hahnemann. 'That sounds like a large bomb?'

In his agitation Hahnemann replied immediately
before the colonel could say a word, addressing Dietrich directly. 'If it is placed in the right position it
could destroy the entire ship.'

'Something's upset their apple cart, all right.' Ford
spoke quietly as he stood alongside Prentice by the
porthole. Their cabin was being methodically searched
by Alpenkorps soldiers who prodded the bedding
gingerly with short-bladed bayonets, opened cupboard
doors as though expecting something to fall out, and
peered cautiously under chair seats without moving
them.

'They're nervy, too.' Prentice watched the searching
process curiously and he thought he sensed a desperate

urgency in their efforts, like men working against a clock. Near the door Sergeant Volber stood directing operations, although his main task, under orders from Eberhay, was to protect the prisoners. During the search more than one man glanced murderously at Prentice who was responsible for the death of one of their comrades, and Volber was present to exercise strict discipline. A moment later the sergeant spoke in German, and when Prentice failed to understand, he waved his Luger to indicate they must move to one side. A soldier who pointedly did not look at them opened the porthole, peered outside, then rubbed a hand round the outer rim as though seeking something which might be suspended there. Satisfied with his search, he closed the porthole and Volber motioned them to take up their former position.

'What the hell's going on?' Ford whispered.

'Don't know – but they're as jumpy as hens with a fox in the yard.' Prentice was glad of Volber's presence: all the Germans carried carbines,* as the technically minded Ford insisted on calling them, and it had been known for a weapon to go off accidentally when aimed at a lethal spot. From the look on the faces of some of these hard-bitten youngsters a carbine could have discharged quite easily in his direction if Volber had omitted to attend the ceremony. Ford continued gazing out of the porthole where he could see on the mainland side of the gulf a chain of pinpoint lights crawling up

---

* Ford was referring to the Gewehr 98 K bolt-action carbine.

the coast road to the north. He pressed his hand lightly on the lieutenant's arm.

'Look – must be our chaps across there.'

'I know, I've seen 'em.' Prentice hadn't relaxed his own gaze from the interior of the cabin. He could feel the deep animosity radiating from the dozen men who went on turning the cabin inside out. One soldier walking past him chanced to let go of his carbine and Prentice had to move quickly. The metal-sheathed butt of the weapon thudded heavily on the cabin floor where a moment before his right foot had stood. If that butt had contacted, it could have crippled him. Volber called out sharply in German and was still barking vehemently when the soldier left the cabin.

'Sounds as though he's going on a charge. With any luck,' Ford added. 'You know, sir, I don't think they really like us.'

'Just be ready to do a quick tap-dance if the occasion arises,' Prentice told him and continued to stare at any man who caught his eye. Yes, Ford had been right: it was a damned queer situation. On board the *Hydra* there must be at least a company of well-trained German troops and some of them expected to operate at high altitudes – he had seen several pairs of skis inside one cabin when they had been taken along earlier for interrogation by that slip of a German officer who spoke English. And behind them, a few miles across the gulf through that porthole, they could see the hooded lights of traffic moving through the night along that vital mainland road to the north. Prentice had no doubt that those were the lights of Allied convoys driving up to the Alkiamon Line, completely ignorant of the fact that the ship whose lights they could see across the water was carrying a German spearhead aimed at Zervos. For by now Prentice had little doubt of the Alpenkorps objective – the Germans on board were on their way to seize that vital monastery observation post overlooking the road Ford was watching through the porthole.

'A whole load of them on the way,' Ford went on, 'I can see lights right up the coast.'

'What the blazes can this lot be looking for?' Prentice wondered out loud. 'And it bothers them. They're sweating.'

'They can melt away for all I care. What I can't make out is why they're still wearing their Mae Wests. It's as calm as the Serpentine outside now.' Ford's description of the gulf had an element of exaggeration because the *Hydra* was still steaming through a moderate swell, but contrasted with the seas off Cape Zervos it could indeed have been the Serpentine. The Aegean, one of the most unpredictable seas in the world, had subsided again.

'I told you, they were nervy,' Prentice replied. Inwardly, he assumed the wearing of Mae Wests was just another example of Teutonic discipline, but it was the object of the search which was nagging at his tired brain. Come to think of it, these boys didn't look as though they'd just got up in the morning. Which was a thought that gave him a certain amount of satisfaction:

if they went on prowling round the ship like this they'd be exhausted before they ever got ashore. The soldiers were trooping out of the cabin when he went up to Volber. 'Speak with German who speaks Englische . . .' he began. It took him a pantomime of gestures to convey that he wished to talk to the little officer who had interviewed them earlier, and when Volber returned he came back with Lieutenant Hahnemann instead.

'What is it?' Hahnemann rapped out. There was tension here, too – tension and irritability in the manner and expression with which he regarded the two prisoners.

'What are you looking for? We might be able to help,' Prentice told him blithely.

The reaction was unexpectedly violent. Hahnemann took a step forward and his right hand rested close to his hip holster. It had been a mistake, Prentice realized at once. The Jerries were more at their nerve-ends than he had realized. He spoke quickly and tersely, letting a little indignation creep into his tone. 'I meant what I said. Why wouldn't I? If I could tell you where it was – whatever you are looking for – it would have saved us having the bedding bayoneted to bits.'

'You will stay here and not send for me again.' He turned away and then looked back. 'Why are you not wearing the life-jackets?'

'Because there isn't a storm any more.'

'You put them on now and they stay on. That is an order. For your safety,' he ended abruptly. They were left alone with the guard while they tied on their Mae Wests again. Prentice was relieved to see that it was the same guard, a thirty-year-old who sat some distance from them with his machine-pistol always aimed in their general direction. A sturdy-faced character, he had shown no exceptional signs of hostility although he was careful never to let them come within ten feet of where he sat.

'I'd still like to know what they were after,' said Ford as he sat down on a pile of massacred bedding. He looked up at Prentice. 'How much longer?'

'About an hour, if they're keeping to the ferry's schedule.' Prentice's watch registered 4.30 AM and the *Hydra* had been due to dock at Katyra at 5.30 AM, a little before dawn. To keep awake he went over to the porthole again for another look at those tantalizing hooded lights of the convoy moving along the coast road. Another hour. Nothing much could happen in that time.

The ten-kilogram composite demolition charge stood on the table. It was enclosed inside a black-painted zinc container about the size and shape of a deep attaché case and there was a web carrying-handle at the top. Inset into the top face were two standard igniter sockets.

'Like that?' queried Dietrich innocently. He gave the impression that this was the first time in his life he had seen a ten-kilogram demolition charge.

'Its twin is hidden somewhere aboard this ship – with the difference that the clockwork time fuse has undoubtedly been attached and set in motion. Show him the fuse, Hahnemann.'

While Burckhardt waited, the engines of the ferry ticked over steadily, unpleasantly suggestive of the ticking of a time bomb. They were alone in the colonel's cabin with the exception of the temporary presence of Hahnemann who had brought in the demolition charge at the Abwehr man's request. As Dietrich had so unfortunately put it, he wanted to see what was going to blow him to kingdom come.

'The fuse,' said Hahnemann.

It was roughly shaped like an outsized egg-cup. Measuring a little over two inches across the top in diameter and six inches in overall depth, the casing was chocolate-brown bakelite, and when Dietrich picked up the device Hahnemann showed him how it worked. The top was a hinged glass lid which had to be lifted to set the clock. Still holding the time fuse, he looked up at the lieutenant.

'And one of these is definitely missing with the charge?'

'Yes. They were in a rucksack at the bottom of the companionway stairs.'

'Not guarded?' Dietrich was looking down at the mechanism.

Hahnemann glanced at the colonel, who nodded. 'There was a mix-up of rucksacks. I'm sure it would never have happened if half the men hadn't been sea-sick. Corporal Schultz thought he had the rucksack with the charges inside with him in a cabin. It was only discovered later that he had someone else's while his own rucksack had been left outside.'

Dietrich ignored the explanation. 'Corporal Schultz is waiting in the passage? Good, I'd like to see him.'

Hahnemann went to the door and let inside a slim man in his late twenties who was clearly not at ease, and his embarrassment increased when he slipped on the polished floor. He glanced at the colonel as he saluted and Burckhardt merely told him to answer questions. He had already had a word with the negli-gent NCO.

'These fuses are totally reliable?' inquired Dietrich. The pink-faced corporal glanced at Hahnemann who told him briskly to answer the question. Schultz was uncertain how much to say and the colonel barked at him to get on with it.

'No, sir, not always,' Schultz began. And having begun he gained confidence and spoke rapidly. 'They have a habit when set of stopping for no reason at all. Then they can start up again of their own accord – again for no particular reason. We do know that they can be affected by jolting or vibrations. They're weird – I heard of one case where a fuse was set to detonate the charge in two days. It was put under a bridge during training and then the man who had put it there died in a motor crash. Everyone forgot about it.' He paused, his eyes on Dietrich who was staring at him fixedly. 'Two years later the bridge blew up. Yes, sir – two *years* later.'

'Thank you.' Dietrich returned the time fuse to Hahnemann who picked up the charge by the handle and left the cabin with Corporal Schultz.

'And where does that get us?' asked Burckhardt.

'It gets us into a worse state of nerves than we were before, I should have thought. You heard what he said?'

'Of course! Which point were you referring to?'

Dietrich clubbed one large fist and began drumming it slowly on the table. It took Burckhardt a moment to grasp that he was drumming in time with the beat of the *Hydra*'s engines. He pursed his lips uncomfortably as Dietrich rammed the point home verbally. 'Affected by jolting or vibrations,' he said.

'We shall not be on board much longer.' He hesitated. It must by now be patently obvious when they were going ashore to anyone who knew the *Hydra*'s timetable. 'Barely an hour. In the meantime the search continues and they may find it.'

'Colonel Burckhardt.' Dietrich was standing up now, his hat in his hand. 'This is likely to be the longest hour of your life. I think I'll go and help them try to find it. You never know – they say heaven protects the innocent.'

As he went along the companionway, hands thrust deep inside his coat pockets, he heard the frenzied clump of nailed boots everywhere. The boots rarely stayed still for more than a short time, as though their occupants were finding it impossible to keep in one place while they continued their frantic search for the missing demolition charge. Inside one cabin he found men with moist faces pushing aside a pile of dark brown hickory skis which could not possibly have concealed the charge. A soldier who didn't look a day over nineteen was peering behind a fire-extinguisher, another impossible hiding-place. There had been tension aboard the *Hydra* ever since the Alpenkorps had arrived, tension initially through the knowledge that at any minute they might be stopped by a British warship, tension because they were aboard the vessel of a country which Germany still officially treated as a neutral in the war. But the earlier tension brought on by the secrecy, by the storm, by the sabotage of a wireless set and the death of one of their men overboard – this tension had been serenity compared with the stark, livid tension which now gripped the *Hydra*'s illegal passengers.

It manifested itself in little ways. The lift of a rifle as Dietrich came round a corner. The kicking over of a bucket of sand by an Alpenkorps soldier hurrying past. The disorganized clump of those nailed boots on the ceiling when he was walking along the companionway of the lower deck. The sentry who guarded Grapos was still at his post, his back to the port-holed steel door leading down to the hold where the Greek was imprisoned. Farther along the companionway Dietrich looked inside the half-open door which led down to the engine-room. He had one foot on the iron platform when a rifle muzzle was thrust in his face, reminding him of the muzzle which Volber had thrust at him as he opened his cabin door when they had taken over the ship. But this time he withdrew swiftly – the muzzle had wobbled slightly. In that brief glimpse he had seen below at least half-a-dozen field grey figures searching among the machinery while another man mounted guard over the chief engineer. The fear was a living mounting thing which he saw in men's faces as he climbed back to the top deck, faces damp, baggy-eyed and drawn with strain as they went on searching amid the ferry's complexities for something no larger than an attaché case. This is a formula for driving men mad, he was thinking as he went on climbing, for slowly shredding their nerves to pieces.

On the open deck it was quieter because there were fewer searchers: Burckhardt had given strict instructions that despite the gravity of the emergency only those men who could cover their uniforms with civilian coats were to be sent up here. Even now he was not prepared to risk a British motor-torpedo boat suddenly appearing and flashing its searchlight over the deck to illuminate men in German uniform. So far as Dietrich could see there were no more than a dozen, hatless men flitting in the shadows. But here again he heard the disjointed hurrying clump of those heavily nailed boots pounding the wooden deck. It was quite dark now, the impenetrable pitch-blackness of the night before dawn, and a cold wind was blowing along the gulf. He leant against the ventilator amidships to light his cigar and a soldier came round the side and cannoned into him. When he saw the silhouette of the hat against the match-flare he apologized and hurried away. Dietrich sighed. Again he had seen the lift of the rifle prior to recognition. He went to the stern and looked over the rail where the screw churned the sea a dirty white colour, stumbled over a piled loop of rope, and went back along the deck to the illuminated safety of the bridge. It was 4.45 AM.

The ten-kilogram composite demolition charge swayed at the end of the rope. The vibrations of the ship's engines shuddered it in mid-sway and the rock of the ship's movements reproduced themselves in the sway itself. The charge thudded regularly against the metal-work as it continued its endless pendulum motion, but the sound of the thuds was camouflaged by the same engine beats which shook it. A man standing close by might not have heard those warning thuds as the charge dangled and swayed and shuddered. The clock was set and the mechanism was ticking, but the most vital sound – the ticking – was muffled by the larger noises. Occasionally the vessel plunged its bows a little deeper into the waters of the gulf and then the charge would strike the metal heavily, its rhythmic sway temporarily upset by the unexpected jolt. For a minute or more it would sway erratically, its pendulum balance disturbed, then it would recover its poise and resume the same even swing backwards and forwards with the regularity of a metronome. It was suspended a long way down the shaft, suspended from an Alpenkorps scabbard which still held its bayonet, a scabbard which had been jammed inside the shaft at an angle which might hold it there indefinitely. And as it went on swaying none of the hatless men who thumped along the open deck in growing desperation had, as yet, carefully examined the ventilator shaft amidships.

Chapter Seven

Sunday, Dawn

'The Greek has escaped – I have instituted an immediate and intensive search of the ship.' Hahnemann reported the news to Burckhardt whom he had found on the bridge standing next to Dietrich. He waited nervously for the colonel's reaction, but Burckhardt, holding a pair of field-glasses, simply looked at him as he asked the question.

'How did it happen, Hahnemann? He was tied up ln the hold and Private Kutzel was standing guard over him.'

'He must have freed himself in some way.' Hahnemann hesitated: the next item of news was bound to provoke an explosion. 'Kutzel is dead – I found him on the floor of the hold with his neck broken.'

'And his rifle?'

Dietrich smiled grimly to himself as he heard the question and he gave the colonel top marks for competence under stress. The weapon, of course, was vital, could make all the difference to the degree of menace posed by the escaped Greek.

'I found that on the floor close to his body . . .'

'Good. He shouldn't be difficult to round up. You

said an "intensive" search, Hahnemann. How intensive? How many men?'

'Fifty, sir.' Hahnemann at least felt confident that he had organized the hunt for Grapos on a sufficiently massive scale, even though there was something else which he dreaded mentioning. He wished to heaven that the Abwehr man wasn't standing there with his hands behind his back, his great shoulders hunched forward as he took in every word the lieutenant was saying. The colonel's reaction gave him an unpleasant shock.

'Fifty? You mean you have taken fifty men off the search for the missing demolition charge?' Burckhardt was facing the unfortunate Hahnemann now, his hands on his hips as he went on bitingly. 'When will you get your priorities right? An explosive with a time fuse has been planted somewhere aboard this vessel, an explosive powerful enough to sink us in the middle of the gulf before we ever go ashore. That, since it appears you don't realize it, is a far greater risk than one unarmed Greek civilian who is probably gibbering with fright in some cupboard. You will tell off no more than twenty men to look for him – the other thirty must immediately resume the search for that demolition charge.'

'He is armed, sir – with a rifle . . .'

'You said you had found Kutzel's rifle.'

'That is correct, sir.' Hahnemann's rigid stance reflected the extent of his unhappiness as he went on stolidly. 'I think the Greek must have surprised Private

Wasserman also when he was asleep in a cabin on the lower deck . . .'

'Asleep!' Burckhardt changed the direction of his attack: what a soldier had been doing asleep during these vital hours was something he could inquire into later. Doubtless Wasserman had sneaked off into the cabin hoping no one would find him there. 'What has happened to Wasserman?'

'He's dead – strangled as far as we can tell. And his rifle and ammunition belt are missing so the Greek must have them.'

Burckhardt paused only briefly while he wished to God that the Abwehr man wasn't listening to all this, but he was still perfectly clear as to what must be done. 'You will still use only twenty men to hunt for the Greek. Issue a general warning that he's armed.'

'I have done that already, sir.'

'Then issue a special warning to those on the open deck – we don't want them starting to loose off at each other.' As Hahnemann hurried away he thought no, that would be the final disaster – to incur further casualties with the men shooting one another. Taking up a firmer stance, he stared ahead to where the searchlight beam shone down the gulf. It was 5.15 AM. A quarter of an hour to disembarkation. Coldly, he catalogued in his mind the risks and setbacks which had bedevilled the expedition since he had come aboard the *Hydra*. A boatload of troops which had been very nearly capsized during the transfer from the *Rupescu*; one soldier sent into the sea by the Englishman,

Prentice; one wireless set sabotaged by smashing the tuning coil; the encounter with the destroyer which had almost proved fatal; a demolition charge of great explosive power planted somewhere in the bowels of the vessel; the escape of the armed Greek; and the death of two more Alpenkorps men during that escape. So three men out of two hundred were dead even before they set foot in Greece. Surely nothing more could happen during the remaining quarter of an hour? Actually, it was likely to be twenty-five or thirty minutes – they were behind schedule with this infernal ferry having to move more slowly because of the danger of mines – and Italian mines of all things. Schnell had insisted on the further reduction in speed to ensure that they sighted them in time. The irony of it was they hadn't seen a single mine since entering the gulf.

'I think I'll go and have a word with Major Eberhay – if I can find him.' Dietrich was already moving away and leaving the bridge to Burckhardt's relief – the large German seemed to dominate wherever he went, to hang over the ship like a prophet of disasters to come. Barely a minute later Sergeant Volber came onto the bridge and the colonel only had to take one look at his face to know it was not good news.

'What is it, Volber?' he rapped out sharply.

'We think Private Diehl may be missing, sir.'

Burckhardt instantly thought of the Greek who was prowling about somewhere with a loaded rifle. 'You *think*? Either Diehl is missing or he isn't? Which is it?'

'We don't know, sir.' Volber lacked Lieutenant Hah-nemann's capacity for telling a complete account quickly, forestalling his commanding officer's questions so far as he could, and the sergeant's habit of replying without explaining was a foible Burckhardt found intensely irritating. He felt the blood going to his head as he forced himself to reply coldly.

'What the devil does that mean?'

'He hasn't been seen for a long time – I've asked several of the men and they all thought he was somewhere else. They're very scattered . . .'

'You've allowed your section to become scattered?'

'We're on the open deck and it takes time to check everyone in the dark . . .'

'Report to me as soon as you can whether he's definitely missing. Definitely, I said, Volber.'

The strain was telling everywhere, Burckhardt thought as the sergeant hurried away. Schnell was being over-cautious, the NCOs were getting rattled, and the men were being steadily drained of their aggressive energies as they plodded round the ship searching for time-bombs and armed Greeks. And soon they would have to fight a campaign. Armed Greeks? The thought reminded him of a few vital questions he had to put to the captain. He took a step forward which placed him at Nopagos' elbow.

'The man callet Grapos has escaped,' he said harshly. 'He has taken a rifle and ammunition – can he use them? Before you reply, remember that he is a civilian with no rights in war and I shall hold you responsible for the death of any of my men if you withhold information.'

Nopagos turned and stared at the German. His skin was lined and pouched with fatigue but he still held himself erect; what little responsibility he still held for his own vessel as its pilot would only cease when they docked at Katyra. He was tempted to tell Burckhardt to go to hell but he sensed something of the tremendous pressure the colonel was undergoing and it seemed senseless to take a risk when they had almost landed. 'He has been able to use a rifle since he was a boy,' he replied.

'But he has something to do with the monastery.' Burckhardt did not understand this at all and his mouth tightened as he held the Greek's eyes.

'He was a novice monk who had no vocation. When he left the monastery it was agreed that he should do odd jobs for them – like going to Istanbul on this ferry to bring back supplies of books and things like that. He has shot birds on the peninsula from an early age. Yes, he can use a rifle.'

'Well?'

'A marksman.' Nopagos gave this reply with a certain relish.

'His limp kept him out of the army?'

'It was his greatest regret. He would be an asset to any army in the world. Has he caused any trouble yet?'

'He has killed two of my men.'

'You see what I mean, then?' For a moment Nopagos

thought he had gone too far. Burckhardt stiffened and a hint of fury came into his eyes and then faded as he regained control. He was careful to keep strict control as he put his next question.

'He knows this ship well?'

'Well enough to hide until we have reached Katyra as you have not found him now.' And with this last thrust Nopagos turned away and attended to his duties once more. But he was not able to resist asking a question which he carefully put in a polite tone. 'Have they found the time-bomb yet?'

'No.'

'So, there is still time.'

This simple comment stung Burckhardt more than anything Nopagos had said previously. He had given Eberhay orders to leave assembly for disembarkation until the last possible moment so they could keep on looking for that missing demolition charge – Burckhardt's greatest fear was that it would detonate just before they landed. He was thinking about this when Schnell, almost exhausted from his long hours over the wheel, straightened up as a soldier ran along outside the bridge and came in breathless. Burckhardt recognized him as one of the two men posted as lookouts as soon as they had passed through the narrows. In his anxiety to speak the man had trouble in getting out his message.

'Mines sighted, sir . . . on the port bow.'

*

The explosion came at 5.45 AM as the *Hydra,* listing to port, her engines beating uncertainly, began the ninety-degree turn which would take her inshore to the distant light of the Katyra landing-stage. They were almost there, Burckhardt reflected as he stood on the bridge behind Nopagos, but the last mile was likely to be the longest of the voyage. The dangers surrounding the expedition were now so overwhelming that his mind had reached the point where it could hardly take in any more – those damnable Italian mines were growing more numerous with every quarter-mile they glided forward; an armed Greek was loose somewhere on board, and a marksman at that; and they had still failed to locate the demolition charge which might detonate at any moment. Lifting his field-glasses to focus on the circle of mines ringing the vessel, he ignored the newcomers arriving on the already overcrowded bridge. Because of the risk of imminent disaster he had ordered the British prisoners to be brought up from their cabin.

'Are we abandoning ship?' Prentice asked quietly.

'No!' Hahnemann's reply was savagely emphatic as his hand guided the lieutenant by the elbow to the rear of the bridge. 'We shall be landing shortly.'

'Through that lot!' Ford sounded incredulous as he gazed over the colonel's shoulder along the searchlight beam which cut cross the darkness. To port and starboard of the illuminated avenue at least four mines floated, metallic spheres which gleamed palely, their surfaces speckled with small shadows – the dreaded nozzles which caused instant detonation on contact.

Burckhardt spoke briefly over his shoulder, instructing Hahnemann to tell them about the missing demolition charge; after all, they were soldiers, so they might as well know the position. With waning enthusiasm, Prentice and Ford listened to Hahnemann and were then pushed to the rear of the bridge, squeezed in between a press of uniformed Alpenkorps troops. Looking to his right, Prentice found he was huddled next to the large German civilian who had come aboard at Istanbul. On their way up from the cabin they had seen him in the distance climbing a staircase and Prentice had inquired who he was.

'Herr Dietrich is with the Abwehr,' Hahnemann had replied with a hint of respect in his voice. Prentice looked up curiously at the huge figure who stared back at him as he lit a fresh cigar with one elbow rested on the shoulder of the corporal next to him. A rum cove, this Dietrich, was Prentice's reaction as he turned to listen to Ford who was keeping his voice down.

'How big did he say that demolition charge was? I couldn't catch all he said in this crush.'

'Ten kilograms. Is that bad?'

'It's not good, I can tell you that straight off. And if it's been dumped near the boilers and they go, too . . .'

He broke off as Burckhardt issued a stream of orders to Eberhay who had appeared at the door to the bridge and then hurried away when the colonel had finished speaking. They were close to the moment of disembarkation, which required disciplined control, and the little major was facing something like near-panic as the troops filed up the staircases. It was then that Prentice saw the Alpenkorps equipment which confirmed his worst fears: he had a glimpse of men with skis of hickory wood passing beyond the bridge. The skis were carried on their backs which also supported rucksacks – which could only mean they expected to be operating in the deep snows on Mount Zervos at the far end of the peninsula. The Alpenkorps' main objective was the natural observation post of the monastery which over-looked the mainland road carrying Allied supplies northward.

'Funny that bomb hasn't gone off already,' he remarked lightly to Ford. He would have liked to feel that he was praying for the charge to detonate, but the truth was that he was sick with apprehension. 'Perhaps the chap who fixed it didn't know what he was doing,' he suggested.

'That's possible, sir. But their time fuses aren't all that reliable – a Jerry we had in the bag told me that. The damned things have a habit of conking out at the wrong moment.'

'You mean they become harmless?' Prentice tried to keep the hope out of his voice.

'Now I didn't say that, did I? Apparently they sometimes stop and then start up again. Vibrations can get them going again as easy as winking. The ship's engines are ideal for the purpose.'

'That's right, cheer us all up.' Prentice did not feel particularly reassured. Ford was an ammunition exam-iner who spent too much of his life fiddling with things

which might go bang in his face at any second –
including enemy explosives and equipment on which
he was also something of an expert. But here on this
German-held vessel he was displaying distinct signs of
nervousness as he pulled at the lobe of one ear and
kept looking round the bridge as though he expected it
to disappear without warning.

'Fasten those straps at once!' Hahnemann had
returned briefly to the bridge and had noticed that
Ford's life-jacket was loose. Every man on the bridge
wore his life-jacket and these cumbersome objects took
up more space and further impeded movement. Prentice had the feeling that he would soon be lifted clear
off the floor if anyone else crowded in on the bridge.
He jerked his head round again to look through the
rear window which gave a view along the deck towards
the stern, a deck which was almost deserted since the
order for uniformed troops to keep out of sight was
still in force. Almost deserted, but not quite. Prentice's
eyes narrowed as he watched sea mist drift past a lamp
near the starboard rail: by its light he saw a short,
heavily built man on the wrong side of the rail, a man
who carried a rifle over his back. Something about the
shape and the movement reminded him of the Greek
civilian who had also come aboard at Istanbul. Grapos,
the captain had called him. Mist blurred the view and
when it cleared the poised figure was gone. He had
dived over the side.

'Seen a ghost, sir?' Ford inquired.

'I've got a crick in my neck if you're referring to my

expression of almost unendurable agony.' Prentice felt sure that at the last minute Dietrich had also glanced through that window, but by then the mist would have blotted out the lonely figure. He was greatly relieved when the German said nothing and continued quietly smoking the cigar which was now adding to the growing foetid atmosphere inside the packed bridge. So Grapos had made a dive for it and was heading for the shore fast. Some people are lucky, he thought, and then he remembered the mine-strewn waters the Greek was swimming through at that very moment and he suppressed a shudder. Despite the number of men compressed inside the confined space it was very silent on the bridge in the intervals between Burckhardt giving sharp orders as officers and NCOs appeared at the door, a silence of suppressed dread which hung over their still heads like a pall as the engines slowly beat out their mechanical rhythm and the *Hydra* continued to turn eastwards.

The bows of the vessel were moving through drifts of white mist which were fogging visibility, yet a further source of anxiety to Burckhardt, who had now left off his civilian raincoat and was dressed in full uniform with the Alpenkorps broad-brimmed cap set firmly on his head. Nopagos stood like a man of wax, his eyes trying to bore through the mist-curtain at the earliest possible moment. Schnell was crouched in a permanent stoop over the wheel, glancing frequently to starboard where the nearest mine bobbed gently less than fifty metres from the hull. At least, he hoped that was the nearest mine. From his all-round view at the rear, Prentice was looking from face to face, noting the gleam of sweat on tightly drawn skin, the nervous twitch of an eyelid, the hands which gripped rifles and machine-pistols so tensely that the knuckles were whitened. These men, all over the ship, were under the maximum possible pressure. They were going into action by dawn. They knew that the sea ahead was alive with mines, and that somewhere, perhaps under their feet, the time fuse was ticking down to zero. If someone had determined to bring well-nigh unbearable pressure on their morale they could scarcely have planned it better than this. He looked to his right again. Dietrich, outwardly the most composed man on the bridge, was still calmly smoking his cigar and looking down at Prentice as though assessing his character and qualities in an emergency.

'Not more than half an hour at the most.' Ford's voice was little more than a whisper, a whisper motivated more by a dislike of breaking the doom-like silence than by a wish not to be overheard.

'Less than that, I imagine. If we ever get there.' Prentice looked again at the landing-stage light which was visible and closer now the mist had temporarily cleared. And there seemed to be light in the east on the far side of the peninsula. Hoisting his wrist upwards, he looked at his watch. Exactly 5.45 AM. Schnell was turning the wheel to straighten course as Burckhardt transmitted an instruction he had received from Nopagos; Dietrich was studying the end of his cigar rather dubiously; a soldier was wiping moisture from his forehead; and Ford was looking round the bridge with quick darting glances when the explosion came.

The silence on the bridge was ruptured by a shattering roar. The *Hydra* shuddered from bows to stern as though struck by a mammoth blow and then wobbled. A wave was carried away from the ferry and swept towards the shore as it gathered up more water in its headlong flight from the vessel. For a few brief seconds it had been as light as day to starboard where a brilliant flash temporarily blinded those who had been looking in that direction. From beyond the open door of the bridge came a babble of panic-stricken voices and the sound of nailed boots scattering across the decks. Stark gibbering panic had seized the ship and on the packed bridge the hysterical murmuring was only silenced by Burckhardt thundering for quiet. He pushed aside Nopagos who had been leaning out of the window to starboard and leaned out himself. The sea appeared to have gone mad as it heaved and bubbled frothily. For a second Burckhardt thought that they had been struck by a torpedo and that a submarine was surfacing. Then the water began to settle. Schnell still held the ship on course, heading for the landing-stage which was coming closer and closer in the darkness and he spoke without looking at the colonel. 'The mine was very close when it detonated.'

'It was a mine, just a mine, we have not been hit . . .' Hahnemann shouted out the news in German and then in English to stem the signs of panic.

'Well, if that doesn't start it ticking, nothing will,' Ford remarked grimly.

'It?' Prentice was still a little dazed with relief as well as shock.

'The demolition charge,' said Ford, whose mind was never far from explosives. 'If the time fuse mechanism had stopped only temporarily that thump was quite enough to get it moving again, believe you me.'

'I was under the impression that we had hit a mine,' Prentice told him icily. 'That's enough to be going on with, I should have thought.'

'Well, obviously we didn't – we're still steaming on course at the same speed. The mine just went off on its own accord rather too close for comfort.' He was having to lift his voice for Prentice to hear him above the shouts on deck as Burckhardt thrust his way roughly off the bridge and went out on deck himself.

'You mean they can be defective, too?'

'Frequently. They can go off without rhyme or reason. On the other hand something else may have bumped into it although I can't imagine what.'

Prentice began to feel slightly ill. He could imagine what else might have bumped into that mine in its frantic efforts to reach the shore. He had a picture in his mind of Grapos diving overboard with that protruding rifle attached to his back, of him swimming among the mines and so easily forgetting the barrel projecting beyond his body. There would be nothing left of the poor devil now. Prentice didn't like to think of what an explosive which could take out a ship's bottom might do to a single human being as it detonated within a few feet of the swimming body.

'I think that little bang has rattled them,' Ford remarked.

'It rattled me,' Prentice replied with feeling. He looked back through the rear window where there was a state of confusion on the deck below. Alpenkorps men in full uniform who had been huddled close to the rail were being sent under cover by Volber who was waving his arms like a man shepherding sheep back to the fold. Within a minute the deck was clear and the babble of voices beyond the open door had ceased when Burckhardt came back to take up his post behind Nopagos. But the damage had been done. Another heavy blow had been dealt at the morale of troops who, on land would have taken the explosion in their stride, but cooped up on the unfamiliar sea the experience was having an entirely different effect. Prentice thought he could see in the faces in front of him a little extra strain, a trace more tension as the cold light from the east died in the false dawn and the landing-stage light at Katyra drew steadily closer.

Schnell was showing great skill as he steered the *Hydra* on the last stage of her perilous course, threading his way between a scatter of mines which floated in the path of the searchlight beam. An oppressive silence had fallen on the limping vessel as she moved through the dark water which was impenetrable beyond the beam, water supporting perhaps a hundred more mines for all Burckhardt could tell. The men on the decks below

were wating – waiting for the final collision with a
mine, waiting for the still-hidden demolition charge to
detonate under them, waiting for the tension-fraught
moment of the landing – although which of these
hazards was uppermost in their strained minds it was
impossible to guess. The engines ticked over monoto-
nously as the ferry slipped towards a blurred shadow
which was the coast.

Plagued by a dozen anxieties, Burckhardt maintained his outward appearance of calm confidence
while inwardly he fretted at the damnably crawling
progress of the vessel. He was already nearly thirty
minutes behind his timetable and he was praying that
the news of the general offensive launched at 5.45 AM
was not yet on the air. It was unlikely – an hour or two
should pass before the world read the reports of the
German onslaught on Greece and Yugoslavia spear-
headed by the Panzers and reinforced with airborne
troops – and the peninsula was still devoid of Allied
troops and wide open to his attack. The whole key to
the operation was a swift dash back along the peninsula
and the capture of the monastery before the Allies had
time to recover their balance. Just so long as there really
was nothing standing in his way – and that they were
able to land safely. He felt the chill of the early morning
air filtering through his uniform and braced himself to
control a shiver as Dietrich appeared at his elbow.

'The inhabitants of Katyra are bound to have heard
the mine explode,' the Abwehr man remarked.

'I realize that,' Burckhardt replied non-committally.

'So there is a serious risk that someone may have phoned through to Salonika.'

'We have attended to that, so once again you can put your mind at rest,' Burckhardt began ironically. Then he paused: they were so close to going ashore that really he was free to speak more openly. 'There is only a single telephone line out of the peninsula, Herr Dietrich, and that was cut several hours ago.'

'Good. But Salonika may wonder why the line has gone dead.'

'Last night's storm will account for that. In a way it was lucky – it has provided an explanation.'

'And you have transport waiting for you as well?' Dietrich inquired genially.

'There are mules on the peninsula. It was impossible to bring them with us but we shall find mules available. The planning has taken into account every possible contingency. As to transport, other arrangements have also been made . . .' Burckhardt trailed off vaguely and lifted his glasses, focusing on a mine which floated, so it seemed, only a few metres off the port bow. The vessel was already changing course to avoid the menace.

'And you expect no opposition?' Despite the atmosphere of suspense on the bridge Dietrich's manner was almost pleasant as he bowed his head to listen to the colonel's reply.

'None at all. There is no one to oppose us – except a handful of fishermen.'

'There are two policemen on the peninsula – or there

were when I was last here.' Dietrich was very close to becoming jocular and good-humoured, a mood he shared with no one else on the silent bridge.

Burckhardt made a great effort to respond. 'I think we can manage if they appear. You come ashore with me, of course.'

'I had assumed that!' Dietrich stared round slowly as though he found it instructive to see the reactions of a company of soldiers about to go ashore into the unknown as dawn broke. He met stolid eyes, tightly shut mouths, and once he caught Prentice's gaze as the lieutenant stared back at him curiously. 'I have my Luger,' he told Burckhardt amiably, 'just in case of trouble.'

'There is to be no shooting!' Burckhardt spoke sharply and for the first time he turned and looked directly at Dietrich. 'My men have strict orders to go ashore quietly. It will increase the element of surprise and their first task is to set up a road-block at the northern end of the village. The first troops ashore will see to that.'

'And when do you expect to take the monastery?'

'Who said we were interested in monasteries, Herr Dietrich? This is a war we are fighting, not a religious campaign.' And having delivered this rebuke the colonel turned away and devoted his whole attention to the lamp which was now so close that they could see it perched at the end of a stone jetty. Under the lamp stood two men, woken up doubtless by the explosion of the mine and anxious to hear what had happened.

They're in for a surprise, Burckhardt was thinking as he saw the Abwehr man easing his way towards the door. I suppose he's checking up on our arrangements for the landing so he can put that in his report to Canaris. Still, with his knowledge of the peninsula he might come in useful yet. Burckhardt looked up as Hahnemann appeared in the doorway when Dietrich went outside.

'Start withdrawing men from the search for the Greek and assemble them for disembarkation,' Burckhardt told him. 'What about the demolition charge?'

'No sign of it, sir. We are still searching . . .'

'Withdraw all men from the search except for those in the engine-room. Any news of the Greek?'

'He hasn't been seen, sir.'

Burckhardt removed the glove he had been wearing from his pistol hand and nodded. 'The Greek doesn't matter any more. Later the search can be continued by the men left to guard the ship.' It was only a minor element in the meticulous plan – guarding the ship to make sure no one tried to take her across the gulf to warn the British. Burckhardt checked his watch. 5.55 AM. Yes, they were thirty minutes late. It would be dawn just about the time they landed; already he could see faintly a low ridge silhouetted against a streak of cold grey light. The countryside in this part of the peninsula was hilly, with a single road to the south which wound its way between the hills until it reached the plateau. From there on the terrain became steadily worse, culminating in the grim wilderness of precipices and sheer ascents of the heights of Zervos.

'You will be responsible for the security of the British prisoners,' he told Sergeant Volber who had just entered the bridge to report that his section was ready for disembarkation. He had already decided that they would be taken half-way along the peninsula and then left there under guard. This obviated any possibility of their being captured and released by a Greek unit which might be sent to the peninsula from Salonika. The information they possessed as to the unit's strength was a little too valuable to share with the enemy. He glanced back at the two men who stared at him with expressionless faces.

'Looks as though they're going to make it,' Ford whispered, 'although I wouldn't bet a brass farthing on the outcome yet.'

'Looks as though *we* might make it,' Prentice corrected him drily. 'And frankly, I wish you hadn't said that – it's asking for that demolition thing to trip its whatnot.'

'There's time yet, sir,' Ford assured him.

Schnell was now having to conduct an awkward manoeuvre to evade a single mine floating dead ahead. He had to steer the vessel round the mine and then alter course afresh to bring the ship up against the side of the jetty. Burckhardt could see that the glowing lamp was a lantern fixed to the top of a low mast and underneath it a small group of figures was huddled. He sent several men off the bridge, ordered the rest to keep in the shadows and joined them. This last mine was causing further delay and he felt the impatience surging up: he wanted to be off this damned Greek ferry, to get ashore and get on with it. And it was not only the timetable which made him curse that so inconveniently placed mine – that object so thoughtfully dropped by his allies was providing more time for the hidden demolition charge to detonate. He prayed to God that it wouldn't happen at the last moment, but a streak of pessimism in his nature made him fear the worst. In war, the chance happenings, the coincidences, were always bad ones. He had learned that in Finland where he had experienced the Winter War as assistant to the German military attaché in Helsinki when the Finns had fought the Russians to a ferocious standstill, in Norway where he had commanded... He spoke quickly in Greek as Nopagos moved to the starboard window. 'Stay by the wheel!'

'If they see me they will be reassured.' Nopagos still stood by the window as he looked over his shoulder. His face was despondent and he looked as though he could hardly stand up: this was probably the last voyage of the *Hydra* and he was bringing home the most terrible cargo he had ever carried. 'I don't want any harm to come to them – if they start to run away...'

'My men have orders not to shoot.' Burckhardt hesitated. The fight had gone out of the captain and it gave a greater appearance of normality if he could be seen clearly on the bridge. 'You can stay there,' he said, 'but you are not to call out to them.'

Dawn was beginning to spread over the peninsula as Schnell edged his way round the solitary mine, and the bleak light showed a landscape still in the grip of winter. The olive trees on the scrub-covered hills were naked silhouettes and along the jetty a coating of frost glittered with the colour of *crème de menthe* over stones green with age. The little group under the lamp which glowed eerily in the half-light stood hunched up with their hands in their pockets and one man was stamping his feet on the stones. An appearance of absolute normality. Another ferry trip ending its voyage quietly as a matter of seagoing routine. Which was very satisfactory, Burckhardt was thinking. Near the end of the jetty, a simple mole which projected straight out into the gulf, the beach was visible, a beach of rocks and stones. And behind the beach a high sea-wall stretched away into the distance. The intelligence people had warned him about that unscalable sea-wall – had emphasized that the only entrance to the village was a gap in the wall at the end of the jetty where a causeway linked the mole with the road into Katyra. Burckhardt was looking beyond the wall now to the short line of two-storeyed houses which were shuttered and still like abandoned villas. The whole place had the look of a resort which is only open during the summer months. It was all going according to plan. They would land without any fuss, occupy the village, set up the road-block to the north, and within an hour the main body of the troops would be moving south into the heart of the peninsula. An officer Prentice had not seen before came on to the bridge to report and the colonel motioned him back into the shadows.

'Major Eberhay reports everything ready for disembarkation, sir.'

'Good. The wireless set is being guarded by two men, I take it, Brandt?'

'Yes, sir. The major saw to it himself.'

'Tell him those civilians on the jetty are not to be brought on board because of the demolition charge. He can keep them on the beach and they can be escorted back into the village later.'

As Brandt left the bridge Burckhardt thought about the wireless set. Until the sabotaged set was repaired it was their only means of communication with GHQ to confirm that the reinforcements could be flown in. It was, in fact, one of the most vital pieces of equipment in the expedition. Without that he would be on his own and there could be the most appalling muddle when they arrived at the plateau. The vessel had almost circumnavigated the pestilential mine and was creeping in towards the jetty where the little group had shifted position. Prentice had moved closer to the window and Burckhardt warned a guard that he musn't get any closer. When he looked to starboard again the jetty was almost under the ship's hull.

*

The lower slopes of the hills were still in darkness as the gangway clattered onto the jetty. Major Eberhay was the first man ashore and a moment later Nopagos joined him, followed by a dozen Alpenkorps soldiers. These troops were unarmed, their collars nearly buttoned to the neck, and one man carried a plaque struck to commemorate the commencement of collaboration between Greek and German peoples. Only the space for the date was left blank. Drawn up in files of threes, they marched steadily along the jetty top in the direction of the causeway which led to Katyra. The plaque was for presentation to the mayor of Katyra. Outwardly, for the first few minutes, the disembarkation had the appearance of an arranged visit as the Alpenkorps paraded away into the distance. Only a band was absent to mark the occasion.*

'No resistance, please! We are overwhelmed!' It was Nopagos who delivered the urgent message to the group of four men who stood stunned under the lamp as the troops passed them. It was not quite the message which Burckhardt had instructed him to deliver but it served the same effect. One man, larger and burlier than the others, took a step backwards as though to move away, but he was restrained by the leading soldier in the next section of troops leaving the ship. The German put a firm hand on the civilian's arm and

_____

* The same technique was practised in Norway where the first unit of invading Germans ashore at Oslo was a brass band which played and marched through the capital to simulate a peaceful visit.

183

ushered him back to the group which stared at the ferry as though hardly able to believe their eyes. The third file of men pouring off the vessel were heavily armed, their rucksacks on their back, their rifles looped over their shoulders, and short bayonets sheathed in leather scabbards by their sides.

From the bridge Burckhardt watched the landing operation with approval and relief. It was all going according to plan. The leading section had already disappeared through the gap in the sea-wall and within minutes would reach their first objective – the mayor's house. It was light enough now to see the Greek flag fluttering in a breeze from a tower behind the wall. He checked his watch again as the file of armed troops began to cross the causeway. Half-way along the jetty the group of four Greeks was being hustled towards the beach while more troops marched past them. Yes, everything was going according to plan. A moment later the firing started.

The firing, which commenced immediately the Greek civilians were clear of the jetty, came at the worst possible moment for Burckhardt. The entire mole from gangway to causeway was dense with disembarking troops and the ski sections were just filing off the ship. It was one of these men, encumbered with the skis over his back, who fell as the first shot rang out. Instantly, what had been an orderly disembarkation became a scene of chaos as the falling soldier crashed into his comrades and caused several to stumble. A second shot rang out and a second man on the jetty fell close to the first casualty. There was a danger of an imminent pile-up of men as the mole seethed with field-grey figures. Burckhardt swore and leaned over the bridge to look down at the open deck below where Hahnemann was issuing quick instructions, shouting to the men to clear the jetty and move inland. A third shot was fired and four men close together half-way along the jetty paused, then began to run towards the causeway, but as they ran one of their number sprawled lifelessly on the jetty floor. Burckhardt left the bridge and made for the open deck. At the top of the staircase Dietrich was staring across the peninsula and as Burckhardt ran past him he noted a trivial detail: for the first time, so far as he could remember, the Abwehr man was no longer smoking a cigar. He was running down the staircase when he heard a fusillade of shots – the Alpenkorps were returning the fire, although what the God they thought they were shooting at Burckhardt had no idea. From his commanding position on the bridge he had been quite unable to locate the source of the attack.

At the bottom of the steps he noted a less trivial detail – the battalion wireless, the last set still in serviceable condition, was stowed against the wall with the flap opened back. An Alpenkorps soldier stood close by guarding the precious equipment. As soon as they had taken Katyra Burckhardt had to send the vital signal, *Phase One completed*. Despite the air of total confusion which now pervaded the vessel where men crouched low behind the rails or ran down the gangway urged on by Hahnemann, the colonel was still thinking clearly and a disturbing idea had entered his mind. Three shots, three casualties. That was the work of a marksman. It was quickly apparent that Hahnemann was disembarking the troops with all speed so Burckhardt, still concerned with his simple calculation, went swiftly back to the bridge where he could see what was happening. He arrived there in time to see more men hurrying along the jetty too close together as the firing continued. A man near the edge stopped as though struck by an invisible blow, tried to stagger forward a few steps, then plunged over the edge. He hit the water with a splash and when the body surfaced it floated motionlessly.

The fusillade continued for several minutes while the Alpenkorps constantly disembarked and ran the gauntlet of the exposed jetty. During the firing Burckhardt ordered the two remaining guards on the bridge to take Prentice and Ford below ready for going ashore. Schnell had left earlier so now he was alone on the bridge as the fusillade ceased suddenly. He waited, turning his eyes now to the lower hill slopes still in the fading shadow of night. Hahnemann had carried out his order to cease fire abruptly and then hold fire for five minutes. Earlier, the colonel had assumed that those shots were coming from behind one of the shuttered windows, but so far he had seen nothing to confirm this. Half-a-dozen men were risking the jetty run again, their bodies crouched low as they ran past the huddled shapes lying on the stones. A single shot split the silence only broken by the thud of nailed boots on paved stone. One man fell. The others ran on, disappearing through the gap in the wall. On the bridge Burckhardt twisted his mouth grimly. He had seen it this time – the muzzle-flash in the hills to the south of the village. The marksman was indeed firing long-distance, and now he felt sure it was the work of one man. He left the bridge and Hahnemann met him at the foot of the staircase with news of the disaster.

'The second set is out of commission . . .'

'What!' Burckhardt was thunderstruck. He felt the blood rush to his head and paused before going on. 'How did it happen?'

'A bullet hit it – all the valves are smashed.'

A soldier was crouched over the set and he kept his head lowered as though afraid to face the colonel. Bending close to him, Burckhardt spoke very quietly. 'You were supposed to be guarding it, Dorff.'

'He could hardly have done anything,' Hahnemann interjected. 'He was by the rail firing off a few shots himself when it happened. He was never very far away from the set. It is just the most appalling bad luck, sir.'

'Bad luck, Hahnemann?' The colonel straightened up and stared at him. 'We have had one set sabotaged earlier in the voyage. Someone planted a demolition charge inside the vessel. And someone, at the beginning, set free the British prisoners. Haven't you grasped it yet that some unknown person is making sure that bad luck does come our way?' He turned as Dietrich walked round a corner and stopped to look down at the wrecked set.

'More?' he asked bluntly.

'A bullet has smashed all the valves. The set is quite useless.' Burckhardt studied the Abwehr man for a moment. 'Herr Dietrich, I believe you possess a Luger. Would you mind showing it to me?'

Without a word Dietrich extracted the pistol from his pocket and handed it to the colonel. While Burckhardt was examining the weapon he stood with his hands deep inside his pockets as he gazed along the jetty where the last troops were hurrying towards the village. It was almost daylight now and the buildings beyond the sea-wall showed up clearly in the pale sunshine. They had a decrepit, unpainted look and several tiles were missing from the shallow roofs which were a dull red colour. Once their walls had been brightly colour-washed but that had been a long time ago; now that the place could be seen properly in the dawn light it had shrunk from a shadowed village of some size to a tiny fishing hamlet of a few hundred people. Burckhardt had checked the gun, had found it fully loaded with seven rounds. He sniffed briefly at the barrel and then returned it. 'Thank you.' He looked at Hahnemann. 'We will go ashore. Tell Volber to bring the prisoners.'

Straightening his tunic, Burckhardt led the way onto Greek soil. Because of the *Hydra*'s list to port, the gangway was inclined at a steep angle, a detail he had overlooked, and he had to run down it onto the almost deserted jetty. Here again, he led the way, walking briskly but without undue haste, pausing to exchange a few words with two medical orderlies who were attending the casualties. One of them looked up and shook his head. Burckhardt resumed his even pace, knowing that men still aboard were watching him from the rails. Behind him came the Abwehr man, hands still inside his pockets, looking towards the south as he trailed the colonel, and behind him followed Prentice and Ford escorted by Volber and a private. At the end of the mole the colonel stopped and called down to Nopagos who was waiting with the other civilians on the beach. 'That Greek, Grapos, what other qualifications had he that you didn't tell me about?'

'He speaks English.'

Nopagos hadn't understood what the colonel was driving at and he saw the German stiffen. Burckhardt's reactions piled on top of one another. Was he being insolent? The question going through the colonel's head had been whether at some time Grapos might have undergone military service, perhaps before he contracted his limp. Grapos spoke English? As he walked on to the causeway Burckhardt tried to recall the sequence of events aboard the *Hydra*. Could Grapos have freed Prentice and Ford? He had been imprisoned in the hold at the time. Had he sabotaged both wireless sets? Was he still on board? Then who was that marksman in the hills . . . Firmly, he pushed the riddle out of his thoughts as he went through the gap in the wall where a sentry had been posted. He saluted as the man jumped to attention.

Behind him Dietrich was taking his time about

walking towards Katyra, dragging his feet until Volber and the prisoners caught up with him. He even stood quite still for a moment while he looked down at Nopagos, and when he continued along the causeway the prisoners and their escorts had passed and were a few paces in front of him. He appeared to be taking a great interest in the view to the south next, staring fixedly at the hills, and then he switched his attention to the sentry by the wall, noting the hand-grenade which hung from the soldier's belt. Finally, he looked back along the jetty to see if anyone else was close at hand. The gangplank was empty and there was no sign of more troops coming ashore. He turned round and called out.

'Volber! I think you're wanted back at the ship.'

The sergeant gestured to the prisoners to halt. They had just passed through the gap and beyond a dusty track wound out of sight past a stone building into the main part of Katyra. Burckhardt had almost reached the bend and Dietrich's words had not been spoken loudly enough to reach him. The sentry looked puzzled and stared at the *Hydra* where a tall figure could be seen at the head of the gangway with its back turned.

'What is it, sir?' Volber took a few paces towards the Abwehr man and his expression was uncertain. In the distance, over his shoulder, the colonel disappeared round the curve in the road which was now empty. Prentice was standing with his hands on his hips while

Ford stared pointedly at the soldier who stood a few paces away with his rifle at the ready.

'I think you're wanted back at the ship,' Dietrich repeated. 'I saw Hahnemann beckoning.'

Volber was in a quandary. He had received explicit orders from the colonel to escort the prisoners personally into the village and he had no inclination to vary from Burckhardt's command by so much as a centimetre. But Lieutenant Hahnemann was the officer who could, and did, make life arduous for him. So he compromised briefly, waiting to see whether the beckoning was repeated from the gangway. Dietrich remained where he was, apparently absorbed in the panorama across the gulf. If one ignored the huddled group on the jetty and overlooked the signs of military invasion, it was an extraordinarily peaceful scene. By early daylight the Aegean was an intense, deep cobalt with a backdrop of misty mountains on the mainland which seemed almost unreal. At the head of the lonely gulf, where the sun caught the water at a certain angle, the sea glittered like mercury, and on the nearby beach small waves, rippled by the breeze, slid gently forward and collapsed.

Volber stirred restlessly. 'I can't wait any longer, sir,' he ventured, and Dietrich nodded as though he understood. He followed the sergeant through the gap and stopped suddenly when he saw, to his right, that two Alpenkorps soldiers stationed behind the wall had been concealed from his view. As he appeared they were looking at the hills to the south, but now they lowered their field-glasses, hoisted their machine-pistols more firmly over their shoulders, and walked back to the gap to take one last look at the vessel which had brought them all the way from Istanbul. Volber paused to have a word with them, making some joking reference to pleasure cruises, but Dietrich noticed that he was staring along the jetty in case Hahnemann appeared and started gesturing. Sighing out aloud, Prentice crossed onto the grass verge and sat down with his back to the wall where Ford joined him. Volber, standing in the middle of the gap with the other three soldiers, was about to reprimand him, when hell opened up on the gulf.

The reverberations of the detonation crashed round the hillsides, roared out across the gulf like a cannonade, and sent a shock wave like a bombardment through the gap in the wall. The demolition charge had reached zero. Dietrich, half-protected by the wall, was thrown sprawling onto the grass and he thought he heard two explosions close together – the charge first, then the boilers going up. The full force of the wave had struck the four Alpenkorps soldiers like a giant hammer and they lay in the road like trampled rag dolls. Only two men were moving feebly and one of them fell limp almost immediately as he lost consciousness. The sentry was bunched up against the outside of the wall in a strangely twisted position. As Dietrich lay on the grass, temporarily deafened by the road, there was a stench of burning oil in his nostrils and Prentice and Ford, whose ears had not been affected, heard debris clattering on the village rooftops like spent shrapnel from ack-ack guns.

For both of them the immensely strong sea-wall had muffled the blast. But Dietrich was recovering quickly. As he staggered to his feet Prentice began to move up behind him with a rock in his fist. The Abwehr man, unaware of what was happening behind him, fished the Luger out of his pocket, looked quickly up the road and along the jetty, and moved towards the soldier who was climbing to his feet in the centre of the road. Prentice, moving soundlessly on the grass, followed Dietrich as he lurched towards the soldier who had now brought himself to his knees and was shaking his head like a dog emerging from a river. He looked up as Dietrich brought the Luger barrel crashing down on his head. He was slumping to the ground when Dietrich tugged the loop of the machine-pistol free. Prentice stared in astonishment, the rock still poised in his hand, but when he saw the machine-pistol he moved forward again. The Abwehr man turned, knocked the unsteady fist aside and thrust the weapon into Prentice's hands. 'This will be more useful – if you can handle the damned thing.'

He had spoken in English and without waiting for Prentice's reaction he hauled another machine-pistol loose from an inert German, tossed it across to Ford, and then extracted spare magazines from the pockets of the two men on the ground. When he stood up he noticed that it was Ford who was familiar with the

machine-pistol and shoved the magazines at him. 'Here
– it looks as though they'd be more use to you. Now,
we've got to get moving pdq. We go that way – along
the wall to the south.'

'Who the devil are you?' Prentice demanded.

'Dietrich of the Abwehr.'

The reply was given ironically as the large man
stared briefly along the jetty wall. The *Hydra* looked
like a refugee from an Atlantic convoy. The funnel was
bent at a surrealist angle and her bows were already
settling in the shallow water. Around the hull men
swam in the sea distractedly as a huge column of black
smoke ascended into the clear sky like a gigantic signal
which would be seen clear across the bay to the
mainland. As he gazed at the wreckage a tongue of red
flame flared up at the base of the distorted funnel. Soon
the whole superstructure would be ablaze and would
go on burning until the hulk was reduced to its
waterline and the *Hydra* was a blackened shell. All
Burckhardt's efforts at preserving an appearance of
normality had gone up with the demolition charge. 'I
thought she'd never blow,' he said half to himself, and
then he saw Nopagos clambering up onto the jetty. The
shock wave must have blown straight over the heads
of the group on the beach. He looked back towards the
town and the road was still empty. 'They'll be coming
soon,' he warned, 'so let's get to hell out of here.'

'Which way? The village is crawling with them . . .'

'Along this wall – five years ago I walked all over
this place. We've got to head up the peninsula . . .'

'But who the devil are you?' Prentice repeated, and when the reply came the Scots burr was even more pronounced.

'I'm Ian Macomber.' He grabbed at the lieutenant's arm. 'Now, if you don't want to get shot, follow me and run like hell!'

Chapter Eight

Sunday, 10 am

By ten o'clock in the morning they had marched almost non-stop through punishing hill country which had caused them either to climb or descend most of the way, and they had still seen no trace of Grapos. It was Macomber who had urged them on mercilessly, insisting that they put as much ground as possible between themselves and the oncoming Germans before they rested. Several times Prentice had tried to talk and ask questions, but on each occasion the Scot had brusquely told him to save his breath for the march. They followed a footpath which twisted and turned as its surface changed, sometimes sand, sometimes rock and often merely beaten earth. A path which led them past olive groves, over hilltops ringed with boulders, and down into scrub-infested valleys where the streams raced with swelling waters. But now they had reached a hilltop where Macomber consented to pause briefly because it gave a clear view back to the north where the road from Katyra came towards them in a series of bends and drops down the near sides of hills dense with undergrowth.

'We can see them coming from here,' Macomber

announced as he perched on a rounded boulder. 'And water is going to be our problem. There isn't much of it on the plateau.'

'This might help,' Ford suggested as he undid his coat and showed a pear-shaped water-bottle attached to his belt. 'I filched that off one of those dead Jerries while you two pulled yourselves together.'

'Ford gets his priorities right,' Prentice remarked, and then stared hard at Macomber. 'Mind if I hear a little more about you now?'

Macomber took a swig from the water-bottle, handed it on to Prentice and grinned faintly. 'I've spent the last fifteen months in the Balkans. Do you think that sounds cushy?'

'Depends what you were doing,' Prentice replied cautiously. 'What were you doing?'

'I'll tell you, then. I'm like Winston Churchill as far as ancestry goes – half-British and half-American. My mother was a New Yorker and my father came from Aberdeen. I spent a third of my early years in the States, another third in Scotland, and the rest of the time travelling round Europe with my parents. My father was a linguistics expert and I inherited his gift for languages.' There was no modesty in Macomber's tone but neither was he boasting; he was simply stating a fact. 'And that's where the trouble started,' he went on. 'Principally my languages are German, Greek and French – which comes in useful when you're in Rumania. I had lung trouble before the war . . .'

'Lung trouble!' Prentice looked sceptical, remembering the tremendous pace the Scot had set up while they were making their dash up and down those endless hills.

'It's cured now – at least so a quack in Budapest assured me. He said it was the pure clean air from Siberia which blows across Hungary in winter that had done the trick. But that lung kept me out of the Forces in 1939, so the Ministry of Economic Warfare asked me to do a job for them. Get your head out of the way, Ford, I can't see that road.'

'What sort of a job?' Prentice asked casually. Without appearing to do so he was trying to check the Scot's story.

'Buying up strategic war materials the Jerries wanted. You'd never believe the funds I had at my disposal. I bought up everything I could lay my hands on and had it shipped out of the Balkans. I had an idea the bright boys foresaw the German *Drach nach Osten* and wanted to denude the place before Hitler arrived.'

'Sounds interesting,' was Prentice's only comment.

'You think so? Just sitting behind a desk and making out orders in quadruplicate for a few thousand gallons of oil or the odd few tons of copper – is that how you see it?'

'I didn't say so.'

'No, but you looked so!' He took out one of his remaining cigars. 'What I don't think you've quite grasped is that I had competitors. Jerry competitors, and they can play very rough, very rough indeed. When I'd survived two attempts to kill me – one in

Györ and one in Budapest – I decided my luck was running out and the time had come to go underground, so I acquired some false papers and set up as a German.' He looked quizzically at Prentice over his cigar, put it back in his mouth and went on talking. 'Don't look so damned unbelieving – false papers can be obtained almost anywhere if you have the money, and I had a small fortune to play with.'

'You set up as Dietrich, then?'

'No, he came later. I called myself Hermann Wolff, and, you know, necessity really did turn out to be the mother of invention. I found myself mixing openly with the German community in Budapest, which in the beginning was simply excellent camouflage, but later when I ran out of stuff to buy up it gave our Ministry brains another idea, a diabolical idea.' He turned again to look over his shoulder at the hill behind, in the opposite direction from where the Germans must come, and this was a gesture he had repeated several times.

'Isn't that the wrong direction to fret over?' Prentice inquired. 'Or could they have got ahead of us on the road while we were doing our cross-country route march?'

'Old habits . . .' Dietrich spread a large hand. 'I've spent so many months looking over my shoulder – because the danger always comes from where you least expect it.' He shrugged and stared at Ford for a moment 'When it comes, it comes.'

'A diabolical job, you were saying,' Prentice reminded him. As he listened he scanned the deserted countryside to the north where a dark smoke column from the burning *Hydra* was still climbing into the brilliant morning sky. They'd see that smoke as far away as Salonika, almost, if the weather visibility was as good across Macedonia. It seemed incredible that a whole German expedition was mustering itself somewhere beyond those hills for a forced march south to Mount Zervos.

'Yes, truly diabolical,' Macomber repeated. 'There were hardly any more strategic supplies I could lay my hands on, but there was a mass of stuff the Germans had bought up which still hadn't been shipped back to the Reich. It was lying around in warehouses and railway sidings, so the Ministry brainboxes said would I have a go at it? Very obliging they were, too – sent out an explosives man to teach me a trick or two about things that go bang in the night . . .' He paused again, detecting a sudden freshening of interest from Ford, but when the ammunition examiner said nothing he continued. 'The trouble again was I was made to order for these sabotage jobs. I picked up information from the German community I was mixing with about what was where – and by then I was accepted in Budapest. We even used German explosives – like ten-kilogram demolition charges.'

'Why not British equipment?' queried Ford.

'Because I was operating in neutral territory and the Hungarian government might not have taken too kindly to British time-bombs being planted inside their goods wagons. Those bombs don't always function according to the book and sometimes they don't function at all. Even when they do, the experts can often piece together a few vital bits and tell the type of bomb that was used and where it was made.' He glanced over his shoulder and grinned again. 'And don't ask me how we got hold of German explosives because that's a state secret.'

'You were pretty successful in passing yourself off as a German even in Hungary then?' Prentice suggested idly. He felt close to exhaustion but his mind was still sufficiently alert to go on checking Macomber's identity so far as he could.

'I knew the Reich well by the time war broke out. In peacetime I'd been a shipping broker – some of my business was with the Reich and I spent a lot of time in Germany before 1939 and sometimes, even then, it was convenient to pass for one of the *Herrenvolk*. The trick is to learn to think like them, to feel you are one of them – and that's something I had to work overtime at while we were on the *Hydra*. I may tell you that was the longest voyage of my life, and it took just twenty-four hours.'

'How did you fool the colonel? That must have taken some doing.'

'The ability to bluff big – nothing else. I took a leaf out of the dear Führer's book there: if you want to believe a lie, be sure it's a whopper. If I'd tried to pass myself off simply as a German civilian, I think they'd have restricted my movements, but the dreaded Abwehr was something quite different. I knew quite a lot about the Abwehr when I went aboard the *Hydra* at Istanbul – in fact, I thought they had somebody on my tail ready to do an assassination act before I could get home . . .'

'You weren't put on that ship deliberately then?' Prentice found it difficult to keep the surprise out of his voice. Ford was emptying the machine-pistol while he tested the mechanism and then re-loaded.

'No, I'd finished with the Balkans and I was on my way to Athens to get a berth to Egypt. The Germans had occupied the whole area and it wasn't possible to operate any more with the key points swarming with their security chaps. I was coming on the direct Istanbul–Athens ferry, but that was cancelled at the last moment. When Burckhardt's lot took over the ship I wasn't completely surprised – the presence of several Germans on the passenger list was something I'd been thinking about ever since I got on board.'

'But why pretend you were the Abwehr?'

'Because I knew how they operated – months ago they'd sent men to Budapest to investigate the sabotage. But mainly because it's the only organization inside Germany today which the armed forces get nervous about. Burckhardt was convinced I'd been put on the ship to check up on how he handled things – which gave me a psychological stranglehold over him from the outset.'

'You make it sound so damned easy.' There was a hint of admiration in Prentice's manner as he sat with his back propped against a boulder and waited.

'Oh, very easy – as easy as moving round inside Hungary and Rumania with top Abwehr agents on your tail. As easy as making frequent trips to wayside railway stations to collect suitcases left by someone you never see – suitcases containing demolition charges. As easy as lugging them across railway lines at two in the morning with engines shunting all over the place and guards with dogs looking for you.' Macomber's voice had risen to a low growl as he glared at Prentice with an intensity of rage which was alarming. 'As easy as going back to your flat late in the evening and noticing that the lock has been tampered with – so you know that inside that darkened flat someone is waiting for you with a knife or a gun or whatever particular weapon they've decided will do the job quickly and quietly. Yes, Prentice, and it was easy on that ship we've just left, too – easy putting those wireless sets out of action with two hundred troops all around you, easy coming into your cabin to cut your ropes to give you a chance to get clear and warn that destroyer . . .'

'I'm sorry,' Prentice said quietly, realizing for the first time the tremendous pressure this man must have lived under for months, catching a glimpse of what it must have been like to go on living alone in the alien Balkans surrounded by enemies while he went on with his deadly work. He supposed that the outburst was the climax of God knew how much pent-up anxiety and living on the nerves endlessly, until it had seemed it must go on for ever. Macomber made no attempt to apologize for the outburst but he smiled wintrily as he smoked his cigar and started talking again.

'Planting the demolition charge was simpler than you might imagine. I just saw it lying with the fuses in a half-open rucksack and grabbed it. There was a little trouble in the dark on deck when I ran into a soldier, but a knowledge of unarmed combat can come in useful. Afterwards, I pitched him over the side like you did your chap. The vital moment was when we'd just come ashore – I'd always foreseen that.'

'Why then?' asked Prentice.

'Several reasons. Burckhardt's whole attention was taken up with the landing and capturing Katyra quickly. Later, he'd have more time to think which is just what I didn't want him to have. Then there was the problem of the other wireless set – I'd messed up the tuning coil with the butt of my Luger but I gathered they might be able to repair the thing. The moment they could wireless for confirmation of my identity I was finished. And you can thank whatever lucky star you were born under that the bomb didn't go off earlier – it must have stopped and then started again.'

'What time had you set it for?' Prentice was taking a great interest in the answer to this question and now he saw Ford looking over his shoulder towards the hill behind them. Macomber's fears were contagious.

'I set it to detonate at 3.30 AM while we were still well down the gulf.'

'Good God!'

A trace of the nervous reaction still smouldered

inside Macomber and he didn't bother to put it too tactfully. 'I'm sure, Prentice, that by now you know there's a war on. There were two hundred German troops aboard who may yet do untold damage to the Allied cause – if I could sink them I was going to do it. And I still will, although how I haven't the slightest idea. You know they're heading for the monastery on Mount Zervos to set up an observation post, I take it?'

'I had an idea that was the objective. I agree we've got to get there first, if we can, but I can't quite see us forming the monks into a defensive battalion to hold off the Jerries. Is there any means of communication there we could use to get in touch with the mainland?'

'Not so far as I know apart from the telephone line to Salonika and that's been cut.' Macomber dropped the half-smoked cigar into the sand and carefully heeled it out of sight. 'But there's always something that can be done as long as you're there – that's something I've learned.' His expression became ferocious as he growled out the words. 'Whatever happens the Germans have got to be stopped from taking Zervos. Hell! If there's nothing else we'll have to set fire to the place to attract attention. There are British troops driving up that coast only a few miles across the gulf. Setting fire to the monastery may be the only solution!'

Prentice stared at the huge figure stooped forward over the boulder and realized that he meant what he said. Previously he had regarded Macomber as an enterprising civilian, with the accent on 'civilian', but now he began to wonder whether the war he had fought in the Western Desert compared with the shadowy, no-quarter struggle the Scot had waged inside the peace-time Balkans. He blinked to keep his eyes open as Macomber clasped both hands tightly and stared again at the road from Katyra with a dubious expression. It was over twenty-four hours since any of them had slept and the strain showed in their whiskered haggard faces; the brain was beginning to slow down, the reflexes to react sluggishly, and these were danger signals. He was about to speak when Macomber made the suggestion himself. 'I think three-quarters of an hour's sleep would work wonders. We may need every ounce of strength we can muster before the day is out but someone must keep watch. He grinned. 'So, if you two are sufficiently convinced of my bona-fides, I'll act as lookout while you get some kip.'

'No, I'll stand watch while you and Ford sleep,' Prentice said promptly. 'You've been through more than us, anyway.'

'Suit yourself,' was Macomber's terse reply. Dropping down off the boulder, he lay on the sand after casting one final look back at the hill behind. The hill looked dangerous was his last thought before he fell asleep.

Macomber was a man who, when he woke up, became instantly alert, all his faculties keyed up for immediate action. The trait had been sharpened during his experience in the Balkans and on waking he had developed another facility – the habit of never opening his eyes until he had listened for a few seconds. Lying on the sand with his back against the rock, he listened carefully to the sounds with his eyes still closed. The scrape of a boot over stone, which told him someone was moving nearby. The quick dull click of metal on metal, which was the movement of a rifle bolt. A coldness down his back was the physical reaction of his brain warning him of danger. Then a voice spoke. Prentice's.

'Don't move, Ford, for God's sake!'

Macomber's prone body was still relaxed and lifeless as he half-opened his eyes. Ford was sitting up on the sand, his suit crumpled, his right hand withdrawing from the machine-pistol which lay close by his side. He had a drugged look and had obviously just woken up. Macomber couldn't see Prentice but the thought flashed through his mind that the lieutenant must have dozed off and during those unguarded minutes a German patrol had arrived. Lying on his side, Macomber's hand was tucked inside his coat pocket where it had rested when he had fallen asleep, and now his fingers curled round the butt of the Luger. The problem was going to be to get in an upright position quickly enough. From the direction of Ford's startled gaze he calculated that the newcomers were stationed behind the boulder he was leant against. But how many of them? The boot scraped again and the shadow of a man fell across the sand in front of where he lay, the shadow of a man and a gun.

'Wait! For God's sake wait!' A note of desperation in Prentice's voice chilled Macomber. 'We can explain – don't shoot!'

The silhouette of the rifle barrel angled lower and Macomber guessed that it was now tilted downwards and aimed at him point-blank. He sensed that the slightest movement of his body would activate the shadow's trigger finger, and while he compelled himself to stay relaxed he felt the stickiness of his palm clutching the pistol butt. A strange tingling sensation sang along his nerves and his brain hung in a horrible state of prolonged suspension as every tiny detail seemed weirdly clear. The appalled expression on Ford's face, the mouth half-open, held as though in a condition of rictus. The wobble of the unknown man's silhouette as he shifted balance to the other foot to take the shock of the rifle's recoil. The flitting motion of some tiny insect hopping over the sand in the shade of the silhouette. Macomber's throat had gone so dry that he felt the most terrible compulsion to cough as a tickle crawled in his throat.

'Do you understand any English at all?' Prentice again, his voice throaty with tension. 'We're on your . . .'

'Yes, I speak English.' A deep-chested voice with a rumbling timbre which sounded familiar. 'Why are you with the German?'

'Look, Grapos,' Prentice pleaded quickly, 'he's not a German. He's British. If you let him wake up and speak he'll talk to you in English as much as you want . . .'

'There are Germans who speak English.' Grapos' tone was unimpressed and savagely obstinate. 'I speak English but I am Greek. He has made you think he is English? We have very little time. He must be killed, now!' The gun silhouette moved again as though the Greek was taking fresh aim and Macomber waited for the thud of the bullet, the last thing he would ever feel. And there was an urgency in Grapos' voice as well as in his words which filled the Scot with foreboding. There was some other danger coming very close, he felt sure of it, a danger the Greek was only too well aware of. Prentice was talking again and this time he was adopting an entirely different tactic, abandoning pleading as he spoke crisply as though he were giving a command.

'Look, I'm telling you, mate. His name is Macomber. Ian Macomber. He's a Scot – that's from the topside a my country – and he's the one who planted that bomb which nearly blew up all those Germans, only it didn't go off in time. He speaks fluent German – a damned sight more fluent German than you speak English. To help us get away he half-killed a Jerry – a German – in front of me. He grabbed a couple of German machine-pistols and gave them to us. Since then he's led the way to where we are now because he knows the country and we don't. And if that isn't enough for you, you can go and dive in the sea again. So stop aiming that gun at him and let him wake up and speak for himself.'

'You are sure of these things?' Grapos sounded

anything but sure of what he had been listening to and the rifle was still pointed down at the inert figure below.

'I'm perfectly sure! Don't you think I can tell when I'm talking to one of my own countrymen? Wouldn't you know when you were talking to a Greek even if you'd heard that same man speaking good German earlier?' Prentice deliberately lost his temper a little, and seeing the look of doubt on Grapos' face he followed up quickly while he had the Greek off-balance. 'And now, for Pete's sake, can he get up and speak for himself? He must be awake now.'

'Yes ... I ... am ... awake.' Macomber spoke slowly and very clearly, resuming his normal manner of speech only when he saw the shadow of the gun move away. 'So can I get up and let you have another good look at me?'

'Yes, you may get up.' Grapos' boots scraped again as he spoke and when Macomber climbed to his feet the villainous-looking civilian was standing several paces beyond him with his weapon still held so that it could cover Macomber with only a fraction of move-ment. A German carbine, the Scot noted. The one he had gone overboard with. The one he had used to shoot down the Alpenkorps men on the jetty. Macomber's hands hung loosely by his sides and he gazed at Grapos without friendship as he asked the question with a single word.

'Well?'

'You look like a German.'

'And you look like a bandit.'

The Greek's eyes flashed. The gun muzzle lifted and was then lowered. He stared back grimly but with a certain respect as he slapped his rifle butt once and then turned to Prentice, ignoring Macomber as he spoke rapidly. 'There is trouble. German soldiers are coming up that hill on the other side . . .' He indicated the hill which had worried Macomber, the hill he had glanced back at so many times. 'When they come to the top they will see you here. We must go quickly.'

'Which way?' asked Prentice.

'That way.' He pointed towards the hill crest over which he had just warned them the Germans were advancing. Prentice took a step forward, stooped to pick up his machine-pistol, which he looped over his shoulder, and then shook his head uncomprehendingly.

'Grapos, you've just said the Germans are coming over that hill, so we'd better push off in some other direction.'

'No. They come this way – so we go this way. You will see. Come! We must hurry.'

'Half a minute!' Prentice was not convinced and his naturally sceptical mind was now wondering whether he could trust Grapos. 'We haven't seen any Germans come along the road down there and they'd have to do that to get over there . . .'

Macomber broke in quickly, relieved to see that Ford's common sense had automatically made him turn round and watch the empty hill crest while the others argued it out. 'Prentice, the Germans were confident they could get hold of mules in Katyra – not enough for all their men, I'm sure, but probably enough to send ahead an advance party. If Burckhardt acted quickly and sent out a patrol on mules in time, they could have passed along that road while we were going across country. In which case some of them would be ahead of us – that was why I kept looking over my shoulder earlier.'

'Theophilous would supply them with mules,' said Grapos. He spat on the ground. 'Theophilous is at Katyra. He has German mother and Greek father, but he loves Germans. It is known for a long time. And Theophilous has mules . . .'

'And undoubtedly would know where to lay his hands on others,' Macomber interjected. 'All right, assuming they're coming up that hill from the far side, where do we go?'

'We go down here and wait.'

'Wait . . .?' Prentice still couldn't understand the Greek's plan but Grapos, without attempting to explain further, led the way down the flank of the hill which was fully exposed to anyone coming over the distant hill crest. From the summit of the hill where they had rested the view into the valley below had been obscured by an outcrop of rock, but as they descended through thick scrub which almost closed over the path they were able to see more clearly. A broad stream on its way to the sea ran along the narrow valley floor and at one point it was crossed by a series of stepping-stones which were barely above the water's surface. On the far bank, perhaps a hundred yards to the right of the primitive crossing point, Prentice caught a glimpse of the dusty track winding its way round the base of the hill towards Zervos. The hill crest, which reared above them now as a hard outline against the cloudless sky, was still deserted. What the devil was the Greek up to? He ran down the path and began talking as soon as he was within a few paces of Grapos who hurried downhill without looking back. 'Where are we going? I want to know.'

'To the pipe.' Grapos spoke over his shoulder without pausing, although he had begun to take a keen interest in the hill crest, staring frequently in that direction as he trotted downwards unevenly because of his limp.

'What pipe? What are you talking about?'

'The pipe takes the floods from the hill to the stream. It was built many years since to stop the waters rushing over the road. We go down the pipe. The Germans will not find us there.'

'How big is it, for heaven's sake?'

'It is big. I went down it when I was a boy.'

'You were smaller, then,' Prentice pointed out urgently. 'And they'll see us as soon as they come over that ridge.'

'That is why we hide. We are there.'

They were less than half-way down the hill when Grapos plunged into a deep gulley. The sides were lined with protruding rocks and it was deep enough to hide them from view completely. Prentice looked back as Ford and Macomber dropped into the ravine and then turned ahead to see Grapos on his hands and knees while he pulled at a clump of scrub with his bare hands. When Prentice reached him he had exposed the entrance to a large drain-pipe of crumbling concrete. The hole was at least three feet in diameter, a dark decrepit opening but large enough to crawl inside on hands and knees. Crouching beside Grapos, Prentice saw that it sloped down at an angle of about twenty degrees, so it should be navigable. Macomber and Ford were also bunched round the forbidding hole which was damp and smelled of decaying fungus, and the fact that there was no light at the end of the tunnel, no visible end at all, did nothing to increase their enthusiasm for the Greek's proposed escape route.

'Where does it come out?' demanded Macomber.

'By the stream. We cross by the stones.'

'And how long is it?'

'Not long.'

'How long is a piece of string?' Prentice muttered under his breath. 'Look, Grapos, we can't even be sure the Germans are coming in this direction. They could easily have changed their minds and be waiting for us farther along that road.'

'They were coming up the hill. You will see. We can see from here.' Grapos climbed out of the end of the gulley and stood behind a dense grove of undergrowth which was taller than a man's height. In places there were gaps in the vegetation which formed natural windows and when the others joined him they found they had a clear view of the hill beyond. Without much expectation of seeing anything, Prentice stared through a tracery of bare twigs, and it came as a shock when he saw figures against the skyline. There were six of them, well spread out, and they started to descend the slope in a semi-circle with the two in the middle maintaining a higher altitude than those on the flanks. Which was correct procedure, Prentice was thinking – the two men in the centre had better observation and could give covering fire to the men below if necessary. He recognized at once the field-grey uniforms and the distinctive caps of the Alpenkorps.

'Why should they choose this area for their patrol?' Macomber wondered out loud.

'Because Theophilous will have told them about the path,' Grapos informed him promptly. 'There are two main ways from Katyra to Zervos – the road and the path. They have come over the road by mule and when they do not find you they turn back – to trap you on the path.' He stared blankly at the Scot while he pulled at a tip of his straggled moustache and his continuing distrust of Macomber was only too obvious.

'They could seal us off inside that pipe with only one man at each end,' Macomber persisted.

'When they reach the stream and cross it, we go into the pipe. They come up this hill and we pass under them.'

'Sounds feasible,' the Scot commented. 'If it works.' Turning round, he renewed his observation of the patrol which was descending the hill slope rapidly;

already they had covered more ground than he would have expected and he reminded himself that these six oncoming Germans were highly-trained Alpenkorps troops, men whose natural habitat was wild, untracked countryside, and who were now operating under ideal conditions. A disturbing thought struck him and he asked Grapos a question quickly. 'I suppose there's no risk that this chap, Theophilous, might have told them about the pipe, too?'

The Greek snorted contemptuously. 'He is not a man who ever walks or hunts – he would be frightened that he gets lost. We wait. When they cross the stream we go into the pipe.'

Macomber moved close to Prentice as he gazed through the dense thicket and he was frowning as though there were something he didn't understand. For a few minutes he watched the patrol, clambering over rocks, sometimes disappearing up to waist-height in undergrowth, but always maintaining their careful formation as they came closer to the stream, then he voiced his doubt. 'I don't like it – Burckhardt is using his men too wastefully.'

'What are you getting at?' snapped Prentice. Still without sleep, he could feel the strain telling and he knew he was trigger-tempered.

'Burckhardt has two hundred men at his disposal to take and hold Zervos. At least he had two hundred when he left the *Rupescu*, he told me. He lost four while on board the *Hydra* . . .'

'Four?'

'Yes, four. There was the man you threw overboard. Grapos killed two more while escaping, and I put one over the side when I was carrying that demolition charge up on deck. His bayonet and scabbard came in useful, by the way – I used them to support the charge inside the ventilator shaft. That's two per cent of his force without adding in those who died on the jetty and when the ship blew up. Yet he feels he can spare another six men to look for us. Does it suggest something to you, Prentice? Something alarming?'

'It suggests he feels he still has enough left to take care of a few monks.' Prentice was having trouble thinking straight. What on earth was the persistent Scot driving at now?

'It suggests to me that he expects heavy reinforcements in the very near future, which isn't a happy thought.'

'You mean by sea? Another boatload in broad daylight?'

'I doubt that. They may use some entirely different method this time.' Macomber found himself looking upwards. The sky was clear blue as far as the eye could see, its only occupants a flock of seagulls sailing high up in the sunlight as they flew away in the direction of Katyra. 'He wouldn't expend a patrol of six men just looking for us unless he was confident more help was on the way.'

'Just what we need at the moment, a Job's comforter,' Prentice muttered irritably. The Alpenkorps were half-way down the hill and they had begun to converge

217

inwards towards the stepping-stones, although as a target they were still spread out over a considerable distance. Keeping his voice down, Macomber had now turned to question Grapos.

'You know the monastery well?'

'I lived there for two years.'

'Is there any other means of communication whatsoever apart from the telephone which has been cut?'

'When they want things, they phone to Katyra. Sometimes they phone Salonika.'

'There is, of course, no wireless transmitter for emergencies?'

'No, nothing like that.'

Grapos was staring through the thicket as he replied without looking in Macomber's direction, and his replies were grudging, but the Scot appeared not to notice his reticence as he pressed on interrogating the Greek. 'You mean there is no other way ... are you listening to me? Good.' Grapos looked at Macomber directly and the brown eyes which looked back were compelling him to concentrate, to remember. 'Is there no other way at all whereby the Abbot can send a message if the phone breaks down?'

'Only the pigeons.'

'Pigeons?' Macomber's voice was sharp. 'You mean he keeps carrier pigeons? Where do they go to when released?'

'To Livai on the other side of the gulf.'

'On the mainland, you mean?'

'Yes. Livai is near Olympus and there are more monks there.'

Macomber nodded and said nothing more while the German patrol continued its descent to the edge of the stream. Even when they crossed they displayed good military caution, only one man moving over the stones at a time until they had all reached the bank below where Grapos and his group waited. As the last man landed on the near-side bank the Greek grunted and moved towards the mouth of the hole. Macomber had earlier noticed that they were standing in a natural water catchment area; above where they stood three small ravines converged into the gulley and he guessed that during bad weather a minor flood must pour into the pipe. A drift of heavy cloud had appeared in the sky and it was coming their way as he followed Grapos. Once again the unpredictable Aegean weather was changing and he prayed there wouldn't be a cloudburst while they were inside that unsavoury-looking pipe. The Greek was on all fours, about to enter the mouth, when he fumbled under his coat, extracted a knife from his jacket pocket, flicked it to eject the blade, then held it upright. The five-inch blade retracted of its own accord. He was putting it into his coat pocket for easier access when Ford rapped out his question. 'Where did you get that?'

Grapos looked over his shoulder and glared at the sergeant. For a moment it seemed as though he wasn't going to reply and then he answered resentfully. 'It is just a knife. My knife.' Ford glanced at Macomber who had immediately detected the note of suspicion in the sergeant's voice and told Grapos to wait a minute. 'It's a German knife,' Ford explained. 'A parachutist's gravity knife. What the hell is he doing with a thing like that?'

'We have to go into the tunnel,' Grapos reminded them sullenly.

'We have to know about that knife, first,' Macomber replied briskly. 'Where did you get it? Come on – I want to know.'

The German patrol must already have started advancing up the hill towards them but the possession of this strange weapon bothered Macomber and he was determined to get an explanation before they followed the Greek inside the pipe. For precious seconds it seemed like deadlock as the three men stared down at the Greek who gazed back at them with a hostile expression. Then he shrugged his broad shoulders, adjusted the rifle he had previously looped diagonally across his back and addressed Macomber. 'I took it from the German I shot.'

'You were miles away in the hills when you fired on the jetty,' Macomber pointed out. 'Just a minute, do you mean one of those Jerries on the boat?'

'No. The man I shot over there.' He made a gesture forwards to the hill the Alpenkorps patrol had just descended. 'There were seven men when I saw them. I shot the man who was to the right and he fell from a rock into the bushes. They did not find him and when they had gone I took the knife.'

'You mean you've alerted this lot! They know someone is close because you've already shot one of the patrol?' Macomber was appalled. He had accepted the Greek's stratagem for evading the Alpenkorps because he had been confident they were only searching hopefully. Now those six highly trained men below *knew* they were stalking someone who couldn't be far away, which meant they would be in a state of total alert.

'Yes,' Grapos confirmed, 'one is shot. When we go through the pipe they will not know we are on the other side . . .'

'So that's it!' Macomber stepped forward and gripped the Greek by the shoulder. 'You want us to go through the pipe and then open fire on them from the other side?'

'We have to kill Germans,' Grapos replied simply. 'When I go to join the army they say I am no good because of my limp. When I have killed many Germans I go to Athens and tell them – then I join the army.'

'Grapos!' Macomber spoke with low intensity. 'We have to get to the monastery before the Germans – in the hope that we can send a message to the mainland in time, or do something to upset them. If the Germans do take the monastery half a division won't shift them – maybe not even a division. Our job is to reach the monastery – to keep out of the way of any Germans we meet on the way, not to fight them.'

'Not fight!' Grapos was outraged. He looked up at Prentice. 'You are a British officer. I was told that when they wanted to know if I knew you. You agree with what this man is saying – this man who pretended he was a German?'

'Macomber's right,' Prentice said quietly. 'We want to get there and the only way we can do that is to dodge them – there are too many to fight. We may achieve a lot more by keeping out of their way.'

'Because it is you who say this.' Grapos glared in Macomber's direction and started crawling down the pipe which left less than a foot's clearance above his arched back. Dropping to his knees, the Scot followed the Greek into the insalubrious hole and the clearance above his back was barely six inches. Prentice, who had decided to bring up the rear, sent Ford down next, took one last look at the gulley to make sure the surface hadn't retained traces of footprints, then went inside himself with his machine-pistol over his back and a fervent hope that the Greek wouldn't start quarrelling with the Scot in this situation. Farther along the pipe Macomber was already finding his great bulk a distinct handicap as he crawled behind Grapos. He had only to lift himself a few inches and he found his back scraping the curved concrete; his contracted elbows grazed the sides of the pipe and his knees were slithering on a film of slime at the base of the pipe as he accelerated his awkward movements to keep up with the Greek's phenomenal rate of progress. The downward slope of the pipe helped him to keep up a certain speed, but he was beginning to dislike the feeling of being shut in as he went on shuffling forward through the total darkness beyond the mouth of the pipe.

Within two minutes he found himself taking great heaving breaths and this was no place for deep breathing – as he penetrated deeper inside the buried pipe the damp smell changed to an oppressive airlessness and the place seemed bereft of oxygen. How the broad-bodied Grapos managed to keep up such a killing pace he couldn't imagine and gradually the sensation of being entombed grew. He had expected his eyes to become accustomed to the darkness but it was still pitch-black and the only sound was the noise of scuffling feet and knees some distance behind him, a sound which reminded him of rats he had once heard scuttering inside a derelict warehouse. He plodded on, hands stretching out into the unknown, followed by the haul of his knees over the scum-like surface of the pipe which he now realized had been embedded in the ground for God knew how long; his hands told him this because frequently the surface of the pipe wall flaked off at his touch and more than once a large piece came away and clattered grittily on the floor. It was badly in need of running repairs but he imagined that when something was built on Zervos it was hopefully expected to last for ever. Nightmare possibilities began to invade his mind – supposing the far end was blocked? The only similar culvert pipe he could remember had been barred at the exit end by an iron grille to prevent small boys swimming in the river from investigating its interior. Grapos had been this way before years ago, but there was no reason why such a grille should not have been fixed more recently. At a rough guess the pipe must be a quarter of a mile long – so what would be the position if the exit were closed? He could never hope to turn round in this confined space and their only hope would be a slow, endless crawl backwards and uphill, a prospect he contemplated with no great relish.

As they went on and the angle of the pipe dipped more steeply, Macomber remembered that the hill slope dropped sharply when it approached the stream. He began to have a horrible feeling that they had taken the wrong decision – that they should never have entered this Stygian cylinder which might be their grave. For a brief second he paused to wipe the gathering sweat off his forehead and then ploughed on, his wrists aching under the weight they had to bear, the palms of his hands sore and tender with groping over the gritty concrete, the pain increasing across his back and down his thighs. When the hell were they going to get out of this blasted tunnel Grapos had led them into so confidently? There had to be a bend soon because only a bend would explain why there was still no light ahead. Unless the tunnel exit was completely blocked: that certainly would account for the continuing state of darkness they were crawling down through. It might also account for the worsening difficulty in breathing.

Macomber was having great trouble in regulating the intake of air now as he shuffled downwards blindly and automatically. But if the exit were stopped up they would be descending into a region of foul and foetid air where breathing might become well-nigh impossible. His great fear now was that they would discover the grim truth too late – that by the time they knew there was no way out they would have degenerated into such a weakened state that they would never be able to summon up the strength needed for the return trip. Years later when they excavated the pipe they would find ... He suppressed the macabre thought and concentrated on keeping going, hands first, then that dreadful, wearying haul forward of the knees which it was becoming an agony to move. His head was vibrating gently and frequently he blinked as brief lights flashed in front of his eyes. He was aware of feeling warmer and he couldn't be sure whether this was an illusion or a symptom warning that something was going wrong with his system. He had moved forward mechanically for so long that his heart jumped with the shock when his outstretched hand touched something hard. The sole of Grapos' stationary boot. Was there a crisis? Had the Greek collapsed on the floor of the tunnel under the murderous physical strain? He called out 'Grapos . . .' Because of the silence which had lasted so long he found he was unconsciously whispering as he called again. 'Something wrong, Grapos?'

The voice which came back out of the darkness was hoarse and breathless. 'We are at the bend. I can see the light at the bottom. When we arrive, you wait inside the pipe. You do not come out until I tell you.'

'All right. You're doing fine.'

Grapos grunted and began heaving himself forward again, on his stomach now because he found this an easier way to progress as the pipe angled downhill more precipitately. Macomber was about to follow when he felt a hand touch his own foot and he called back over his shoulder. 'Nearly there, Ford. We can see the end of the tunnel. Pass it on.' There was a considerable element of exaggeration in his statement but it seemed a reasonable moment to send back a cheerful message. As he rounded the bend, Macomber was able to appreciate the extent of his exaggerated optimism: the pipe was angled downwards at an increasingly nerve-wracking pitch and the blur of light in the distance was little larger than a sixpence. They were probably barely half-way down the hill slope. He was easing himself round the bend when his right knee contacted a particularly slippery patch and before he knew what was happening he lost balance and crashed heavily against the tunnel wall. He felt it crumble under his impact and a large piece of concrete slithered into his thigh followed by a shower of loosened earth. In places the damned thing was little thicker than paper. Calling back to warn the others, he crawled forward again with a sensation of moving down a chute. The brief pause had hindered rather than helped – his knees were wobbling badly and he expected at any moment to keel into the wall for a second time. When the accident happened it was so unexpected, so unforeseeable and bizarre, that it took away Macomber's breath. He had just caught up with Grapos and was within inches of his rearmost boot when the uncanny silence inside the tunnel was shattered by a ripping, cracking sound. Little more than a foot beyond Grapos' head the tunnel roof splintered, caved in and exposed a small hole – and thrust down through the hole was an Alpenkorps boot with a leg showing to the knee.

Macomber froze as Grapos lay rigid, his face inches away from the point where one of the Alpenkorps patrol had trodden through the rotting roof of the ancient pipe. Sufficient light percolated through the small aperture for him to see the pattern of large nails on the sole of the boot. Scarcely daring to breathe, he watched the leg withdrawing. For a few seconds it was held fast by the smallness of the hole when the boot tried to free itself, then it disappeared upwards, leaving the small aperture with ragged concrete edges. Still on all fours, Macomber prayed that the others behind him would lie still, that they had realized something had happened, that they would understand the desperate need for preserving total silence.

Grapos was still lying motionless on the tunnel floor, unable to reach the rifle looped over his back and having the sense not to attempt that dangerous manoeuvre. With agonizing slowness the Scot eased his tender knees forward a few more inches, wondering whether the hole was large enough for the invisible German to peer down and see Grapos, but he doubted whether that was possible. The Greek should be just far enough from the hole to go undetected. But how bright would that Alpenkorps man be? Would it occur to him to investigate the pipe, to kick in a little more of the crumbling roof? Originally, the pipe must have been laid just under the earth's surface, but over the years the rain had probably washed away some of the pro- tecting soil until only a thin layer had remained. He found it an uncanny feeling to be lying there cooped up inside the narrow space, buried just underneath the hill slope and knowing that not three feet above them there was probably a German standing, undecided what to do about this phenomenon. Or had he gone away and climbed farther up the hill over their heads, cursing the pipe and not giving it another thought? He would have his orders to maintain the line of the sweep and German discipline gave little scope for personal initiative. But these were Alpine troops, men very different in training and background from the average breed of Wehrmacht footslogger. Their training taught them to use their heads, to think for themselves.

All these rattling thoughts passed through Macom- ber's brain as four men lay absolutely still inside the pipe while two of them – Prentice and Ford – had even less idea of what was happening because they had been farther back. All they knew was that the wriggling, advancing worm of feet and heads had unaccountably stopped after that weird breaking sound had travelled back up the tunnel. Instinct alone, or perhaps a tele- pathic sense of emergency, prevented them from calling out to ask what had gone wrong. Macomber felt the

boots resting against his knuckles begin to wriggle and
he understood the signal – Grapos wished to move
back a little farther away from the hole. To avoid the
risk of two men's movements, Macomber simply
perched both hands a little higher up the tunnel wall
and the legs wriggled back underneath his own hoisted
body, then stopped moving. He had made no sound
during his short passage backwards but Macomber
wished to heaven that he knew what had caused the
Greek to retract that short distance. Was it in anticipation of something? The next moment he had confirmation that he had guessed correctly – a heavy
instrument was hammered against the ragged rim of
the aperture. Fragments clattered on the floor of the
pipe and then the steel-plated butt of a rifle came half-
way inside the pipe as a piece collapsed unexpectedly.
The German was enlarging the hole to get a better
view.

Macomber felt Grapos' body tense and then relax
almost immediately – he had been about to seize the
rifle butt and jerk it downwards out of the unseen hand
holding it. Had the Alpenkorps man been alone it
would have been a worthwhile action, but Grapos had
remembered in time that the German was not alone on
the hill slope. Grimly, Macomber waited for the hammering to be resumed, for the hole to be enlarged to a
point where they must be seen, but as the seconds
passed the hammering was not resumed and there was
an unnerving stillness beyond the aperture. Apparently
the soldier was now satisfied that it was simply a

deserted culvert and he had continued uphill with the sweep. Or was this too comforting an explanation of the lack of activity above that tell-tale hole? Had he, in fact, seen Grapos? Probably not – Grapos had moved farther up the tunnel just in time. The complacent thought had hardly passed through Macomber's head when he realized how fatally he had been wrong, realized that the German was still standing there just above them and that this was a man who was going to make sure of the business with very little expenditure of effort. The expenditure of a single hand-grenade, in fact.

The stick-like object fell through the hole and landed on the floor of the pipe. Macomber knew at once that they were going to die, that the grenade would detonate under perfect conditions. Inside that confined space the blast would be enormous with only a fraction escaping through the aperture; the main part of the explosion would be concentrated and funnelled along the pipe in a searing wave of bursting gases which would tear them to pieces. Prentice at the rear might just survive – survive with ruptured ear-drums as the hellish noise roared over him. Macomber felt Grapos stir under him and knew what he was trying to do, but the Greek was sprawled along the floor in a near-helpless position and he would never manage it in time. The Scot's hand closed over the grenade as he pivoted, taking his whole weight on his left hand to give him hoisting room. Gripping the throwing-handle and knowing that he held death in his fist, he looked

upwards, calculated in a split-second and then jerked
his hand, praying that the missile wouldn't catch the
rim of the hole and come bouncing down again. The
grenade sailed up through the aperture's centre and
vanished as Macomber instinctively huddled over
Grapos who now lay perfectly still. The detonation
echoed back to the prone men as a hard thump like the
thud of a rubber hammer against an oak door. Macomber let out his breath and then nearly fell over as
Grapos scrambled out from underneath him, half-stood
up, pushed his head through the hole and heaved with
his shoulders to force his way through the fractured
rim.

What the devil was he up to now? The manoeuvre
took Macomber completely by surprise. Was the Greek
on the German side, was he taking this last chance to
get out of the tunnel and reach his friends? Still
standing in a half-crouched position with his head and
shoulders only above the rim, Grapos was doing something frantically with his hands and arms. Below him
Macomber held the Luger aimed at the lower part of
his body while he tried to work out what Grapos was
trying to do. He waited a whole minute and then the
Greek lowered himself back inside the tunnel, pausing
on his knees to reach up outside the hole while he
hauled clumps of vegetation over the aperture. His
hands were streaked with blood and when Macomber
caught a glimpse of the prickly undergrowth he understood – he had been clawing and arranging a screen of
vegetation to conceal the hole from the rest of the

Alpenkorps patrol. Grapos sagged into an awkward sitting position and wiped his streaked hands carefully underneath his coat while he took in great gasping breaths of air. When he could speak he looked at Macomber and his former mistrust had gone as he dragged out the words. 'The German is dead – the bomb must have landed at his feet. He is alone . . . the others will come and will think the bomb went off by accident . . . with luck. If they do not see the hole . . .'

'You covered it completely?'

'I think so. If they search they will find it – but why should they do that if they think the bomb exploded by mistake? They will see it is not in his belt.'

'Thanks,' Macomber said simply. 'Think you can make it to the end of the tunnel? Good. And now you'd better be extra damned careful how you emerge.'

'I will manage.' Grapos wiped hair away from his face and stared at the Scot. 'And thank you – that bomb came within centimetres of my nose – if it exploded here I would have no head now . . .'

'Get moving – those Germans will be here any minute.'

In spite of their cramped state the four men made speedier progress down the last stretch of the tunnel and then waited at the bottom until Grapos signalled that all was clear. Like the Alpenkorps, they crossed the stepping-stones singly, and in less than five minutes they came out from the undergrowth on to the deserted road to Zervos. Grapos grinned as he hoisted his rifle over his shoulder prior to leading the way. 'It will be good from now,' he informed them. 'We are in front of the Germans.'

'I wouldn't count on that,' Macomber replied sharply. 'I've got a nasty idea something very peculiar is going to happen between here and Zervos.'

Chapter Nine

Sunday, Noon

The advance guard of the Alpenkorps was in sight and since they were mounted on mules it could only be a matter of time before they overtook anyone moving on foot. Perched on the crag which hung over the road a hundred feet below, Macomber closed the Monokular glass which Prentice had returned to him and looked down at the roadside where Grapos waited for the oxen-carts coming from Zervos. It had been agreed that it would be better if he questioned the peasants riding on the carts alone and the three of them – Macomber, Prentice and Ford – had climbed up from the road to keep out of sight. For the Scot this had been a welcome opportunity to see a long distance back over the way they had come, although the view could have been more encouraging.

'I hope Grapos isn't going to take all day arguing the toss with those peasants,' Prentice said irritably. Lack of sleep was making it increasingly difficult to keep his eyes open and now it was only will-power which sustained his movements. The trouble was that he had missed even the short rest the others had enjoyed before Grapos had appeared on the hilltop.

'He may get some news from them – or at least find out where we can get some food,' Macomber pointed out.

'I couldn't eat a thing. And that lot following us hasn't put any edge on my appetite either.'

'It shouldn't take them too long to get here,' observed Ford. 'They'll drive those mules till they drop – and mules don't drop all that quickly.'

Macomber forced his sagging shoulders upright and began speaking rapidly. It was clear that Prentice was in such a low state that a few minutes of pessimistic conversation might be more than enough to sap his remaining resistance, so he deliberately instilled a rough vigour into his voice. 'We're standing on a good lookout point to check the geography of the area so you know what lies ahead of us. It's about ten miles from Katyra to the plateau, and the plateau itself is about six miles long. Then there's about another four miles from the far end of the plateau up to Zervos. That last four miles is pretty appalling – you climb up a winding road from the plateau which zigzags all over the place – so if we can conscript some mules for ourselves, we'd better do it. Grapos may manage to fix that up – I gather he knows just about everyone on the peninsula.'

'You mean we have another ten miles to do before we get to the monastery?' Prentice started to sit down on a rock and then remained standing; he had the feeling that if he relaxed he might never get up again. 'I don't see us getting there today,' he said firmly.

'Burckhardt will get there today – I'm sure that's the

key to his whole timetable. And if you look over there I rather think you'll see Mount Zervos in a minute.'

From their elevated position at the top of the crag they had a panoramic view over the peninsula and to east and west the Aegean was in view, still a brilliant blue across the gulf where they could see the mountains on the mainland above the vital road the Allies were using. The surface of the water glittered in the sunlight and when Macomber scanned it with his glass he thought he could make out small dark specks amid the calm cobalt, the specks of Italian mines floating in the gulf. The mainland was still half-shrouded in mist but here and there the sunlight caught the tiny square of whiteness which must be the wall of a building. To the north a dark column of smoke still hung in the sky from the burning *Hydra*, but the plume was less well-defined now and less smoke drifted upwards to maintain its density. And it was in that same direction where a distant file of men on mules advanced towards the crag at a seemingly snail's pace, a file which was telescoping as the head of the file went down inside a dip in the white streak of road.

To the south a fleet of heavy clouds drifted low over the peninsula, but the clouds were thinning rapidly as they drifted out across the gulf beyond Cape Zervos and, as Macomber had predicted, the mountain slowly emerged from the clouds like a massive volcanic cone, a cone whose slopes were white with snow to the triangular-shaped summit. Prentice stood watching the mountain appear with a sense of awe – had they really a dog's chance in hell of scaling that giant and reaching the strategically vital monastery before the Germans took it? Borrowing Macomber's glass again, he focused and saw that the clouds had never really covered the peak; they had smothered the plateau and intervened between the mountain and the view from the north. So the met men had been right – Zervos was hardly ever obscured by the weather and once Burckhardt was established up there he would have a continuous view of the supply road. Prentice felt temporarily over-whelmed – overwhelmed by what was at stake and by the apparently insuperable problem of arriving on Zervos in time.

'It's not so good to the east, though,' Macomber warned them soberly. 'At this time of year the weather comes from that direction and I don't like the look of what's on the way.'

To the east the sea was still visible, a grey ruffled sea rapidly disappearing under a fresh formation of dense cloud banks which had a heavy swollen look. There was very little doubt that extremely dirty weather was coming, heading for the section of the peninsula they would have to cross. Prentice stared again southwards where the mountain was now fully exposed to its base, and when Macomber told him to focus on a certain spot he thought he saw a tiny rectangle of rock perched close to the sea. 'If you're looking at the right place,' the Scot told him, 'that's the monastery. It's pretty high up, as you'll see.'

'Pretty high. Well above the snow-line, in fact.'

Perhaps a mile farther on from the crag the last remnants of cloud were now clearing from the edge of the plateau which rose abruptly from the foothills like a wall. Again Macomber pointed out a certain spot and Prentice found the road which climbed up to the tableland. On the eastern side of the plateau a wisp of smoke eddied into the sky as it was caught by a strong wind and there appeared to be a huddle of buildings under the smoke. 'That's the village of Elatia,' Macomber explained in reply to Prentice's question. 'We shan't go near that – a spur track runs off the main road to reach it.'

'Main road? Some main road!' Prentice handed back the glass and looked down to where the oxen-carts had stopped below while Grapos talked to several peasants who had gathered round him. At one moment Grapos gestured vigorously towards Katyra and Prentice guessed that he was warning them about the approaching Germans. Shortly afterwards something like panic gripped the gathering. Three of the four oxen-carts filled up with the peasants and began to leave the road to drive straight across the fields which stretched away from the base of the hill. One wagon got stuck as its wheels caught in the ditch and the shouts of the passengers urging the beasts to make greater efforts echoed up to the crag. The fourth cart, empty, remained standing in the road as Grapos stared up at the crag and waved both arms furiously to summon them down. As they started their descent Macomber took one last look northwards and saw the tail of the

Alpenkorps column sliding out of view. When it emerged in sight again it would be that much closer to the crag and to Mount Zervos.

'The news is bad – very bad,' Grapos greeted them. 'The Germans attacked my country and Yugoslavia at 5.45 this morning. They say the forts at Rupel have held the first attack.'

'They said the Maginot Line would hold all attacks,' Prentice muttered under his breath. 'Why have they left this wagon?' he asked out loud. Grapos had turned the cart round so that now it faced away from the Alpenkorps.

'For us! They are going into the fields to escape the Germans so that it did not matter that they knew you were here. With this we can save our strength and some of us can sleep. I know where we can get food and clothes.' He looked at Ford and Prentice. 'With those clothes you would freeze to death on Zervos.'

'Any other news, Grapos?' Macomber inquired quietly. 'And how do your friends know about the German offensive? The telephone line was going to be cut.'

'It has been cut since last night. They heard the news on the wireless.' Grapos' manner had become openly hostile as though he resented the question, and Prentice thought Oh, Lord, those two are at it again! 'I tell you the truth,' the Greek added vehemently.

'Of course you do,' Macomber replied, completely

unruffled. 'But I deal in fact and I like to know the details. Where can we get the food and the clothes?'

'At a house where the road climbs. We must go . . .'

'Just a minute! You know this family well?'

'There is no family. There is one man and I have known him many years. He would be in the army fighting but he is old. And he has no German mother – if that would really worry you, Mr Macomber.'

'Then let's get moving. This will be a chance for you to get some rest, Prentice. Make the most of it. I have an idea it may be the last chance you'll get!'

The inside of the ox-cart was carpeted with straw and Prentice, who sprawled full-length after bunching up the straw into a makeshift palliasse, had fallen asleep almost as soon as the cumbersome vehicle started moving. Grapos held the long whip which signalled the animals that it was time to work again and they began lurching forward over the dusty road at a laboured pace across a small plain. The foothills continued on their right, hiding the gulf from them, but they became lower as the wall of the plateau crawled towards them with infinite slowness. It would have been at least as quick to march on foot but Macomber felt that Prentice must recuperate even though the Alpenkorps on mules must inevitably close the gap between them, and the cart provided a means of rest for all four men. Although convinced that it was crucial to conserve their energies for what might lie in front of them, the slow-motion pace of the cart irritated him almost beyond endurance. The wagon was drawn by two long-horned oxen which plodded along sedately as the ancient wagon creaked and groaned as though it might fall apart at any moment. They were coming close to the wall of the plateau when Ford asked Macomber his wry question. 'Anything worrying you – anything in particular, I mean?'

'Well, this ox-cart for one thing. It's not exactly the Orient Express.' He stared ahead as Grapos, who stood between them, glared in his direction. 'For another thing, I can't work out how we're going to communicate with the mainland forces in time to warn them of what is happening here. In time,' he repeated. 'Once Burckhardt has established himself on the heights no one will ever shift him – the place, the position, everything, makes it a natural fortress. But the thing which bothers me most of all is the size of his force – I'm absolutely certain that he's expecting massive reinforcements.'

'Hard to see how – unless they sneaked in by sea again. Could they land somewhere over there?' Ford pointed towards the eastern coastline which was still clear, although out over the Aegean the clouds were continuing to mass.

'There's no way inland. The cliffs go on until they reach the delta area in the north. But I can't see them risking a sea-going expedition twice – and this one in broad daylight. They can't be expecting to break through from Salonika in time or else they wouldn't have sent Burckhardt in the first place . . .' Macomber trailed off and stared ahead as he put himself in the colonel's position and tried to imagine his next move. Ford was standing with his back to the way they were going so he could watch the road behind but so far it stretched away emptily as far as he could see.

When they reached the base of the plateau wall Grapos took them inside a single-storey stone house concealed by a grove of cypresses and there the owner, a man in his seventies, divided among them the meal he had just prepared for himself. The food was strange and strong-tasting and consisted of balls of meat rolled inside the leaves of some unidentifiable vegetable. He offered to cook more but Macomber said they had no time and they ate with relish food they would normally have rejected as inedible.

Macomber was keeping watch by himself just beyond the cypresses while he drank *ouzo* from a large glass when he saw them coming. His Monokular brought them closer – Alpenkorps on mules, a file which extended back into the distance and which was a far more formidable force than he had imagined from his earlier sight of them. He ran back into the house to find Prentice and Ford trying on two ancient sheepskin coats the owner was providing and then exploded when the lieutenant started to write the man's name in a notebook so they could send him payment later. 'Prentice, you may have just signed that man's death warrant! If the Germans catch us and find that . . .'

'Of course! I must be half-asleep,' the lieutenant replied apologetically. He went to a stone sink and began setting fire to the page prior to washing away the embers. The room was stone-paved and stone-walled. A hideous place to spend seventy years of one's life.

'And we have about half a minute to clear out of here,' Macomber rapped out.

'I'm just burning a death warrant, as you so aptly pointed out.' Prentice had recovered his normal composure after the sleep in the cart and there was a faint smile on his face when he stared back at the large Scot. 'How close would you say?'

'Two miles. Maybe less.'

'Close enough, I agree. We'll have to hike it up to the top of that plateau. I hope you can walk faster than a mule, Ford.' He dropped the blackened paper into the sink and poured a stone jugful of water over the mess, pushing it down the drain with his finger. 'There's no way up except the road, I suppose?'

'No other way,' Grapos told him.

'Right! The road it is!' He turned to the old man. 'Tell him he has our grateful thanks for his hospitality. I rather fancy it would be a mistake to offer money for the food?'

'A mistake,' Grapos agreed abruptly. He was looking through the open doorway towards the road and hoisted his rifle higher as he moved towards it.

'Tell him also,' Macomber intervened, 'that when the Germans arrive and ask about us, he's to say he saw us get off the wagon we'd obviously stolen and run up the hill. If he tells them something they're more likely to leave him alone. Tell him also to wash up three of those plates and glasses and just leave his own dirty. They'll be looking for things like that. And don't forget the thanks.' He waited while Grapos poured out a stream of Greek and the old man kept shaking his head as though it were nothing, and he was relieved to see as they left that the old man was already starting to wash the dirty plates.

When Macomber looked back as they started to climb the hill, the line of mounted troops was already appreciably closer and he knew that they must hide soon or be captured. With the Scot in the lead they ascended the winding road at a slow trot, but long before they reached the top they were slowing down badly. The gradient was steep and wound its way between huge boulders which seemed on the verge of toppling down the rugged incline. Groves of bare olive trees studded the hill slope and the frequent twists in the road soon hid them from the plain below, which had the advantage of hiding them from the Alpenkorps mule train, but had the disadvantage of preventing them seeing how close their pursuers were drawing. Cover was what they needed, Macomber was telling himself, and he was tempted to leave the road altogether and hide on the hill slope, but this would mean throwing in the sponge: the Alpenkorps would ride past and continue on to Zervos. I'm damned if I'm giving up as easily as that, he thought, after surviving that voyage from Istanbul.

'I'd say we have another thirty minutes left – at the outside,' Prentice called up to him.

'At the outside,' Macomber agreed. Thirty minutes before the leading Alpenkorps troops overhauled them. It was beginning to get a bit desperate and he was pinning all his hopes on seeing a chance to escape when they reached that plateau which stretched six miles to the base of the mountain. This was one area where he had very little idea of the topography because when he had travelled this way five years before it had been drenched in mist while they drove over the tableland. The stitch in his side was getting worse as he forced his legs to keep up the route-march pace and now each thud of his boots on the road pounded up his side like a sledgehammer. To counter the pain he stooped forward a little, cursing inwardly as Prentice caught up with him.

'Take it easy, Mac, you'll kill yourself. You're streaming with sweat.'

'Time is running out – we had a head start on them and we've lost it. We'll have to make a quick decision when we reach the top.' The effort of speaking was a major strain now but he was damned if he was going to give up. Keep moving, you'll work it off! Prentice was walking alongside him now and this gave him a pacemaker to keep up with. He forced himself to resist the impulse to look at the ground because this brought on greater fatigue. Straightening up, he stared at the ridge they were approaching. Was this the rim of the plateau at long last? He had thought so hopefully with three lower ridges and had been disappointed each time. In his state of extreme pained exertion the plateau above was now taking on the character of a promised land, a haven where there must be some salvation from the relentless Alpenkorps coming up behind.

He was hardly aware of the landscape they were passing as the pain grew worse and pulled at him like a steel wire contracting inside his body. Boulders, olive groves, clumps of shrubbery moved past in a blur as he fixed his eyes on the wobbling ridge moving down towards them as they turned another bend and then another. Despite his robot-like condition he was conscious that the air was cooler, that a breeze was growing stronger, and this gave him fresh hope that they were close to the head of the tortuous road which went on and on forever – another bend, another stretch of white dust, another bend . . .

'Must be nearly there – with this wind,' Prentice commented.

Macomber only grunted and stared upwards. Was he breaking the grip of the stitch? It seemed a little less agonizing, a little less inclined to screw up his muscles into complex knots. It left him quite suddenly and with the realization that he had conquered it he began to take long loping strides which Prendice could hardly keep up with. He wiped his face dry as he walked and then accelerated his pace, feeling a sense of triumph as he saw only sky beyond the lowering ridge. They were almost there! Revived by the small quantity of food and the wine he began moving faster still as the gradient of the road lessened, leaving Prentice behind in his anxiety to catch his first glimpse of the plateau.

There must be no hesitation here – they must decide swiftly what they were going to do and do it. There might even be a convenient farm at the top. With a lot of luck there might even be bicycles – he had seen men cycling when he had visited Katyra before the war. A cycle should be a match for a mule. They needed some form of transport which would take them the six miles across the plateau, something which would put them well ahead of that blasted mule train of Burckhardt's. He put on a spurt, came over the top and the plateau lay before him.

The disappointment was so crushing that he stood quite still until Prentice reached him. A classic table-land spread out into the distance, an area of flatness devoid of any form of cover for several miles. In fact, he could hardly have imagined a region less suited for them to escape the Alpenkorps. The road was a surprise, too: a highway of recently laid tar which ran straight across to the mountain, the land greenish on one side and brownish on the other. They must have started the highway from the peninsula tip, a highway which in due course would be extended to Katyra.

'Not quite what we're in the market for,' Prentice remarked.

'It might as well be the sea for all the good it is to us.' Macomber glanced over his shoulder. 'How's the Greek?'

'Had a bit of trouble with his limp coming up. Ford stayed back to keep him company. What's exciting them now, I wonder?'

Ford and Grapos had appeared but they were standing together on an outcrop of rock a short distance from the road as they waved their hands with a beckoning motion. Prentice left Macomber gazing bleakly at the plateau and went back to the outcrop. The ground he scrambled up was dry and gritty, which confirmed that the storm of the night before must have blown itself out somewhere near Cape Zervos. And there was a trace of excitement in Ford's voice as he called down, 'Hurry up or you'll miss it.'

'Miss what?'

The sun which shone on the back of Prentice's neck as he hauled himself up on the rock had no warmth in it and the coldness of the light breeze was a reminder that they were approaching a zone of low temperature. Standing beside Grapos, he adjusted his sheepskin coat. It was too big and flopped off the shoulders; Ford, who was wearing another coat belonging to the same man, fitted far more comfortably inside his sheepskin. Had the Greek possessed a third coat? The thought had never struck Prentice during the flurry to get away from the house. Following the line of Ford's pointed arm he could see the top of the house now, its faded red tiles so levelled by the height that it looked flat-roofed. And only a few yards beyond the cypresses the head of the Alpenkorps column was approaching the foot of the hill road. 'There they come,' said Ford, 'the first of the many.'

'You're sure they are the first? There may be more of them already coming up the hill.'

'No, sir. You and Macomber were in such a perishing hurry to get up here I don't imagine you ever looked back – but we caught sight of them more than once and that's the head of the column.'

Prentice was surprised. Earlier he had been startled to find German troops in front of them when they came over the hilltop near the pipe, and now he was surprised at how long it had taken them to reach this point since he had glanced back when they rushed out of the house below. He waited for two or three men to turn aside and enter the house, but the column went straight past and vanished as it began to mount the hill road. The wagon had been left behind the cypresses, which also concealed the house, and the Alpenkorps were going to ride up the hill without ever realizing its existence. With a feeling of relief he jumped down from the platform and hurried back to where Macomber still stood, stood like a man of stone as he gazed upwards, his hands inside his coat pockets, the expression on his face so grim that it recalled his impersonation of Dietrich.

'What's the matter?' asked Prentice. He tilted his head. 'What's that – I can hear something?'

'The reinforcements – Burckhardt's reinforcements. By God, I expected something but I hadn't expected this. They must have half the Wehrmacht up there coming in.'

The sky to the north-east was still clear, more than clear enough for them to see the huge aerial armada which was descending on Zervos. The steady purr of

their engines grew louder as they flew over the peninsula at a height of less than a thousand feet and they
were close enough already for Macomber to see that
they were three-engined machines with an iron cross
on the fuselage and the swastika on the tail. 'Transport
planes,' Ford said in his ear. 'They'll very likely have
parachutists aboard.' In the distance, flying even lower,
came more planes and these were towing other
machines with different silhouettes. Macomber was
focusing his glass on them as Prentice spoke.

'The Alpenkorps have just started to come up the
hill behind us.'

'They'll take Zervos before nightfall. There's nothing
to stop them,' said Macomber.

'Unless this airborne crowd is heading for the mainland,' Ford suggested without much conviction.

Macomber stared through the glass, holding his head
tilted back as the planes flew in closer. The aircraft
towing other machines were losing height rapidly while
the transport planes circled above the plateau, their
engines a muted roar. There were no Allied fighters to
intercept them, of course, although a flight of Messer-
schmitts had now appeared: the bulk of the over-
strained RAF was supporting the Greek war in Albania
and even these formations were few and far between.
With a feeling of appalled helplessness they watched
the aerial fleet droning casually over the plateau like a
flying circus putting on a show before an invited
audience, although the only audience to watch this
display of Luftwaffe air power was the group of four

men on the plateau rim. There were probably between twenty and thirty planes, but it was the thought of what they might contain which frightened Prentice. 'Those machines they're towing are gliders,' said Ford. He saw Macomber nod in confirmation and now the shadows of the planes were flitting over the level surface of the plateau, a perfect landing ground for putting down an airborne force. A moment later a cluster of black dots sprayed from one of the transport machines and the dots became cones as the parachutists floated downwards. A machine detached itself from its powered carrier and the gliders started to come in to land.

The four men were retreating from the plateau towards the hillside above the road when Macomber called out. 'Wait a minute, Prentice! Something's going wrong with this one.' A glider detached from its powered transport was wobbling unstably as it headed for the earth and had the appearance of being out of control as it descended towards the rim of the plateau close to where Macomber waited. An ugly, ungainly beast, it was twin-tailed and the fuselage was squat, suggesting great carrying capacity.

Half a mile along the road more parachutists were floating down over the brownish ground which seemed to be the main landing area and the sunlight caught their tilting cones – white for parachutists and various colours for the 'chutes supporting supply containers.

Only one transport plane had attempted a landing to the left of the road and his machine was propped at a dangerous angle with the nose well down and its tail angled in the air. On the other side of the road two transports had already touched down safely and a third was just coming in.

'That plane on the left will be in trouble,' Prentice said tersely. 'It's marshland on that side.'

'How do you know that?' Macomber asked quickly.

'Because I persuaded the pilot to make a detour and fly over here on our way to Istanbul. We'd been discussing Zervos before I left Athens and I wanted to see what the place looked like. He told me that the green area was marshy . . .'

'Those transport machines are JU 52/3s,' Ford interjected professionally. 'I've heard they can carry mountain guns . . .'

'This is hardly a good time to start cataloguing German equipment,' Prentice snapped. 'I say we'd better get out of here – and fast.'

'And this brute of a glider coming towards us is a Gotha unless I'm very much mistaken,' Ford continued, and then found he was alone as the others ran back towards the boulders and scrub at the top of the hill. As he followed them he could hear the whine of the wind rising and the steady beat-beat of more transports coming in. Ford, who had a fatalistic streak in his make-up had little doubt that this was the end of the line; they would spend the rest of the war in some German prison camp, unless they were shot in the process of being captured. He was close to the first boulders when the machine-pistol slipped off his shoulder and he had to turn back to pick it up.

The huge Gotha assault cargo glider was flying down at an unpleasantly acute angle less than a hundred yards away. If it wasn't very lucky it was going to miss the rim of the plateau and go crashing down onto the plain below. Fascinated by the spectacle of the imminent disaster he stayed out in the open. Macomber seemed similarly affected because now he came out from behind the rocks and stood close to Ford as the massive glider swooped down, tried to level out at the last moment, and then thudded into the soft earth a bare hundred feet away.

'For God's sake get under cover, you idiots!' Prentice shouted from behind them. Ford, the spell broken, turned to go, but Macomber still waited as he gazed at the machine. The shock of landing had righted the fuselage and now the whole of the nose of the aircraft was lifting back like an immense hood. A soldier stood near the entrance as the aperture yawned larger, exposing a vehicle like a large car which waited to emerge. The German was moving unsteadily as he climbed behind the driver's seat and he paused to wipe something which might have been blood from his forehead. The engine started up and the vehicle began to move slowly out of the nose with a rattling sound as the driver slumped over the wheel as though he could hardly hold himself up. There was little doubt that he had been badly knocked about by the crash-landing.

Prentice, who had come out from cover with Grapos, spoke over the Scot's shoulder. 'If we could just grab that . . .'

'Exactly what I was thinking, but there are bound to be more men inside.'

Ford grabbed his arm and his voice reflected a rare excitement for the phlegmatic sergeant. 'It's a bloody half-track! Look!'

The clanking sound grew louder as the vehicle came out with painful slowness and the dazed driver remained still unaware of their proximity. Capless, he was wearing the uniform of the Alpenkorps, but it was the vehicle itself which Macomber was staring at as he put his hand inside his coat pocket and began to move forward purposefully over the grass. A long vehicle without any roof, its body was painted a drab olive-grey and at the front it was supported by two normal wheels, but there were no wheels at the rear; instead it was held up by two large caterpillar tracks. As Ford had said, a half-track – half-tank, half-car. The grinding of the tracks was muffled as they moved down onto the grass and now the driver lifted his head to see where he was going and saw Macomber standing a few feet away. The Scot spoke swiftly, rapping out the words in German.

'Brake! Colonel Burckhardt is here. He needs this vehicle at once!'

The driver reacted automatically to the command in German, braked, then stared hard at the man who had

given the order. His eyes travelled over the Scot's
shoulder to where Prentice and Ford were moving
forward while Grapos watched the road behind. As he
made a sudden movement to reach something Macomber pulled out the Luger and struck him across the
temples. He had the door open and was hauling the
soldier out before he had sagged to the floor while
Prentice and Ford ran to either side of the open mouth
of the glider. Heaving the driver out onto the grass
with one hand while the other still retained the Luger,
he looked up as another German soldier appeared at
the open nose, his rifle at the ready. Two shots were
fired within the fraction of a second. The first, fired by
the soldier, struck Ford. The second, fired by Macomber, entered the German's body as Prentice ran round
the back of the vehicle, arriving at the moment when
the Alpenkorps man slumped down in the space
between the rear of the tracks.

'Heads down!' it was Prentice who shouted as he
snatched a grenade dangling from the fallen German's
belt. The grenade sailed into the interior of the glider
and detonated near the back. A moment earlier Macomber had caught a glimpse of movement from inside the
plane, but when he raised his head after the thumping
explosion there was no further sign of activity aboard
the Gotha. Ford was holding onto the side of the tracks
as he stooped forward on his knees, but he was trying
to clamber up as Prentice and Macomber reached him.
The passage of the bullet was marked by a neat tear on

the right shoulder of his sheepskin coat. Prentice had an arm round his chest and was helping him to his feet as Macomber spoke.

'Get him aboard quick! I'll have to try and drive this blasted thing – they'll be on to us in a minute.'

Ford was upright now, one arm clutching Prentice round the waist for support as he clambered inside a cut-out aperture which was the rear-door of the half-track. He spoke through his teeth to Macomber. 'Drives like a car ... any car ... the tracks move with the wheels.' Macomber was turning to go to the front when he saw the distinctive Alpenkorps cap on the head of the soldier slumped between the tracks. He scooped it off and rammed it down over his own head as Grapos arrived, running at a shuffling jog-trot with his rifle between his hands.

'The mules are here,' he gasped out. 'Coming over the hill quickly. I think the first man ...'

'Get in, for God's sake.'

Prentice had successfully manoeuvred Ford into one of the benches behind the two front seats and Macomber was behind the wheel as Grapos climbed aboard. Brake, clutch-pedal, gear-lever – it *looked* like an ordinary car. Ford told Prentice to shut up a minute and leaned forward. 'An ordinary car, Macomber, that's all it is – for driving, anyway.' He sagged back against the bench seat as Prentice grabbed at a first-aid kit attached to the rear of the driving-seat and then the vehicle began moving forward over the grass towards the road.

The tracks clanked gently as they revolved over the field and the vehicle had a feeling of great stability.

Macomber was concentrating on three things at once – on getting to know how this queer monster worked, on keeping an eye on the hilltop over which the Alpenkorps might stream at any moment, and with what little attention he had left he cast quick glances to the south where the road ran past the landing zone. The sky was littered with a fresh wave of falling parachutists and another transport plane had just come to a halt after a bumpy landing. Dammit, he said to himself and speeded up. The half-track reached the road at the moment when the leading Alpenkorps soldier crested the rise on his mule.

Hahnemann! Macomber felt certain it was the German lieutenant on that animal. He must have been hurled overboard into the sea when the *Hydra* blew up, must have been one of those men swimming in the water. The thought darted through his brain as it all became a kaleidoscope and he reacted with pure instinct. Two more men on mules appeared behind Hahnemann. Parachutists hitting the earth, their 'chutes landing and pulling sideways. A giant glider cruising in to land on the brownish area. The steady throb of planes' engines overhead mingling with the urgent shouts of the men on the mules. Still feeling like a man towing a caravan, he turned the wheel and the half-track climbed onto the road. As its great metal tracks ground their teeth into the hard tar they set up a jarring vibration sound and the unexpected barrage of noise panicked the mules. There was more shouting, frantic now, as the animals headed across the hilltop, threading their way nimbly among the boulders and away from the strange machine. Macomber completed his turn, hunched his shoulders, pressed his foot down, and the half-track began to build up speed as the wheels spun and the tracks churned round faster and faster, half-deafening its passengers with the pounding beat of metal on tar.

'How fast can it go?' shouted the Scot.

'Twenty ... thirty ... forty. Fifty would be pushing it.' Ford had his arm out of the sleeve now and was taking off the right side of his jacket as he replied. There were three rows of bench seats across the vehicle behind the front seats and Grapos occupied the rear position. He had aimed his rifle at Hahnemann but the half-track had lurched at the wrong moment, almost throwing him off, and he hadn't fired a shot. Now there was no target – the mules and their riders were lost somewhere inside the tangle of boulders. He swore colourfully in Greek when Macomber shouted over his shoulder for him to get down on the floor out of sight – Grapos was rather too distinctive a figure for his liking at the moment.

Ahead more transport planes were droning in the sky as they waited their moment to come down, and already the plateau to the right of the road had the look of a disorganized military tattoo. So far there were no troops close to the road but a few hundred yards away parachutists were grappling with the supply containers and a number of men were already armed with machine-pistols. Several looked up as the half-track roared past and their uniform was very different from that of the Alpenkorps, so different that they might have belonged to another army. They wore pot-shaped helmets not dissimilar to diving helmets, smocks camouflaged with mottled dark green and brown, and overall trousers which gave them a deceptively clumsy appearance, but there was nothing clumsy about their movements as they began to form up in sections. Macomber, having got the feel of the vehicle, was now sitting very erect so his Alpenkorps cap was prominently on view and frequently he drove with one hand while he waved with the other to the men assembling in the field, a performance which Prentice witnessed with some trepidation. It was typical of Macomber, he was thinking, to carry the bluff to its utmost limit.

'Look out!'

Prentice shrieked out the warning. Like Macomber, all his attention had been fixed on the airborne force's landing area and it was only by chance that he glanced to the left. A Gotha assault glider released from its tow-rope was coming in to land from the east. It was already flying very low, perhaps twenty feet above the ground, flying on a course which would take it directly across the road just ahead of the speeding half-track. Prentice guessed that the pilot was desperately trying to maintain flight long enough to take his machine beyond the marshland area and it was horribly clear that the two very different forms of transport were headed on a collision course. Macomber had time to slow down but nearby a drawn-up section of parachutists was marching steadily towards the road. If he slowed, stopped, they'd get a damn good look at who was inside the vehicle and they had machine-pistols looped over their shoulders. Without hesitation he accelerated and it became a race towards destruction.

His shoulders hunched again, he watched road and oncoming glider. It was an uncomfortably fine calculation – known speed of half-track against estimated speed of glider, with the added element of the plane's angle of descent. The half-track was now thundering down the road, which had begun to slope, at a pace which alarmed Prentice, the tracks rotating madly under increasing tension as the moving metal smashed its way forward with a rattling cannonade of sound. Across the green field the glider grew larger as it maintained its course unerringly and lost more height. He must be mad, Prentice was thinking. Macomber's going to try and beat the bloody thing, to sneak past ahead of it! The glider was so close now that he wanted to close his eyes, to look away, but he felt a terrible compulsion to stare at the oncoming machine which now seemed enormous.

'We won't make it,' said Ford who had now become aware of what was happening, and Ford was good at this sort of hair's breadth calculation. Prentice would have felt even less happy had he known that exactly the same thought was pressing down on Macomber, and now it was too late to think of reducing speed. The converging projectiles were so close that he would probably smash into the tail of the glider as it passed. The only answer was a little more speed.

The downward gradient of the road was increasing as he pressed his foot harder and prayed – prayed against two catastrophes. He had heard somewhere that if you drive a tracked vehicle too fast a caterpillar could break loose, freeing itself from the small wheels over which it revolved and leave the vehicle altogether. If that happened at the speed they were moving at now there would be very little hope of survival. Grimly, he kept his foot down, his mind totally concentrated on the straight road ahead, the tortured gyrations of the overstrained tracks, and that huge drifting shape about to move across his bows. Prentice had one arm steadying Ford while the other hand gripped the side of the vehicle as the glider lost more height and cruised forward barely six feet above the plateau and less than fifty yards from the road. Grapos, lying resentfully on the floor with his feet under a bench and his back against the rear of the vehicle, had the shock of his life when he looked up and saw the bulk of the Gotha loom up. The half-track raced forward, Grapos involuntarily ducked, and the wing of the Gotha passed over the rear of the vehicle, landing a short distance beyond the road.

Prentice sagged against the back of the bench and stared at the back of the huge Scot, his lips moving soundlessly. Macomber was already slowing down to a safer speed, expecting some uncomplimentary comment from his passengers, but the occupants of the bench were stunned, so he was saved an argument. In the distance a transport plane was stationary close to the road and Macomber whistled under his breath when he saw something which looked like a part of a field-gun coming down a ramp through a large opening in the fuselage. 'How is Ford?' he called out over his shoulder.

'Ford is surviving,' Ford replied.

'The bullet grazed him,' amplified Prentice who was now fixing a bandage to his final satisfaction. 'He's lost a bit of blood and he looks like Banquo's ghost but the fresh air will probably tone him up a treat.'

'There's a plane ahead with something coming out – better try and identify it so we know what we're up against.'

'We can see what we're up against,' Prentice told him bluntly. 'The cream of the Wehrmacht. And I suppose you've seen there are more half-tracks over to the right? One's just nosed its way out of that Gotha which just missed us.'

'Do you think we're nearly clear of them?' asked Ford and there was a note of anxiety in his voice.

'Not much ahead as far as I can see. Why?' Macomber had detected the anxious note and was wondering what had struck the technically minded Ford.

'Because we've been lucky so far – it's wireless communication that worries me. If the Alpenkorps who came over the hill can send a message ahead we may have a reception committee waiting for us.'

It was a point which had worried Prentice but he

hadn't seen any point in raising new problems at this particular juncture. So far they had got away with their audacious dash along the fringe of the assembly area, and this didn't entirely surprise him: the Germans had just landed on enemy territory and were taken up with carrying out a certain vital routine – collection of weapons from the supply containers, the unloading of heavy equipment from the gliders and transport planes, and the assembling of the men into their units. They had no reason, when their attention was so divided, to see anything strange in one of their own recently landed half-tracks speeding along the road to Zervos. But wireless communication was a different matter.

'We may be lucky,' said Macomber. 'I made a mess of both of Burckhardt's wireless sets and if he hasn't got that tuning coil fixed he'll have to wait until he finds one with this airborne mob. Now, watch it, Ford.'

He had been travelling at little more than twenty miles an hour to give the tracks a rest but now he began to build up speed again as they approached the transport plane which had landed little more than a hundred yards from the road. Men were scurrying round the machine and he saw beyond it another plane which had been hidden from view. Close to the aircraft stood a complete field-piece. Ford twisted sideways on the bench as they roared past and this time, to Prentice's relief, the Scot did not attempt his cheerful waving act. The planes were receding behind them when Ford spoke.

'They're 75-mm mountain guns – just what they

need where they're going. And I saw several 8-cm mortars. This lot is really going places.'

'Some of the half-tracks will haul the mountain guns?' Prentice inquired.

'Yes, that's it. And they'll carry troops aboard as well. They've landed a beautiful heavy-nosed spearhead for the job.'

'Why send Burckhardt's expedition at all?' Macomber asked.

'That's very necessary,' Prentice explained, 'for a variety of reasons. First, if they hadn't had this patch of clear weather the airborne force could never have landed at all and then Burckhardt would have had to do the whole job himself. Second, I can see now that it was vital for them to land men at Katyra to seal off the peninsula . . .'

'And third,' interjected Ford, 'there's a limit to how much a glider or transport can carry. You can have heavy stuff – the mountain guns, the half-tracks – or you can have men, but you can't have both. So it's my bet Burckhardt's expedition is bringing in a sizeable portion of the manpower while the airborne fleet brings in the heavy stuff. Together, it makes up a beautifully balanced force.'

'That's the second time you've used the word "beautiful",' Prentice complained. 'Frankly, I can't see one damned thing that's beautiful in what's coming to us.'

'Just a professional observation, sir,' Ford explained blandly.

'I think we've left them behind,' Macomber called

out. 'It looks as though those two planes landed closest to Zervos.'

The road stretched away across the plateau and still ran straight as a Roman road, a perfect highway for the advance of the German invaders. They were much closer to the mountain now but it no longer rose from its base with majestic symmetry; a heavy cloud bank from the east was drifting across the lower slopes and the peak had a lop-sided look. The disturbed Aegean was no longer visible from the plateau and another formation of low cloud was gradually obliterating the tableland itself. The road was sloping upwards as it climbed towards the mountain wall and Macomber could feel a distinct drop in temperature as the wind grew stronger. The worsening of the weather was a development he viewed with some disenchantment; his photographic memory for places vividly recalled that murderous stretch of road farther on which zig-zagged up the flank of the mountain, a road twisting and turning over precipitous drops as it ascended into the wilderness.

At least Burckhardt's tracked spearhead wouldn't be able to do a Le Mans over that course, but the trouble was he had to take the half-track up the same road. The gradient was increasing more steeply as Prentice called out to him.

'How are we off for petrol?'

'We had a hundred litres – a full tank – when we started, so that's the least of our problems.'

'The pilot of the glider would insist on a full tank

before he took off,' Ford pointed out helpfully. 'That minimizes the risk of something going wrong during the flight – an explosion, even.'

Prentice groaned half-audibly. 'And talking about trouble, I don't much like the look of that dirty weather blowing up from the east.'

'Is the Greek still on the floor?' Macomber asked. 'He can get up now if he is and give us his opinion – a Met forecast, in fact.'

Prentice glanced round and lifted his eyes to heaven. Grapos was sprawled on his side with the rifle cuddled in his arms and he was fast asleep. The coil of Alpenkorps climbing rope, which earlier he had pulled from under a bench and examined with interest, lay with a German army satchel at his feet. How anyone could kip down on top of those vibrating tracks passed Prentice's comprehension. 'The Greek,' he announced in a loud voice, 'is in dreamland.'

'Well, wake him up,' Macomber commanded brutally.

Disturbed from his slumber, Grapos sat on the bench behind Prentice who put the question about the coming weather to him. He stared across the plateau, pulling absently at one corner of his moustache and then feeling the stubble on his chin. Then he stared ahead to where the mountain was fast losing itself behind the vaporous pall which was drifting across the plateau in front of them. As he watched, the mountain disappeared. 'It is bad,' he said. 'It is very bad. The worst. There will be much snow within the hour.'

'Exactly what makes you predict that?' Macomber called back to him sharply.

'It is from the east. The clouds are low. They are like a cow with calf – swollen with snow . . .'

'First time I've heard of cows with snow inside them,' Prentice commented in an effort to lighten the pall Grapos himself was spreading over them. But the Greek was not to be put off by unseemly levity.

'The sea has gone from the plateau – that is another sign. The top of the mountain has gone – another sign. As we climb it will get worse and worse. It will be very cold and there will be a big fall of snow.'

'Thank you,' said Prentice, 'you're fired! We'll get another Met forecaster from the BBC.'

'You ask me – I tell you. There may be landslides on the mountain. There will be ice on the road . . .'

'And the sea shall rise up and encompass us, so we'd better find a Noah's Ark,' said Prentice in a kind of frenzy. 'For Pete's sake, man, we asked you for a weather forecast – not a gipsy's warning of doom. Now can it!' And he looks a bit like a gipsy, the old brigand, he thought as Grapos glared at him resentfully and then gazed stolidly ahead as though drawing their attention to the appalling prospect which lay before them. 'That answer your question, Mac?' he called out.

'I think so. Further outlook unsettled.'

It was the reference to ice on the road which most disturbed the Scot. He would have to take this cumbersome half-track up a route which, five years before, a car had found difficulty in negotiating in good weather, because during that trip only the plateau had been blotted out by low cloud. It would make it equally hazardous for Burckhardt, of course, so it really depended on which way you looked at the problem, but Macomber was going to be in front with the Germans coming up behind. He changed gear as the gradient increased again and they were moving at little more than twenty miles an hour when Prentice asked if he could borrow the Monokular glass. He kept it for only a short time and then handed it back as he spoke.

'You were right, the outlook is unsettled – behind us. A half-track is coming after us like a bat out of hell. It could be Hahnemann aboard, but I'm only guessing, of course.'

'How many men?' Macomber was already trying to coax a fraction more speed out of the vehicle.

'Three or four. I couldn't be sure. He's on the flat at the moment so he'll have to slow down when he starts coming up.' Ford and Grapos twisted round on their benches and saw in the distance the half-track coming towards them at speed. Macomber was watching what appeared to be the crest of the hill they were climbing and beyond it the cloud hid the base of the mountain which must be very close. He would have to outdrive Hahnemann up that devilish road: the snag was he would soon be slowed down by the mist while the German could drive full-tilt up to this point, thus narrowing the gap between them to almost zero. The weather was certainly not their friend at the moment. He drove up steadily, reached the crest, and immediately the road turned and dropped into a dip between dry-stone walls where it turned again. The oxen were massed at the bend.

There were three Greek peasants with the animals which had accumulated at this point, and they were shouting their heads off and flailing the beasts with birches made of slim stems. So far as Macomber could see as he drove down towards them their efforts were only adding to the confusion and the road was well and truly blocked. With the thought of that other half-track tearing towards them he pulled up his own vehicle inches from the chaos of animals and drovers. 'Sort them out, Grapos! Get them moving and damned quickly! They can shove them on to that bit of grass by the next bend till we get past. Then tell them to block the road again.' He waited while Grapos got out of the vehicle and began shouting at the drovers, who, at first, simply shouted back. An ox rested its horned head on the side of the half-track and stared at Ford with interest. Grapos continued his shouting and gesticulating match with the drovers and Prentice felt his temper going. A minute later the animals were still milling round the vehicle and Grapos was still conducting his verbal war with his countrymen. Something snapped inside Macomber. He stood up, pulled out his Luger and fired it over the heads of men and beasts. The animals panicked and began to trot off down the road, followed by the drovers who penned them into the grassy area while the half-track grumbled past them.

'You told them to block the road again?' Macomber

shouted back to Grapos who had resumed his seat on the bench.

'I told them the Germans were coming and they must make them wait.'

Macomber swore violently to himself: mention of the Germans coming would undoubtedly frighten the drovers so much they'd keep their animals penned up off the road until the second half-track had passed. They had closed the road to him but he felt sure they would open it to the Germans. Something pretty drastic had to be done to widen the gap between the two vehicles. The road was straightening out once more as it went down a hill between high earthen banks, so he accelerated. The half-track built up speed rapidly under the pressure of his foot and he felt a coldness on his face as the road flew away under him. The mist was floating aimlessly and as it drifted to and fro he caught glimpses of the mountain wall rising up like an immense fortress bastion. Here and there pinnacles of rock spurred upwards and then vanished as the mist closed in again. Glancing at the speedometer, he saw that they were moving at the equivalent of fifty miles an hour and he was well aware that only the weight and stability of the racing tracks were holding them on the road. When the mist parted again momentarily he saw a stone bridge at the bottom and the old route came back to him: beyond the bridge the road veered to the right and then started its fierce climb up the mountain. Within a minute or two he would be reduced to crawling pace as he attempted the first acute bend and the realization of this fact made him exert a trifle more foot pressure.

Behind him Ford was white-faced with the aftermath of his wound, but Prentice was white-faced at the speed they were travelling as he clung tightly to the arm of the bench seat which was shuddering so violently that he was scared the screws attaching it to the floor might soon shake loose. Grapos had wedged himself in against the side of the vehicle, and when Prentice glanced back he thought he saw for the first time a flicker of uncertainty in the Greek's narrowed eyes. Ford's reaction was brief but significant: he leaned forward, stared at the speedometer, then braced his back against the bench. In his determination to out-distance the following half-track Macomber seemed to be going far beyond the bounds of a calculated risk as he drove steadily downwards, the high earthen banks sliding past them in a blur, the sound of the pounding tracks confined inside the sunken road like the noise from a stamping mill, and now the revolving metal was developing a disconnected rhythm which brought Prentice's raw nerves to screaming point. Was the Scot intent on killing every man aboard?

The mist had rolled like a grey fog over the gulley below, temporarily blotting out the narrowing distance between the rushing half-track and the bridge, and it was only when the greyness dispersed briefly that Macomber grasped his mistake, understood that he had overestimated his margin of safety badly, saw the bridge – with the right-angled turn beyond – soaring up towards him, alarmingly close. He began to lose speed knowing that he was too late, that the half-track must still be moving too fast when the moment came to swing the wheel, to turn to the left sharply over the bridge and then turn to the right even more sharply once he was across it. He lost more speed, lost it dangerously quickly, and behind him his three passengers – Grapos now on his feet, grasping the rear of the bench which seated Prentice and Ford – were like frozen men, men who had lost all ability to move even as they stared petrified at what lay ahead of them, knowing that they were going straight through the bridge wall into the river below.

Chapter Ten

Sunday, 2 pm

Too late to brake, too late to reduce speed – by orthodox methods. Macomber veered to the left suddenly, immediately veered back to the right, straightened up again. At the speed they were moving the huge tracks at the rear responded a fraction later, as he had intended, and the left-hand caterpillar cracked into the earthen bank with shattering impact, jerking Prentice's bones almost out of their sockets as the caterpillar partially acted as a brake. The vehicle bounced smartly off the bank and a flurry of earth minced up by the revolving track showered over them as the other bank rushed towards them. Macomber had veered to the right now, then to the left, straightened up again, but this time the collision was far more violent and the wheel nearly leapt out of his hands, which would have brought on final disaster, but somehow he maintained his grip as the vehicle shuddered wildly, wobbled uncertainly, still holding its equilibrium as more earth burst in the air and rained down over them. The trouble was he had overdone it this time.

The right-hand caterpillar was acting superbly as an improvised braking system, had lost him a great deal of lethal speed, but the track rammed against the bank had become trapped and now it was rotating furiously inside the earth as it desperately tried to break free. Macomber was holding the wheel with a ferocious grip which signified more than an attempt to regain control – it also signified his fear that the track would come loose, break away altogether from the vehicle. Above the roar of the engine a new sound screamed out, a sound of churning metal rasping over rocks embedded inside the bank, a hellish sound which went on and on as the track revolved frantically and clouds of earth and loose stones soared above them. Then it freed itself and the half-track leapt forward down the natural gradient while Macomber wrestled to keep control, to lose more speed without tipping them over as the right-angled bridge rushed up to meet them. He hit the ice patch at the moment when he felt he might just make it.

The ice patch, starting at a point where part of the earth bank had collapsed into a ditch, was several inches thick, so instead of breaking under the enormous weight of the vehicle it propelled the half-track forward like a sledge sweeping over a skating-rink. Macomber turned the wheels, felt them take on a life of their own, as they hurtled down on the leftward turn over the bridge. He swung the wheels farther to the left, praying for the massive tracks to act as a sheet-anchor, then they were half-way round the bend with the tracks continuing the sweep behind them and Macomber had the feeling some irresistible power had taken hold of their tail as the momentum of track weight carried them farther and farther sideways. The wheels were half-way up the bridge when the right-hand track smashed into the stone wall, a dry-stone edifice of boulders unsealed with mortar. The impact of steel against stone was mind-shattering: Prentice was hurled along the bench, stopped by the side of the vehicle as Ford cannoned into him, and only Grapos, still upright, held his position by the lightness of his grip on the rear of the bench. A few feet beyond them, Macomber took less of the shock, but the impact sound was deafening as the track battered the wall open, tumbled huge boulders into the river below, and then they were suspended over the brink, half the right-hand track in the air over the drop. Prentice shook his head to fight down the stunned sensation, peered over the side and saw he was looking down into the river thirty feet below, a foaming torrent which carried along half-submerged floats of greenish ice. He felt the half-track tremble, begin to tip backwards gently. They were going over . . .

At the last moment Macomber had braked. A swift glance over his shoulder showed him the appalling danger – the jagged gap between the boulders, the greenish swirl, a third of the vehicle in mid-air, so probably at least half the equilibrium, then he, too, felt the tremble, the insidious lifting motion beginning. He released the brake, depressed his foot. The engine throbbed, built up power; something bumped gently in front. Christ, the wheels had left the ground, had just returned to the road surface! Something had locked onto the vehicle, holding it fast. He felt the floor rising under him again as they started to tip backwards again, the wheels clear of the ground. They were going to somersault over, the track weight no longer a sheet-anchor as it performed the function of a fulcrum to see-saw the half-track down into the roaring torrent. Mist like smoke drifted over the bridge, obscuring the view like a London fog, the clammy moisture settling on Macomber's sweat-stained forehead. His instinct – of self-preservation – urged him to leave the wheel, to jump for it onto the road still beside him – but for once he ignored the instinct, knowing that the others would go over the edge with the vehicle. He remained rigid behind the wheel, pressing his foot down still farther as the caterpillars revolved furiously among the scattered boulders, metal clashing so savagely with stone that Prentice saw flint-sparks fly in the mist. It lasted perhaps twenty seconds – the final skid, the smash into the wall, the first lift of the vehicle, the brief return to firm ground, the second more nerve-rasping tilt. It was the left-hand caterpillar Macomber was counting on, the track less thrust out over the drop, the track whose treads still clawed at firm ground, and now the gamble began to work as the caterpillar shifted the mess of boulders and grated its way forward inch by inch – dragging the other track with it until that also gained a firmer grip and did its part in heaving the vehicle farther on to the bridge, farther away from the yawning gap. Macomber felt it coming, felt the wheels hit the road again, released some foot pressure just in time as the vehicle surged free, and in freeing itself the right-hand track let go of a section of wall which had leaned outwards under the shock of the initial impact. Above the growl of the engine they heard a muffled splash as a whole fresh section of wall dived into the river and Macomber steered the half-track over the bridge and started to take the right-hand turn, then braked. He looked back, his engine still running.

'Jesus ... I thought that was it ...' Prentice wiped his damp face while Ford licked his lips and held his wounded shoulder where it had cannoned into the lieutenant. Grapos, recovering more quickly than the others, had his rifle gripped in his hands as he stared backwards the way they had come, the way the pursuing half-track would come. 'Not much point in hanging about here, is there? Let's get moving,' Prentice demanded irritably.

'There might be a point in waiting here for them.' Macomber stared back at the wrecked wall. The vanished section was perhaps twenty feet wide and he was seeing it as the Germans would see it when they reached the bridge, his mind racing while he tried to estimate their likely reaction when they reached the bottom of the hill. The mist, which had thinned but still swirled over the bridge, made the devastation look even worse, like the aftermath of a battlefield. He looked forward again to where the road turned to go up the mountain: the road turned right sharply, but to the left, where the bridge ended, a rock slope continued up from the road and disappeared behind a clump of trees only half-seen in the greyness. A gentle slope which looked firm enough, firm enough to take up the half-track. 'I want you all to get out and take up position for when they arrive. We'll fight it out here,' he said abruptly.

'What the hell for?' Prentice was vehement. 'If we go on we should keep ahead of them with a bit of luck . . .'

'Up that mountain road?' Macomber was twisted round in his seat again where he could face Prentice and his expression was grim. 'Look, I've been up that road once before – it's just about wide enough to take this thing, it zigzags backwards and forwards up the mountain with a sheer wall on one side, a sheer drop on the other, and higher up it may be covered with shot ice. There's even ice in the river behind us. We'll be crawling up that mountain like a man going up on his belly . . .'

'We'll still be in front,' Prentice persisted obstinately, 'and if we have to, we may discover a better spot to ambush them . . .'

'Not as good as this.' The Scot was eyeing the left-hand slope speculatively. 'And we're more likely to get the element of surprise here – they'll think we went over with that wall.'

'Not when they look over and see nothing there, they won't . . .'

'So, we'll have to make sure that by the time they discover their mistake it's too late.'

'You'll have to hide the half-track,' Ford pointed out

soberly. 'It would give the whole game away if they can see . . .'

'That's the guts of the thing.' Macomber extracted one of his three remaining cigars, lit it quickly. 'They won't spot it until it's too late if I can work this the way I see it.' He took several puffs and then pointed up the slope. 'I'll be up there inside those trees and I don't want anyone opening fire too soon. They'll come down that road, maybe a bit more slowly than we came down it, and they'll see the ice patch, which will slow them down even more, give them time to spot that smashed-up wall. But they won't stop on the ice – they'll keep on coming and pull up on the bridge to have a look. That's when I come down out of those trees. Then you can shoot as long as your ammunition lasts out.'

'You're going up that slope?' There was an incredulous note in Prentice's voice. 'You'll never make it – you must be bonkers even to attempt it . . .'

'What are you beefing about?' Macomber growled. 'You're not coming with me – and I'm just beginning to get the feel of this gadget. I could even get to like it. Now, for God's sake get moving – they'll be here any minute.'

Partly because he felt they had lost too much time to continue up the mountain, partly because he sensed the agreement of Ford and of Grapos, who had dropped into the road and was already looking for a good vantage point, Prentice reluctantly helped Ford out of the vehicle, and as soon as they were in the roadway Macomber let off the brake and began driving forward.

The slope was a little steeper than he had anticipated but once the tracks gripped its surface he felt them steadily pushing the vehicle up the ascent. The mist was thickening again when he had climbed sixty feet above the bridge and he switched on his lights to see where he was going. The beams were blurred cones and the lights reflected off tiny particles of moisture as they penetrated the trees, showed up a massive slab of rock beyond. Tilted at an angle of perhaps thirty degrees, sagged back heavily against his seat, he steered the half-track cautiously between two tree-trunks, pulled it up with its nose inches from the slab, looked back and swore. The one essential of the ambush was a clear view of the bridge and the mist had closed over it, blotting it out completely. If it didn't shift before the German half-track arrived he was impotent, powerless to help, and the other three would have to fight it out alone. He took out the cigar, moistened his lips and waited with the engine ticking over. Another calculated risk – that the motor of the German vehicle combined with the mist would muffle the sound of his own engine. What the devil was keeping Jerry?

Waiting was an activity – if doing nothing can be termed activity – Macomber had some experience of. Waiting in the shadows of a warehouse on the Danube while he checked the supplies going aboard a barge; waiting beneath a manhole cover while a German soldier patrolled the street above; some of his most gruelling hours during the past fifteen months had been spent waiting. But at the moment waiting didn't suit him; it gave a chance for the fatigue to make itself felt, to settle in his weary limbs and his over-strained mind, and he wondered how much more he could take before his final reserves were drained. Even the slow-motion coils of mist which drifted below as he remained twisted round in his seat seemed to add to the appalling tiredness which was becoming his permanent condition. He blinked, thinking he saw a man creeping up through the mist, but it was only the vapour assuming strange shapes, and then, above the murmuring throb of his own motor, he heard the sound he had been waiting for.

The half-track proceeding cautiously down the hill echoed weirdly through the fogged silence, a distant engine sound combining with a more distinctive noise – the rattle and grind of the descending tracks. And still the bridge was lost, might be a dozen miles away for all he could see of it through the dense pall which smothered the slope so that now it might have been late evening or early morning. Had he known this was going to happen he could have stopped lower down, relying on the mist alone to conceal his presence, but it was far too late to alter position, so all he could do was to wait and hope – hope that damned mist would thin in time. The clanking sound was closer now, the half-track still moving slowly, as he had foreseen it would. His hand went towards the brake, clutched it, and he had forgotten he was smoking as he stared fixedly downwards, trying to make up his mind whether the mist had thinned just a little. His eyes were feeling the strain of staring in one direction and a dull ache was building up behind his temples as the clanking noise grew louder, still a muffled ratchetty sound, but definitely louder. They'd be at the bottom any moment now, turning onto the bridge. It wasn't going to work, there was going to be a tragedy down there, Macomber felt it in his chilled bones, a chill brought on by a feeling of almost unbearable frustration which twitched at his nerves. I may be responsible for the death of three men, he thought.

A breath of wind touched his face as he heard the engine sound slow – they had reached the bottom, they were turning the corner. He suddenly realized his lights were still on and switched them off quickly. A blunder like that would have lost him his life long ago. Pull yourself together, for Christ's sake, this is going to be tricky enough as it is without going to sleep on the job. A noise like gently falling water came from above as the wind rustled the trees, then the mist began to retreat rapidly, to dissolve back down the slope as the wind parted it in melting eddies. He stiffened, his side rigid against the seat, straining to see what was happening down there. Had a voice drifted up from below? He was frowning ferociously, still trying to decide, when the mist cleared from the bridge and he saw the German half-track turning the first corner as it lumbered up to the bridge and stopped, broadside on to the destroyed wall, stopped in the position Macomber had prayed it would stop. Four men inside, and the man standing up by the driver was Hahnemann. Too far away to see clearly, but Macomber knew it was Hahnemann, knew it for a certainty from the way he moved. Now!

He released the brake, accelerated, reversed down the slope at gathering speed as the tracks churned and slithered their way down, the revolutions increasing with every yard of the descent. Had they reacted instantly, remained cool, taking deliberate aim before they fired, they might have killed the Scot, freed the half-track's steering so it would have careered in a different direction. But Macomber had counted on the element of surprise, on the element of terror which can freeze men's minds for vital seconds, on the view as seen from the bridge which a moment earlier had seemed so deserted, on the view seconds later as they heard the harsh grind and thunder of the descending tracks and saw the tank-like projectile coming out of the mist and roaring down on them. Still twisted round in his seat, both hands locked to the wheel, steering by feel alone, Macomber turned the direction of the onslaught a fraction, aiming the half-track square at the vehicle below. He saw Hahnemann react at last, saw him haul out his pistol from his holster, raise it, take deliberate aim, then collapse as Grapos, secreted behind a rock above the bridge, fired at the same moment as Prentice pressed the trigger of his machine-pistol. Hahnemann's three companions ducked, or fell, Macomber had no idea which, as the tracks bounded over a flat boulder and changed direction round the end of the bridge, smashing with enormous force into the side of the German vehicle parked by the gap. The collision was tremendous, a jarring shock which knocked Macomber backward into the wheel, and only his anticipation of what was coming prevented his being impaled on the steering column as he braked at the last moment, a split-second problem of timing since he needed all the force of the rushing descent to strike the half-track before he tried to escape following it to destruction. The battering-ram blow slammed the German vehicle half-way over the edge as one of the Alpenkorps men scrambled dazedly to his feet, acted intuitively and threw himself over the brink, only to be followed seconds later by the half-track which dropped sideways and buried him when it plunged into the river. A burst of water jumped up to bridge height, subsided, and Macomber, turning painfully round saw that his own vehicle was perched on the brink, but perched safely. He was lying forward over the wheel, taking in great gulps of mist-laden air when Prentice reached him. 'Are you all right, Mac?'

'I think so. Stand clear a minute.'

Afterwards he could never remember his automatic action of driving forward slowly and turning the half-track so it faced towards the mountain road before he braked, switched off the engine and staggered out onto the road where Prentice held him as his legs almost gave way. 'I'm not too bad ... I'll survive. I want to see ...' He stumbled over to a piece of the remaining wall and leant heavily against it while he looked over. The half-track, upside down, had been caught by two huge boulders thrust above the water, but as he looked down it lost its balance, tipped over sideways, wallowed briefly three-parts submerged and then sank. Bubbles coming up from it reached the surface and were then whipped away in the fast-flowing current, so he couldn't be sure whether his eyes had played him a trick. The sunken vehicle gave up one last memory, the uniformed body of an Alpenkorps man who came to the surface and then was swept away downriver, towards Molos, towards the Gulf of Zervos. 'Poor devil,' Macomber muttered, then he straightened up, still using the wall for support. 'There'll be others on the way, so we'd better get on – up the mountain.'

Chapter Eleven

Sunday, 2.30 pm

The ledge which supported the road was dangerously narrow – as Macomber had predicted they were hemmed in between a vertical wall of rock to their right, a wall which climbed high above them, while to their left the abyss fell away to unknown depths, unknown because the mist below prevented them from seeing how far down the drop continued. They were fifteen minutes' driving time from the wrecked bridge – no great distance considering he had been compelled to move up at a rate of only a few miles per hour – but in that time they had climbed steadily and Macomber calculated that soon they would have ascended a thousand feet, one thousand nerve-crushing feet. Before they had left the bridge Prentice had offered to take over the wheel, but the Scot refused the suggestion. 'I think I've a little experience of handling her now,' he had remarked drily, conferring a feminine status on the most unfeminine-looking object imaginable. 'You might even say I've had a crash course in coping with a half-track.'

'Crash is the word,' Prentice agreed humorously, 'and that's why I'm wondering whether you're in fit state to drive it up the mountain.'

'If I'm not, you should have time to nip off the back.'

Prentice was recalling this last optimistic remark as he stared over the side to where the world dropped away into nothingness. The tracks were grinding irritably over the shale-strewn road as he leaned forward to speak directly into Macomber's ear. 'You'll watch it, won't you, Mac? This isn't too good a place for nipping off anywhere.'

'You could slip over, too, even if you made it – you've seen what's coming up?'

Prentice stared ahead and was joined in his stare by Ford and Grapos who shared the same bench seat. Up to this moment the road had a dull, powdery look, but ahead it gleamed with a sinister sheen – a sheen of ice which coated the surface from wall to brink. 'That doesn't look too funny,' Ford remarked thoughtfully as he recalled vividly what had happened to the half-track when it hit the ice patch on their way down to the bridge. 'Think we can make it?' Prentice asked softly, subconsciously seeking reassurance.

'It may be all right,' Macomber replied non-committally as he edged the vehicle forward. 'Nothing's ever as bad as you think it's going to be – once you try it.' But his confident reply, deliberately delivered in that form to keep up the morale of his passengers, hardly corresponded with his misgivings. Further evidence that they were climbing steadily was provided by the equally steady drop in temperature and already the mist drifting over his windscreen was lingering, settling to form streaks of blobbed ice. There was no wind worth speaking of at this height yet; just a relentless fall in temperature which caused the Scot to pull the scarf a little tighter round his neck, a purity of cold which inhibited speech and made a man want to sink into the stillness of the mountain. The tracks rumbled forward under them as the ice came closer and Macomber cursed their bad luck – this hazard had presented itself at the very moment when the ledge was narrowing so there was barely a foot of free space on either side of the lumbering vehicle.

He was finding it more difficult to handle in the confined space – no leeway for even the fraction of an error and the concentration required every second was beginning to sap his last reserves of energy, to dull the keenness of his nerves just when he needed every ounce of alertness he could summon up. The vehicle moved on, passing into the ice zone as Macomber sat up straighter, every fibre of his consciousness keyed up for the first sign of slipping, the first hint that the tracks were in trouble – because it was the tracks which would get them through if they survived this ordeal, their weight which would hold the vehicle on the ledge – and conversely it was their malfunction which could bring about the final disaster, the slither backwards which he might not be able to control, ending in their dropping over the precipice, hauled down by the weight which had earlier saved them. Above the low clatter he heard a new sound, the chilling prickle as the tracks moved onto the ice, followed immediately by a crackle like breaking glass. He let out his breath: it was all right, the ice was breaking. He had to keep up this gradual pace and the tracks would anchor the vehicle while the wheels crossed the treacherous surface, then the tracks would fracture it to allow their own safe passage. Within a minute he was frowning, knowing he had miscalculated dangerously, that his remark that nothing was as bad as you expected was incorrect – things could be worse, infinitely worse. It was the *feel* of the half-track which warned him, something he was becoming familiar with, because now they felt to be moving over a permanent smoothness. The grip of the caterpillars into the road he had noted farther down was missing. They weren't gripping any more – they were moving upwards over a second more solid layer of ice beneath; only the surface had cracked. And he was coming to a bend. And he could see the first of the snow, white streaks garnishing the gleaming surface. Prentice leaned close to his shoulder, careful not to distract him, to keep his tone moderate and calm.

'Look, Mac, I think we have a problem. We're still moving over ice. The stuff must be inches thick.'

'I know. You'd better all move onto the rear bench – just in case.'

'I appreciate the suggestion . . .' Prentice was speaking with studious calm, a calm he was making a certain effort to assume, '. . . but I don't think that would help. If we start to go we'll go backwards, so I don't foresee any rush to leave by the rear exit.'

He was right, of course, Macomber thought pessimistically; they were totally boxed in – by the wall, the abyss, and by the danger of the vehicle starting to slide backwards. Their options were also critically limited in another direction which Prentice probably hadn't grasped yet: Macomber dare not risk braking – stopping on this glass-like surface – because once he stopped they would face the almost inevitable peril that when the half-track tried to move forward again the caterpillar would revolve uselessly over the ice, the first stage in the final slip-back. Boxed in, unable to stop, compelled to move up and up whatever faced them, Macomber began easing the vehicle round the shallow curve, his eyes switching constantly from one point to another – from the curving wall to the extension of the road ahead in case it narrowed even farther. He sat very still behind the wheel, his mind filled with the clanking sound of the turning metal, the curve of the sheer wall which went on and on, the sharp edge where the road ended and the blurred abyss began.

Behind him Prentice sat motionless on the bench in the position nearest to the drop, with Ford in the middle and Grapos seated close to the wall, a wall the Greek viewed with increasing disenchantment as it insidiously moved nearer to his right shoulder: the ledge was contracting. Perched above the brink, Prentice's gloved hand gripped the side of the vehicle as though attached to it and he felt the vibrations of engine and tracks passing up his arm, felt the freezing air numbing his cheeks, felt the tremble of the half-track when it wobbled as it passed over an ice-coated unevenness. The crackling sound, the thinly-iced layer crumbling under the weight, came to him above the engine's purr like the sputtering of a log fire, the symbol of warmth while he slowly froze into a state of immobility, and he couldn't take his eyes off the ribbon of ascending ledge which gradually unwound as the road climbed higher and higher. How much more of this could Mac stand? An audacious gamble – like the reversing of the half-track down the slope to hit the Germans on the bridge – he had grasped this side of the Scot's character; but this murderous, mind-killing creep up the ice-bound mountain, this was something else again, something which made him regard the Scot with far greater awe. And he must be nearly asleep over that wheel . . . He pushed the thought out of his head quickly. It frightened him too much. Glancing at the others, he saw Ford's hands clasped rather tightly in his lap, his face wooden, whereas Grapos was leaning forward, watching the road intently as though expecting a fresh hazard any second. To take his mind off watching the road Prentice pulled out the looped rope from under the bench, saw that at one end a grappling hook was attached, and when he opened the Alpenkorps satchel he saw more climbing equipment – another rope, pitons, a hammer. As he shoved satchel and rope back under the bench something damp flaked his face, dropped into his lap. It had started snowing.

The snow started falling heavily as they navigated a

fresh turn in the road and a rising wind met them, a
bitter wind which blew the flakes into a turmoil so they
danced above the ledge, driven this way and that in
disconcerting flurries. For Macomber the coming of the
snow was the final straw, the ultimate hazard. He had
kept the half-track on the ledge, maintaining an even
space on either side as it narrowed, as he found himself
increasingly compressed between wall and brink; maintaining an even speed as it balanced itself delicately on
the solid ice, but he had accomplished this gruelling
task with a reasonable visibility. Now this only asset
was taken away from him as blinding snow fogged his
vision, pasted itself over the windscreen, blurred wall
and precipice edge to mere silhouettes whose exact
location he could no longer rely on. He switched on the
lights and they sent out short-lived swathes penetrating
only a few yards inside the frenzy of the snowstorm
which was growing rapidly more violent as the wind
rose to a moaning howl and the men on the bench seat
behind him bowed their heads to shield themselves
against the onslaught of the elements. Grapos, his chin
dug into his chest, was peering warily to his right
where the rock face seemed to be closing in; if they
collided with that at the wrong moment it could veer
the vehicle outwards and over the drop, and Macomber, seated on the other side of the half-track was less
able to judge their distance from the wall than from the
brink. In the faint hope that he might be able to issue a
warning in time, the Greek lifted his head, ignored the
whipping snowflakes which stung his skin and stared

ahead through half-closed eyes. No doubt about it – they were appreciably closer to the wall.

This slight change of position was not a mistake on the Scot's part as Grapos feared; it was a deliberate act to try and reduce a little the overwhelming danger they now faced. Unsure from moment to moment of the precise position of the abyss edge he had turned in nearer to the mountain, knowing that if they struck the rock face he at least had a chance to recover, and knowing that if the tracks tipped over the edge there would be no chance of survival at all. Macomber had seriously considered halting, but they were still passing over solid ice and they were still moving up a steepish incline, so if he could keep going until the storm died away the hazards were probably a fraction less danger-ous than the hazards of stopping – to say nothing of the fact that somewhere not too far behind them Burck-hardt's force must already be making its own way up the mountain road. And the possibility of finding himself stationary on the ice-bound ledge as armed men, more than likely men equipped with mortars, came round a corner in his rear was not a contingency which appealed to him. He turned his head slightly, shouted to make himself heard above the howling wind. 'Any idea how much farther, Grapos?'

'One kilometre beyond the big bend.'

'How far to this ruddy bend?'

'Soon – very soon now.'

'How do you know in this stuff?' Macomber bawled out sceptically.

'Because of the gash.'

Gash? The Scot glanced quickly to his right and saw for the first time a break in the endless mountain wall, a fissure scarcely wider than the breadth of a man, and beyond the gyrating snow he had a glimpse of a narrow tumble of water which fell almost vertically and which was frozen solid in mid-air. Then it was gone. Jesus, the temperature must be low up here. As he looked ahead again the road began to turn round the mountain, and it went on turning, which forced him to keep the wheel swung over permanently to the right, but at least this was an improvement on the zigzags he had encountered lower down, hairpin bends he doubted he could even have attempted if the snow had come then. He drove on, up and up, following the continuing curve of the wall, peering from underneath his Alpenkorps cap brim as his gaze switched from brink to wall and back again to brink, and so great was his concentration that it was a few minutes before he realized there had been a change in the weather. It was still snowing but the wind had dropped, fading away to a chilling stillness as the curtain of snow floated down almost vertically in the windless atmosphere. For the hundredth time he brushed his hand over the windscreen to clear the snow: the wipers had packed up some time ago and his hand was equally effective for removing some of the freezing snow which was steadily adhering to the glass at either end of the screen. And now the headlights penetrated farther, giving him a safer view of what was coming up – and they were only about one kilometre from safety according to Grapos. The thought had barely passed through his head when he stiffened, felt his hands grip the wheel more tightly. A short distance ahead a boulder rested against the inner wall, a boulder rounded and partly covered with snow, and as the headlights moved nearer he saw its massive size, that it was only partly protruding from a ravine similar to the one they had recently passed, that it must have tumbled down the ravine and then become jammed in the exit immovably just before it crossed the ledge and swept down into the abyss. The dream of safety receded as every turn of the tracks took them closer to the emergency. Macomber weighed up the chances quickly – the boulder appeared firmly jammed inside the ravine, they were within a kilometre of easier going, there appearing to be just sufficient room for them to squeeze past, but it would take them to the edge of the precipice.

'You'll never make it, Mac . . .' It was Prentice's strained voice which spoke, but the Scot maintained the same even pace as he called back to them.

'Prentice, get to the back and watch the tracks – the outside one. If I'm going over, signal Ford by waving your hand. Ford! You warn me by clapping a hand on my left shoulder damned quickly, too!' He heard feet moving back along the floorboards. Someone slipped in the snow and swore as they saved themselves. On his own initiative Grapos went back to watch the inner track which had to pass the boulder. Macomber reduced speed to a point where he feared the engine might stop altogether and the snow-covered obstacle crept closer and seemed to magnify itself hugely as he steered away from the mountain wall to give himself maximum clearance, which involved placing the left-hand track on the very edge of the precipice.

The half-track crept forward through the deepening gloom, because now the snow drifting down had made it seem almost like night, and his headlights reflected weirdly off the ice covering which had formed over the mountain wall. It was like living through a bad dream, Macomber thought wearily – the drifting snow which he no longer brushed away from the windscreen, from his weighted coat; the uncanny silence, the muffled throb of the engine, the creak of the turning tracks, the blurred cones of the headlights, and now that frozen gleam off the rock wall. Inside his gloves his hands had hardly any feeling left, his feet were losing contact with the rest of his body, the dull ache in his forehead was fogging his mind, and he had the strange sensation that he was disembodied, that his limbs belonged to someone else, that he was reacting like an automaton. Perhaps his judgement had gone, he was attempting the impossible, and they would end up plunging into that abyss which could easily go down for a couple of thousand feet. He blinked, bit his lip, pushed the defeatist thoughts out of his mind and glared ferociously ahead as the trapped boulder moved closer and closer and the outer track revolved along the rim of the ledge. They were within yards of the obstacle now, would attempt to slide past it within seconds.

At the rear of the vehicle Prentice was leant half over the side as he followed the progress of the caterpillar which was starting to inch out over the precipice as they began to pass the boulder. It was a frightening sight – a portion of the moving belt suspended over the drop – and he was on the verge of signalling to Ford when he decided to wait a few seconds longer, to see whether the position deteriorated. On the far side, mid-way along the half-track, Grapos was gazing down as the boulder with equal intensity while the inner track churned slowly forward, drew alongside it and shaved snow from its encrusted surface. Glancing over his shoulder towards Prentice he frowned at the lieuten-ant's precariously poised position and then looked down at the boulder again. The main section of track was beginning to slide past it. Prentice, leaning over the outer edge, was supporting himself with one hand only to give himself the best possible view of what was happening, and the fact that his head was almost upside down probably brought on the attack. He was in the same position, staring intently as an inch of track revolved in mid-air, when the dizziness swept over him and he knew he was going to faint. Muddled, disorientated, he felt the quick movement of his right foot slipping over a patch of snow at the same moment as he heard the first grind of the vehicle against the boulder. His balance went completely, both feet sliding under him as Grapos lurched across the half-track, grasped his right arm and jerked him backwards. Prentice fell heavily, caught the back of his head on the bench and sprawled on the floorboards.

Macomber was concentrating on the precipice brink, his hands gripping the wheel, his foot ready to apply a little pressure, when he heard the scraping sound of the inner track contacting the boulder. He waited, his nerves strung up to fever pitch, waited for the hand to descend on his shoulder warning him to brake, and when nothing happened – confident that Prentice was still checking the outer caterpillar – he continued forward. The vehicle was shuddering unpleasantly as the scraping developed into a grinding sound and he suppressed the urge to glance back. His job was driving, not observation, but again he was obsessed with the mounting fear of what would happen if the caterpillar disengaged from the vehicle, leaving it with only two wheels and a single track which must cause a state of fatal disequilibrium within seconds. The half-track shuddered again and the vibrations travelled up the steering column while he resisted the temptation to steer the front wheels, which were now well past the boulder, in towards the mountain wall. Then the shuddering and grinding noise ceased at the same moment. He drove a few yards farther forward and turned the wheel, taking the half-track away from the edge. Within minutes the road was fanning out, becoming wider as the weather began to clear and the snow drifted down more slowly, soon to stop altogether. To his right the mountain wall moved away from him, the road followed it at a distance, and on his left the precipice faded away where the ground sloped more gradually. He increased speed, experiencing a sense of exhilaration.

'Soon we shall see the monastery.' It was Grapos who spoke with hoarse confidence as he stood behind the Scot and stared over the windshield. 'We go down, pass a big rock, and there it is.'

'How are the others?'

'Prentice fell down and struck his head, but he is conscious again and Ford is helping him.'

Macomber glanced over his shoulder and saw Prentice seated on the rear bench with his head between his hands and Ford beside him. The lieutenant looked up, caught the Scot's frowning expression and waved back encouragingly. 'I'll be OK in a minute – how much farther before we see something?'

'Not far. Take it easy while you can.' Macomber looked up at Grapos. 'That rock you mentioned – I seem to remember it hangs out over the road, doesn't it?'

'Yes. We pass it – we see the monastery.'

They were travelling downhill but the view to the south was obscured by a snowbound slope as they lost altitude rapidly, descending into a bowl with wintry hills sweeping down on all sides. Along the ridges the wind whipped up the snow in flurries which eddied briefly and then vanished, but the sky above was a clear cold blue and the sun shone palely and without warmth. Macomber thought he had never seen such a bleak landscape, a wilderness where savage rocks reared up in strange shapes which reminded him of the wastelands of Arizona. They were close to one of these weird rock formations – the only one which towered above the road – when Grapos' hand gripped his shoulder tightly. 'There is someone up there – up on the crag.' Macomber looked up a second too late and they were already moving into the faint shadow the rock cast across the road. He slowed down, braked under the lee of the rock, and followed Grapos out of the half-track, flexing his stiffened fingers which had become almost locked to the wheel.

They had climbed only a few feet when the Greek pulled the Scot close to the rock and whispered. 'I go up this side – you take the other and wait. If he hears me coming he will go down your side – you wait and he meets you.' Macomber nodded, scrambled stiffly back down through knee-deep snow to the road, gestured to the other two men to stay where they were, and made his way under the looming rock. The far side was a steep slope covered with harder snow where the east wind had blown over it, and he had climbed less than fifty feet before he came up behind a large boulder which provided a perfect ambush point. With his Luger in his hand he settled down to wait, and while he waited he stared out at the panoramic view.

The monastery was in sight. Mount Zervos, remote above the vagaries of the weather was fully exposed to view. Crouched behind his boulder, Macomber saw that it was as he remembered it – the huge bluff shouldered out from the mountain, hanging over the sea on one side while on the other it plunged hundreds of feet to the lake below. The walls of the monastery rose vertically from the summit of the bluff; four windowed slabs like giant watch-towers linked together by battlemented walls. They seemed to grow up out of the rocky bluff as they sheered upwards and were silhouetted against the sea with the mainland beyond, the most remote and ascetic hermitage in all Europe – and the ultimate objective of Colonel Burckhardt.

The sea was grey and choppy but comparatively calm as the last of the snowstorm crossed the gulf. Macomber doubted whether the snow had even reached the bluff this time, so once again the monastery had retained its unimpaired view across the sea to the mainland supply road. Below where he waited the ground receded away to the lake, a stretch of water at least half a mile wide, a lake frozen solid. The road went down to the eastern shore, turned along the northern edge of the ice-sheet, and then vanished before reappearing at the far end, close to the sea at the point where it began its unseen ascent to the bluff. A good half mile of the road was lost, blocked completely by an immense mass of snow heaped up against the slope below Macomber. This was drift snow, probably anything up to thirty feet deep, snow blown there recently by the high wind and which would strangle any type of powered vehicle attempting to drive through it. He stared down at the frozen lake, a sheet of water which must have frozen steadily thicker throughout the long winter. Was it solid enough to support half-tracks and mountain guns? A rattle of disturbed stones beyond the boulder warned him that someone was coming.

'Do not shoot! Please!'

Grapos' voice. Macomber lowered his Luger, stood up and saw the Greek leaning against the rock face with his rifle hoisted harmlessly over his shoulder. 'What's wrong?' he asked sharply.

'He is dead. Come, you must see.'

'Who's dead?'

But the Greek had turned back and was scrambling up again through the snow, using one hand to lever his limping foot more rapidly up past the rock. Macomber swore at his ambiguousness and went up after him. When he arrived at the top, receiving the full blast of the wind in his face, Grapos was staring down at a flattened projection just below which spurred out over the road, and Macomber found he could see down past the spur into the half-track where Ford still sat on the rear bench while Prentice stood in the road gazing up at them with his machine-pistol at the ready.

The uniformed figure on the spur lay sprawled over a machine gun. His attitude was that of a soldier watching the road from the north, the road they had just driven down in the half-track, but despite the presence of the two men above him he remained in his life-like posture until Grapos reached down and prodded him with his rifle tip. The uniformed figure went over sideways and ended up on his back with his face staring at the sky, a face with a rigid look and an unnatural bluish tinge. The poor devil had frozen to death at his post. Macomber gazed down at the Alpenkorps uniform, the stiffened Alpenkorps cap which still clutched the head, the weapon which still stood mounted in position, the barrel encased in ice and frozen snow so that it had the appearance of a glass gun. The Germans were already on Zervos, had already penetrated the monastery.

Chapter Twelve

Sunday, Zero Hour

The attack on the monastery was planned, agreed in detail, and each man knew the part he had to play. The plan was Macomber's, a plan which relied on audacity, on an eruptive breakthrough into the heart of the sanctuary, and it was based on the unproven assumption that only a small number of Germans had taken over the place in preparation for the arrival of Burckhardt's army. It was also based on Grapos' intimate knowledge of the interior of the monastery, knowledge which Prentice had transferred to his notebook as a series of ground-plans which showed the layout. It was the basic assumption which still worried Prentice as he closed the book and tucked it inside his pocket.

'If there are more men up there than we think, we haven't a hope,' he warned.

'I agree,' Macomber replied briskly, 'but it's logical. They must have arrived as civilians – the only safe way they could travel before war was declared – and in that case a large party would arouse suspicion. They only faced the monks, so a few of them could do the job.' He checked his watch. 'And we've spent twenty-one minutes working this out, so we'd better get moving before

Burckhardt lands on our tail. God knows there's enough to do in the time . . .'

He had kept the engine ticking over during their discussion; now he released the brake and the half-track began moving down towards the lake. Behind him the others were seated on the floor of the vehicle, their backs against its sides and their heads crouched forward, so from a distance it appeared that only Macomber, still wearing his Alpenkorps cap, occupied the vehicle. As they rumbled downhill at a steady pace the caterpillars whipped up the soft snow and cast it into the ditches on either side, and within a few minutes they had driven past the point where the road entered the massive snowdrift, had crossed a stretch of uneven ground and were pulling up at the eastern end of the lake to give Macomber a chance to study the ice. He would have liked to conduct a reconnaissance, to attempt walking out over the ice, but time was short. He had little faith in the Germans being held up for long by that boulder on the mountain ledge: with their manpower and the equipment they carried they would soon shift it higher up the ravine, and since he had negotiated the formidable road the weather had improved. German luck again. The wind, bitter and penetrating, whined eerily across the frozen sheet and he could see snow powder blowing over the dulled surface, but was Grapos right – right in his conviction that the prolonged winter had solidified the ice to a depth which would support the enormous weight of a half-track? He turned in his seat as though looking back up the road and saw Prentice's anxious face staring up at him. 'You think we might make it?' the lieutenant inquired.

'Only one way to find out.'

'I have told you,' Grapos repeated hoarsely. 'In winter the monks take their ox-wagons over the lake when the road is blocked.'

'As late in the year as this?' Macomber asked critically.

The Greek hesitated and Ford, disliking the hesitation, looked at him quickly. Grapos cleared his throat before speaking again, but his voice was confident. 'It is not usual – but five years since we also have the bad winter and then they take the wagons across in April. That was also the time of the great landslide – the avalanche. Much snow had fallen all through the winter and when the spring comes the mountain comes alive . . .'

Macomber lit his last but one cigar, then interrupted the Greek's flow of words. 'Let's hope it's as thick as it was five years ago, then. And now I'd appreciate it if the League of Nations debate could be adjourned – this is going to take a little concentration.' He released the brake, exerted a little foot pressure and they were moving out over the ice.

He kept his speed down to a crawl, to less than ten miles an hour as the tracks rumbled hollowly over the ice sheet and their treads ground into the surface with a brittle sound which tingled his nerves. It was almost spring, the time of the year when the ice would

imperceptibly begin to thin, to lose that extra inch of
solidity which might make all the difference to whether
they crossed safely or plunged through shattered ice
into the depths below. And the depths were something
which didn't repay thinking about. During their discussion the Scot had asked Grapos about the depth of the
lake and his answer had not exactly raised anyone's
morale. 'Fifty metres. More deep in places,' had been
the answer. Fifty metres. More than one hundred and
fifty feet of sub-zero water below the frozen floor they
were crossing. The right-hand track wobbled gently as
it mounted an area of unevenness in the ice and then
there was an unpleasant crushing sound as the track
squashed the tiny ridge. Inside the vehicle Prentice,
with his back against the right-hand side, felt the slight
incline, followed by the trembling fall. His heart leapt,
his hands locked round his machine-pistol and his eyes
met Ford's. The staff-sergeant had an opaque look, but
Prentice saw the flicker of fear as Ford observed the
brief contraction of the lieutenant's eyebrows. Then the
half-track was rumbling forward smoothly again while
Prentice flexed his fingers and let out his breath, breath
expelled like a small puff of steam in the chilled
temperature inside the vehicle.

The ordeal was probably more mind-wracking for
the men concealed on the floor than for Macomber,
because hidden away inside the half-track they couldn't
see where they were going or how far they had come
and they experienced everything by feel alone, leaving
their imaginations free to conjure up the most frightful

possibilities. At least Macomber had a task to accomplish, a vehicle to steer; but for him the pressure built up in other ways. He had intended keeping close to the shore, driving past the immense snowdrift as he followed the line of the invisible road, but shortly after moving onto the lake he had taken an irrevocable decision, plagued by the desperate shortage of time. So he had changed his mind and was now heading on a course which would take them along the diameter of the circle – straight over the centre of the lake.

The half-track was rumbling smoothly on, wobbling only occasionally, a wobble which was probably only the natural sway of the unwieldy vehicle, although for Macomber it had an unpleasant similarity to the bowing of weakened ice under a great weight, when he noticed the paler colour of a huge area of ice towards the centre of the lake. His lips tightened – he was on course to cross directly over this strangely discoloured section. In early winter, when ice had formed, it must have formed first at the fringes along the shore before creeping inwards until eventually it had encompassed the entire lake. So the ice in the centre was the freshest, the youngest, probably the thinnest. The wheels were close to this distinctive section when he changed direction, steering a curve which would take him beyond this possibly treacherous zone. He only hoped to God he had turned in time, that he wasn't already moving over ice only a fraction of the thickness of what they had already crossed. With an effort he resisted the urge to reduce speed – the advantage now might lie in crossing this area as swiftly as possible – but he also resisted the succeeding temptation to increase his speed over ten miles an hour, since faster movement might intensify the danger.

The distant shoreline crawled nearer with agonizing slowness. The huge snow-covered bluff to their left where the rock rose vertically from the lake slid behind them as they drew level with the rampart walls of the monastery. And now Macomber saw that there was someone at the summit of the lofty tower which overlooked lake and sea, a tiny, faceless figure too minute to be identified as monk or German soldier, and the Scot blessed his foresight in arranging for the others to conceal themselves on the floor. The sun was low, casting the interior of the half-track in deep shadow, so even a lookout with field-glasses would see only a German half-track driven by one man, a man in a nondescript coat with an Alpenkorps cap rammed down over his head. You see what you want to see, Macomber told himself, so with luck a German lookout would see one of his own vehicles sent ahead to test the stability of the ice. He sucked in a deep breath of chilled mountain air to revive his flagging reserves. God he was tired, he was so damned tired! Within the next few seconds he was stirred into petrified alertness.

He was within two hundred yards of safety, coming closer to the shoreline where the road emerged from the snowdrift, when he felt the vehicle begin to tremble, saw the ice sheet ahead of him tilt and quiver prior to the moment of fracturing fatally, realized that the huge

COLIN FORBES

weight under him was beginning to drop . . . His hands
tightened on the wheel, his foot pressed down on the
accelerator – reflex actions he was unaware of and the
sagging motion of the half-track quickened. He was
speeding forward over the ice when he grasped what
was happening – happening to him rather than to the
vehicle: he was suffering a violent attack of giddiness.
He leaned back hard against the seat, sucked in quick
gulps of the pure air, felt his lungs expanding, his head
clearing, and then he was closing the gap between lake
and road, keeping his foot pressed down regardless
and with only one idea in his mind – to get clear of this
bloody lake come hell or high water. The wheels
bumped over rock-hard ruts, the half-track drove forward through frosted grasses which broke off and
scattered like pine needles as it moved onto the road,
and it was soon ascending until it was lost from the
view of the monastery under the leaning overhang of
the bluff towering above them. Macomber pulled up,
left the engine running and rested on the wheel. His
eyes were still open when Prentice scrambled to his
feet and laid a hand on his snow-covered shoulder.

'You've made it! Are you all right, Mac?'

'Give me a minute . . . Look down there . . .'

The words came out in gasps and while he struggled
to get a grip on himself Prentice extracted the Monokular from his coat pocket and focused it out over the
gulf. In the distance to the south a lean grey vessel was
approaching with smoke streaming from its stack and
a clear wake to stern. A British destroyer was heading

for the peninsula. Her deck was crammed with troops and Prentice fancied he recognized the individualistic hats the Australians wore – Australians and some New Zealanders probably, steaming directly for Cape Zervos where the tortuous track led up the cliff face.

'It's packed with troops,' Prentice said quickly. 'Aussies and Kiwis. God, if only they'd get here in time.'

'They won't!' Macomber was recovering and he clambered unsteadily out of the vehicle to stand by the lieutenant. 'Burckhardt should make it within the hour and . . .' He looked back at Grapos who was seated on a bench beside Ford. 'How long do you reckon it would take a man to come up that cliff track?'

'Three or four hours. It would depend on the man. Mules find it difficult.'

'There you are,' Macomber said grimly. 'And they haven't even landed yet – won't for a while. That's always assuming they're heading for the cape – they could easily be bound for Katyra.'

'Lord, no!' Prentice was appalled. 'If only we had a Verey pistol – or even a mirror.' He turned to the others. 'It would be just too damned convenient if anyone had a mirror, I suppose?'

It was too damned convenient; no one possessed a mirror. Macomber brushed snow off his leather coat and began walking stiffly downhill the way they had come, and every step jarred his cramped body, cramped with sitting behind the wheel, cramped with the tension of crossing the lake. Feeling as though at any moment he might keel over and fall in the snow, he reached the point where the road turned under the bluff to continue along the shore, and with Ford at his heels he came round the corner. He stopped abruptly, holding back the sergeant with his hand. 'There you are – that shows how much time we've got. Sweet Fanny Adams.' The bluff loomed above them, and above that rose the sheer climb of the monastery wall, terminating in the high tower which reared like a pinnacle in the sunlight. But it was across the lake where Macomber was staring, his face bleak as his lips chewed briefly. Round the flank of the snow-covered slope on the distant shore a small dark bug-like object was crawling forward. The first half-track had arrived already.

'You were right,' Prentice said tersely as he peered over their shoulders. 'Those chaps on the destroyer will never make it.'

Macomber turned round, talking as he started back towards the half-track, his weary feet scuffling through the snow. 'We'll go ahead with the plan exactly as we arranged. We've got to find some way of warning that destroyer – if they land men and start them up that track with Jerries in position at the top of it there'll be a massacre.'

'Burckhardt will know he can cross that ice when he sees our track marks,' Prentice called out, panting up behind him. The Scot had temporarily recovered his vitality, spurred on by the sight of Burckhardt's arrival, and he was moving uphill with rapid strides as he shouted over his shoulder. 'He'll see nothing. The wind has practically obliterated the marks we made, so he'll have to make his own recce. Which gives us extra time. Not bloody much of it, though.'

Taking a last quick look at the oncoming destroyer, he climbed back into the half-track, glanced to his rear to make sure they were all on board, and then began driving uphill. For a short distance the road fell away steeply to the west – to their right – where the mountain slope sheered down towards the wind-ruffled Aegean far below, while on their left the toppling wall of the bluff leaned over them. The road was deep with snow, soft snow from the recent fall, and streaks of whiteness smeared the bluff's wall. Across the gulf Macomber could see the ship-wrecking chain of rocks extending towards him from the mainland, ending in the saw-tooth which had so nearly destroyed the *Hydra*, and beyond the rocks he could see the mainland itself where Allied troops would be moving up the vital supply road. Then another rock wall closed off the view and they were ascending a narrow, twisting canyon on the last lap of their long journey to the monastery.

He had ascended perhaps two hundred feet, con-fined between the narrowing walls of the canyon which climbed vertically above them, when he saw a trail of cloud creeping over the road ahead, blotting out what lay beyond. Switching on his headlights, he reduced speed as they slipped inside the vaporous mist; ice-cold drizzle chilled his face and there was a sudden drop in temperature as he crawled round a bend and went up a steep incline. The headlights penetrated the cloud just sufficiently for him to see what was happening, to see where the road turned yet another bend as it spiralled up towards the summit of the bluff, and now water was starting to run down the snow-packed road and the snow itself was melting to slush. He drove on up through the drifting cloud, feeling his clothes grow heavier as the damp clung to him, feeling the tracks slither once and then recover stability as they ground patiently upwards while he grew cold and miserable and sodden and it seemed as though the elements were flinging one final ordeal in his path almost within sight of their objective. Behind him the others had taken up position. Grapos stood at the rear of the vehicle, the Alpenkorps rope looped over his shoulder, while Prentice and Ford huddled on a bench close to him, their weapons gripped between their hands as they watched the Greek who stood facing the way they were going. Macomber turned another bend, saw the road levelling out, switched off his headlights, and heard the hammering of Grapos' rifle butt. The signal to halt.

He braked, left the engine running, and the tang of salt air was strong in his nostrils as the cloud began to thin and pale sunlight percolated through the haze. Grapos dropped off at the rear between the tracks and was followed by Prentice and Ford who went after him and vanished in the cloud. Behind the wheel, Macomber was wiping moisture off his watch-face while he timed five minutes exactly. The mistiness, which would have masked his onslaught until the last moment, was receding rapidly as the cloud left the peninsula and floated out over the gulf. He grimaced, saw ahead the final rise in the road which hid him from the monastery, checked his watch again. At four minutes and thirty seconds the cloud had dispersed completely, but again that would have been too damned convenient. Now for the break-in, the final effort – with everything staked on one vicious surprise attack.

With the cloud gone he was bathed in the cold bright sunlight of winter and he could see the Aegean to his right, but rising ground shielded the destroyer from view, he could see the stark triangle of Mount Zervos, a peak of whiteness where the light caught the snow crystals, but the monastery was still invisible; and he could see the deep, trench-like gulley along which Grapos had led the other two men, but they had disappeared. He checked his watch: ten seconds to go. Reaching inside his pocket he dragged out the Luger from the sodden folds and laid it on the seat beside him. Five seconds left. His hand clutched the brake, waited, released it. He was off.

He accelerated rapidly, mounted the rise, crested it. The road ran straight to the monastery which rose up less than two hundred yards away. He took in the impression in a flash. The towers and the wall linking them were lower on this side. The greenish shell of a dome, which he remembered was the church, showed beyond the wall-top. The ancient gatehouse, a tumble-down wooden structure which appeared to lean back against the stone for support, was in the centre of the wall. Three or four storeys up wooden box-like structures were attached to the stonework, protruding from the wall like giant dovecotes, each structure faced with tall shutters which led out to a small balcony. The ground between the crest and the monastery was bare and level with huge boulders strewn close to the left-hand section of the monastery. Mid-way to the gatehouse he swerved off the road, crossing open ground in a sweeping half-circle, which brought him back on the road again with the half-track's rear presented to the monastery. So far he had seen no sign of life and the place had a derelict look. He changed gear, began reversing towards the closed gate which barred his way, twisting round in his seat as he kept one eye on the road, another on the gateway rushing towards him as he built up speed and the monastery came closer and closer.

He saw out of the corner of his eye movement on the roofed-in, railed walk which spanned the first floor of the gatehouse, the movement of a field-grey figure steadying himself as he took aim, and he knew something had gone fatally wrong. The Alpenkorps cap was not enough to make the German pause, or had he spotted one of the others at the last moment – Macomber had no idea which – but he knew that within seconds the German would open fire, that he must ignore the threat of almost certain death, that the rifle would be discharged at point-blank range if the man had the sense to wait only a few seconds longer when he couldn't possibly miss, firing down from his elevated position at a target moving rapidly closer under his gunsight.

During the final rush up to the closed gates Macomber became aware of everything around him – the snow-covered ground where rocks poked up through the whiteness, the shabbiness of the small balconies where decrepit paint exposed the mellow woodwork, the open-necked collar of the Alpenkorps soldier on the gatehouse who was steadying himself against the wall as he aimed his rifle, the rotting timbers of the large double gates, the mildewed-looking dome of the church vanishing from view as the wall rose up and screened it, the high-powered throb of the engine, the metallic grind of the whirling tracks . . .

He heard the report of the rifle above these sounds, a sharp crack, the first shot fired in the coming encounter – the shot fired by Grapos from behind a large boulder. The German on the balcony was stood immediately over the roadway and he staggered forward as the bullet penetrated, reached out a hand to steady himself on the frail balcony rail, sagged forward with his full weight, which was too much for the support, and he fell through it at the moment the half-track smashed through the gates, tearing both loose from the upper hinges so they toppled inwards and the vehicle stormed over them and continued reversing under the archway and into the vast courtyard beyond. Macomber blinked with relief, heard something thud down behind him, glanced back swiftly and saw the

317

dead German folded over the second bench. The half-track roared on inside a stone-paved square which was larger than he remembered it, a square with a plane tree in the centre, the church to the right, an ancient stone well beyond the tree – a square large enough to accommodate a small army, overlooked on all sides by windows and arcaded walks which ran round the inner walls at each floor level. The vehicle was charging towards the tree when he reduced speed, changed gear, went forward and began thundering round the square, turning the wheel erratically as though the half-track had gone berserk. His Alpenkorps cap was prominently on view, as was the German soldier behind him, a soldier impossible to identify from his crumpled position. Macomber completed one circuit, heard the sound of shots, described a wild S-bend tour round the church and reappeared suddenly from the other side as he headed into the square again and accelerated afresh. For anyone inside the monastery the speeding half-track had become a hypnotic focal point – a focal point to divert their attention for vital seconds from what might be happening elsewhere.

When Grapos jumped from the stationary half-track as the cloud dispersed from the bluff he plunged straight into the gulley leading away from the road and towards the monastery, a ravine seven feet deep which hid the hurrying men from any possible observation from the monastery walls. He ran forward in a crouch, his rifle between his hands, the rope looped from his shoulder. He was heading for one of the towers which protruded out from the wall, so that the side farthest from the gatehouse formed a right-angled corner which couldn't be seen from that direction. Behind him came Prentice with Ford close at his heels. The staff-sergeant's shoulder still throbbed with a dull ache but he could use the lower part of his arm and, more important still, he could use his machine-pistol if he held it awkwardly.

Close to the wall, Grapos paused and lifted himself half-out of the gulley at a point where a large boulder hid him from the gatehouse. This was the position he must take up to cover Macomber when he had arranged the ascent of his companions. Dropping back into the gulley, he ran forward again and clambered out where the ravine ended at the base of the wall. They were now hemmed in by the corner, invisible from the farther extension of the wall unless someone came out onto a balcony. Ford took up a position where he could observe the receding wall while the lieutenant gazed upwards, his machine-pistol hoisted. It took Grapos less than a minute to prepare the rope for throwing, a rope weighted at the tip by the metal hook, and when he hurled it upwards and inwards the hook trapped itself on the floor of the projecting side-balcony twenty feet above them. Taking a long breath, Grapos jumped up the rope, held on, swayed briefly like a pendulum as he tested its resistance, then dropped to the ground again and glared at Prentice.

'It is good – but you must be quick. You remember the way?'

'Perfectly!' Prentice glanced at his watch, looped the machine-pistol over his shoulder, began to climb the rope hand over hand, his legs stiffened, his boots pressed against the roughened stonework as he half-hauled, half-walked himself up towards the balcony. The shaky structure trembled a little under his progress, but he ignored the warning of its instability, climbing faster as he got the hang of the ascent. If the bloody thing came down, it came down. Neck or nothing now. His face eased up to balcony level and he saw the hook firmly embedded between the open floorboards. One final heave and he was clutching the shaky rail, hauling himself over the top, standing on the floor with the closed shutters behind him. He propped the machine-pistol against a post where he could reach it easily, looked over, saw that Ford had already tied the rope round his body and under his armpits. As he started to haul up the sergeant Grapos was slipping back inside the gulley and running along it to take up position behind the boulder.

Hauling up Ford proved strenuous: the sergeant tried to help by splaying his feet against the wall, but he was unable to lift himself by his hands which were concentrated on gripping the rope, so the lieutenant had to haul up his full weight length by length, the rope taut over the balcony rail which was shuddering under the pressure, the floor quivering under his feet as Grapos' warning flashed through his mind. 'The balcony has not been used for many years because it is dangerous . . .' Sweating profusely, his arms almost strained from their sockets, his legs trembling with the arduous exertion, Prentice saw a tangle of dark hair appear, a hand grasp the floor edge, and then the railing gave way, collapsed inwards like broken matchwood. He jerked in more rope, his back pressed hard into the shutters, his feet driving into the floor as he heaved desperately and Ford was half-dragged, half-scrambled his way through the smashed rail and ended up on his knees on the balcony. The sergeant was still recovering his breath, blood was still oozing from his left hand where the wood had gashed it, while Prentice untied the rope, released him from it, and then dropped the rope end down to the ground for Grapos to use later. 'All right, Ford?' he croaked, leaning against the shutters as he reached out for the machine-pistol.

'Just like the obstacle course at Chester, sir.' He stood up cautiously and unlooped his own weapon. 'But maybe I need a refresher course. We'd better get inside – I can hear Mac coming.'

The clattering rattle of the approaching half-track was in their ears as Prentice dealt with the process of getting in. He used his machine-pistol butt to club the latch and the woodwork splintered swiftly under his third blow. Without realizing that the shutters opened outwards, he used his shoulder to go through them, head tucked well in as he rammed his body against and through the breaking shutters with such force that the impetus took him half-way across the room before he could pull up. He hardly saw the room: faded religious murals on the stone walls, a cloth-covered table, an ikon; then he reached the varnished door and opened it with great care. The musty odours of the unused room were in his nostrils as he peered both ways along a deserted corridor and from beyond the balcony he heard the grumble of the oncoming half-track. They'd cut the timing pretty fine. Beckoning to Ford, he ran down the passage to his left. It was like running through a cloister – wooden archways at intervals and large windows to his right which looked down on the square below – and the only sound in the monastic silence, now the walls had muffled the half-track's approach, was the sound of his clumping boots as he ran full tilt for the staircase at the end. He paused briefly when he arrived at the corner, looked to his right where another deserted corridor ran along the second side, glanced up the empty staircase and ran up it, turning at a landing before running up the second flight. On the second floor an identical view faced him – corridors stretching away from the corner in two directions. To his right, at the far end, Ford, who had just emerged from his own staircase, raised a thumb. Prentice returned the signal and went over to the nearest window, hid himself behind a section of the wall and waited.

In less than thirty seconds he saw the half-track coming backwards into the yard, but gave the vehicle only a brief glance as his eyes searched the windows across the square at different levels. His waiting time was very short – the half-track had entered the square, had reversed direction and started driving forwards round the square below them when a window opposite opened and two German soldiers leaned out to stare down at the half-track's mad career round the square. Prentice raised his machine-pistol, thrust the muzzle sharply through the glass, and the shattering noise was lost in the long burst as he sprayed the window steadily, saw the Germans crumple and disappear as movement higher up caught his eye. Through an open window on the top floor another German was aiming his rifle downwards at Prentice when Ford's machine-pistol opened up with a murderous rattle, one much shorter burst, short but lethal. The German with the rifle lost his weapon and followed it down into the yard below as Macomber sped towards the church. A burst of answering fire from farther along the top floor hammered Prentice's shattered window as he jumped back behind the wall. He heard Ford's weapon replying as something moved behind him. He swung his gun round, knowing the magazine was almost empty, and the muzzle pointed at Grapos who froze at the top of the stairs. He must have come up the rope like a charge of electricity.

The explosion came as Prentice, inserting a fresh magazine, was grinning crookedly at Grapos. The grenade landed mid-way along the corridor between Ford and the lieutenant, but Grapos had seen it fly in through a window and was sheltered behind the stair-case. 'Jesus, this is getting rough,' Prentice muttered half to himself. He knocked a shard of glass from his sleeve, staring down at the Greek who stood with his rifle and the rope looped afresh over his shoulder, and started to move round the corner into the next corridor. Ford, protected by a section of wall, was firing again across the yard as the German on the top floor opposite changed tactics. He must have assumed that there were men spread along the side corridor because suddenly a stream of bullets began shattering every window along the passage Prentice was about to move into. Glass was strewn over the floor, bullets scarred the inner wall while the lieutenant, safe behind the wall in the next corridor he shared with Ford, waited for the barrage to cease. The next grenade landed closer to Ford, sent a fresh shock wave in both directions, and for the first time Prentice grasped what was happening.

A German had entered the corridor below them. Knowing the enemy was on the floor above, he hadn't risked coming up a staircase: instead he was leaning out of a lower window while he tossed grenades upwards and inside the second-floor windows. It was only a matter of time before he chose the right aperture for his deadly missiles. Prentice hesitated, reviewing the situation. Macomber couldn't fire on the German while he was driving the half-track round the square at that pace, and the plan called for him to keep up this diversion whatever happened. The fusillade along the next corridor ceased briefly and Grapos called out, 'I will deal with him . . .' He gestured along the corridor and then downwards, took out his knife and ran down the passage before disappearing inside a room mid-way along the building.

The room which the Greek had entered also had a balcony, and it was towards this he ran after closing the door as a precaution against a grenade landing in the entrance. Thrusting open the shutters, he went into the sunlight and the firing in the square was muffled to a quiet rattle. It took him a matter of seconds to jam the hook down between the floorboards, to throw the rope over the edge, then he was slipping down the rope which dangled past the first-floor balcony below. His boots scraped the rail, felt their way inside it, and he slithered the last few feet on to the balcony. Inserting his knife blade between the ill-fitting shutters, he forced up the latch, fingered open the left-hand shutter gently and went inside the half-darkened room. The inner door was closed and he listened with his ear pressed against its panel for several seconds before gripping the handle with his left hand. The right hand held the knife ready for throwing as he eased the handle to the open position, stood to the opening side of the door and flung it back against the wall. When he went into the corridor he saw that the lone German had changed his position and was standing by the window below where Prentice was sheltering. The German had a grenade ready for throwing when he saw Grapos, changed his mind instantly, and hoisted it for a throw straight down the corridor. The knife left Grapos, sped along the passage, struck the soldier a second before he threw. He staggered, dropped the grenade, crashed into a window, one hand clutching his arm. The grenade detonated at his feet.

Macomber, hearing bullets ricocheting off a bench behind him, had driven the half-truck behind the church. His role as a diversion was over and it was time to give a hand with his Luger, so he drove out once more, pressed his foot down and headed for the ramp leading up into the arcaded walk on the eastern side of the square, the side where most of the Germans had appeared earlier. The half-track surged forward at an angle across the square and he was turning the wheel as he went up the ramp, swung round into the corridor, and realized too late it was a fraction narrow for the passage of the vehicle he had intended driving the full length of the arcade. The ground floor was enclosed from the square by a railing only and it was the left-hand caterpillar which encountered this railing, churning it to pieces as it rasped its way forward. The first stone pillar it met was the obstacle it refused to overcome; instead the track parted company with the vehicle, disengaged itself completely and whipped across the square as an intact ring. Macomber had braked at the moment of impact and he jumped over the windscreen, landing on the bonnet and sliding off on to the floor as the vehicle settled at a drunken angle. The engine sputtered and died. He wondered why there was no more shooting.

After waiting a minute, he hobbled slowly along the

corridor and stopped at a short flight of steps leading down into the square at a point half-way along the arcade. Shattered windows everywhere, some starred with pieces still intact. And no sound of gunfire. The silence which had descended on the monastery seemed uncanny as he saw Ford peering out from the second floor, risking a quick look-round before withdrawing his head with equal abruptness. Macomber waited a little longer, but there was no sign of the enemy except for the crumpled figure in Alpenkorps uniform which had toppled from the fourth floor early in the battle. The German in the half-track had long ago been thrown to the floor by one of the Scot's wilder swerves. Still cautious, he made his way along the arcade, turned the corner at the bottom, and walked along the second side. Grapos met him at the foot of the staircase and nodded towards an impressive figure standing a few steps up. A man as tall as Macomber, a vigorous seventy-year-old, he was dressed in the long robes and the flat-topped hat of a dignitary of the Greek Orthodox Church. It was the Abbot of Zervos.

'I found him locked inside his room on the second floor,' Grapos whispered as Prentice appeared on the stairs behind the Abbot.

Macomber spoke in English, remembering from his visit five years earlier that the Abbot understood this language, and he wanted the lieutenant to hear what was said. 'We need information quickly, Father. How many Germans are there here?'

'There were ten men,' the Abbot began crisply. 'They

arrived by car yesterday evening disguised as civilians, but they had their uniforms with them. There were three cars . . .'

'Just a moment, please.' Macomber held up his hand and looked at Prentice. 'Any idea how many you've accounted for yet?'

'Seven,' the lieutenant replied. 'I've been round the building with Ford and checked . . .'

'Eight then, including that frozen lookout – or nine with the man on the gatehouse . . .'

'*Seven*,' Prentice repeated firmly. 'I've included both those Jerries in my count . . .'

'There are three men on the north tower,' the Abbot intervened urgently, crossing himself. 'Captain Braun, who commands this unit, spends a lot of time up there with two other men. They have organized an observation post on the roof of the tower and I think they are watching the mainland road. They have a telescope, a wireless transmitter and a mortar gun . . .'

'A mortar!' Macomber looked up the staircase at Ford who had come round the corner with his machine-pistol tucked under his good shoulder. Despite his wound he looked the coolest man in the group as he stopped and listened to the Scot's question. 'Ford, could a mortar on that high tower cause the destroyer any trouble?'

'It depends. If it's an 8-cm job like the ones I saw on the plateau things could get pretty sticky. Mind you, the range would have to be right and the mortar man would have to be good – but being in the Wehrmacht he probably is. If he's damned lucky and drops a bomb down the stack into the boiler-room – well, you saw what happened to the *Hydra* . . .'

'We'd better get up there bloody quick,' Macomber snapped. He turned to Grapos. 'You know the way up, so get us up there . . .'

The Abbot intervened again, fingering the crucifix suspended from his neck. 'This is a holy place and should never have become a battlefield, but the Germans have only themselves to blame and they have invaded my country. Captain Braun has taken over my bedroom on the fourth floor as his office – Grapos will show you the room I mean – so he may be inside there rather than on the tower.'

'I doubt it – after all this shooting.' Macomber frowned and thought for a moment. 'On the other hand none of you have been seen in the square since the firing stopped, so Braun may just have assumed we've all been wiped out.' He looked again at the Abbot and spoke quietly but firmly. 'And now I want you to go back to your room on the second floor and stay there, whatever happens.' He was following Grapos up to the first landing when he turned for a final word with the Abbot. 'What's happened to all the monks who live here?'

'They have been locked up inside the refectory – across there.' The Abbot pointed across the square towards the church. 'There is plenty of room for them . . .'

'So it's best they stay there for the moment,' Macomber

broke in briskly. 'Wait here until we've gone and then go to your room, please.' He turned to Grapos. 'There are only three of them but this could be the most dangerous job of the lot. Let's get going.'

They ascended to the third floor without incident and Macomber led the way with the Greek one step below him. The Scot was desperately worried about what might happen if the destroyer came within range before they reached the tower, but he still went up cautiously, pausing at each landing to listen carefully, climbing the stairs like the others on the soles of his boots, so they made very little sound as they approached the fourth floor. Macomber had reached the landing, was about to peer round the corner, when he heard footsteps coming along the top floor. Gesturing to the others below, he waited. The footsteps arrived at the top of the staircase, then faded. Macomber ran up the last flight, saw an empty corridor stretching away, a short passage to his left, an iron-studded door in the stone wall at the end of the passage, a door which must lead to the tower and which was open. He went silently down the short passage and listened at the open door, looking up a stone spiral which vanished round a corner in the gloom. He arrived just in time to hear someone hammering sharply on a wooden surface in a certain way, a signal which doubtless identified the new arrival. Metal scraped over metal as a bolt was withdrawn, nailed boots climbed the last few steps, a trap-door slammed shut and the bolt rasped home again.

'Who was it?' Grapos whispered in his ear while Prentice and Ford kept a watch on the corridors. Macomber waved a hand to make the Greek shut up and started up the spiral, feeling his way in the darkness with his hand on the roughened wall. The steps were dangerously narrow, fading into nothingness at the inner edge, and when his head touched something he knew he was at the top. He retreated down several steps and switched on his torch. The trap-door was a massive slab of wood, so close-fitting that no hint of daylight had shown through in the darkness. We'll never break through that, he thought, and went back down the spiral.

'We can't shoot our way up on to the roof,' Macomber informed them quietly, 'there's a trap-door like a piece of teak up there. Prentice, let's take a quick look at the Abbot's bedroom and see what drags the brave captain – if it is Braun – out into the open. Ford, you stay here while Grapos watches the lower stairs. If someone starts coming down this spiral, join Grapos, and we'll take care of ourselves.'

They approached the bedroom tentatively in case a guard had been left inside, but the room was empty. The windows looked out over the mountain and the only furniture was an austere bed, a wooden table and a chair. A wireless transmitter rested on the table with a pair of headphones laid neatly behind it close to the chair. 'So that's it,' Macomber commented. 'He's transmitting to Burckhardt from here now. He must have found the roof inconvenient. I'm damned sure he thinks we've all been killed – he hasn't even locked the door.'

'Couldn't,' Prentice pointed out laconically. 'There's no keyhole. Do you think he'll be back?' He was looking out of the window but the wall of the tower cut off any view down to the lake.

'I hope so. It's our only chance of getting up to that tower roof. I'd give anything now for a ten-kilogram demolition charge. Placed under that trap-door it would blow the whole roof into the lake. We'll have to work something simple out in case he does come down again. I expect he might – those headphones look as though he's expecting to use them again in the near future.'

This time Macomber let Prentice make arrangements for Braun's reception because he wanted to hold himself in reserve for what he proposed to attempt if Braun came down again. While Ford watched the staircase, Prentice and Grapos took up ambush station on either side of the doorway leading up to the spiral. Macomber waited at the end of the stone passage with his Luger ready for an emergency. It was a simple-seeming operation like this which could so easily go wrong. They waited and the minutes passed as Macomber wondered whether Braun was now permanently stationed on the roof, whether having radioed a warning of the attack on the monastery he was now going to sit tight until the first half-tracks poured into the square below. Or would he venture once more down the spiral to send a further message about the destroyer's progress? In the silence he heard his wrist-watch ticking and then he heard something else.

Something which thudded hollowly from the interior of the spiral. The trap-door had been opened very quietly this time, had then been closed with less sound than previously. Macomber stared down the passage to where Grapos waited pressed against the wall, his knife held by his side, to where Prentice waited on the other side of the doorway, his forehead moist although the temperature was low inside the stone passage. There was a long pause when they heard nothing and Prentice began to think it was a false alarm, but the Scot thought differently and could almost sense the presence of someone listening inside the spiral before he came out. Then a boot scraped over stone, the muzzle of a machine-pistol stabbed out of the doorway and a uniformed captain of the Alpen-korps came out behind it. Prentice grabbed with both hands as Grapos lunged with the knife, but the German swung round with a swift reaction which made Macomber take a step forward. The lieutenant had one hand pressed over his mouth, the other locked round his throat when the German swung so unexpectedly, tearing the hand free from his throat. Grapos had little better success when his knife hit the wrong target, was deflected along the barrel of the machine-pistol and skidded over the German's hand, which made him let go of the weapon but had no disabling effect. The German flung his whole weight on Prentice, catching the freed hand between himself and the bare wall, and the lieutenant thought his knuckles were broken as Grapos lunged a second time and the knife went home. Braun sagged, collapsed on the floor, and when Macomber checked his pulse he felt nothing. Captain Braun had become a permanent casualty.

'I'm going straight up,' Macomber said quickly. 'We're running out of time and they may think Braun's forgotten something if I go up now. Grapos, if I can get that trap opened, can get even half-way on to the roof, you follow . . .'

He was mid-way up the spiral when the pain caught him across the back, a sharp stabbing pain which locked him immovably for several seconds: he must have twisted something when he'd leapt out of the half-track. He suppressed a groan, felt Grapos bump into him, and forced himself up the last few steps. With the Luger in his right hand, his fingers felt the trap-door to check his whereabouts, then he rapped confidently on the underside of the lid in a certain way, the way Braun had rapped. There was a pause, long drawn-out moments when he thought the stratagem hadn't worked, followed by a rattling sound as the bolt was withdrawn.

It went wrong at once. The trap-door opened slowly and there was no one to shoot at as daylight flooded down into the spiral. When the gap was wide enough he ran up the last few steps, aware of an unforeseen handicap – the trap was being opened from behind him by someone he couldn't see. He reached the stone-paved roof and half-turned round, only to find himself again temporarily immobilized in that position by the fierce pain which seared his back and cramped his movement, making it impossible for him to aim the Luger at the kneeling corporal who slammed down the trap and pushed the bolt home. The falling slab of wood had struck Grapos on the shoulder, leaving Macomber isolated on the roof with the two Germans. The corporal, still on his knees, was reaching for a pistol lying on the stones beside him when Macomber threw his Luger. The weapon smashed into the corporal's temple and he fell over sideways, his fingers still closed over the pistol as he lay still, facing the sky with his eyes open. The other soldier had been standing by the wall looking out over the gulf when Macomber came onto the roof, his body crouched as he pressed his eye to a powerful field-telescope mounted on a tripod, while close by a short, squat-barrelled mortar was set up on its own tripod near a pile of snub-nosed shells. Heavily built, the German's open collar exposed a thick neck, and he was only taken by surprise for a few seconds, then he dropped to his knees and began tugging furiously to free something caught under the canvas which cushioned the mortar bombs. It came free as Macomber wrenched himself into action and reached him.

The German, still on his knees, swung round with the machine-pistol and the Scot grabbed at the muzzle in mid-swing. Instead of pulling at the weapon, which the German expected, he pushed viciously and the soldier lost balance, letting go of the gun as he fell over backwards, but his elbows saved him from sprawling over the floor. Still in pain, Macomber made a mistake, thinking he had enough time to reverse the weapon and get a grip on it. He was still fumbling when the German came to his feet and went for his throat, and the momentum of his charge carried Macomber back against the waist-high tower wall. He couldn't even attempt to use the gun which was compressed between their bodies as they grappled fiercely and Macomber felt himself being pushed remorselessly backwards over the brink. The soldier was a few inches shorter but he was in prime condition and ten years younger, and the Scot was very close to the end of his physical resources. With the gun penned between them, the German had both hands locked tightly round Macomber's throat and now, as his back arched over the wall screamed with pain, he felt his air supply going. A momentary panic gripped him as he started to tip over the drop, the rim of the wall hard against the small of his back and acting as a fulcrum for the German to lever him down to the lake far below.

Knowing that he was winning, the soldier ignored the gun, squeezing his hands tighter and tighter as Macomber's face changed colour. The Scot's hands still held the machine-pistol and he managed to force it sideways, but he still couldn't use it. Had the German continued his pressure he would have sent Macomber over the edge within seconds, but he saw the gun come loose and released his right hand to grab at it, confident that the Scot was done for. And Macomber was almost done for – the German was holding his throat with only one hand but he had quickly inserted his thumb into the Scot's windpipe and his victim began to choke. Get rid of the gun! The message raced through Macomber's brain and he jerked feebly but with just sufficient force to snatch it out of the hand clutching the dangling strap. He let go and the machine-pistol disappeared over the edge.

As the thumb pressure increased reddish lights sputtered in front of his eyes and he felt his last remaining strength ebbing away. This was it. Nothing else left. His right hand fluttered, felt hair at the moment when the German's nailed boot ground down his instep. Pain shrieked up his leg like an electric shock and he was seized with a spasm of blind fury which sent fresh adrenalin through his veins. He grabbed a large handful of hair, clawed his hand, twisted it and dragged it sideways with all the energy he could muster, hauling at the hair as though to tear it out by the roots. The thumb pressure slackened, was released. Macomber sucked in a gasping lungful of cold mountain air, knowing that within seconds the brawny German would recover. Releasing the hair, he clawed his hand again and, as the soldier's face reappeared, he struck. The savagery of the onslaught unnerved the German and he propelled himself backwards away from the wall to save his face, catching the heel of his boot on an uplifted stone. He was fighting to restore his balance when Macomber's bull-like charge, head down, punched into his stomach, driving him headlong across the roof. The Scot was following him when his right foot tangled with a leg of the telescope's tripod and he crashed forward on his chest as the telescope toppled, broke away from its tripod and rolled over the roof. Macomber had hauled himself up on all fours, his chin sticky with blood where it had grazed the stones, when he saw that the wall had saved his opponent. The German had slapped his hands hard down on the wall-top to halt his momentum when Macomber, close to him, whipped a hand round his right ankle and lifted. The German made his second mistake. Acting by reflex, still off-balance, still groggy from the pile-driving blow in the stomach, he lifted his other foot to kick Macomber in the face. Elbow hard into the roof, the Scot hoisted as high as he could, no more than a few inches, but a fraction more of the German's weight was now poised over the brink than over the roof. The imprisoned foot jerked upwards out of Macomber's grasp of its own volition and the soldier was propelled outwards and downwards as the Scot climbed to his feet. The scream came up as a fading wail and he was just in time to see the minute spread-eagled figure strike the ice hundreds of feet below.

Using the wall for support, he made his way over to the trap-door, kicking out of the way an opened notebook, the book they had used to record the passage of Allied supplies up the mainland road. Stooping painfully, he pulled back the bolt, but he let them open it, and when the lid lifted it was being raised by Grapos, with Ford below and Prentice bringing up the rear. It was the staff-sergeant who made the first comment. Seeing the crumpled corporal lying on his back he stared curiously at Macomber. 'We didn't think we'd see you alive again, but I thought there were two of them.'

'One went over the side ... you'd better look down here quick.' He was still holding on to the wall support and he looked haggard as he gently massaged his throat and stared down at the lake. 'Burckhardt's nearly here . . .'

Burckhardt had moved with great speed: his force was already arrayed and moving far out onto the lake, so that as the Scot gazed down from the great height of the tower he had the sensation of watching a diorama in a war museum. Six half-tracks, spread out widely over the ice like toy models, led the advance, followed by Alpenkorps and parachutists on foot. Farther back more half-tracks crawled forward and each of the weird vehicles carried only its driver – to minimize casualties if the ice broke at any point Burckhardt had shrewdly emptied the half-tracks of all superfluous passengers. Several light ack-ack guns and 75-mm mountain howitzers, unlimbered from the half-tracks which had hauled them up the mountain road, were being drawn bodily over the ice, two men to a gun, and Macomber noticed that round all the vehicles and guns there were unoccupied areas of frozen lake – the men on foot were nervous of the weight this equipment was imposing on the lake's surface. The sense of looking down on a scale model was heightened by the heavy silence which had fallen over the mountain as the wind dropped, and no sound of the advancing army reached the watchers on the tower. Macomber looked at the staff-sergeant who was also gazing down at the threatening spectacle.

'Any hope at all, Ford – by using the mortar? It is an 8-cm, isn't it?'

'Yes. You mean break the ice under them? We can try, but I can't feed the mortar with this shoulder.' He looked across at Prentice who was nursing his swollen right hand. 'And neither can he. Grapos' shoulder is temporarily numbed from the blow it took from that trap-door.' He looked doubtfully at Macomber, who instinctively straightened up from the wall. 'Can you cope?'

'I'll have to. And we'd better get moving.'

Macomber looked back out to sea. The mounting crisis was of the worst possible magnitude. The destroyer had turned to come in closer, to steam directly for the cape, and within a matter of minutes it would have vanished under the lee of the peninsula prior to commencing landing operations. If Burckhardt reached the monastery he would not only have achieved his objective – he would be in a position to slaughter those troops as they wound their way up the cliff-face track. What on earth had warned Athens that something was wrong? He dismissed the question as academic and began a quick count of the snub-nosed shells lying half covered with canvas while they waited to service the mortar. Thirty bombs. It didn't seem many, not nearly enough. He rammed his last cigar into his mouth and chewed at it as Ford, the calmest man on the roof, stood by the parapet, turning his face sideways to gauge the strength of the fading breeze, screwing up his eyes against the sun as he estimated distances and trajectories. While they waited for the staff-sergeant to complete his calculations Macomber helped Prentice to fix his hand in a makeshift sling with the aid of his scarf, a hand which was swelling ominously, and he watched Burckhardt's progress tensely as he attended the injury. The half-tracks were crawling steadily forward like mechanical bugs – bugs which were now almost two-thirds of the distance across the lake as they approached the road up to the monastery. And even from the great height he looked down on them, Macomber could at last hear a faint purring sound travelling up through the cold mountain air, the purr of engines and caterpillar tracks grinding over the ice.

'That must be Burckhardt – in that car.' Prentice had looked up after testing the sling, and Macomber focused his glass quickly to where the lieutenant had pointed with his good hand. A compact open car, strangely shaped, was driving over the ice slowly as it reached a position mid-way between the distant shore and the leading half-tracks. Ford left the wall, lurching unsteadily towards the mortar as he made his comment.

'It will be a Kubelwagen. The car, I mean. Looks a

bit like a squashed bucket close up – they'd bring that in by glider. Now, I need your help, Mac.'

First, they had to move the mortar, to drag it round away from the sea so that its muzzle aimed out over the lake, and then Ford, with considerable difficulty, cradled a bomb in his arms and showed Macomber what he must do. 'There are three basic things to remember – don't put a bomb down the barrel nose first, or else we can all say good-bye; slide it in – don't push; and keep your hands out of the way afterwards if you want to hang on to them. I'll try and give you a demonstration, and then you're on your own – I've got to be by the wall to see what's happening . . .'

'They're going up the mountain, too!' Prentice, who had again borrowed the Scot's Monokular, was focused on a point beyond the bluff as he shouted out. Colonel Burckhardt was proving himself an excellent tactician and was leaving nothing to chance: the greater portion of his force was assembled on the lake, but beyond the distant shore two straggled lines of dots were ascending the lower slope of Mount Zervos itself as ski troops made for the monastery by a different route. Seeing those two lines climbing higher, already disappearing behind the bluff, Macomber guessed the route they would follow. The southern shore of the lake was blocked by the bluff climbing vertically from the water's edge, but ski troops could ascend to a point above the bluff and then cross the mountain slope above it, until they reached a position where they could ski

342

downwards over a slope which ended close to the monastery entrance. The snowbound mountain had an overloaded look above the bluff and Grapos, who also guessed at their route, spoke grimly.

'They will need care and luck up there.'

'Why?' demanded Macomber.

'The thaw is coming – the time for the mountain to move.'

'You mean an avalanche?'

'Yes.'

'We'll worry about them later.'

Ford completed his demonstration for the Scot's benefit. Replacing the bomb on the canvas, he then crouched down to make a careful adjustment to the angle of fire, went quickly back to the wall to check the target, and returned to the mortar to adjust it again. Macomber, in a rising fever of impatience to get the thing firing, also went briefly to the wall for a final appraisal. The Kubelwagen was moving closer to the front line, halting frequently for a few seconds, presumably while Burckhardt had a word with his troops. The six half-tracks in front were now three-quarters of the way across the lake and within minutes they would have reached firm ground. Feeling automatically for a match to light his cigar, he brought out his hand empty; this was going to be tricky enough as it was without smoke getting in his eyes. He went back to the mortar, checked to make sure that the blood on his hand was dried, wiped both hands briskly on his handkerchief, and then stooped to lift the first bomb as Ford took up position by the parapet and warned Prentice and Grapos to stay in their corners.

Prentice had the best view, squeezed into the north-east corner where he looked down on the entire lake. The first bomb went away seconds later, soaring out over the wall, diminishing rapidly in size as it described an arc and landed on the ice ahead of the leading half-tracks. Prentice's teeth were clenched with anxiety as he watched its fall. He saw a brief spurt of snow where the projectile hit. Then nothing happened. Nothing. His eyes met Ford's as the sergeant pressed his hands harder on the wall, his face expressionless.

'It didn't go off,' said Prentice bitterly.

'No. It must have been a dud. Let's hope the whole batch isn't. I hear there's a lot of sabotage in German factories.' He looked over his shoulder at Macomber who stood ready with a fresh bomb, gave a brief order. 'Fire!' The second bomb was away, vanishing to a pinhead. It landed close to the dud, followed by the sound of detonation, a burst of snow. Prentice swore out loud. The ice had remained intact. Was it too solid for penetration? The fear was in all their minds and Prentice's hopes hadn't been high from the beginning. 'Fire!' Ford had rushed to the mortar to make a frac-tional adjustment before returning to the wall and giving the order. The third bomb soared through its parabola, curved to its descent. It landed close to the leading half-tracks and the distant thump echoed back to the tower as snow flew in the air with the burst of the bomb. An area of black shadow fissured the lake as ice cracked and disintegrated and water opened up under three half-tracks. 'Fire!' The fourth bomb spread the fracturing process as the three half-tracks disappeared almost simultaneously. One moment they were there and then they were gone, swallowed up as a new lake spread, a lake of ice-cold water. Over fifty metres deep, Grapos had said. So the half-tracks were now settling one hundred and fifty feet below the lake's surface. 'Fire!' Ford had made a further minor adjustment before he rushed back to the wall, his head thrust forward as he scanned the whole lake and Macomber, already drenched in sweat, fed in a fresh bomb. At this stage even Prentice, who could see everything happening, had not grasped the magnitude of the plan the precise Ford had devised for the destruction of the entire German force.

The fifth bomb sped out over the wall, almost too fast for the eye to follow, descended, struck the lake in the middle of the three surviving half-tracks closest to Zervos. Another spray of snow flashed upwards, another thump reached the distant tower, and then a huge area of ice cracked. Prentice gazed in astonishment as a sheet of ice became a temporary island separated from the rest of the frozen lake, a sheet supporting the three half-tracks and a group of Alpenkorps gathered behind them. The island's existence was momentary. The sheet fissured in all directions, broke up and sank. With the Monokular screwed hard against his eye, Prentice saw one half-track at the outer edge of the ice go down, wheels first, the tracks tilting upwards into the air, and then the whole vehicle slid out of sight under the ink-dark water which had appeared. The chances of a single man surviving in those sub-zero waters was nil. 'Fire!' The next bomb landed farther to the right, just reaching the ragged rim of the still-intact ice, detonating while still above the water-line. Figures beyond the rim were thrown into confusion, some falling and some scattering in a hopeless search for safety. The whole ordered array on the lake was beginning to change, to falter, to break up into a vast disorganized chaos as Ford increased the rate of attack, frequently adjusting direction or angle or both as Macomber, the pain in his back now stabbing at him non-stop, his clothes sodden with sweat, his bruised body protesting with growing aches, worked away methodically stooping, grasping, lifting, feeding the barrel.

'Fire!' This bomb travelled much farther, the zenith of its parabola far higher above the lake, the descent point more distant. Prentice pressed the Monokular into his eye, focusing it on the Kubelwagen. He heard the thump and saw the snow dust at almost the same moment – dust which immediately rose behind Burckhardt's vehicle. The whiteness surrounding the car dissolved, became pitch-black water, and as the vehicle went straight down Prentice saw there were still four people inside. Burckhardt was drowning, surrounded by his own men. The fresh area of sinking ice stretched out towards the monastery road, tilting as men on top of it ran in all directions trying to escape. Prentice saw one man run straight off the edge into the water and as he took the glass away from his eye the ice sheet went under. A huge channel of dark water, perhaps a hundred yards wide, separated the frozen area of the lake from the road on the western shore leading up to the monastery.

'Fire!'

Ford had again made an adjustment and Prentice saw that the mortar's barrel was pointing at an extreme angle, saw also the bomb cradled in Macomber's arms nearly slip as the Scot forced his wearied body to further effort. The bomb coursed out over the lake, became a tiny dark speck against the whiteness below, and landed close to the distant eastern shore on the far side of the scattering troops. The thump was fainter. A fresh channel of water opened up, starting at the shoreline and spreading inwards towards the centre as three more bombs landed and black dots scurried over the diminishing white surface. Two mountain guns vanished. A half-track driving to the rear to escape the cannonade drove straight over the edge. More than a third of the attacking force on the frozen lake had disappeared and for the first time Prentice grasped the painstaking cleverness of Ford's plan. He had quartered the lake systematically in his mind and was destroying it section by section in such a way that he inflicted the maximum amount of damage, commencing with the vital section near the road up to the monastery, working backwards, and then over-leaping to destroy the ice near the far shore. His ultimate objective was to compress the surviving Wehrmacht force on a huge island of ice caught between water to east and west, the snow-drifted road to the north, and the sheer wall of the bluff to the south.

'Fire!' The bomb landed uselessly in clear water. 'Fire!' Prentice's glass was focused just beyond the most recent dropping point and he saw two puffs of snow as the bomb bounced across the ice and detonated in the midst of a crowd of German troops fleeing towards the bluff. At this point some of the more quick-witted Alpenkorps were escaping. Using their climbing ropes, they had begun to scale the precipitous bluff face, realizing that only suspended in air would they be safe from the rain of missiles pouring down on them. Ford now turned his attention to the section of frozen lake which bordered the snow-drifted road. A large number of troops and a mountain gun were heading for the drift zone when the falling bombs began to shatter their escape route, driving them back on the huge remaining sheet of ice which covered perhaps a third of the lake. 'Fire!' Prentice removed the Monoku-lar, dropped it into his pocket. The fatigue of staring through the glass made him rub his eyes and then dab them with his handkerchief, and all the time the bombardment was continuing as Ford concentrated on the huge island of ice covered with marooned Germans. 'Fire!' 'Fire!' 'Fire . . . !' Prentice lost count of the number of bombs Macomber slipped down the barrel, and the rate was increasing as Ford built up the barrage and Macomber, wiping his hands frequently on his trousers for fear of dropping a bomb, summoned up his last reserves of energy and went on feeding the mortar with fresh ammunition.

When Prentice looked out across the lake again he was astounded at the changed scene. The lake, which had so recently been a white plain, was now a dark sheet spattered with what, from that height, looked like slivers of snow, but which were really large spars of floating ice. The central island had almost disappeared and there was only a handful of men still marooned on a small patch of whiteness. Macomber fed in more bombs, surrounded the ice islet with five fountainheads of spurting water. Five misses. The next bomb landed dead centre on the remaining floe, fragmented it, tipped the survivors choking, drowning, sinking into the chill water. Perhaps a dozen Alpenkorps men still clung to the bluff which they were ascending slowly, but the invasion force on the lake had been annihilated.

'Like a target range,' Ford said. 'Unique.'

'Not quite,' Macomber reminded him. 'There was also Austerlitz.'* In response to the shake of the sergeant's head, he replaced the bomb he was holding on the near-empty canvas and went stiffly over to the parapet. 'And now we've got to face that lot.'

There were three bombs left on the tower roof when Macomber made his grim remark and pointed out over

---

* At Austerlitz Napoleon destroyed a Russian army by firing at a frozen lake and drowning the enemy crossing the ice.

the wall. Unlike the others, whose whole attention had been concentrated on the lake below, the Scot had been observing with increasing anxiety the ski troops' progress. They had now climbed the slope to an altitude well above the bluff and were coming forward in a line which curled over the flank of the mountain. The leading man was less than a quarter of a mile away as he sped closer towards the monastery. Grapos hobbled out from his corner and gripped Macomber's arm.

'You make avalanche,' Grapos said urgently. 'Where the dark hole is . . .'

'He means that hollow in shadow,' Prentice interjected. 'Why there?' Macomber had already gone back to the mortar, was helping Ford to shift the weapon's position, then waiting, cradling another bomb in his arms as the staff sergeant checked the mountain slope and changed the angle of fire.

'Because,' Grapos explained, 'that is where the Austrian ski man started the avalanche. We had warned him not to go – but he laughed at us. I was standing on this roof watching him. He comes down over the hole and the avalanche begins. The mountain comes alive.'

'We'd better try it, Ford,' Macomber said quickly. 'It's a gamble, but it's the only one we've got. A hundred bombs could miss them all considering the speed they're moving at.'

He waited, still cradling the bomb, while Ford reconsidered the angle of fire and made a further adjustment. The reaction was setting in, his arms and legs felt like jelly, and he knew he might collapse on the roof at any moment. For God's sake stop fiddling with that mortar, man, and let's get on with it! Ford nodded – to indicate he was satisfied – and Macomber let the first one go. Because the mountain slope rose above the tower he was now able to see what was happening and he saw the bomb hit the snow some distance above the hollow.

'Damn!' It was the first display of emotion Ford had shown since they had begun firing the mortar. The shot was wide and he knew it was his fault – not enough care taken over the initial preparation. And there were no bombs to waste this time on ranging shots. He adjusted the angle of fire as Macomber picked up the second bomb. The missile went away. Macomber saw this one land below the hollow, close enough to the Alpenkorps column to provoke a sudden swerve in the well-spread line – the section leader had not overlooked the lesson of what had happened on the lake – but no more than a swerve. Ford bit his lip as Macomber encouraged him. 'Third time lucky.' The staff-sergeant looked dubious – too high last time, too low this time. And only one more to go. But he kept his nerve: the first two shots had bracketed the target above and below, so now they must drop one mid-way beween the two points. He took a deep breath, adjusted the barrel very carefully, then nodded to Macomber. The final bomb burst on the mountain a short way above the hollow.

It was very quiet on the tower and the four men stood perfectly still while they waited. Behind them the sea was empty, the destroyer had disappeared; below them the lake was still and lifeless; above them rose the peak of Zervos, crisp-edged against the palest of skies. The mortar barrel gaped upwards, as harmless now as a piece of old scrap iron, something they might as well tip over the wall so that at least the Alpenkorps would never use it. Probably it was imagination, but the Scot fancied he heard the swish of oncoming skis as he stood with his eyes fixed on Mount Zervos. He blinked and looked again, unsure whether his eyes had played him a trick. He had been watching the hollow but now he transferred his gaze higher up the mountain to a point near the summit where something had attracted his attention. Was there a gentle ripple of movement, so gentle that his eye might never have noticed it but for his fading hope? There seemed to be a trembling, a hazy wobble close to the peak. Slowly, like the rolling back of a sheet, the snow began to move in a long wave, the wave stretching the full width of the slope as it surged downwards, gathering height as it swallowed up more snow. And now Macomber heard something – a faint growl which gradually swelled and deepened to a sinister rumble as he saw fresh signs of something terrible happening. The slope was shifting downwards at increasing velocity, a moving slope at least a mile wide as the wave mounted higher, picked up momentum and thundered down on the Germans like a tidal wave. The mountain had come alive.

The slope seemed like a living thing as it seethed and rolled towards the lake far below, a whole mountain erupting sideways, the wave curling at the crest, the snow-slide roaring down, the rumble a tremendous sound in their dazed ears, a sound like the eruption of a major volcano, blowing its lava flow up from the interior of the earth. The Alpenkorps tried to scatter at the last moment – some ski-ing downhill, some whipping across the slope, all trying to race the wave which bore down on them and for a brief moment in time they were like a disturbed nest of ants scurrying away from catastrophe. Then the wave arrived, swept over the broken line, engulfing them, burying them, carrying them down the slope and over the bluff face where it cascaded down the precipice like a vast waterfall and washed away the men still ascending it before it plunged down into the depths of the lake. Prentice shouted his frantic warning as the wave reached the bluff's brink – the leading skier, not yet overwhelmed by the avalanche, had stopped, unlooped his rifle from his back, was taking aim at the roof of the tower. Macomber, his gaze fixed on the bluff, heard the shout too late. He was dropping to the floor when the bullet thudded into him and he was unconscious before he sprawled over the stones.

The Australian doctor had underestimated Macomber's vitality, so he came out of the drugged state at the wrong moment, the moment when they started to take him down the nose of Cape Zervos, strapped to a stretcher, powerless to move, but conscious enough to think, to remember, to experience to the full the unnerving ordeal of being transported in the prone position down a track a mule might jib at. The track, no more than a rather broad path, was the route from the cliff summit to the base of the cape where the Allied troops had landed. It was a fine morning, the sun was shining, there was not a trace of sea mist, so his downward view was unobscured as his life balanced in four hands – two holding the rear of the stretcher, two supporting the front. The stretcher tilted downwards at an angle of forty-five degrees as the two men carrying him found the way increasingly dangerous – ascending a precipitous zigzag can be difficult, descending it may prove impossible. The Scot thought the unobscured view was impressive – a sheer drop seaward to the ruffled waters of the Aegean far below, a glimpse of a lower level of the zigzag, perched on another brink. And in his invalid state, Macomber had lost his head for heights.

He watched the uncertain gait of the man in front through half-closed eyes, half-closed because he was determined they shouldn't realize he had come awake – even a small surprise like that at the wrong moment could make a foot stumble, a hand lose its grip, could cause the stretcher to leave them and send him vertically down to his grave as the stretcher turned over and over in mid-air before it mercifully reached the sea and the waves closed over him. Cursing his over-vivid imagination, he tore his mesmerized gaze away from the trembling distant waters and tried to concentrate his mind on what had happened, on what Prentice had told him when he first recovered consciousness. 'He got you in the shoulder ... the bullet's out now ... the quack says you'll be all right ... they'll be taking you to Athens.'

Macomber wasn't sure what day it was as he went on staring at the back of the man below him, but he remembered other things the lieutenant had told him. The Australians had come up this hellish track like demons. With the New Zealanders. They had dragged up dismantled twenty-five-pounder guns by brute strength, had reassembled them on the heights, were now in full command of Zervos. The blowing up of the *Hydra* had warned them something was seriously wrong; the great cloud of black smoke rising over Katyra had forced a quick decision – the sending of a destroyer laden with troops. I wish I had one of those bloody German cigars, Macomber thought as the man behind him tripped and the stretcher wobbled uneasily. They should have let Grapos take the rear. But at least the bearer had held on firmly, had regained his balance quickly. They went slowly down another section, then another, poised over sheer drops, the only sound a slithering of boots over the treacherous ground. Time stopped for the Scot, went into a state of suspension, so that it seemed to go on for ever. They were close to the half-ruined jetty at the base of Cape Zervos, but still a hundred feet above the sea, when the man in front stumbled over a hidden rock, fell sideways onto the track, saving himself by cannoning against a boulder and completely losing his grip on the stretcher.

Macomber's legs hit the earth with a bump. He braced himself for the long spiralling fall.

The rear of the stretcher sagged a foot, then steadied and was held there by two hands only until the other man climbed to his feet, started to apologize, then stopped as he saw the look in the eyes of the man holding Macomber. He lifted the stretcher again and they went on down the track to where the launch moored by the jetty waited to transport the Scot to the destroyer anchored farther out. Macomber delayed his official awakening until he was rested on the jetty wall, then he twisted his head round to say thank you. Grapos' whiskered face stared down at him. 'I come with you,' he said simply. 'Now they take me in the Greek army. Yes?'

AVALANCHE EXPRESS

For Jane

Author's Note

I wish to put on record my admiration for and gratitude to the late Sir William Collins CBE who encouraged so many authors – including myself – and who was, I believe, one of the greatest publishers of the century.

Contents

Part One

The Sparta Ring

Chapter One

Basel and Zürich, Switzerland

It was Wednesday – dangerous Wednesday – and as always the first Wednesday in the month. It was Wednesday, December 1, a bitter cold day with the snow deep in the streets of the ancient Swiss city that throughout history has been the centre of so much intrigue.

VAGONE-LETTI.

MOSKWA-MINSK-BREST-WARSZAWA-BERLIN

FRANKFURT-HEIDELBERG-BASEL.

The destination plate on the side of the single sleeping car on Gleis 1 – Track 1 – conjured up a romantic and dangerous journey. Standing by itself in Basel Hauptbahnhof, its passengers recently disembarked, it had a lonely and alien look, almost a sinister touch when you read the destination plate. For the sleeping car this was the end of the line. Each week this single sleeping car, constantly unlinked and attached to different trains, made its way from the heart of the Communist empire to the centre of Western Europe.

It had left Moscow at four in the afternoon of

Monday, November 29 – the day the Soviet Politburo had met to assess the vast military manoeuvres conducted personally by Marshal Gregori Prachko. It had arrived at Basel Hauptbahnhof at 9.20 a.m. The time was now 9.45 a.m. The staff had left the sleeping car, which stood empty on its deserted track. Outside the nearby station restaurant were two men in dark hats and overcoats, taking no apparent interest in the sleeping car. The smaller, more heavily built man smoked a French cigarette while he tried not to show his distaste for the unfamiliar tobacco.

'No action yet,' he murmured in German.

'Patience, Gustav,' his taller, slimmer companion replied. 'Waiting is our profession.'

Inside the restaurant at a table close to the door an English girl checked her watch as she sipped a cup of coffee she didn't want. She had already paid her bill and was ready to leave at any moment. Everything about Elsa Lang was unattractive. She wore a shabby, military-style raincoat, and a large, floppy hat concealed most of her dark, stringy hair. A large pair of ugly horn-rimmed glasses hid most of her face. Her shoes were worn and scuffed at the toes; her suitcase was scratched and a dismal grey colour. She went on sipping her coffee until her watch registered 10 a.m. Then she moved as the second hand reached the vertical.

Picking up the suitcase, she shuffled out of the restaurant, walking past the two men in dark coats and hats. The younger, heavily built man glanced at her and then away. She walked slowly, round-shouldered as though her case was heavy, peering nearsightedly about her. Gustav, who had lit a second Gauloise – he had a compulsion to smoke even strange tobacco when under tension – gestured toward her back.

'What a mousy-looking cow,' he sneered to his companion.

'Keep your eyes where they should be,' Walther Fischer snapped in a whisper.

At least, that was the name shown on the passport he carried in his pocket, the passport carefully fabricated in the forgery section housed in the basement of KGB headquarters in Dzerzhinsky Square, Moscow. Fischer was beginning to worry. The station was filling up with passengers to catch the Transalpin Basel–Vienna Express and other trains. The two men moved forward to try and keep the sleeping car under observation while Elsa Lang paused amid the swirling crowd as though bewildered.

At the same moment a short, plump man in a white steward's jacket appeared from the direction of the station exit and under cover of the crowd walked rapidly to the rear entrance of the sleeping car from Russia. He walked purposefully, as though he had every right to be there, and disappeared inside. Fischer, the taller of the two men, craned his head over the crowd and saw what had happened.

'Someone's gone aboard,' he whispered. 'Dressed like a steward.' He grabbed his companion, who had started to move forward, by the arm. 'Not yet. Wait for him to get off. We shall have to do something about that white jacket . . .' He took off his dark coat, folded it over his arm, waited.

Inside the sleeping car the white-jacketed steward worked quickly, moving straight to the third compartment. Once inside, he closed the door, opened up the corner washbasin, and thrust his right arm deep inside the large waste-disposal channel that emptied the basin. The cassette was fixed to the side with waterproof tape and he swore under his breath as he wrestled to tug it loose. At any moment a Swiss rail guard might come aboard and normally the cassette came away more easily. Taking a firm grip, he wrenched hard and it was in his hand. He stripped the relics of the tape off the cassette and shoved them in his pocket.

Outside in the station more and more passengers were filling up the entrance hall as the steward emerged and walked quickly toward the exit. Fischer and Gustav moved at the same moment, shouldering passengers out of their way. The steward brushed past Elsa Lang, who was caught up in the turmoil of hurrying passengers, and continued toward the exit as the two men caught up with him. At that moment the crowd thinned out suddenly, leaving only one man, of medium height with a droopy moustache, who stood leaning against a wall absorbed in his newspaper. Fischer pressed a 9 mm Luger pistol hard

6

into the steward's back under cover of his folded overcoat.

'Run for it and you're dead. Now, move over here . . .'

They eased the steward into an empty part of the hall to the right of the exit. 'Put on this coat,' Fischer ordered as he slipped the Luger back into his jacket pocket. As the pale-faced steward obeyed, Fischer kept glancing toward the man with the droopy moustache and glasses, who was still apparently absorbed in his newspaper. 'Now, get into that Mercedes by the kerb,' Fischer ordered. 'Rear seat . . .' They went out into the snow; after the rush of passengers the street was almost deserted except for an unmarked laundry truck parked a few yards ahead of the Mercedes.

In the rear seat of the car Gustav ran expert, searching hands over the steward while Fischer climbed in behind the wheel of the rented car and twisted around in his seat. 'I can't find a damned thing except this,' Gustav reported. He showed a handful of waterproof tape, all twisted and torn.

'Search him again – and be quick about it. We're going to miss the express . . .' Under cover of the seat back Fischer wrapped a woollen scarf around the barrel of the Luger. It would help to muffle the shot when he killed the steward. The travelling rug in the back draped over the body should delay its discovery, and the car had been rented in Mannheim, Germany. That was where the Swiss police would make their first inquiries, and while they were pursuing them Fischer and his companion would have reached Vienna aboard the Transalpin.

In the station hall Matt Leroy, the droopy-moustached American dressed in English clothes, was walking slowly past the exit, idly smacking his folded newspaper against his trouser leg. The driver behind the wheel of the unmarked laundry truck saw the signal in his rearview mirror, spoke briefly to his companion beside him, got out, and walked back with a roll of clean towels in his hand. Leaning inside the front window of the Mercedes, he spoke quietly in German as Fischer jerked around to face him.

'Get out of the car and step inside the back of that truck.'

Fischer stared at the end of the roll of towels the laundryman was holding, stared at the gun barrel just inside the roll. 'And I'll take that first if I may . . .' With his left hand the man in overalls scooped up the Luger from Fischer's lap and slipped it into his pocket. Gustav, in the rear seat, was looking at another gun concealed inside a screwed-up towel held by the second man in overalls who had jerked open the rear door. The steward had already relieved him of his automatic.

From inside the station hall Matt Leroy watched the four men enter the rear of the laundry truck, watched the doors close as the steward climbed in behind the wheel and started the engine. Only when the van was on the move did he run inside the station and then slow to a quick walk as he saw the big clock, which registered 10.08 a.m. Two minutes before the Transalpin departed for Zürich nonstop.

Inside the rear of the laundry truck Fischer asked his question to distract his captors' attention as he felt the vehicle moving. 'What did he collect? And how did he lose it . . .' He was still speaking when he tried to knee the nearest man in overalls in the groin. The laundryman jerked away from the blow, swung his pistol barrel in an arc that connected with Fischer's skull. 'Very stupid.' He nodded once and smiled at Gustav. The second laundryman crashed his own pistol down on the back of Gustav's head. Each blow had been lethal; both men were dead on the floor of the swaying van.

Soon after daylight on the following day a Swiss policeman, patrolling the shores of the river near the thundering roar of the Rhine Falls below Schaffhausen, observed a large cabin trunk that had become jammed between two massive boulders as the swollen river frothed and tumbled past it. Four hours were needed to bring a police boat equipped with a lifting crane and grapple into position below the falls. Another hour was needed to claw the trunk out of the cauldron of boiling water. Ashore, when they opened the trunk, they found the naked bodies of two men crammed inside, and there were no means of identification. Both men had died from a heavy blow to the skull.

When Matt Leroy walked slowly past the exit whipping his folded newspaper against his leg as a signal to the driver of the unmarked laundry truck, Elsa Lang was boarding first-class car 43 of the Transalpin Basel–Vienna Express, due to depart at 10.10 a.m. The corridor was deserted as she slipped inside a washroom and locked the door. She then moved very swiftly, taking off the shabby raincoat, her scuffed shoes, and her horn-rimmed glasses and floppy hat. A moment later she had detached her black wig, exposing fair hair, which she quickly combed.

Perching her dull grey suitcase on the toilet lid, she unzipped the outer cover to reveal an expensive pigskin case beneath. Opening the case, she took out a pair of Gucci shoes, slipped into them, and took out a matching Gucci handbag and a sable coat, which she put on. The detachable outer case cover she packed quickly under expensive lingerie, together with the wig, hat, raincoat, and discarded shoes. Locking the case, she used her make-up kit and studied herself briefly in the mirror. The horn-rimmed glasses went inside the Gucci handbag. The Elsa Lang who emerged from the washroom was unrecognizable from the dowdy girl who had entered it only minutes earlier.

Not only had the change of clothes altered her

entire appearance; as she moved along the corridor to her reserved seat she was slimmer, taller, for she walked without a slouch, and her way of moving – which so identifies a man or woman – had also changed. She walked with a brisk, springy step, reached the empty compartment, and went inside. To keep the compartment to herself she took off the sable, spread it out on another seat, and perched the Gucci case on a third. Sitting down, she crossed her slim, elegant legs and checked her watch: 10.08 a.m. The express was due to depart in two minutes for Zürich on its long journey to Vienna. Opening her handbag – where the cassette the steward had slipped to her was concealed in a zippered compartment – she took out an ivory cigarette holder, inserted a cigarette, lit it, and took a deep, long drag.

'Christ,' she said to herself, 'butterflies in my stomach again. Will I never get over the tension at moments like this?'

Then she remembered what Harry Wargrave had once told her. 'When you lose the tension you get out of this business – you need that to keep the reflexes razor-sharp ...' The recollection was some comfort as she forced herself to relax, to sit back in her seat and feel her pulse rate returning to normal.

It was even of more comfort when she saw Matt Leroy walk past her window on the platform to board the car higher up. God, she thought, he left it late this time; I wonder why? The express started moving, gliding out from under the huge vault of the

Hauptbahnhof into the falling snow as it headed east on the fast one-hour lap to Zürich.

The Swiss ticket collector arrived a few minutes later as the express was speeding through Switzerland. He took his time about examining her ticket; he was a man who appreciated feminine beauty. And this one is a beauty, he was thinking as he clipped the ticket and glanced at her again. Level grey eyes looked back at him with the hint of a mischievous smile. The bone structure of her face was striking; a well-shaped nose, a full but firm-lipped mouth, and a jaw that suggested character and determination.

'A pleasant journey, madame,' he said in careful English. He shrugged as he looked out of the window. 'In spite of the weather . . .' He left the compartment. An observant Swiss, Elsa Lang thought as she put the round-trip ticket back inside her purse. '. . . madame.' He had noticed her wedding ring, although the truth was she was still very much single at twenty-eight. Another detail Harry Wargrave had insisted on. 'Married women attract just a shade less attention than a single girl travelling alone.'

Outside in the corridor the inspector was checking the round-trip ticket of the American, Matt Leroy, who stood leaning against the passenger rail smoking a cigarette. 'I asked for a smoker reservation,' he remarked casually. 'And they gave me this,' he lied. He gestured to the empty nonsmoking compartment behind, where his holdall bag lay on a seat. From Leroy's accent the inspector assumed he was dealing with an Englishman: an accent Leroy had perfected during his two years attached to the American Embassy in Grosvenor Square as security officer. Also, the American wore a camel-hair coat purchased in Savile Row.

'Plenty of room in smoking compartments,' the inspector suggested as he clipped the ticket.

'Doesn't matter,' Leroy assured him. 'It's not far to Zürich.'

He had actually booked the nonsmoking seat to place him close to Elsa Lang. As the inspector moved along the train Leroy checked his watch and touched his droopy moustache. It was always a tight schedule and once again he was hoping to God the express would reach Zürich on time. And the fact that, like Elsa, he was travelling on a round-trip ticket he would never use was just a further detail insisted on by the Englishman Harry Wargrave. 'It gives the impression you're going back to Basel,' he had pointed out. 'Just in case the wrong person is close to you . . .'

At 11.12 a.m. promptly the express pulled into Zürich Hauptbahnhof. Elsa Lang was already standing with her case at the end of the coach ready to get off quickly. Hurrying through the ticket barrier, she carried her own case to the cab rank that faces the Hotel Schweizerhof across the street and stepped inside the first waiting cab. Only when she was inside did she give the instruction to the driver in a low, soft voice.

'Zürich Airport. And I'm late for my flight . . .'

Following her off the train, Matt Leroy had taken a different route. Sprinting along the wide side hall past the baggage counter he had the keys of the Citroën in his hand as he reached the car parked at the end of the station. The ignition sparked at the first touch – the car had been left for him only a few minutes earlier – and he drove around to the front of the Hauptbahnhof in time to see Elsa's cab leaving. She was peering out of the window so he could spot her. At a discreet distance he followed her to the airport, ten miles outside the city.

Leroy, thirty-four years old, had a deceptive studious appearance, but there was a steely alertness in his manner as he peered ahead through his silver-rimmed glasses to keep Elsa's cab in sight. Frequently he glanced in his rearview mirror to make sure no vehicle was tailing them. His task, reinforced by the back-up team at Basel who had disposed of the steward's interceptors, was to see that Elsa Lang reached Zürich Airport safely. And as on their previous monthly trips it was with a feeling of relief that he saw her cab pull up in front of the airport building, saw her step out of the cab with her Gucci suitcase and hurry inside the building. Leaving the Citroën outside, he followed her in.

It was with a further feeling of relief that, inside the reception hall, he saw a tall, dark-haired Englishman standing by a bookstall apparently studying the

14

paperbacks. Leroy sighed, his task once more completed. Harry Wargrave was taking over.

At thirty-seven Harry Charles Frederick Wargrave had lived three lifetimes compared to the average man of his age. He was six feet tall, slim and easy in his movements, and his eyebrows were as dark as his dense thatch of hair, eyebrows often raised slightly as he regarded people with a quizzical stare. His nose was long, his cheek-bones prominent, his mouth wide with a hint of humour at the corners. Everything about him as he stood waiting by the bookstall wearing a military-style raincoat suggested a casual, easy approach to life, an 'I don't give a damn' manner. More than one person had lived to regret this assessment. Some had died.

At nineteen Wargrave had gained his wings as a Navy pilot – at that time the youngest pilot in the British Navy. He held a separate certificate for flying choppers. He had driven motor torpedo boats and sometimes described himself as a 'mechanical nut. I see something new with an engine and I have to learn to drive or fly the thing . . .'

Transferred later to naval intelligence with the rank of commander, he had been attached to the British Embassy in Washington to help track down spies inside the States who were passing to Soviet Russia technical secrets Britain had shared with America. But all of this had only been a beginning. Fluent in French, German, Italian, and Serbo-Croat, he had later still been seconded to the British Secret Service – still the best in the world despite certain novel writers' attempts to portray it as a club of professional idiots.

After service in various parts of Western Europe – a period when he came to know well all the top security and counter-intelligence chiefs – Wargrave was dispatched to the Balkans. Based in Athens, he engaged in activities that were still shrouded in mystery. 'The biggest killing ground in the world,' he once called the Balkans. 'If a man can survive there he can survive anywhere . . .' At thirty-six he had retired and emigrated to Canada, where, on the investment advice of millionaire industrialist William Riverton, he had multiplied his small capital by ten. On retiring he had explained his philosophy in typical pithy fashion.

'Like a racing driver, in this profession you get out before you're forty or you're dead . . .'

Now he stood by the bookstall at Zürich Airport, well aware that Elsa Lang was checking in for her flight, that the receptionist had already placed her case on the conveyor belt that would carry it to the waiting aircraft – although he had not once looked in her direction. He checked his watch: 11.37. A very tight schedule, but once again Elsa, bless her, had made it. And Wargrave had always insisted the schedule must be very tight. In an earlier argument with Matt Leroy he had overruled the American's apparently quite reasonable objections.

'There's no goddamn margin for error,' Leroy had protested. 'We have the minimum time to grab the cassette off the sleeping car. Elsa has only minutes to catch the Transalpin express. The express has to arrive on schedule at Zürich to give her any chance to reach the airport in time to catch her flight . . .'

'Precisely,' Wargrave had agreed laconically.

'That's all you have to say, for God's sake?'

'The faster the fox moves, the less chance the hounds have of picking up its scent, Matt.' Wargrave had grinned sardonically. 'A tight schedule makes it tricky for us – but even more tricky for the enemy. Ever watch a falcon dive on its prey? It swoops like lightning, then it's up and away. We're that falcon . . .'

Wargrave was on the verge of moving away from the bookstall to join Elsa's flight – time was running damned short now – when he was aware that Matt Leroy was standing next to him as the American picked up a Harold Robbins novel. Nothing in Wargrave's easy stance hinted at the tightening of his nerves. Leroy had strict instructions to approach him only in an emergency. Over the public address system they were already making the last call for Swissair Flight 160.

Leroy bought the paperback and then laid it on top of some magazines while he took his time over pocketing his wallet. Wargrave called the girl back and bought a copy of the same novel. He didn't pick it up as she laid the paperback alongside Leroy's copy. Paying for it, he waited until the girl moved to serve another customer, picked up Leroy's copy, and then began running for the final departure gate Elsa had already passed through.

In the first-class section aboard the Swiss DC-10 aircraft Wargrave chose a seat on the opposite side of the aisle and one row behind Elsa Lang. She sat staring out of the window with her long legs crossed, a symphony in nylon he thought agreeably as he fastened his seat belt. And that was another little detail he had instructed her in when they had first started this monthly routine a year earlier.

'On the plane always sit with your legs crossed ...'

'Really?' she had inquired ironically. 'Is it likely that I'll lose my official virginity thirty thousand feet up over the Atlantic?'

'I have to confess my opportunities would be limited,' he had assured her. 'But if anyone catches me watching you, the sight of your legs will be all the innocent explanation they'll need.'

'Or maybe you're simply exploiting your duties for overt sexual purposes?'

Not for the first time in dealing with Elsa Lang, Wargrave had been lost for a reply. He was thinking about this as he studied her legs and then the other passengers while the machine built up throbbing power and then began taxiing toward the main runway. Which is the wrong priority, he reminded himself: the other passengers first, then Elsa's legs. And once in the air he must pay a call to the washroom to extract and read the message Matt Leroy would have slipped inside his paperback.

Outside the airport building, cosily parked in the Citroën with the heater going full blast, Leroy smoked a cigarette, waiting for the plane to take off. It had stopped snowing but the sky was low and heavy with swollen overcast, the threat of more snow to come, and it was only December. Already the long-range forecasters were beginning to mutter about the most bitter winter in Europe for many years being on the way. And that after the hottest and most prolonged summer in living memory when drought had smitten Western Europe and even in southern England temperatures had soared into the nineties. 'That's what they call compensation, I guess,' Matt told himself. Looking up, he saw the plane.

The DC-10 climbed rapidly, spinning out a dirt trail behind it. Then it was gone, swallowed up in the dense overcast. But Swissair Flight 160 was not bound for the United States or Britain, as might have seemed normal if the operation had been carried out three years earlier. Instead, its destination was Montreal, Canada.

Chapter Two

Montreal and Washington

On the tenth floor of the Baton Rouge Building in Montreal the elevator doors opened at 3.30 p.m. local time and Elsa Lang stepped out, followed by Wargrave carrying her case. It was still Wednesday, December 1. Glancing both ways along the corridor, Elsa walked briskly to a door that carried a plate bearing the legend *Riverton Corp, Inc.* Opening it, she faced a girl receptionist behind a huge slab desk. It was Wargrave who spoke.

'We're expected . . .' He spoke with an American accent, he did not take the cigar out of his mouth as he spoke, and he wore dark glasses. 'Mrs Perkins and Clyde Wilson. Mr Riverton expects us . . .'

Elsa Lang was wearing her dark wig and horn-rimmed glasses, which she had put on while Wargrave drove her in the rental car from the airport. The receptionist didn't give her a second look as she spoke into the intercom and then told them to go in. Elsa led the way through the familiar door and Wargrave carefully closed it behind them as a compact, poker-faced man rose from behind a desk much smaller than the receptionist's.

'Glad to see you back.'

That was all William Riverton, the legendary Canadian millionaire industrialist, said as he walked with a slow, deliberate tread to unlock a door at the side of his office. Seventy-three years old, Riverton had controlled one of the most secret counter-espionage organizations in the Western Hemisphere during the Second World War. Even now there was a magnetism about this extraordinary man, a suggestion of enormous willpower in his impassive face and slow-moving eyes. Wargrave watched the old warrior with something close to affection as the Canadian unlocked the heavy door and stood aside to let them enter.

The large room beyond the door was windowless, illuminated by overhead fluorescent tubes. On one wall a series of clocks showed the time in different parts of the world – Zürich time, Bucharest time, Moscow time . . . The atmosphere was over-heated.

'Sit down, you must be tired. How did it go? Coffee?'

The voice was American, the speaker a fifty-five-year-old, well-built man of medium height with thinning grey-white hair, a finely-shaped forehead, and a welcoming smile that radiated assurance and good humour. Only the eyes were searching, as though seeking signs of strain, any hint of trouble. Julian Haller embraced and hugged Elsa, helped her off with her raincoat, grinned as she took off the wig and glasses.

'That's an improvement,' he commented.

21

'Thanks, Julian.' Elsa gave him her warmest smile. 'And coffee would be heaven – I'm jet-lagged out of my mind.'

'Timed it perfectly, didn't I?' Julian Haller grinned as he poured coffee from the pot, then added cream just the way she liked it. 'There's a large scotch for you, Harry, on the side table,' he went on. 'Ed phoned in your arrival from the airport.' As he handed her the cup he glanced across the room where Wargrave was inserting the cassette he had extracted from Elsa's handbag into a tape recorder. 'Why the hurry?' he asked quietly.

'A wee spot of bother at Basel,' Wargrave replied. 'It looks as though someone is breathing down Angelo's neck – two men with guns grabbed Neckermann after he had passed the cassette to Elsa.'

Elsa twisted around in her chair. 'You never tell me anything,' she accused. 'You had plenty of time to tell me on the way here in the car . . .'

'You were tired. I thought it could wait.' Wargrave continued reporting to Haller, who lit a cigarette. The American's smile had vanished as he listened to the Englishman with intense concentration. 'Leroy did well – very well,' Wargrave commented. 'He spotted what was happening and his back-up people rescued Neckermann.'

'And the two men who grabbed him?'

'At the bottom of the Rhine would be my guess,' Wargrave said lightly. He went on talking quickly as he saw Elsa wince. 'I'm going to play the cassette from our unknown Russian friend, Angelo. Ready?'

There was a sudden feeling of tension inside the room as the cassette spools revolved, as the familiar voice began speaking clearly in English, a hoarse, whispering voice obviously disguised, speaking to them from Moscow, over four thousand miles away – a voice they now knew could belong only to a senior member of the Soviet Politburo.

The voice of the man they knew only by the code name of Angelo had finished speaking. There was an appalled hush inside the room. It was the most terrifying signal Angelo had ever sent. Elsa, normally so outwardly calm and relaxed, sat tense and rigid, the burning cigarette between her fingers momentarily forgotten. Haller sat motionless behind his desk, his head turned slightly to one side. Wargrave, the coolest of the trio, removed the cassette and looked at Haller.

'So, the next move is?'

'You'd better catch the first plane to Washington. I'll warn Bruno you're on the way . . .'

Opening a drawer in his desk, the American checked flight times, checked the clock on the wall that showed Montreal time. 'If you move very fast indeed, Harry . . .'

'I'm on my way.'

Haller unlocked the door leading to Riverton's office with his own key and Wargrave put on his dark glasses as he hurried out. He gave a little two-finger salute to the Canadian industrialist, who nodded without speaking. Sixty seconds later, Wargrave was behind the wheel of his rental car.

Driving just within the speed limit, he reached the airport in time to board the next flight for Washington. As the plane took off and disappeared inside another heavy overcast, Wargrave relaxed in his seat, but he was careful not to close his eyes in case he fell asleep. He had the cassette inside his breast pocket and the jet lag of the Zürich-to-Montreal flight was hitting him. For the next few hours he was going to have to forget about sleep. Harry Wargrave was on his way to see Bruno – the code name for Joseph Moynihan, President of the United States.

At Dulles Airport, James Ryder, a large, paunchy American, went through the usual routine. Wearing dark glasses and a vicuña coat, which suggested a person of some importance, he stood with a suitcase in his hand watching the arrival board, which showed the Montreal flight had just landed. Mingling with passengers from the flight, he strolled toward the airport exit and waited while passengers boarded the airport bus. He went on waiting while others took cabs, looking impatiently at his watch as though annoyed at the late arrival of his own vehicle.

Ten minutes later a blue Cadillac pulled in by the kerb. Ryder stood quite still while a tall man dressed in chauffeur's uniform climbed out from behind the wheel, walked around, and opened the rear door. Ryder climbed inside without a word of thanks and settled himself in the back as the chauffeur returned behind the wheel.

'OK, let's go. Make it snappy,' Ryder ordered and began reading a magazine he had taken from his pocket.

Through the heavy traffic of early evening they drove to the White House, and during the whole journey no word was exchanged between the two men. Arriving at the White House, both men showed the Secret Service operative the special passes signed by Joseph Moynihan himself. There were no further formalities; they were immediately escorted to an ante-room that led directly to the Oval Office. And as instructed, the Secret Service man left them alone in the room, locking the door on the outside.

Ryder sat down in a chair and pulled the magazine from his pocket as Harry Wargrave removed his peaked cap, straightened his uniform jacket, and knocked on the door leading to the Oval Office. Not even the chief of the Secret Service detachment that guarded the President was aware that it was the chauffeur who was the important visitor.

On leaving the aircraft at Dulles Airport, Wargrave had gone straight to a room set aside for his use, a room to which he held the only key. Inside he had

quickly changed into the chauffeur's uniform waiting
for him. Then he had hurried to where the Cadillac
was parked and had driven it around to where Ryder
was waiting for him. Ryder was a 'blind' – he had no
idea who Wargrave was and he assumed the Englishman was a Canadian. A member of the presidential
Secret Service entourage, Ryder carried out the orders
given to him personally by the President without
question – and without informing his own chief of
what he did. President Moynihan himself opened the
door in response to Wargrave's knock, ushered him
inside, and closed the door.

'Some kind of emergency, Harry?' Moynihan asked
crisply.

'In our opinion, yes, Mr President.'

Wargrave walked to the desk where the tape
recorder was waiting and inserted the cassette. Joseph
Moynihan, six foot one and informally dressed in shirt
sleeves, went back behind his desk and poured a large
scotch. He pushed the glass over toward Wargrave.
Moynihan was an impressive figure, and not only
because of his height and build.

Round-faced, he had quick-moving blue eyes and
he was rarely still for more than a few minutes.
Radiating vitality, his expression was constantly
changing when he spoke and his manner was blunt
and direct. At forty-one he was the youngest man to
occupy the White House this century; he was also the
most anti-Communist President since the Russian
Revolution. Perching his buttocks on the edge of the

desk he listened with folded arms as the man they had code-named Angelo began speaking.

'Angelo reporting ... a major emergency faces Western Europe ... Marshal Prachko has just completed the most massive military rehearsal for the invasion of Germany, France, Holland, and Belgium ... The plan assumes Soviet tanks will enter Hamburg thirty minutes from Z hour ... within forty-eight hours three major bridgeheads will have been established across the Rhine. One hundred and sixty Soviet divisions will be deployed ... including one hundred fully mechanized, fifty tank, ten airborne ... Advance armoured elements will reach the Channel ports seven days from Z hour ... Operation Thunderstrike was carried out between Kazakhstan and the Ukrainian border over distances that precisely reproduced those the Red Army would cross in Western Europe ...'

Angelo went on to describe in terrifying detail how Operation Thunderstrike had been conducted. Taking a transparent map of Western Europe, the Soviet High Command had superimposed it over an equivalent area of western Russia. The river Volga had become the Rhine. Signposts – unreadable to American spy satellites orbiting three hundred miles over the area – had been erected reading *Paris, 30 km, Hamburg, 45 km, Calais, 80 km*, pointing toward the Russian city that was the equivalent distance.

One Soviet army group had represented the NATO opposing force. The main attacking Red Army groups, outnumbering NATO by three to one or more – as

27

they did in reality – had been commanded by Marshal Prachko himself. So overwhelming had been the onslaught, so swift its speed of movement, it was assumed the American President would feel it pointless to launch a retaliatory nuclear strike.

As the cassette came to the end, Angelo's final words were spoken in a deep and forceful voice. 'It is vital immediately to make a huge demonstration of American power to deter Marshal Prachko and his supporters, who are on the verge of achieving a majority in the Politburo . . .'

Briefly there was the same hush inside the Oval Office as had descended on the room in the Baton Rouge Building in Montreal when the tape had ended. But only briefly; as Wargrave switched off the machine Moynihan stood up from the desk where he had stayed perched throughout the recording.

'I think we can term this a major emergency,' Moynihan commented. 'Reports from satellites that have come in confirm major military manoeuvres have taken place in the area Angelo specifies. They couldn't tell us what he has told us, of course. And then there's the laser problem – scientists here and in Moscow reckon they're on the verge of a breakthrough.'

'A breakthrough to where?'

'Someday, maybe very soon, laser beams projected over long distances will be able to divert missile guidance systems – which means any missile fired will fall back on the original launch point. Result One?

End of the nuclear deterrent. Result Two? The Soviets will feel free to use their ground forces in Europe without fear of nuclear retaliation . . .'

'So what's the answer?' Wargrave inquired.

'This.' Moynihan pressed a button on his intercom. 'Ed, call an immediate meeting of the National Security Council. One hour from now. I don't care where the hell people are. Get them here . . .'

Inwardly Wargrave sighed with relief – relief that it was Joseph Moynihan who was sitting in the White House. How many previous Presidents would have taken a decision so quickly, would have acted with such determination? As though to confirm his unspoken thoughts, the President hitched up his slacks and spoke tersely.

'That meeting is just the formality. I've already decided what action must be taken. And Sparta has done a great job. I say that to you personally, Harry.' He held out his hand and shook Wargrave's. He had a strong grip. 'And you can pass on the same message to Julian Haller . . .'

The enormous power of Moynihan's reaction became apparent to Wargrave twenty-four hours later back in Montreal. By night, three US airborne divisions with all their equipment emplaned at Fort Worth, Texas, aboard a vast fleet of Lockheed C–5A transport planes. At the White House, Moynihan sat up all night in his shirt sleeves phoning the Chancellor of West

Germany, the Prime Minister of Great Britain, the President of France, and the NATO commander in Brussels. And all the time the giant transport planes were taking off, heading east across the Atlantic for the European mainland. Flight schedules were timed for maximum psychological impact – to raise the morale of Europe.

At nine o'clock in the morning – at the height of the rush hour – Londoners hurrying to work were startled to hear a thunderous roar in the sky above them. Looking up they saw the endless stream of US aircraft flying just below cloud level, a vast sky train of planes that came on and on. Less than sixty minutes later the same immense air cavalcade passed over Brussels and within a further hour the airborne force had landed in West Germany. To ram the point home, Moynihan made a brief television broadcast beamed worldwide by satellite, a broadcast made in his typical direct language.

'Let no one make any mistake – the American defence frontier lies along the West German border where it adjoins the Soviet prisoner states. As to what has just landed in the Federal Republic, well, there's plenty more where that came from . . .'

'Sparta has done a great job . . .'

President Moynihan had been referring to the Sparta Ring when he congratulated Harry Wargrave in the White House, to the special intelligence unit based outside the United States in Montreal, Canada. To explain how this unique outfit came into existence, it is necessary to go back a year earlier – to the time when Vice-President Moynihan had recently assumed the presidency after his predecessor was killed suddenly in a skiing accident in Colorado.

Chapter Three

Prague, Czechoslovakia

At that moment in history Matt Leroy – who later guarded Elsa Lang on her monthly journeys from Basel to Zürich Airport – was just completing his tour of duty as security officer at the American Embassy in Prague. It was December 8, the weather was mild, although snow had fallen in the High Tatra, and the American ambassador was holding an evening reception for certain Soviet Politburo members visiting Czechoslovakia. For Leroy his last night in Prague before returning to the States the following day looked eventful.

'My first chance to see the top enemy at close quarters,' as he confided to an aide.

The ambassador was not so enthusiastic. He had just received a personal instruction from Joseph Moynihan, who had recently succeeded as President, a message couched in typically pithy terms, which were later to become so familiar. 'Don't play footsie with the Kremlin crowd. A firm politeness is the order of the day. And on no account initiate any toast to their goddamn fake détente . . .'

As he circled among the guests under glittering chandeliers, Matt Leroy had a vague look while he held a glass of bourbon he sipped at occasionally. In fact he was examining everyone present with the utmost care, missing not even the smallest detail. Among the senior Politburo guests was Anatoli Zarubin, minister of trade and commerce. It was Zarubin who pounced on Leroy, clinking glasses with the American.

'To continuing détente, my friend,' Zarubin proposed in perfect English.

'To détente,' Leroy agreed without enthusiasm.

Zarubin was a small, dark-haired Russian with a neat moustache and a cheerful manner, and was reputed to be something of a ladies' man. Despite his doubts Leroy had found himself liking the talkative, joking minister, who expressed a fanatical devotion to the jazz of Dave Brubeck. 'I have all his records, play them over and over again,' he chattered on. '*Take Five* – that's my all-time favourite...' Leroy had found other Soviet guests less likeable.

The party was warming up by nine o'clock and the vodka was flowing most freely in the vicinity of Marshal Gregori Prachko, Soviet minister of defence. Prachko, a large, barrel-chested man of fifty-eight, had arrived in full uniform and covered with row upon row of medals. 'Enough to stock a First Avenue pawnshop,' Leroy thought sourly. He was quite obviously trying to get everyone else drunk, insisting upon toast after toast.

'Détente! Détente! Is there anyone here who refuses to drink that toast with me? Then let him show himself as the enemy of peace!'

Leroy studied him unobtrusively, noted the brutal nose, the aggressive jaw, the bristles of hair projecting from ears and nostrils. 'All of the bastard he's supposed to be,' he was thinking. 'And God help the men who serve under him.' Leroy kept circulating slowly, looking for one particular man, a man, oddly enough, whose appearance he had no description of. Was it possible that somewhere among the large crowd Colonel Igor Sharpinsky was present?

Deputy chief of the KGB, Sharpinsky was a shadow to Western security chiefs, so much so that he had been nicknamed Colonel Shadow. Literally all that was known about him was that he existed and Washington's dossier on him occupied only one page containing a few lines. Even the few lines were vague and insubstantial. 'It is rumoured that he is the KGB officer who liaises with GRU, Soviet military intelligence ... It is believed that at different times he has served with different Soviet embassies in the West under assumed names.' And that was about it.

A moment later Leroy saw another senior Politburo member who was not his favourite pin-up. Surprised – this man had not appeared on the advance guest list – Leroy pretended to sip more bourbon while he watched one of the most feared men in the world: General Sergei Marenkov, head of the KGB. The secret police chief was hovering at the edge of the crowd as though observing everyone present.

Wearing a dark blue business suit, Marenkov was a short, stocky man of fifty-five with wide shoulders.

He stood quite still, his strong-jawed face showing no expression. As he gazed around the room from under bushy eyebrows, he seemed to be cataloguing everyone at the reception, which probably was exactly what he was doing, Leroy thought. Unlike his mysterious deputy, Colonel Sharpinsky, Washington had a dossier three inches thick on Marenkov. The general was known to have an encyclopaedic memory. 'I'll bet he knows every man inside our embassy – what his job is and when he pees,' Leroy told himself.

Marenkov suddenly started moving slowly around the fringe of the crowd. By now the room was filled with noise, loud voices, the never-ending clinking of glasses, with Anatoli Zarubin tirelessly chatting and joking. Leroy seized his opportunity as Marenkov was passing him. He lifted his glass. 'Peace and goodwill, for God's sake, General.' Marenkov said something in Russian, and clinked glasses, and his brown eyes stared hard at the American, then he moved on. It had not been a too friendly encounter but Leroy had not been able to resist the chance to study the KGB chief at close quarters – even if only for a few seconds.

By the end of the evening Leroy felt he had achieved nothing. Certainly he had caught sight of no one who might be Igor Sharpinsky, no one who kept close to Marenkov. It had been interesting, something to put in his final report, but nothing more. The shock came when the party was over.

*

Returning to his room after midnight to complete his packing – he was due to catch the morning plane to Frankfurt – he felt in his jacket pocket for his cigarettes and stiffened. Tired with the anticlimax that so often ends a party, Matt Leroy became suddenly very alert. Inside the pocket his fingers touched something unfamiliar, something that shouldn't be there. He slowly drew out a sealed envelope. On the outside was written in English capital letters FOR THE PRESIDENT'S EYES ONLY.

Leroy got to bed that night much later than he had expected. Waking up his technical assistant, he had the envelope subjected to a series of tests. It was negative for explosives, for any kind of poison. He had the envelope, still sealed, X-rayed and the clear outline of a cassette showed up on the film. On the outside of the cassette someone had scratched the letters *A.N.*

'Where did you get it?' West, the technician, inquired at one stage.

'It was delivered to me,' Leroy replied and left it at that. 'Incidentally, this is top security – so you mention it to no one after I've gone . . .'

Back in his bedroom at 5 a.m., his packing completed, Leroy sat propped up against his pillow fully clothed while he thought. He knew the envelope could only have been slipped into his pocket – and very skilfully – by someone at the reception. He had put on a fresh suit only minutes before the reception had started. The only possible conclusion – fantastic as it seemed – was that the envelope had been slipped to him by one of the Russians at the reception. And right under the eyes of General Sergei Marenkov, head of the KGB. He shuddered at the thought. Whoever it was must have an incredible nerve. Or maybe he was desperate.

But the more he thought about it, the more plausible it seemed. It was no particular secret that he was ending his tour of duty, that he was on his way back to the States – a fact that would certainly be known in Soviet circles. So someone had taken this fact into account, that the cassette would stay in Prague for only a few hours after it had been passed to him.

'And how the hell do I get it into the President's hands?' he asked himself.

It was typical of Matt Leroy that he should suspect the need for the utmost secrecy, which meant bypassing his own chief in Washington. He had still not solved the problem when he landed in Washington the following day. Instead, the problem solved itself.

Twenty-four hours after Matt arrived in Washington the Chancellor of the Federal Republic of Germany flew in as President Moynihan's guest. And Matt Leroy was invited to the White House reception to report direct to the German Chancellor on his assessment of the political situation inside Czechoslovakia. It was not an idea that greatly appealed to Leroy's chief, Chuck Grant.

'Why the hell he can't take his briefings from me God alone knows,' he informed Leroy savagely.

'Maybe he likes on-the-spot reports,' Leroy suggested with an owlish blink of innocence.

But it was President Joseph Moynihan who liked on-the-spot briefings. As he remarked in typical unorthodox fashion to one of his aides, 'It's the man in the field who knows. The bureau desk johnnies over here love interpreting intelligence. For "interpreting" read "fouling it up." It's their rationale for holding down a job that probably isn't needed anyway.'

At the Washington reception, Leroy was introduced to Moynihan, who took him by the arm to guide him to the Chancellor. 'Just a moment, Mr President,' Leroy said quickly. In a few words he explained about the cassette. 'I have it on me,' he continued quickly in a low voice. 'It could be dynamite . . .'

'Really?' Moynihan gave a great big beaming grin. 'Dynamite, you said? I'll look forward to opening that.'

'I've had it checked for explosive content,' Leroy said hastily, 'both here and in Prague.'

'I assumed that – I was joking. Now, do you think you could slip it into my pocket as skilfully as it went into yours in Prague? And the place is crawling with Secret Service men . . .'

'Done, Mr President.'

'You have one hell of a nerve coming direct to me with this – bypassing your superiors.'

'I would agree with your evaluation of my action,' Leroy replied.

'And your name is Matt Leroy? Correct? I might just need an insubordinate bastard like you in future. Some people,' Moynihan went on with the ghost of a smile, 'call it initiative. And now we'll go and talk with our distinguished guest.'

Late that night Moynihan listened to the cassette alone in the Oval Office. The unknown man who had made the recording opened by saying that his code name in future would be Angelo, that he would communicate only by cassette, that the authenticity of each cassette would be shown by the letters *A.N.* he would scratch on the outside. He then gave information about Soviet policy, about the views of the most influential members of the Politburo, about the present Red Army order of battle in Eastern Europe.

What followed was even more extraordinary. He gave the President instructions that an entirely new intelligence unit must be set up outside the borders of the United States to transport cassettes from Europe to North America. 'Your existing intelligence agencies have been exposed and destroyed by your own press and Congress in a way the Soviet KGB could never have achieved,' the voice continued in English. 'To protect me you must set up this special unit, commanded by an American, I suggest, but staffed by Europeans – they will be operating in Europe, remember. Because they are islanders, British personnel may well prove to be the most reliable . . .'

And so it went on, giving details that cassettes would be dispatched by the Moscow Express concealed in the sleeping car that arrived in Basel, Switzerland, on the first Wednesday of each month. More details followed – the compartment number in the sleeping car, the precise place of concealment. On each Friday following the arrival of a cassette on Wednesday receipt of the cassette should be acknowledged over the Voice of America programme beamed to Eastern Europe – by the playing of a record he would specify and which was to be played at 5 p.m. Moscow time. Receipt of this first cassette was to be acknowledged by playing Count Basie's *One O'Clock Jump*. The cassette ended with a warning.

'No attempt must be made by any of your special unit personnel to identify me. That is mandatory. As to my motives, these are my own affair. The next cassette will travel aboard the Moscow Express sleeping car that reaches Basel on . . .'

The previous President, a consensus man, would undoubtedly have consulted the Secretary for Defense, the new CIA chief Moynihan had appointed to try and revive this organization, and God knew who else. But Angelo had judged his man correctly. The following morning Moynihan made certain discreet inquiries without revealing the reason for them. At the end of the day he was convinced that the top-secret data given over the cassette were genuine, that Angelo could only be a member of the Soviet Politburo. He sent for Julian Haller of the National Security Agency.

Moynihan, an ex-Navy man, had known Julian Haller since the Vietnam War and they had remained friends ever since. Haller was also a Navy veteran – he had served aboard the USS *Savannah* during the Second World War and had later been transferred to naval intelligence. It was in this capacity he had first met the man who one day by accident became President. 'Haller,' Moynihan was fond of saying, 'is one of the few men who really tell me what the score is. He isn't normal – he has no political ambition . . .'

Julian Haller listened in absolute silence while Moynihan told him what had happened, that he proposed to go along with Angelo. 'The information in that cassette you have listened to can only come from a senior member of the Soviet Politburo,' Moynihan pointed out. 'I've had it checked out.'

'It could just be a subtle trap,' Haller warned. 'To influence you with false information – giving you enough genuine data to fool you.'

'I've considered that. Angelo has given too much.'

'It would seem so,' the cautious Haller replied. 'And he has predicted certain things which – if they come true – would reinforce our confidence. What do we do now?'

Moynihan, dressed in slacks and an open-neck

shirt, stood up and assumed his favourite position, perching his backside on the front of his desk in the Oval Office. 'First, Julian, let me tell you something of my philosophy. My predecessor tried the soft option with the Soviets – with everything. Open government was his call. Let's all be buddies and love each other. Rot!' He took a quick drink of scotch and banged the glass down on the desk.

'He was a sincere man,' Haller suggested dubiously.

'He was naïve. The people only feel secure when they have strong, honest leadership – both qualities are equally important. The whole of the Western world has been sinking into a state of neurosis – almost a psychotic state – of fear.'

'So how do we remedy that?' Haller inquired.

'I'm not a nice guy . . .' Moynihan's mobile features formed a grin. 'I'm a cynical bastard who believes only a strong lead will cure that psychosis – and stop the Soviets in their tracks. Leonid Sedov is no Stalin, but just so long as we present a weak profile he has to go on pushing, pushing – otherwise Marshal Prachko and his lackeys will take over in the Politburo. They may do so even yet – unless I can outmanoeuvre them – and God, it's going to help me if I have an ear inside the Kremlin – Angelo's ear. There's something else,' he added casually.

'Top-secret? Sure you want to tell me?'

'Yes to both questions. It will help you realize just how vital your secret unit could be. Not yet, but when the time is ripe, I'm thinking of offering to conclude with the People's Republic of China a mutual defence treaty.'

'That would be something else again,' said Haller, startled.

'It would put the squeeze on the Soviets.'

'So what do we do now?' Haller asked again.

'You disappear. Officially you retire from the NSA. You get the hell out of the States and set up this special unit. Angelo is right – the existing agencies are busted flushes for this kind of work. Certain congressmen, certain newspaper reporters have gone too far – they have destroyed our intelligence shield.' Moynihan's face darkened and he hammered his clenched fist on the desk. 'Meantime the KGB goes marching on in full strength and power – spying, sabotaging, subverting – and all with the full backing of the Politburo. When I took on this job, I swore on oath to defend the United States – and by God I'm going to do it!'

'The CIA is being reorganized—'

'CIA. Club of International Amateurs! That's what those initials stand for in my book.'

'It could all be called pretty unconstitutional if ever it leaked,' Haller warned again.

'I've thought of that. Any President who – for the sake of his country's security – won't risk personal impeachment isn't fit to sit in this chair.'

'That's certainly a novel interpretation,' Haller admitted. 'Canada is the place,' he went on briskly.

'And can I use your name to get the cooperation of William Riverton, the Canadian industrialist? He was concerned with Allied intelligence in the last war and could provide the cover we need – maybe even the base?'

'Do that. I know him. Give the old warrior my best wishes.' Moynihan paused. 'Isn't this going to play hell with your domestic life? All the time this operation lasts you won't ever be able to set foot in the States. What about Linda?'

Haller had a stable marriage; he had been married for thirty years to Linda, who was a fashion designer in New York. Using the Metroliner service, they spent as much time together as they could even though they worked in different cities. It was Moynihan who answered his own question. 'We'll find some way of financing frequent trips to Montreal for her. Now, what about personnel?'

Haller grinned. 'That could come easy. There's a friend of mine called Harry Wargrave, a Britisher. Ex-naval intelligence, and he's got top US security clearance. I see him as the link man between Montreal and here – maybe something more than that. He's in Canada now, fishing in the Lake of the Woods area.' The grin broadened. 'He's thirty-six. And he thinks he's retired.'

Chapter Four

Montreal, Zürich, Moscow

Under the energetic impetus of Julian Haller, the special unit to bring Angelo's cassettes out of Europe to North America was set up in seven days. But despite Haller's energy, this was only made possible by the cooperation of the Canadian millionaire William Riverton. Haller's interview with the Canadian was surprisingly short. Sitting behind his desk in the office on the tenth floor of the Baton Rouge Building, Riverton read Moynihan's letter of introduction only once.

'I have to burn this,' he informed Haller, who sat smoking opposite him. 'Back in a minute.' When he returned to sit down again, Haller felt compelled to apologize.

'This is asking a great deal—'

'My understanding is,' Riverton interrupted, 'that you are to set up a highly secret intelligence unit aimed against the KGB. That is all I will know – or wish to know. Correct?'

'Correct.'

Riverton went on speaking rapidly, staring straight ahead as though Haller were not there, and the

American listened in fascination. He could almost feel the waves of intense concentration inside Riverton's brain as the Canadian solved problem after problem before Haller had even raised them.

'You need a base that is absolutely safe. Beyond that side door to my left is the suite of rooms I used in the Second World War. They will be at your disposal for as long as you need them. I will immediately have installed electronic devices that will defeat the most sophisticated bugging systems available to the KGB. On the roof of this building is a complex of radio antennae I use to communicate with my network of worldwide companies. I can supply you with the most advanced transmitter. My entire communications system will be available to you.'

'We could import our own equipment,' Haller began.

'Unwise. Nothing should cross the border. The man whose letter I have just burned suggested supplying funds through a series of untraceable bank accounts.' Riverton smiled for a second and then resumed his poker-faced expression. 'All accounts can be traced if you dig deep enough. I will put the sum of one million dollars in an account for you to draw on as you see fit—'

'Which will have one day to be repaid,' Haller interjected.

'Never. One question. Will personnel of your unit be coming here regularly?'

'I foresee certain people – two or three – arriving at

monthly intervals only. They will probably be the same people.'

'Warn me the day before if you can. I will change around my receptionists outside – I have offices in other parts of the city. That way the same girl will never see these people twice . . .'

Installed in Riverton's suite of offices, Haller made a series of phone calls. Harry Wargrave was the first man the American brought into Montreal. Warned in advance that discretion should be observed, the Englishman arrived wearing Canadian clothes and he spoke to the receptionist in a Canadian accent. It was a knack of Wargrave's to pick up in a few days the local accent of whatever part of the world he might be in.

'I need Elsa Lang,' the tall, dark-haired Englishman said crisply when Haller had explained the situation. 'She will be the courier who brings out the cassettes – a girl attracts less attention. Her father was a British admiral, she speaks French, Italian, and German fluently, she has a lot of nerve, and since she once worked under me with naval intelligence at the Washington Embassy she has top security clearance.'

'You will come out of retirement to help, then?' Haller asked as he watched the Englishman closely. Wargrave gave a lopsided grin which the American remembered; it normally indicated Wargrave was under stress. 'Something's gone wrong?' he inquired quietly.

'When you phoned I was on the verge of marrying

an Irish-Canadian girl. I told her a job had cropped up I was considering that would take me away pretty regularly – your job, I was referring to. She flared up and said I stayed at home or forget the marriage. So I said we'd forget it . . .'

'I don't like this, Harry.' An exceptionally humane man, Haller was troubled and he lit a cigarette – he was a three-pack-a-day smoker – before he went on. 'Maybe if you went back you could make it up with her. God knows, you've had a bellyful of this type of work—'

'You've missed the point,' Wargrave snapped tersely. 'She had a lucky escape. I was already getting bored – sooner or later I would have got restless for something more exciting than nine-to-five behind a desk. You know me . . .'

'If you say so . . .'

The next recruit was Haller's choice – Matt Leroy might be an American, but he had plenty of experience of European underground warfare against the Soviets. And during a stint at the American Embassy in London he had perfected an English accent that enabled him to pass himself off as British. Also he had triggered off the whole operation by bringing back the cassette from Prague.

And there was another detail Haller had not overlooked in connection with Prague. West, the technician who had tested the sealed envelope slipped into Leroy's pocket at the Prague reception for explosives and poison, had already been flown out of

48

Czechoslovakia. At the moment in Washington, West was aboard an aircraft for his next posting – the most remote part of the United States Moynihan could think of. Fairbanks, Alaska.

But Haller still had to interview and approve one of the key people who would form part of the unit operating inside Europe. Wargrave had already received a positive reply to his cable inviting Elsa Lang to fly to Montreal and she was due to arrive that afternoon.

'Elsa is a natural for this one,' Wargrave had assured him, but Haller was reserving judgment. An Anglophile, the American wondered whether she would measure up in his eyes.

In London, exactly one week before Harry Wargrave arrived in Montreal, Elsa Lang was driving her Ford Escort automatic from Pinewood Film Studios back to a block of flats on the edge of Regent's Park. She was excited, on top of the world, exceeding the speed limit when she dared, impatient when traffic lights stopped her less than a quarter of a mile from her destination. Glancing to her right, she briefly caught the eye of a young man pulled up alongside her behind the wheel of a Porsche.

'Doing anything tonight, luv?' he called out.

He saw a fair-haired girl of twenty-seven, grey-eyed and with superb bone structure, a hint of hauteur in her expression that immediately aroused his hunter's instinct. Under her powder-blue cashmere sweater firm breasts were silhouetted, and he shrugged regretfully as she turned away and stared at the traffic lights. Then she was turning left away from him and passing Madame Tussaud's waxwork museum. She was almost there; within minutes she would be using the key in her handbag to let herself into Jerry's flat.

It was Friday afternoon, only three o'clock but almost dark – so dark that cars were travelling with their lights on. Elsa glanced at the passenger seat beside her where the black case containing her film make-up kit lay. For a year now she had been chief make-up girl at Pinewood and this was how she had met Jerry Gifford, the production manager she was going to marry. But her glance fell not on the make-up case; affectionately she had looked at the small package tied in silver ribbon, the package that contained the jewelled tiepin that was her engagement present for Jerry.

Parking her car by the kerb, she checked the doors, got out holding the make-up case and the package, locked the car, and glanced up at the windows of the fourth-floor flat where Jerry lived. She frowned briefly, then smiled to herself. Curtains were drawn across the windows; he must have woken late and had a hell of a rush to get to Pinewood this morning. He was working on a different film from her and she hadn't seen him all day. Deliberately she hadn't sought him out to let him know her boss had allowed her to leave early. She wanted to be inside the flat when he arrived, to surprise him.

Outside the flat door she inserted the key, turned it, walked half inside, and paused. The stereo was on in the living room, playing a Spanish love melody. Jerry must have got back early. Closing the door quietly behind her, she heard something else above the stereo sound. Voices. From behind the half-open bedroom door. She froze. Her face lost all its colour. Without making a sound, she walked slowly toward the door, forcing one foot in front of the other.

She felt she was sleepwalking, that this couldn't be happening. She could recognize both voices now. Jerry's. And the girl was Sheila, the six-foot redhead from Texas, her roommate. Like someone hypnotized, she paused close to the door, listening. Sheila said, 'You like it like this?' Then giggled. Elsa felt as cold as ice, heard Jerry use foul, erotic words he had never used in her presence even in bed. Sheila responded with equally filthy language, which didn't so much shock Elsa.

She took one brief look through the door, closed her eyes, and backed quietly away. The bedclothes were all on the floor, the two naked figures were writhing as one. The full shock would come later, she knew. She placed the wrapped package with the tiepin on the living-room table, the package that contained the card carrying the words *For Jerry, from Elsa with all my love.* By its side she dropped her key to the flat. Then she left, quietly closing the door behind her for the last time.

She drove back to her own mews flat in Chelsea on automatic pilot, the flat she shared with Sheila Colston, stopping for traffic lights, moving forward again without being aware of what she was doing. All reflex actions. She still felt terribly cold as she turned into the cul-de-sac, as the wheels wobbled over the cobbles. The mews seemed horribly empty when she got out of the car, but contrarily she was also thankful: she couldn't have faced some meaningless chitchat with one of the neighbours.

Inside the four-room flat – living-dining room, kitchen, two bedrooms – she poured herself a neat scotch, put it to her lips, then poured it down the sink, untouched. Going into her bedroom, she closed the door, took the photo of Jerry, and put it into a drawer. From the same drawer she took the loaded Smith and Wesson and lay down on the bed.

Elsa Lang, twenty-seven years old, her carefully combed fair hair spread over the pillow, lay on the bed staring up at the ceiling, the .38 Smith and Wesson revolver close to her right hand. Before lying down she had made herself up in front of the dressing-table mirror, not really seeing herself at all as she applied the last touch of lipstick. And she had done one more thing before lying down. Emptying the loaded revolver, she had spun the chambers and inserted two bullets at random, then spun the chambers once more.

She was going to aim the muzzle at her temple three times, spinning the chambers after each aim – if she were still alive. And if she had survived after pressing the trigger for the third time she would go on living. Somehow. Which gave her a three-to-one chance. Or did it? She was too keyed up – or too empty, she wasn't sure which – to work out the odds.

At four in the afternoon it was dark inside the bedroom even with the curtains still drawn back. As she lay there, images of her past life came into her distraught mind. Her schooldays at the Godolphin, the exclusive public school near Salisbury. The ridiculous straw boaters with red bands. The navy-blue cloaks, red-lined and with hoods worn when they moved about inside the grounds. She remembered so well the evening she had been late leaving for supper, seeing ahead of her a column of cloaked and hooded figures wending their way from the boarding houses through the twilight toward the school, along the paths between the trees and the grass. Just like a coven of witches, she had thought.

She had hated school, with its lack of privacy in the dormitories at night, the emphasis on the team spirit. Even in those days she had been a loner – and alone – seeing her parents only at vacations. She had never revealed this to her father, Admiral Sir Geoffrey Lang, chief of naval intelligence. And since then she had met so many girls who would have given their back teeth to go to the Godolphin! Including her roommate, Sheila. Her hand clutched the familiar butt of the revolver. Time to press the trigger for the first round.

Later, that god-awful secretarial college where they taught you nothing except how to be a lady. Except that she had perfected her languages. Elsa had a natural talent and liking for foreign languages. Then the never-to-be-forgotten night when she had pleaded with her father only a few months before he had died. Her mother, whom she had never known, had died when she was born.

'So you want me to get you a job in naval intelligence?' he had growled over his bifocals.

'It would be different,' she had pleaded without hope.

'Bore the pants off you,' he had replied. Then he had given her one of his rare smiles and hugged her shoulder. 'Still, if that's what you want . . .'

Everything had changed from that moment: life had savour. After a stint at the Admiralty she had earned swift promotion and been attached to the Paris Embassy. She had travelled all over Europe, sometimes acting as a courier, which was very unusual for a girl in those days. Then, out of the blue, had come the posting to Washington – and Harry Wargrave, Commander Harry Wargrave, RN, who controlled naval intelligence in the United States. Her hand tightened on the butt of the revolver.

It was Harry who had given her the gun after a cipher clerk had been kidnapped from the French

Embassy by the KGB. Or so it was assumed: his mutilated body had later been found in a used-car lot. It was Harry who had taken her to the FBI target range and trained her to be a crack shot. She certainly shouldn't miss at this range . . .

She aimed the muzzle at her temple calmly. The metal felt cold against her skin. She wasn't supposed to possess the weapon – she had no permit. But at the end of her tour of duty in Washington she had flown back with secret papers and diplomatic immunity that bypassed the metal detectors at Kennedy Airport. No one had asked her for the weapon when she had resigned, bored with the idea of working once more at the Admiralty.

'Never aim a gun unless you intend to fire if necessary . . .'

It was Harry who had told her that. Since leaving Jerry's flat near Regent's Park, Elsa had steeled herself not to cry; now, at the remembrance of Harry Wargrave, of his kindness and friendship, a single tear formed in her right eye, ran down her cheek. Something else he had once said came back to her.

'Life is never a bed of roses. Everyone has their ups and downs. If you get a big down, forget all that public school balls about not showing emotion. All right, do it in private – but let go just once. Cry it out of your system – but never give up. Never! Never!'

She let go of the gun and herself, twisting her slim body as she sobbed and sobbed into the pillow for all of ten minutes. Then, drained of emotion, she got off the bed and went to the bathroom to clean herself up. This time she looked directly at herself in the mirror. 'Get a hold of yourself, you stupid idiot,' she told her mirror image.

She emptied the revolver of cartridges before she wrapped it in newspaper and put it into the rubbish bin. And before she did that she broke the firing pin with a hammer so the weapon was useless. The cartridges she would drop into a letter-box later; harmless, they would be collected by the postman, who would doubtless hand them to the authorities. Strange that the memory of Harry Wargrave had brought her back to sanity.

Sheila did not return to the flat that night. Instead she phoned Elsa the following morning, her Texan accent nervous, unsure. 'Elsa, I'm so sorry – it just happened, I don't know how . . .'

'I shall be out of the flat between ten and noon,' Elsa replied. Her voice was crisp and devoid of emotion. 'So you have two hours to get over here, collect your things, get out.'

'That's not much time—'

'And leave the rent money on the sideboard,' Elsa informed her in the same calm voice. She replaced the receiver, ate a quick breakfast of coffee and toast, and was out of the flat before ten.

The following morning the postman delivered a package. She knew what it contained before she opened it and she dropped the tiepin from Jerry in the rubbish bin – the contents of the previous day, including the revolver, had already been collected by the dustman. By now the weapon would be pulp in the crusher. There was no note with the tiepin.

'Gutless swine,' she murmured.

She had already phoned Pinewood Films, giving them her resignation. She never wished to see the damned place again. Making herself up in front of the mirror, she took a lot of trouble over the process, then surveyed the result. She knew she was attractive to men. And she had made up her mind how she was going to live her life from now on. She was going to play the field, manipulate men, lead them on, and then drop them when they were crazy over her. She was going to be a thoroughgoing bitch, get her own back. It could even be fun – playing the deception game as once she had played it professionally with naval intelligence in Washington.

Above all, she was going away somewhere. Paris? Rome? It didn't make much difference. Five days later the long and cryptic cable from Harry Wargrave arrived, offering her the chance of a job. '. . . Something like the old days,' was the only clue he gave her as to its nature.

Within an hour of receiving the cable she was calling at the Midland Bank branch in Piccadilly to collect the money he had cabled her. The Pan Am office was only a few paces from the bank and she immediately booked a first-class seat on the first available flight to New York. The cable had instructed her to fly there first, then take a transfer flight on to Montreal.

'Round-trip or one-way?' the booking clerk had asked her.

'A one-way ticket,' Elsa replied firmly.

Smartly dressed in a two-piece navy suit and a cream polo-necked sweater, Elsa Lang sat in a chair Haller had drawn up for her alongside his own. It was typical of him that he had not confronted her from behind his desk, that he had introduced an air of intimacy to put her at her ease. Wargrave sat some distance away, staring at the large wall map of Europe.

'Film make-up girl is a long way from naval intelligence,' Haller suggested with a broad smile. 'Without going into details yet, this is a tough job.'

'You mean you haven't even taken the trouble to check my dossier?' Elsa demanded and her tone was sharp. Still staring at the wall map, Wargrave repressed a smile. Haller was going to get more than he had bargained for.

The American met her grey eyes, her unsmiling face, opened a drawer, and dropped a dossier on the desk. 'There it is – I know it backward. But you could have lost your touch,' he suggested gently.

'Lost my fanny,' Elsa blazed crudely. 'And before we go any further, I need to know who I would be working under. You or Harry Wargrave? Even if you decide to take me, I'd then have to decide whether I'd accept the offer – and the question of my boss could be crucial . . .'

She was still staring hard at Haller and the American was careful not to show she had rocked him back on his heels. My God, he thought, she's checking *me* out, wondering whether *I* measure up. He had no way of knowing what Wargrave had immediately realized: Elsa Lang had weighed up Julian Haller as a man who responded to a challenge, and within minutes of meeting him for the first time.

'You would take all your instructions direct from Wargrave,' the American assured her quietly. 'Incidentally, I also know my job,' he added mildly. 'Would it have made a difference had it been otherwise?' he inquired.

'Bet your sweet life it might,' she responded. 'What do I know about you, Mr Haller? We might prove incompatible,' she added with a quirkish smile. She crossed her very desirable legs and Haller looked at them. 'It's a more comfortable position,' she remarked. 'I'm not trying to sex you up . . .'

Wargrave turned his head away, almost choked as he repressed a grin. Haller stared at Elsa's legs a little longer, and then he beamed broadly and Elsa chuckled softly. 'You'll want to know why I'm interested in returning to my old work, I imagine?' she suggested.

'It would help some,' the American admitted. 'Cigarette?'

'Not while I'm on the grill, thank you. I had over a year at the film make-up job,' she explained carefully. 'Once I'd met all the types there were to meet I developed itchy feet, maybe a desire to do something more ... *meaningful* is an awful word, but' – she smiled ironically – 'probably it expressed my meaning.'

For the next ten minutes Haller cross-examined the English girl, using every trick in the book to bring to light a weakness, something that might make her a dangerous liability in an emergency. And gradually – when she had indicated that she really wanted the job – he gave her some hint of what she was involving herself in, watching her closely for any sign of doubt or uncertainty.

A past master at the art of probing character, Haller was unable to fault Elsa, whom he was rapidly coming to like – even more important, to trust. With one hand stroking her crossed leg she answered every question directly and with composure, her eyes meeting his levelly, and only once did her hand freeze for a second, a reaction that neither man noticed.

'You've never thought of getting married?' Haller asked casually.

'Often,' Elsa replied instantly. 'But so far I've never met the right man.' She was careful not to glance in Harry Wargrave's direction as she replied.

Haller lit a fresh cigarette and sprang his shock question. 'Can you use a gun? You may have to.'

'Yes. I'm most familiar with a .38 Smith and

Wesson. In Washington, Harry took me to the FBI range and I practised a lot. At that time the KGB had kidnapped a cipher clerk from the French Embassy – he wanted me to be able to protect myself . . .'

It was Wargrave, a veteran of Balkan intrigue since his tour of duty in Athens, who had suggested the name for the unit just before flying across the Atlantic to organize the European end with Elsa Lang and Matt Leroy.

'We need a code name for this outfit,' Haller had pointed out. 'The President will be Bruno. What will we be?'

'Why not the Sparta Ring?' the Englishman had replied. 'It has a hard, stoic sound – and these monthly trips to Basel are going to call for something like stoic qualities. But the main thing in its favour is that it has a Greek sound. If ever a whisper of the name reaches the KGB it will divert their attention away from Switzerland.'

'Sparta it shall be . . .'

For the next twelve months the operation flourished. In Basel, Wargrave had organized a backup team for Matt Leroy. One of them was Peter Neckermann, an ex-police sergeant of the German *Kriminalpolizei* the Englishman knew and trusted. Neckermann played the part of the white-jacketed 'steward' who boarded the sleeping car to retrieve the cassettes. Wargrave chose Neckermann's protectors from other men he had known for many years; one was a French Secret Service man who had retired early, the other a Dutchman recommended to him by General Max Scholten, chief of Dutch counter-espionage. All three men were dedicated anti-Communists, and none of them knew what the operation was really all about. Wargrave ran Sparta totally as a close-ended unit.

Operating regularly inside Switzerland, he even kept the activities of Sparta a secret from his old friend Colonel Leon Springer, assistant-chief of Swiss counter-espionage. Here Wargrave was taking a calculated risk, as he once explained to Haller in Montreal.

'Sooner or later Springer is going to hear of our regular trips to Zürich and Basel. He knows me well. He'll instantly suspect an espionage operation.'

'We'll have to risk that,' Haller had replied. 'We know now beyond any shadow of doubt that the information coming in from Angelo is priceless. It's uncanny – it's almost as though Bruno were sitting in on every major Politburo meeting.'

'And Angelo has to be Anatoli Zarubin . . .'

'From his pictures he looks like a charmer,' Elsa interjected as she looked around the windowless room that always gave her a feeling of claustrophobia. 'I bet I'd fall for him,' she added wickedly with a glance in Wargrave's direction.

'If a girl isn't fussy . . .'

Despite Angelo's warning in the first cassette there had inevitably been speculation about Angelo's identity behind the closed doors of the room adjoining Riverton's. 'He is the most civilized, cosmopolitan member of the Politburo,' Wargrave had pointed out. 'Everyone who has met him finds him reasonable.'

'He's the polished idol the Kremlin wheels out every time it seems the West might be getting suspicious of the détente racket,' Haller growled. 'That's his main job – to throw smoke in our eyes.'

'Getting back to Colonel Springer,' Wargrave persisted, 'I may one day feel the time has come to contact him. I don't have to give him even a whisper of what is happening.'

'Use your own judgment – the European end is yours.'

The American's final comment was a reference to the fact that he never left Montreal – that the whole European operation was always handled by Wargrave, Elsa, and Matt Leroy. Wargrave had stood up to leave when Haller indicated that it was not his final remark. His expression was grim as he told them of an incident in Moscow that had been reported to him by an undercover Russian agent working for the West in a minor capacity.

'Anatoli Zarubin – whom we are damned sure now is Angelo – often visits the Moscow railyards in his position as minister of trade and commerce – with the apparent purpose of speeding up dispatch of goods to the West. They need the hard currency, of course – so his visits would seem normal.'

'Which is when he slips the cassettes inside the

sleeping car on the Moscow Express,' Elsa pointed out.

It had been three o'clock in the afternoon of Monday, November 1, in Moscow when the incident Haller told them about had taken place. The temperature was ten degrees below freezing point, it was as black as night, and the rails were coated with ice as Anatoli Zarubin, heavily muffled in a fur coat and hat, walked alone in the marshalling yards alongside the Moscow Express minutes before it was due to move into the station prior to its departure for the West.

Climbing aboard the sleeping car that two days later would reach Basel in Switzerland, Zarubin began inspecting the compartments. It was known in the Politburo that he had a fetish for neatness and cleanliness. 'The express is a mobile propaganda weapon,' he often explained. 'The West will judge us by our trains and civil aircraft they see.' Zarubin continued toward the front of the sleeping car, then stopped. A figure, no more than a glimpse of a shadow, had emerged from a compartment ahead and slipped off the coach. Walking more quickly, Zarubin arrived at the car door, which was swinging in the dark. He looked out and froze with shock.

A shot rang out, deafeningly loud in the silence and the dark, then a second shot. So close that for a moment Zarubin thought he had been hit. He dropped to the track and crouched low. To his right a man walking with a lamp doused the light and vanished behind a line of freight cars. Still crouched low, Zarubin was suddenly blinded by a powerful torch shone direct in his face. He waited for the third shot that would kill him.

'Oh . . . it's you, Zarubin . . .'

The voice was that of General Sergei Marenkov, head of the KGB. 'Come over here and look at this,' Marenkov continued grimly. Still dazed, Zarubin walked slowly alongside the express to where Marenkov stood over a crumpled body with his pistol still in his hand. The KGB chief shone the torch down onto the face of the man he had shot. 'It's Starov of the GRU,' he explained in a hard voice. 'He's a saboteur – see that grenade in his hand? He was going to attach it to the coach.' Marenkov frowned suddenly and looked at Zarubin. 'What were you doing here?'

'Checking the coach.'

The man with the lamp neither of them had seen was now over three hundred metres away, already wording in his mind the report that would later reach Washington before it was passed on to Julian Haller.

Inside the room on the tenth floor of the Baton Rouge Building in Montreal, Wargrave had listened in silence as Haller finished his account of the incident at the Moscow marshalling yard. 'It could have been a coincidence – Marenkov being there at the same time as Zarubin.'

'Except that I've had two other reports of our friend General Marenkov poking his nose around those freight yards on other occasions,' the American replied. 'There's a time limit on Angelo's survival and that time limit could be running out.'

The next date for collection of another cassette was Wednesday, December 1. It would be the twelfth cassette Sparta was picking up. On Tuesday, November 30, Harry Wargrave was staying at the Hotel Schweizerhof in Zürich. And at that moment he had no inkling that this cassette would contain the news of Marshal Gregori Prachko's Operation Thunderstrike military manoeuvres, the news that would decide President Moynihan to send overnight to West Germany the huge airborne force.

Elsa Lang and Matt Leroy were already in Basel, staying once again at a different hotel in the city ready for the morning pickup. On Wargrave's instructions they never stayed at the same hotel twice. And the Englishman had just taken a serious decision: he was going to see Colonel Leon Springer of Swiss counterespionage. Was it instinct that prompted the decision? Or was it Haller's recent reference to the fact that soon they could be coming to the end of the Sparta road? He wasn't sure. He just knew that when he had followed his instinct in the past he had always been proved right.

It was noon when he entered Springer's small,

cramped office on the second floor of the building that overlooks the river Limmat. He had phoned from the hotel and the Swiss had made an immediate appointment. He rose from behind his desk and came forward to shake the Englishman's hand.

'Welcome to Switzerland, Harry. Times are a little less tense since last we met,' he commented in excellent English.

Thirty-three years old, Colonel Leon Springer was the very opposite of the cold, precise Swiss so often caricatured in newspaper reports. Slimly built, he had the nose of a predatory hawk, smiled constantly, and was fond of cracking jokes during moments of crisis. Smartly dressed in a dark blue suit, the Swiss was amiable and talkative, a man who moved restlessly and chain-smoked. Fingering his neat moustache with one hand, he poured coffee with the other.

His reference to the last time they had met recalled to Wargrave a major incident in his career as he sat down in a comfortable leather armchair and accepted the cup of strong coffee. At that time he had helped Springer track down a Communist spy ring operating out of Geneva. Three of the Soviet agents had died, two of them shot by Wargrave himself.

'I'm passing through Switzerland now and again on business, Leon,' he remarked. 'I should have called on you earlier.'

Sitting back in the swivel chair behind his desk, Springer again stroked his moustache as he gazed out of the window where snow fell gently over the ancient buildings and spires of one of Europe's most beautiful cities. Wargrave observed the gesture with a sense of heightened alertness; it indicated the Swiss was under some stress. 'So you have deserted your old love for the more peaceful world of business?' Springer inquired. Do I detect a hint of scepticism, Wargrave wondered.

'Not so peaceful,' he replied easily. 'Business can be just as wild a jungle and the same law applies – the survival of the fittest.' He sipped his scalding coffee. 'The only difference is they don't shoot at you – not often, anyway.'

'The survival of the fittest?' the Swiss repeated. 'And vis-à-vis the Soviets, that is a lesson many of our Western politicians still have to learn – before it is too late, I pray fervently. At least I thank God that Joseph Moynihan is sitting in the White House.'

'I couldn't agree more . . .' Wargrave switched the conversation, anxious to steer it away from Moynihan. 'How is life for you these days? Brigadier Traber is thriving, I hope?'

Springer's sharp eyes blinked: the Englishman had given him just the opening he was seeking. 'I will pass on to him your best wishes.' He paused. 'We would both thrive more if we could solve a very worrying problem. I suppose that if I asked you to give us a hand with it, you would say you were retired – to the world of business,' he added significantly.

'Just spell out the problem, Leon.'

'You have so many contacts, Harry, so many people who are indebted to you from the old days. Could you still call on one of them to come here and investigate a tricky situation?' He paused again. 'It is only fair to say the risk could be total – and I would not want to know the name of the person you chose . . .'

'I said spell it out.'

Springer's manner underwent a change. As he leaned forward across the desk, the eyes above the beaky nose became alert and intense. 'We have reason to believe a major Communist cell is operating in the strategic Andermatt area. One of my men checking in that town was recently found dead inside the Rhône Glacier – inside one of the ice tunnels. He appeared to have died from natural causes – until my forensic people found the tiny hypodermic puncture at the base of his skull. We still don't know what poison was injected.'

'But it proves something is going on up there in the mountains?'

'Exactly. The trouble is I need a fresh eye to look over the Andermatt area – a non-Swiss who, because he is a stranger, may see something we would overlook. It is not something I would press you to do – even more since it will involve calling in one of your friends—'

'Consider it done.'

Wargrave swallowed his hot coffee in three gulps. He had no wish to linger with the shrewd colonel, much as he liked him. Too much conversation could be dangerous. When he left Springer's headquarters he was well satisfied: he had explained his frequent visits to Switzerland and had cemented his relationship with the Swiss counter-espionage organization by agreeing to help it.

The moment the Englishman had left the building, Springer called his chief, Brigadier Arthur Traber, on the scrambler phone. On that day Traber was visiting his headquarters in Bern, the Swiss capital. 'Any development on the Andermatt front?' he inquired as he heard Springer's voice.

'Wargrave has at last called on me. I knew he would – sooner or later. He's covering his frequent visits here. The important thing is he has agreed to send someone to Andermatt.'

'Any idea who?' Traber asked.

Springer chuckled before he replied. 'You don't really expect that he told me that, do you, sir? He's a lone wolf, which is what makes him so effective. He's capable of keeping three balls in the air at once without anyone knowing. But he may well succeed where we have failed – he's done it before.' Springer chuckled again. 'He told me he was in business these days.'

'The intelligence business?'

'I'm certain of it. What I don't understand is these monthly visits to Zürich. He arrives from Montreal on the first – or last – Tuesday of each month, takes a room – always at a different hotel – spends the night here and catches the Wednesday flight back to Montreal. Why Montreal?'

'You tell me.'

'I can't. Our people at the airport check him in and out, and that's it. But I suspect it could be high-level, very high-level indeed . . .'

Wargrave went back to the Hotel Schweizerhof by a devious route in case he was being followed. It was unlikely, but long ago deviousness had become second nature. Taking a cab to the Quaibrücke – the last bridge before the lake – he paid off the driver, waited until a tram was about to leave, and jumped aboard at the last moment. A few minutes later he jumped off again just as the automatic doors were closing and walked rapidly up the Bahnhofstrasse to the Hotel Schweizerhof.

Immediately when he reached his room he placed a long-distance call. He had to wait a long time; he smoked several cigarettes while the call was routed through a series of European exchanges. At three in the afternoon – lunch had been sent up to his room – the phone rang. He spent less than three minutes talking in a roundabout way clearly understood by the person at the other end of the line. 'Andermatt, yes,' were the last words he spoke before replacing the receiver. And even Wargrave did not realize that he had just made one of the most decisive phone calls of his career.

*

It was Tuesday, November 30, when Wargrave made his phone call. On the following morning, Wednesday, December 1, Elsa Lang took the twelfth cassette from Peter Neckermann, the white-jacketed 'steward,' in the crowded Basel station only seconds before Neckermann was abducted by the two KGB men – the men who ended up inside a cabin trunk trapped in the Rhine Falls at Schaffhausen.

And it was this twelfth cassette that carried Angelo's urgent warning about Marshal Prachko's Operation Thunderstrike. It was this cassette that decided President Joseph Moynihan to dispatch overnight to West Germany the huge airborne force in the giant C–5A transport planes as a warning to the Soviet Politburo. The repercussions of the twelfth cassette were enormous and worldwide.

The emergency meeting of the Soviet Politburo was summoned for eight o'clock in the evening, Moscow time, of Friday, December 3. One by one the fleet of black Zil limousines turned into the Kremlin gateway. Each driver, a KGB man, wore a flat, short-brimmed fedora hat and a heavy blue overcoat. Leonid Sedov, First Secretary, was the earliest arrival, coming from his apartment in the nine-storey building at 26 Kutuzov Prospekt. General Sergei Marenkov, who occupied the apartment above Sedov, was next to arrive, followed a few minutes later by Anatoli Zarubin, minister of trade and commerce.

The last to arrive, at three minutes to eight, was Marshal Gregori Prachko, as always in full uniform, his insignia of rank glittering on his shoulder boards, his chest ablaze with his rows of medals. Why did he always arrive last, the cynical Leonid Sedov wondered. To make a dramatic entrance, of course. He opened the meeting the moment Prachko had eased his great bulk into his chair.

It was an acrimonious, bitter meeting as the moderates clashed violently with the hard-liners, and for once the moderates had the ammunition to launch an all-out attack on Marshal Prachko and his supporters. For a whole hour Prachko listened in unaccustomed silence as the offensive was mounted against him.

'You have provoked the Americans into taking action ... The morale of the Western capitalist countries has been lifted to unheard-of heights ... You have weakened the chances of our comrades in France and Italy infiltrating their way into the governments of those countries ... Your sabre-rattling has backfired, has put us back a whole decade ...'

Prachko, no mean political tactician, deliberately waited until the offensive was petering out and, like an expert general, launched his counter-attack. He made a great show of opening a folder and extracting a typed report, which he placed before him on the highly polished table. As he began speaking, the lights from the chandeliers overhead reflected off his medals.

'I have here a highly secret report prepared by Colonel Igor Sharpinsky, deputy to my comrade

General Marenkov, who also has a copy. As you know, Colonel Sharpinsky acts as liaison officer between the GRU and the KGB – he therefore felt the subject was so dangerous to the security of the state that he should supply this report to me—'

'One moment!' It was Leonid Sedov, First Secretary, seated at the head of the long table, who intervened. Sedov, sixty years old, was a well-built man of medium height with thick greying hair and an oddly shaped jaw – it was rumoured he had recently been operated on for some undisclosed illness. He turned to General Marenkov, head of the KGB, who sat watching Prachko from under his bushy eyebrows with an impassive stare. 'General Marenkov, would you prefer to deal with this report yourself?'

'I have no objection to the marshal revealing its contents. As he has just said, its gravity can hardly be exaggerated.'

'Then I will continue,' Prachko growled. 'Operation Thunderstrike was carried out hundreds of miles from our border with the NATO forces – so even under the terms of so-called détente it was not necessary to inform NATO of the operation. And there was no way in which American orbiting satellites could guess the true purpose of the manoeuvres. They cannot yet read signposts from the air,' he went on sarcastically. 'And yet within days of its completion the American President reacts by sending a huge reinforcement of troops to Europe—'

'Excuse me,' Sedov interrupted, 'but I cannot see where all this is leading. Could you get to the point?'

'Only someone sitting at this table could have informed Moynihan.'

Having dropped his bombshell, Prachko sat back as all hell broke loose.

'That is slanderous, mad,' Anatoli Zarubin protested.

'You go too far,' observed Pavel Suslov, the thin-faced party theoretician. He also, like Zarubin and Marenkov, had attended the Prague reception at the American Embassy over a year earlier when the original cassette had been slipped into Matt Leroy's pocket. A quiet man, his presence had largely gone unnoticed. Sedov, who spent half his life preserving the balance between the moderates and the hard-liners, intervened again.

'You will need far more evidence than that to back up what you have just alleged,' he said grimly.

'It is here.' Prachko produced a thick wad of papers out of his folder. 'Sharpinsky has produced a meticulous analysis of our actions and American reactions over the past year. Time and again Moynihan has anticipated our moves. It is all here and points to only one conclusion – a top-level informer.'

Marenkov leaned forward. 'I have read the report,' he said abruptly. 'I find it not only disturbing – I find it convincing. I propose a task force should be formed at once to investigate this matter – that it should be directed by the First Secretary, myself, and Marshal Prachko—'

'We should all have access to that report,' Zarubin snapped.

Sedov intervened for the third time. 'I propose that General Marenkov's suggestion should be put to the vote.'

By a narrow majority Marenkov's proposal was carried. The meeting broke up in some confusion and members were still arguing as they left the room. Three men only remained behind – Leonid Sedov, Marshal Prachko, and Marenkov. The hunting down of Angelo had begun.

Chapter Five

Montreal

'This time I want you to take great care – Sparta is soon going to blow up in our faces. I can smell trouble coming,' Julian Haller went on as he warned Wargrave and Elsa in the room next to William Riverton's office in the Baton Rouge Building.

It was Monday, January 3. On Wednesday, January 5, they would be in Switzerland again to pick up the thirteenth cassette from Angelo. Elsa Lang felt sure it was the weather that was depressing Haller. Europe was now reeling under the worst winter for over forty years as blizzards raged and one airport after another was closed down. She tried to joke the American out of his black mood.

'Unlucky thirteen? I didn't know you were super-stitious, Julian. And you an agnostic – shame on you.'

'Fly over in that frame of mind and you'll fall flat on your face,' Haller snapped. He regretted the out-burst as he saw Elsa's expression. 'Look, I've been in this game a long, long time. I can sense when an operation that's gone smoothly for months could turn sour.'

'He's got a point, Elsa,' Wargrave warned. 'Those

two KGB types turning up in Basel last time weren't a good omen.'

'Matt dealt with them,' Elsa flared. 'We knew it wasn't going to be easy right from the start.'

'I admire your spirit,' Haller said quietly. 'But I've had more reports that Marenkov keeps checking the Moscow railyards – and that is one tough, very smart professional. He's onto something.' He leaned forward over his desk and spoke very emphatically. 'He's found the end of a piece of string and he'll go on and on till it leads him to something. We're sitting over four thousand miles away from General Sergei Marenkov and I can feel him moving, probing.'

'We'll watch it,' Wargrave said. 'Wednesday afternoon we'll be back with another cassette. Just don't sit here worrying your guts out. OK?'

The next forty-eight hours were a nightmare for Julian Haller. His wife, Linda, had come up to Montreal from New York and he was glad about that – and sorry at the same time. A cool, soothing woman, Linda Haller made regular visits to the Canadian city, where Riverton had arranged a contract with a fashion firm to explain her visits. She had no idea of the existence of the Sparta Ring and had long ago accepted that there were many things her husband couldn't discuss with her.

'There's a crisis coming up, isn't there?' she asked him in the middle of the night when she got up and found him helping himself to a glass of milk from the refrigerator.

'Let's just say at the moment I'm not having the time of my life.'

'You'll solve it. You have before.'

'Other people are involved. Good people.'

'Then I'm not going to say try and get some sleep, because I know you won't. Let's sit up and play Scrabble.'

'You always beat me,' he grumbled.

She wrapped an arm around his neck. 'Tonight I'll let you win . . .'

Wednesday afternoon the flight from Zürich was delayed by bad weather. Outwardly composed, Haller was worried stiff. He did something he had never done before: he went into Riverton's office and asked if they could chat to pass the time. The millionaire waved a hand to a chair and began talking about his experiences in the Second World War. He told the American a story about how he had once sat up thirty-six hours waiting for news of a girl who had been parachuted into France and hadn't sent the signal reporting her safe arrival.

'I nearly went mad with the waiting,' Riverton went on quietly, not looking at Haller, 'but the waiting is always the worst in this business. I was fond of this particular girl – she had a lot of guts and a great sense of humour. She was a little like the girl who comes here each month . . .'

Haller was astonished. Without a word being

exchanged the Canadian seemed to have read his thoughts, and Haller also had grown fond of Elsa Lang. 'What happened to the girl you are talking about?' he asked.

'After thirty-six hours the signal arrived – she was safe. Incidentally, that girl of yours came in here one day and we had a long talk. Nothing about her work, of course,' he added quickly. 'Did you know that just before she came over here to join you she was on the verge of getting married?'

'No.' Haller had not even realized Elsa had ever talked to Riverton. Thinking about it, he wasn't entirely surprised: Riverton was one of those rare men people confided in; it was something indefinable in his personality.

'She had a raw deal,' Riverton went on. 'She was very much in love with this film production manager. I gather he was older than her – but she's the sort of girl who'd be attracted to older men. Everything was fixed – wedding date, where they would spend their honeymoon. Then she arrived at his flat early one evening. The fool hadn't locked the door and the bell was on the blink. She walked in and found him in bed with her best friend. That's why she accepted whatever job you gave her – to get the experience out of her mind.'

'And I never knew . . .'

'Would you have taken her on if you had? She's clever – she kept it quiet.' Riverton turned to stare hard at the American. 'And if you ever let her know

I've told you I'll kill you with my bare hands. But bear it in mind if your operation gets tough.' He looked up as Elsa Lang came into the room, followed by Wargrave.

'Sorry to burst in on you,' Elsa said quickly, 'but the girl outside said you were alone and we knew Julian would be worried . . .' She stopped as Riverton answered his intercom. 'It's all right, Miss Russell, I was expecting these people.'

Haller was already leading the way through the side door into the concealed suite of offices. Closing the door, he swung around. 'Ed never phoned in your arrival from the airport.'

'There's some kind of foul-up with the telephone system,' Wargrave explained as he took the thirteenth cassette from Elsa and started inserting it into the tape recorder. 'And our flight was badly delayed – in Europe only Milan, Zürich, London, and Schiphol airports are still open. The weather is unbelievable. A blizzard is raging over most of the continent. I hope to hell it's quietened down in time for our February trip.'

Haller began organizing the coffee percolator for Elsa, who had taken off her fur cap and dark wig. There were flecks of snow on her raincoat even though she had dashed from the car into the Baton Rouge Building. The American poured a large scotch for Wargrave and placed the glass beside the tape recorder.

'Any interference this time at Basel?' he asked quietly.

81

'Not a quiver,' Elsa replied as she sank into an armchair. 'The whole operation ran as smooth as silk.' She lit a cigarette while Haller poured coffee. 'Thanks, Julian, I could drink it by the gallon – it is cold, cold out there. We saw the Saint Lawrence frozen solid as we came in.' She took a gulp of the coffee. 'That's much better. I wonder what Angelo has to tell us this time...' She stopped talking as the familiar, hoarse voice began speaking. Before Angelo had spoken for a minute she froze despite the warmth of the room.

'My usefulness here has come to a sudden end ... I must ask you to make immediate arrangements to airlift me out of Romania this coming Saturday, January 8, without fail ... The emergency is total...'

Wargrave stopped the recording and stared at Haller, who calmly lit a fresh cigarette; it was an instinctive reaction to take the tension out of the situation. Elsa had lost all her colour; Wargrave stood by the recorder with both hands splayed on his hips, his cheekbones very marked, his eyes half closed as his mind raced. 'Bruno is available, I assume,' he said quietly.

'Bruno is not available,' Haller told him, referring to President Moynihan by his code name. 'He flew suddenly to Peking today. He won't be back for a week, so we're on our own.'

'So it's up to the Turtle,' Elsa said with a forced smile. The Turtle was the nickname she had invented for Julian Haller because he wasn't afraid to stick his neck out, to take major decisions without referring them back to the White House.

'Looks like it,' the Turtle agreed. 'As one of our revered past Presidents once said, the buck stops here.' He looked up at Wargrave. 'Set the machine again – let's hear the worst.'

Angelo continued reporting: evidence had accumulated over the months that an informer existed at a high level; finally the source of the leak had been narrowed down to someone inside the Soviet Politburo. A triad of three men – Leonid Sedov himself, Marshal Prachko, and General Marenkov – had been entrusted with the tracking down of the informer. And just as had happened with the first cassette received a year earlier, Angelo again laid down precise instructions as to how he should be rescued.

'... an airstrip just west of Bucharest ... map reference ... landing time for rescue aircraft 11.30 a.m. local Romanian time, repeat local Romanian time ... co-operation of certain Romanian personnel assured ... expert pilot required ... confirm agreement this arrangement by playing Dave Brubeck's *Take Five* Voice of America programme 1700 hours Moscow time Thursday, January 6, repeat Thursday, January 6 ... Any delay will be quite fatal ...'

The recording ended with a repetition of the warning that any delay would be fatal. Elsa reached over and took a large swallow from Wargrave's untouched glass of scotch. The colour came back into her face as she spoke slowly, determined to keep her voice steady.

'Today is Wednesday. He asks to be airlifted out Saturday. It's impossible.'

'It presents difficulties,' Haller agreed.

'Difficulties?' Elsa almost choked.

Wargrave had said nothing as he walked across to the wall behind Haller's desk where a large-scale map of Europe hung. Using the ruler he had taken from the Turtle's desk, he began making measurements, checking distances. One distance he checked carefully was the flight route from Milan to Bucharest; then, using a flexible rule, he double-checked the same distance on a large globe in the corner. Tapping the rule against his teeth, he hummed a little tune while he made calculations on a scratch pad, then looked up at Haller. 'I need an up-to-date European rail time-table – and all the airline timetables.'

'Will do.'

Haller disappeared into a room beyond that Elsa and Wargrave had never entered. Inside sat a Canadian ex-seagoing radio operator Riverton had found for Haller, a man whom the millionaire knew as utterly trustworthy and who had once worked for Canadian intelligence. On one table rested a transmitter, on another the coding machine Haller personally operated. As an added security precaution the Canadian had never been permitted to see Wargrave or Elsa. In the room Haller had just left Elsa was arguing with the Englishman.

'Wednesday today, Saturday he expects to be taken out – three days and we're here in North America. You'll never manage it.'

'In seven days the Israelis planned and executed the Entebbe operation. We have co-operation at the Bucharest end – so in three days it should be possible.' He gave his lop-sided grin. 'It damn well has to be possible.'

He spent the next few minutes studying the time-tables Haller had brought back, making more notes on his scratch pad. Haller watched him in silence, smoking a fresh cigarette and drinking a glass of milk. The Englishman stretched his aching shoulders and looked at the American. 'It will be a close-run thing, as one of our more celebrated generals once said, but I can do it. At the moment the only airports in Europe still open are London, Schiphol near Amsterdam, Zürich and Milan. According to the met people, Milan may close down soon and there's a question mark over Zürich, so we may have to bring Angelo out by train—'

'By train!' Haller was appalled. 'For God's sake, we have to fly him out here direct to the States. If it is to be done, it is to be done quickly or not at all,' he paraphrased Shakespeare.

Wargrave shook his head. 'You've never been to Europe bar one brief trip to London, have you, Julian? Like so many Americans you think of movement only in terms of by car or by flying. In Europe they have the finest train system in the world, expresses that move at eighty miles an hour. The Atlantic Express may be the answer.'

'I don't like it,' Haller snapped.

'You don't have to – you may just have to accept it if Milan and Zürich close down at the wrong moment.'

'And if they do?' Haller demanded belligerently. 'What's with this Atlantic Express?'

'The position that may face us is quite simple,' Wargrave explained. 'The blizzards raging over Europe have bypassed one country only – Holland. So we can count on Schiphol Airport staying open. The Atlantic Express leaves Milan late in the afternoon for its ultimate destination – Amsterdam. It passes through Zürich, so if Milan is closed to flying and Zürich stays open we can fly out Angelo from there.'

'And supposing Zürich is closed down?'

'Then it's the long haul aboard the express all the way to Amsterdam.' Exasperation began to show in Wargrave's voice. 'For Christ's sake, I can get total co-operation from every security service in each country the express passes through. Face it, Julian, that train may be the only way to get him out fast. And we'll need aircraft standing by at both Zürich and Schiphol to fly to the States. Any more damned roadblocks you want to put in my way?'

Haller's quick mind had digested the information Wargrave had provided and, characteristically, he immediately changed tack.

'Cool it, Harry. Point taken. I don't know how I'm

going to do it in the time, but I'll have a Boeing standing by at Schiphol, another one at Zürich.'

Wargrave's expression was grim as he made his next demand. 'I'll want full control of the whole operation,' he warned.

'On a day-to-day basis I'm willing to concede—'

'*Full* control,' Wargrave repeated. 'Europe is my backyard.'

'OK,' the American agreed. He tapped a file on his desk. 'And I know why it's Bucharest. On Saturday a Soviet delegation is visiting Romania to try and patch up differences between the two countries. The make-up of the delegation is interesting . . .' He drank more milk slowly.

'Oh, come on,' Elsa protested, 'don't keep us in suspense. Who is in the delegation?'

'The report reached me this morning. Led by Anatoli Zarubin; another delegation member is Pavel Suslov, the Soviet party theoretician. Saint Marx himself.'

'Surprise, surprise,' Elsa commented. She glanced at Wargrave. 'How the hell do we get Angelo from Bucharest to Milan?'

'By airlift,' the Englishman explained. 'First we borrow a Hawker-Siddeley 125 jet from a wealthy Italian playboy I know – oddly enough he's a violent anti-Communist. It's about eight hundred miles to Bucharest from Milan, another eight hundred back again. The HS 125 has a 2,600-mile range – which leaves plenty of fuel to spare.'

Haller was twisted around in his chair, staring at the wall map of Europe. 'Why not fly Angelo direct to Zürich?'

'Because it would take me too close to the Hungarian border – the Russians might send up interceptors to shoot us down. Also, the weather being what it is, I can't risk crossing the Swiss Alps.'

The American was still staring at the map. 'If Zürich Airport does close down, it's going to be a damned long train haul clear across Europe.'

Wargrave nodded and looked grim as he glanced at Elsa. 'It will be a nightmare – and literally, because the express will travel through the night. I suppose you both realize that once Angelo is out of the Balkans General Marenkov will mobilize the entire KGB–GRU underground apparatus to kill him before we can fly him out to the States? It will be like threading our way through a minefield. But I still say it can be done. Damn it, it has to be done.'

Haller had not overlooked Wargrave's glance at Elsa. 'It won't be necessary for Elsa to come on this trip,' he said firmly.

'Like hell it won't,' Elsa replied quietly. 'I was in at the beginning – I'm going to be in at the end.'

'It's up to her,' Wargrave suggested mildly. 'But she could come in very handy.'

'I forbid it,' Haller snapped.

'I thought I had full control,' Wargrave remarked. 'And this is no time to break up the team. Incidentally, we have to fly straight back to Europe tonight.' This time he didn't glance at Elsa, who kept her expression blank; she was still feeling the effects of jet lag from their flight across the Atlantic a few hours earlier. 'There's an Air Canada flight this evening that gets us into Schiphol tomorrow afternoon,' Wargrave went on. 'From there we fly on to Zürich and then on to Milan, where we touch down tomorrow, Thursday evening.'

'Isn't that rushing it a bit?' Haller inquired.

'It gives me Friday in Milan to organize final arrangements. And I can do that better from Europe than I can from here. Saturday morning I fly the jet to Bucharest to pick Angelo up from the airstrip.'

'You're flying the jet yourself?'

'I've flown that very machine several times before on trips with my playboy contact.'

'I hear the Italian girls are quite something,' Elsa murmured.

'And he has the pick of the bunch,' Wargrave assured her. He tore the used sheets off his scratch pad and looked at Haller. 'Now, we have to use every minute before we catch that evening flight to Schiphol. I've got a whole series of cables that have to be encoded and sent to various European security chiefs alerting them – Scholten in The Hague, Franz Wander of the German BND, Colonel Springer in Zürich, and Colonel Molinari of SIFAR in Milan.'

'Alerting them?' the American queried.

'That I may need their help – just that. Nothing about Angelo, of course. Not yet, anyway. They may have to know after I've got him out of Romania . . .' He was writing on the pad as he spoke. 'This could develop into something pretty murderous if we have to bring Angelo all the way by train to Schiphol. And don't forget to tell the Voice of America to play that record *Take Five* to warn Angelo we're coming for him.'

'As if I would.' Haller leaned back in his chair, looked at the ceiling, and said something that stopped Wargrave scribbling his signals. 'There's one more little detail I omitted to mention. A third member of the Soviet Politburo is accompanying that delegation to Bucharest . . .'

'That's right, save the best bit till last,' Elsa joked.

'General Sergei Marenkov, head of the KGB.'

Part Two

Escape Route

Chapter Six

Schiphol, Zürich, Milan

Leaving Montreal aboard Air Canada Flight 866, which departed at 9.35 p.m. on Wednesday, January 5, Wargrave, Haller, and Elsa crossed the Atlantic overnight. At London Airport they changed to their connecting KLM Flight 128, which took them on to Schiphol outside Amsterdam. For Elsa – as for Wargrave – it was the second time she had crossed the ocean in twenty-four hours and her mind was dizzy with fatigue.

'I don't think my internal clock will ever tell the right time again,' she remarked to Julian Haller, who sat alongside her as they approached the Dutch coast.

'You should have got some sleep.'

'Very funny, Turtle,' she replied acidly, 'I damn near woke you up to share my misery. You slept like a dog.'

'Always do,' Haller replied complacently.

Elsa peered out of the window to look down on Holland as the plane lost height. The flat landscape was barely streaked with snow, as though some giant had scrawled chalk marks across the fields. But there was a fierce wind coming in off the North Sea that was hurling giant waves against the dikes. As she looked down she saw drifts like white smoke, which were wave spume caught up in the wind. Two rows behind them, Harry Wargrave occupied a corridor seat where he could keep an eye on his companions. Then the warning lights came on, seat belts were fastened, and the plane was landing.

General Max Scholten, chief of Dutch counter-espionage, was waiting for Wargrave in the security office at the airport and the two men met alone. 'Big trouble?' the Dutchman inquired as he warmly shook Wargrave's hand.

'In a word, yes. How are things here?'

'The situation could become explosive – literally,' the counter-espionage chief replied as he lit a cigar.

General Scholten, one of Wargrave's closest friends, was a small, sixty-year-old man who looked ten years younger. Plump-figured, with a comfortable paunch, he had a cherubic, pink-complexioned face, twinkling blue eyes, and the cheerful smile of a contented man. His cherubic appearance had been the downfall of more than one spy he had amiably interrogated until he had caught his target in a contradiction. His appearance also concealed the fact that he was the most ruthless anti-Communist security chief in Europe. 'You do not converse with a viper,' he had once told Wargrave in his impeccable English. 'You creep up behind it and chop its head off with an axe.'

Wargrave glanced around the bare room, which held only a table and two hard-backed chairs. The interrogation room, he guessed. 'What explosive situation?' he asked.

'I have a whisper – very reliable – that the Geiger Group is about to cross into Holland. I have already alerted the Venlo Team.' He puffed at his cigar. 'The trouble is it is only too easy to cross the border into Holland . . .'

'They're bad news,' Wargrave commented.

The Geiger Group of terrorists had created havoc in West Germany during the past year. Banks had been robbed, hostages taken, a leading German politician kidnapped; they had even attempted to blow up a major power station. And all in the name of the movement of World Freedom and Revolution, whatever that might mean. Wargrave doubted whether the terrorists even knew themselves.

'I think they are financed by the KGB,' Scholten remarked quietly. 'By remote control, of course. The problem is to prove it. That would plaster mud all over Comrade Sedov's face.'

'Why are they coming here?'

'The Germans have made things too hot for them – so they move on to what they hope will be a softer target. I would dearly love to get them in the sun-sights of the Venlo Team.' Scholten was referring to the special team of snipers he had personally organized for just such an eventuality. 'But you haven't come here to listen to my problems. What are yours?'

'We are over here to bring out a key anti-Communist agent,' Wargrave said carefully. 'We may bring him aboard the Atlantic Express. I can tell you more later with coded signals – we'll use the Scarab system.'

'A big fish?' Scholten asked casually. 'Or do I talk too much at this stage?'

'A big fish – one that could draw a lot of KGB fire because of the information he is carrying.'

Scholten's blue eyes gleamed. 'If you bring out the Soviet underground apparatus in an attempt to assassinate him, that could give us a unique chance to chop off the viper's head.'

'As long as mine doesn't get chopped off in the process, you bloodthirsty old bastard,' Wargrave said amiably. 'And the plane—'

'Your American friends' Boeing 707 landed ten minutes ago – just ahead of your own flight. It is now at a remote part of the airport under heavy guard. And now, since your Swissair flight for Zürich does not depart until 1640, perhaps we could have a drink with your friends – if it is not breaking security. I would like to meet that attractive girl . . .'

Wargrave was amused. He had left the aircraft alone and Haller and Elsa were now waiting in the transfer lounge. Scholten's eyes twinkled. 'I saw her glance back at you in a certain way when you were coming down the aircraft steps. She likes you very much.'

'Let's go and have that drink – with my friends,' replied Wargrave.

*

In the transfer lounge Haller had just received a message handed to him by an armed courier from the American Embassy in The Hague. Before leaving Montreal, Haller – with no way of communicating in code with President Moynihan – had taken the desperate expedient of phoning a trusted friend in the American Embassy at Ottawa.

He had asked for a simple message to be sent to Moynihan – at that moment flying over the Pacific aboard Air Force One on his way to Peking. The message had read: *Our friend is leaving for fresh woods and pastures new*. It had been signed *Turtle*, the nickname the President knew Elsa Lang had given Haller.

The message had been handed to Moynihan during his first meeting with the Chairman of the People's Republic of China. Towering over the short, tough man who controlled the destinies of over eight hundred million people, the President had instantly understood the message – that it meant Sparta was on its way to bring out Angelo and transport him to the United States.

The news could hardly have arrived at a more opportune moment. Scheduled to spend ten days in China, Moynihan immediately grasped how much the arrival in Washington of Anatoli Zarubin, a senior member of the Soviet Politburo, would impress the hard-headed Chairman – and in the fact that he would be able to reveal that for over a year he had benefited from a direct pipeline into the Kremlin.

Waiting until he was back at the American

Embassy, changing for the great banquet to be held that evening in his honour, Moynihan drafted a short reply to The Hague embassy, ordering the ambassador to send it by courier to meet the flight Haller had told him he was taking to Holland. And this was the message Haller was reading while Wargrave was talking with General Scholten.

Timing perfect. But utmost speed essential. Repeat essential. Bruno. Haller's reaction was relief mingled with grimness. The enormous stakes at issue were escalating hourly.

General Scholten's statement that the Geiger Group was about to enter Holland was not entirely accurate. At the moment the Dutchman was talking to Harry Wargrave at Schiphol, Rolf Geiger, the terrorist chief, had already established his headquarters in Amsterdam.

It is still not generally known by the public that most terrorist organizations operating in the West are financed – and often armed – by the Soviet KGB or GRU, however indirect the links may be. And contact was often maintained through East Berlin.

For Soviet Russia the policy paid high dividends. By creating ceaseless ferment in the West it allowed Soviet propaganda to contrast conditions in the West with the 'peace' inside Russia, a 'peace' maintained by the tight police state control exercised by the vast KGB apparatus. The Geiger Group of terrorists that had carried out so many violent incidents inside the German Federal Republic was a prime example of this policy.

Rolf Geiger posed as a German anarchist, but his real name was Dikran Kikoyan, his real nationality Armenian. Born at Yerevan, midway between Lake Sevan and the Turkish border, he was a dedicated Soviet agent who manipulated his group of terrorists so skilfully that they had not the least inkling they were controlled by the Soviet GRU. And Kikoyan was hardly the public's idea of a terrorist chief.

A small, dapper man in his early fifties, he was lean-faced, with a long nose and a neat dark moustache that matched his carefully trimmed hair. In London he would have been known as a snappy dresser and he was quite a ladies' man with his courtly manner and capacity for making girls laugh. At this moment he was standing by the third-floor window of an old house in Amsterdam overlooking a canal while he recalled his interview with Colonel Igor Sharpinsky in East Berlin three weeks earlier.

'It is no longer safe for you to continue operations in the German Federal Republic,' the soft-spoken KGB chief had explained. 'This alone confirms my decision that you should move on to Holland.' He pushed across the table where the two men sat a copy of the West German newspaper *Die Welt*.

'You have to expect casualties,' Kikoyan replied almost insolently as he crossed his carefully pressed trouser legs and stared out of the window of the second-floor office of KGB headquarters in East Berlin. God, what a monstrosity the place was, he thought as he gazed at the concrete blockhouses that served as apartment buildings.

'The newspaper,' Sharpinsky repeated, his pale eyes gazing blankly from behind his rimless glasses, eyes that terrified most of his subordinates. Kikoyan – Rolf Geiger – was not in the least intimidated by Sharpinsky, whom he disliked intensely. As he had once remarked to his assistant, Erika Kern, 'The ghoul makes a vocation of himself, puffed up like a pouter pigeon with his own power.' He lit a cigarette as he glanced at *Die Welt*.

The newspaper's headline story was about the Geiger Group's failed attempt to rob a bank in Hamburg. There was a large picture of one of the dead terrorists clad in his sinister 'uniform' – his head covered with a woollen ski mask with slits for the eyes, his body clothed in a windcheater and ski pants – all in black. Geiger himself had chosen the uniform as the group's trademark. 'The clothes alone create an impression of terror,' he had once explained.

'So we move into Holland,' Geiger remarked, wiping a speck of cigarette ash from the sleeve of his expensive business suit. 'That can be accomplished overnight – I have already foreseen you would decide this and have the necessary contacts in Amsterdam.' He tapped his gold-topped cane against a leg of Sharpinsky's desk, which further irritated the Russian. 'You have the diamonds I asked you to provide?' He checked his Patek watch. 'The Intourist bus will be leaving soon for Checkpoint Charlie, so we'd better get on with it.'

'One thing at a time.' Sharpinsky controlled his cold fury with an effort. He would have liked to have disciplined this Armenian dandy severely, but Geiger had been too successful, was too highly regarded by Marshal Gregori Prachko himself. Geiger proceeded to infuriate him even further by taking the words out of his mouth.

'As in the Federal Republic, we have a double task. One,' he tapped his cane hard against the desk leg – 'to create havoc and terror with a series of kidnappings of prominent Dutch figures, bank robberies, explosions in The Hague and Amsterdam?'

'Correct,' Sharpinsky replied in a distant tone.

'Two, we must reconnoitre strategic objectives ready for sabotage when the Red Army moves. The Maas bridge that carries the main rail link between Belgium and Holland, the dikes which hold back the sea, the Phillips works at Eindhoven...' Geiger checked his watch again. 'Do I really have to go on? And where are the diamonds?'

Tight-lipped, Sharpinsky opened a drawer, took out a small black cloth bag, and spilled a small fortune in diamonds on the desk. 'Thank you,' Geiger said with exaggerated politeness. Unscrewing the top of his cane, he pulled out a thin spool of rolled cardboard from the hollow cane; then he extracted several pieces of silk from a pocket, wrapped the diamonds, inserted them inside the cane, and pushed back the cardboard spool before replacing the top of the cane.

'Rather amusing,' he remarked. 'We use the products of the capitalist system to help destroy it.' He did not need Sharpinsky to tell him that the diamonds had been smuggled by a devious route from South Africa via Angola to Moscow.

'Which route are you using to reach Amsterdam?' the Russian asked, still staring at the dapper little man facing him. Geiger's quick dark eyes had hardly met his once since the interview had started, as though to emphasize his contempt for Sharpinsky's attempt to intimidate him.

'From West Berlin I fly to Frankfurt,' he replied easily. 'From Frankfurt another flight to Paris – then the Trans-European Express direct to Amsterdam. Customs checks on that train are nonexistent—'

'I do know that.' Sharpinsky stood up to indicate the interview was ended, but Geiger was already on his feet, slipping on his Savile Row overcoat. For the first time Geiger stared hard at the Russian, smoothing his moustache with one manicured finger before he spoke. 'And I would prefer it if you did not summon me to East Berlin again for a long time. I know you have arranged for the Intourist guides to keep the other tourists from West Berlin in the department store until I rejoin them inconspicuously – but the risk is, in my opinion, unnecessary.'

Three weeks later in Amsterdam, Geiger recalled his cold conversation with the KGB deputy chief as he stood by the window gazing across the canal to a line of warehouses opposite, where chains with hooks hung five storeys up just above double doors. Once they had been used to haul cargo up inside the warehouses. He swung around quickly as a girl came into the almost dark room.

Erika Kern, an attractive, dark-haired girl with a full figure, was thirty-two and a native of East Germany. Cold-faced – which added to her attractiveness – she was the only other member of the terrorist group who knew it was controlled by the GRU. The rest – 'peasants,' as Geiger sometimes referred to them – had the idea they were fighting for the world liberation of oppressed peoples – which did not include citizens of Russia.

'The diamonds are sold?' she inquired.

'So easily – this is Amsterdam.' Geiger pointed to an executive's case on a table, and when she opened it the case was filled with neatly stacked Dutch guilder banknotes – untraceable funds to finance Geiger's activities.

'No more interference from Sharpinsky, then,' Erika remarked. Geiger nodded, little knowing how wrong he was – and with no suspicion of the huge emergency already building up.

The great blizzard continued to rage over Europe. On television viewers watched dramatic pictures of the river Elbe in Germany frozen from bank to bank, watched the snow ploughs fighting a losing battle in Austria, saw the Swiss skating on Lake Zürich for only the third time this century. And Swissair Flight 793 from Schiphol to Zürich was pure hell. Once over the German border, the DC–9 flew into ceaseless turbulence along with heavy snow. Elsa stopped looking out of the window and Haller stopped reading his novel. Behind them again, Wargrave sat with his hands clasped in his lap as he checked his watch frequently. He had a vital call to make as soon as the plane touched down at Zürich.

Leaving the plane at the airport, he was met by a police official who offered to escort him to Springer, who knew he was coming in on this flight. 'Give me a minute,' Wargrave said, 'I just want to call my fiancée.'

Dialling the Andermatt number, he had to wait only a few seconds before the call was answered; he had cabled Andermatt before he had left Montreal. He spoke very quickly, asked a few questions, then gave brief instructions. By his watch the call had lasted less than three minutes. Then he let the police-man take him to Springer.

He gave the Swiss colonel exactly the same infor-mation he had given Scholten at Schiphol, but he added something extra. 'I have someone in Andermatt and they may be getting somewhere. Too early to say exactly where yet.'

'I am profoundly grateful.'

'There is something else. In case of emergency I

have given them your open number – without telling them who they will be speaking to. They will ask for a Mr Gehring and say Leros is calling. If that happens, can you arrange for them to be put through immediately to yourself – or to Brigadier Traber, if you're not there? I'd like any message Leros passes to you – however cryptic – to be passed on to me urgently. By then you'll know how to communicate with me.'

'Leros calling Mr Gehring,' Springer repeated. 'Our switchboard operator will be informed it is a top-priority call if it comes through. And now?'

'I'm catching the 1925 Swissair flight to Milan. What's going to happen will happen in the next forty-eight hours.' Wargrave looked out of the window, where snow was falling heavily. 'Has the Boeing from the States arrived yet?'

'It is due within two hours – soon after your flight for Milan departs. We shall take great care of it,' he promised. He paused as he lit a cigarette. 'This agent you are escorting out of Europe – he is of very great importance, may I ask?'

'Possibly the most important since the war.' Wargrave decided to be a little more frank with Springer than he had been with Scholten; the Swiss security chief was going to feel the heat earlier than the Dutchman – and if Zürich Airport stayed open they would never even move into Holland. 'My plan is to bring him here aboard the Atlantic Express Saturday night – the day after tomorrow – because by then we predict that the Milan Airport will be closed.'

'As quickly as that? Then it might be wise if I issued a discreet alert?'

'It might be wise,' the Englishman agreed. 'We shall set up our own communications unit on the express to keep in constant touch with you – Colonel Molinari in Milan is giving me his full co-operation. And I'm just wondering whether it might be a good idea if you arranged something rather special for me when the express reaches Chiasso.' He outlined the plan and Springer immediately agreed.

'Be careful, be lucky,' the Swiss colonel instructed as he took his leave of the Englishman.

The moment he was alone Springer used his scrambler phone to call his chief, Brigadier Traber, in Zürich. He reported briefly what he had been told, then added a comment. 'It could be this is the opportunity we have been waiting for – to flush out the main Communist sabotage teams the Soviets are holding in reserve for an emergency. Had you better consult with Bern?'

Without realizing it, Springer was adopting an almost identical attitude to that of Scholten in Holland. There was a pause on the phone before Traber replied; when he did he startled his deputy. 'I don't think I need bother Bern yet. Saturday you said? That means over the weekend when most ministers will be away from their desks and not too easy to contact. We may handle this on our own, Leon . . .'

The revolt of the European security chiefs against

their more cautious government ministers was
beginning.

Five minutes after Wargrave had made his brief phone
call from Zürich Airport to the Swiss ski resort, Robert
Frey left the Hotel Storchen in Andermatt and drove
his Volkswagen van westward out of the town to the
farmhouse that was his home several kilometres along
the road toward Gletsch. Even with chains on his
wheels he drove carefully; it was night and the roads
were like skating rinks. Turning off the road, he pulled
up in front of the steep-roofed building and went
inside.

Frey, a huge man with a weather-beaten face, a
world-famous mountaineer and the dominant citizen
in Andermatt, was met inside the polished, wood-
block hall by his assistant, Emil Platow, a short, wiry
Swiss who seemed even smaller as Frey loomed over
him. 'Anything to report?' Frey inquired.

'News has just come in from Athens – about your
girl friend, Anna Markos.'

'So?'

'Nothing tangible. She lives in an expensive apartment. It is rumoured the rent is paid for by a Greek
cabinet minister . . .'

'So, she is his mistress. Now give me the meat.'

'That's all,' Platow replied with some embarrassment. 'And the fact that two days ago she visited the

Rhône Glacier area with another tourist, René Marchais – the French skier who is so good on the slopes—'

'Marchais talks a lot when he drinks,' Frey remarked. 'I was listening to him in the bar at the Storchen the other night.' He frowned and listened carefully as the sound of a distant rumble came from somewhere outside, a rumble of falling rock. About five kilometres distant, he estimated. The whole area was fragile with potential avalanche slides.

'So,' he concluded sarcastically, 'we have learned more about Anna Markos here in Andermatt than you have gleaned from Athens. Great work, Emil, great work . . .' He strode off into his study to pour himself a stiff drink.

What Emil Platow had failed to discover was that five days earlier, in the morning, Anna Markos, a strikingly handsome and well-built Greek woman, had driven with René Marchais in her hired Renault to Gletsch at the foot of the Rhône Glacier. It was only nine o'clock when Anna pulled up outside the tiny railway station at Gletsch as she saw a police patrol car approaching from the other direction.

'Nice to have company – even if only the police,' she remarked, glancing around the desolate wasteland of snow. Sunlight was reflecting off the mighty glacier to the north, a greenish reflection from what looked like a tidal wave of ice about to plunge down into the valley below.

Réne Marchais, the slim, boyish Frenchman who

had picked up Anna at the Hotel Storchen, grinned. 'I was hoping the only company I would enjoy today would be yours . . .' So far he had failed in his efforts to coax her inside his bedroom but he was confident it was only a matter of patience and time. The approaching police car pulled up and the driver got out to speak to them; he glanced at the pair of skis in the back of the Renault.

'It could be dangerous skiing, sir,' he warned. 'The snow is unstable, to say the least.'

'This is René Marchais,' Anna interjected with a warm smile. 'He is well known at Chamonix as one of their stars.' She looked up at the mass of ice to the north. 'Isn't it up there where they discovered a dead man in one of the ice tunnels?'

The Swiss studied her. Normally it was not a subject he would have discussed, but his wife was away visiting relatives in Lausanne and he welcomed the chance to chat with such an attractive woman. He, too, looked up at the silent glacier.

'Yes, it is a mystery we have yet to unravel – how he came to be there.' He shrugged. 'Probably we shall never know what happened . . .'

'Was there no one about at the time? He died alone – in this wilderness?' Anna chattered on.

'Only Robert Frey's helicopter,' the policeman replied. 'He had landed near here to check the snow-fall – it is one of his duties to keep an eye on the avalanche situation.'

'And he saw nothing?'

'No, that is what increases the mystery – from the ground he might have seen nothing, but checking from the air he was bound to have seen anyone else in the area. It was entirely deserted at the time.'

Anna continued staring at the remote glacier. 'I always love a mystery – you can start imagining what might have happened . . .' She caught the change in the Swiss's expression. 'I'm sorry – it must have been rather horrible.'

'I would not advise you to drive any farther,' the policeman warned them. He looked again at the skis. 'Nor would I advise anyone to ski – even if they do come from Chamonix,' he added tartly.

Anna turned the Renault and followed the police car back to Andermatt as Marchais grumbled in his boyish way. 'They are so cautious, these Swiss. I shall certainly ski from Andermatt, whatever they say. I find that story of the body in the ice tunnel fascinating.'

'I'm not sure they liked us talking about it,' Anna replied.

'It would make a good topic in the evening over a drink. Who was the mysterious man? What was he doing inside the glacier? Was it an accident or was he murdered?'

'Your imagination is running away with you,' Anna told him in her excellent French. 'And unless you promise to drop the subject I will not join you for that drink this evening.'

'My lips are sealed,' Marchais promised with exaggerated solemnity.

Two days later René Marchais was killed while skiing on the slopes above Andermatt. The police were not satisfied with the results of their investigation; they began treating it as a case of homicide.

'Maybe we should have gone by train,' Elsa said brightly.

Her double scotch had jumped off the fold-out tray as the aircraft bucked and then dropped over the Swiss Alps. The scotch spilled all over the sleeve of the Turtle, who sat alongside her. Taking out a handkerchief, she began to sponge the sodden sleeve. 'My, my, Mr Haller, you smell like a distillery. And all these months I thought you were teetotal.'

'You wouldn't like just to pour the next one over me instead of down your throat?' Haller growled.

Behind them Harry Wargrave occupied his normal seat two rows back, the gangway seat where he could watch his two companions and move fast in an emergency. As the turbulence increased, he congratulated himself on his decision not to cross the Alps, not to fly direct from Bucharest to Zürich. The HS 125 executive jet waiting for him in Milan was twin-engined, an excellent plane – but not one to cross the Alps in a raging blizzard.

Like Elsa, Wargrave had now made two flights

across the Atlantic in twenty-four hours and the double jet lag was hitting him like a hammer. Haggard-faced, his cheekbones showing sharp against the skin, he thanked God he would get two nights' sleep in Milan – Thursday and Friday – before his hazardous Saturday flight to Bucharest. And again, like Elsa, he had not slept a wink on the flight from Montreal to Schiphol.

His brain had been racing over the problems ahead, over the multitude of details to be organized. At this stage it was so damned tricky – people like Springer and Molinari had to be told enough to prepare for what was to come without revealing the big secret: that it was a senior member of the Soviet Politburo they were bringing out. As the plane lost height for the approach run into Milan he watched Julian and Elsa talking, their heads close together.

'If Milan Airport stays open we may be able to fly back to Zürich,' Haller murmured.

'That would solve a lot of problems,' Elsa agreed lightly. 'Fingers crossed, hope and pray . . .'

As she was speaking, the aircraft dropped without warning into an air pocket and her stomach flipped again. Outside the window nothing could be seen through the pall of falling snow and Elsa was wondering if they were going to have to land blind, to go through the hazardous process whereby the pilot was talked down with the aid of radar. Christ, I hope not, she thought as the warning lights came on and she leaned over to fasten Haller's seat belt with her deft fingers.

'Someone could lose a little weight,' she teased him as she snapped the belt over the hint of a paunch. Then she fastened her own belt and stubbed out her cigarette with steady fingers. The truth was Elsa Lang was scared stiff of flying, a fear she had concealed from everyone – even from Harry Wargrave, who thought he knew Elsa better than anyone.

The Swiss plane landed at Milan Airport at 8.05 p.m. It was still Thursday, January 6. In less than thirty-six hours Wargrave was due to take off in the Hawker-Siddeley 125 executive jet on his flight to Bucharest to pick up Angelo. At the airport Haller was impressed by Colonel Molinari's organization; discreetly bypassing all customs and immigration formalities, they were hustled inside the back of a large plain van without windows. The interior of the vehicle belied its plain exterior.

Fitted with comfortable, leather-armed seats, well heated against the bitter night chill outside, they relaxed as the van left the airport by the cargo entrance. In the front seat Molinari sat behind a small table using a radio telephone into which he spoke rapidly in Italian. Haller had no idea what he was saying but Wargrave and Elsa, who spoke fluent Italian, gathered he was reporting their imminent arrival to their destination.

'This vehicle is quite something,' Haller remarked as the Italian completed his call and swung around to face them.

'It is a command truck,' Molinari replied in English, 'mainly used in antiterrorist operations. I am taking you to a special base we rarely use that will be at your entire disposal.'

'How far from the station – Milano Centrale?' Wargrave asked.

'Two kilometres – your signal specified somewhere close.'

Colonel Luigi Molinari, the SIFAR chief, was a typical north Italian in appearance; born forty-three years earlier at Piacenza, he was short, stockily built, with a hard, round-shaped head and a calm, wary manner. Haller was impressed by him also; he exuded an air of competence and toughness. His next remark and action confirmed the impression. 'You specified weapons,' he told Wargrave. Opening a large case on the floor, he lifted out a .38 Smith and Wesson special and looked around. Both Haller and Elsa held out their hands at the same time.

'Ladies first . . .'

Molinari handed the gun and a package of ammunition to Elsa. Stooping again, he brought out a Colt .45 with another package and gave it to Haller. To Wargrave he gave two Sten guns with spare magazines, and Haller frowned. 'Pretty conspicuous, difficult to conceal, hardly the latest in armament,' he commented.

'Three criticisms in less than thirty seconds,' Wargrave replied. 'That's pretty good.' Taking an empty holdall from his case, he stowed the weapons inside. 'But these are for my flight to nowhere.' He phrased the reply carefully – Molinari had not been given the slightest clue as to the destination of the HS jet. 'As to its history, I have never known the Sten to jam.'

'I have alternatives,' Molinari remarked. 'Take your pick.' Haller left his seat, watching his balance as the truck swayed around a corner, slapping his hand against the wall. 'It's armoured, isn't it – the truck?' he queried, and Molinari nodded. Inside the case was a minor arsenal: German Lugers, Walthers, Belgian Browning automatics, several Colt .45s, two Webley-Fosberys, and even a couple of machine pistols.

'Enough to start a small war,' Haller commented, 'but I guess we have what we need.'

'I have the impression you may start a small war,' Molinari replied.

He opened a small window in the front of the truck that looked into the cab, picked up a microphone, and spoke into the instrument. 'You might like to see this,' he told Wargrave. Extracting a map, he handed it to the Englishman. 'This shows the location. Study it and burn it after we have arrived.'

Behind Wargrave Elsa and Haller peered through the little window, which gave them a clear view beyond the truck's windshield. They were driving down a narrow cobbled street in a poor area of the city, with a wall of unlit buildings on either side. The truck had slowed as it bumped over the cobbles, and it had stopped snowing for the moment. In the glare of the headlights they saw they were moving down a cul-de-sac; at the end the way was barred by a pair of enormous wooden doors large enough to let inside a massive hay wagon, which was probably what had once passed through them a hundred years earlier. The truck rumbled on. Elsa tensed. They were going to smash straight into those massive doors. At the last moment – in response to Molinari's warning phone message – the doors swung inward and the truck rumbled into a huge stone courtyard and stopped. Men immediately closed the doors behind them. They had reached the base.

The courtyard they stepped into when the rear doors were opened was entirely enclosed by ancient six-storey buildings, but Wargrave noticed there was an alternative exit through another pair of doors opposite those they had entered by. Molinari led the way up a curving stone staircase, carrying Elsa's bag as she clutched the sable close under her chin; the night air was bitter. She looked around curiously at the second-floor room he led them to.

It was split-level and had a strange semicircular window at floor level, which Molinari immediately drew a curtain over. In the middle of the large room a huge old-fashioned green stove was radiating waves of heat and the furniture was heavy and dark. 'I'll show you to your bedroom,' the Italian said to Elsa. 'You must be tired and there is an adjoining bathroom. A meal will be served in about half an hour,' he went on in Italian – earlier Elsa had suggested they converse in his language. 'And this will help to soothe the tension of the flight.' He picked up a bottle of Chianti. 'It's one floor up. This way . . .'

Returning to the room below where Wargrave and Haller were waiting, Molinari became brisk and businesslike, seating them around a table where scratch pads and ballpoint pens were laid at intervals. 'I gather from your signal,' he said in English to Wargrave for Haller's benefit, 'that you are bringing out a key Communist agent?'

'The HS 125 jet—' the Englishman began.

'Is already waiting at Milan Airport.' Molinari smiled thinly. 'Your lady-chasing friend Aldo Martino was only too ready to oblige you. My own men are guarding it. When do you leave?'

'Saturday morning, 0730 hours. I expect to be back about 1330 hours. I'll need transport to bring my passenger back here for a change of clothes. I can't give you exact measurements – can you get hold of a large selection in various sizes? A vicuña overcoat would help – I want him to look wealthy—'

'We'll pay for all this, of course,' Haller interjected.

'Including the jet charges?' Molinari inquired with a straight face. 'Martino is charging fifty thousand dollars per hour.'

'Fifty thousand dollars!'

'He's joking,' Wargrave hastily assured the American. 'Once Mr X has changed I'll drive him to Milano Centrale. The schedule is tight but we want to take him to Zürich aboard the Atlantic Express – unless Milan Airport is still open and we can fly him there.'

'That is very unlikely,' Molinari replied. 'My met people tell me the airport will close down within twenty-four hours. You may have trouble taking off in your jet.'

'I have to take off, come hell or high water, but we must assume from what you've just said it will be the Atlantic Express. Now I'm going to ask a lot.'

'Anything you wish, Harry. Remember, I owe you.'

At that moment Elsa Lang came downstairs and one of Molinari's men guarding the building showed Matt Leroy into the room. Leroy gave Elsa a little salute and turned to Haller. 'Sorry I'm late – when I came in on the train from Basel I spent time mooching around Milano Centrale. Seemed a good idea to familiarize myself with the layout.'

'That's all right,' Haller replied. He included Elsa in his glance. 'You'd both better sit in on this – I'll fill you in later on what you've missed.'

'It's a giant of a station,' the droopy-moustached American warned. 'Anything could happen there.'

'My men will be everywhere,' Molinari assured him. 'In uniform to put on a show of force – and in plain clothes, too.'

Wargrave began speaking rapidly. There was so much to be done, so little time. 'I want two extra

Wagon-Lit sleeping cars attached to the rear of the Atlantic Express – reserved for our exclusive use. You managed to get the communications equipment I requested, Luigi?'

'It is waiting at Milano Centrale,' Molinari replied.

'I want a complete communications unit set up in the Wagon-Lit – the second one, not the rear car. We have our own operator who will run that, a man called Peter Neckermann. I gave him your number and he—'

'He is at this moment installed in a room on the third floor here – next door to the room where we have our own communications outfit.'

'That's going to save time,' Wargrave commented. 'I'll have some urgent signals to send within the next hour. Going back to the express, I want a direct telephone installed from the communications compartment in the Wagon-Lit to the train driver. Can you manage all this?'

'We will manage it.' Molinari continued scribbling shorthand notes on a pad. 'Twenty-four hours is ample time and we have more. Next?'

'Now we come to the moment when I land back at Milan Airport with our passenger. I'd appreciate your help in throwing out a smoke-screen to cover our tracks.' He went into details and Molinari said he saw no problem there. The Italian also suggested a second diversion, which they immediately agreed.

Everyone was smoking and already a blue cloud hung around the single overhead lamp above the table. Elsa, changed into a blue woollen dress that hugged her neck, sensed the tension in the room. 'We come back here with the passenger, I take it?' she asked. 'His appearance must be changed before we reach Milano Centrale – I've brought my film make-up kit.'

'Come back?' Haller repeated in an ominous tone. 'And where did you think you were going?'

'I'll be flying in the jet with Harry,' she informed him. 'We've already agreed—'

'You will not!' Haller hammered his fist on the heavy table. 'I absolutely forbid it. That flight will be one of the most dangerous—'

'You think I'm some damned butterfly?' Elsa flared.

Wargrave intervened quietly. 'She may come in useful—'

'She won't!' Haller snapped. 'Because she won't be in that plane. If he agrees, Matt can go—'

'Matt just agreed,' said Matt owlishly.

Wargrave shook his head, still speaking in his quiet, laconic tone. 'Matt I need to keep looking around Milano Centrale. He has a flair for spotting something out of place. As for Elsa, she speaks fluent French – the second language where we're going to – and a girl can provide a distraction at just the right moment.'

'I'm not happy about this at all,' Haller snapped again.

'But then I'm running this end of the operation, Julian. Remember?'

'A woman agent,' Molinari suggested soothingly, 'can complement a man with great skill – especially when they have worked together for some time, as I can tell these two people have.'

Haller glanced at Matt Leroy, who was staring into space. 'Don't look at me,' Matt said. 'Elsa is a big girl now.'

'And now, before we eat,' Wargrave said crisply, 'I'd like to go up and see Peter Neckermann alone if I may.'

'I will show you the room,' Molinari replied. Neither man looked back into the smoky room below as they ascended the stairs; there was an atmosphere they preferred to ignore. Elsa sat flushed with annoyance, Haller was brooding, and Matt had resumed gazing into space.

Alone with Peter Neckermann in the third-floor room, Wargrave began giving him instructions as he wrote out a long signal. Neckermann was the ex-*Kriminalpolizei* sergeant who for twelve months had played the dangerous role of the white-jacketed 'steward' who retrieved the cassettes from the Moscow Express sleeping car in Basel. A small, well-padded man of fifty-two, he had a gnome-like face, thick brown hair, and a perpetually mild expression.

But Neckermann's appearance was deceptive. Just prior to retirement he had been off duty and driving his car along the Konigsallee in Düsseldorf when he had run into the Geiger Group rushing out of a bank they had just raided. Driving onto the sidewalk, he

121

had headed straight for one terrorist, who stopped
and aimed his machine pistol at Neckermann point-
blank. Neckermann had pressed his foot down, the
wind-shield had shattered, and unscathed he had
ridden over the terrorist. And for several years he had
served at Wiesbaden as radio operator in the communications division.

'You have to be very careful with this signal,'
Wargrave warned. 'Transpose it into one-time code
using pages one to one hundred in this book.' He
handed to Neckermann a copy of Somerset Maugh-
am's *The Moon and Sixpence*. 'And here are the technical data you need.'

It was Springer who had only a month earlier
remarked to his chief, Brigadier Traber, that Wargrave
was a lone wolf. And this signal the Englishman was
carefully keeping a secret between only himself and
Neckermann. The signal was going to a senior
member of the Yugoslav Politburo.

Julian Haller deliberately held back his announcement
until after dinner, until after Molinari had left to make
the many arrangements he had to organize. Alone
with Elsa, Matt, and Wargrave, he sipped the
occasional glass of wine he allowed himself. Putting
the glass down on the table, he looked around with a
smile.

'One final detail I ought to mention. On this operation we're going to need all the backup we can

muster. So I've arranged for another outfit to supply an extra man, a Phillip John. He's a killer—' He saw Elsa's expression and changed the description. 'A crack shot, that is. He's coming in from Genoa tomorrow.'

Wargrave suddenly became tense and leaned forward over the table. 'Could I inquire from what other outfit?' he asked softly.

'CIA.' Haller looked apologetic. 'Now don't start worrying, for God's sake. He's British – and he's kept strictly for backup, so he's not known. And he was the only one near enough to call in at such short notice.' Haller took a deep drag on his cigarette, watching the Englishman for signs of doubt. 'He can apparently shoot the wing off a bee at fifty yards. He could even be better than you,' he added with a grin.

'The CIA has no idea why we need him, I suppose?' Wargrave queried.

'Good God, no!' Haller's reaction was explosive. 'Just that I need him for a local job. Just as they have no idea Sparta exists. I asked in my old capacity as a National Security Agency man.'

'I'll want a quiet talk with him before I decide,' the Englishman warned. 'And when he arrives I'd like him sent straight to me – before he has time to get his bearings.'

Elsa smiled to herself. Mr Phillip John was going to wonder what had hit him; in the past she had seen Wargrave subject a new recruit to intensive interrogation. Haller tried again to reassure him.

'We shall have two Wagon-Lits to guard – and if it does turn out we have to go all the way to Schiphol we'll have to organize a duty roster so people get a little sleep. An extra man could make all the difference.'

Wargrave thought about it. A backup man was not a normal field agent. He was held in reserve for very special operations and there was a ban on engaging the same backup man more than three times in a year. That way he was least likely to become known to the KGB. 'I have heard of Phillip John,' he remarked.

'You have?' Haller was startled. 'Not through Molinari?'

'Definitely not!' Wargrave stubbed his cigarette. 'Let's just say I have my sources – which don't in the least put Phillip John at risk. And, as you say, we may need all the help we can get.' He checked his watch, took Molinari's map showing their location over to the stove, lifted the lid, and burned it. 'I think it's time for bed now,' he remarked.

'Bed I like,' Elsa agreed. She caught Wargrave's expression. 'They do have a separate room for you,' she told him saucily and yawned.

'Tomorrow will be a packed day – checking details,' Wargrave warned. 'Saturday will be something else again – it's a long way to Bucharest and back . . .'

Chapter Seven

Bucharest

At precisely 7.30 a.m. Saturday, January 8, Wargrave's HS 125 jet took off from Milan Airport and disappeared inside the heavy overcast. Strapped into the co-pilot's seat beside the Englishman, Elsa Lang had a large-scale map of the Balkans spread over her lap. She had flown with Wargrave before in Cessna aircraft and had displayed a flair for navigation, often locating features on the ground, checking the flight route, and helping to keep them on course.

'What happens if we don't get the right landing signal when we arrive?' she inquired.

'We turn back and head like hell for home.'

As always, in the final cassette Angelo's instructions had been very precise. On approaching the airstrip outside Bucharest, the runway lights would come on and a signal lamp would flash repeatedly: three longs ... one short ... three longs ... And Angelo himself would be identified by two silver letters pinned to his coat lapel. *A.N.* The aircraft gained height rapidly, heading east for Belgrade, which lay on the direct route to Bucharest.

'Did Phillip John pass inspection?' Elsa asked.

'Winchester and Cambridge. Then a spell with a London merchant bank. It all bored him stiff, so he went after something more exciting. He's got that,' Wargrave commented dryly. 'A quiet man, which I liked. Reflexes like a top racing driver's. I tested him with the old trick – place a gun on the table between us and when I use a certain word in casual conversation he goes for the gun.'

'Who won?'

'His hand reached the butt first.'

'He beat you?'

'My hand was on top of his, pinning him down.'

'What is he like. Handsome?'

'Five foot ten tall, a hundred and fifty pounds in weight, white-faced, curly brown hair, very controlled in his movements. A professional.'

Crossing the Yugoslav coast in a snowstorm, Wargrave made his first contact with the Belgrade government's radar scanners. Through the microphone headset he spoke to them in Serbo-Croat briefly. During his years in the Balkans, Wargrave had made some good friends and one of them was Stane Sefer, chief of the Yugoslav security police. It was to Sefer he had sent his secret signal via Peter Neckermann on Thursday evening. Late on Friday he had followed this up with a phone call to Belgrade requesting Sefer's permission to overfly Yugoslavia 'on an urgent mission.'

'Our radar will track you in and out,' Sefer had

promised. 'And in this weather you'll need us to keep you on course.'

The lean-faced Stane Sefer had asked no questions, but he had guessed that Wargrave was on his way to fly out an agent working against the Russians. And like the whole Yugoslav government, Sefer was only too ready to support anyone helping to hold back the massive surge of Soviet power. No one in Belgrade was under any illusion that Yugoslavia could well become the Red Army's next objective – after the occupation of Romania, whose independent leaders were equally wary of the Bear's intentions.

It was another bad flight – flying blind all the way across Yugoslavia – and without the help of Sefer's radar tracking stations, which guided Wargrave to the Romanian border, he might not have made it. Beside him Elsa Lang sat studying her map, constantly trying to catch a glimpse of the ground, trying to look as though it was all in a day's work. During the first hour the neat scotch she had swallowed just before she boarded the jet had helped, but it was a three-hour flight to Bucharest and the anaesthetic quality of the drink had long since worn off.

'At least it looks as though we've kept our flight secret,' she remarked at one point.

Elsa might have felt less sanguine had she been able to witness an episode at Milan Airport soon after the jet had taken off. In the control tower Toni Morosi, a sallow-faced assistant air traffic controller,

complained to his chief of bowel trouble and was
allowed to leave the tower. Instead of heading for the
men's room, the supposedly stricken Morosi went to
a pay phone and dialled a Milan number. The call was
answered immediately by the man at the other end.

'Russo here,' Toni Morosi said quickly. 'A Hawker-
Siddeley private jet took off at 7.30 flying on an
easterly course.'

'What makes that significant?' the sombre voice
demanded.

'It was waiting all Friday in a special hangar
heavily guarded by security troops.'

'Who was on board?'

'No idea.'

'Keep me informed of developments.'

The connection was broken as Morosi mopped his
forehead and hurried to the men's room to sit on a
seat for a few minutes before returning to the tower.
The man inside a Milan garage who had received
Morosi's message later encoded it and included the
information in a signal he sent on his powerful transmitter to Moscow. Because he saw no special significance in the message he delayed the transmission.

'There's the river Arges.'

Elsa was peering down out of the window at the
flat Romanian plain, checking landmarks against her
map. The jet was now flying at fifteen hundred feet
and for the past half hour she had located landmark

after landmark. They had been lucky; once over the Yugoslav border and out of touch with Stane Sefer's radar tracking stations they had run into clearer weather. The plain below was a white landscape but it was no longer snowing in this part of the Balkans.

'We should soon be there,' Wargrave replied. 'Keep a close lookout for those landing lights.'

It was close to 11.30 a.m., Bucharest time, which was one hour ahead of Milan time, and as they drew closer and closer to the Romanian capital Elsa felt the jangle of her nerves growing worse. She glanced at Wargrave, whose expression was intent but calm. Sensing her glance, he smiled reassuringly. 'Not every girl gets a trip to the mysterious Balkans – and all expenses paid, too.'

'Better get ready,' Elsa replied.

Behind them was a roomy cabin that could comfortably seat six passengers, and Wargrave suspected there could well be more than one passenger coming aboard – Anatoli Zarubin had a wife and daughter and it seemed unlikely he would leave them behind. The equipment Elsa was collecting off the seat behind her was less reassuring than Wargrave's remark. Resting the Sten gun and spare magazines where the Englishman could snatch them off her lap, she picked up her own .38 Smith and Wesson and laid that also in her lap. Then – dead ahead in the semi-dark of the wintry day – the airstrip lights flared.

'Watch for the flashing lamp signal,' Wargrave warned.

Strung up to the highest pitch of tension, Elsa stared down as Wargrave dipped the nose of the machine steeply. What was waiting for them down there? They were landing in the middle of a Communist state – a state that had often showed its mistrust of Moscow, but still Communist. 'Don't forget the A.N. symbol Angelo said he'd be wearing,' she recalled. And that was a damned unnecessary remark, she thought; as if he would forget. I must get my nerves under control. Then the signal lamp began flashing. Three longs . . . one short . . . three longs . . .

Wargrave reduced speed as the parallel lines of lights flew toward them, there was a bump as he hit the runway, then he was taxiing the jet, losing speed as fast as he dared, having no idea of the length of the runway. The jet stopped and Elsa peered out of the window on her side, seeing nothing. God, she thought, I want to go to the bathroom. Wargrave kept the motors running and looked out of his window.

'Funny, doesn't seem to be anyone about . . .'

'But someone turned the lights on.'

'So someone has to be here,' Wargrave agreed.

He took the Sten gun from her and she grasped the butt of her Smith and Wesson. Just holding the weapon gave her a little comfort. What the hell was going on out there in the semi-dark? Suddenly Wargrave switched on the searchlight mounted on the nose of the jet. The light stabbed the darkness, showed up clearly a man walking toward the plane along the runway, a short, stocky man with wide shoulders, wearing a heavy fur coat and no hat.

He came on, walking sturdily, carrying a briefcase. At the first flash of the light he had thrown up a hand to shield his eyes, but now he had removed his hand and walked with his head lowered. As he came close his face became clearer, a strong-jawed face with bushy eyebrows that Elsa recognized from the many photos of him she had studied. She gasped.

'My God, Harry! It's a trap, a damned trap.'

The man coming toward them – who had almost reached the aircraft – was General Sergei Marenkov, head of the Soviet KGB.

Chapter Eight

Bucharest, Vienna, Milan

Wargrave realized instantly that it was hopeless. He could try and fly straight out again, but the runway ahead wouldn't give him the space to take off, there was no time to turn the machine, and in any case they would have the aircraft ringed with machine guns, maybe even small field pieces. It didn't stop him trying. A hostage might just get them out of the trap, a hostage of the importance of Marenkov. Throwing open the door, he waited until Marenkov stood below it looking up at him.

'Don't move a finger, General,' he shouted above the roar of the jets. He spoke in German, not expecting to be understood, but the Russian would understand the Sten aimed point-blank at his chest.

Marenkov made a waving gesture, indicating that the automatic stepladder should be lowered. Wargrave hesitated, then told Elsa to press the button. The power-operated staircase emerged and slid to the ground. Marenkov started to climb the steps and then stopped as Wargrave gestured with the gun and shouted.

'Hold it there.'

'What is wrong with your bloody eyesight?' the Russian bawled back in English.

'Christ!' Elsa whispered in Wargrave's ear. 'His lapel. For God's sake, look at his lapel!'

Marenkov was now himself pointing to his right coat lapel in which two silver letters were pinned. *A.N.* Wargrave gazed at them bleakly. He leaned out of the machine and Marenkov took a step upward and leaned forward also until their faces were almost touching.

'What does it stand for?' Wargrave demanded.

'Angelo. I am Angelo. We must leave quickly. My friends run the most terrible risk – take me on board and fly me the hell out of here.'

Figures in fur coats had now appeared out of the near-dark and Wargrave was sure that one of them was Ion Manescu, chief of the Romanian secret police. Scarcely a minute had passed since Elsa had recognized Marenkov, but in that short time Wargrave's brain had been racing, recalling the whole saga of Angelo. He could have kicked himself for not suspecting the truth earlier. Lowering the gun, he reached out a hand and hauled the Russian aboard. He didn't even have to give the order to Elsa; she had already pressed the button and the automatic staircase retracted. Wargrave slammed the door shut as Marenkov scrambled into one of the front passenger seats and leaned forward to shout.

'You are at a turn-around point, a large circle. Turn your machine left through one hundred and eighty degrees and take off in the direction you landed. It should be done quickly.'

'You think I intended staying for tea?'

It was as Marenkov had described: he was able to turn the jet in a slow semicircle and then he was facing back the way he had come, looking down the runway between the parallel lines of lights. He began taxiing past the lights, built up speed, the lights raced past in a blur, and then he left the ground and was climbing rapidly, heading west for the Yugoslav border and Stane Sefer's friendly radar stations.

Hindsight. Always useless. But from start to finish the Angelo operation had all the marks of a professional, of a man skilled in the craft of espionage at the highest level. And Anatoli Zarubin, Soviet minister of trade and commerce, had not qualified for that kind of work. It's always what is under our noses we do not see, Wargrave thought wryly. Once he glanced back at General Marenkov, who stared back at him from under his bushy eyebrows with his arms folded, his face expressionless. As he looked ahead, the one thing Wargrave could not fathom was why a man like Marenkov had done this thing. Why?

Sergei Mikhail Loris Marenkov was twenty when he found himself fighting behind the enemy lines in the Ukraine in 1941 as a partisan leader. He showed natural gifts of leadership and by 1943 he was an assistant commissar attached to a tank unit at Kursk.

It was Nikita Khrushchev, a fellow-Ukrainian, who adopted him as a protégé and arranged his exceptional promotion. After the war a KGB talent-spotter – recognizing his talent for organization, his encyclopedic memory and his industry – recruited him for the secret police.

Marenkov had only to read a page of a report once and it was committed to memory for all time. In his mind he could carry hundreds of names and addresses and telephone numbers, any amount of statistical data, and he never forgot a face or a name. His progress up the stepladder of power was rapid for another reason: he never attached himself to any power faction, so he was trusted by all. Then, at the age of forty-five, Sergei Marenkov got married.

Irina Marenkov, a slim, frail-looking beauty, was entirely different from her husband. Intensely political, she had already begun to have doubts about the system before she married Sergei. Alexander Solzhenitsyn's writings completed her conversion. She decided that the Soviet state was a sham, had become a near-military dictatorship under the growing influence of Marshal Gregori Prachko and his Politburo supporters. She sowed the first doubts in her husband's mind.

But Marenkov himself was also beginning to worry about the way the system was developing. He personally detested the swaggering, overbearing manner of his colleague Marshal Prachko, but carefully concealed his feelings. He knew that the Soviet arms buildup far exceeded what could ever be needed for defence against the West. Then Colonel Igor Sharpinsky was appointed his deputy.

It was some time before Marenkov realized that Sharpinsky was Prachko's protégé, manoeuvred into position as his deputy to increase the power of the GRU – Soviet military intelligence. Sharpinsky's official task was to liaise with the GRU, but secretly he supported Prachko's every move. Then Marenkov came home to his apartment at 26 Kutuzov Prospekt late one night to find Irina dead. She had taken an overdose of sleeping tablets and left a brief note. *As a suspected dissident, I have become a liability to you. I love you too much to destroy you. Instead, I destroy myself.*

Marenkov, who had never shed tears before, wept for an hour. For three days he stayed alone in the apartment, refusing to see anyone. Then he launched his investigation. It took him only three more days to discover that during his absence in East Germany a campaign of rumours had been spread accusing Irina of subversive activity. The source of the poisonous rumours was Colonel Igor Sharpinsky.

The secretive nature – among other qualities – that years earlier had led Marenkov into the KGB now served him well. Overnight – he stayed up until dawn taking the decision – he decided to work against the perverted system that had destroyed his wife, that was destroying his country. He became Angelo.

A highly intelligent man, Marenkov knew that

sooner or later time would run out for him. There had been the unnerving incident in November in the Moscow freight yards when – only a minute after he had placed the latest cassette aboard the sleeping car – he had stepped off the coach to face Captain Starov of the GRU about to board the sleeping car to examine it. With characteristic decisiveness he had shot Starov twice and then placed in his dead hand the grenade he always carried in his pocket, the grenade he would have withdrawn the pin from and blown himself up with if he had ever been discovered and faced with imminent arrest.

When the triad of Leonid Sedov, Marshal Prachko, and himself was formed to track down the high-level informer, he found he occupied the macabre role of hunting down himself. To gain a little time he gave the impression that he suspected Anatoli Zarubin, whom from the beginning he had seen as a useful cover. He had even exploited Zarubin's known liking for American jazz when he asked in the cassettes for certain jazz records to be played over the Voice of America station acknowledging safe receipt of the cassettes in Washington. And it was this pretended suspicion of Zarubin he had given as his reason for accompanying the Soviet delegation to Bucharest.

And now he was eight thousand feet over Yugoslavia in a jet piloted by an Englishman, knowing that every kilometre of his long journey to the United States would be fraught with danger – that the entire forces of the KGB and the GRU would be mobilized to kill him and his protectors. It would not be a safe journey.

Within minutes of Wargrave's being airborne again, a small convoy of cars left the Romanian airstrip and headed back at speed for Bucharest. When the news broke of Marenkov's flight, Ion Manescu, chief of the secret police, planned to launch an official investigation. His report would show that unknown capitalist agents had airlifted the Russian out of Romania. Anxious to return to the capital, Manescu, noted for his furious driving, sat behind the wheel of the lead car and soon outdistanced the other vehicles.

Alone in the rear car, one of his subordinates, Leo Ionita, pulled up at a villa behind a railed wall, ran inside and made a brief call, then ran back to his car. Accelerating, he reached Bucharest only a short distance behind Manescu, stopped again, and ran into the hallway of a large block of apartments. There he spoke a few brief words to a member of the Soviet Embassy who was waiting in response to the phone call. Minutes later, the Russian drove straight to his embassy.

As in Yugoslavia, so in Romania there was a hard core of Stalinists who secretly supported Soviet Russia. Leo Ionita was one of these secret Stalinists. Within minutes of his Russian contact's reaching the embassy, a short, urgent signal was transmitted to

Moscow reporting General Marenkov's departure. Within minutes of this signal reaching Moscow, a fresh signal was transmitted from KGB headquarters at 2 Dzerzhinsky Square to Vienna, where Colonel Igor Sharpinsky was paying one of his frequent visits to the Austrian capital. He heard of Marenkov's flight from Romania while Wargrave was airborne, still a long way from Milan.

It was 11 a.m. Vienna time – one hour behind Bucharest time – when the Moscow signal reached the Soviet Embassy in the Austrian capital. As usual, Sharpinsky had arrived in Vienna armed with a diplomatic passport under an assumed name. With the signal on the desk in front of him, he sat in his second-floor office staring through the lace curtains into the street below. It was snowing heavily and passers-by muffled in overcoats and scarves were trudging through the snow with their heads down.

Colonel Igor Sharpinsky stroked the thinning hair over his high domed forehead and behind his rimless glasses his eyes were motionless, hardly aware of the people in the street as his mind raced, checking over a whole series of contingencies he might have to deal with. Despite his deceptively mild appearance he was one of the most dangerous and able men in the Soviet Union; at this moment on a wintry morning in the ancient Austrian capital he knew he was at a crossroads in his career.

He was in the position of a gambler who stakes everything on one throw. The prospect did not daunt him; Sharpinsky was an audacious man who had not reached his present post without taking risks. And unlike his recent chief, General Sergei Marenkov, he had never disdained intrigue. He was an only child, born in Leningrad; his father had been a captain in the GRU. Exploiting this connection, Igor had worked his way up the ladder of power by switching his allegiance from one power faction to another according to who was winning and who was losing. Had he been born in the West he would undoubtedly have ended up as chief executive of one of the major multinational companies where a premium is placed on successful intrigue.

Sharpinsky had been one of the few men who had spotted Gregori Prachko's potential before the Soviet marshal's lightning climb to supreme power. He had carefully attached himself to the military meteor and his gamble had paid off. Prachko had secretly exerted his influence to place Sharpinsky in the key post of deputy to General Marenkov for liaison between the KGB and the GRU. And it was Sharpinsky who had been sent to various key embassies in the West under a series of aliases to report on the real state of Western defence. It was these reports – officially submitted only to Marenkov but with a second copy quietly submitted to Prachko – that had convinced the Soviet marshal that the time was approaching when Western

Europe could be conquered without the risk of American intervention.

On receipt of the brutal signal from Moscow, 'Seek out and destroy Marenkov,' a lesser man might have leaped into action, issuing a stream of orders. Sharpinsky had sat calmly thinking for some time while his cold, logical brain sifted the possibilities, while he tried to think himself into the minds of the opposition. And he refused to allow the fact that he was desperately short of time to hurry or disturb him. Only when he had analysed the problem to his satisfaction did he take action.

Pressing a button on his desk, he summoned his deputy, Rudi Bühler, the East German who directed the GRU sabotage units in Western Europe. Quietly he gave him certain instructions, which Bühler put into operation over the phone. After he had made a series of calls, Bühler put down the receiver and looked at Sharpinsky, who was still staring out of the window.

'Golchack is still at Annagasse 821. A team is on the way there now, backed up by a motorcyclist who will report to us the moment they have done the job. Air reservations have been made on the Zürich flight. But why Zürich?'

Forty years old – ten years younger than his chief – Rudi Bühler was a heavily-built man of medium height, but unlike Sharpinsky there was something gross about the East German. And unlike the smooth-skinned Russian's, his heavy, pugnosed face had a leathery complexion. Before replying to the question Sharpinsky left his desk and took several agile steps to a wall map where a series of pins traced a course across Yugoslavia.

'First, among a sheaf of routine reports that came in this morning from Milan was mention of a British jet taking off in an easterly direction . . .'

'I don't follow—'

'Listen and you might learn something,' Sharpinsky replied in his soft voice. 'Second, reports from Yugoslav agents at radar-scanning stations refer to the jet's course continuing across the Romanian border in the general direction of Bucharest . . .'

By 'Yugoslav agents' Sharpinsky was referring to certain Stalinists who regularly sent Moscow reports through secret transmitters, Stalinists who waited for the day when the Soviet Union would absorb Yugoslavia.

'I begin to see,' Bühler commented. 'This links up with the machine our Romanian agent reported had airlifted Marenkov out of the country.'

'You are learning,' Sharpinsky told him dryly. 'But there is far more: our camera-carrying satellites orbiting over the Balkans are at this moment tracking the jet's course and so far it is heading back along the same course – to Milan.'

'I still don't understand why we go to Zürich,' Bühler persisted.

'Because they will try to take him there from Milan

aboard the Atlantic Express. Agents in the freight yards at Milan yesterday reported a lot of security activity – and two special Wagon-Lit coaches are to be attached to the Atlantic Express leaving Milan late this afternoon.'

'Why not fly him from Milan to Zürich?' Bühler objected.

'Because I have just heard that Milan Airport has been closed down to all traffic,' the Russian replied. 'We can hope that the jet will crash, but we must assume they have chosen a skilled pilot who will land the jet blind. If he succeeds they will certainly not attempt another flight. And Zürich Airport is still open – from there they could fly him direct to the United States. He must – whatever the risk – never reach Zürich.' Sharpinsky glanced at his deputy. 'So now you know – proceed with checking the Annagasse operation.'

Bühler left the room, once again impressed with the painstaking deductive processes of his chief, and when he had left, Sharpinsky permitted himself a thin smile of satisfaction. Because the Russian was something of a showman who took every opportunity to impress his staff with his extraordinary brain. The reason why Sharpinsky knew that Marenkov was definitely scheduled to travel aboard the Atlantic Express was, in fact, far simpler.

Only a short time before Sharpinsky had summoned Bühler to his office a gloved hand had lifted the receiver in a telephone booth in Milan Central

Post Office to take the call he had placed to a number in Vienna. The owner of the gloved hand had spoken rapidly in German to the Hungarian in Vienna after identifying himself as Patros.

'They plan to transport the agent aboard the Atlantic Express leaving Milan this evening ... the two rear Wagon-Lit coaches ... the last coach will carry the agent ...'

The phone call from Patros was brief and he was worried that only now had he been able to slip away to make the call. Also he had no idea of the identity of the Soviet agent who was working for the West. The gloved hand replaced the receiver, and after paying for the call the individual who had used the code name Patros hurried out of the Post Office.

In Vienna the Hungarian, who occupied a flat close to the Soviet embassy – who was unknown to the Austrian security services to have any connection with the Russians – took the message straight to Colonel Sharpinsky. It had been as simple as that. And Wargrave's jet was still on its way to Milan.

During the next hour Sharpinsky composed a long series of signals in his careful script. While he wrote he listened to Beethoven's *Emperor* Concerto, which he had put on his record player. It seemed appropriate to the scale of the operation he was about to launch, which included use of major GRU sabotage units in the West held in reserve for the time when the Red Army invaded Western Europe. The message from Moscow had been explicit, a heady directive for a less-balanced man than Igor Sharpinsky: 'You have full power to activate the entire GRU apparatus if necessary . . .' His task completed, he spoke into the intercom.

'Send me the duty officer from the coding section.'

While he waited, Sharpinsky took a suitcase from a cupboard that had remained packed for months in case of an emergency. Every three days a woman KGB officer unpacked the case, spread out the clothes, and later repacked it. The contents were innocent enough – winter clothing (a similar case was packed with summer wear), a rare book carefully wrapped in silk, and the latest copy of a catalogue from Sotheby's, the London auctioneers.

'Come in,' Sharpinsky called out as someone knocked on the door. Leo Scoblin, assistant cipher clerk in the basement code room, entered. A thin-faced man of thirty-five, Scoblin walked with a slight limp. Sharpinsky handed him the signals inside a sealed envelope; it was only after Scoblin had left the room that the Russian noticed that the two airline tickets for Zürich brought in earlier by Bühler were lying face up on his desk. He placed a notepad on top of them; even the smallest lapse of security annoyed Sharpinsky, a perfectionist.

In the basement the chief cipher clerk immediately began encoding the signals for rapid transmission to secret transmitters in various parts of Europe. There were signals to Zürich, Basel, Milan, Mulhouse, and

Amsterdam. But the longest signal was for transmission to Andermatt, Switzerland.

The signals to Basel and Zürich arranged for the coming arrival of Sharpinsky in Switzerland. The message to Milan was received by a transmitter operating inside a garage close to Milano Centrale, the station from which the Atlantic Express would depart that same evening. In Mulhouse, Yuri Gusev, star executioner, received his orders. And in Amsterdam, Rolf Geiger, leader of the Soviet-controlled terrorist group, was instructed to stand by in readiness for possible urgent action.

In Andermatt, where Sharpinsky's signal had been decoded, an expert hand was tapping out a signal on a transmitter concealed behind a roll-top desk. The signal was on its way to Franco Visani, the chief Soviet GRU agent in Lugano, the Swiss tourist resort just north of the Italian border and on the main rail route from Milan to Zürich. It gave instructions for the organization of an attack on the Atlantic Express – with special reference to the rear Wagon-Lit.

Immediately when he had decoded the signal Visani left his apartment, went to a nearby hotel, and made a series of phone calls. He spoke in a cryptic way and left the hotel as soon as he had completed his task. It was unlikely the calls would ever be traced, but if they were they would lead only to an anonymous hotel phone.

*

At this stage of the huge operation Sharpinsky was mounting to kill Marenkov before he could leave Europe, the most important signal was the one transmitted to Milan. Just as in this great Italian city Molinari had set up his own secret base, so had the GRU. The Soviet military intelligence unit was also located only a few kilometres from Milano Centrale and was controlled by an Italian with the code name of Sappho. Ever since he had served a spell of duty at the Soviet Embassy in Athens, Sharpinsky had developed a liking for Greek code words.

Sappho ran his thirty-man unit from the cover of a garage in a side street, a garage from which he operated a small fleet of radio-controlled cabs. It was Sappho whom Toni Morosi, the assistant air traffic controller at Milan Airport, had phoned, warning him of the take-off of the HS 125 jet under maximum security conditions. Now Sappho, a bony-faced man, lean-bodied, and with an abundance of suppressed nervous energy, was discussing the decoded signal with his deputy, Ugo Sala.

The word 'deputy' was misleading; Sala, short and carrying a lot of weight, a forty-year-old man with a large head and a wide, aggressive mouth, had – unlike Sappho – undergone a course of training in Moscow. Technically, he outranked Sappho, but the two men worked well together. Sitting in the living room of the small apartment above the garage, Sala listened while Sappho explained.

'Marenkov has gone over to the West. Yes, I know

it is incredible – certainly heads will roll in Moscow, so let us thank God we are here. From now on he will be code-named Peter. And where do you think Peter is at this moment?'

'Don't play games at a time like this,' Sala replied with unaccustomed irritability. He was badly shaken and doing his best to conceal it. 'I gather we are involved?'

'At this moment,' Sappho said slowly, aiming for maximum shock effect, 'he is aboard a British jet, which we estimate will land at Milan Airport at between one and two this afternoon.'

'Then why thank God we are here?' Sala demanded. 'It puts us in the firing line. What do we do – attempt to kidnap him back?'

Sappho shook his greying hair. 'The order is more drastic.'

'That means we have to kill him – if we can?'

'Before he can board the Atlantic Express tonight. Just who is involved we are not sure – or they have not told me. Probably a combined Anglo-American operation. I want you to track him from the airport to the station.'

'You are not sure, then, he will be taken to the Atlantic Express?' Sala pounced.

'My instructions are to prepare for any eventuality. They may just change their escape route at the last moment. If we fix ourselves on just one plan we may be fooled. That we cannot afford.'

Sala lit a small cheroot; his mind was moving into

high gear. 'If he does go through Milano Centrale that might be the best place to get him – if we can detect him.'

Sappho shook his head again. 'I disagree. Already I have heard that the station is swarming with Molinari's security men. I have something else in mind – but your job is to ensure which route they take when they leave the airport.'

'I'll use one of the cabs, then – that way I can keep in radio touch with you.'

'Exactly. Use the special waveband – and simply refer to him as the passenger.'

Sala stood up and stubbed out his cheroot. 'They really have dropped one in our lap this time,' he commented.

Inside his office at the Soviet Embassy in Vienna, Sharpinsky was changing into the winter clothes he had taken from the suitcase kept in the cupboard. Dressed again, he took off his rimless glasses, replaced them with a pair of thick pebble glasses, and studied his new appearance in a mirror. The face that stared back at him bore little resemblance to Igor Sharpinsky. Satisfied, he put the pebble glasses in his pocket, replaced them with the rimless pair, and sat down at his desk as he checked his watch. Soon he must leave with Bühler for the airport but first he needed to have confirmation from the motorcyclist that the Annagasse operation had proceeded smoothly.

Sharpinsky had much to feel satisfied about. He had alerted agents all along the route the Atlantic Express would follow from Milan to Amsterdam. He very much doubted whether he would need the services of the Geiger Group in Holland; the net had been spread and he was confident Marenkov would be dead before the train ever reached the German border. But it was this exceptional thoroughness that had carried Sharpinsky to his present position, and now he felt almost excited as he contemplated what success in this mission might mean for him personally.

Inside the Soviet Politburo the division between the hardliners and the moderates was finely balanced and First Secretary Leonid Sedov was desperately trying to restrain the growing power of Marshal Gregori Prachko, the leading hardliner. Only recently Prachko had confided in his protégé, Sharpinsky.

'Pavel Suslov is wavering – soon he may join us.'

'You will still be one vote short of a majority,' Sharpinsky had pointed out. 'And Anatoli Zarubin will never join you.'

'I am not thinking of that two-faced, spineless pro-Westerner,' the barrel-chested Soviet marshal had replied savagely. 'All he can think of is creeping to the Americans. I am referring to Marenkov.'

'Marenkov?' Sharpinsky had been startled. 'He never takes sides. He is nothing more than a policeman.'

'Who may yet resign, retire – he has not been the same since his wife committed suicide.'

'You are wrong – he is tougher than he has ever been; I work under him . . .'

But now Prachko had been proved right, even if not in the way he had foreseen. And if Sharpinsky was appointed head of the KGB in succession to Marenkov, the West would face the most aggressive Politburo since Stalin's day. The issues at stake were indeed incalculable.

Heinz Golchack, the Austrian rare-book dealer who lived at Annagasse 821, caught Swissair Flight 433 from Schwechat Airport with only minutes to spare. The flight took off at 1325 hours – the last to leave before the airport was closed down. Leaning back in his seat, Golchack studied the Sotheby catalogue through his pebble glasses as the DC–10 climbed. He was courteous but a little vague with the hostess when she asked him what he would like to drink. 'Have you any . . . Schnapps? I am not a very good air passenger, you see . . .'

'Certainly, sir. Don't worry – I'll bring it quickly.'

Back in the galley the stewardess commented to her friend that it was a change to have a polite passenger aboard in weather like this. 'He's rather a dear,' she went on as she poured the drink, 'the typical absent-minded professor.'

Which was rather strange, since less than two hours ago at Annagasse 821 Heinz Golchack had received a visit from two men heavily muffled in scarves and fur-lined overcoats, with their hats pulled well down over their foreheads. He was expecting one man, not two. Thirty minutes earlier a man had phoned explaining that he was a private collector of rare books from Munich, and could he call to see Golchack?

'I have brought a friend,' the shorter of the two men remarked as Golchack stood in the doorway of his isolated fifth-floor apartment.

'Please come in. I have some coffee on the stove so . . .'

Heinz Golchack, a short, well-built man, was a fifty-two-year-old bachelor who lived alone and was something of a recluse – Vienna has many similar people – and he valued his privacy so much he cleaned the apartment himself. He was walking toward the kitchen when the shorter man who had phoned struck him a savage blow on the skull from behind with a rubber truncheon. Golchack was dead before he slumped to the floor.

His two visitors then became very active. His attacker took out a gauze cap and wrapped it over the dead book dealer's skull to prevent blood seeping onto the carpet. His companion consulted a list and checked off items as they were dealt with. A suitcase taken from the bedroom was packed with the clothes Golchack would have needed for a trip. His shaving kit was collected from the bathroom, his passport from a drawer.

While one man packed the case his companion

emptied the coffeepot he found on the stove, washed and dried it, and stowed it away in a cupboard together with the two cups Golchack had put out. Just before they left, the man who had killed Golchack took a typewritten slip from his pocket and left it on a desk. The slip was from a Swissair printed pad and typed on it were the departure and arrival times of Flight 433 to Zürich.

Locking up the apartment with keys taken from Golchack's pocket, they carried his body and the case down a back spiral staircase and shoved them into the rear of the old Mercedes they had parked in the cobbled interior yard on arriving. Then they drove across the yard and out through the massive double-doored exit leading into Annagasse. A motorcyclist parked by the kerb watched them go, kicked his starter, and drove at speed back to the Soviet Embassy to report completion of the job.

In an isolated part of the Vienna Woods the two men backed the Mercedes up an old track until they reached the rim of a deep bowl in the snows. It took them less than five minutes to heave the case into the bowl, topple the body after it, empty cans of gasoline, and ignite it with a gasoline-sodden rag. When the flames had died to a smouldering, oily stench they shovelled snow over the relics. They then drove back to the Soviet Embassy.

It had all been planned months earlier when agents had spotted Heinz Golchack as a likely candidate for an identity switch in an emergency. During one of

Golchack's rare visits to Salzburg they had used skeleton keys to enter his apartment and photograph his passport, which was then duplicated in the laboratory on the top floor of the Soviet Embassy, duplicated except for the photograph, which had been changed. Heinz Golchack was now a charred corpse in the Vienna Woods. Heinz Golchack was also a passenger aboard Swissair Flight 433 on his way to Zürich.

Chapter Nine

Milan and Zürich

When Wargrave's executive jet crossed back into Yugoslav air space Elsa's role as navigator ceased; from now on Stane Sefer's radar scanners were guiding him back toward Milan. She decided to take the opportunity to seat herself beside their Russian passenger to brief him on what would happen when they reached Milan.

The bushy-eyebrowed KGB chief swivelled in his own seat to stare at her and she met his gaze, surprised to see in his brown eyes an unexpected human expression. 'You enjoy flying?' he inquired quietly, watching her closely.

'Love it,' Elsa lied instantly. 'Especially when I have so much confidence in the pilot.'

Immediately she regretted adding the last remark. A curious expression appeared briefly in the penetrating brown eyes; Marenkov glanced ahead at Wargrave and then looked at her again. Instinctively she knew he had detected in her tone something of the concealed affection she felt for the Englishman. God, this one is quick, she thought; I'm going to have to watch myself.

'I hate flying,' Marenkov replied. 'It frightens me every time I board an aircraft.' The plane lurched at that moment, then dropped a hundred feet before Wargrave regained control. With the Russian staring at her, Elsa made a supreme effort to look unconcerned as her stomach flipped. Marenkov took a flask from his coat pocket, unscrewed the flask, and handed it to her as he leaned forward and whispered.

'I think you are a brave little liar,' he told her. His large left hand squeezed her arm as he offered the flask with the other. 'Neat vodka. Drink some – but slowly. Come, I insist,' he went on. 'The only way to fly is drunk...' He grinned and she found the grin attractive and comforting.

Taking a swig, she swallowed the fiery liquid. Already she was beginning to understand how this tough-looking Russian had risen to become chief of the world's most feared secret police. It was not simply hardness, as she had imagined; he possessed a most unusual insight into human nature. Within minutes of their meeting he had penetrated two of the secrets she had successfully kept from everyone else – her paranoid fear of flying and her affection for Harry Wargrave.

'Drink a little more,' he urged as she started to hand back the flask. Meekly, she obeyed the suggestion. His hand was still gripping her arm reassuringly. When she returned the flask he upended it and took a great swallow. 'You see,' he told her with another smile, 'I also take the medicine I recommend to others. Now, tell me about Milan . . .'

Comforted by the vodka, comforted also – strangely enough – by the stocky, wide-shouldered man by her side, she began briefing him crisply, keeping it short and to the point, determined to impress him with her own competence. To her surprise she found the Russian was a man who could listen without asking questions and she had the impression he was memorizing every single word she said.

Once, as the plane lurched again, her coat fell open to the knees and he glanced down at her legs approvingly but without a trace of lechery in his steady brown eyes. Hastily she covered them up. He smiled again, a warm smile that transformed his normally bleak, watchful expression.

'You have beautiful legs,' he remarked simply. 'So had my wife, Irina . . .'

'I heard about her,' Elsa replied quietly. 'I'm sorry – I know she . . .' Not knowing what to say next, she said nothing.

'Know she committed suicide,' the Russian completed the sentence for her. His mouth tightened, his eyes became grim. 'Technically, that was so. In fact she was driven to kill herself – which is another way of saying she was murdered. It is one reason why I am now sitting beside such an attractive girl aboard this plane,' he ended softly.

Only a short time later the plane began to lose height rapidly and Wargrave warned them they were approaching Milan. The Russian handed Elsa his flask again and gratefully she took another swig of vodka. Hell was coming up again; she loathed landings as much as she detested takeoffs.

Caspar is aboard.

'Jesus Christ!' Julian Haller muttered the imprecation to himself as he read the signal Molinari had just handed him in Milan Airport control tower, the signal Wargrave had just radioed in from his approaching jet. Before the Englishman had taken off from Bucharest they had, at Wargrave's suggestion, made a list of all members of the Soviet Politburo and given them code names. 'We are, after all,' Wargrave had pointed out, 'assuming that Angelo is Zarubin – suppose he is someone else? I'll want to let you know at the earliest possible moment.' And Caspar was General Sergei Marenkov.

'I have bad news for you,' Molinari continued. 'The air traffic controller says it is impossible to bring in your jet in this weather.'

They were standing by themselves, out of earshot of the tower staff. Haller took a quick decision. Inevitably all the security chiefs whose territory Angelo would pass through would have to be informed of his identity. He stared hard at Molinari. 'I can tell you now Wargrave is bringing in a senior member of the Soviet Politburo. We have to get him to the States. The passenger I'm talking about is General Sergei Marenkov, head of the KGB.'

The tough Italian SIFAR officer stared back at him, nodded his head, and walked straight over to the chief controller, a sharp-eyed man in his early forties. 'You will talk that jet down.'

'Impossible!'

Molinari was not a man normally given to dramatics but the situation could hardly be termed normal. Extracting his revolver, he laid it on the controller's desk. 'That says you will talk him down. This is a national emergency. Or do you lack the guts?' he inquired softly.

'That is an insult,' the controller flared.

'For which I will offer my abject apologies – when you have landed that jet safely.'

'I can only try . . .'

'Do better than that – succeed.'

Wargrave lifted the angle of descent slightly, less than he would have liked but the grave danger was that the jet would stall. The Milan controller was still talking him down, seeing him only as a falling blip on the radar screen, and under his desk the controller's left-hand knuckles were white and bloodless. Behind him Molinari stood absolutely motionless, his eyes fixed on the blip which represented three lives at extreme risk. Beside him stood Julian Haller, shoulders hunched forward, an unlit cigarette in his mouth. Haller had compelled himself to stay in the control tower – he would much have preferred to wait inside the security room where he couldn't see what was happening. For the twentieth time he cursed himself for allowing Elsa Lang to accompany Wargrave.

In the co-pilot's seat Elsa froze like a zombie. Normally the large swallow of neat vodka she had taken from the flask Marenkov had offered would have made her tight. But it had no effect; she might just as well have drunk water. Now the Russian leaned forward in his seat to give her a reassuring squeeze on her shoulder. He was also watching the altimeter. There was a jerky bump. The jet had touched down. Again the blur of lights – far more fogged than on the Bucharest airstrip – sweeping past, then gliding. The jet slowed, stopped. They released their seat belts. Wargrave swung around and reached for the Sten gun.

'Drop flat on the floor,' he ordered the Russian.

'What's wrong?' Elsa snapped.

'Too many vehicles coming . . .'

'And the Soviet satellites will have tracked our course from Bucharest,' Marenkov warned from the floor of the cabin.

The instrument panel clock registered 1.57 p.m. Outside, it was almost dark. Through the gloom the headlights of numerous vehicles were rushing toward the stationary machine. Fire trucks, three ambulances,

and the armoured truck that had taken them to
Molinari's secret base when they landed at Milan the
previous Thursday. The armoured truck arrived first.
Its lights played over the aircraft and then it pulled
alongside, leaving space only for the automatic staircase to be lowered. Wargrave pressed the button,
threw open the door as the driver of the truck got out
and shone a torch up the staircase.

'Drop that damned light,' Wargrave roared in
Italian.

The driver dropped the torch in sheer astonishment
and fright. Wargrave made him mount the staircase
and demanded his identity card. 'We have come to
pick you up,' the man protested. 'The airport is ringed
with troops.' Ignoring the protest, Wargrave checked
the identity card, handed it back.

'We're travelling with you in the cab,' Wargrave
informed the driver. 'Three of us. And I'll drive while
you guide me.'

'There's hardly room – we have armed guards in
the back to protect you . . .'

Elsa went down the staircase first at a run and
waited for Marenkov, who scrambled down with
great agility, clutching his briefcase, with Wargrave
close behind him. They climbed up into the armoured
truck's cab and Wargrave shooed the driver ahead,
climbed behind the wheel, and slammed the door
shut.

'This is my truck,' the driver protested again.

'So I want to be behind the wheel in case one of

161

those vehicles out there is the wrong one,' Wargrave snapped. 'Now – guide me. Which way to Molinari?'

'Head for the tower – those lights you can just see.'

Wargrave already had the armoured truck moving, driving at accelerating speed as fire trucks and ambulances swerved to avoid his onward rush. 'You're crazy,' the driver protested. 'You and your passenger' – he glanced curiously at the man between Wargrave and Elsa who was muffled in his fur coat with the collar turned up so it was impossible to see his face – 'would be safer in the back. That was the whole idea . . .'

'Crazy?' Wargrave gave a bitter grin without a trace of humour. 'Crazy enough to land on an ice-bound runway when your controller said it was impossible. Crazy enough to know that if a reception committee is somewhere on this airfield they will expect us to be in the back, not here. And where now? I said guide me, for God's sake.'

'Between those two flashing lights.'

The carabiniere driver shrugged at this madman as he pointed toward two lights that were just visible, that winked on and off at frequent intervals. It was snowing heavily, visibility was appalling, and Elsa was flicking snowflakes off her coat. Across her lap lay the Sten gun and her .38 Smith and Wesson. Behind the armoured truck one of the ambulances was following closely and in the murk, under cover of the rumble of the armoured truck's engine, Wargrave wasn't aware of its presence.

Only as they came nearer did Wargrave realize that visibility was so bad the small winking lights were actually large searchlights, each mounted on an army vehicle spaced to leave a passage between them for the armoured truck. As he drove closer he could see beyond them the vague shapes of a large convoy arranged in a large semicircle – police cars, motorcycle outriders, and a second armoured truck that was an exact replica of the vehicle Wargrave was driving. He slowed down as his headlight glare picked out a group of waiting figures, one of them Molinari, he thought, the other Julian Haller. Immediately to his right the airport tower loomed and visibility was clearing. He stopped. Behind him the ambulance stopped, its headlights focussed on the rear doors of the armoured truck.

The rear doors of Wargrave's truck were thrown open as the four armed carabinieri inside prepared to leap out and run to the front. There was a sudden hideous rattle of machine-gun fire from the stationary ambulance as a hail of bullets sprayed the interior of the truck ahead. The four carabinieri never had a chance; within seconds they were dead. The ambulance began reversing away from the carnage of ripped bodies.

Standing beside one of the searchlight trucks, Molinari reacted instantly speaking rapidly into the walkie-talkie he held in his hand. One of the searchlights swivelled, lit up the ambulance in its massive glare. Out of nowhere a light tank appeared, grinding forward on its tracks until it hit the ambulance, toppling it over sideways. One man only appeared from the far side of the overturned vehicle and started running. The tank's machine gun chattered briefly. The running man jumped off the ground as though jerked by a string, fell, and lay still on his back.

'Don't move!'

Wargrave shouted the warning as he gripped the Sten and poked the muzzle out of his window. On the far side of the cab Elsa aimed the Smith and Wesson out of her window and found she was aiming it point-blank at Colonel Luigi Molinari.

'Get out this side – quickly!' the SIFAR chief ordered.

They jumped out just as the searchlights were doused on Molinari's instruction over his walkie-talkie, hands grasped them by the arm and hustled them inside the back of the second armoured truck, the doors were slammed shut, and Molinari pressed a switch that illuminated the interior. He led Elsa to one of the leather-armed chairs. 'Coffee?' he suggested. 'Strong?'

'Black as the devil, please.'

Molinari gave Marenkov only one quick curious glance and then poured coffee from a flask. 'We wait here for a while, of course,' he said to Wargrave. 'Thank God you weren't in the back – and a requiem for my poor carabinieri. How did you guess?'

'I didn't, but I was suspicious. I saw three ambu-lances. Three people aboard the jet coming in, so one ambulance, yes. Two, still feasible. Three seemed one too many. If we'd had a radio communication in the cab I'd have warned you. And thank God you armoured the wall between the rear and the cab – I heard bullets thudding against my back . . .'

'We do our best,' Molinari replied.

There was a short silence while they all drank coffee in quick, long gulps. Reaction was setting in. General Marenkov, relaxing in his chair, seemed the calmest person present. 'I am greatly sorry about your men,' he told Molinari. 'I fear it is only the beginning.'

'I'm Julian Haller,' the American interjected grimly. 'I will be the man in charge of your debriefing when we reach the States. But a few names and addresses for Molinari might be in order right away – in view of what has just happened.'

'Absolutely no debriefing until you land me safely in America,' the bushy-eyebrowed Russian replied brusquely. 'That is the normal procedure.' He paused and turned to Molinari. 'For you I make an exception. KGB personnel in Milan I can give you – but not the GRU people, who have, I know, built up a powerful apparatus here. Are you ready?'

Molinari produced a ballpoint pen and sat behind the small fold-out table at the front of the truck, which held a telephone, the coffee flask, and a scratch pad. Expecting the Russian to take a list from his briefcase, unaware that this contained only the latest Red Army order of battle, he was startled as Marenkov leaned back in his chair, half-closed his eyes, and began

reeling off a list of names and addresses from
memory.

In the control tower Toni Morosi, assistant controller,
had watched the arrival of the armoured truck, had
witnessed what followed. He walked over to the chief
controller, who was still recovering from the stress of
talking down the jet followed by the bursts of gunfire
outside the tower. 'I'm feeling terrible,' Morosi complained. 'My stomach's getting worse. Could I go
home?'

'You'd better push off, then,' the controller told
him.

He was irked by Morosi's frequent visits to the
men's room during the morning, and in any case the
airport was closed for an indefinite period. When he
left the control tower, Morosi's health seemed to take
a sudden turn for the better as he hurried to a pay
phone and dialled the Milan number. Again the
sombre voice of Sappho answered almost
immediately.

'Russo here,' Toni Morosi announced. 'The jet
landed safely at 1357. An armoured truck brought the
passengers to the tower.'

'And then?'

'There was a shoot-out. The passengers weren't
hurt.'

'You're certain of that?'

'I saw it all from the tower,' Morosi snapped. 'I don't make mistakes, you know. They transferred the passengers to another truck. It should be leaving soon now.'

'You know what you have to do,' the voice interrupted.

'Of course.'

'Do it.'

The armoured truck left by the main airport gate, preceded by two police cars. A third police car followed close behind. And a few minutes before the first of the two police cars moved through the gate three motorcycle outriders had ridden ahead of it. In that weather – on an early January afternoon – they had the highway almost to themselves. Almost.

Sitting behind the wheel of his Renault, which he had parked a short distance from the airport exit, Toni Morosi sat beating a nervous tattoo on the rim of the wheel. He had the heater on and ten minutes later he was nearly asleep. It was the highpowered purr of the three motorcycle outriders leaving the airport that jerked him into alertness. Morosi watched them disappear in a southerly direction and tried to start the engine. It took him seven attempts before the engine fired, then he kept the motor ticking over and waited. Two police cars swung out of the gate and again turned south, followed by an armoured truck. The cautious Morosi waited a few seconds longer and then was damned glad he had as the third police car appeared and sped after the truck.

'Looks like Genoa,' he murmured to himself and drove after the convoy, keeping the tail-light of the rear police car just in sight. It was going to be a long drive.

It was exactly 1435 hours when Colonel Molinari's convoy left Milan Airport and headed south through the wintry afternoon in the general direction of Genoa. In the airport security room he was informed over the radio that a Renault – it was difficult to be sure even though the police officer in the rear car was using night glasses – appeared to be following the convoy. '*Bene*,' was his only comment as he switched his transceiver to a fresh waveband and began speaking rapidly.

It was exactly 1450 hours when a second armoured truck emerged from the Milan Airport exit, but this departure differed in several respects from the earlier one. First, it turned in the opposite direction, heading straight for the centre of Milan. Second, it was entirely unescorted as it moved at speed – almost dangerous speed – along the snowbound highway. Behind the wheel Wargrave glanced in the rearview mirror and saw nothing but the deserted road. 'It might just work,' he remarked to Elsa Lang, who sat beside him in the passenger seat.

'You could sound more confident,' Elsa suggested.

'In this business I always assume the worst,' Wargrave replied amiably.

Beyond the armoured wall behind them Julian Haller was sitting with General Marenkov and four plainclothes SIFAR men, who had automatic weapons across their laps. The Russian again seemed the calmest passenger as he went on reading an Agatha Christie novel Elsa had loaned him. Was it fatalism, Haller wondered? Or was it simply that years of living with the pressures of his job had trained Marenkov never to show his emotions? The truck rumbled on at speed into the centre of Milan.

Behind them Ugo Sala maintained a careful distance between the truck and the radio cab he was driving. Earlier he had waited in a side road close to the airport exit while he observed Molinari's convoy turn south, followed shortly afterward by Toni Morosi. 'And I've come up with four aces,' he told himself as he moved closer to the truck. It was safe now to close up; there was more traffic about.

Behind the wheel of the truck Wargrave again glanced in his rearview mirror. He was nearing Molinari's secret base where they had been taken when they had landed in Milan. He was also moving more slowly because of the traffic and the trams. Less than a minute later he looked in the rearview mirror again. 'Trouble?' inquired Elsa.

'We're being tailed by a cab, I think.'

'Lots of cabs about . . .'

'This one appeared soon after we left the airport.'

'One cab looks like another. How can you tell?'

'He parked it only half under cover – one side of the bonnet is thick with snow, the other barely smeared.'

'What do we do?'

'Lose him.'

Elsa checked her watch. 'It's 3.30. The Atlantic Express leaves at five past five – and I have to work on Marenkov to change his appearance. We can't chase all over the city.'

'Maybe we won't have to.'

In Milan, trams have the first priority; you give way for a tram. Wargrave was approaching an intersection, the road ahead was clear, he pressed his foot down. Elsa glanced to her right and stiffened. 'Look out – trams!' The first of a whole convoy of trams was crossing the intersection as Wargrave rammed his foot down to the floor. Appalled, Elsa saw the first tram looming just beyond her window, its bell ringing frantically. The truck roared on. Pedestrians turned and froze in horror. The tram driver, still ringing his bell nonstop, braced himself for the collision. Wargrave stared ahead, his foot still hard down. Inside the back of the truck the SIFAR men, hearing the bell ringing, gripped the arms of their seats. The tram driver stared in disbelief as the rear of the truck passed him in a blur and the tram sailed on.

Inside his radio cab Ugo Sala swore foully as he

braked so savagely he would have gone through the windshield but for his safety belt. As it was, the stop made him gasp. Still swearing he waited as the convoy of trams proceeded past, masking the view ahead completely.

Reaching the turn-off into the dead-end street, Wargrave swung the wheel. He had slowed down but he was still moving fast down the narrow street, rattling over the cobbles as he reached with one hand for the microphone Molinari had used on their earlier visit to the base. 'Ronco coming in, Ronco coming in . . .' he repeated in Italian, using Molinari's code word. Elsa tensed as she saw the massive double doors ahead remain closed while Wargrave continued toward them at speed.

'For God's sake, we can wait,' she snapped.

'Not until that cab reaches the end of this street and sees us.'

The huge doors, still closed, rushed toward them as Wargrave went on repeating the warning message over the microphone. Here we go, Elsa thought. He was within twenty yards of them when they swung inward rapidly and he drove on into the courtyard and braked. In the rearview mirror he saw them close again. They had arrived.

As the last of the trams passed, Ugo Sala drove forward, saw that the truck had vanished, and slowed down while he glanced to left and right as he passed side streets. It took him only a few minutes to realize that he had lost the vehicle. Pulling into the kerb, he spoke into the mike, which was not tuned to the normal cabdriver's waveband.

'Rome Three calling. Rome Three calling. Passenger now dropped. Repeat, passenger now dropped . . .'

'Where are you?' a voice answered, Sappho's voice calling from a garage that was the headquarters of a small radio cab rental firm.

'Via Pisani.'

'Then it's Milano Centrale. Proceed there at once and await arrival of passenger . . .'

Chapter Ten

Zürich

At precisely 1435 hours – when Molinari's deception convoy was leaving Milan Airport – Colonel Igor Sharpinsky, in his assumed identity of Heinz Golchack, landed aboard Swissair Flight 433 at Zürich in a snowstorm. Among the passengers who filed off the aircraft behind Golchack was Rudi Bühler, who had travelled separately. At Passport Control the Swiss officials checked papers with their usual thoroughness. The official facing Golchack glanced at the short, well-built man standing before him and then looked at the passport photograph.

'Could you please remove your glasses for a moment, sir?' the official requested politely.

'Of course. I'm sorry,' Golchack replied vaguely.

He removed the pebble glasses, which he was not wearing in the photograph, and the official had a shock. The face matched the photo – as far as any passport picture matches its owner – but without the glasses the Swiss found himself looking into one of the most penetrating pairs of eyes he had ever encountered: blank, still eyes. Golchack noticed that – as with the other passengers – the official made a quick note of the name and passport number, and then he was asked for his home address. He had no way of knowing that this was the first stage of the alert Colonel Leon Springer had issued to all entry points.

'Thank you, Mr Golchack. Are you staying long in Switzerland?'

'One or two days, then I go to Germany.'

Outside the airport hall Golchack ignored the airport bus other passengers were boarding and summoned a waiting cab. 'The Baur au Lac Hotel, please.' Settling back with his case on the rear seat, Golchack waited until they had driven a short distance from the airport, checked his watch, and then asked the driver to pull up for a moment. He seemed to be drawing attention to himself. Outside, the snow was falling heavily, the cab's windshield was frosting over, and only the fan shape kept clear by the wipers enabled the driver to see where he was going. 'I have been thinking,' Golchack explained in excellent German, 'is there a train I could catch which would take me on to Bonn? If so, I think I will return to Zürich later.'

'At 3.30 a train leaves for Germany. We should get you there in time.'

'Take me to the Hauptbahnhof, then. Please hurry – as far as that is possible.' Golchack smiled vaguely, gesturing outside the window at the weather.

Arriving at Zürich Hauptbahnhof, Golchack paid off the driver, noted that his cab had already picked up another fare, and walked into the huge hall of the

Hauptbahnhof where a series of rail tracks ended. Then he did a curious thing; after waiting a moment he glanced across to where a man leaning against a news-stand stood apparently gazing into the distance, and descended an escalator leading to the underground shopping mall.

Carrying his case, he walked across the mall and mounted another escalator on the far side, which carried him up to the street on the opposite side to the Hauptbahnhof. As he trod on the rubber mat at the entrance of the Hotel Schweizerhof the automatic plate-glass doors slid aside and a wave of heat met him. At the reception desk he presented his passport for filling in the registration form.

'You have a double room with bath reserved for me.'

The receptionist consulted a card index. 'Yes, Mr Golchack. The reservation was phoned through from Vienna. Room 201 . . .'

The professorial-looking guest took his time over filling in the form, printing everything in careful capitals. By the time he had completed the formality, Rudi Bühler, who had followed in his own cab, had entered the reception hall. Also, the man who had stood by the news-stand in the Hauptbahnhof had come into the hotel and was studying some jewellery in a showcase.

'Room 201, you said?' Golchack repeated for Rudi Bühler's benefit.

'Yes, sir. The porter will show you to your room.'

'Have you . . . a railway timetable I could consult first?'

Patiently, the receptionist handed over the time-table and Golchack moved farther along the counter to study it while Rudi Bühler quickly filled in his own registration form. In the hall behind them the man from the Hauptbahnhof news-stand was still examining the showcase jewellery. Then, as if by chance, all three men moved toward the elevator at the same time, accompanied by the porter carrying Golchack's and Bühler's cases.

The elevator was small and the four men were just able to squeeze inside it together. As the elevator ascended to the second floor the man from the news-stand held his room key in his hand with the number showing. Room 207. The porter assumed the three men were strangers as the elevator stopped at the second floor. 'You are on the third floor,' he explained to Bühler. 'I shall only be a moment.'

The guest for Room 207 entered his own room as Golchack proceeded along the corridor with the porter. Alone inside Room 201, Golchack allowed time for Bühler to arrive at his own room and return to Room 207. Checking the bathroom, he went back into the large double bedroom and peered through the heavy lace-curtained windows that overlooked the Bahnhofstrasse. He was staring down into the richest street in the world, the street where all the big Swiss banks had their main branches. It was still snowing as a tram passed below his window, and sparks flashed as the overhead traction brushed the frosted wires. Checking his watch, he opened the bedroom door, saw that the corridor was deserted, locked his door, and walked along to Room 207. He rapped on the door in a certain way and Bühler opened it a fraction, then let him inside. Golchack wasted no time on greetings.

'Everything is set up?' he inquired in German. He looked around the room. 'I want to send several signals immediately.'

'I am ready when you are, sir.'

Heinrich Baum, the man who had waited by the Hauptbahnhof news-stand, was a Swiss dentist from Basel. A compact thirty-year-old, Baum was lean-faced, sported a pencil-thin moustache, and had a brisk manner. He opened a black case resting on a table. When he first opened the case it appeared to contain a set of dental equipment. Pressing two concealed catches, Baum elevated a telescopic aerial and inserted three plugs into sockets, and the disguised transceiver was ready for transmission.

'Two signals have come in for you,' he informed Golchack, 'one from Milan and the second from Moscow.'

With a feeling of relief Golchack took off his pebble glasses and replaced them with his normal rimless pair so he could see to read clearly. The Milan signal was brief. *Peter landed safely. Interception failed. Everything indicates he will travel aboard Atlantic Express departing Milan 1705 hours.* He handed the signal to Bühler.

'We arrived here just in time,' he commented.

The Moscow signal was briefer. *Now use total apparatus to destroy Peter.* Although unsigned, Golchack knew this signal had been sent by Leonid Sedov himself and Marshal Prachko. Again he handed the signal to Bühler, carefully keeping his voice flat and toneless.

'All the GRU sabotage units are now at our disposal.'

'Let's hope we don't have to go that far.'

Golchack glanced at him with his pale blank eyes and Bühler wished he had kept his mouth shut. Hurrying to the bathroom, he burned both signals, flushing the embers down the toilet. In the bedroom Golchack took three slips of paper from the Sotheby's catalogue and handed them to Baum. He had written out the three signals while he waited in his bedroom for Bühler to reach Room 207.

'Send them in the sequence I have indicated,' he instructed. 'Encode the first, send it, then the second, and so on.' He turned to Bühler as the sabotage chief returned to the room. 'Let me have a look at the map.'

Bühler opened up a large-scale map of Switzerland he had brought from his room and spread it out over the double bed. Golchack bent over the map, took out a pen, and ringed two areas, being careful not to mark the map. 'At one of these points between Milan and Zürich we eliminate Peter.' He spoke quietly as though discussing a business transaction. Bühler was staring at the second location Golchack had ringed.

'We would attempt even that?'

'If necessary, yes. I have already alerted Andermatt. The destruction will be enormous – but so long as we destroy Peter what does it matter?'

While they talked, Heinrich Baum was already starting to transmit the first, very brief encoded signal. And before he began transmitting he had set a small pinger clock for two and a half minutes. It was unlikely that Swiss radio-detector vans would be in the vicinity, but Golchack never took a single unnecessary risk. Working together, it would take two radio-detector vans at least five minutes to take a fix on a secret transmitter – to plot from two locations the cross-point of the radio beams indicating where the transmission was coming from.

And Baum's signals had only to travel a few kilometres to the place where the main Soviet transmitter was based. Beyond the east bank of the river Limmat that divides the ancient city of Zürich the land rises rapidly to the Zürichberg, a heavily wooded hilltop that in summer is the favourite relaxation spot of the Zürichers. In winter it is deserted and few people wander along the winding tracks lined with great walls of log piles. It was close to the Heubeeri-Weg track that a large mobile trailer was parked.

Officially, Professor Georg Mohner, the well-known Swiss meteorologist who occupied the mobile trailer alone, was studying weather patterns, and the interior of the trailer was crammed with meteorological equipment. What Mohner, a tall, thin, ascetic-looking man, did not advertise to the rare visitors to his well-heated trailer was the concealed power-operated aerial that could be elevated – and withdrawn swiftly – at the push of a button. Nor did he show them the exceptionally high-powered transmitter which, from the heights of the Zürichberg, could send signals all over Europe.

Within two minutes of receiving the first signal from Baum at the Hotel Schweizerhof, Mohner had elevated his own aerial and was transmitting long-distance. And, like Baum, he had set his own time-clock for two and a half minutes. The first signal went to Milan, the second to Moscow. The third – and longest – was transmitted to Andermatt.

In Room 207 at the Hotel Schweizerhof, Golchack checked his watch. It was exactly 4 p.m. In an hour's time the Atlantic Express would start its long journey from Milan with its ultimate destination Amsterdam. And already the secret Soviet base Golchack had set up inside Switzerland was geared for action.

It was exactly 4 p.m. in Vienna when Leo Scoblin, assistant cipher clerk in the code room at the Soviet Embassy, came off duty. Hurrying out of the Soviet Embassy as fast as his limp would allow him, he climbed behind the wheel of his Volkswagen. The engine was cold and it was only at the eighth attempt that the motor fired. Sighing with relief, he drove off at speed, weaving his way through the traffic, his hands gripping the wheel tightly.

Perhaps it was the heavy traffic, maybe it was his sense of extreme urgency, that made him take only cursory glances in his rearview mirror. Certainly he never saw the old Mercedes following him, a vehicle occupied by the same two men who earlier that afternoon had in the Vienna Woods cremated the body of a rare-book dealer called Heinz Golchack.

It was to Leo Scoblin that Colonel Igor Sharpinsky had handed the sealed envelope of signals before leaving Vienna to catch his plane for Zürich in the guise of Heinz Golchack. It was Leo Scoblin who had noticed on Sharpinsky's desk the two air tickets to the Swiss city. And it was the meticulous Sharpinsky who had ordered a watch to be kept on Scoblin, but only as a precaution.

Reaching the main Post Office, Scoblin limped inside and whispered across the telephone counter the number he wanted. The girl did not hear him first time and he repeated the Zürich number in a slightly louder voice, but still softly enough to make it impossible for anyone else to hear him.

'You will have to wait,' she informed him. 'I will call out the booth number.'

'Just say "your Zürich number,"' he pleaded.

In a fever of impatience he was careful to conceal, he sat on one of the benches with his back to the wall. The system wasn't very satisfactory from Scoblin's point of view. For an international call you gave the girl the number and then waited until the call was connected and she called out the booth number you could take the call from. Leo Scoblin was no amateur – he had chosen a seat in the open – but he failed to notice the quiet entry of the two men from the Mercedes who took up a position in a shadowed part of the hall out of his range of vision.

He had to wait ten minutes and then the girl shouted out the message. 'Your Zürich call is on the line. Take it in Booth Three.'

Scoblin limped quickly toward Booth Three, which was near the Post Office exit. Closing the door carefully behind him, he lifted the receiver and spoke rapidly in German. 'This call is very urgent. Kramer speaking. Paul Kramer. Put me through to Arthur Petersen. Please hurry.'

'One moment, please.'

The girl operator at Brigadier Traber's counterespionage headquarters reacted quickly. The names she had been given were top-priority and she plugged in immediately to Traber's private line. 'Mr Paul Kramer on the line for you, sir – from Vienna.'

'Put him through.'

'Paul Kramer here.'

'Petersen speaking . . .' Traber, a small, plump man of fifty-five with quick-moving eyes, found he was gripping the receiver tightly. The line was good and he sensed the extreme tension in the voice far away to the east in Austria, a voice he only heard very occasionally. The voice began speaking quickly.

'I heard the news two hours ago but I have only just been able to get away. Crocodile is coming. He is on his way to Zürich . . .'

Inside the telephone booth Leo Scoblin heard the squeak of the badly oiled hinges as the door opened behind him. He had no time even to turn his head as the short-bladed knife was plunged up to the hilt below his left shoulderblade. At the other end of the line Traber heard a short gulp. 'Hello,' he said. When there was no reply he replaced the receiver. He felt slightly ill. Leo Scoblin, the Israeli agent, had been a nice chap. And Crocodile was the code name for Colonel Igor Sharpinsky.

More than that – just before he took the call a signal had come in from Harry Wargrave in Milan informing Traber that the 'key anti-Communist agent' the Englishman had referred to on his way through Zürich was General Sergei Marenkov, head of the Soviet KGB. 'All hell is about to break loose,' the Swiss said to himself. Picking up the phone, he asked to be put through immediately to Springer.

Springer was at that moment at security headquarters in Lugano, southern Switzerland. It had been decided that Springer would watch over the Atlantic Express's progress along the section of rail track south of the Gotthard; north of the Gotthard Brigadier Traber would take over. Traber got through on the scrambler phone very quickly.

'Leon,' he opened the call bluntly, 'I have just heard from Wargrave that the passenger they are bringing through is General Marenkov of the KGB.'

'God Almighty . . .'

'We may need his help, too. Brace yourself – there is more to come. I have also just heard from an impeccable source that Crocodile left for Zürich about two hours ago.'

'Any more details?' Springer asked quickly.

'None. I fear the source was chopped in mid-conversation.'

'This,' Springer pointed out, 'may be a once-in-a-lifetime opportunity for us – the entire Communist underground sabotage apparatus could surface to wipe out a huge target like Marenkov. I suggest a red alert throughout the entire country with all leave cancelled.'

'My next move,' Traber assured him. 'Now I must get off the line. Good luck at your end.'

Breaking the connection, Traber began making a series of phone calls. From what Leo Scoblin had told him, Sharpinsky must have come in by plane. His first call was to Zürich Airport security.

'I want an immediate list of all passengers who came in on Swissair Flight 433 from Vienna. I want to know where they are now. Check the airport bus. Track down all cabdrivers who picked up passengers off that flight. When do I want the list? On my desk thirty minutes from now!'

Chapter Eleven

Milan, Moscow, The Hague

It was 4 p.m. Saturday, January 8, when Heinz Golchack had set up the Soviet base at the Hotel Schweizerhof in Zürich. It was 4 p.m. in Milan when Wargrave, returning to Molinari's secret headquarters behind the massive closed doors at the end of the cul-de-sac street, dispatched a series of coded signals to various European security chiefs. They had been prepared in advance, and his radio operator Peter Neckermann had only to substitute the name 'Marenkov' for 'Zarubin.'

These signals were sent to Brigadier Traber in Zürich, to Captain Franz Wander of the German BND in Wiesbaden, to General Max Scholten, Dutch counter-espionage chief in The Hague. While he was sending these warning signals the tempo of the whole operation was accelerating and there was a sense of extreme urgency inside the building Molinari had placed at Sparta's disposal. The Atlantic Express was due to depart from Milano Centrale at 5.05 p.m.

In her bedroom Elsa Lang was transforming Marenkov's appearance with the aid of the make-up kit she always carried, using the expertise she had acquired during her year's stint with the film company in London as make-up girl. Marenkov, a white overall draped over his shoulders, sat patiently in a chair as she trimmed his bushy eyebrows and changed his hairstyle. Again the Russian seemed the calmest person in the building.

'You'll have trouble turning me into a film star,' he joked as he stared at his own image in the wall mirror.

'Well, you may not be Gregory Peck,' she responded, her hands working busily, 'but you could pass as Lee Marvin if you were taller.'

'He's a villain – like me.'

Elsa grinned as the Russian shook with laughter. 'Keep still, you oaf, I've work to do.' A curious relationship had developed between the Russian and the English girl since, detecting her morbid fear of flying, he had passed her his flask of vodka during the nightmare flight from Bucharest. It could hardly be called friendship, but each felt for the other a certain affinity, the affinity of people who conceal a deep loneliness. Elsa had lost her husband-to-be just before joining Sparta; Marenkov had lost his wife.

'Now, clothes . . .' Elsa said briskly.

Molinari had excelled himself in the short time at his disposal, bringing to the building a whole selection of winter clothes in various sizes and styles, including three vicuña overcoats. Marenkov tried on several suits quickly until Elsa was satisfied with a dark blue business suit. And one of the vicuña coats fitted him perfectly. He struck a pose in front of the mirror. 'I think I'm going to enjoy myself in America,' he remarked genially.

'We're travelling as husband and wife,' she went on briskly. 'You're George Wells, an oil executive working for Shell International – there is such a man, but at present he's in Venezuela. The fact that the Atlantic Express is bound for Holland where Shell has its headquarters makes the role even more convincing. We're travelling first-class, of course, and will share a sleeping compartment.'

'Ten years ago and I might not have behaved myself.'

She smiled her appreciation of the compliment and then became businesslike again. 'Your tie needs straightening.' Competent fingers occupied themselves briefly with the tie. 'We're very well fixed . . .' She had to explain she meant wealthy. '. . . hence the expensive clothes. Your passport will be ready before we leave.'

As soon as Elsa had completed changing his appearance Marenkov was photographed and one of Molinari's technical experts in the basement attached it to the passport – a document that had been prepared in advance, omitting only the photo and details of height and colour of eyes. Elsa gave him the passport and two ticket folders.

'We need tickets?'

'To pass through the barrier at Milano Centrale – everything must look normal in case anyone is watching.'

She swung around as she heard the door opening, slid her hand inside a half-closed drawer, and grabbed the Smith and Wesson. Marenkov, moving with extraordinary agility, took hold of a full bottle of wine by the neck, raised it ready to throw, and stood in front of Elsa. In the doorway Harry Wargrave surveyed them with his hands on his hips.

'Not bad,' the Englishman commented, studying Marenkov's changed appearance. 'In fact, quite remarkable. You have about fifteen minutes – we want to reach Milano Centrale just before the express departs.' He left the room and Elsa spoke severely to the Russian.

'I am supposed to be guarding you. From now on you do exactly as I say.' She pointed to the two folders he held in his left hand. 'The tickets are for Amsterdam in case we have to go all the way through to Schiphol if Zürich closes down, which I hope it doesn't. The sleeper reservations are for Coach 4, the rear Wagon-Lit – the first one we come to beyond the ticket barrier. But we actually board the Wagon-Lit beyond, then walk back.'

'Wargrave has organized this well,' Marenkov commented.

'One more thing,' Elsa went on. 'The easiest way to recognize a man – or a woman – in disguise is by their walk. You walk with a heavy, deliberate tread. You've got to alter that. Now let's practise – walk around this room and I'll criticize. And remember, the danger point could be Milano Centrale before we get on the train . . .'

At 4.15 p.m. a droopy-moustached figure wearing glasses and a raincoat was wandering around the vast concourse of Milano Centrale, a rail terminal that in size rivalled Frankfurt Hauptbahnhof. Built of marble with huge pillars and a soaring vaulted roof overhead, it resembled a majestic mausoleum rather than a rail terminal. And as he continued wandering around with a folded newspaper in his left hand, Matt Leroy was worried.

By now very familiar with European stations, he didn't like the look of Milano Centrale. It was too big, there were too many places where snipers could hide. Not that there was so much really to worry about with Molinari controlling the security, he reminded himself. Mingling with the passengers already boarding the Atlantic Express – many of them Italian workers returning from their New Year's holiday at home to jobs in Switzerland and Germany – was a small army of SIFAR men in plain clothes.

More than that, there were a large number of uniformed carabinieri putting on a deliberate show of open force. And high up behind office windows, Matt knew, were stationed three of Molinari's well-trained snipers armed with rifles and telescopic sights. The folded newspaper the American held in his left hand was not there by accident; every SIFAR man in the station knew he might use it to casually point in a certain direction, to indicate something that had aroused his suspicions.

One man Matt Leroy did not notice was a short man carrying a lot of weight who had a wide, aggressive mouth. Ugo Sala, the Italian who had followed Wargrave's truck from the airport and had then lost him when the convoy of trams barred his way, was standing outside the restaurant drinking a cup of coffee close to the barrier beyond which the sixteen coaches of the Atlantic Express spread away into the distance.

Unlike Toni Morosi, the assistant air controller who had followed Molinari's deception convoy south toward Genoa, Ugo Sala, a senior KGB operative, had visited Soviet Russia and while in Moscow he had several times seen General Sergei Marenkov at close quarters. Glancing up at the station clock, he saw the time was 4.35 p.m. In thirty minutes the Atlantic Express was due to depart.

In Amsterdam, Rolf Geiger swung his cane jauntily as he walked nimbly along the cobbled street beside the silent canal; he avoided the diabolically uneven and narrow sidewalk – far too easy to slip and find yourself tumbling down one of the flights of steps leading to basement entrances. He had just visited the famous red light district where surprisingly attractive girls displayed their wares in picture windows.

Geiger was well aware he could have enjoyed himself with Erika Kern; more than once she had indicated this. But like Harry Wargrave, strangely enough, Geiger never mixed business with pleasure, never made love to one of his subordinates: it led to complications that could be dangerous. Turning up the steps leading to the building where he had set up his headquarters, he inserted the key in the lock and paused.

One hell of a gale was blowing in from what the Dutch called the West Sea. Geiger could hear behind him the sinister clank and scrape of the hanging chains as they rattled in the gale high up on the warehouses opposite. It took some force of wind to move the ancient iron. Inside, he climbed the incredibly narrow and twisting staircase to the third floor and was met by Erika Kern as he opened the apartment door. One look at her face told him something had happened. She spoke the moment he had closed and locked the door.

'We are on standby alert.'

'What the devil do you mean?'

'A signal has just come through from Sharpinsky in Vienna. All units are to stay where they are pending further orders.'

Geiger checked his watch, his jaunty manner now businesslike and alert. 'That's damned bad timing –

we're in the middle of moving into Holland. Now, let's just think . . .'

Erika, a trained radio operator who dealt with the transceiver hidden in the basement, brought him up to date with her normal efficiency. 'I have contacted Wojna at Willich. I was in time to tell him to stay there for the moment.'

Jacek Wojna was the leader of the main terrorist unit, a huge Pole who carried out the raids Geiger planned. And Willich was a small German village, little more than an estate of new houses, midway between Düsseldorf and the Dutch border. It had originally been chosen as the German centre of operations by Geiger because of its isolation and its proximity to the Dutch border as an escape route in an emergency. Erika Kern had lived in one of the houses, pretending to be Jacek Wojna's wife.

'They still have the gasoline truck and the ambulance hidden away,' Geiger recalled. 'I could do with some coffee,' he added and went on talking while Erika attended to the percolator. Behind the drawn curtains it had started to rain and the storm lashed at the window.

'They will bring out the explosives – and themselves – inside the truck,' Geiger continued as he sat on a couch and lit a cigarette. 'That way they will easily cross the border. The ambulance they will leave behind.'

It was six months since they had hijacked both vehicles in West Germany, killing the drivers and secreting the vehicles for a raid they had never carried out. The small dapper man sat very still while Erika made the coffee and she was careful not to say anything. He was, she knew, trying to anticipate the reason behind Sharpinsky's totally unexpected signal.

'The signal said nothing else?' he inquired eventually.

'No, just to stand by.'

She stopped speaking as the door opened and Joop Kist, a small, thin-faced man of thirty, came in, his raincoat dripping. From beneath the raincoat he produced a Nikon camera equipped with a telephoto lens. Ignoring Erika, he spoke to Geiger. 'I have photographed the Maas bridge – two whole films,' he said with a touch of pride.

'The guards didn't see you?' Geiger inquired sharply.

'Of course not. Shall I develop the film in the basement? Tomorrow I can go to Eindhoven to photograph the Phillips works.'

'Develop the films by all means,' Geiger agreed amiably. 'But don't be in such a hurry to rush about all over the place – wait a few days before you do the Eindhoven job.'

Erika waited until Joop Kist had left before she made her remark. 'I'm not sure I trust him. There's something not quite right about Kist.'

Geiger was amused and smiled. 'Just because he's our newest recruit you don't have to get nervous. He's Dutch – so he speaks Dutch, which none of us does, and we are in Holland. Already he has proved invaluable in making the initial contact with our illicit diamond dealer friend.'

'My instinct has not always been wrong,' Erika flared.

'Of course, he hasn't shown immediate interest in your sexual attractions,' Geiger commented. His voice sharpened. 'I had him thoroughly checked out, you know that. A month ago he shot a policeman who almost died. He was carrying the gun when he joined us and I had someone break into police records to photograph his file. The ballistics record of the bullet they took out of that policeman matches the gun he brought with him.'

Erika poured coffee into a cup and handed it to Geiger with a cold expression. 'I want to go and check the transceiver, if you'll excuse me.'

'By all means,' Geiger agreed equably. He was still smiling as she left the room with her lips pressed tightly. In an hour her annoyance would have evaporated, and this was Geiger's way of reminding her who was boss. She was a strange girl, he thought as he sipped his coffee – promiscuous in a discriminating way. Geiger often suspected that her main motive for accepting her dangerous task in the West was to get away from East Germany where her liking for swift, ferocious affairs would never have been tolerated.

Taking out his passport, he glanced at the document. The Western world knew him as Leo Sanchez, wealthy Argentinian playboy who moved around on the fringes of the international jet set. He was best known in Paris, where he had lived for three years, directing the Geiger Group's outrages in Germany by remote control. His picture had even appeared in the gossip columns of a London paper. 'Be conspicuous and wealthy and no one will suspect you,' he had once told Erika. And she had certainly not relished the move to Amsterdam; in Paris she had left behind too rich a variety of lovers.

Finishing his coffee, he began to wonder about the unexpected signal from the man they called in Moscow the Silent Colonel, Igor Sharpinsky. Something was on the move somewhere and Geiger had a premonition he wasn't going to like it; certainly he didn't like the long arm of Sharpinsky reaching out again so quickly to rest a hand on his shoulder. Could it, he wondered, be something to do with the sudden dispatch of the huge American airborne force to Germany? President Joseph Moynihan was still an unknown quantity, but this action suggested he could be formidable.

At Dutch counter-espionage headquarters in The Hague a call had just come through for Scholten. Major Sailer, his assistant, took the phone call and then put his hand over the receiver before he spoke to his chief. 'A man called Panhuys wants to speak to you urgently – he's used the special number.'

'Scholten here,' the general said calmly as he took

the phone. 'Are you safe? Good.' He listened without saying anything more except good-bye at the end of the brief conversation. Then he turned to Sailer.

'The Geiger Group have arrived. And that information is top secret. Now we come to the difficult part – the waiting . . .'

It was night at Willich, the tiny village midway between Düsseldorf and the Dutch border where the Geiger Group had their temporary headquarters. Outside the isolated village flat fields deep in snow spread away in all directions. The village was little more than an estate of good-class houses recently built, each with its own backyard. Inside one of the houses, which was built on several levels, Jacek Wojna, the burly, six-foot-tall Pole the neighbours knew as Erika Kern's husband, was cleaning an Uzi sub-machine gun in the living room as he spoke to Gaten, a short, wiry Norwegian.

'I don't know what Geiger thinks he is doing – holding us up here at the last moment just when we were moving on to Holland.'

'Geiger always has his reasons,' the bony-faced Gaten replied cautiously. He was reassembling a German automatic weapon. The small armoury of weapons inside the house was a mix of many countries, but none of the weapons was Russian. It was a careful policy of Geiger's to use nothing that might link them with the Soviet Union.

'Stop creeping up Geiger's arse,' Wojna snapped brutally. 'I'm the boss around here and you'd better not forget it.' He aimed the gun at Gaten and the Norwegian stiffened as Wojna's finger curled around the trigger. He pressed the trigger and laughed as Gaten jumped. 'You really thought I had one up the spout, didn't you?'

'I'll be as glad to get out of Germany as you,' Gaten assured the Pole. 'And do you have to play with guns like that?' He had trouble keeping a quiver out of his voice; the Pole was quite capable of shooting one of his own team the moment he decided anyone was expendable.

They were talking in French, their only common language, and Gaten had been born in Bergen. A Norwegian anarchist, he had worked on the oil rigs, and Geiger was holding him in reserve for the day when the order came to sabotage the giant floating platforms in the North Sea that were flooding oil and gas into Scandinavia and Britain.

'You checked out the ambulance and the gasoline truck this afternoon?' Wojna demanded.

'They are safe in the barn,' Gaten told the Pole.

'Hell, I could have guessed that!' Wojna threw down the gun and reached for a bottle of gin on the couch beside him. 'Are they ready for instant movement, is what I'm asking you. Do I have to spell out every question like talking to a bloody three-year-old?' He took a deep swallow from the bottle.

'The tanks are full of gas – I tested the ignition and

they both fired first time. They're well insulated with canvas over the hoods and I left the oil heaters burning.'

'I'll bet it's still like a goddamn refrigerator inside that barn,' Wojna grumbled. He looked around the living room and spat on the carpet. Already there were signs everywhere that the house was now occupied only by men; dirty glasses littered a table, empty liquor bottles lay on the floor and on chairs. When Erika Kern had lived there the place had been kept as neat as a new pin, and she would have given them hell if she could see its condition now.

'This place is a pigpen,' Wojna snapped. 'Finish assembling that shooter and then get things cleaned up. And don't forget to keep your gloves on.' Not that Wojna gave a damn about cleanliness, but it was his way of enforcing discipline on Gaten.

'I'm not the bloody housekeeper,' Gaten began; then he saw Wojna's expression. 'All right, if you insist.'

Both men were wearing cotton gloves – something Erika Kern had ordered before she left for Amsterdam. 'I've cleaned the place for fingerprints,' she had warned Wojna, 'so you see everyone wears their gloves while they're still here.'

Upstairs in the bedrooms four more men were sleeping; it was part of Wojna's system that his men slept in shifts so some of the terrorists would be fresh for action at any hour of the day or night. And screw it, Wojna thought as he took another swig from the gin bottle – when are we going to see the action? He little guessed he would have one more job to do inside Germany.

At 6 p.m. in Moscow – still only 4 p.m. in Zürich and Milan – the three Soviet Politburo members charged with the responsibility of identifying the secret informer now faced a different and more terrifying task. At Marshal Prachko's urging the signal had gone out to Sharpinsky to use the entire Soviet apparatus in Western Europe to stop and kill Marenkov. And Anatoli Zarubin had replaced the former head of the KGB as the third member. It was, oddly enough, the moderate Zarubin who had supported Prachko's suggestion, but he had phrased his support carefully.

'Since Sharpinsky, your personal protégé,' the small, dark-haired Russian reminded Prachko, 'failed to suspect his own chief in time, then I suppose we must give him his head to try and remedy his gigantic error.'

Prachko, bristling like the hairs protruding from his ears and nose, grunted and kept silent. It was First Secretary Leonid Sedov who brought up the fearful question. Sedov, who held his position by balancing the moderates against the hard-liners in a tightrope act, was secretly pleased with Zarubin's reaction. If there was a great disaster the responsibility could be dropped squarely on Prachko's barrel chest.

'What action should we take,' Sedov inquired, 'about all the key KGB agents in Western Europe –

agents whose names and addresses Marenkov carries in that remarkable memory of his?' He paused. 'I am thinking particularly of West Germany . . .'

Seated at the long polished table under the chandeliers in the Kremlin, no one spoke for a minute. It was a blockbuster question. Ten years earlier most of the four thousand Communist spies in the Federal Republic had been West Germans; later they had been found to be unreliable and had laboriously been replaced by dedicated East German Communists who had to be provided with fake identities – not a process that could be accomplished overnight. And now these enemy agents were being tracked down by the West German analyst, Dr Richard Meier, with the aid of a giant computer in Cologne known as NADIS.

Into NADIS were fed the behaviour patterns of suspected Soviet agents – drop points for the collection by other agents of secret material, money movements out of suspect bank accounts, clandestine meeting points between agents – and from the computer print-outs Meier was able to relate apparently unconnected persons and events. If to this operation was added Marenkov's lists of names and addresses, the German BND could organize a vast dragnet scooping up the entire Soviet underground apparatus. It would take at least a decade to rebuild the apparatus. It was Leonid Sedov who broke the silence.

'If Marenkov should escape,' he suggested, 'might it not be better if the agents had been evacuated –

later they could infiltrate back into West Germany. It takes at least five years to train an agent,' he reminded them.

'You suggest we send out a preliminary alert?' Prachko asked.

'This is perhaps more your province,' Sedov suggested smoothly.

Marshal Prachko was trapped and he knew it. If he said no and there was a catastrophe he would be blamed. If he said yes – evacuate them – and it proved unnecessary he would also be blamed.

'Only a preliminary alert,' he said at last, hedging his bets.

'And with your protégé Sharpinsky in charge of the operation to destroy Marenkov,' Zarubin observed slyly, 'how can we fail?'

Zürich Airport has closed down.

The grim signal from Brigadier Traber reached Wargrave only fifteen minutes before he was due to take Marenkov to Milano Centrale. He showed the signal to Julian Haller in the odd split-level room with the semicircular window they had first entered on arrival at Molinari's secret headquarters. The American read it and pursed his lips, a rare betrayal of emotion under stress.

'That means we have to go all the way,' the Englishman remarked. 'All the way across Europe to

Holland, since Schiphol is the only airport still open. Which gives the KGB more time to wipe out Marenkov . . .'

'Any extra precautions?' Haller inquired tersely.

'Plenty.' Wargrave glanced at his watch. 'Molinari has installed a scrambler phone on the third floor, thank God. I'm going to be using that until the moment we leave here. And one more thing, Julian . . .' He gave the American specific details as to how the Russian was to be guarded on the train. 'And now I've got to make those phone calls.'

On his way up, Wargrave stopped on the second floor to give more instructions to Phillip John, the backup man Haller had brought in from the CIA. The new British recruit to Sparta was giving his 9 mm Luger pistol a final check when Wargrave entered. Five feet ten inches tall, thirty-three years old, white-faced, Phillip John had curly brown hair and level blue eyes that stared straight at the person he was talking to. He merely glanced up as his visitor came into the room and went on checking the weapon before he inserted it inside his spring-loaded shoulder holster.

'Alarm bells ringing?' he asked casually.

'What makes you think that?' Wargrave inquired.

'I've learned to sense atmospheres.' John smiled faintly. 'And I did hear you come up those stairs at a hell of a lick.'

'Zürich Airport has closed down. So it's all the way to Schiphol.'

'That should be fun.'

'I hope that last remark doesn't indicate your general attitude to the task before us,' Wargrave said slowly and deliberately.

'No point in getting into a lather.' John had a soft-spoken voice and his whole manner was easy and casual. But his movements had been anything but casual when they had played who-grabs-the-gun first to test his reflexes, Wargrave recalled. Even John's clothes were casual; he wore a black-and-white-check sports jacket, carefully cut to conceal the Luger under his left armpit. He smiled at the tense expression on Wargrave's face.

'I rather like the look of that girl agent of yours,' he remarked. 'With her along, the trip will pass in a flash.'

'And that's another thing,' Wargrave continued in the same even tone. 'If I catch you fooling around, I'll break your arm.'

'No problem,' John assured him easily. 'But I have eyes that can see and she has a superb pair of legs. Or haven't you noticed?'

Wargrave ignored the remark, gave him detailed instructions, and left the room. On his way upstairs he felt faintly annoyed with himself. Surely he couldn't be jealous of this good-looking character he had seen chatting with Elsa?

For the next few minutes, alone in the third-floor room with the scrambler phone, he was very busy. His first call to Brigadier Traber gave him a shock.

The Swiss counter-espionage chief in Zürich interrupted him.

'Yes, the met people expect our airport to remain shut down for days. And there's more bad news – I have every reason to believe that Colonel Igor Sharpinsky is at this moment somewhere in Zürich. I'm looking for him now – but with no description of his appearance, the outlook is not promising.'

'He'll be directing the operation to kill Marenkov.'

'I'm certain of it. Any news from Andermatt – from your agent? That could be crucial, since Andermatt sits on top of the Gotthard tunnel the Atlantic Express has to travel through,' Traber reminded the Englishman.

'Not a word. These things take time. But don't forget I've given my friend your number and the code name is Leros. If you get a message from Leros rush it through to me – it could be a cryptic message but I'll understand . . .'

Wargrave's next call was to Captain Franz Wander of the German BND, who was waiting in Wiesbaden. Wander had already received the coded signal warning him Marenkov was the passenger and characteristically had taken action. 'In a few minutes I shall board a train for Basel,' his cheerful voice told the Englishman. 'I have already been in touch with Traber and I will take over security from there while you're passing through Germany. What's that, Harry? Sharpinsky is in Zürich? I don't like the sound of that . . .'

'No one does,' Wargrave admitted.

'One more thing,' the German went on. 'When it becomes clear to the Soviets that you're getting Marenkov safely out I foresee an attempted exodus of their key underground agents – so I have ordered a full alert along the border with the East. Oddly enough, this terrible blizzard makes it easier for us to clamp down on all crossing points. We could net a huge haul.'

'When we're getting Marenkov safely out,' Wargrave repeated. 'I like your confidence – believe me, it's going to be a bastard.'

The call to Springer in Lugano – the Swiss had left a message saying he had moved there – was briefer. Wargrave simply checked that the special arrangements he had earlier requested to be made at Chiasso would be carried out. 'A flatcar will be attached to the rear of the last Wagon-Lit,' the Swiss colonel assured him.

In The Hague, General Max Scholten, cherubic-faced and plump, was talking to his assistant Major Jan Sailer, who was the very opposite in appearance to his chief. Six feet tall, thin-faced, and wearing a perpetual expression of anxiety, Sailer was giving Scholten the latest reports on the movements of the Geiger Group of terrorists. Towering over his short chief, the thirty-seven-year-old Dutchman shook his head dolefully.

'Rumours, nothing but rumours – nothing solid I can get my teeth into . . .'

'But all suggesting the Geiger Group is coming into Holland? Right?'

'That's about it.'

He waited while Scholten took the call on his scrambler phone from Milan. He had already received Wargrave's coded signal that Marenkov would be aboard the Atlantic Express. And he knew that Zürich Airport had closed down – which meant that Marenkov would eventually be airlifted out of Schiphol by the Boeing 707 standing by – if Marenkov survived. And he also knew that the Germans had closed the eastern border to shut the door against an exodus of key underground agents in that direction.

'We look forward to seeing you in Amsterdam,' he concluded his conversation with Wargrave. 'If necessary I can communicate with you aboard the Atlantic Express. One final word. Take care!'

Putting down the phone, Scholten stood up and walked over to the window. The rooftops of the distant Parliament Buildings were streaked with snow, no more than that. The great European blizzard was still bypassing Holland. And one virtue that Scholten possessed was the ability to see two moves ahead in the game.

'Do you remember reading that in 1951 the Soviet agents Burgess and Maclean were taken off from Dunkirk aboard the Soviet freighter *Marya Ulyanova*?' he asked suddenly.

'I think I heard about it, yes,' Sailer replied. He couldn't understand his chief's remark at all.

'The interesting thing is that history may repeat itself,' Scholten continued. 'I have just heard that the 17,000-ton Soviet freighter *Maxim Gorky* has just passed Heligoland in the German Bight and is proceeding south through heavy seas. Soon she will be off the Dutch coast.'

'Really?' commented Sailer, still not seeing in which direction his chief's mind was moving. 'She's going to have a rough passage – the glass is falling rapidly.' Which was true: a Gale Force Eight was building up and alerts had already gone out to watch the dikes where huge waves were battering the sea defences. Less than forty-eight hours earlier Elsa Lang, looking down from the KLM aircraft flying them from London to Schiphol, had seen the white froth of the waves hitting the Dutch coast. 'Incidentally,' Sailer inquired, 'have you informed the minister of recent developments?'

'Not yet.' Scholten turned away from the window and smiled. 'After all, it is Saturday and we do not wish to disturb his weekend prematurely.'

The truth was that – like Brigadier Traber in Zürich – Scholten had not the slightest intention of communicating with his government. The revolt of the European security chiefs against their indecisive politicians was accelerating.

In Room 207 at the Hotel Schweizerhof in Zürich it was 4.30 p.m. when Heinz Golchack also heard that

Zürich Airport was closed down. He had taken the simple precaution of asking his deputy, Rudi Bühler, to phone the airport to inquire about a flight to Germany. He reacted instantly to the news.

'That means they will have to take Peter all the way to Schiphol in Holland. Just in case he reaches here alive we will make further preparations.'

Golchack wrote out two further signals for encoding and transmission by his radio operator, Heinrich Baum, to Professor Mohner's mobile trailer on the Zürichberg, where, in turn, Mohner would retransmit them to their ultimate destinations. The first signal was to senior GRU operative Yuri Gusev, at that moment in Mulhouse, France, close to Basel. The second signal was to Rolf Geiger, controller of the Geiger terrorist group in Amsterdam.

At this moment, as the great blizzard continued to rage over Europe, the ether was alive with signals radioed from one transmitter to another, legal and illegal. And half an hour before the Atlantic Express was due to leave Milan on its long journey two great opposing forces – the Western security systems and the combined KGB–GRU apparatus – were moving on a collision course.

At 4.35 p.m. Sparta was ready to move Marenkov to Milano Centrale and aboard the Atlantic Express. Alone in a third-floor room with Molinari, Wargrave was checking last-minute arrangements with the

SIFAR chief. Phillip John had already left for the station in his own car with Peter Neckermann, Wargrave's radio operator, who would control the special communications unit Molinari had installed in the second Wagon-Lit.

'All clear?' Wargrave asked.

'Absolutely. It is very ingenious,' Molinari agreed. 'I wish you exceptional luck.'

'Time to get moving . . .'

In the split-level room Elsa was waiting with Marenkov, who was carrying her Gucci case. 'You look too expensive for me to keep,' Wargrave commented. Elsa assumed a snooty pose, twirling on her Gucci shoes, showing off her sable and matching Gucci handbag. 'I'm quite sure you couldn't afford me,' she told him saucily. She slipped her arm inside Marenkov's. 'This gentleman, as you can see, is far more my style.'

The Russian was the very image of the successful tycoon in his vicuña coat, handmade shoes, and smart, snap-brim hat. To demonstrate that he had learned his lesson he took a few brisk, light-footed paces around the room – so different from his normal heavy, deliberate tread. Elsa clapped her hands, applauding the performance. Wargrave nodded his approval as he moved toward the door leading down into the courtyard where the Mercedes 450 was waiting. Half his mind was on what was happening in the room, the other half checking to make sure he had forgotten nothing. And alone upstairs after talking to Molinari he had made one last call, but this time not on the scrambler phone. It had been a booked call he had arranged earlier through the Milan exchange, a call to Andermatt.

Chapter Twelve

Andermatt, Switzerland

At 4.40 p.m. Robert Frey put down the receiver of the phone in the bar of the Hotel Storchen in Andermatt and looked up as a woman came down the stairs into the hall beyond. 'Anna, I have a large bloody mary waiting for you,' he called out.

'Drink it yourself – maybe it will choke you.'

Andermatt is a winter ski resort, a small town of white-walled, steep-roofed houses with one main street, standing at the head of a long valley that leads to Gletsch and the Rhône Glacier. Its hostels and hotels were packed with a cosmopolitan crowd of visitors. Among those who had recently returned from the ski slopes was Anna Markos, a striking-looking woman of thirty-eight with a full-bosomed figure that at this moment was occupying the full attention of Robert Frey. The Greek woman stood at the entrance to the bar with her hands on her hips, teasing Frey.

'Come on,' he commanded in French, 'stop clowning about.'

Carrying his own drink and the bloody mary, he went over to a couch to one side of an open fire where half a tree trunk blazed and crackled. Sprawling in front of the fire, he crooked his finger at her. Anna Markos shrugged her well-shaped shoulders, walked into the bar, and, avoiding the empty place beside Frey, settled herself in a chair opposite him.

'Why do we always have to fight?' Frey demanded.

'Because you think you only have to crook your finger and any woman will strip naked and lie down for you.'

'Many have enjoyed that pleasure.'

The *après-ski* crowd was filling up the hotel and bar, faces flushed with their exertions on the slopes, with anticipation of the wild evening to come – French, German, Scandinavian, a few British (the Swiss franc was hard on their wallets).

Anna Markos stripped off her ski jacket, ignoring Frey as she stared around at the crowd. Taking off her ski cap, she shuffled her long black hair loose and presented her profile to the huge Swiss as she briefly checked her appearance in a wall mirror. It was a magnificent profile with a superb aquiline nose, high cheekbones, and a prominent, well-shaped jaw. And now he could see more clearly the thrust of her breasts against the tight azure blue shirt, the outline of her long, powerful legs, which she crossed with slow deliberation. Reaching across for her drink, she evaded the clutch of his hand and drank half the contents of the glass in one deep gulp. Her large black eyes flashed at him over the rim of the glass.

'And this doesn't even buy you an introduction.'

'And yet we have known each other for over—'

'We were never introduced – you intruded on my privacy,' she rapped back ironically.

In force of personality and appearance Robert Frey, famous Swiss mountaineer, matched Anna Markos. Frey dominated the town of Andermatt, engaged in all its activities; and the winter sports season was the climax of his year. Over six feet three tall, a large bearlike man of forty-five with a great beak of a nose and a shaggy mane of dark hair, Frey exuded physical vitality and enjoyment of life. He was something of a local hero.

As a mountaineer, Frey had climbed all the major mountains in Switzerland, including all the faces of the killer Eiger. An expert skier, a skilled pilot, he was also a geologist and an expert on avalanches; he was a member of the Federal Snow and Avalanche Research Institute located on the Weissfluhjoch eight thousand feet above Davos. At this time of the year he was always on the move: taking up his helicopter to check on the snowfall, searching for potential avalanche zones; running his ski school for the cosmopolitan collection of visitors; throwing himself into the *après-ski* revels after dark.

It was after dark that the joking, back-slapping Swiss was in his element. Robert Frey, separated from his wife, had a large appetite for women, and seldom an evening passed when his appetite was not satisfied with a fresh conquest. Anna Markos was – so far – one of his few failures. The healed slash down his right-hand cheek bore witness to Anna's vicious defence of her body when he had trapped her in a bedroom. So he wanted her all the more; sitting sprawled before the log fire, he stared at her magnificent thighs and pictured the moment when they would be pinned under his great bulk.

'Dreaming dreams again?' Anna inquired caustically.

Robert Frey did not reply as he glanced at a couple of French girls who had just entered the bar, stared at him insolently for a moment, and then ordered drinks. From the discothèque in the next room pop music began playing and several couples started jiggling. Things were just beginning to warm up. He sighed, finished his drink, and stood up. Bending down, he took hold of Anna Markos' chin in his great paw. She stared up at him contemptuously.

'I will see you later this evening, my beauty.'

She said nothing as he strolled away, taking his parka off a hook and donning it as he went out into the night and climbed behind the wheel of a Volkswagen van. As he drove off Anna Markos left her drink, pulling on her fur-lined ski jacket while she crossed to the hotel exit and peered out. At five o'clock it was pitch-dark and in the gently falling snow the lights in the windows of the small town were a blurred glow. She hurried to unlock her rented Renault and get behind the wheel. In the distance Frey's red tail-light was vanishing as she started her engine.

Following it along the narrow street where couples

strolled with skis shouldered like fearsome weapons, she pulled in to allow two army vehicles to pass her. Glancing back, she saw soldiers armed with automatic weapons peering out from between the drawn-back canvas covers. Another army truck was parked in a side street. Was there some kind of military exercise in progress, she wondered. Anna Markos had no way of knowing that from his Zürich headquarters Brigadier Traber had just issued a partial alert throughout the whole of Switzerland.

Driving on, she reached the abrupt end of the town. Beyond ran the rule-straight valley, which eventually led to Gletsch and the Rhône Glacier; it was inside the ice tunnels of this glacier that Colonel Springer's agent had recently been found murdered. Pulling up off the deserted road, she got out of the car, took a monocular glass from her pocket, and focused it. The view through the single lens was none too clear but the lights in the huddle of farmhouse buildings helped, and the snow was stopping. She was in time to see Robert Frey's van turn in through the gateway. Above the huddle of buildings rose the radio antennae that helped Frey keep in touch with the avalanche institute above Davos.

As she stood alone by her car, what Anna Markos could not see was the powerful pair of night glasses trained on her from a window in the farmhouse. Emil Platow, the short, thin Swiss of forty with brown hair and sideburns, lowered the night glasses as Robert Frey strode into the darkened room and threw off his parka. He stood silhouetted in the light from the hall. 'What the hell is going on?'

'That woman friend of yours drove after you. She's stopped just beyond the end of the town. It's the second time. I think she's observing us through glasses.'

Without a word Frey took the night glasses from Platow and gazed at the distant parked Renault, at the shadowy figure standing beside it. Impossible to make out the face, but the posture, the general outline of the figure – and the car – were familiar. Platow went on speaking.

'I spotted her in the same position about this time two nights ago.'

Frey lowered the glasses, closed the curtains. 'Put the damned lights on,' he snapped. Going across to a cupboard when the room was illuminated, he took out a bottle and poured himself a glass of wine. He stood drinking it before he spoke.

'Well, I agree – it looks as though we've found our spy.'

Chapter Thirteen

Milano Centrale

Matt Leroy passed through the ticket barrier and climbed aboard the second Wagon-Lit at 1655 exactly – ten minutes before the train was due to depart. Moving back toward the rear of the train, he began checking each compartment. On Track 5 at Milano Centrale the Atlantic Express stretched away into the distance, a sixteen-coach train. At the rear were the two Wagon-Lit sleeping cars specially attached and reserved for the use of Sparta.

Beyond these were the two normal Wagon-Lit coaches and beyond them three first-class ordinary coaches. The rest of the train was made up of second-class coaches – already mostly filled – and the restaurant car. Inside the second rear Wagon-Lit, Leroy took charge of three keys handed to him by a SIFAR man dressed as a rail inspector. All the keys were the same and they locked the end door of the coach, sealing off the last two coaches from the rest of the train. Reaching the last compartment, he rapped on the locked door in a certain way. Peter Neckermann opened it a fraction and then wider.

'Got everything you need?' Leroy inquired.

'The radio equipment is most superb,' the German replied in his careful English.

Leroy glanced inside. There was so much equipment it reminded him of the control panel of a Boeing 747. Giving Neckermann a little salute, he proceeded on to check the rear coach. In about five minutes Mr and Mrs Wells – Marenkov and Elsa Lang – were due to arrive.

Beyond the main concourse in the lower hall at the foot of the escalators Phillip John stood close to the exit. Once he checked his watch and then began marching up and down to keep warm as more passengers ascended into the huge station. He kept glancing down the via Pisani, looking for a dark blue Mercedes 450 automatic.

Behind the wheel of the Mercedes, Wargrave could see the vast silhouette of Milano Centrale coming closer as he kept a steady but not too fast speed. Over to the left loomed the lozenge-shaped giant of the Pirelli Building, and behind him Elsa sat next to Marenkov. Nobody had spoken since he had driven out of the courtyard of Molinari's secret headquarters and he decided it was time to ease the tension.

'Molinari is already at the station controlling the security operation,' he told Marenkov. 'Elsa will lead you into the main hall and up the escalator into the concourse. Resist the temptation to hurry – the place is crawling with guards although you won't see them. I'll come after you and wait at the top of the escalator to make sure no one is following.'

'A well-organized operation, Mr Wargrave,' the Russian commented. 'So far . . .'

'For the vote of confidence, many thanks,' Wargrave observed dryly.

'I merely wished to sound a warning note,' Marenkov replied quietly. 'Somewhere they will make their first attempt – it could be within the next few minutes.'

'That's right,' Elsa said brightly. 'Cheer us up.'

'Whatever happens when we pull up, you just go straight on into the station,' Wargrave instructed. 'Whatever happens,' he repeated.

He turned the Mercedes, swung it close in to the kerb, and stopped the car. A porter opened the rear door with unusual speed; at least, the SIFAR man was wearing a porter's uniform. Taking the Gucci suitcase, he moved off up the steps. Marenkov was just following Elsa Lang out of the car when the incident happened. Two cars approaching the station collided with a grinding crash. The Russian stiffened. 'Come on – diversion,' Elsa whispered as she took his arm. 'All according to plan.'

All hell was breaking loose where the two cars had hit each other. The drivers were outside their vehicles, gesticulating, shouting as uniformed carabinieri ran toward them. Everyone's attention was diverted in that direction; several late passengers paused to watch the commotion. Elsa and her temporary husband were already at the top of the steps, moving into the lower hall, walking past Phillip John and three carabinieri with rifles in their hands, stepping onto the deserted escalator, which carried them up into the concourse.

'Track 5,' Elsa said as they stepped off the escalator. At that moment, as they started toward the ticket barrier, a sleepy porter driving a luggage truck almost drove into Elsa. The Russian moved with great agility; grabbing Elsa around the waist, he hauled her clear and then, as she took his arm, he walked with several heavy, deliberate paces at his normal walk. It was the near-accident that had put him off his stroke. Recovering, he brisked up his pace, walking with a quick, light-footed tread, the tickets in his hand as they approached the barrier.

Outside the restaurant Ugo Sala, the KGB agent, was standing while he drank his second cup of coffee to keep out the bitter cold. He had been watching the prosperous-looking couple without much interest until the luggage truck incident. Now he froze. While training in Moscow he had seen Marenkov on several occasions and Ugo Sala was an astute observer. He had noticed the change in the walk and as he watched the man in the vicuña coat he was sure of his identity even though the change in appearance was astonishing.

Had Sala been carrying a gun – which he was not – and had he been a good shot – which he was not – he might have tried to shoot Marenkov. Not that he would have succeeded because two SIFAR plainclothes men with their hands in their pockets were standing only a few metres away. Instead he left the station and hurried to his parked cab. Once inside with the door shut he used the radio telephone.

'Rome Three calling. Rome Three calling. Passenger has now boarded train . . .'

At the bottom of the escalator Phillip John stood waiting with Harry Wargrave while Mr and Mrs Wells, the Shell International oil executive and his wife, disappeared from view as they walked on into the concourse. Behind them outside the station the commotion caused by Molinari's staged accident continued. 'You look tired,' John said. Wargrave glanced at the white-faced marksman. It had been a simple statement, as though John didn't really give a damn.

'Time enough to feel tired when we reach Schiphol,' Wargrave replied tersely.

But John was right. Wargrave felt bone-weary from the feet up. He had stayed up half Friday night double-checking plans with Molinari, and only a few hours ago he had flown all the way to Bucharest and back. The lower hall was deserted now; the carabinieri had disappeared, the last passengers had scrambled up the escalator. The two Englishmen were alone as Wargrave lit a cigarette, said, 'See you,' and stepped onto the slow-moving escalator. Phillip John would board the Wagon-Lit independently.

As the escalator carried him up, Wargrave stood

casually with one hand on the rail, waiting for his first glimpse of the concourse beyond. Elsa and Marenkov should just about be passing through the ticket barrier. Reaching the top, he stepped off and then paused, moving a few feet to his right until he stopped in front of the downward-moving escalator. Elsa and Marenkov had just passed through the ticket barrier and were walking toward the entrance to the second Wagon-Lit.

At the bottom of the escalator Phillip John whipped his 9 mm Luger out of his shoulder holster, took swift aim, holding the pistol in both hands, and fired a single shot. Wargrave fell backward, collapsing onto the moving escalator, which slowly carried his slumped body back down into the lower hall.

Elsa and Marenkov heard the single shot; still holding the Russian's arm, she looked back in time to see Wargrave slump, to see his crumpled body slide slowly out of view as the escalator carried it down. Her grip tightened on Marenkov's arm. She had a feeling of constriction in her throat, she felt sick with shock, then her training asserted itself.

'We go straight on board . . .'

Matt Leroy was waiting at the entrance to the second Wagon-Lit and started to ask a question, but Elsa interrupted him. 'I need to see Julian immediately.' Leroy, whose orders were to stay by the only open door to the two rear sleeping cars, told a SIFAR man in the corridor to escort them. Haller was waiting for them in Compartment 3 – he had left the secret base with Molinari a few minutes ahead of Wargrave to check for himself security arrangements at the station – and the smile on his face vanished as he saw Elsa's expression.

'Oh, Julian – they've shot Harry. He was at the top of the escalator when . . .' Her voice broke and it was Marenkov who wrapped an arm around her waist and lowered her to a seat as the American stood up quickly. 'Lock this door,' he snapped, 'and only open it for the special knock.' Marenkov locked the door; Elsa stiffened herself and took the Smith and Wesson from her handbag. She laid it on the seat beside her.

'I'll be all right,' she told the Russian, 'and I still have a job to do.'

Marenkov sat beside her and spoke with unusual gentleness. 'In Russia we have a saying: tears wash away all tensions.'

'No tears . . .'

Outside, Julian Haller was striding along the corridor with a grim expression. All the blinds were lowered in the rear two Wagon-Lits to shield the coaches from the platform. At the end of the second coach Matt Leroy was still waiting by the open door. 'Wargrave has been shot,' Haller informed him. 'Stay where you are,' he ordered as Leroy turned toward the door. 'No one leaves the train.' At that moment Phillip John climbed aboard and faced Haller.

'You've heard the news?' he asked quietly.

'That Wargrave has been shot? Yes. How is he?'

'They took him to the Swiss Red Cross place here.' John paused. 'I have bad news, I fear. Harry Wargrave is dead.'

Haller stared at him, his expression devoid of emotion. He knew already the reaction would come later. 'How did it happen?' he demanded. 'Have they got the killer?'

'Not so far. I was at the foot of the escalator when someone fired a single shot. I couldn't see where it came from. Must have been an expert sniper. The station is swarming with carabinieri and SIFAR men. They've closed off all exits and Molinari has taken personal control of the search operation.'

'Take over here from Leroy,' Haller ordered. 'Shut that damn door and allow no one else aboard. You come with me,' he told Leroy. 'Mount guard outside our compartment.' Taking a deep breath, he went back to Compartment 3. If you have a lousy job to do, get it over with quickly, he told himself. He would have liked to have a word with Molinari but the express was due to leave shortly. In response to his special knock the door was opened a fraction by Elsa and through the narrow opening she was pointing her Smith and Wesson at him. All exactly as per Wargrave's specific orders, he thought sadly. Her eyes searched his as he came inside and locked the door.

'Is he alive?' she asked quietly.

Haller shook his head. She sat down very erect, holding the gun in her lap, staring at the compartment wall. Haller squeezed her shoulder, lit a cigarette, and inserted it between her lips. 'I hate this bloody outfit,' she said tonelessly. Marenkov, tactfully, folded his arms as he sat beside her and said nothing. She hates me now, he was thinking – if I had stayed in Russia the man this girl secretly loved would still be alive.

It was only two minutes before the departure of the Atlantic Express when the late passenger appeared, carrying a small bag in one hand while the other held the cane to help him walk. Six feet tall, he seemed shorter as he hobbled along with a stoop, his shoulders bent. He wore a heavy astrakhan fur coat, which gave the impression of a heavy-built man, and a Tyrolean hat with a tiny red feather in the hatband. His hair was shaggy and grey and he peered ahead through a pair of bifocals. Despite his slight limp he moved surprisingly quickly with an odd, shambling gait. From behind the window of the closed door Phillip John guessed his age at sixty and never gave him a second thought.

Boarding the third Wagon-Lit coach, the passenger presented a ticket in the name of Joseph Laurier and the attendant ushered him to a double sleeping compartment reserved in this name. Laurier spoke not a word to the attendant, who heard him lock the door on the inside. 'A sourpuss,' the attendant thought as he returned to his post at the end of the coach. There was always one on every trip.

A minute later, the express, hauled by a single Bo-Bo 111 electric locomotive – a sixteen-coach train weighing over seven hundred tons – glided out from under the immense vault of Milano Centrale, rattled over the maze of switches and gathered speed as it headed north. The station clock registered exactly 1705 hours.

Part Three

Avalanche Express

Chapter Fourteen

Chiasso, Lugano

The coaches swayed from side to side as the express built up speed crossing the flat, snowbound plain of the Po. In one hour it would reach Chiasso, the Swiss border point. Inside his double sleeping compartment in the third Wagon-Lit, Joseph Laurier, the last man to board the express, lifted the blind to look out into the night. The lights of Milan's outer suburbs had gone; by the light of a rising full moon he saw snow falling on the endless plain. Unlike most passengers who have just boarded a train, Laurier seemed restless.

Closing the blind, he left his compartment and began wandering toward the front of the train with his shuffling tread. Walking slowly, gripping the handrail to keep his balance, he passed through the two normal Wagon-Lits and then peered into each compartment as he progressed from coach to coach.

Sometimes passengers looked up as he passed, but from his vague glance no one guessed that he was noticing every single person aboard the express. Moving through the dining car, where tables were being laid – the first dinner sitting was at six o'clock –

he continued his slow progress toward the front of the train. Long before the express was approaching Chiasso he had walked the full length of the train and back again to his own compartment.

In the communications compartment at the rear of the second Wagon-Lit, Peter Neckermann removed his headphones and looked up at Matt Leroy. 'I have reported to Springer again that everything is OK so far.'

'OK?' Leroy stared at the gnome-like little German who spoke good English. It was one of the qualifications that had enabled Neckermann to obtain his old job as international radio operator with the *Kriminalpolizei* in Wiesbaden. 'OK?' Leroy repeated. 'With Harry Wargrave dead?'

'You saw the body?' Neckermann inquired.

'For Christ's sake, no – I wasn't allowed to leave the train.'

The droopy-moustached American was irritated. Neckermann had been a friend of Wargrave's and he had shown no emotion on hearing of the Englishman's death. These goddamn Europeans, Leroy was thinking. Stiff upper lip and all that crap.

'Did Haller or anyone else see the body?' Neckermann persisted.

'No.'

'I see . . .'

Unsure whether he could control himself, Leroy left the communications compartment and went back to Compartment 3, where Haller and Elsa were guarding Marenkov. Phiilip John stood aside to let him enter the rear coach. 'You look as though you've swallowed a bee,' the Englishman commented in his soft voice. 'Missing the Coca-Cola?'

Leroy punched him on the arm none too gently. 'I did just that, fellow, so watch the smart remarks. And your extra nipple is showing.' He tapped John's shoulder holster. There was a blur of movement and Leroy found himself staring into the muzzle of the Luger. 'OK,' he conceded, 'so you're red-hot with the shooter.' As he disappeared into the rear coach John slipped the gun back in place and unfastened the top button of his coat, which had tightened it to expose the outline of the weapon. John was a man willing to learn from anyone.

Knocking on the door, Leroy faced the set procedure – the door opened a fraction, Haller stared out holding a Colt .45 and let him inside. Leroy was relieved to see that outwardly, at least, the atmosphere of gloom had lifted. Everyone was making an effort. Marenkov was playing a game of solitaire with a pack of cards; as he entered, Elsa reached over and moved a card into place.

'Neckermann just reported again to Springer,' Leroy informed Haller.

'We'll reach Chiasso soon,' the American commented.

He lifted the blind a fraction as the express passed Como station and then lowered it. He had no way of knowing that outside in the night the passage of the express was being observed from the fourth-floor window of an apartment block close to the railway line. Inside the darkened room the owner of the apartment watched the long glowworm of lights speeding past. Closing the curtains, he switched on the light, opened a closet, and pressed a concealed catch, and a flap dropped open revealing a high-powered transceiver. He began transmitting.

As the express approached Chiasso, Joseph Laurier lay reclining on his berth inside his sleeping compartment in the third Wagon-Lit. Checking his watch, he became restless again. He swung his long legs onto the floor, took the bone-handled knife he had kept under his pillow, and slipped it down inside the thick sock of his right leg. The train was slowing down as he slipped on his astrakhan coat and Tyrolean hat. As the express stopped, he picked up his cane.

It was 6.05 p.m. when the Atlantic Express stopped at the Swiss border point, where there were huge marshalling yards, and where Swiss Passport Control and Customs board trains. And it was no longer snowing. After the steady rumble of the fast-moving wheels an uncanny hush descended on the interior of the train. Outside, the platform was deserted. Inside Compartment 3 Elsa picked up her revolver and rested it in her lap.

'You are expecting trouble?' Marenkov inquired.

'It's Chiasso. Every stop is a potential danger point.

Would you mind not playing with your cards until we're moving again? I don't want any distractions.'

'Then you will have to conceal your legs – if you wish my attention not to be distracted.'

Elsa forced a faint smile: the Russian was trying to cheer her up at a moment of tension. Haller had gone out into the corridor to keep watch and she felt her sole responsibility for guarding Marenkov – and again intuitively he had sensed her mood.

Outside on the platform, Joseph Laurier was trudging up and down alongside the third Wagon-Lit like a man who feels the need of fresh air after an overheated train. And he saw signs of growing activity. Three new passengers appeared from the waiting room, all men and all well protected in fur coats. Obviously travelling together, and carrying cases, they entered a second-class car and slammed the door shut. Laurier watched them and then turned to look toward the rear of the platform.

A huge canvas screen over seven feet high blocked off the platform near the end of the express. Somewhere in the distance Laurier could hear the rumble of approaching wheels. He glanced to his left again as a fourth passenger emerged from the waiting room and strolled toward the express, a far more striking-looking person than the three nondescripts who had boarded the second-class car.

Hatless even on that bitter cold evening, the newcomer was six foot two tall, wore a long blue coat, and was smoking a pipe. As he passed close by,

Laurier observed his prominent cheekbones, his strong nose, the neat moustache as black as his thick hair, his hard jaw, and the dark, alert eyes. He walked with a steady, controlled tread and everything about the man suggested hidden reserves of strength. Tucking his slim executive case under his arm, he tugged with both hands at the semi-frozen door handle and disappeared inside a first-class car.

For about ten minutes nothing more happened and then there was a resounding thump and the express shuddered. Something had been attached to the rear of the train. Laurier climbed back on board and a few minutes later, leaning out of the window of his compartment, he saw a dozen uniformed Swiss Passport Control and Customs officials boarding the train. Which was most unusual, Laurier reflected; normally only two men from each service came onto northbound trains at Chiasso.

Inside Compartment 3 Elsa was startled as the train shuddered under the heavy thump. 'What the hell was that?' she asked Haller, who had just returned to the compartment.

'Some kind of shunting, I guess. There's a big marshalling yard here.'

A few minutes later the express began moving again, heading for the eastern shore of Lake Lugano and the causeway that carried the railroad over to the west bank. And no one inside Compartment 3 was aware of the significance of the great thump that had hit the train. Attached to the rear of the last Wagon-

Lit was a flatcar – and perched on the flatcar, held down by snap chains, was a large Alouette helicopter, its rotor blades folded parallel with the flatcar.

'I think I'd like a bit of exercise,' Elsa said. 'Do you mind?' she asked Haller. 'I'm getting claustrophobia locked up inside this compartment.'

'Just so long as you stay inside the rear two Wagon-Lits,' the American replied.

'It's not just the exercise . . .' Elsa had opened her case and was putting on her dark wig. 'It might be an idea if I had a look at the passengers – I could just spot something.' She put on her horn-rimmed glasses and the military-style raincoat she had always worn while waiting to collect the cassettes from Necker-mann in Basel. 'No one is going to recognize me looking like this. At least, I jolly well hope not,' she added in mock indignation.

'Well, take care,' Haller said reluctantly. 'Maybe it is a good idea,' he added.

Haller had changed his mind quickly. Not because he really thought she would spot anything significant – but it might help to release some of the tension out of her system after the shock of Wargrave's death.

It was Harry Wargrave Elsa was thinking about as she moved along the swaying corridor and waited while Phillip John unlocked the door of the second car. Planning out the journey back in Milan, Wargrave had given her an instruction. 'After Chiasso put on your Basel gear and take a walk through the train. Take a good look at the passengers – you might spot someone. You suggest it – Julian will jump on me if I do.'

Several cars ahead of her, six men dressed in Passport Control and Customs officer uniforms were just entering the compartment occupied by the trio of men who had boarded the train together at Chiasso. The three swarthy-faced men looked up in surprise at this invasion and then produced their passports. The compartment was so crowded now it was difficult for anyone to move.

'Baggage! ' snapped one of the officials.

Heaving down a case off the rack, he snapped the catches open, stared inside, and whistled. Inside the case on top of some clothes were three Walther pistols. One of the Italians grabbed for a pistol and was knocked back against his seat by a chopping blow from a Swiss. A second Italian tried to punch another Swiss in the groin, and a fist slammed into his jaw. Within a minute all three men were handcuffed and two more cases had been opened. Again one of the Swiss whistled and showed the contents to his companions.

'Explosives, too. Hand grenades, gelignite sticks . . .'

Elsa entered the corridor of the car as the first Italian was brought out and hustled toward the front of the train. Walking more slowly, she saw the second two handcuffed Italians escorted from the compartment and taken away in the same direction. As she passed the compartment one of the Swiss inside pulled down the blind, but not before she had seen the open case on the seat with the pistols lying inside. Turning around, she went back toward the rear of the express to report what she had seen to Haller.

Walking into the Wagon-Lit ahead of the two sealed cars at the rear, she saw a grey-haired man with a cane emerging from a sleeping compartment; then he changed his mind and went back inside. Still walking rapidly, she passed the compartment, noticed that the door was only half-closed, heard something, started to turn. A hand grasped her around the throat, a second hand gripped her handbag as she reached for the gun and dragged her savagely back inside the compartment. 'Try to scream and I'll throttle you,' a voice hissed in her ear.

Half-choked, Elsa went on fighting inside the compartment, kicking viciously behind her, aiming for her captor's shins. The handbag containing the gun was wrenched out of her hand. Laurier gave her a hard shove in the back that sprawled her face down on the berth. Slamming the door shut, he locked it as she spun around on her back and prepared to launch herself with one hand crooked in a claw. Then she froze with shock as Laurier pulled off his grey wig and glasses.

'You really wouldn't want to kill me? Or would you?' Harry Wargrave inquired quizzically.

She stared up at him, all the colour drained from her face. Wargrave grinned down at her. 'Sorry I had to knock you about, but I had to get you in here fast – someone could have been coming down the corridor.'

'What . . .' Her voice choked, this time with emotion. 'God, I thought you were dead.'

'That was the whole idea – I fixed it with Phillip John and Molinari. It was John who fired the shot – deliberately just nicking my shoulder. He's a crack shot, thank God. Then they rushed me to the Swiss Red Cross unit in the station. I changed into this outfit in a room next door and boarded the express with a minute to spare. Cigarette?'

She ignored the extended packet, her expression bleak. 'I couldn't ask why you did all this, I suppose?' she asked in a strangely icy tone.

'Something's wrong aboard this express – I can't put my finger on it yet. I needed to work alone without Haller breathing down my neck. And I wanted to check all the passengers without being recognized. I've been in this business a long time and I reckon the KGB have my picture.'

'You didn't warn me,' she said very quietly.

'I couldn't.'

'You bastard!' She stood up suddenly, swung her right hand, and struck him hard across the face. Then she gave way, buried her face in his chest as he hugged her to him. 'Harry, you bastard ... bastard ... bastard.' Her body, thrust against his, was trembling and shuddering. He lifted her chin until their eyes met. 'No tears,' he warned. 'You have to go back to Haller looking normal. No swollen eyes.' He held her tight until the trembling quietened, and then held her at arms' length. Her grey eyes were glossy but she had fought back the tears. 'Good girl.'

'I'm a mess.' She turned away and studied herself in the wall mirror. Her black wig was awry; her horn-rimmed glasses had fallen onto the floor in their struggle, but they were unbroken. She fixed herself while they went on talking. 'You said no tears – you mean I'm to go back and not let them know?'

'Exactly that, for the moment.'

'Julian is pretty broken up about you. He hasn't said much but I can tell. Surely you can't suspect *him*?'

'Julian Haller is the best operative who ever came out of Washington. Just trust me. At this stage a man on the outside – outside the sealed coaches – could be a distinct asset.'

He wasn't telling her everything, Elsa guessed, but by now she had accepted the situation. Harry Wargrave – always unorthodox, a loner – had so often been proved right in the past. 'But Phillip John knows,' she pointed out.

'Only that I'm alive. He thinks I'm still back in Milan, running the operation by remote control. And,' he went on gently, 'I couldn't warn you – are you sure you could have reacted convincingly when you heard the news if you'd known the truth?'

'No,' she admitted. 'Do I come along and see you secretly every now and again?'

'Definitely. And at regular intervals. I need to know anything that happens in the rear Wagon-Lits. One more thing: at any time Traber may transmit an urgent signal to me from Zürich. The signal will come from someone called Leros. That you get to me fast.'

'Your radio operator, Peter Neckermann, thinks you're dead – at least, I think he does.' She frowned. 'You didn't tell him? No? It was funny – I went in to see him and, come to think of it, he took the news very coolly.' She smiled faintly and looked at Wargrave with a hint of pride. 'As though he didn't believe they could knock you off that easily.' She glanced at herself finally in the mirror and put on her horn-rimmed glasses, then turned to face him. 'If I really looked like this would you ever notice me?'

He took hold of her chin and kissed her full on the mouth. 'And that's something else you don't report back to Julian,' he said with mock severity. 'He doesn't believe in cohabitation between agents.'

'I'd better go,' she said hastily. 'Oh, God, I nearly forgot to tell you. Three assassins came on board at Chiasso, but Swiss security nabbed them.' She told him quickly what had happened and Wargrave's reaction surprised her. Listening with half-closed eyes, he then questioned her.

'A bit obvious, wasn't it?' he commented. 'The KGB are better than that. It stinks to high heaven of a diversion – something to put us off our guard.' His tone became urgent. 'Try and convey to Haller that your instinct tells you we're moving into a danger zone. The arrest of these three thugs may make him relax.' He rapped an irregular tattoo on the basin. 'Knock like that when you come back – then I'll know it's you. And for God's sake get the message over to Haller – I sense big trouble coming.'

As the Atlantic Express stopped at the station of Lugano, perched high above the city, three different pairs of radio detection vans were patrolling the streets below. The vehicles were under the direct control of Springer from his local headquarters in the tiny Piazza Cioccaro.

'If some secret transmitter is going to radio progress to the Soviet base Sharpinsky has set up in Zürich, that transmitter has to be near the station,' Springer informed his deputy, Captain Theodor Horner.

Horner, a short, round-shouldered man of forty with reddish hair and eyebrows, was looking down from the second-floor office into the deserted square. Surrounded with ancient stone buildings, on the western side was the entrance to the funicular that climbed to the station. 'And what progress would it report?' he inquired.

'Lack of progress,' Springer replied cryptically.

'And now I'm going to meet the express. It is due two minutes from now.'

Running downstairs, the agile colonel waited while the guard opened the front door, and then hurried across the beautiful little square to where the funicular was waiting for him. The doors closed the moment he stepped inside and the car ascended through the tunnel to the station. 'Lack of progress . . .' Springer had already been informed by Peter Neckermann's radio aboard the express that three Italians armed with weapons and explosives had been arrested. First round to us, he was thinking as he stepped out of the car and walked onto the Lugano north-bound platform. The Atlantic Express glided past him, halted.

No passengers were waiting to board the train. Springer wondered whether Wargrave might step off to have a word; on Haller's specific instructions, the Englishman's 'death' had not been reported. The American saw no reason to send negative news at a time like this. The Swiss watched while a train door opened; two men in uniforms stepped out followed by the three handcuffed Italians, who had to be helped down the steep drop. Another uniformed officer left the train and the three Italians were hustled away to three waiting police cars.

On the far side of the road, almost out of sight, a green Volkswagen was parked without lights. Springer waited until the express started moving again, glanced across at the Volkswagen, which he imagined belonged to one of the night rail staff, and went back down inside the funicular to the Piazza Cioccaro. Within a matter of minutes his staff would be subjecting the Italians to intensive interrogation.

Slumped behind the wheel of the green Volkswagen, Franco Visani, assistant manager of one of the smaller banks in Lugano, a small, portly Swiss of forty-seven, watched as the three handcuffed Italians were hustled inside the police cars. He went on watching as he saw a slim civilian return to the funicular and wondered who he was. Waiting a little longer until the police cars had gone, he switched on his lights and ignition and drove rapidly down the curving road into the city.

It took him only three minutes to reach his apartment. Once inside he opened the wall closet that contained a concealed transmitter and began sending his prepared signal. Visani was a supremely confident man. Although he checked his watch, he omitted to set his time clock for two and a half minutes. He ignored his training. In any case, this was a maximum priority signal and he had to complete it. Also, he was a slow, pedantic operator.

Springer had just returned to his second-floor room, after chatting briefly with the guard downstairs, when two radio detector vans working in conjunction began picking up Visani's coded signal. Inside each van the operators turned their aerials with care, plotting their courses until they crossed, pinpointing the transmitter's location. A phone rang inside Springer's operations room. Horner listened for a moment, then replaced the receiver.

'A transmitter. In the Piazza Dante, for God's sake.'

Springer ran down the stairs for the second time within ten minutes. Accompanied by three men dressed in civilian clothes like himself, he continued running along a side street. When he reached the Piazza Dante uniformed policemen were already there. One had used a skeleton key to gain admittance.

'The fourth floor, I think,' he informed Springer. 'One of my men is up there already.'

On the fourth floor a skeleton key was used again. Two policemen with drawn pistols burst into the apartment and Springer followed calmly with his hands in his coat pockets. Visani was just ending his transmission, had just signed off and was closing the cupboard. He turned to face the policemen's pistols. Keeping out of sight, Springer caught sight of the Communist agent's face in a wall mirror. He withdrew from the apartment and returned to the Piazza Cioccaro to tell Horner.

'Franco Visani, of all people! I have already sent out a call from a police car to pick up all his known associates. I suspect we have just cracked a major cell. I wonder what signal he sent?'

Springer might well have felt less happy with his success had he known the contents of the signal Franco Visani had just transmitted to Mohner's mobile trailer on the heights of the Zürichberg – a signal that

in turn Mohner had retransmitted to the Hotel
Schweizerhof.

*Deception operation has just been completed. Three men in
handcuffs taken off Atlantic Express by police at
Lugano . . .*

In Room 207 at the Hotel Schweizerhof, Heinz
Golchack read the signal and grunted. It was hardly a
model of conciseness and he made a mental note to
reprimand Visani through his immediate superior. He
handed it to his deputy, Rudi Bühler.

'It's working,' Golchack remarked placidly. Checking his watch, which registered 7.10 p.m., he walked
over to the large-scale map of Switzerland spread over
the bed and indicated a certain point on the railway
between Lugano and Bellinzona, the next stop. 'It will
happen there.'

'We should be out of here in half an hour, then,'
Bühler replied.

'We shall see.' In any case, Golchack was thinking,
I always have another card up my sleeve, something
that even Bühler knows nothing about. As a piece of
insurance it was useful to have a trained assassin
aboard the train.

Chapter Fifteen

Vira, Bellinzona

Height: six foot two; colour of eyes: black;
name: Jorge Santos. Citizenship: Spanish.

At Lugano the Passport Control and Customs officials had entered the first-class compartment occupied by the fourth passenger who had come aboard at Chiasso. The tall Santos sat in his corner seat with his long legs stretched out while the Swiss checked his passport and then handed it back to him. Relaxed, still smoking his pipe, the Spaniard stared back at the official with unmoving eyes while he drew a thumbnail across his dark, neat moustache.

'Where are you travelling to, sir?' the Swiss inquired.

'I go all the way to Amsterdam,' Santos replied in careful French.

There is something magnetic about this passenger, the Swiss was thinking, some feeling of pent-up tension despite his casual posture. He felt uncertain but could not pin down the reason for his uncertainty. And the official in uniform was one of Springer's men. A search of the Spaniard's case by his colleague in Customs uniform produced nothing unusual.

'Thank you, sir.'

The two officials withdrew and proceeded along the train. Puffing gently at his pipe, Santos glanced out of the window where three men in handcuffs were being escorted out of the station. During the lap from Chiasso, Jorge Santos had observed several things. A rather drab-looking girl with dark hair and glasses had passed his compartment, glancing in. He had the impression she was looking for someone. And then a late-middle-aged man with shaggy grey hair and carrying a cane had passed, who also glanced in.

Soon after the Swiss officials had left, Santos stood up, opened the door, saw the corridor was empty, and slipped inside the next empty first-class compartment. His movements were anything but casual as he reached under a seat, wrenched loose the 9 mm Luger attached with adhesive tape, and slid it inside his pocket. Returning to his own compartment, he sat down again in the corner seat, stretched out his legs, and puffed contentedly at his pipe.

At the small military sub-unit just back off the road that led across the high plateau on the way from Lugano to Bellinzona, the uniformed Swiss guard stamped his feet to keep them from freezing. God, what a night to be on duty! Behind him was a closed gate in a high barbed wire fence protecting the huddle of concrete buildings which, basically, were a series of sheds where army vehicles were stored. Then he stiffened and unlooped the rifle off his shoulder.

A large Mercedes travelling along the deserted snowbound highway had suddenly turned off and headed for the gate. Blinded by the headlights, he jumped to one side and then the car drew alongside him and halted. The driver climbed out, a tall, loose-limbed man wearing a heavy overcoat who had his right hand inside his pocket as he began speaking rapidly in Italian. The guard interrupted him.

'This is military property. You are not allowed—'

'For God's sake, it's my daughter. And you have a phone.' He pointed to the overhead wire the car had stopped under. 'Look in the back. She's desperately ill – we need a doctor, a hospital, and quickly . . .'

The guard glanced at the man in the front passenger seat, then peered into the back where a man in the rear seat had lowered the window. The Swiss guard had a daughter of his own, but it was not a child he saw next to the man, it was a dark-haired girl in her late twenties, a girl doubled over in pain as she grasped her stomach and groaned horribly. He was still looking inside when the tall driver rammed a knife deep into his back. The soldier collapsed, dead.

The next stage of the operation proceeded with a precision that might well have been admired by a Swiss military commander. The girl, suddenly perfectly fit, jumped out of the car with a pair of wire cutters and proceeded to cut a hole in the wire fence large enough for a man to walk through. The tall driver climbed onto the roof of the car, took the long-handled wire cutter handed to him by another of the men, and severed the overhead phone line. The man who had sat by the girl in the rear bent over the soldier's body and relieved him of his military great-coat and cap.

Three minutes later there was a furious hammering at the guard-house door beyond the wire fence. The off-duty Swiss soldier inside who was sleeping with his legs perched on a chair woke with a start. Befuddled with sleep he still had the presence of mind to pick up his rifle before he opened the door. Outside, a Swiss-uniformed soldier he assumed was Giulio stood bent over holding a limp girl in his arms. 'What the hell . . .' He was still speaking when the girl shot him with a Mauser pistol. Dropping to the ground, she rushed inside, crossed an empty room, and stood in the doorway of an inner room where a third Swiss soldier was reaching for the phone. She shot him twice.

'Was that necessary, Luisa?' the man in uniform asked.

'It was quickest. Now, get on with it.'

The dark-haired Luisa had a very pointed chin, sharp eyes, and a dominating manner. Urging the three men to hurry, she checked her watch. It was 6.50 p.m. In four minutes the Atlantic Express would reach Lugano. Satisfied that they were moving fast enough, she rushed back to the hole in the fence.

Six minutes later all three men were wearing the uniforms of the dead Swiss soldiers, two of them ill-fitting, but this was a detail that would be noticed only in the light and at close quarters. None of the three men aboard the army vehicle they were now driving through the gate they had unlocked – using one of the keys hanging from the guardroom wall – had any intention that they would be seen at close quarters. The vehicle they had taken from one of the sheds was a light Jeep mounted with a heavy machine gun – mounted on a swivel so it could be fired at any angle.

The Mercedes had already left the army post manned by only three men – as the attackers had known long before they arrived. With Luisa behind the wheel, the car was speeding along the highway northward; to her right ran the rail line over which the Atlantic Express would pass on its way to Bellin-zona. In the distance she could just make out the square silhouette of the signal tower at Vira. Pulling up on the deserted highway with a violent jerk of the brakes, she flashed her headlights on and off, on and off, on and off . . .

Inside the signal tower Emilio Valenti, a short, frog-faced man who had been surreptitiously staring south down the highway for the past ten minutes, saw the flashing headlights. He walked back up the tower to where his colleague was bent over the control panel. Signalman Carli was giving his full attention to the control panel; the Atlantic Express was due to pass over his stretch of the line. 'Cigarette?' Emilio suggested. His colleague shook his head; he had one burning in the ashtray by his side, a fact Emilio had already observed. Emilio took a deep breath, hefted the heavy wrench he was holding, and brought it down on the back of Carli's skull. Carli, killed instantly, was still sliding to the floor when Emilio pressed a button on the control panel. On the northbound track a signal at green turned to red.

Snatching up his coat, Emilio put it on as he left the signal tower and hurried down the steps. Panting, he ran like a rabbit across the track and over the verge to the highway as the Mercedes arrived. Pulling up with a screech of brakes, Luisa screamed at him. 'Not the front door – get in the rear.' She was moving again before he could shut the door.

'I think I killed him . . .' Emilio began nervously.

'Shut your mouth, you creep. I've got a job to do.'

In the rearview mirror she could see the lights of the Jeep slowing down. And half a kilometre behind her the three men in the Jeep could see the lights of the Atlantic Express approaching as they parked by the roadside.

'The last Wagon-Lit, remember, Marco,' the man behind the wheel of the Jeep reminded his companion. 'We know he's in that car.'

'Think I don't know my job?' Marco snapped. 'You handle the driving – I'll handle this.' He took a tighter grip on the heavy machine gun as the driver switched on the ignition.

'Why are you so nervy?' Haller demanded. 'They took off that bunch of thugs at Lugano. Sure, they'll try something else later.'

'I've just got this feeling,' Elsa persisted. 'Call it a hunch, call it what you damn well like – I've got this feeling something nasty is about to happen . . .'

The express had left Lugano, was now picking up speed as it approached the plateau beyond the city which the railway crossed before it began descending the great drop to Bellinzona, where the track clings like a thread to the mountainside. Inside the compartment Haller sat alongside Elsa while Marenkov stood with his back to the window, easing the stiffness out of his limbs. With the blind closed, from outside the train the Russian's bulk made a perfect silhouette. He was watching Elsa closely.

'What happened while you were going through the train?' he inquired softly.

'I saw those three gunmen being arrested.'

'I think you saw – or experienced – something else. Am I wrong?' Marenkov held up a warning hand. 'Think before you speak. I am a man who respects a clever woman's intuition.' As he spoke Marenkov was thinking of his poor, dead wife, Irina; of the times when she had sensed coming shifts in the Moscow power factions and had warned him.

'Thanks,' Elsa replied somewhat ungraciously. Marenkov was beginning to get to know her a little too well. Risking what must seem a touch of insolence, she looked sideways at Haller. 'I just think we can't afford to relax for a single second.'

'What the hell makes you think I'm relaxing?' the American snapped. 'We're running a deadly gauntlet all the way to Schiphol. What I can't understand is what's got into you at this particular moment.'

'Fear,' Marenkov said quietly. He was still standing with his back to the window, still watching Elsa curiously. 'I can always smell fear.' The Russian shrugged and gave up his probing of the English girl. 'The express is slowing down,' he remarked.

Haller checked his watch, although he knew they couldn't possibly be approaching Bellinzona yet. 'Must be a signal against us,' he commented.

In the main signal tower at Lugano the chief signalmaster, Alois Reiter, a forty-year-old man with restless eyes, was staring at his control panel. He was staring at the Vira stop signal, a stop signal for which there was no reason. Another man might have hesitated while he thought of reasons, might have phoned the Vira tower. Instead Reiter instantly obeyed instructions. He dialled a number that put him straight through to Springer's headquarters. Horner took the call, listened briefly, put his hand over the receiver, and reported to Springer.

'There's an unexplained stop signal on the line – the tower near Vira. The express will be halted in less than two minutes from now.'

Springer's reaction was electric. 'Warn Haller – major alert.' He glanced at a map on the wall, turned to another officer. 'Red alert for sector 431. All vehicles to be stopped – civilian, police, military, the lot. Set up roadblocks around the entire sector. Seal it off. Nothing moves in or out.'

'Military vehicles, too?' the officer queried.

'Everything, I said,' Springer snapped. 'Everything that moves. And don't forget the Locarno airstrip.'

The officer was already using the phone, issuing a stream of orders. All over sector 431 Swiss Army and security units began moving through the night, helicopters were taking off, light army planes were moving out of their hangars. And, using the transceiver himself, Horner was sending out the top alert. *Guisan . . . Guisan . . . Guisan . . .* The name of the Swiss commander-in-chief during World War II who had, at a critical moment, ordered total mobilization of the Swiss armed forces against the vehement objections of his government. In Traber and Springer the spirit of Guisan still lived.

The Atlantic Express was hardly moving when there was an urgent rapping on the door of Marenkov's compartment. Unlocking the door, Haller opened it a fraction. In the corridor Matt Leroy found himself staring into the muzzle of Haller's Colt .45. 'A top alert just came over the radio,' Leroy snapped.

'Get back to the end of the car.' Haller stepped out to run along to the communications compartment in the next Wagon-Lit and saw Peter Neckermann – against all orders – standing in the corridor. 'Guisan,' Neckermann shouted. 'Guisan – Guisan . . .'

Haller swivelled on his heel, went back inside the compartment, where Marenkov was still standing with his back to the window. 'Down on the floor,' he rapped out, grabbing the Russian, pushing him down. Elsa was already on the floor as Marenkov sprawled alongside her. 'Under other circumstances I would appreciate this position,' he told her. Realizing he was reassuring her, she took his hand, squeezed it. 'They'll handle it.'

'We can be sure of that,' Marenkov replied, concealing the extreme tension he was feeling.

Haller had left the compartment and Elsa reached up to lock the door. The express was now stationary as the American ran along the corridor to where Phillip John stood on guard. He grabbed the Englishman by the arm. 'Come with me,' he ordered and went inside an empty compartment. Switching off the lights, he raised the blind a few inches, then all the way. He couldn't see anything that attracted his attention. It wasn't snowing, the sky was clear, and a full moon shone down on a deserted highway that ran close to the railroad track. Haller lowered the window and a wave of ice-cold air filled the compartment. He glanced north, saw the red light, looked south, and dropped to a kneeling position.

'Here they come . . .' He had hardly spoken when they heard the drum-fire rattle of a machine gun. In the stillness of the night the sound was appallingly loud. 'An army Jeep,' Haller said quickly. 'Aim for the driver. Stop him. Get the driver . . .'

John squeezed in front of Haller, calmly took up a position huddled in the corner, and steadied his Luger, aiming for a point on the highway the Jeep had not yet reached. The machine-gun cannonade was a roar now, ripping across the windows of the rear Wagon-Lit as it drove along the highway. The man behind the gun was an expert, moving the barrel up and down a fraction as he sprayed the Wagon-Lit. John waited, his Luger steady, his body motionless. A hail of bullets thudded into their compartment and then the Jeep came into sight as it passed the window. John fired three times in rapid succession. The rattle of machine-gun fire ceased as the Jeep drew level with the second Wagon-Lit. Then it disappeared into the night, heading north along the highway.

'Missed them. Damnation,' John said bitterly.

'Moving target,' Haller commented sympathetically. He had jumped up off the floor, aimed his Colt .45 out of the window, fired one shot. The Jeep's machine gunner slumped over his weapon. Haller ran back down the corridor, used the special rap on the door, which was opened by Elsa, her revolver aimed through the gap. Marenkov was on his feet and behind him the blind was ripped to pieces, the window shattered. Had he remained standing a minute longer he would have been dead a dozen times over. The Russian crunched glass as he stepped forward.

'My congratulations on your security system, Mr Haller. Were any of your men hit? No? Thank God for that. They will, of course, make a fresh attempt to kill me, but I am considerably reassured by this little happening.'

Haller kept the surprise out of his expression. The Russian seemed the calmest person in the Wagon-Lit. At the far end of the corridor Haller saw Leroy giving a thumbs-up sign, indicating that the second Wagon-Lit had escaped unscathed as the Jeep had fled off down the highway. 'We're moving into the next car,' he told Marenkov. 'Elsa, escort him there.' He stared over their shoulders through the smashed window into the night. 'And that's a damn fast reaction . . .'

Along the highway a convoy of Swiss military vehicles had appeared and was stopping. Troops armed with automatic weapons leaped from the trucks and fanned out to surround the halted express.

From his Lugano headquarters Springer had already dispatched chief signalmaster Alois Reiter and two other railmen by fast car to the tower at Vira. By now the whole of sector 431 was alive with military and security vehicles on the move. Roadblocks had been set up. Large choppers were landing troops at strategic points. The entire wartime antisabotage system was in operation and one unit had already reached the military sub-post where the gang had hijacked the Jeep. By radio they reported back to Springer the finding of the bodies of the three dead Swiss soldiers. The colonel ordered that the news be immediately circulated to all units operating in sector 431.

The three Communist agents who had sprayed the express had abandoned the Jeep inside a copse of trees and were riding in the Mercedes with Emilio Valenti, the signalman who had stopped the express. Behind the wheel sat Luisa, her face tense as she drove at high speed along the northbound road leading to Bellinzona. With a deserted highway ahead, she rammed her foot down; the speedometer needle crept up to a hundred and eighty kilometres, a dangerous speed on the ice-patched road.

'You'll kill us at this speed,' warned Marco, who had used the machine gun, who had been shot by Haller in the forearm.

'Shut your trap.' Luisa spoke as though in command. 'You did your job, now I'll do mine – get us away.'

She skidded as she took a bend, the car started to go out of control, she fought with the wheel, regained control, accelerated along the next stretch. Behind her she heard Marco gasp. 'Scared?' she inquired. 'Then open the door and get off.'

'There's a chopper coming toward us,' the loose-limbed man beside her remarked. 'How soon before we change cars?'

'Three minutes. Maybe four. Then we lose the bastards. In half an hour we'll be at the airstrip.'

'The longest half hour of our lives,' screeched Marco behind her. 'Mother of God! Look ahead . . .'

The Mercedes was moving at top speed down an incline with wooded verges on both sides. Ahead was a roadblock made up of police cars parked broadside on. As Luisa lost speed a searchlight came on, shining direct in her eyes. Ducking her head, she lost more speed, turned onto the verge, moved into reverse gear, backed, turned, and started to drive back the way she had come. Then she swore foully and jammed on her brakes.

An army tank had emerged from the trees, was now holding the centre of the highway as the barrel of its long gun was depressed and then held in a fixed position aimed point-blank at the car. Luisa reached for her pistol in the dashboard alcove. At the same moment a soldier smashed open the window by her side and aimed his rifle. The rear windows were broken, rifle muzzles poked inside the car.

'Stay exactly where you are,' a voice shouted in Italian.

The doors were hauled open. The four men put up no resistance but Luisa began clawing and kicking at the officer, who had grabbed the pistol from the alcove. Dropping the pistol, he struck her a savage blow with the back of his hand and she fell back against the wheel. She was bleeding, groggy, barely half-conscious as he dragged her out. 'That will teach you to murder Swiss soldiers,' he said calmly. 'Handcuff the bitch,' he ordered a subordinate.

Many kilometres away down in the Lake Maggiore delta, army vehicles making a routine check on a private airstrip had surrounded a light plane. The pilot put up no resistance. Within thirty minutes, Colonel Springer had destroyed the key Lugano Communist underground sabotage apparatus.

The Atlantic Express was moving again, heading for the great drop where the rail track clung to the mountainside as it descended to Bellinzona. Elsa rapped on the door of Wargrave's compartment. He opened it a fraction, let her inside, and relocked it. 'Fun and games,' he commented. 'They didn't get Marenkov, of course? Cognac?' He offered her a metal flask. 'You look as though you need it.'

She studied the Englishman as she drank from the neck of the flask. He was still dressed as Joseph Laurier, wearing his shaggy grey wig and bifocals. Even allowing for the disguise, he looked damned tired.

'No, they didn't get Marenkov,' she confirmed. 'Nor anyone else – although I don't see how you could be so confident.'

'The time element. The express had stopped a

whole minute before the machine gun opened up. It was an unscheduled stop and Haller is no fool. Tell me about it.'

He listened intently, noticing once again how Elsa could compress a complex incident into a few words. She had taken off her black wig and glasses as though she wanted to make herself as presentable as possible for him. 'So you were right,' she said as she ended her report; 'those three so-called assassins who came on board at Chiasso were a diversion – to make us drop our guard before the real professional attack.'

Wargrave shook his head. 'Not so professional as I feared. They botched the job. Well planned up to a point – but they missed their opportunity.'

'Really?' Sometimes she thought Wargrave was a little too sure of himself. 'Well, all right, how would you have done it?'

'Machine-gunned the whole Wagon-Lit as the express was still slowing down – it could have been done in a fast-moving Jeep. They gave Haller just enough time to react. You say John tried to shoot the driver? Roughly what distance was there between the window and the Jeep?'

'We were about fifty metres away from the highway. Julian said the Jeep took its time – moving at about twenty miles an hour.'

Wargrave made the same comment as Haller. 'But it was a moving target – and at night, too. How is Marenkov being guarded, by the way?'

'Exactly as you specified.' She stood up to fix her

261

wig and glasses. 'I'd better get back – Julian let me out to see what was happening farther up the train. Most of the passengers are pretty jittery. Inspectors are going through the cars telling everyone it was a Swiss Army exercise – no one has seen what happened to the rear Wagon-Lit, of course. I don't think everyone is swallowing the story.'

Wargrave produced a thin spool of cardboard used for sewing thread. 'One more thing. When we stop at Bellinzona step out on the platform with this concealed in your glove. A man in Swiss railroad uniform will approach you and warn you to get back on board, that the train will soon be leaving for Airolo. In French. Slip him this spool. It's a message for Springer.'

'He knows about Joseph Laurier?'

'No, but you told me Julian hasn't reported my supposed demise.' He squeezed her arm. 'And watch it. That Vira attack was just for openers.'

'More is on the way?'

'You can bet on it. Colonel Igor Sharpinsky has yet to serve up the main course.'

Elsa looked at the tiny spool Wargrave had given her to hand over to Springer's man at Bellinzona. 'Why not get Peter Neckermann to send a signal? I can pretend the signal is from me.'

'Because the message asks for a fast double-check to be made on Neckermann himself.'

*

In Lugano Springer had taken one of his split-second decisions that so often startled his subordinates. He had decided to board the Atlantic Express at Bellinzona. Leaving Horner in charge, he was driving through the outskirts of the city, heading for a military airstrip that had already been alerted. And before his sudden departure he had issued fresh instructions.

'I want radio detector vans patrolling every place the express stops at between here and Zurich – Bellinzona, Airolo, Göschenen . . .'

'You think we may repeat our success here in Lugano?' Horner suggested.

'Sharpinsky will need to know what is happening so he can plan his next move. That means a Soviet agent aboard the train must in some way pass a message – or indicate by a gesture – whether Marenkov is still alive. After the attack at Vira I am sure some signal must be passed at Bellinzona.'

'I will arrange it.'

'We will extend the operation,' Springer hurried on. 'Between here and Zürich very few passengers will leave the train. Those that do are to be followed by unmarked police cars.'

'I will arrange that also.'

'And if any locals are hanging around a station when the express arrives, they are to be followed also.'

Springer was thinking about these instructions as he accelerated, knowing that he was short of time. At least the train would be delayed at Bellinzona while the shattered rear Wagon-Lit was unhitched, with the flatcar behind it. Then they would have to bring back the flatcar with the Alouette helicopter aboard and link it to the express again. And why had Wargrave asked him to have the chopper hauled behind the train?

As he approached the airstrip Springer felt he had some cause for satisfaction. He had heard that Franco Visani, who had operated the secret Communist transmitter in the Piazza Dante, was showing signs of weakening under interrogation. 'Before the express reaches Basel I could just unroll the entire Soviet underground network,' he told himself. 'The farther the train goes the more moles will emerge from their burrows.'

The military pilot of the light aircraft, who had seen the headlights of Springer's car approaching, had his engine tuned up as the colonel left his car, ran toward the machine, and climbed into the passenger seat. Equipped with skis, the aircraft moved down the runway, lifted off. Again Springer checked his watch. With a bit of luck he would make it.

The hard-faced woman wearing a shabby coat and hat stood in the shadows of the hall of Bellinzona station as the Atlantic Express pulled in and stopped. At the southern end of the platform a large canvas screen had been erected, a screen similar to the one at Chiasso that had masked the attachment of the flatcar with the Alouette. The screen meant nothing to her – she was watching for something quite different.

Unusually, many windows were lowered even though the night was bitterly cold; restless passengers, unconvinced by the story of a 'Swiss military exercise,' wanted to see what was going on. The woman's eyes sharpened as a door opened and a passenger descended to the platform. Joseph Laurier, wearing his astrakhan coat and carrying his cane, began to walk idly up and down the platform. A moment later her eyes switched as another door opened.

Clad in her sable and Gucci shoes, clutching her Gucci handbag, Elsa Lang strolled along the platform near to the entrance hall, paused to light a cigarette. Noting the attractive fair-haired girl's clothes, the woman's mouth pursed. Then someone else got off the train and her eyes switched again.

Phillip John, looking like a male model in his smart camel's-hair coat, strolled along the snow-crusted platform watching Elsa, his left hand tucked in his pocket. His right hand – his gun hand – swung free. A moment later Jorge Santos, the six-foot-two Spaniard, smoking his pipe, descended to the platform near the station exit. Elsa watched him as he stood staring around, studied the confident way he held himself, his striking face, which reflected an almost animal magnetism. God, she thought, what a handsome brute. She had glimpsed him earlier inside a first-class compartment but she had not realized how tall he was. Santos caught her eye for a second and glanced away. His pipe had gone out. Very deliberately he bent down, lifted a foot, and knocked his pipe against the sole of his shoe to empty the relics.

'Madame Wells?' Elsa turned and faced a man wearing Swiss railroad uniform. 'It might be best if you got back on board. The express is due to depart shortly,' he murmured. They were very close together as she passed over the spool Wargrave had given her and he took it from her with such skill no one noticed the exchange. Leaving her, the Swiss walked back into the darkened hall. Elsa lingered on the platform – getting straight back onto the train might appear a little obvious.

The Swiss dressed as a railroadman had just reached the exit when a car pulled up and Springer, muffled in a scarf, stepped out. 'Is the Atlantic Express still here?' the colonel asked the railroad man. 'It will be here at least ten minutes,' the man replied as he slipped the spool to Springer. Walking into an office that had been reserved for his use, the colonel closed the door and nodded to one of his staff, Major Jurgen Thall, who was waiting for him. Extracting the message from the spool, he read it quickly and handed it to his subordinate.

'Top priority to Captain Franz Wander of the German BND. He should by now be waiting at security headquarters in Basel. The answer must – *must*,' he emphasized, 'come to me over the radio telephone aboard the express. It has to bypass Peter

Neckermann, the radio operator on the train. And I want the reply thirty minutes from now . . .'

Walking back into the hall and out onto the platform, he passed a woman in a shabby coat and hat who was being questioned by one of his men in a Swiss rail inspector's uniform. 'Can I help you, madame?' he had suggested a moment earlier.

'I have been waiting for my husband,' the woman explained. 'This is the five o'clock express from Milan?'

'This is the Atlantic Express, yes, madame.'

'Surely he should have got off by now?'

'Assuredly,' Springer's man agreed. 'You are certain he was travelling on this train?'

'He expected to – unless he was delayed by a business meeting.'

'Then he must have been delayed. You will see, he will arrive in the morning.'

'I'm sure you're right. Thank you.'

The shabbily clothed woman walked back through the hall and outside to where an old Fiat was waiting by the kerb with a man behind the wheel. She got inside next to him and closed the door and he drove off. 'He gave me the signal,' she said. 'They didn't kill him. Marenkov is still alive somewhere on the express.'

On the Bellinzona platform Joseph Laurier was still limping restlessly about, but Jorge Santos had returned aboard the train. Now he stood leaning out of a window with his dead pipe projecting from the right-hand corner of his mouth. Elsa was walking back to the rear Wagon-Lit with Phillip John trailing a few yards behind her. At that moment Springer appeared from the hall, followed by his assistant Major Thall, crossed the platform, and entered the train.

Nothing in Laurier's expression or movements betrayed his extreme surprise. He had recognized the colonel instantly, had caught the brief glance Springer gave to the north – toward the Gotthard the express would soon be approaching. Had Springer foreseen – as Laurier had – that soon the Atlantic Express could be moving into a gigantic geographical trap as it climbed the mighty gorge where the mountains on both sides closed in like pincers on the rail track?

Behind the canvas screen at the end of the platform the Swiss railroad staff, working with their normal speed and efficiency, had already unhitched the bullet-riddled Wagon-Lit and the flatcar. Backing them onto the side spur to Locarno, they had separated the two cars and had brought back the flatcar carrying the Alouette helicopter, linking it with the Wagon-Lit now occupied by Sparta. Laurier climbed aboard the train, gave one last glance toward the Gotthard, closed the door. One minute later the Atlantic Express left Bellinzona.

*

A short time before, as the woman in the shabby coat and hat left the station hall and climbed into the Fiat, one of Springer's men made a note of the car's number. As the car drove off he shook his head at the driver of a police car parked by the side of the station. With the snowbound streets of Bellinzona deserted at this hour it would be impossible to follow the Fiat without being detected.

After leaving the station the Fiat drove less than a kilometre before it turned inside an open garage. The doors were shut immediately by a waiting man. Hurrying up inside his apartment, followed by the woman, who was lighting yet another cigarette – she was a chainsmoker – the driver opened up the transmitter concealed inside the television set and began sending one of two signals prepared in advance. Unlike his banking colleague in Lugano, Franco Visani, the driver sent his signal to the Zürichberg in less than two minutes, so the patrolling detector vans did not get a fix on him.

Less than an hour later, traced by the car registration number, the couple were under arrest and subjected to intense interrogation. Deprived of food, allowed only water to drink – but, above all, deprived of tobacco – it was the woman who cracked. Eighteen men and women comprising the Bellinzona Communist underground sabotage apparatus were apprehended. But that was sixteen hours later. The vital factor was the signal that had been sent to Zürich.

Chapter Sixteen

Zürich, Andermatt

At 7.45 p.m. in Zürich Traber received a signal telling him that the Atlantic Express had just left Bellinzona. He passed on the news to his assistant, Major Kurt Dobler, who sat at another desk in the same room. Dobler, an alert man of forty with a lean face and long jaw that gave him a foxlike appearance, got up from behind his desk and marked the time next to Bellinzona on a wall map.

'Any further developments on the passengers from Vienna who came off Flight 433?' he inquired.

Traber himself had handled the check in his search for Colonel Igor Sharpinsky since the tragically broken call from Leo Scoblin in Vienna warning him that Crocodile – Sharpinsky – was on his way to Zürich. Holding his pen poised over the passenger list, the counter-espionage chief shook his head.

'We have traced most of them and they appear genuine. I've just heard that this Heinz Golchack checks out.'

'Wasn't that the Austrian passenger who changed his destination?'

'That's right. We found the cabdriver who picked

him up from the airport. Apparently Golchack asked him to take him to the Baur au Lac, then decided instead he would catch a train for Bonn. It sounded an odd note to me, so I phoned Lorenz in Vienna and asked him a favour. Lord knows he owed me one.'

'What happened?' Dobler asked.

'Lorenz co-operated more than I could have hoped for. He went with some of his security men to Golchack's apartment, let himself inside, and checked the place. Golchack wasn't there but they found a Swissair printed slip giving the times of Flight 433 to Vienna. So, that's that.'

With an expression of resignation the portly Swiss used his pen to cross out one of the few remaining names on his list, that of Heinz Golchack.

Peter still alive. Still aboard Atlantic Express. Positive.

In Room 207 at the Hotel Schweizerhof in Zürich – less than two kilometres from Traber's headquarters – Heinz Golchack read the signal that had just been relayed from Bellinzona. He checked his watch: 7.45 p.m. Taking off his rimless glasses, he began polishing them, although they were perfectly clean. Bühler, his heavily-built, pug-nosed deputy who knew his chief so well, noted the gesture. Golchack was beginning to feel the pressure.

'It is a disappointment,' Bühler ventured.

Golchack glanced at him briefly with his pale eyes and the East German wished he had not spoken.

Replacing his glasses, Golchack studied the map of Switzerland spread over the bed. On a nearby table his transistor radio was on, the volume turned down low; it was important to hear the news bulletins, to be sure that Zürich Airport remained closed. Taking out his pen, Golchack ringed an area on the map, again without marking it.

'Bellinzona was merely Phase One,' he said calmly. 'Now we will launch Phase Two . . .'

Without moving, Bühler stared at the area Golchack had ringed. He was, after all, GRU chief of sabotage operations in Western Europe. This time he did not allow Golchack's stare to intimidate him. 'That means uncovering one of our main sabotage plans if it ever comes to invading Switzerland.'

'So?' Golchack inquired softly.

'I thought I would just mention it . . .'

'So you have mentioned it – for the record in Moscow later, no doubt,' Golchack continued in the same mild tone. 'And I will consider whether to include it in my own report – that you hesitated at a decisive moment.'

'You misunderstand me,' Bühler said hastily.

'That I will also consider later – whether I misunderstood you, Rudi.' Golchack held his subordinate in suspense to discipline him, walking over to the window to stare down into the street. It was snowing very heavily, a dense white curtain of snow that blurred the view. Zürich Airport would certainly remain closed. Turning around suddenly, he issued a crisp order.

'Send the signal to Andermatt. Phase Two. Immediately!'

At his headquarters Brigadier Traber was taking short puffs at his small cigar. He was not satisfied. Ever since the days before the Russian Revolution in 1917 Switzerland had been a refuge for Communist agents because of her neutrality – ever since Lenin had waited in Zürich with his comrades, hoping for revolution to break out in a Western country; Russia had been low on his list of priorities. So the Russians were very familiar with Switzerland, which Swiss security never forgot. Picking up his phone, Traber asked to be put through on the scrambler radio telephone to Springer aboard the Atlantic Express.

It was no secret in Swiss military circles that the brilliant Springer was being groomed to take over from Traber on his retirement, that he had Traber's full backing. When the call came through Traber explained the position to the colonel.

'My suggestion is that we start again from zero in Zürich,' Springer said briskly. 'Send out teams with the Flight 433 passenger list to all hotels – to check the registration lists.'

'One hell of a job,' Traber commented. 'There's so little time.'

'Start at once,' Springer urged. 'Put every available man on the job. If there's one chance in a thousand of our tracking down Sharpinsky we mustn't miss it.'

'I'll start at once,' Traber promised.

'One other thing: send out every possible radio detector van. Sharpinsky has to have radio communication to keep control of this operation I'm convinced he's personally directing . . .'

'Consider it done.'

'And put a pair of vans close to the Hauptbahnhof,' Springer went on. 'It worked at Lugano and it could just work in Zürich. Incidentally, has any message come in from Wargrave's agent Leros in Andermatt?'

'Negative.'

Ten minutes later one of Traber's radio detector vans was parked in a side street just below the first-floor restaurant of the Hotel Schweizerhof.

Less than three hours earlier in Andermatt, as Anna Markos stood by her parked Renault watching the farmhouse through her monocular glass, it was the closing of the curtain by Robert Frey that warned her she had been seen. Climbing back inside the car, she drove the short distance back to Andermatt, reversed the Renault in the narrow street, and left it where it could not possibly be seen from the farmhouse. Then she walked back to the edge of the town and waited.

Clad in her ski jacket and tight ski pants, she felt the bitter east wind slice through the back of her fur-lined hood like a knife. But Anna had endured the Athenian winters and Greece is closer to the Siberian winds than Andermatt. Keeping close to the corner of the last house in Andermatt, she continued her watch on the distant farmhouse, then checked the time: 5.30 p.m. The Atlantic Express should now be halfway between Milan and Chiasso. Then she heard the sound she was waiting for.

The throb of the helicopter's motor was faint but distinct in the cold night; as on earlier occasions at this hour she noted how quickly Frey's men had manhandled the chopper out of the barn that housed the machine. Angling up her monocular glass, she saw the whirr of its rotors as the Sikorsky helicopter climbed, following the snow-blurred silhouette more by its lights than its bulk.

It flew straight down the valley toward her, gaining height all the time, passing over Andermatt at an altitude of one thousand feet as it headed east in the general direction of the Gotthard and the giant Wasserhorn peak. Later, Robert Frey would return to enjoy the *après-ski* revels, but now he was attending to more serious duties, checking the general avalanche situation before he made his routine report to Davos.

Brushing snow off her clothes, Anna Markos climbed back behind the wheel of her Renault. She had left the engine running; in temperatures like these it often took five minutes to get the damned thing started again. Driving at speed along the deserted valley road, she pulled in around the back of the huddle of farmhouse buildings, which were in darkness. Not a light anywhere. It was a risk she was taking, but if a guard had been left behind she would say she had come out to visit Frey.

At the rear of the farmhouse she found a back door with glass-panelled windows. Thrusting her gloved hand against a pane, she crushed the glass and felt inside. She was surprised to find the key had been left in the lock; had it not been she would have used the skeleton keys in her pocket. And it was not amateurishness that had caused her to smash the glass pane first; Anna wanted her break-in to be discovered later.

She explored the interior of the deserted farmhouse with the aid of a torch, moving from room to room until she came to Robert Frey's study, the room on the western side where Emil Platow, Frey's assistant, had earlier watched her through a window with his pair of night glasses. Here she spent longer.

A large oblong-shaped room measuring about fifteen by twenty feet, the polished wood-block floor was carpeted with expensive Persian rugs. In one corner on a steel table stood the transmitter Frey used to communicate with the avalanche institute near Davos. She read a few words typed on a printed form next to the transmitter. *Slow build-up of snow on the Wasserhorn. No sign of a dangerous situation developing so far . . .*

– It was a desk built into a wall that eventually attracted her attention. Dropping the flap, she studied the interior. In the pigeonholes were two books on mountaineering, but otherwise the desk was remarkably free of the papers and clutter normally found inside such a piece of furniture. Anna's deft fingers began feeling around inside the pigeonholes, probing, pressing. Suddenly the index finger of her right hand pressed in against something. There was a faint machine-like hum and the entire pigeonhole structure slid toward her over the dropped flap. Behind was a second transmitter.

It could just be a spare, a backup in case the main transmitter broke down, she speculated. And it was an advanced design, possibly secreted against the possibility of vandals breaking into the farmhouse. Just possibly ... She pressed her finger inside the same pigeonhole and the false front retreated back into its original position, concealing completely what lay behind it.

For a whole minute she stood in front of the desk. She had closed the flap. Then she did a curious thing. Taking hold of one of the teardrop earrings she was wearing, she held it in her hand and used the torch to find a bare patch of wood-block floor. Dropping the earring, she left the farmhouse by the back door, climbed into her Renault, and drove back to Andermatt.

Once inside her bedroom at the Hotel Storchen, she went to the drawer containing her jewel case, unlocked it, and took out a bracelet and a string of imitation pearls. Adding to these her other teardrop earring, she screwed up her collection inside her large motoring glove, left the bedroom, and went downstairs. The bar was unusually crowded for that hour and Anna thought she sensed a feeling of tension, a lot of nervous laughter and heavy drinking. A lithe, quick-smiling Frenchman got up hurriedly from a table and came toward her. It was Louis Celle, a friend of René Marchais, who had recently been killed on the ski slopes. And this time he was not smiling.

'Anna, come and have a drink with me,' he pleaded.

'Sorry, Louis . . .' She kept her gloved hand tightly closed. 'I have to go out for a few minutes.' She genuinely regretted her need to refuse him; he looked so miserable.

'I went along to the police station again,' Louis continued. 'Did you know they are not satisfied that René's death was an accident? At my urging they checked with Chamonix, and they know he was an expert skier.'

'You know how sorry I am.' Anna kissed him on the cheek. 'But who can tell? Even the most expert skiers can—'

'It was an easy slope,' Louis insisted. He gestured toward the bar. 'Everyone is talking about it. Hardly anyone will go on the slopes now.'

'Because of René?'

'Well, not entirely.' Louis hesitated. 'Since then conditions have deteriorated and people are beginning to fear avalanches. They say a snow build-up is developing.'

Anna stroked his cheek. 'Go back and have a drink, Louis. Maybe later I can join you . . .'

Leaving the hotel, she paused a short distance from the exit and listened. It was bitterly cold and very dark, but overhead the sky was clear again and the tip of the moon appeared behind a mountain. But what had caused her to pause was a low, sinister rumbling sound, which echoed from one side of the valley to the other. Avalanche sounds. No wonder most tourists were steering clear of the slopes.

In a deserted side street she found a drain coated with ice. The distant rumble continued as she used the heel of her boot to smash the ice and dropped the jewellery between the drain slots. And as she walked back to the Storchen she could hear the familiar voice in her mind. 'Detail, Anna – never overlook the small detail that can kill you . . .'

After taking off in his Sikorsky helicopter, Robert Frey had pointed its nose straight for the giant Wasserhorn peak, which rose above the Gotthard railroad track far below. Beside him sat Emil Platow, who peered down as they passed over the glittering lights of Andermatt.

'I hear the police are investigating René Marchais's death,' he said and something in his tone made the huge Swiss piloting the machine glance at him sharply.

'You are losing your nerve?' he inquired quietly.

'Of course not.' Frey's question had shaken Platow

badly; it was not safe for a member of Frey's organization to betray any sign of demoralization. In fact, it
could be damn dangerous. 'It's just that all Andermatt
is talking about the accident . . .'

'So there's nothing to worry about – and the police
can never prove it was anything but an accident. But
it was necessary,' Frey said calmly as he increased
altitude. 'I realized that when Marchais was talking
his head off in the Storchen bar about my chopper
being the only thing around when they found that
counter-espionage agent's body in the glacier tunnel.'
The subject went clean out of his mind as he
manoeuvred the machine toward the Wasserhorn
summit.

Among all the top GRU agents who controlled
secret sabotage apparatuses in Western Europe, Frey
was – in the opinion of his master, Colonel Igor
Sharpinsky – the cleverest and most ruthless, with the
possible exception only of Rolf Geiger. Why had the
Swiss, who already enjoyed so much prestige as a
mountaineer internationally, betrayed his country for
over fifteen years? Certainly he was no perverted
idealist; he had read very little Marxist theory, which
he thought a thundering bore. His dual motives for
his treachery were far simpler.

Shrewdly, as he believed, weighing up the likely
outcome of the endless struggle between the Communists and the West, he was convinced that in the
end Soviet Russia must win because of its superior
and aggressive leadership. As he had once remarked

to Platow, 'Since Churchill, Adenauer, and de Gaulle there has been no leader worth a damn in the West.' Recently he had begun to have doubts since President Joseph Moynihan had taken over in the White House, but it was too late to turn back now.

The second motive was Frey's greed for power. He revelled in the fact that he personally controlled a secret organization, that within the past few hours he had sent to Franco Visani, the Soviet agent in Lugano, detailed orders for an attack on the Atlantic Express. Now, losing altitude as he prepared to land on the summit of the Wasserhorn, he was checking on the second, far vaster contingency plan Sharpinsky had suggested in his signal to Frey from the Hotel Schweizerhof in Zürich.

With expert touch he landed the machine carefully on the centre of the flat-topped peak, well clear of the brink. Adjusting his snow goggles after switching off the motor, he opened the door and dropped to the ground, followed by Emil Platow, who carried the measuring instruments.

From the summit the view was intoxicating in its moonlit grandeur, but Frey hardly noticed it, nor did he approach the brink from where he could have looked down on the railroad track over which the Atlantic Express was due to pass later that evening. The two men worked quickly, measuring the depth of the recent snowfall, and then climbed back into the machine, which was airborne again within minutes.

'My God,' Platow exclaimed as the helicopter

headed back for Andermatt. 'Another fifty centimetres of snow since the last check – the whole slope could start a gigantic slide any moment.'

'So if we have to resort to the ultimate weapon the timing is perfect,' Frey replied calmly. 'And don't start worrying about Davos – nothing like that has fallen in Andermatt. So they won't suspect the report I send in ...'

At 6.15 p.m. Robert Frey's Sikorsky landed again at the farm. It was Emil Platow who discovered the break-in. Frey had entered by the front door and gone straight to his study, where four other members of his sabotage team were waiting. Throwing down his parka on a chair, he sat down to write out for the avalanche institute above Davos: *No further appreciable build-up of snow on the Wasserhorn. Have compared last year's records and if these can be taken as standard ...*

Frey became aware that someone was peering over his shoulder. Looking up, he saw Erich Volcker, a short, fat, bald-headed man of forty-five standing behind him. 'Damn it, I can't write out this damn report with you standing there watching me,' he boomed.

'Sorry.'

'There's been a break-in.' Emil Platow came running into the study in a state of great excitement. 'Someone was here – must have been before you arrived,' he said, looking at the four other men. 'A pane in the back door is broken.'

'Calm yourself, Emil,' the huge mountaineer reprimanded.

Standing up, he put his large hands on his hips and looked around the room, noted that the desk flap was closed, let his eyes go on wandering. The other five men, dominated by his presence, remained quite still, quite silent. Frey's eyes continued his search, moving across the furniture, then they dropped to the floor. He took two long paces, stooped, stood up dangling the teardrop earring from his fingers. He smiled at Erich Volcker.

'I know this. Foolish of her to leave her calling card, wasn't it?'

Chapter Seventeen

The Gotthard

In its awesome grandeur this gigantic gorge that carries the main north–south rail link from nordic Europe to the Mediterranean south is one of the wonders of the world, rivalling the Grand Canyon in Arizona. As the rail track continues its endless climb, passing through spiral tunnels turning through three hundred and sixty degrees as the ascent goes on, crossing bottomless ravines and gulches, the immense Alpine peaks close in on either side.

Awe-inspiring in summer, it has an atmosphere close to terror in winter. High up on the near-vertical slopes millions of tons of snow hang poised – often needing only the passing of a single skier to bring them down. Close to Airolo, the small town at the end of the strategic tunnel passing under the Alpine range – passing under Andermatt – huge crags overhang the rail track. At frequent intervals the track is lined with great steel snow barriers. This is avalanche country.

It was the Gotthard that worried Wargrave. It was the Gotthard that so concerned Springer that he had flown from Lugano to board the Atlantic Express at Bellinzona. And in the guise of Joseph Laurier, Wargrave was still restlessly moving about the train. Ahead in the otherwise deserted corridor he saw the six-foot-two-tall Spaniard, Jorge Santos, leaning against the passenger rail while he puffed at his pipe. He paused next to Santos, hanging his cane by the handle on the rail.

'You, too, my friend, find this a disturbing journey – and soon we shall move into a region fit for the Greek gods, a veritable Olympus,' Laurier remarked in fluent French.

Santos' black eyes glanced at the newcomer sharply, then he shrugged. 'These long train journeys by night are full of stress.' He paused, puffing on his pipe. 'And that strange business after Lugano when the express stopped. A Swiss inspector told me it was an army exercise. You believe that?'

'I think it was something far more sinister,' Laurier replied. 'I can recognize live machine-gun fire when I hear it.'

'And now we are moving into the Gotthard,' Santos remarked. 'A frightening place.'

'Who can tell what may happen on a night express?' Laurier mused. 'So many strangers all crammed together for so many hours.' He glanced at the profile of the man standing beside him, a striking profile with its aquiline nose, its high cheekbones. 'I am travelling all the way to Amsterdam on this trip,' he remarked. 'Are you?'

'All the way. So it will be a very long night . . .'

*

There was a growing tension inside the express as it headed up a gentle incline on its way to the great gorge. In the dining car they were serving the second sitting and more drink was being consumed than food. Passengers in their compartments who might have been settling down for the night sat up staring out of the window at the moonlit landscape. In the rear Wagon-Lit food was being served to the occupants from a compartment that in Milan Molinari had had converted into a makeshift galley.

'Why could not food have been brought along from the dining car?' Marenkov inquired as he sank his teeth into a pizza.

'Because poison is one of the weapons of the KGB,' Haller replied bluntly.

'Don't you like pizza?' Elsa asked the Russian.

'I can eat anything,' Marenkov replied ambiguously.

Springer sat opposite him, eating his own pizza off a cardboard plate and drinking coffee from a cardboard cup. He had already asked the Russian for a list of KGB agents in Switzerland and Marenkov, glancing at Haller, had tapped his forehead. 'The moment I am aboard the Boeing at Schiphol, the moment that aircraft is thirty thousand feet over the Atlantic, I will provide all the information you need.'

'I need it now,' Springer told him sharply. 'It is, after all, for your own protection.'

'It is the normal procedure,' Marenkov replied brusquely. 'It is my passport to America – the information I carry in my brain. All previous KGB agents who have fled to America have waited until they set foot on United States soil before they talked—'

'It's useless,' Haller interjected. 'I've been through all this with the general earlier – and as he says, it is normal procedure.'

Springer's face was set and grim as he stared at Marenkov, who looked back at him impassively. Elsa decided it was time to defuse the rising tension between the two men. 'Do let him get on with his food,' she said lightly to the Swiss colonel. 'We've got enough on our plates,' she punned, 'without fighting among ourselves.'

They had finished their meal when Matt Leroy knocked on the door. 'Colonel Springer is wanted on the radio telephone urgently,' he announced. He looked at the relics of the meal. 'Nice to see no one is going hungry,' he remarked. Haller looked appalled. 'God, it's time you changed duty with John – drag him out of his compartment and then get back here and eat.'

Elsa, complaining of stiffness, accompanied Springer to the communications compartment; she had guessed this signal could be the reply to Wargrave's request for a double-check to be made on their radio operator, Peter Neckermann. And since Springer had earlier been told by Haller of Wargrave's 'death' in Milan she didn't want the reply to be passed on to Haller. Inside the communications compartment the gnome-like Neckermann had just finished his own meal. Springer took the call on the phone and without looking at Neckermann said 'yes' several times and finally, 'You are sure?' Breaking the connection, he took Elsa into the corridor and waited until he heard the German lock the door on the inside.

'I don't understand what's happened,' he said gravely. 'I had a message signed by Wargrave at Bellinzona and Haller says he died in Milan. The message said I was to give you the reply. That call was from my chief, Brigadier Traber, in Zürich. He has heard from Captain Wander of the German BND, who is now waiting to take over the train's security in Basel. Peter Neckermann is cleared. Wander says he would vouch for him with his life.'

'Don't tell Haller – or anyone. I'll join you later.'

'As you say . . .'

Springer had a curious expression as he studied Elsa for a moment, an expression that could have been a hint of hope. 'I thought Haller's story was odd,' he murmured. 'I leave the entire matter in your hands.'

Phillip John had replaced Matt Leroy as guard at the forward end of the Wagon-Lit as Elsa approached him. The Englishman, smart and cool-looking as ever in his check sports jacket, smiled faintly. She had the impression that during his rest period he had freshly shaved. 'Can't keep away from me?' he chaffed her.

'Strange as it may seem, by making a massive effort I can manage it for an hour or two,' she replied. 'And now perhaps you would let me into the next car.'

'What for?'

'Because I damned well say so,' she rapped back.

'The lady only has to ask – her request is granted,' John replied, not in the least fazed. He reached up and made a show of straightening the dark wig she had donned before leaving Haller's compartment. Then he perched her horn-rimmed glasses higher on her nose. For a second his hand touched her cheek. 'Sooner or later, when all this is over, you and I ought to—'

She passed through the door he had opened without replying, heard him lock it, and hurried to Joseph Laurier's sleeper. Inside the compartment Wargrave checked the position of the bone-handled knife he had earlier slipped inside his right sock before he opened the door and let her inside. She told him about the signal clearing Neckermann and he nodded. He was still wearing Laurier's shaggy grey wig and bifocals and again she thought he looked horribly tired.

'What about food?' she asked. 'You got something in the dining car, I hope?'

'No.' He gestured toward his case. 'I brought a flask of coffee and sandwiches from Milan. What is the atmosphere like back in Marenkov's compartment?'

'Lousy. Springer tried to get a list of Swiss KGB agents out of Marenkov and he wouldn't give. Haller is acting as peacemaker. But there's something more.'

Lighting a cigarette, he placed it between her lips as she sat on the berth. 'What is something more?'

'Tension – getting worse all the time. Only Phillip

John, who's on guard duty, by the way, seems unaffected, the cocky bastard. The trouble, as I see it,' Elsa continued, crossing her legs and taking off her hornrims, 'is nothing more has happened. It's getting on their nerves – the waiting, the inaction. And yet they feel sure something big is coming. They're worried about the Gotthard.'

'Me too.'

Turning off the light, Wargrave lifted the blind. The express was climbing steeply now, moving around endless curves as it headed toward distant Airolo. And the big mountains were closing in on the train, great peaks; Wargrave had to crane his neck to look up and see their moonlit summits. Out of the shadow of a ravine a long spear of ice hung motionless in the night, the spear of a huge waterfall frozen in midair. The wheel rumble changed as the express moved onto a bridge spanning a dark drop. He lowered the blind, switched on the light. 'Any met reports come in?' he asked. 'I'm thinking of the weather north of the Gotthard.'

'Terrible, Springer says. A raging blizzard. It's just this section between Airolo and Chiasso where it's stopped snowing – and that isn't expected to last for long. Oh, and just to cheer you up: a *föhn* wind's expected here soon.'

'I think it's started already – you can feel it hitting the side of the train.'

Wargrave was stripping off his grey wig. Removing his bifocals, he tidied himself up, combing his hair briefly. Elsa watched him with concern now she could see his real appearance. 'God, you look tired – your eyes are bloodshot. When did you last sleep?'

'Can't remember,' Wargrave said cheerfully. It was Saturday night. Friday evening he had been up until the middle of the night going over operational details with Molinari. Saturday morning had brought the arduous flight to Bucharest and back, including two rather tricky landings. And since boarding the Atlantic Express he had not slept a wink. He checked himself in the wall mirror. 'Back to normal – that's better.'

'Why are you dropping the Laurier cover?' she asked.

'Because the time has come to emerge into the open – from what you've just told me morale back in the Wagon-Lit doesn't sound too good.'

'Is that all?' she asked quietly. 'You're expecting something to happen, aren't you? And you'll give Julian one hell of a shock. He'll blow his top,' she warned.

He took her by the shoulders. 'Just stop fretting and get back to them. Don't say a word about me. Not one word.'

'If you say so . . .'

Wargrave waited a few minutes to give her time to get back to the compartment and then opened the door. Peering both ways to make sure the corridor was empty, he walked back along the car, which was swaying around another endless curve. At one point he raised a blind and the ice-bound walls of the Gotthard loomed in his face, their dark shadows flecked with more spurts of waterfalls frozen in the moonlight. Pausing by the locked door to the rear Wagon-Lit, he lit a cigarette, then rapped in a certain way.

Phillip John opened the door, holding his Luger pistol in his right hand. His white face showed shock, then he recovered and slowly slid the Luger back inside the spring-loaded holster. Wargrave put a hand against his chest and gently pushed him back against the toilet door.

'Don't I gain entry?' he inquired mildly.

'I thought you were still in Milan . . .'

'Will-o'-the-wisp, that's me,' Wargrave told him amiably as John relocked the door. 'People never know where I'm going to turn up next – it's helped to keep me alive all these years. Let's have a chat while we're alone.'

They were hemmed in the narrow space between the end of the car and the toilet door, out of sight of the corridor beyond, which was empty. 'Why, in the name of God?' demanded John. 'There's been a wake going on for you ever since we left Milan.'

'Because it was necessary, old man,' Wargrave explained, mimicking John's public school accent. He saw a flush of colour in the white face. 'And now it's time to bring up the reserves – me. We have a job to do. There is what used to be called a fifth columnist in this car. KGB or GRU man to you.'

'In this car?' John said slowly. 'You have to be

joking.' He stared at Wargrave. 'No, you're not joking. Who is he?'

'I don't remember saying it was a he.'

John stared hard again, a flicker of surprise in his eyes for the second time. 'You can't possibly suspect Elsa Lang? I gathered she's been with your outfit since way back when.'

'The best moles have been on the inside, implicitly trusted by their employers for a long time, John. It is the key to their success. Surely you've learned that by now?'

'Elsa Lang? I'm staggered. Jesus Christ, Haller will go berserk when he hears.' He frowned. 'You really do have proof? You have the reputation of never trusting anyone.'

'I have proof.' Wargrave stubbed his half-smoked cigarette under his foot and immediately lit a fresh one. The train was rocking from side to side as it negotiated a long, steep curve. Peering out of the window, Wargrave could see the glow of the front cars behind the engine, the flash of the overhead traction wires.

'What are you going to do about the Lang girl?' John asked.

'Nothing.'

'But you said you had proof . . .'

'I said that, yes,' Wargrave agreed laconically. 'But I didn't mention Elsa was the agent. You were the one who brought her name up. The GRU put a man aboard.'

'The GRU?'

'Definitely. Marenkov would have recognized a KGB man. He is one of Colonel Igor Sharpinsky's people. Neckermann was a prime suspect – he had access to the communications system.'

'Was?' John inquired.

'Yes. He was cleared only a few minutes ago. Springer gave Elsa a message to bring to me. You see, John,' Wargrave went on affably, 'I was certain when I heard that machine-gun gang at Vira riddled the rear Wagon-Lit. Only the rear Wagon-Lit, mark you – not the second one Marenkov and Elsa boarded at Milan. They *knew* he was in the rear car.'

John looked thoughtful and leaned back against the toilet door. 'It is suggestive,' he admitted. 'So who is the candidate for the GRU man?'

'You are.'

'You must be out of your crazy mind.'

'Because you're a marksman,' Wargrave explained.

'Then I could have killed you at Milano Centrale.'

Wargrave shook his head. 'You knew you couldn't do that. You knew Colonel Molinari was in on the fake shooting. And you wanted to get aboard the Atlantic Express. Incidentally,' he went on, 'if you had shot me and tried to run, three of Molinari's trained snipers had you in their gunsights all the time you were in the hall – just as a precaution.'

'Crazy like a fox you are . . .' John's mouth twisted in a sneer. 'Why haven't I shot Marenkov by now?'

'Because you haven't had one single chance. Every

time that compartment door opens, someone's revolver is aimed point-blank at you. Haller's, Elsa's – it makes no difference. And you're a professional, John – you know if you fired at them the reflex of their trigger finger would get you. I made very special arrangements to protect Marenkov before I came aboard.'

'This is all pure speculation,' John protested. 'You said you had proof – show me your bloody proof, you bastard.'

'Vira,' Wargrave replied simply. 'Elsa described to me exactly what happened. From a stationary position you aimed your Luger at a target of three men moving at no more than twenty miles an hour. You fired three shots. You missed with every one.'

'It was a moving target.'

'At the range of fifty yards. Three men bunched together. You were waiting for them. And Haller shot one of them. You aimed to miss your own men.'

John, the man who had phoned Vienna from Milan, using the code name Patros, to warn Sharpinsky that Marenkov would be aboard the Atlantic Express, sighed. 'This is beyond me. I need a cigarette, too . . .' His right hand slid inside his jacket, started to withdraw the Luger at speed. Wargrave's hand holding the cigarette pressed the burning end down on the back of John's wrist. John winced, let go of the gun, which slid to the floor as he hit Wargrave a hard, chopping blow on the side of the neck. A little late, Wargrave realized John was ambidextrous, that he could use his left hand with the same force and agility as his right. Fog swam in front of his eyes as John kneed him savagely in the groin, but Wargrave anticipated the attack and turned, taking the blow in the side of his leg. He aimed a blow at John's lower belly, but John also turned and took the impact on his hip.

As they struggled, confined in the small space between the toilet and the outer door, Wargrave was still groggy from the unexpected blow, seeing his opponent as a blurred figure, and John was stronger than he had expected. Suddenly, John lowered his head and butted Wargrave hard in the face while he pressed down the handle of the door, which flew open. Wargrave fell outward into the night, but as he fell his left hand reached upward, grabbed at the top of the door, and then he was hanging in space by one hand from the swinging door.

The express had just started to cross another curving bridge spanning a deep gorge, which yawned below Wargrave. Only the swing of the train stopped his hand from being crushed by the door smashing back against the side of the train. The swing began to move the door inward again. John waited, the Luger he had rescued from the floor in his hand. He had no intention of shooting Wargrave – the sound of a shot could never be explained. Wargrave was simply going to disappear. He had a reputation as a loner, so who would be surprised when he vanished again? All this went through John's quick brain as he waited to hammer the Luger barrel against Wargrave's half-frozen knuckles, to smash those knuckles.

The door swung slowly toward John as Wargrave groaned with pain, reached out, and then dropped his hand and doubled up. John watched clinically, his white face showing no excitement, nothing. The door swung closer and John raised the barrel of his Luger, his eyes on the clenched knuckles that were all that held the Englishman from oblivion. He aimed the barrel with deliberate care. The door swung in. Wargrave's right hand holding the knife he had hauled from his sock lunged, entering John's stomach. The express lurched. John fell out the door; his body missed the guardrail and plunged over a hundred feet to the almost frozen river in the gulch below. He landed on his back and slow-moving water creeping down from the high Alps froze over him, forming first a thin film of ice. From the express, Wargrave, clambering safely back inside the corridor, looked back at the gulf before he closed the door. His nose was running with blood from where John had butted him. Twelve hours later, Swiss troops who arrived at the bottom of the gulf found a macabre sight – John spread on his back staring upward, embalmed in ice. They had to use electric power drills to get at him.

Chapter Eighteen

The Wasserhorn

In the side street alongside the Hotel Schweizerhof in Zürich the radio detector van operator was smoking a forbidden cigarette to keep himself awake. Ever since the van had arrived there had been no sign of illegal signals being transmitted in the district. A kilometre or so away a team of Traber's men was checking a hotel's register; they had four more hotels to visit before they arrived at the Schweizerhof.

In Room 207 Heinz Golchack mopped beads of perspiration off his high-domed forehead. Certainly it was hot inside the well-heated room but it was more than temperature that was causing Golchack to sweat. In a very short time a historic 'natural' catastrophe of gigantic proportions was about to take place in the Gotthard. Not that this concerned Golchack. The only question in his mind was, would it kill General Sergei Marenkov?

And he was aware of the rising tension in his two companions, a tension he pretended not to notice. It was Heinrich Baum, his radio operator, he was most doubtful of. Baum, after all, was a Swiss. Let him sweat, Golchack thought. And Golchack was a man who always hedged his bets. 'Never rely on a single plan,' he was constantly drilling into his subordinates. 'It is always vital to have a backup . . .' Aboard the Atlantic Express, Golchack had two secret back-up men.

One of them – Phillip John – had been infiltrated into the CIA three years earlier. John had actually carried out several executions on behalf of his American employers to cement his credibility. In the meantime he had waited for the moment when Golchack would order him to act on behalf of his real employer, the GRU. It was by no means unlikely that John would be able to seize the opportunity to wipe out Marenkov at some stage of the journey.

'Baum,' Golchack said suddenly, 'when I tell you, these two signals are to be transmitted.' He handed the Swiss two slips of paper. 'The shorter one for Basel is to be transmitted first. Then you send the Amsterdam signal. Encode them.'

Golchack forced himself to sit still in a chair as he thought. He had dedicated his life to climbing the rungs of the Soviet ladder of power. Although he had never married, he was not indifferent to the attractions of women, but he had satisfied his natural urges in brief encounters that held no danger of distracting him from his life's ambition. And even after ordering the massive Andermatt Phase Two operation he was still hedging his bets.

The long signal to Amsterdam worried him a little – it was perhaps a little too lengthy for safe

299

transmission – but it was necessary. It gave very
detailed contingency instructions to Rolf Geiger, head
of the Geiger terrorist group, now close to the Dutch
border. And, of course, there was always the second
backup man aboard the Atlantic Express. There was
always Nicos Leonides . . .

Nicos Leonides. In certain Balkan circles the name
kept men awake at night: prominent anti-Communists
who thought they heard a footfall on the stairs, men
who feared they might have been 'put on the list,' as
the phrase was so innocently termed. It would have
been quite wrong to use the designation 'hit man'
where Leonides was concerned. The crude phrase
conjures up a picture of a hired killer who completes
contracts to kill an individual for a large sum of
money. Leonides, a dedicated Communist from Salonika, only terminated the lives of well-known anti-
Communists. The curious thing was that his employer
– Colonel Igor Sharpinsky – had never met him.

Leonides had first offered his services to Sharpinsky when the Russian was pretending to act as military attaché at the Soviet Embassy in Athens under an
assumed name. And Leonides always communicated
by phone through public call boxes. At first sceptical,
fearing a trap and mistrustful of Leonides's idealistic
protestations, Sharpinsky had ignored the Greek's
offer to serve as an executioner. Several phone calls
later, the Russian had agreed to Leonides's suggestion

that it might be 'convenient' if the editor of a certain Athens newspaper, a late-middle-aged man, should be eliminated.

Three days later the sceptical Sharpinsky was astonished to read that the Greek editor's car had been discovered burned out at the foot of a steep cliff and half-submerged in the sea, the body washed away by a storm. Two years and three deaths later, Sharpinsky was convinced that he had an ideal human weapon for emergencies. Shrewdly – since the targets were always suggested by Leonides – Sharpinsky guessed that the Greek combined his Communist dedication with personal vendettas. So typical of the Balkan peasant mentality. But by a devious route there had always been a line of communication whereby the Russian could contact the Greek. And fortunately, at just the right moment, Nicos Leonides had been in Milan. He was now aboard the Atlantic Express.

Sprawled in the corner seat of his first-class compartment, his long legs crossed at the ankles, Jorge Santos relit his pipe and glanced up as Harry Wargrave hurried past along the corridor on his way to see Phillip John. Like Wargrave, the Spaniard had not eaten in the dining car; he had brought with him aboard the express a bottle of wine and some food, which he had just finished consuming.

Puffing at his pipe, he checked his watch, then

changed his position to ease the stiffness out of his limbs. There was, he sensed, an air of uneasiness aboard the train, which was now moving much more slowly as it climbed the great ascent toward the distant Gotthard tunnel. Outwardly at least, Jorge Santos was one of the most relaxed passengers aboard the Atlantic Express.

'I still think you might have told me, Harry.'

Elsa was using a gauze pad from her first-aid kit to wipe blood from Wargrave's nose when Julian Haller, grim-faced, had issued his second rebuke. They were sitting in the Wagon-Lit compartment – with Marenkov and Springer – and Wargrave was quite unrepentant, even aggressively so.

'It worked,' the Englishman snapped. 'I winkled out the GRU man they'd placed on the inside. And don't forget,' he went on emphatically, 'that before we left North America you agreed I would control this end of the operation.'

'You could have trusted me . . .' Haller began again.

'Too much play-acting would have been involved,' Wargrave insisted. 'You had enough on your mind as it was. So let's stop wasting time and get on with the next stage of the operation.'

'Which is?' Springer inquired.

'I'm taking off in that Alouette chopper you've got aboard the flatcar. Elsa's coming with me. And I need that special radio you brought onto the train, Leon – to keep in communication with the express while we're aloft.'

'That's out,' Haller snapped. 'Taking Elsa . . .'

'Do I have to remind you once more, Julian,' Wargrave inquired quietly, 'that I'm running the European end?'

'Why use the Alouette now?' Springer asked curiously. 'I have troops placed at strategic intervals along the line between here and Airolo.'

'Maybe because I'd like to check the points between the intervals.' Wargrave grinned sardonically as Elsa put away the gauze. 'If you don't like that, call it sixth sense – nothing has happened for a while now and I reckon Sharpinsky is due to make his next attempt very soon.'

Marenkov had remained silent during the discussion but the mention of his deputy, Colonel Igor Sharpinsky, stirred him. It was only recently that Haller had decided to tell him of the GRU man's suspected presence in Zürich. 'I agree with Mr Wargrave,' he said quietly. 'It has been too quiet for too long. Like him, I sense something is going to happen.'

Fifteen minutes later Wargrave helped Elsa across the swaying gap from the rear of the Wagon-Lit to the flatcar where the Alouette helicopter, guarded by a unit of Swiss troops, was chained down. Climbing up inside the cabin, Elsa reached down for the automatic weapon and spare magazines a Swiss soldier handed up to her. 'Good luck,' he called out in French.

Elsa was dressed in ski pants, a fur jacket with the hood pulled over her head, and fur-lined boots – all of which she had borrowed from one of Springer's ski troopers aboard the train. Already on board the machine and sitting in the co-pilot's seat was Springer's Swiss radio operator, Max Bruder, a short, thin man who spoke English. Wargrave was the last to climb on board and settle himself in the pilot's seat as two Swiss soldiers on the swaying flatcar bent down, ready for his signal to release the snap chains.

From the open door of the rear Wagon-Lit Springer, his face chilled with the cold, was watching anxiously. He was alone – Haller had stayed behind in the compartment to guard Marenkov while Matt Leroy patrolled the corridor. And the Swiss colonel was none too happy about the manoeuvre Wargrave was about to attempt. He had to gauge the moment of take-off with unnerving precision. The flatcar was swaying considerably – the maximum sway is always with the last car of the express. He had to build up sufficient lift-off power for instant elevation the moment the snap chains were released. He had to avoid any risk of stalling the motor, which would bring him crashing down on the flatcar – or on the track behind it. And there was a strong sidewind blowing from the east.

Behind him in the heated cabin Elsa found herself clutching the automatic weapon tightly as Wargrave started the motor, as the rotor above them started to spin erratically and then increased into a steady whir. Glancing down, she saw her white knuckles in the glow from the instrument panel. The machine was throbbing with power, straining to lift off. She took a deep breath, forced herself to relax. At that moment Wargrave raised a hand, dropped it, signalling for the release of the snap chains. The flatcar chose this moment to give a sudden lurch and a gust of wind beat against the side of the machine.

'Oh, God . . .'

The machine ascended vertically, was above the train as the side wind beat against the fuselage with such force that the chopper was hurled westward. Then Wargrave regained control and Elsa peered down out of the window. The lights of the Atlantic Express were visible far below, a curving chain of lights as the train moved around yet another endless bend. Elsa relaxed back in her seat, adjusted her headset, checked her watch. It was 8.15 p.m. She spoke into the microphone under her chin.

'What is that huge peak in the distance – way over to the north-west?'

'That,' Wargrave replied, 'is the Wasserhorn.'

It was 8 p.m. in Andermatt when a heavy farm tractor hauled Robert Frey's Sikorsky out of the barn among the huddle of farm buildings west of the ski resort; Anna Markos had been mistaken when she had assumed Frey's team manhandled the chopper into the open. As the machine emerged, Robert Frey stood beside his deputy, Emil Platow, towering over him.

'Hurry it up,' Frey ordered the tractor driver. 'We don't have all night to do the job.'

He climbed up inside the chopper as the tractor driver released the machine, which was equipped with skis. Emil Platow and four other men jumped into the machine behind him. And within three minutes Frey, sitting in the pilot's seat, was airborne, gaining altitude rapidly as he headed southeast toward the huge summit of the Wasserhorn, which overlooked the Gotthard railroad track.

The lights of Andermatt passed below them as Frey continued on course. He had already informed the avalanche institute at Davos that he had decided to make one final check because there had been a rise in temperature of several degrees. *A routine precaution* ... his signal had worded it. Behind him the cabin was crowded – and not only with the five-man team, which included his explosives expert, Emil Platow. Sometimes a very small quantity of explosives is used to set off a minor snowslide to prevent a dangerous accumulation later. But the machine was carrying almost a ton of gelignite, was, in fact, a veritable flying explosives depot as Frey continued to head for the massive peak of the Wasserhorn.

*

A short time before Robert Frey had driven at speed from Andermatt to board the Sikorsky he had visited Anna Markos in her bedroom at the Hotel Storchen. Anna was sitting in front of her dressing table, apparently making herself up for the *après-ski* revels, when someone knocked on her door. Getting up, she went over to the door and spoke through it. 'Who is there?'

A deep, familiar voice replied. 'It's me, Robert. Robert Frey.'

She unlocked the door, let him in, and returned to the dressing table, watching the huge, shaggy-maned Swiss as he stood behind her looking at her mirror image with open admiration. Bending over her, his hands clasped her ample bosom and squeezed. 'And who did you think it might be? I have a rival?'

'Dozens.' Her nails clawed at his exploring hands and he removed them with a grunt. For a moment in the mirror she caught an expression of near-savagery in his face as he wiped a streak of blood from one hand, then he smiled and shrugged. 'Someone has stolen my bits and pieces of jewellery,' she informed him. 'Look.' Opening the drawer, she lifted the lid of her empty jewel case. 'I took them off yesterday evening, and tonight when I came to put them on . . .' She shrugged her well-shaped shoulders. 'I know they are not valuable – but even so . . .'

'You should inform the police. I'd go right away if I were you. The station is very close – take the first street on the left after you turn out of the hotel.'

307

'You think so?' she asked doubtfully.

'In Switzerland the police take theft very seriously. Let me help you on with your coat.'

She slipped on a thick sweater and let him help her into the coat. 'They'll get annoyed if you don't report a theft,' Frey said easily as he accompanied her downstairs. The bar was packed, filled with smoke and the sound of raucous pop music. He went with her to the exit and repeated the directions. 'I would come with you but I'm expecting a phone call from Davos,' he remarked casually.

He remained standing outside the hotel entrance as she walked away, rubbed his face vigorously as though the keen bite of the wind was chilling him, then got into his Varu and drove off at speed toward the farm. A few yards up the street a Peugeot stood parked without lights. Behind the wheel Erich Volcker noted the signal Frey had made by rubbing his face and waited until Anna Markos had disappeared down the side street. Then he switched on his lights and tried to start the engine.

Walking slowly down the deserted side street, Anna Markos pulled up her ear muffs; now she had full use of her acute sense of hearing. The street was dead straight and narrow, so narrow it allowed the passage of only one vehicle. On either side of her the houses were shuttered and silent and flakes of gentle snow drifted lazily down. In the night hush the only sound was the crunch of her boots on the crusted snow. And this, she knew, was not the way to the police station.

Then she heard the car turn into the street behind her. She began walking more quickly, her long, powerful legs covering the ground at speed. She was careful not to run: one slip on the ice and she would be finished. Behind the wheel of the Peugeot sat a grotesque figure. Erich Volcker was short and very fat, but it was hard fat. He had plump legs and small, neat feet. His round skull was entirely hairless and his pouched lips tightened as he trapped the Greek woman in his headlight beams. Taking a deep breath, he pressed his foot down.

Anna Markos heard the change of the engine sound. In the lights of the car she saw a few paces ahead a large round rock lying by a doorway. She risked running the few paces, stooped, picked up the rock, and swung round. Behind his wheel Volcker stared in astonishment as he saw her turn and face him. He kept his foot down. The rock sailed through the air, and struck his windshield a smashing blow, and the glass crazed. One moment he had ten-tenths vision, the next second he was blind. Holding the wheel steady, he looked out of the side window and watched the walls of the houses rushing by, maintaining the same distance from them, waiting for the bump and thud as he rolled over her.

Pressed inside the doorway, Anna watched the car flash by her, proceed on down the street, slow at the end almost to a crawl as it turned a corner and disappeared. She went back swiftly up the street the way she had come and turned right into the main street, where there were lights, people. As she re-entered the Storchen there was the same curious smile on her face as when she had collected the jewellery to throw it down the drain.

Anna Markos, the agent Harry Wargrave had sent to Andermatt, was a very brave woman. Suspecting that Robert Frey was the head of the Communist cell operating from Andermatt, she had not been sure. At the risk of her life she had sprung a trap using herself as bait – and now she was sure. The attempt to murder her had proved her case. As she entered the crowded reception hall, Louis Celle grasped her arm.

'Come and have a drink, Anna. For a start . . .'

'Louis, I'm looking for Robert Frey.'

'He just drove off.'

'In which direction? Do you know?'

'Yes, he went that way . . .'

Louis waved his arm toward the west, toward the cluster of farm buildings beyond Andermatt where the helicopter was housed. Anna ran upstairs, locked herself inside her bedroom, and used the phone to call Göschenen station for the second time in an hour.

'Can you tell me when the Atlantic Express is expected to reach Göschenen?'

'There has been a delay, madame, but the express is making up time. We expect it here at 8.49.'

'So if I catch the 8.31 from Andermatt on the Schöllenen I should be in time?'

'Assuredly, madame – it is a connection.'

It took Anna Markos much longer to get through to the Zürich number she had memorized. The girl who answered the phone at the other end merely repeated the number. 'This is Leros calling,' Anna said quickly, 'Leros calling Mr Gehring. It is very urgent.'

'One moment, please . . .'

Behind his desk at counter-espionage headquarters in Zürich, Traber stiffened when he heard who was calling. It was the very first time Wargrave's agent in Andermatt had approached him. 'Put him straight through,' he replied. He was even more surprised when he heard the voice of a woman speaking to him in faultless German. 'I'm Gehring, yes,' he said immediately.

'Please give a name urgently – very urgently – to Mr Roose. You heard me – to Mr Roose? The name is Robert Frey, Robert Frey. Repeat it, please. That's right . . .'

The connection was broken before Traber could reply. Mr Roose was Harry Wargrave. The reference to Robert Frey the Swiss counter-espionage chief didn't understand at all; Frey was one of Switzerland's most respected citizens. But Traber did not waste time on speculation. Pressing a button on the intercom, he asked to be put through to the duty officer of the communications section. Within three minutes the signal was on its way to the communications compartment in the Wagon-Lit at the rear of the Atlantic Express.

Robert Frey was a perfectionist, never satisfied, and he was not satisfied now with the progress of his sabotage team although they had, in fact, worked swiftly since disembarking from the Sikorsky perched at one end of the rocky plateau that formed the summit of the Wasserhorn. The initial shovelling away of snow to reach the hardcore ice layer below had not taken long; the wind from the east that had caused a near-disaster when Wargrave was taking off from the Atlantic Express flatcar had scoured the summit of the Wasserhorn almost clear of snow, leaving only a thin coating.

'Hurry it up,' Frey ordered. 'Move your bloody muscles – we're behind schedule.'

'We're damn well not,' Emil Platow murmured to the man he was working with as he checked his watch.

'What was that, Emil?' Frey demanded, his huge figure looming over the stooped Platow.

'We're on schedule,' the Swiss snapped irritably.

'This part we can hurry over. The next part, no. Do you never use that bonecase you call a brain?'

And Frey was right. At distant intervals, they had

shovelled open five separate holes. Now they were beginning to use the drills powered by the portable generator on board the helicopter. Cables trailed like lifelines from the Sikorsky to the drills the team were using, drilling through the ice core deep into the rock of the mountain summit. It was a calculated risk, using the drills, but the sites chosen were well back from the precipitous edges of the plateau.

Frey had chosen the drilling sites long ago – and Frey knew something he had not included in the reports he passed on to Davos after each flying expedition to check the stability of the mountain slopes high above the Gotthard. Zigzagging across the Wasserhorn was an immense fracture, a fracture whose depth Frey had once privately checked with seismological equipment. The chief of the Communist cell based in Andermatt knew that the apparent impregnability of this giant towering above the Gotthard railway was flawed.

The drilling completed, they began the mind-chilling climax to the operation, the lowering of the explosives into the prepared cavities. Frey himself supervised this part of the operation; while Emil Platow handed him the small dome-shaped shells, he gently lowered them into position. The other four men carried the explosive shells gingerly from the chopper. As Frey lowered the last one inside its cavity, all that remained was to link up the electrical system that would cause detonation – at intervals of several seconds rather than simultaneously. Frey was aiming for nothing less than a chain reaction; as one part of the mountain shifted, so it would release the next section, and then the next – until the deep fracture opened up and sent half the mountain down onto the railroad track in an avalanche of unprecedented magnitude.

'There's a chopper coming,' Platow said suddenly.

Frey looked up; Platow surpassed his chief in only one quality: the exceptional acuteness of his hearing. And Emil Platow was right. A chopper was coming toward the Wasserhorn.

Wargrave's Alouette helicopter was now a long way north of the Atlantic Express as he followed the line of the railroad, still uneasy and not sure what he was looking for. A movement of civilian vehicles, a movement of men, something that shouldn't be there? In the moonlit night the view ahead was fantastic – in the distance he could see the panorama of the main Alpine line, half-obscured in clouds and the terrible weather north of the Gotthard.

Behind him Elsa was swivelling her night glasses through a wide arc to the northwest. She paused, her lens locked on the Wasserhorn peak. She waited a moment before she spoke; Wargrave liked people to be certain before they expressed an opinion. Then she lowered her glasses and spoke into the mike below her chin.

'There's a chopper landed on the Wasserhorn.'

314

'Are you sure?' Wargrave demanded.

'If I hadn't been sure I wouldn't have said so. And I think there are several men moving about on the peak.'

'That is the Wasserhorn,' Max Bruder, the Swiss radio operator, confirmed.

'Report it to Springer,' Wargrave snapped. 'I want a top priority check – which means a reply within minutes. Repeat: within minutes.'

Wargrave changed course away from the railroad track, heading directly for the huge summit gleaming in the moonlight. Behind him Elsa inserted a magazine into her automatic weapon and released the safety catch. Bruder was sending his signal. Elsa reached for a spare magazine and laid it in her lap. Wargrave was straining to see what was happening on the summit. In less than a minute he saw that Elsa was only too damned right. There was a chopper – and men moving around it.

Aboard the express Springer reacted instantly on receiving the signal. Through Neckermann he was urgently contacting army headquarters at Andermatt. There was only a brief interlude before the reply to his query came back from Andermatt. As usual, before taking off in his Sikorsky, Frey had informed the local military commander of his flight to check the snow situation. Springer read the reply and dictated a signal for immediate transmission to Wargrave.

Chopper on the Wasserhorn commanded by Robert Frey, the highly respected and able mountaineer. His departure

for routine avalanche check passed and approved by military
commander at Andermatt. Springer.

'So that's that,' Elsa commented as she read the
signal Bruder had handed her. 'False alarm. And I've
taken us away from the rail track. Sorry, Harry.'

'You must never apologize for vigilance, Elsa,'
Wargrave said sharply. 'It could have been
something.'

'Robert Frey is a remarkable man,' Max Bruder
commented as Wargrave changed course again to
head back for the railroad track. 'I met him once – it
was an honour to shake the hand of such a man.'

'Some sort of local hero?' Elsa inquired.

'Only one of the world's top mountaineers,' Wargrave replied. 'Now let's go on checking the track.'

'The chopper's going away,' Emil Platow said, unable
to keep the relief out of his voice. 'Funny – it wasn't
an army machine. No markings . . .'

'Some idiot civilian pilot lost his way, trying to find
the airstrip,' Frey replied.

'At this time of night?' Platow beat his gloved
hands around his body to bring back the circulation.
It was bitterly cold but the view was magnificent, a
vast panorama of range upon range of snowbound
peaks. From where he stood perched on a boulder
Platow could see, far below, the glint of the moon on
great spears of ice, great waterfalls frozen in midair,

dark shadows that hid the gashes of bottomless gorges.

'You worry too much,' Frey remarked as he made a connection with two wires. When he had finished, it would merely require the turn of a single switch on the control box to set off the series of massive detonations. Completing the connection, Frey glanced at his watch. They were ahead of schedule. By only a few minutes, but they were ahead of schedule. And only because he had driven hard his well-trained team. Now nothing could save the Atlantic Express.

Nor was Robert Frey worried about the aftermath of the huge catastrophe he was precipitating. In all probability the Bern government would appoint him inspector in charge of the investigation later; once the avalanche started to roll, who would remember the muffled sound of the previous detonations on the peak – even assuming they were heard? And should anything go wrong, Frey already had his escape route planned.

'I think I can see it coming!' Platow called out.

'Are you sure?' Frey queried as he joined Platow on the boulder.

'For God's sake, of course I'm sure!'

'Then tell the others to get back on board the chopper fast. Move, man, move!'

Almost delirious with nervousness and excitement Platow scrambled across the plateau to pass on the order to the other men, who stood in a huddled group as though seeking warmth from each other against the penetrating cold. On the boulder Frey lifted the glasses slung around his neck and focused them down the Gotthard. And Platow was right. The distant lights of the Atlantic Express had appeared around a bend far below.

The Alouette had almost returned to a position above the railroad track when Bruder reported that an urgent signal was coming through from Springer aboard the train. Taking down the message, he handed it to Wargrave, who glanced at it and then swore. The words came clearly through to Elsa, craning her neck to look down at the railway.

'Bloody hell . . .'

Message from Leros, the signal read, *Robert Frey. Repeat, Robert Frey.*

'Those men on the Wasserhorn,' Wargrave snapped – through the microphone his voice crackled with urgency – 'it's a Communist sabotage team.'

He had already changed course violently, swinging the Alouette sideways so Elsa had to grab the arm of her seat to keep her balance, accelerating as he changed course, as he ascended, building up a speed of eighty miles an hour as the rotor system above them whirled into high gear while he headed directly back for the Wasserhorn summit. The whole cabin was suddenly charged with tension as Bruder, bewildered, protested.

'But that is Robert Frey . . .'

'Able and respected mountaineer,' Wargrave said viciously, recalling Springer's earlier description. 'Elsa, get ready to gun those men down – every single man on that peak. Shoot to kill.'

Elsa reacted instantly: dropped her night glasses and grabbed her automatic weapon. They were approaching the mighty peak at great speed as she lowered a window and the cold, bitter night air flooded inside the heated cabin. Kneeling down, she rested the barrel of the weapon on the window edge as her face froze, as the machine rocked and swayed in the turbulence of the sudden ascent that was taking them to a height above the peak. It was going to be damned difficult to aim at anything under these circumstances, she was thinking. Wargrave seemed to read her thoughts as he continued climbing, his cheekbones sharply outlined in the glow from the instrument panel.

'Spray them – elevate the gun up and down a fraction and then sideways back and forth a fraction. Only a fusillade will get them.'

On the Wasserhorn summit four of the men had almost reached the stationary Sikorsky, running across the light snow in their anxiety to reach the machine, but the fifth running man had stopped, turned, and pointed upward. A shot rang out, then another, both of them missing Wargrave's chopper, which was now descending toward the summit. Elsa let loose a long tracer burst, moving the muzzle in a slight arc.

On the peak bullets riddled across the snow, reached Emil Platow, who had fired. He slumped in the snow. Twenty metres away Frey cursed the stupid, crazy reaction of Emil, bent down to the control box, and turned the switch. For a moment nothing happened. For a moment even the supremely confident Frey wondered whether the electric circuit had failed. Then he felt the first tremor, the first terrifying rumble. He ran toward the helicopter and then stopped, his mind blank for several seconds, unable to take in what he saw.

The Sikorsky with the four men aboard it toppled as the rock under it collapsed. Frey had miscalculated the extent of the accumulated detonations. For a second or two the Sikorsky remained poised on the brink, then it went down. Smashing against a crag, it broke off the rotor system, losing the whole system as the fuselage with the men inside spun down the mountain until – hundreds of feet down – it struck a protruding crag. The machine detonated, exploded in a brilliant flash of flame, vanished in a whirl of disintegrating fragments. By pure chance only Robert Frey was left alive on a tiny platform of surviving rock, staring up at the Alouette hovering over him.

'I want that man alive,' Wargrave snapped. 'Lower the hoist cradle, Elsa.'

He had no need to give instructions to Max Bruder, who was already radioing Springer. *Avalanche coming . . . Huge avalanche heading for railroad track.*

Started by Frey ... Repeat, avalanche heading straight for express ... From the Wasserhorn ... the Wasserhorn ...

From the hovering machine they had distinctly heard the explosive detonations, followed by the terrible rumble as the Wasserhorn came apart at the fracture, sending millions of tons of snow and rock in a slow, gradually increasing slide of mammoth proportions. From the air, it was like watching an ocean inclined at an angle of forty-five degrees in motion as half the mountain came apart and began its gigantic descent to the Gotthard far below.

Elsa, who during her stint at the Washington Embassy had flown in helicopters with Wargrave when he had taught her to use the hoist, was already lowering the harness cradle from the open door while Wargrave held the machine in a hover above the relic of the summit. It wasn't easy; the cabin was littered with equipment, with pairs of short skis, sticks, and climbing boots. At one moment she damn near fell out of the door as her foot tripped over a rope with a large grapple hook.

'Just stay aboard,' Wargrave commented through his mike.

'Just let me concentrate on the job,' Elsa flashed back. 'You might keep the bloody machine level, for a start . . .'

Wargrave smiled briefly. Elsa Lang was on form, full of guts and spit, which was just as well considering what she was trying to do. He almost issued a

warning about how to handle Frey when he reached
the cabin, then decided to keep his mouth shut. The
swaying hoist cradle was now within feet of the huge
Swiss mountaineer, swaying backward and forward.
Unnoticed by Elsa, who was concentrating on her
tricky job, Frey took a small .22 pistol out of his coat
pocket and rammed it barrel first up the tight cuff
wrapped over his left wrist. Then he reached up,
grabbed the swaying cradle, held it while he adjusted
and fixed the straps firmly. Then he signalled with an
upward gesture.

Elsa began hauling him up as the helicopter continued its hover and Frey swayed below, coming up
closer to the machine foot by foot. Max Bruder was
continuing to send his urgent warning signal to Springer nonstop. Below, the mountain continued its vast
collapse, spreading as it gathered momentum, spreading a kilometre-wide wave of falling rock and snow,
heading for the tree line, the fir forest that lay in its
path. Below that, far below, the Gotthard railroad
track still gleamed in the moonlight as the Atlantic
Express came closer and closer.

'Another minute and he'll be aboard,' Elsa
reported.

'I want him alive – but watch the bastard. I can't
help you.'

Wargrave was none too happy about what they
were attempting. On the one hand he had guessed
how important it could be for Springer to be able to
interrogate Robert Frey – Anna Markos's message had

indicated she had identified him as the top Communist agent in Andermatt. On the other hand he was worried that, confined as he was by his need to control the machine, Elsa was going to have to deal with the mountaineer on her own.

Elsa was preoccupied with the last tricky stage of getting Frey inside the cabin. Using one hand, she detached her headset and microphone. Her Smith and Wesson was ready – tucked inside the top of her ski pants. It was up to her to cope with this giant Swiss on her own and now she could see his face clearly as he stared up at her. Was there a flicker of surprise when he saw that it was a girl who was hauling him to safety? She kept her eyes fixed on the large, hawklike nose, the eyes she could hardly see behind the snow goggles he wore. Something warned her this was a formidable man, that she had better be pretty damned careful.

Then she was swinging the cradle inside through the open door and Frey was aboard. Glancing around, the mountaineer saw the pilot, trapped by his need to control the machine, the radio operator next to him absorbed in repeating his urgent signal. His right hand tugged at his left cuff to extract the pistol as the girl slammed the door shut. The pistol stayed where it was, caught by the tightness of his sleeve. Elsa faced him with the Smith and Wesson in her hand and then the machine lurched, and threw her against the side of the cabin, and she dropped her weapon. Frey hurled his whole bulk against her, throwing her on her back at the rear of the cabin, falling with her, pinning her down underneath him. His right hand grasped her throat, squeezed.

As she lay pinned under the great bulk of Frey, Elsa's right hand scraped over the floor, felt the grapple hook, grasped it, and hooked it around Frey's thick neck. Startled, he let go as he felt the point pressing against his throat. Half-choked, her eyes blazing with fury, she screamed at him in French, 'Get off, back off me, or I'll rip your fucking throat open . . .'

Frey was frightened – and not only by the piercing point of the hook pressed against his throat. The look in the girl's eyes was terrible. She would do it. He knew she would do it. 'Back off slowly – but very slowly,' Elsa hissed through her teeth. Frey climbed up slowly as Elsa came up with him, holding the grapple at his throat. Then he felt the barrel of a gun rammed hard into his back and heard Max Bruder's voice.

'One mistake and I'll blow your spine to pieces.'

Within two minutes they had Frey bound and tied with his wrists behind him. Elsa, who had jerked Frey's .22 pistol from his cuff, was none too gentle as she tied the final knots. Then she rolled him to the back of the cabin, leaving him face up so he could breathe. Before she left him she bent over him with the hook. 'One peep out of you and I'll use this. Understand?'

Wargrave had already swung the machine in a half

circle and was heading out across the Gotthard valley at high speed for the train. At that time he had no idea he had captured the chief Soviet sabotage agent inside Switzerland; nor did he know that Colonel Springer, receiving the news from Bruder, had already sent two top priority signals to Andermatt and to Brigadier Traber in Zürich. Within hours patrol cars, armed with lists of Frey's known friends and associates, were speeding through cities as far apart as Geneva and Lugano; officers were knocking on doors in the middle of the night, taking people in for intensive interrogation. Within five days the entire Frey sabotage ring had been rounded up. But at the moment all Wargrave was concerned with was the steady fall of the mighty avalanche toward the railroad track as the Atlantic Express continued up the incline.

Chapter Nineteen

Avalanche

Robert Frey was a brilliant organizer who believed in taking out insurance against the possibility that even the best-laid plans can go astray, and the operation to destroy the Atlantic Express – adapted from the Communist contingency plan to block the Gotthard in wartime – hinged on precise timing, on the express being in the right place to take the full force of the avalanche he had unleashed from the Wasserhorn.

So at intervals along the track – and always at places where the express would be moving slowly up a major incline – he had placed individual members of his widespread sabotage organization. Frey had calculated carefully the likely course of the avalanche, the section of the track it would take out. It was essential the express should be moving over that selected portion of the track when the avalanche struck. And it was because these were single men spaced apart that Wargrave had found it impossible to spot them from his aerial survey.

Springer reacted with his usual energy and decision when he received the first warning of what was coming from Wargrave's helicopter. In the compart-

ment he occupied next to the compartment containing
Marenkov and Haller, he bent over a map with his
assistant, Jurgen Thall. 'The Wasserhorn is there.' He
drew a circle over a stretch of track. 'If the avalanche
reaches the track I estimate it will hit somewhere
inside that ring.'

'And we are now travelling just about in the middle
of it,' Thall pointed out.

'A little nearer to the northern end of the danger
sector,' Springer replied. 'Get on the phone to the
engineer – tell him I need maximum speed.'

Thall left the compartment, ran down the corridor
to the communications section where a special phone
had been installed to link them directly with the
engineer's cab. Alone inside his own compartment,
Springer switched off the light, raised the blind, and
lowered the window. Ignoring the blast of cold air, he
stared out at the terrifying moonlit spectacle.

There was no dramatic roar, no rushing momentum, only the steady slide of a whole mountain on the
move toward the railroad track. It was like a great
wave coming toward him in slow motion, a tidal
wave of tumbling rock and snowslide, a slide of
millions of tons of snow. As Springer watched, it
reached the top of the tree line, the first trees of a
great fir forest spreading down the lower slopes. Like
an oceanic tidal wave it simply passed over the firs,
and Springer knew that under that white wave great
trees, scores of years old, were being crushed to pulp
like matchsticks. Then he saw something that made

COLIN FORBES

him freeze. The slide reached an immense crag. Instead of pouring over it, the slide jerked the crag off the mountain and took it down with the mounting torrent. Springer then realized this was no ordinary avalanche, huge though it might be: the Wasserhorn was flawed; this was an avalanche to make history. He turned as Thall slammed open the door.

'We can't get through to the engineer.'

'Why the hell not?'

'He's not answering.'

At that moment the slow-moving express, lumbering up an incline, lost more speed, then stopped. A few seconds later it began to creep backward down the incline, back down into the sector of maximum danger.

There were two men inside the cab of the Bo-Bo locomotive hauling the Atlantic Express up the incline. They had little to do except watch the gauges, check the signals ahead. And the throb of the motor had muffled all sound of the oncoming avalanche. Enrico, the chief engineer, was cleaning his hands with a rag when Frey's man jumped aboard, hauling himself inside the cab. Enrico stared in disbelief as the man struck his colleague a brutal blow over the head with the barrel of his gun, splitting his skull. The man aimed the gun at Enrico. 'Turn around.' The chief engineer turned around and the saboteur struck him a grazing blow, which he imagined had eliminated

Enrico, who sank to the platform, dazed and only half-conscious. Frey's man, Anton Gayler, studied the controls briefly, then moved a lever, then two more levers after the express had stopped. The Atlantic Express started moving backward.

Gayler, a short, burly man with buck teeth, had no fear he would be caught in the avalanche; on the eastern side of the track, only a short distance away, a driver was waiting behind the wheel of his Fiat with the engine running, waiting to pick up Gayler and drive him up the eastern side of the gorge well clear of the avalanche. As the express continued its slow retreat down the incline, Gayler peered out of the western side of the cab. Several uniformed men were running up the track toward him. One of them, a civilian, was streaking far ahead of the others. Gayler took aim with his gun.

'Get troops to the cab,' Springer ordered as he pushed past Thall into the corridor. But it was the colonel who was first out of the train, opening a door at the end of the car, dropping onto the lower step and then jumping carefully from the slowly reversing express to the track. He had fourteen coaches to pass before he reached the locomotive as he streaked along the track, his nine-round .32 Browning automatic in his hand. But he had one advantage in his race against time – the express was moving backward past him, hauling the locomotive steadily toward him.

He was close to the motor when he saw the silhouette of a man lean out of the motor cab, a silhouette without railroad cap or uniform, a silhouette that aimed something at him. Springer ducked as he continued running, heard a shot, then a second shot as gravel spurted up beside him, Springer suddenly stopped running, whipped up his automatic, calmly gripped it in both hands, and fired. Something – it was the gunman's pistol – spun out of the cab and fell on the track.

Inside the cab Gayler, the knuckles of his right hand shattered and bleeding, swore and stumbled to the other side of the cab. Using his left hand, he lowered himself from the cab to the track and stumbled across the verge onto a nearby road. A dozen yards away stood a Fiat with a driver behind the wheel and the car's engine running. Gayler gasped with relief at his luck in getting off so close to the escape vehicle.

Aboard the train on the east side a compartment window had been lowered. There were no lights inside. A shadow of the upper half of a man appeared at the window, which was shielded by the train's bulk from the moonlight. A hand protruded. As Gayler stumbled on toward the parked Fiat a single shot was fired and Anton Gayler fell dead in the road. A second shot was fired. The man inside the Fiat slumped dead behind his wheel. It was marksmanship of the calibre the dead Phillip John had been reputed to possess.

The shadowy figure withdrew from sight and the window closed.

The express was still moving backward when Springer climbed into the cab. He took in the scene at a single glance: one man probably dead; Enrico, the chief engineer, stirring feebly on the floor as he slowly recovered from the grazing blow. Springer knelt beside him, shook him none too gently.

'Get a grip on yourself – quick. I have to get the train moving forward at speed ... an avalanche is coming. Get a hold on yourself, man, for God's sake. How do I do it – get the express moving forward?'

Enrico made a supreme effort, sat up with his back to the cab, and began pointing. Springer reached for one lever. A shake of the head. A gesture. Springer reached for another lever. Enrico nodded, tried to call out, 'Careful ...' Springer moved the lever and the express jerked to a grinding halt. More gestures. Springer's hand moved from lever to lever until Enrico nodded. The stalled express began moving slowly forward, so slowly Springer was appalled at the lack of pace. Two Swiss soldiers had boarded the cab after him and one was trying to apply first aid to Enrico. But the engineer, a sturdy man from Basel, waved him aside and clambered to his feet to help Springer.

'Who are you?' he asked.

'Military intelligence.' It was not the answer Springer would normally have given but he wanted to impress the man with a sense of extreme urgency. 'I want the motor opened full throttle,' Springer said vehemently. 'An avalanche is heading straight for us.'

'Could be dangerous on this stretch . . .' The engineer was moving the controls despite his warning; perhaps it had struck him that avalanches can be even more dangerous. The wheels began to move a little faster; Springer felt the vibrations of enormous power quivering the plate under his feet. The engineer had reacted totally to his instruction and the Atlantic Express started to crawl up the steep incline, but still agonizingly slowly, rumbling over threads of bridges spanning great gulfs, swaying as it swung around great curves, as the needles on the gauges shuddered. Several needles, Springer noticed, had passed above red markings, indicating the tremendous pressures building up. He went over to the western side of the cab.

The great forest had gone, obliterated under the tidal sweep of the oncoming avalanche which was level with the train, less than one kilometre away now, the vast wave of tumbling rock and snow so high that Springer had little doubt it was going to overwhelm the express. Normally it would have stopped in the narrow valley floor, but this time too much was coming, too high, too fast . . .

Many thoughts raced through Springer's mind as he watched the disaster coming closer: about his wife, Clara, and his eighteen-year-old son, Charles, a student at Lausanne University – both of whom would be at home now in their Zürich apartment, whom he might never see again. And then he realized the true magnitude of what was approaching – it was a *triple* avalanche that fiend Frey had unleashed to kill just one man – never mind about the other three hundred and fifty souls on board the express . . .

At first he had identified what he knew was the fall of a major powder-snow avalanche, which makes little more than a hissing sound as it slides downward, a vast wave of snow glistening in the moonlight with a certain majestic splendour. But now above the rumble of the labouring locomotive he heard a sound like thunder reverberating among the peaks that warned him that gigantic quantities of ice were on the move. And as if this were not terrible enough, he could see huge rocks bounding down amid the white dust of the powder snow. It was also a rock avalanche.

September 11, 1881. The village of Elm overshadowed by the Plattenbergkopf. Millions of tons of rock had fallen, a great wind had preceded the impact, whirling people into the air, carrying whole houses into space, smashing others to pieces under the shock of the blast wave. That, too, had been a rock avalanche. And there were three hundred and fifty people on board the express, Springer thought again. Oh, my God . . .

Throughout the length of the train stark panic had gripped the passengers, who filled the corridors despite the efforts of the Swiss railroad staff and security men to keep them inside their compartments. The thunderclap of the ice fall completed the panic. Some, in their terror, opened doors and dropped to the track, running back past the train as though escape lay that way – when they were running *toward* the avalanche.

It was even more frightening at the rear of the express where, with the lights turned out, Haller and Marenkov stood looking out of the window. And Julian Haller, glancing at his watch, thought of his wife, Linda. In New York it would be 2.35 p.m., local time. She would be working in the fashion design office on Madison Avenue. Would he ever see her again? He doubted it. At least she would benefit from his generous pension rights. Suddenly a girl with long hair came running past them under the window – running toward the avalanche – her face distorted with terror. Marenkov leaned out, grabbed her by the hair. As she screamed, he used his other hand to grip her under the armpit and hauled her bodily up inside the compartment. He slapped her across the face to stop the hysterics. Haller opened the compartment door and faced Matt Leroy, who was on guard outside.

'What's happening?' Leroy demanded.

'Nothing much,' Haller replied with bitter irony. 'Take this girl back up the train; hand her over to one of the security people and tell him to keep her inside a compartment.'

334

On the western side of the track, railroad officials and men from Springer's detachment had rounded up most of the fleeing passengers, were pushing them back on board the slow-moving train with the aid of other passengers, who helped hoist them aboard. Haller returned to the window beside Marenkov and saw something horrific. From distant houses in the path of the avalanche people were running. In the moonlight both men saw a child rushing down a field, pursued by a woman, presumably its mother.

As the child continued running, a boulder descended from out of nowhere and crashed down on the child. Haller felt physically sick as he watched the distraught mother reach the boulder, running her hands over it in a hopeless attempt to move it – the rock must have weighed a quarter of a ton. The American glanced at Marenkov and his gall rose as he saw the impassive expression on the Russian's face. He could have hit him. Then Marenkov spoke in a low growl.

'The bastards . . .'

'Your people,' Haller snapped.

'Kindly inform Springer,' Marenkov continued in the same growling tone, 'that as soon as he is ready I will provide a complete list out of my head of every KGB agent in Switzerland. The GRU people I do not know . . .'

In the corridor of the first-class car next to the third Wagon-Lit Jorge Santos stood among a crowd of people staring out at the avalanche. He had noticed something, and as he stood with his dead pipe clenched between his teeth he was trying to make a calculation. The two eastern faces of the Wasserhorn were angled toward each other, separated by a gulch, so now two separate waves of the avalanche were advancing toward each other. If they met in time, their massive collision might just halt the entire landslide.

Inside the Alouette, five hundred feet above the avalanche, Wargrave had noticed the same phenomenon. Holding the chopper in a hover, he was now engaged in a highly dangerous task. Among the equipment Springer had put aboard the helicopter at the Englishman's suggestion was two hundred kilos of gelignite; as long ago as the previous Thursday Wargrave had foreseen a situation where he might need to bomb a hostile vehicle approaching the express. Wargrave had now assembled the explosive cylinders on his lap into one large bomb, which he had fused. If he could slow down the right-hand wave of the avalanche it might give time for the other wave to collide with it.

'You should know,' he warned Elsa and Max Bruder, 'that this is highly tricky. It's a short fuse – it has to be – and if it detonates too early . . .'

'There are several hundred people aboard that express,' Elsa said quietly. 'Only four of us up here . . .'

Her throat felt parched and she was sick with fear

as Wargrave opened the window, ignited the fuse, and dropped the homemade bomb. The moment he had dropped it Wargrave elevated the chopper at maximum speed. The bomb detonated the second it reached the ground just yards ahead of the right-hand wave. It slowed the wave for only seconds, but by then the left-hand wave met it in frightful collision. The sound of the impact reached them inside the Alouette as the chopper rocked under the shock wave, as a storm of snow hurtled up and enveloped the Alouette. Then the snow dust cleared and Wargrave was descending toward the train.

The avalanche ended in the normal cone shape. A tongue of snow swept over the track behind the express, flooding over the track just below the overhead traction wires, too weak now to bring down the traction pylons. The Atlantic Express continued on its way, heading for Airolo, the last stop before it entered the Gotthard tunnel.

Chapter Twenty

Schöllenen Trap

Immediately after phoning Traber in Zürich from Andermatt to send her warning signal – the signal that had been instrumental in saving the Atlantic Express from destruction – Anna Markos had packed her case in her room at the Hotel Storchen. She estimated she just had time to catch the 8.31 train from Andermatt to Göschenen, where she would wait to board the Atlantic Express.

Before leaving the room – she had earlier paid her bill – she took one precaution. Feeling under her left armpit, she checked to make sure the sheathed knife concealed there was easily extracted. Unlike Elsa Lang, who had been trained to use pistols and automatic weapons by Harry Wargrave on the FBI shooting range in Washington, Anna was a child of the Balkans, where women use knives.

And again unlike Elsa, the daughter of a British admiral who had been educated at the Godolphin public school in Salisbury, Anna had been brought up in the back streets of Athens. She was only seven years old when both her parents had been killed by the Communists at the time of the Greek Civil War –

the war the Greek anti-Communists had partly won owing to the military aid sent by President Truman. And in the Balkans passions are stronger and last longer than in the West. Since she had been eighteen years old Anna had devoted her life to fighting the underground Communist apparatus. It was in Athens that she had originally joined forces with Harry Wargrave.

Going out the back way to the garage, she removed the blanket she had draped over the hood of her rented Renault to prevent the engine freezing up. Within two minutes she was driving it out of the archway and into the main street. It was only a short distance to the station just beyond the eastern outskirts of Andermatt but she drove carefully. This was not the moment to skid into a wall. There were one or two other cars about, and a hundred yards behind her a small grey Fiat followed at a discreet distance. Behind the wheel sat the fat, bald-headed Erich Volcker, the man who earlier had unsuccessfully tried to run her down in a side street.

Anna was heading for the Schöllenen railroad, which descends from Andermatt to Göschenen on the main Milan to Zürich rail route. It is one of the strangest and most sinister railroads in Europe. With a gradient of 1 in 5½, it creaks and rumbles its way down over a rack-and-pinion system as huge cogs suspended below the coaches turn over the ratchet rail. In less than three miles it drops over a thousand feet and the journey takes fifteen minutes.

In that time it grinds its way down through a series of tunnels and avalanche shelters and at one point crosses the river Reuss where that ferocious stream plunges and winds its way through the terrible gorge and over a great waterfall. Travelling it by day is a weird experience; by night the experience becomes eerie and frightening as the grind of the slow-moving cogs reverberates and echoes inside the dark tunnels.

At intervals windows in the rock and short open stretches outside the tunnels reveal an awesome view – the drop into the gorge, the tumble and froth of the foaming torrent below. At the moment the Reuss was frozen. As Anna pulled up outside the station she was not surprised to see that apparently she was the only passenger. In a week's time the train would be crowded with returning vacationers. Leaving the Renault parked outside – she could inform the car rental people later – she went into the booking hall to buy her ticket.

'You will have about three minutes to catch the train at Göschenen,' the ticket clerk informed her. 'Hurry across to the main station when you get down.'

'Thank you,' Anna replied in German. 'I know the way – I came up only two weeks ago.'

Choosing a compartment in the middle of the short train, she perched her bag on the seat ready for a quick exit and sighed with relief. She had got away from Andermatt in one piece. And she had done the job: she knew who was controlling and directing the secret Communist cell from Andermatt. Then the door was opened and a man climbed inside as the train began to move. Sitting down in the seat diagonally opposite to her, Erich Volcker took out a cigar and paused.

'You mind if I smoke my cigar, miss?'

Anna glanced at him and shrugged her shoulders without replying as she looked away. The grinding of the cogs was beginning and she had the feeling the strain on the train was enormous as it angled downward, that maybe the cogs would slip and the train would plunge down through the tunnel. It was an irrational fear; she knew the Swiss rack-and-pinion system was an engineering marvel, that in its whole history it had never failed to operate smoothly and safely.

'Some people do object to cigars,' Volcker continued as he puffed until the end was a glowing red.

Anna was tense and her nerves were strained. In that brief glance she had noted a great deal about Erich Volcker, had observed his hard fatness, his obscenely bald head, and his small watchful eyes. Some men who were bald have a magnetic attraction for women; Erich Volcker did not fall into this category. And she was suspicious. Why, when the train was empty, had he chosen this compartment?

It could be that she faced nothing more harmless than an amatory approach from this hideous man. That was an experience Anna Markos was only too familiar with. And when Volcker had tried to drive her down in the Andermatt side street before she

COLIN FORBES

smashed his windshield she had no chance to catch even a glimpse of the driver with the headlights glaring in her face. Surreptitiously she checked her watch. Another thirteen minutes alone with this creep. And he was carrying no baggage. Was he a railroad official going home? If so, why was he not in uniform? With an unencouraging expression of arrogance on her face, Anna went on checking the possibilities as the train ground down through another tunnel. Through a cavernous window in the rock she caught a moonlit glimpse of the icebound river Reuss.

'You have had a pleasant holiday, I hope?' Volcker persisted in his throaty voice as he moved to the seat opposite her. 'Everyone has a great time in Andermatt.'

Anna Markos stared directly at him for the first time, her full lips curled in an expression of contempt as she loosened her fur coat as though feeling the warmth of the compartment. She noted his very large hands, the backs of his fingers sprouting black hairs. He could use some of that up top, she was thinking. She sat with her own hands clasped casually in her lap as he went on staring back at her while he pulled on the cigar until the end was again a fiery, glowing tip. Then he removed the cigar from his mouth, leaned forward quickly, and stabbed the burning end on the back of her right hand to shock her – to throw her off balance for a few seconds.

At least, that was what he tried to do. Anna's hands moved with a movement so quick it was a blur. She

342

knocked the cigar out of his hand, there was a shower of sparks, some of which touched his cheek. 'You bitch...' His huge hands grasped her around the throat, half-encircled her strong neck in a vicelike grip. His long fingers held her like a restricting necklace, his thumbs jammed deep into her windpipe. She clawed the right side of his fat face, drew blood as she carved a deep gash, but Volcker ignored the pain, knowing it would take only thirty seconds. Twisting around on the seat, she dropped backward, but he held on and came down on top of her with the whole of his bulk. Her vision was swimming, she felt her consciousness ebbing away.

With a sudden violent movement she swung her powerful body sideways off the seat, carrying him with her, and he landed underneath her on the floor of the compartment with her on top. But still he held on with his strangling grip. She could feel the cog-wheel vibrations coming up through the floor as the train made its laborious twisting way down the Schöllenen. With a supreme effort of will she stopped herself fainting. Volcker's fat, bald-headed silhouette was a fading blur.

With her right hand thrust between them, she seized the handle of the knife, jerked it clear of his throttling embrace. Gritting her teeth, she gripped the knife with all her strength and thrust it upward and deep into his side. He let out a muted, animal-like gulp and his hands left her throat. There was a peculiar thudding sound. Panting for breath, Anna hauled herself back up on the seat. The sound was the thudding of Volcker's tiny feet on the compartment floor. The sound stopped. Volcker lay very still, his eyes open and staring.

Anna checked her watch: 8.40 p.m. Six minutes to Göschenen. Bending over the dead man, she heaved and strained to extract the knife. It took all her strength to free the weapon. Using a large handkerchief she found in one of his pockets, she wiped the handle clean of prints, after donning a pair of gloves. Then she wiped the blade clean of blood, mopped up a few spots off the compartment floor, and stuffed the handkerchief back into his pocket.

Inside his wallet she found a card with his name on it. Printed under the name in German were the words 'aircraft mechanic.' Another visiting card bore the name of Robert Frey. She replaced the wallet and stared out of the window. The train, still moving at a snail's pace as it continued its steep descent, had moved out of the tunnel and was passing under an avalanche shelter. Below the shelter roof the railroad track was open – there was a sheer drop, a glitter of ice a long way down. She unlatched the door, left it bobbing gently against the door frame with the cogwheel vibration.

Standing behind the dead man, she stooped and hoisted him by the shoulders. He seemed to weigh half a ton as she hauled him upright, her hands under his armpits, and forced the body forward until it was touching the opened door. Her chest heaving with the exertion, she took another deep breath and pushed with all her strength. The door flew open; Volcker dropped through the opening, missed the track, and fell out of sight into the gorge. The compartment was suddenly icy cold with the night air flowing in. Leaning out, looking to her left, she saw a fresh tunnel coming up. She hauled the door inward and closed it.

After a quick check of the compartment floor for traces of blood, she checked her appearance in the mirror. Her neck was bruised and swollen. Opening her case, she took out a scarf and wrapped it around her neck, refastened her fur coat, and pulled up her hood. Taking a lipstick from her handbag, she applied it freshly. That made her feel much better. Then she remembered the cigar. She found it smouldering under a seat and pitched it out of the window.

As the little train emerged from the end of the tunnel and stopped alongside its own special station she was standing by the door. At Göschenen, north of the Alps, a blizzard was raging. She checked her watch: 8.46 p.m. Once again a Swiss train had arrived precisely on time. Picking up her bag, she opened the door, stepped down into the snowstorm, and hurried across to the main station. She gave not a single glance backward to the mouth of the Schöllenen tunnel.

Chapter Twenty-one

Göschenen, Zürich

By the time the Atlantic Express had reached Airolo, Wargrave, guided by his Swiss radio operator, Max Bruder, had landed the Alouette at a nearby airstrip ringed by what seemed to be half the Swiss Army. Springer drove the short distance to the airstrip and, as Robert Frey was taken off the machine, he faced hostile and armed men – so hostile that Springer himself escorted the hitherto respected mountaineer to a police van. Weather conditions being so appalling north of the Gotthard, the chopper would be useless, so it was left at the airstrip. Springer then drove Wargrave, Elsa, and Bruder back to the waiting express, which started up as soon as they were on board.

The train had only just commenced its ten-minute journey through the Gotthard tunnel when Wargrave called what he termed 'a council of war' in the Wagon-Lit compartment where Marenkov remained under guard. Besides Elsa and Julian Haller, Springer was present. It was Wargrave who opened the meeting with a typical remark. 'I suspect that what has happened so far may only be the beginning. As they say on British Rail, after the soup the worst is yet to come . . .'

'What I do so love,' Elsa interjected, 'is your eternal optimism.'

'My eternal realism,' the Englishman corrected her with a laconic smile. 'We know that Traber has reported the arrival of Colonel Igor Sharpinsky in Zürich and I don't think that gentleman is going to give up easily.'

'I can give you a description of him,' Marenkov said suddenly.

Springer stared at the Russian; since the avalanche a radical change had taken place in Marenkov's attitude that he would provide no information until he was airborne and on his way to the States. 'That we could use,' the Swiss agreed. 'In the West he is known as Colonel Shadow because no one has ever been able to photograph him.'

'And I could build up a sketch from your description,' Elsa suggested. She was already taking a large notepad from her case. 'When I was make-up girl with a film company I used to pass my spare time sketching people.'

'Leave that for a few minutes,' Springer suggested. 'We have almost two hours before we reach Zürich. There is a mystery I do not understand. The man who attacked the engineers in their cab was shot – once by myself, but I only winged him. He managed to escape from the cab on the other side of the train and was making his way to a waiting car when someone shot him dead. That same someone then shot dead the driver of the escape vehicle.'

'One of your people?' Haller inquired.

'No. That is the whole point – I have checked. But one of my people who was scanning the express from a crag on the eastern side says both shots were fired through an open window by someone on board the express.'

Wargrave stirred in his seat. 'Any idea what range the shots were fired from?'

'The report I have received estimates the first shot was at a range of about one hundred metres – and the saboteur who was killed by a single shot was moving at the time. As for the man behind the wheel of the car, the range was even greater.'

'That's some shooting,' Elsa exclaimed.

'Precisely,' Springer interjected. 'Which is exactly what worries me – we have, somewhere among the three hundred and fifty passengers aboard the express, an outstanding marksman. Who is he? Why is he on the train?'

The train roar as it moved through the tunnel was very loud and Elsa had to raise her voice to make herself heard. 'But if he shot down two of Sharpinsky's men he has to be on our side.'

'I admire your recognition of the obvious, your logical turn of mind,' Wargrave remarked dryly. 'I find it so reassuring.'

'I have the strangest feeling someone is cocking a

snook at me,' Elsa replied caustically. 'It couldn't be I'm displaying an element of naïveté, I trust?'

Wargrave grinned as she glared at him. 'Naïve, you're not. But the unknown marksman could have an excellent reason for shooting down those two men – if he were sufficiently ruthless. By killing them he ensured that if caught they would never talk under interrogation. It could also mean something else more sinister . . .'

'That he is important,' Springer said quietly. 'Important enough to have the power to shoot down his own people to protect his identity.'

'Then the list of possible names is very narrow,' Marenkov suggested.

'Narrow it,' suggested Haller.

'Boris Volkov. Simovitch, the Bulgarian. Leitermann, the German from Leipzig. All of them are KGB marksmen of exceptional calibre.'

'I go along with that,' Haller said. 'The question is: which one is sitting within fourteen cars of where we're sitting now?'

Marenkov shook his head. 'Leitermann is in the United States waiting for an assignment. Within ten minutes of the Boeing's taking off from Schiphol with me aboard you will have details and he will be under arrest.' He waved a hand as Haller started to speak. 'No, that is what was agreed – a complete debriefing to start once I am over the Atlantic. Volkov is under treatment in a Moscow clinic for a liver complaint. I cannot add to the list GRU personnel because I don't know them.'

'So that leaves Simovitch,' Haller pointed out

Wargrave intervened. 'Simovitch was secretly killed in Brussels eighteen months ago by the British Secret Service.'

'Which cancels out everyone you have mentioned, Marenkov,' Haller observed irritably.

'Not quite,' the Russian replied. 'There is a fourth man.' He turned to Wargrave. 'You once operated in Greece?'

'If you say so.'

'Then you may have heard the name Nicos Leonides?'

'No.'

'He is Sharpinsky's favourite executioner – although, as far as I know, he has worked only in his native Greece. I have no description of him – but it is a possibility.'

'And no description of any kind – even a reference to his habits, likes, dislikes?' Elsa inquired.

'Nothing.' The Russian stared around the compartment and his expression was grim. 'Of one thing I am certain – so much is personally at stake for Sharpinsky that when he learns I am still alive I am convinced he will board the express himself at Zürich.' The Russian clenched his fist. 'You can count on it.'

'So we need your description of him quickly,' Elsa said emphatically.

'That may not help – he is a master of the art of

disguise, a natural-born actor. But he will board this train before it leaves Switzerland – I stake my life on it.' He smiled without humour. 'In fact come to think of it, that is what I am staking – my life . . .'

Wargrave left the compartment and moved up the train away from the Wagon-Lit as it approached Göschenen. Unlike previous night trains bound for Holland, the new Atlantic Express would be continuing north to Zürich instead of bypassing the city and heading northwest for Basel via Lucerne. And despite all the efforts of Swiss rail officials to reassure passengers, there was still a sense of nervous tension aboard the train after the avalanche experience.

As he passed compartments Wargrave noticed that some had the blinds drawn where people were trying to get some sleep, but in others passengers were still wide awake, staring fearfully out although they could see nothing but the tunnel. As it approached the exit and Göschenen station, the train slowed down, then glided past the platform and stopped. A snowstorm was raging and the platform was deep with a white carpet as a single passenger climbed aboard.

Anna Markos had a first-class reservation and she was relieved to see the compartment was empty. In the next compartment Jorge Santos watched her pass as he sat alone, his long legs still sprawled, his pipe between his teeth. When the express began moving again he stretched, stood up, and went out into the corridor. He stood for a moment outside the next compartment where Anna Markos was taking off her coat, displaying in profile her magnificent figure. Glancing sideways she caught sight of Santos observing her. The Spaniard gave her a wink. She turned her back on him and when she sat down, crossed her legs, and looked again he had gone. Two minutes later Harry Wargrave entered her compartment, closed the blinds on the corridor side and sat down opposite her.

'Thank you, Anna,' he said simply.

'My message – it reached you?' Like Wargrave, she was conversing in little more than a murmur.

'In the nick of time, thank God. I can tell you now – you probably saved the train from total destruction. Frey set off an avalanche from the Wasserhorn.'

'Oh, my God . . .'

'You saved us all, Anna,' Wargrave repeated gently. 'Was it very tough in Andermatt?' He leaned forward. 'You look strained. Something happened, didn't it?'

Anna shrugged. 'Yes, something happened.' Very briefly she described her experiences and the expression on Wargrave's face grew grimmer as she continued. 'I got on to Robert Frey partly by instinct. Also by luck and digging.' She took a deep drag on her cigarette. 'He was just a bit too much the local hero. But that proved nothing. I checked on who was near the Rhône Glacier the day Springer's agent was found dead in the ice tunnel. Robert Frey's chopper had landed at Gletsch nearby early that morning. Still not conclusive . . .'

She described what had happened since. '. . . Even the hidden transmitter in his farmhouse wasn't conclusive. There were no code books left lying around, of course. So, as I told you, I set myself up as human bait . . . when he guided me into that deathtrap of a street, I knew.'

'And the man on the Schöllenen who tried to kill you,' Wargrave reminded her. He squeezed her right leg above the knee so hard his grip hurt. 'For Christ sake, your brief was to take care, not to push it over the edge.'

'But you admitted I saved the express, Harry. We took chances in Athens, remember . . .' His hard grip on her leg comforted her. There was a time when she had suggested they became lovers and Wargrave – reluctantly – had told her it was madness for agents to become emotionally involved. She had seen his point but even now, with his hand gripping her, she felt the old feeling. 'What do I do now I'm here?' she asked as he released his grip.

'Stay under cover. I'm not telling anyone about your being on the train – I may still need a secret back-up.' He leaned forward and gently removed the scarf from her neck. He winced when he saw the bruising, which had now developed into ugly blue welts.

'That needs medical attention.'

'Later. It's a little sore but I'll survive. Is there anything else I should know?'

'Yes. Colonel Igor Sharpinsky is somewhere in Zürich.'

'That bastard! God knows we spent time trying to track him down in Athens a hundred years ago.'

Wargrave explained how Traber had heard that Crocodile – the code name for Sharpinsky – had arrived in Zürich and that Marenkov was convinced the KGB colonel would board the express at Zürich. 'But at least we do have a description of him,' he went on, 'and Elsa Lang is building up a sketch portrait that may help.'

'He is very clever, very ruthless,' Anna warned.

'Even so, for all we know, Traber may already have tracked him down.'

The gigantic Wasserhorn avalanche that might have engulfed the Atlantic Express just missed it ... The train is now proceeding on its way to Zürich ...

It was 8.40 p.m. in Room 207 at the Hotel Schweizerhof when Heinz Golchack switched off his pocket-size transistor radio, which had just broadcast the news flash. Aware that Rudi Bühler and Heinrich Baum were watching him, Golchack kept his face expressionless as he polished his rimless glasses.

'What the hell do we do now?' Bühler demanded aggressively when he could stand the silence no longer.

'We destroy that map for a start . . .'

He waited while Baum was burning the map in the bathroom and then waited again as Baum hurried back to receive a signal that was just coming in from Moscow via Mohner's transmitter on the Zürichberg. He read the signal in silence and went to the bathroom to burn this message himself. When he returned, his high-domed forehead was glistening with sweat.

'Send the short signal to Basel,' he instructed Baum, 'then the long one to the Geiger Group in Amsterdam.' The signal to Basel was going to Yuri Gusev, the GRU executioner, who had now arrived in that city from Mulhouse in response to Golchack's earlier signal.

Heinrich Baum, the Swiss dentist from Basel, looked dubious. 'The Amsterdam signal is a very long one,' he suggested tentatively. 'Can we not abbreviate it?'

Golchack stared at him with his pale eyes, but the Swiss stared back defiantly. They had been locked away inside the room for five hours now without food and only a flask of coffee Bühler had brought to drink from. Golchack, who was a teetotaller – 'Alcohol clouds the brain and distorts judgment' – ate very little and saw no reason why his subordinates should not conform to his habits. But there was a feeling of claustrophobic tension in the room and Baum would have given anything for a brief walk along the Bahnhofstrasse, even in the snowstorm that was enveloping the city.

'If it had been possible to make it shorter I would

have done so,' Golchack replied coldly. 'Are you questioning my instruction?' he inquired softly.

'Of course not.'

'Then why are you not already sending the signals?' Golchack inquired in the restrained voice Baum found so unnerving. The Swiss sat down in front of his transmitter and began sending the shorter signal to Basel.

The operator in the radio detector van parked in the side street under the second-floor restaurant of the Hotel Schweizerhof reached for the radio telephone that put him in direct communication with Traber's headquarters. It was Traber himself who answered the call.

'We have a radio fix, sir.' He was careful to keep the excitement out of his voice. In an emergency Traber did not appreciate any display of emotion. 'The Hotel Schweizerhof. Yes, sir. Positive.'

'Continue listening. I'm coming myself . . .'

The police patrol team checking hotel registers had just arrived at the Schweizerhof when the plump figure of Traber, puffing a small cigar and with hands thrust deep inside his overcoat pockets, walked into the reception hall. Behind him followed six of his men, also in civilian clothes and all of them armed.

'Anything?' Traber asked, glancing at the register.

'Heinz Golchack never went on to Germany,' one of the policemen said quickly. 'He's registered here – Room 201.'

'I see.' Traber took another puff at his cigar. 'Any other arrivals since lunchtime, say?'

'Heinrich Baum, a dentist from Basel – Room 207. And a Rudi Bühler – also from Vienna, whose arrival could coincide with Flight 433 – in Room 316.'

'Golchack's room first,' Traber ordered. He looked at the receptionist. 'Passkey, please. And if anyone in the hotel tries to use the phone – no matter from which room – your switchboard is temporarily out of action.' He turned to the hotel porter, who was lapping up every word. 'Take us to Room 201 first.'

The two policemen remained in the reception hall as Traber ascended in the elevator with two of his men while the other four went up the staircase. Outside Room 201 Traber waited while one man inserted the key quietly, turned it, and then burst inside holding his pistol, followed by his colleague. When they found the room unoccupied they proceeded along the corridor to Room 207, registered in the name of Heinrich Baum. Again they adopted the same procedure, but here the outcome was different.

Heinrich Baum had just finished sending his overlong signal to Amsterdam, was just closing up his disguised transmitter, when the door burst open. He grabbed for his pistol lying next to the transmitter and was still turning around when Traber's man shot him dead. He fell to the floor, his right hand dragging with him the encoded Amsterdam signal. Previously he had destroyed the signal to Basel. Traber stooped down and retrieved the piece of paper.

'Pity we couldn't have interrogated him,' he remarked.

'And God knows how long it will take our cryptanalysts to decipher this, if ever. It's probably Soviet one-time code. Unless the code book is here . . .'

'Sorry, sir,' the man who had shot Baum apologized, 'but he was reaching for his gun.'

'You did well. And I can't say I'm sorry to see a dirty Swiss traitor get his.'

A brief search produced no sign of any book, but in the bathroom Traber sniffed. 'Smell of burning. Previous signals going up in smoke and down the toilet, of course.' They found that Room 316 – registered to Rudi Bühler – was also empty and Traber then went back down to the reception hall. His tone was crisp when he spoke to the receptionist.

'Golchack and Bühler have gone. Surely you would have seen them if they left by the front entrance? My men are searching the hotel but I'm not optimistic.'

The receptionist looked doubtful. 'Unless they left when my colleague took over the desk for a few minutes while I used the bathroom. That was less than a quarter of an hour ago . . .'

Less than fifteen minutes earlier Heinz Golchack had indeed left the hotel, explaining to the temporary receptionist that he had a migraine and that the night air might help to clear it. During this brief chat Rudi Bühler had also slipped away through the exit. Leaving the hotel, Golchack had walked the few yards to the escalator that led down to the underground shopping mall.

At that hour the underground cavern was deserted and he had quickly taken off his pebble glasses and slipped them into his pocket. From another pocket he had taken an old peaked cap of the type worn by chauffeurs and pulled it well down over his head. Crossing the shopping area, he had mounted another escalator that brought him out onto the other side of the Bahnhofplatz from the Schweizerhof, and hailed a cab.

'Pelikan-platz, please,' he had instructed the driver in faultless German.

Getting out at the Pelikan-platz, he had waited until the cab disappeared before crossing the road and walking at speed through a series of side streets. Even though it was snowing heavily Golchack was enjoying himself. He loved the city of Zürich with its spires and ancient buildings and twisting streets, just as he loved Vienna for the same reasons. He would, in fact, have happily lived in the Swiss city for the rest of his life. And the girls were marvellous, with their erect walk and their slim figures. There was nothing like it in Soviet Russia. Then he arrived at Lindengasse 451, a villa near the end of a deserted cul-de-sac.

Taking a key from his pocket, he opened the door

and went inside. At the top of a flight of steps in the split-level hall a tall, dark-haired girl in her mid-thirties met him. She was holding an automatic, which she slipped back inside her handbag as she recognized her visitor.

'Get rid of that, Ilse,' he ordered.

He had handed her the passport made out in the name of Heinz Golchack. She took him into a large, heavily curtained room full of sombre furniture and antiques. Taking off his snow-covered cap and coat, which showed he had been outside recently, he handed these also to her; then he sat down and took off his soaked shoes. 'And get rid of that lot, too. What time will the express arrive?'

'The last time I phoned the Hauptbahnhof – ten minutes ago – they said 2233 hours. Expected departure time is 2300 hours.'

'Then we shall have to hurry – there is a lot to do. I am going aboard the Atlantic Express.'

'The security cordon at the Hauptbahnhof will be massive, Mr Volger.'

Mr Volger ... Travelling from Vienna to Zürich, Colonel Igor Sharpinsky had assumed the identity of a real person – poor Heinz Golchack, rare-book dealer whose cremated relics were now hidden in a bowl of snow in a remote part of the Vienna Woods. Now he was temporarily assuming the identity of Edward Volger, Swiss antique dealer, who did *not* exist but whose pretended existence had been carefully built up by Ilse Murset, an expert in antique dealing.

In the quiet backwater of the Lindengasse no one took much notice of neighbours, but it was understood that Edward Volger spent much of his time abroad, that he was something of an eccentric, a night owl who returned to the villa late and worked through the early hours. On the odd occasion – always after dark – a man somewhat resembling Sharpinsky in build had been seen hurrying into the villa, but it had been established he was rarely at home.

Taking away the wet clothes and shoes, Ilse returned with a dressing gown and slippers, which Sharpinsky put on; he then settled himself in a chair behind a desk covered with invoices. It was most unlikely the police would check this address, but if they did they would find Edward Volger attending to his business affairs. 'Is everyone here?' Sharpinsky inquired. 'Good. Then bring them in and we will make plans to deal with Traber's massive security cordon.'

And it was not by chance that Sharpinsky had moved from the Hotel Schweizerhof just before the Swiss security men had arrived. On the rare occasions when Igor Sharpinsky operated abroad underground he never stayed in one place for more than five hours. As he waited for Ilse to fetch his subordinates from upstairs the Russian thought grimly about the signal from Moscow Baum had handed him before he left to the Schweizerhof. *All key agents now being advised to leave Western Europe . . .*

The signal was a terrible blow to Sharpinsky

COLIN FORBES

because it implied that Moscow was contemplating the possibility that he might fail in his attempt to kill Marenkov. And the fact that the signal was unsigned told him it had been dictated by Leonid Sedov himself. They had heard over the radio that the avalanche had not destroyed the Atlantic Express.

At 8.40 p.m. in Zürich, when Sharpinsky had heard the news that the Atlantic Express had survived, it was 10.40 p.m. in Moscow when First Secretary Leonid Sedov sat in session with the other two Politburo members charged with handling the Marenkov crisis – Marshal Prachko and Anatoli Zarubin. Prachko, normally so aggressive and confident, was strangely silent as they digested the news. It was Zarubin, the small, dark-haired minister of trade with his sophisticated manner, who subtly turned the blame on Prachko.

'Your protégé does not seem to be shining in this supreme emergency,' he suggested amiably. 'So far all he has done is to uncover our main underground sabotage apparatus inside Switzerland.'

'He had to try something,' Prachko bridled, pulling at the hoglike bristles protruding from his nostrils.

'He also had to succeed,' Zarubin observed. 'How much longer do we allow him before they fly out Marenkov and he starts uncovering all our agents – men it has taken years to train and infiltrate? I am thinking particularly of West Germany,' he added.

362

'Sharpinsky will think of something,' Prachko blustered.

'But if he doesn't?' Leonid Sedov intervened as he rubbed his jaw. The recent operation had left him with a tickle that irritated him in moments of tension. His voice was firm and decisive as he stared directly at Marshal Prachko. 'Is this not the time to order a general evacuation of all our key agents from West Germany, France, and Belgium – before it is too late? They can always return later.'

'My information,' Prachko replied, playing for time, 'is that the German border controls on the east have been alerted and fully mobilized. And in this weather it will be even more difficult for them to slip over the frontier into the German Democratic Republic.'

'Then they will have to try and reach the freighter *Maxim Gorky*, which is now proceeding south from the Baltic and will soon be off the Dutch coast.'

'If that is *your* recommendation,' Prachko agreed slyly.

'No!' Sedov's voice was sharp. 'As minister of defence, it is your advice we seek.'

Prachko was trapped and he knew it. There had already been a débâcle in Switzerland that could be laid at his door and now he was faced with two impossible alternatives. If he said no and Marenkov reached America, the Communist underground apparatus in Western Europe would be shattered. If he said yes, the agents would escape but it would take time to infiltrate them back into Western Europe. He opted for what seemed the less dangerous alternative.

'I recommend they should be evacuated.'

Zarubin, he noted, recorded in a minute that the decision was that taken by the minister of defence. He didn't like it but there was nothing he could do about it. He made one final comment.

'At this moment Sharpinsky is probably making plans that will eliminate the traitor Sergei Marenkov . . .'

Chapter Twenty-two

Zürich Hauptbahnhof

It was 9.10 p.m. – less than two hours before the Atlantic Express was due to depart from Zürich – when Sharpinsky sat looking at three photographs on the desk in the living room of the Lindengasse villa. He had already given specific instructions to four men, who had left the villa, and now he was alone with Ilse Murset he felt the tension rising inside him. The waiting was always the worst part, but everything had been dealt with. And Rudi Bühler should by now be in Basel waiting to board the Atlantic Express later.

When Bühler had left the Schweizerhof Hotel a few seconds ahead of Sharpinsky he had crossed to the Hauptbahnhof and caught a train for Basel. The hotel receptionist would have provided Traber's men with his description – if they had by now tracked down the temporary Soviet base – and it was only prudent that he should leave the city immediately. As Sharpinsky studied the three photographs, Ilse's slim white hand touched his neck.

'What can the photographs possibly tell you?'

'Study the enemy,' Sharpinsky replied. 'Looking at

these pictures, I believe it is possible to foresee how these men will react under pressure.'

The first photograph, the least clear, was of Springer, the brim of his hat pulled low, a picture taken with a telephoto lens from a window in the Bahnhofstrasse. The second picture – much clearer – was General Max Scholten, chief of Dutch counter-espionage, his cherubic face easily identifiable, and taken outside the Hotel Astoria opposite the railway station in The Hague. The third, taken several years previously in Athens, was of Harry Wargrave. Sharpinsky's finger stabbed at the third photo. 'That man is the most dangerous.'

'You feel tense . . .' Ilse's fingers continued to caress the Russian's neck. 'Shall we go upstairs?' Her tall, slim figure was taut as she unzipped the front of her dress. The Russian hesitated; he checked his watch.

'There's no time to go upstairs.'

'Then let's do it here on the floor.'

Two of the men who had left the villa immediately on receiving Sharpinsky's instructions walked to a Citroën parked farther down the street. Klaus Jaeger, tall and heavily-built, a native of East Germany, got behind the wheel while his smaller, slimmer companion, Hans-Otto Nacken, also from East Germany, sat beside him. Both of them were carrying faked West German papers. Within a matter of minutes they were approaching the Hauptbahnhof.

Jaeger did not pull up in front of the Hauptbahnhof; he took the Citroën around to the end of the station and parked it in the shadows. Leaving the car, both men strolled into the station through the side entrance past the baggage counter. For the sake of appearance Jaeger was carrying a case. They spent several minutes while they walked around studying the Swiss rail porters who were waiting for the arrival of night trains.

'That one over there,' Jaeger said as he stopped and lit a cigarette. 'He's just about the right height and build.'

Separating himself from Jaeger, Nacken walked over to the porter, who was a short, well-built man of a similar physical make-up to Sharpinsky. 'I see from the indicator board that the Atlantic Express isn't due to leave till eleven o'clock. I've got my times mixed up – so I'm due for a long wait. The board is correct, I suppose?'

'Yes, sir. And it's a miracle it's making up time. Have you heard the news?'

'What news?'

'There was an avalanche south of the Gotthard – the worst this century, they say. It almost overwhelmed the express.'

'My God! No, I hadn't heard. Well, at least there won't be one between here and Basel.' He offered the porter a cigarette. 'Must be boring work for you – hanging around here all night. How much longer do you have on duty?' he asked casually.

The porter took a deep drag on the cigarette. 'I go off at eight in the morning. You get used to it.'

Nacken chatted for a few minutes and then drifted away, putting his left hand in his coat pocket. It was the signal Jaeger, watching from a distance, had been waiting for. He walked over to the porter. 'Can you fetch my other bags from the car? It's parked at the end of the station.' He dumped the case he was holding on the porter's trolley and followed him. They were moving along an ill-lit cavern past the baggage storage department and no one else was in sight.

Reaching the Citroën, Jaeger opened the rear door after glancing around to make sure no one was about. 'The bag in there,' he explained. 'Be careful, it's heavy.' As the porter leaned inside, Jaeger took a small steel truncheon encased in leather from his pocket, leaned over the porter, and smashed it down on the man's skull with considerable force. The porter collapsed, dead.

Nacken appeared from the shadows and helped to heave the body completely inside the back of the car. 'The trolley,' Jaeger reminded his companion as he pulled a travelling rug over the corpse. Nacken moved the trolley back against the wall into the shadows. It would be needed later. Then they were both moving into the front seats, closing the doors quietly, and Jaeger drove away over the Limmat bridge.

He drove to a quiet part of the lake beyond the Quaibrücke and pulled up by the shore under a copse of trees, switching off his engine and lights. It took the combined efforts of both men to undress the dead man, to divest him of his uniform, cap, and boots. Jaeger took his wallet, checked with his torch to make sure the porter's rail pass was inside. 'That's it,' he said. 'Now, let's lose him.'

They fastened heavy chains around the body – the chains from the case Jaeger had warned the porter was heavy – and between them carried the body to the edge of the lake. At this point the ice on the lake was thin and the water below was sixty feet deep. Swinging the body between them, one man holding the shoulders, the other the feet, they cast him down. The weighted corpse broke through the ice with a splintering crunch and sank.

Getting back behind the wheel of the car, Jaeger drove to the Quaibrücke, crossed it, and headed for the Lindengasse. They now had what they had been sent for, a railway porter's uniform, and the porter would not be notified as missing by his wife – if he had one, Jaeger thought callously – until long after the Atlantic Express had departed. After all, as he had told Nacken, he was not due off duty until eight in the morning.

The second team of two men who had been dispatched from the Lindengasse at the same time as Jaeger and Nacken had a simpler task. Getting into another car, they drove to the western side of the city until they reached a large garage in an industrial suburb. One of the men got out, opened the double doors, and then closed them after the car had been driven inside. It pulled alongside a huge furniture truck that carried on its side the legend *Möbel – Salzburg*.

Getting out of the car, the driver switched on the garage lights and took a case out of the car. When he opened it the case contained nothing more sinister than liverwurst sandwiches and a flask of coffee. 'No alcohol,' Sharpinsky had warned. 'If I find you have disobeyed me you will be recalled at once.' The second man went to a wall phone and dialled a number. It was Ilse Murset who answered.

'André here,' the man reported. 'The consignment is now ready for delivery.'

'Understood!' Ilse broke the connection.

Inside the garage the men who had phoned Ilse climbed up into the cab of the furniture truck, pulled aside the canvas cover, and checked the load. Here again the truck contained nothing more sinister than a full load of furniture, but it was very heavily laden and the tail gate at the back tilted outward at a perilous angle. Also there was a curious cable and pulley device that linked the tail gate through the full length of the truck to the cab.

'Alfred, here are yours.'

The man in the cab threw down some overalls, climbed down from the cab, and made his way to the back of the garage where there was more room. Within a few minutes, both of them dressed as furniture delivery men, they sat down on a bench to consume their sandwiches and coffee. At regular intervals the driver checked his watch.

As soon as they had delivered the porter's clothes to Lindengasse 451 Jaeger and Nacken drove off again in the Citroën and recrossed the Quaibrücke. But this time, instead of proceeding south along the lake shore, they drove north along the banks of the river Limmat and then turned uphill along the main road toward the Zürichberg. They were driving through an expensive district of neat villas and well-kept gardens when Jaeger swung the wheel and turned into a drive.

Behind them a man who had been waiting in the bitter cold closed and locked the wrought-iron gates. Pulling up in front of the two-storey villa where icicles hung from a balcony, Jaeger switched off the ignition and alighted from the car. 'Check the limousine,' he ordered Nacken. 'And above all check the engine.'

A severe-faced woman of fifty who had heard the car arrive opened the front door, let Jaeger inside, and closed it. She had her hair tied back in a bun and wore a long dark dress that gave her the appearance of a housekeeper. 'All your clothes are ready for you in the main bedroom,' she informed him.

'Get rid of this.' Jaeger handed her his identity card. 'And where is the passport?' They were speaking to each other in fluent Russian. The woman took a passport from her pocket and handed it to him. He checked it quickly. The Soviet diplomatic passport, carrying his own picture, was in the name of Boris Volkov; rank, captain. He went upstairs to change.

The business suit laid out on the bed was Russian in style and made of Russian cloth. He even changed into Russian underclothes, shirt, tie, shoes, and hat. When he went back downstairs he found Nacken had already changed into his own uniform, that of a Soviet chauffeur. 'The car,' Jaeger said, 'I want to check it for myself.' Following Nacken, he entered the garage by a door directly from the back of the villa.

Inside the garage stood a gleaming Mercedes that had recently been polished to a glasslike sheen. And that won't last long in this weather, Jaeger thought. The car was carrying diplomatic plates, those of the Soviet Embassy in Bern. He made Nacken get behind the wheel to test the ignition and the engine fired immediately. Satisfied, Jaeger went back into the house and dialled the number of Lindengasse 451. Again it was Ilse Murset who answered the call.

'Bernard here,' Jaeger reported. 'The collection is now ready for delivery.'

'Understood!' Ilse broke the connection.

'All the arrangements are complete,' she told Sharpinsky as she zipped up the front of her dress. 'Everyone is in position and I will be ready to drive you to the Hauptbahnhof.'

Colonel Igor Sharpinsky, sitting only in his shirt, nodded.

'Soon now, Traber,' he said. 'Very soon now . . .'

*

The Atlantic Express was making up lost time rapidly as it continued its nonstop descent north of the Gotthard through a blinding snowstorm. In the motor cab of the powerful Bo-Bo locomotive, Enrico was being assisted by a fresh chief engineer Springer had insisted should accompany him from Airolo. It was not an arrangement that pleased the sturdy Swiss from Basel.

'It takes more than a bump on the head to knock me out,' he grumbled as he watched the gauges and checked the signals. 'And we are going to make Zürich on time. Damn it – my reputation is at stake.'

Inside the compartment of the rear Wagon-Lit where Marenkov was under guard the atmosphere was tense and growing worse the closer they came to Zürich. For the third time – to Julian Haller's intense irritation, but he was now feeling very fatigued – the Russian repeated the same remark.

'I am convinced that Sharpinsky will board the express at Zürich . . .'

'Will attempt to,' Elsa corrected him. She held up the portrait of Igor Sharpinsky in her notepad that she had built up from Marenkov's description. 'Now, for the first time, we know what he looks like.'

The stocky, wide-shouldered Russian waved an impatient hand. 'That won't help – I keep telling you he is a genius at altering his appearance.'

'Don't be so pessimistic,' Elsa snapped back. 'I told you I spent a whole year as film make-up girl changing actors' appearances. If anyone can spot him coming on to the train, I can.'

This both Wargrave and Springer, who also sat in the compartment, had agreed. So the plan was that when the train arrived at the Hauptbahnhof Elsa would stand close to the ticket barrier examining everyone who came aboard. And the Swiss colonel, at least, had reason for satisfaction: Marenkov had already out of his encyclopedic memory provided a list of names and addresses of all KGB agents in Switzerland – although not of the GRU agents, whom he knew little about.

'Which areas outside Russia did Sharpinsky work in when he was attached to different embassies under various cover names?' Wargrave inquired.

Marenkov checked off the posts on his fingers. 'Paris, for six months. London, for another six months. Washington, for two years. Athens, for a year. Finally, The Hague, for another year.'

'So presumably in languages he is fluent in Greek, French, English, and American?'

'I was under the impression the last two were the same language,' Haller interjected tartly.

'We all have our illusions,' Wargrave replied with a grin. 'Am I right, General?'

'Correct,' Marenkov replied. 'Sharpinsky is a remarkably accomplished linguist – it was one factor in his being moved around so rapidly, in his swift rise to become my deputy. Unlike most Russians he is a natural cosmopolitan. He is fluent in German, also,'

he added. 'He spent some time in East Berlin maintaining contact with terrorist groups.'

Haller stretched and yawned. 'Well, we'll just have
to wait and see what happens when we get to Zürich'
– he checked his watch – 'which will be soon now.'

'Sharpinsky will come aboard this train,' Marenkov
repeated obstinately. 'I know him.'

'When the time comes, let's just hope I know him,
too,' Elsa said fervently as she studied her sketch.

The Atlantic Express, its cars crusted with snow,
glided inside the huge cavern of Zürich Hauptbahnhof, moved alongside Gleis 4, and stopped. Traber's
security ring mounted around the station was one of
the tightest he had ever organized. Inconspicuous in a
heavy coat and a shallow-brimmed hat, he stood near
the ticket barrier puffing at his short cigar as passengers began filing off the express, haggard-faced from
fear and lack of sleep. But it was not the passengers
getting off that Traber was quietly studying; it was
the huddle of passengers waiting to board the express.

Thirty security officials, armed and in civilian
clothes, were at various points inside the Hauptbahnhof. There were also an unusual number of uniformed
police strolling around the concourse. Outside in the
snow a dozen patrol cars with reinforcements were
parked at strategic points, all of them in radio contact
with Traber's assistant, Major Kurt Dobler, who stood
close to his chief with a compact walkie-talkie in his

hand. Showing his identity card in the palm of his hand, Springer came through the barrier to meet Traber.

'How are things aboard the express?' Traber murmured.

'Tense. But under control. Our VIP is convinced that Sharpinsky will try to board the train.'

'Seems unlikely now you have a description.' From the express Springer had informed his chief that Marenkov had told them what the KGB colonel looked like. 'On the other hand,' Traber continued, 'we have not yet located the main Soviet control base.'

At the barrier there was exceptional security. Alongside the ticket collectors stood security men waiting to check passports and just behind them stood a group of uniformed police. A few yards to the right a second barrier was open – reserved for porters to take luggage aboard. Each porter was stopped while a dog handler allowed a German shepherd to sniff out explosives to check the baggage.

'Who is that attractive girl in the fur coat waiting on the far side of the barrier?' Traber inquired.

'One of us. Elsa Lang. She may be able to recognize Sharpinsky if he tries to board the express.'

On the far side of the barrier, her fur hood pulled up against the cold, Elsa stood smoking a cigarette, studying the waiting passengers openly as though waiting for a friend she had arranged to meet. From her experience as a make-up girl she knew how easily a person's appearance could be transformed. So she was concentrating on height and build, looking for a short, well-built man. Forget everything else, she reminded herself – moustaches, beards, clothes, apparent age – fix your eyes on what can't easily be changed. A civilian near to her moved closer, spoke behind his hands as he lit a cigarette.

'Security. Colonel Springer told me about you. If you see him, tell me – even if you only think it might be him. Don't look at him again.'

'I know my job.'

'I can tell that already. And move well away from me as soon as you finger him. There could be shooting.'

'Thank you for the warning,' Elsa replied more graciously from behind her handkerchief, her eyes still fixed on the crowd penned behind the barrier.

Leaning out of the window from his first-class car, Jorge Santos was still smoking his pipe. Only someone who knew him well would have noticed something slightly odd as he stood there with the window down, watching the last of the passengers disembarking, who were passing through the barrier. Normally he smoked with his pipe clenched at the right-hand corner of his mouth; now the pipe was projecting from the left-hand side. A few paces from where he stood Wargrave opened a door and stepped down onto the platform. He took up a position where he could cover Elsa Lang, his hand inside his overcoat pocket gripping the Smith and Wesson.

On both sides of the barrier the security men had a

sense of waiting for an imminent emergency as passengers began moving through the barrier slowly while their passports and tickets were checked. And porters were now passing inside their own separate barrier, waiting while the German shepherds sniffed the baggage. At the moment a large furniture truck carrying the legend *Möbel – Salzburg* was moving along the east bank of the river Limmat. The driver checked his watch and swung the huge vehicle over the bridge leading direct to the Hauptbahnhof.

'Nothing so far,' Traber murmured. Major Dobler was just receiving a message on his walkie-talkie. 'My God!' he muttered. 'Are you certain? Check it with Bern. Top priority . . .'

'What has happened?' Traber asked calmly as Springer moved closer.

'A Mercedes with Soviet diplomatic plates has just drawn up outside. One passenger – here he comes.'

Striding into the station, his back erect, walking with a distinctly military bearing, was a tall, heavy-built man wearing a fur coat and hat. Behind him one of Traber's men removed his own hat, a signal to alert his chief. The new arrival joined the line.

'What the hell is going on?' Springer hissed.

'I don't like it,' Traber replied crisply. 'Keep your eyes open.'

When the passenger from the Soviet diplomatic car reached the security officials the line stopped and there seemed to be some confusion. Another security official slipped quietly away from the barrier and hurried over to Traber. 'What do we do, sir? He's carrying a diplomatic passport. Military attaché at the Soviet Embassy in Bern. A Captain Boris Volkov . . .'

'Who?' Springer exploded. 'Boris Volkov is a top trained assassin! To hell with his diplomatic passport. Delay him at the barrier.' He stopped as there was an appalling crashing sound from the front of the station. Outside the Hauptbahnhof the large Salzburg furniture truck had run up onto the sidewalk. Inside the truck's cab the driver had released the cable attached to the tail gate, which collapsed, spilling out a torrent of furniture on top of a line of people waiting for cabs. The scene that followed was too horrific to describe as men and women buried under the heavy furniture began screaming. From under a wardrobe a woman's projecting hand shook feebly and then fell still. Inside the station all eyes turned in the direction of the sound, all except those of Springer, who continued to watch the barrier where Klaus Jaeger, in the guise of a Soviet captain, was protesting violently.

Through the second barrier a short, well-built porter, whose trolley had just been checked by a German shepherd, pushed the trolley along the platform, his cap pulled down over his forehead. As he passed Jorge Santos, who was still leaning out of the window, he glanced briefly sideways at the Spaniard and then moved on down the platform with the single blue suitcase he was carrying.

'Can you not recognize a diplomatic passport when you see one?' Jaeger was shouting in German. 'My embassy will hear of this, I promise you.'

He was still protesting when the security official disappeared with the passport. Reaching Springer, he handed the passport to the colonel. 'It looks genuine,' the official commented.

'I don't give a damn if it's gold-plated,' Springer told him viciously. 'He's not going aboard that express. Go and tell him it doesn't seem genuine, that we're checking with Bern.' He looked at Traber. 'And it's going to take an incredible amount of time to get through to Bern . . .'

'A lot seems to be happening all at once,' Traber observed, looking toward the front of the station where Major Dobler had run to check the furniture truck incident. 'Almost as though someone planned to divert our attention.'

'To give time for Volkov to slip aboard, of course,' Springer snapped. Then he frowned. 'No, that can't be right. If this man was Boris Volkov himself he would never use his own name. There's something here that I don't understand – don't trust . . .'

The Hauptbahnhof was in an uproar. Police cars had converged on the furniture truck where people trapped under the deluge of furniture were still screaming. An ambulance, its siren screeching, pulled up alongside the truck. The driver and his mate, the perpetrators of this brutal diversion, had been confident they could escape in the resultant confusion.

Diving down an escalator leading to the underground shopping mall, they separated, heading for different escalator exits. Each man emerged on the far side of the Bahnhofplatz with a pistol in his hand.

They found themselves facing a mixture of passersby and policemen. To make more confusion, they started firing at random and several pedestrians, running for cover, collided with policemen. But two policemen ignored the confusion, raised their own pistols, steadied them with both hands, and took careful aim. Each of the policemen fired twice. The truck driver was still running when he fell dead. His mate died five seconds later.

Inside the Hauptbahnhof, Klaus Jaeger. still playing his role of a Soviet military captain, stormed up to Springer and snatched the diplomatic passport out of the Swiss's hand. 'You will hear more about this from Moscow,' he shouted. 'It may well cause a major diplomatic incident with your government.'

Springer let him go with the passport as Jaeger walked swiftly back to his parked limousine, where Nacken, dressed in his chauffeur's uniform, had remained behind the wheel of the Mercedes. As Major Kurt Dobler returned to report about the furniture truck horror Springer grabbed the walkie-talkie off him and began speaking rapidly, his voice now matter-of-fact.

'I want all unmarked cars and trucks – repeat, unmarked – to follow the Soviet limousine on a shuttle system. Follow, but do not intercept. And all available radio detector trucks will carry out the same instruction. Now, move it!'

He handed the walkie-talkie back to Dobler and looked at Traber. 'May I leave it to you now, sir? I'd better get back aboard the express.'

Even as Nacken – with Jaeger sitting in the back – drove the Mercedes away from the Hauptbahnhof, the huge dragnet Springer had set in motion was operating efficiently. A laundry truck that had taken the Zürichberg route was actually driving ahead of the Soviet limousine when the driver saw its head-lights in his rearview mirror. His colleague beside him reported its position over the radio and detector vehicles followed them up the road toward the Zürichberg.

Arriving at the villa on the hillside – confident that he had not been followed because there were no cars behind him – Jaeger turned in between the wrought-iron gates, which again were promptly closed behind them. Inside the villa Nacken, who doubled as radio operator, started sending the previously encoded signal on a transmitter to Mohner on the Zürichberg inside his mobile trailer. The signal informed Moscow that Colonel Igor Sharpinsky had boarded the Atlantic Express.

Within ten minutes two radio detector trucks close to the Zoo at the top of the Zürichberg crossed their beams at a point on the Heubeeri-Weg track inside the woods on the summit. Mohner, the much-respected meteorologist, had just completed sending his overlong transmission when he heard a knock on the door of his mobile trailer. When he opened it, security officers were facing him with pistols in their hands.

'I wondered how long it would be before you came,' he said.

Promptly at 2300 hours the Atlantic Express began moving out of Zürich Hauptbahnhof on its way to Basel and West Germany. In various compartments the considerable number of fresh passengers who had come on board were settling themselves, listening to the story of the avalanche from travellers who had boarded at Milan. As the platform slid past him, Jorge Santos, still leaning on the open window, noticed a porter's trolley standing by itself on the platform. His mouth tightened as he raised the corridor window and made his way back to his own compartment. As with many other compartments, the blinds were drawn on the corridor side and it was only when Santos opened the door that he saw the man sitting in his corner seat in the otherwise empty compartment. Santos went inside and closed the door, his pipe still in the left-hand corner of his mouth.

'Hello, Nicos,' Harry Wargrave said. 'I thought the moment had come for us to link up.'

'I agree,' Nicos Leonides replied. 'Colonel Igor Sharpinsky has just boarded the express . . .'

Chapter Twenty-three

Basel, The Hague

Three years earlier in Athens it had been Harry Wargrave's idea that Nicos Leonides, secretly a dedicated anti-Communist, should try to penetrate the Soviet Balkan underground by offering himself as a private Communist executioner. 'I have a strong whisper that Sharpinsky is a member of the Soviet Embassy staff here in Athens,' he had explained. 'Try and get to him.'

'It will take time and ingenuity,' Leonides had warned.

'So we will provide him with bodies,' Wargrave had gruesomely suggested, 'bodies of prominent anti-Communist Greeks he would like to see dead.'

Working at the time for the British Secret Service, Wargrave had typically run this private operation on the side while he continued with his regular work. Over a period of time Wargrave and Leonides – once the Greek had persuaded Sharpinsky over the phone to allow him to prove himself – had provided three major executions, three 'bodies.'

The first 'victim' had been the late-middle-aged anti-Communist editor of a leading Athens newspaper, only one of Leonides' many personal friends – and in the Balkans friends are much closer than in the West. Realizing that in any case he was a target for Soviet gunmen, the editor had readily fallen in with the plan. His burned-out car had been discovered at the foot of a steep cliff after a stormy night and it was assumed the body had been washed out to sea. Instead, the 'dead' editor, a widower, had secretly been transported by motorized caïque to one of the more remote Greek islands, where he was still enjoying his unusual retirement.

In due course two more 'victims,' both of them friends of Leonides in the clandestine Greek anti-Communist underground, had agreed to co-operate – again, both of them widowers, so there were no family complications. One, an ageing politician, had 'died' in a plane that had crashed into the sea after a bomb explosion – but only after the politician piloting the plane had earlier parachuted from the aircraft over land. The third, a senior security chief on the verge of retirement, had 'expired' when his car exploded after he turned on the ignition. The relics of the body discovered spread over a wide area were those of a corpse Leonides had stolen from a morgue.

All three Greek 'victims' were now living on the remote Greek island: living off the proceeds of a major bank raid that Leonides himself had pulled off without injuring a soul. And Nicos Leonides had established himself in the eyes of Sharpinsky as a singularly effective executioner who stage-managed 'accidents' that could never be traced back to Soviet sources.

It was Harry Wargrave who, before leaving Montreal on his flight to Europe to rescue Angelo, had cabled Leonides to fly to Milan and phone the Vienna number Leonides had been given if he wanted to contact Sharpinsky. The KGB colonel had fallen for the bait and ordered Leonides to board the Atlantic Express – to kill Marenkov as soon as the opportunity arose.

'I suppose he's still counting on me,' Leonides told Wargrave with an ironic smile as he sat down facing the Englishman in his compartment aboard the Atlantic Express.

'How do you know he's just come aboard?' Wargrave asked sharply.

'Because I was instructed that at Zürich Hauptbahnhof I must signal from the train window whether Marenkov was still alive – by keeping my pipe in the left-hand corner of my mouth.'

'So who is Sharpinsky?'

'I have no idea.' Leonides spread his hands in a gesture of resignation. 'I watched carefully and none of the passengers coming on board took any notice of me. That was my mistake . . .'

'What mistake?'

'I think he came through the barrier disguised as a porter.' Leonides described the solitary trolley he had seen on the platform as the express moved out of the Hauptbahnhof. 'A porter always takes his trolley away with him,' the Greek pointed out. 'By now he will have transformed himself into one of the numerous passengers who came aboard. What do I do next?' he asked abruptly. 'And what about Anna in the next compartment?'

It was Anna Markos, Leonides' sister-in-law, who had formed part of Wargrave's secret cell in Athens – whose sister, once Leonides' wife, had been killed during a Communist bomb outrage in the centre of Athens. I have a great deal of hate going for me, Wargrave thought as he stared back at the tall Greek.

'You both stay under cover,' he decided. 'Incidentally, I assume it was you who shot those two saboteurs when the express was stopped at the time of the avalanche?'

'My very meagre contribution to our combined efforts so far,' Leonides replied.

'Yes, you both stay under cover,' Wargrave repeated. 'I have a hunch that before this thing is finished I may have to adopt some rather unusual, not to say totally illegal, methods. So let us assume for the moment that we are all back in Athens.'

'It is my intention to kill Sharpinsky once he is found,' Leonides said quietly. 'I want no exchange of this man for one of our people in prison inside Russia. I want to kill him. Is that quite clearly understood?'

Wargrave stood up and his face was bleak. 'And until we reach Schiphol and get Marenkov aboard that waiting Boeing to fly him to the States I am in complete control of the operation and give all the orders. Is that clearly understood, Nicos?'

'I regret to say – yes.'

Inside the single sleeping compartment reserved in the name of Waldo Hackmann, American citizen – the compartment had been reserved from Lugano – Colonel Igor Sharpinsky had divested himself of his porter's uniform. From the blue case he had carried aboard the train he changed into fresh clothes and had stuffed the porter's uniform inside a strong plastic bag weighted with bricks. Pulling down the window, ignoring the blast of cold air that flooded inside the compartment, he waited until the express was crossing a bridge over a river and then hurled the plastic bag out. It fell a long way down before it hit thin ice, broke through the surface, and sank. Closing the window and lowering the blind, Sharpinsky turned up the central heating to warm up the compartment before any Swiss officials arrived.

Now he was dressed in a checked sports jacket and slacks of American cut, his cheeks plumped out with cottonwool pads; his head had been shaven bald by Ilse Murset before he left Lindengasse 451. He tried on his horn-rimmed spectacles and checked himself in the mirror. Under his check sports jacket – the label inside bore the name of a Fifth Avenue store – he wore a very thick sweater, which gave him a portly appearance. He lit a large cigar, took out his American passport, and checked it. He was now Waldo Hackmann, a dealer in Old Master paintings from Boston.

His case, which he had left on the berth, carried several labels with a much-travelled look. The Hôtel Georges Cinq, Paris; the Dorchester, London; the Ritz-Carlton, Boston; and the Mark Hopkins, San Francisco. He had just finished checking his appearance when there was a knock on the compartment door. Hackmann opened the door and faced the sleeping-car attendant.

'This compartment was booked in the name of a Mr Waldo Hackmann, due to board the train at Lugano,' the attendant explained.

'I'm Hackmann,' Sharpinsky replied in a perfect American accent. 'I came on to Zürich by another train yesterday – change of schedule.'

He presented his passport and ticket as a Swiss passport official appeared behind the attendant, reached past him, and began examining the document. Sharpinsky noted that besides checking the document the official was writing down the name and passport number. He looked up at the passenger. 'And your home address, sir?' Sharpinsky gave him an address on Beacon Hill, Boston. As the door closed and he was left alone, Sharpinsky took a deep drag on his cigar. As he had anticipated, a very thorough check of every passenger was now taking place. And probably, soon, they would be checking with the United States . . .

*

COLIN FORBES

Returning from Nicos Leonides' compartment to the Wagon-Lit at the rear of the express, it had been Wargrave's idea that an immediate check should be made on all passengers who had come aboard at Zürich. Waldo Hackmann's credentials were among the first to be subjected to this scrutiny.

From the communications compartment operated by Peter Neckermann an immediate signal with Waldo Hackmann's details was sent to Interpol headquarters in Paris, where a special night staff was waiting on duty at Traber's request. From Paris the information was instantly relayed to FBI headquarters in Washington; in the American Capital it was 5.15 p.m., Eastern Standard Time. A phone call was immediately put through from there to local FBI agents in Boston.

Agents Crammer and Hinds drove at once to the Beacon Hill address Hackmann had provided, even though a check in the telephone directory had shown a Waldo Hackmann living at the address. The house in the quiet street of old and picturesque dwellings seemed to be empty, but Crammer and Hinds had strict instructions. Opening the front door with skeleton keys, they explored the interior. It was Crammer who found in a wastebasket a crumpled carbon copy of Hackmann's European schedule.

Saturday, January 8, Zürich; Sunday, January 9, Amsterdam; Monday, January 10, Paris; Tuesday, January 11, Brussels . . .

The request for the check from Washington had

been marked 'brief – urgent,' so Crammer immediately reported back to Washington, from where a reply was sent to Paris and then to Neckermann aboard the Atlantic Express. And no one suspected that the real Waldo Hackmann, a Communist sleeper, acting on instructions Sharpinsky had originally sent from Vienna before he left for Zürich, was at that moment spending a pleasant weekend at the St Regis Hotel in New York, where he had registered under an assumed name. The Atlantic Express was approaching Basel when Springer crossed Waldo Hackmann's name off his list of suspects.

Three hundred and fifty miles north of Basel the 17,000-ton Soviet freighter *Maxim Gorky*, the new pride of Soviet Admiral Gorshkov's spy ships, a vessel fully equipped with the latest sophisticated electronic devices and bound from the Baltic for the African state of Angola, was changing course. The vessel's captain, Joseph Morov, had received an urgent coded signal from his home port, Leningrad, ordering him to anchor off the mouth of the Rhine near Rotterdam. The ship was ploughing through heavy seas as he discussed this new instruction with Commissar Valentin Rykin, who had also received his own signal.

'How long do we have to wait, I should like to know,' Captain Morov demanded. 'I am responsible for the safety of this ship and the glass is falling rapidly.'

Rykin, a short, broad-shouldered man with a thick thatch of black hair who outranked even the ship's captain, gave a shrug. 'Twelve hours, maybe. Then we reverse course and head back for Leningrad at full speed.'

'At full speed! In this weather!'

'That's your problem. You must be prepared to take on board a large number of key agents who may arrive in powerboats at intervals – possibly even pursued by Dutch torpedo boats.'

'We shall be in Dutch territorial waters. If their coastguard people wish to come aboard—'

'They will be stopped,' Rykin snapped. 'I have already ordered machine guns to be mounted.'

'You must be mad,' Morov protested. 'You can't open fire on Dutch ships – it will cause an international incident.'

'Only if necessary . . .' A huge wave hit the bridge and Commissar Rykin was hurled against the woodwork as the vessel's bows were submerged under green foaming sea. Rykin recovered his balance and stopped himself rubbing his badly bruised elbow; a Soviet commissar was indifferent to pain. 'Only if necessary,' he repeated. 'In any case Holland is a toy state,' he sneered. 'How many tank divisions can they muster?'

It was midnight as the Atlantic Express approached Basel. It was also midnight in The Hague as General

Max Scholten at Dutch counter-espionage headquarters stood staring out of the third-floor window
of the old building that overlooks the Hofvijver Lake
in the middle of the city. The Gale Force Eight blowing
in the North Sea was whipping the surface of the lake,
creating a turbulence similar to that in the mind of the
Dutch security chief. His aide, Major Sailer, put down
the phone and reported the news.

'The Atlantic Express reaches Basel in five minutes'
time – and Marenkov has survived so far.'

'Which explains the reports I am getting from
Germany and France that top Soviet agents are beginning to run – and in this direction apparently. The
Germans have sealed off their eastern frontier with
the Zone.'

'And you mentioned you had heard the Geiger
Group of terrorists is definitely crossing our border
into Holland,' Sailer reminded his chief. 'Not that
there is any connection . . .'

'I wonder . . .' In the distance the cherubic-faced
Dutch security chief could see the dim outline of the
Houses of Parliament. Sailer joined him by the
window. 'Do you not think we should inform the
minister, perhaps . . .'

'At this hour?' Scholten demanded in mock horror.
'And it is the weekend – almost Sunday morning. No,
I will handle this myself.' He stopped speaking as
Sailer answered the top-priority phone where the line
was being kept permanently open. Sailer listened,
said thank you, and replaced the receiver.

'The long-range marine radar people have just picked up that huge Soviet freighter, the *Maxim Gorky*. They say she has changed course, that she is heading direct for the mouth of the Rhine.'

Scholten glanced at a wall map of Western Europe. 'Now I do really wonder – I sense a pattern emerging that may link the Atlantic Express with that freighter. I want to speak to Harry Wargrave on the express.'

'But the express doesn't pass anywhere near the mouth of the Maas.' (Sailer was referring to the mouth of the Rhine.) 'It travels direct via the Rhineland to Amsterdam.'

'Alert all the torpedo-boat patrols,' Scholten ordered.

As the Atlantic Express stopped at Basel Hauptbahnhof, Wargrave was talking to General Max Scholten over the radio telephone from Neckermann's communications compartment. It was a long conversation and when he said good-bye he privately thanked God that at the end of the line – controlling the Dutch sector – was one of the most dedicated security chiefs in Europe, despite Max Scholten's outwardly cherubic appearance.

And Neckermann had been very active sending signals since they left Zürich. One signal had gone to Captain Franz Wander of the German BND who was waiting at Basel Bad Bahnhof – the station beyond the Hauptbahnhof where German Passport Control and

Customs board all trains bound for Germany. Even if intercepted by secret Soviet monitors, the message would have meant nothing to them. It read: *Inge is on board Atlantic Express. Please board train and effect arrest as soon as on German soil.* Translated, the signal referred to Marenkov as Inge, indicating he was still alive, and asking for total security precautions to be taken over from the Swiss.

Two minutes later the express moved in under the roof of Basel Hauptbahnhof and stopped. Inside his compartment Waldo Hackmann had lifted the blind and turned off the lights and was sitting in the dark. It so happened that his window was facing the wired-off 'cage' inside which passengers waiting to board the train were kept after they had passed through Swiss Customs.

Hackmann's teeth clenched tight on the fresh cigar he had not lit as he studied the people inside the cage. Among them he could clearly see Yuri Gusev, the GRU agent he had summoned from Mulhouse, and, standing well apart from the Russian, Rudi Bühler, who had earlier caught a train from Zürich to Basel. Bühler, heavily built and of medium height, had changed his appearance. Wearing French clothes, he was dressed in a long raincoat that seemed to add to his height, and inside his pocket he carried a passport identifying him as Pierre Masson, commercial artist.

Yuri Gusev was a short, large-chested man with big feet and he carried a suitcase. Expensively dressed, he had a Swiss passport in the name of a

Geneva bank official who existed and he had arrived at the last moment. Convincing in demeanour, he had been hustled through into the cage by a tired Customs man who had not checked his case. A minute later the cage was opened and the new passengers came out onto the platform and headed for the waiting express.

Boarding the express, Gusev, star executioner of the GRU, went straight to the sleeping compartment number he had received in the radio signal sent earlier to Mulhouse by Sharpinsky from the Hotel Schweizerhof. Waldo Hackmann opened the door while he was still rapping on it, let Gusev inside, and closed and relocked the door. Gusev wasted no time as the pseudo-American began talking. Opening his suitcase, he took out a Swiss railway inspector's uniform and changed into it rapidly.

'Peter is in the rear Wagon-Lit,' Hackmann told him as Gusev pulled on his uniform trousers. 'He is well guarded – you can wait until the express is moving, until they are lulled into a feeling of overconfidence. They must be very tired.'

'No!' Gusev was abrupt, certain in his reply. 'We strike immediately – at Basel Bad Bahnhof the German BND are bringing aboard a small army.'

'Here at the Hauptbahnhof?' Sharpinsky was startled, forgot for a moment that he was travelling as Waldo Hackmann, and had replied in Russian although hitherto they had conversed in French. Inwardly he cursed himself for the slip, which he would not have forgiven in a subordinate.

'The psychology of the situation is simple,' Gusev explained as he put on his inspector's cap and checked his appearance in the mirror. 'Swiss security is about to hand over to the Germans – subconsciously they feel their job is done, that they can relax.'

'I still think it is too early,' Hackmann snapped in French.

Gusev overrode his remark, talking at the same time as the KGB man. '. . . There is a lot of confusion while the express is here at the Hauptbahnhof. Passengers are getting on and off. There is a lot of movement – a fluid situation that I can take advantage of. Have I ever failed you yet?' he demanded as he straightened his uniform jacket.

'If you are sure . . .'

'I am more than sure – I am certain. I have been thinking of nothing else since I received your signal. Peter will be dead and I will be off the train before it leaves here.'

'Get on with it – but do not fail,' Hackmann snapped. 'I will check the corridor—'

'Not necessary,' Gusev told him. 'I am a Swiss official in uniform checking tickets. No one will think it odd if they see me leaving your compartment.'

Opening the door, he listened for a moment, stepped out into the corridor, and Hackmann locked it behind him. He was glad the executioner had gone. Yuri Gusev had built up a formidable reputation and was something of a law unto himself; on his record of success he could afford to be. So highly was he rated

that on two separate occasions he had been interviewed by Marshal Gregori Prachko himself. Hackmann lit his cigar and reminded himself that at the
first opportunity he must throw Gusev's suitcase –
which now contained the business suit he had
divested himself of – out of the window.

The moment he had left Hackmann's compartment
Gusev walked toward the rear of the train, standing
aside to let passengers move along the corridor as
they struggled with their cases to find their compartments. As he entered the second Wagon-Lit, the coach
linked to the sleeping car where Marenkov was under
guard, he came face-to-face with one of Springer's
security men in plain clothes.

'Have any new passengers entered this car?' the
security man asked him in German.

'That is what I have been sent on board to check,'
Gusev replied in the same language. 'I have plenty of
time before the express leaves the Hauptbahnhof. I
was told you would have a list of passengers who
came on board earlier. Is that so?'

The security man reached in his pocket and produced a list of names. 'Give it back to me before you
get off the train.'

'And if I do find someone not on the list?' Gusev
inquired. 'Who needs to know?'

'I do. Be careful not to alert any fresh passenger,'
the security man warned. 'Just find me, give me the
details – I will take it from there.'

Gusev's reference to the list of passengers had been

an inspired guess, but he was very familiar with the efficiency of the Swiss security system. It was typical of the Russian executioner to take such a bold line. Unlike his professional colleagues of lesser calibre, Gusev was not a man who believed in intricate planning; an opportunist by nature, his technique was the swift, unexpected thrust – to take full advantage of the element of surprise. As he had once boasted to Sharpinsky, 'There is not a security establishment in Europe I could not walk inside.'

'Walk in . . .?' the KGB deputy chief had queried sceptically.

'Confidence is the key. You give the impression that you belong there – aggressively so if challenged.'

And it was true. Only six months earlier Gusev had penetrated one of France's top nuclear centres to kill a defected Soviet scientist. Now, as the express waited in the Hauptbahnhof, he walked steadily along the corridor toward the locked door leading to the rear Wagon-Lit.

Ahead he saw a woman passenger who had just boarded the train; behind her, a second Swiss security official again in plain clothes. You learned to recognize the breed. The short, large-footed Russian stopped the woman. 'May I see your ticket, madame?' he requested in German.

'Can't it wait until I have found my compartment?' the middle-aged woman, who was carrying a case, demanded irritably.

'Your ticket, please,' Gusev repeated firmly.

The security man squeezed past them as Gusev inspected her ticket. 'Thank you, madame.' He handed back the ticket and the reservation slip. 'Your compartment is four doors along.'

Arriving at the locked door to the rear Wagon-Lit, Gusev slipped inside the toilet, pushed the lock across to show the 'engaged' sign, and waited with the door almost closed. A minute later Haller came down the corridor, rapped on the locked door in a certain way, and was admitted by Leroy, and the door closed again. Gusev waited, checking the second hand of his watch, then emerged, glanced back along the deserted corridor, and repeated the same rapping signal.

Leroy was opening the door, his revolver in his hand, when Gusev fired the small gas pistol through the aperture. The pellet of tear gas exploded in Leroy's face and he was aiming his weapon blind when Gusev flung the door wide open and hit him on the side of the skull with the barrel of the pistol, knocking him out. The amount of gas ejected by the specially designed pistol was small – enough to put the victim out of action briefly but not enough to affect the man who fired the pistol.

Closing the Wagon-Lit door behind him, Gusev stepped over the unconscious Leroy and peered along the next corridor. At this moment Wargrave was still inside the communications compartment, talking to Scholten in The Hague. Haller had entered the compartment containing Marenkov and Elsa and was reporting the latest news.

'They're checking everyone coming on board – double-checking them, that is. They have already made one check while the passengers waiting to board were inside the wire cage.'

'So nice Springer is still alert even though his job is nearly over,' Elsa remarked. 'He gets off at Basel Bad Bahnhof, I assume?'

'Correct,' Haller agreed. 'Then the German people come on board and we'll be in equally good hands there – Franz Wander is one tough character. Since his appointment the KGB have had it rough in the Federal Republic. Where is Harry now?' he inquired.

'Still in the communications compartment.' Elsa put her hand over her face to suppress a yawn. God, I'm whacked, she thought; if only I could snatch an hour's sleep.

Marenkov, who had stood up behind Elsa when Haller rapped on the door, still looked remarkably fresh and restless. 'Since Sharpinsky didn't get on the train at Zürich, I'm convinced he will board the express here,' he said dogmatically.

'Springer checked the passengers inside the cage. I think I'll go along and have a word with Harry,' Haller replied. Elsa opened the door for him and closed it as the American walked down the corridor, rapped on the communications door, and disappeared inside.

Gusev, who had been waiting out of sight at the far end of the car, watched Haller walking away, entering another compartment. The moment the American was gone he padded along the corridor. His large feet moved quite silently as he moved with a cat-footed tread. He knew which compartment Haller had left – the window blind facing it was very slightly askew. He moved steadily along the corridor, not slowly, but neither was he hurrying as he listened carefully.

Reaching the compartment door, he did not hesitate for a second, repeating the rapping signal Haller had used to gain admittance to the car when he was hidden inside the toilet. The door began opening. Behind it Elsa stood with her Smith and Wesson and behind her stood Marenkov. She had opened it only a few inches when the pellet from Gusev's gas pistol hit her chest and exploded, sending the vapour into her eyes. The door was flung wide open by Gusev, who had dropped the gas pistol and was pulling the Luger from his shoulder holster with lightning speed.

Temporarily blinded, Elsa was trying to aim the Smith and Wesson when Marenkov hurled her aside onto the berth and leaped forward. His powerful left hand grabbed Gusev's gun hand, twisted it brutally, and smashed it against the door jamb, once, twice. Gusev felt his wrist break, the gun slip from his hand. He dropped to his knees; his left hand, pulling a knife from beneath his uniform jacket, lunged the blade forward and upward. Considering the pain he was feeling, the knife thrust was extraordinarily swift, a flashing blur. Then he felt Marenkov's right hand lock around his left wrist as the Soviet general, bending down, again smashed his hand against the door jamb three times in rapid succession. Gusev's second wrist was broken and the knife fell from his nerveless fingers.

Marenkov was not finished with him yet. Using both hands, he hauled the broken Gusev up, grasping him under the armpits, and literally threw him out of the compartment. Gusev crashed against the metal passenger rail and slumped to the floor, then made one final effort to get to his feet again. Inside Marenkov's mind all the pent-up frustration and hatred he had concealed since his wife's suicide flooded out like a dam bursting. 'Give me a gun,' he had demanded of Haller hours ago and the American had refused. Farther along the corridor Wargrave had emerged from the communications compartment and now he watched, a revolver in his hand, unable to shoot for fear of hitting Marenkov.

As the incredibly tough Gusev clambered to his feet Marenkov smashed a fist into his face, driving his head back hard against the passenger rail; then, using both clenched fists, he hit Gusev blow after blow, and when the executioner sank to the floor for the second time he kicked him with vicious force in the skull and trampled on him. Wargrave grabbed him by the arm. 'For God's sake, that's enough – he's dead . . . dead . . . dead . . .'

The Russian turned and went back into the compartment, where an appalled Elsa was swabbing her eyes with a handkerchief she had dampened under the tap; appalled that she had failed in her task, as she believed. 'That was for Irina,' Marenkov said quietly, the ferocity ebbing away. 'Are you all right? For a moment I thought he had killed you . . .'

'He would have done – except for you.'

Confusion filled the corridor outside. Leroy, recovered from the attack, was equally appalled at what he regarded as his own failure. It was Haller who calmed them down, who sent Wargrave to warn Springer of what had happened. On the platform outside, Waldo Hackmann, who had left the train as though to get some exercise – but in fact to be ready to leave the Hauptbahnhof if Gusev's lightning attack succeeded – was close to the rear Wagon-Lit compartment when the corridor blind, carelessly shut, flew up. Standing by a porter, he saw for a brief moment General Sergei Marenkov outlined by the light from inside the train – recognized his recent chief, despite the trimmed hair, by his bulk, by his movement as he bent over a girl sitting on a berth. Then Haller hauled down the blind and fixed it properly.

A few minutes later Hackmann witnessed the stretcher that Springer had arranged to be brought being carried off the train with a blanket drawn over the stretcher's occupant, who he knew could only be Yuri Gusev.

Returning to his sleeping compartment, Hackmann closed the door in a state of shock and stared at the single glove on his berth. The glove told him that Rudi Bühler had successfully come aboard the express. Sinking down onto the berth, he lit a fresh cigar and stared at the opposite wall. Having counted so much on the previously flawless record of Yuri Gusev, he was left now only with Bühler, who was certainly no trained assassin. And Nicos Leonides – whom he had seen for the first time at Zürich because he knew which window to look for when he had slipped on board the train disguised as a porter – no longer had the KGB colonel's confidence; otherwise he would have done the job before now.

As the train moved out of the Hauptbahnhof on its way to Basel Bad Bahnhof, Sharpinsky took a decision. The only possible solution now was for the Geiger Group to destroy the entire Atlantic Express, taking Marenkov with it.

Chapter Twenty-four

Germany, Amsterdam, The Hague

'Look, for God's sake – Cruft's Dog Show!'

Standing beside Matt Leroy, Elsa stared out in amazement at the scene on the snowbound platform as the train stopped at Basel Bad Bahnhof. On the platform stood forty German shepherds, each with its handler, straining at their leashes as though they couldn't wait to board the express.

'I don't get it,' Leroy replied as the doors of the three Wagons-Lits were opened and the dogs scrambled on board. It was Captain Franz Wander of the BND, a large, smiling-faced German who spoke English with a Cambridge accent, who explained his tactics to Julian Haller and Wargrave inside the compartment next to the one where Elsa was guarding Marenkov.

'It is just after midnight. For most of the time the train will be travelling through Germany it will be night – and this means there will be no good reason for people to be moving about the train. I can average three dogs to patrol the corridors of each car. That will keep the passengers in their compartments. I want total control of movement until you cross the Dutch border.'

'You could get a few complaints,' Haller observed with a dry smile.

'Complaints I can deal with.' Wander, very smart in a grey business suit despite his bulk, grinned broadly. 'We shall tell them there is a bomb scare – that the dogs are here to sniff out explosives.' He looked at Wargrave. 'Any objections, Harry?'

'None.' Wargrave spread his hands. 'Brilliant, I call it. We might even get a night's sleep.'

'Some people in the non-sleepers will want to go to the bathroom,' Haller remarked.

'We shall royally accompany them there and back – with a dog . . .'

Prepare contingency plan to destroy Atlantic Express. Wait for fresh signal before taking action. Skiros.

It was midnight in Amsterdam – the Atlantic Express was about to stop at Basel Hauptbahnhof, and a few miles south in The Hague Scholten had just heard of the change of course of the *Maxim Gorky* – when Rolf Geiger stood by the third-floor window of the old house in Amsterdam checking in his mind the plans he had made in response to the signal he had received earlier.

'Skiros' was the code name for Sharpinsky and the signal had been dispatched by the Swiss dentist, Heinrich Baum, from the Hotel Schweizerhof. As Geiger peered down between the almost closed curtains a police patrol boat puttered under an arched bridge and passed below along the canal beneath the building. Behind him his new recruit, Joop Kist, the thin-faced Dutchman, was talking on the phone to Amsterdam Central station. Kist said thank you and replaced the receiver.

'They expect the Atlantic Express to arrive here at ten in the morning,' he reported.

'Good. Send Erika to me and stay downstairs on guard until I call you.'

Closing the curtain, Geiger was sitting behind a desk when Erika Kern, his dark-haired confidante, came into the room. Despite his disbelief in Erika's mistrust of Joop Kist he still felt it wise to let the Dutchman know as little as possible about what he was planning. He came straight to the point as the girl sat provocatively with her superb pair of legs crossed. She never stops trying to rouse me, he thought cynically.

'Everything is arranged in case we have to go into action?' he inquired.

'Yes,' Erika replied crisply. 'First the express will have to be diverted through Belgium to ensure it crosses the Maas bridge. That is arranged.'

'Go over it again.'

'Jacek Wojna and the others are still waiting at Willich and they have been ordered to stand by for imminent action. They have the explosives, of course – so it only needs one brief signal for them to move.'

'They know the exact section of the railway embankment to blow up north of Düsseldorf?'

'Wojna has already reconnoitred the area – he may be a brute but he has the unit under tight control and he can be relied on to do the job.'

'He will have to move very fast, and the weather in Germany is appalling.'

'That will help him,' Erika replied in her most soothing tone. 'Half the police are out trying to rescue people from cars caught in the snowdrifts.'

'It sounds reasonably satisfactory,' Geiger commented. A meticulous planner, he took nothing for granted, least of all success. 'So if we are ordered to blow up the embankment the authorities will have to divert the express at Cologne via Brussels. It will continue toward here via the Maas bridge.'

'Did you enjoy your walk earlier?' Erika inquired softly. She was only too well aware that Geiger had paid a visit to the red-light district and there was a hint of malice in her question.

The Armenian reacted instantly. Getting up from behind his desk, he walked around it and slapped her hard across the face, then returned to his chair. Erika said nothing, showed nothing in her expression, although inwardly she was delighted. At long last she had provoked the Armenian, and although she would have preferred Geiger to have sprawled her on the couch and whipped up her skirt, it was a step in the right direction. Erika enjoyed being manhandled.

'And the main base here?' Geiger asked in an even tone as though nothing had happened.

'The barn near Dordrecht is ready for them when

they cross the border with enough explosives to blow three bridges sky-high. The whole express will go down into the river. What about uniforms?'

'The normal ones.' Geiger was referring to the group's standard operational clothing – black ski masks, windcheaters, and ski pants. He smiled as he fingered his moustache. 'If we are seen we want to leave our trademark.'

'You do trust Joop Kist?' Erika inquired doubtfully.

'He is another peasant, an idealist, but he speaks Dutch, which is invaluable now we are here. In any case, I have seen to it that he knows very little of our plans.'

'I'm still worried about him. If there is an emergency and I am proved right?'

'Shoot him,' Geiger told her cheerfully.

The Atlantic Express was speeding through blizzard-stricken Germany as Elsa Lang made her way back from the front of the train toward the rear Wagon-Lit, almost exhausted now. It had been her own idea that, with the sketch of Colonel Igor Sharpinsky firmly fixed in her mind, she would check the passengers in the faint hope of spotting the KGB colonel. As she entered the next Wagon-Lit, Waldo Hackmann – after giving the attendant at the end of the car a large tip – was turning around to walk back to his compartment with a glass of brandy in his hand.

Their eyes met for a moment and then Hackmann

walked on ahead of her and disappeared inside his compartment. As she passed the closed door Elsa automatically noticed the number. Compartment 19. She had noticed nothing familiar about the passenger. Passing one of Captain Wander's doghandlers, she patted the animal, returned to one of the empty compartments in the rear Wagon-Lit, and said good-night to Matt Leroy, who was on guard.

'Pleasant dreams,' the droopy-moustached American wished her.

'I'm going to sleep like a dog.'

She flopped onto the lower berth in her clothes and fell instantly asleep. But she did not have pleasant dreams; instead she stirred restlessly as she experienced nightmares. She was at Basel Hauptbahnhof, collecting yet another of those bloody cassettes . . . She was landing at the Bucharest airstrip with Wargrave, seeing Marenkov instead of Anatoli Zarubin approaching the plane . . . hearing the burst of machine-gun fire at Milan Airport as the fake ambulance fired into the back of the armoured truck where she sat in the cab with Wargrave and Marenkov . . . More machine-gun fire as she lay on the compartment floor at Vira while the Jeep riddled the train . . . watching the avalanche wave coming closer until it overwhelmed her and she woke up. Sighing with relief, she lay listening to the thudding of the express's wheels taking them to Schiphol, to safety . . .

*

At 2.30 a.m. the express was approaching Karlsruhe, where it would stop briefly. Inside Compartment 19 Sharpinsky was sipping the last of his brandy as he talked to Rudi Bühler, who had entered the compartment ten minutes earlier when the German dog-handler was temporarily absent from the corridor.

'You have to get that signal transmitted,' Sharpinsky told his deputy. 'You have to get off at Karlsruhe – a car will be waiting for you – get to the house and make sure personally the signal goes off immediately to Amsterdam. Any questions?' He spoke as though there couldn't possibly be any.

'It is a very long signal,' Bühler commented as he examined the encoded message the Russian had handed him. 'If the Germans are using radio detector vans . . .'

'At this stage we are all expendable,' Sharpinsky told him brutally. 'Including myself,' he added frankly.

'You propose to stay aboard the express, then?'

'Until the very last moment – in case I can do the job myself. Although that I doubt, with all those damned dogs the BND have put aboard the train.'

Bühler glanced at his chief, who had spoken with his normal self-restraint. He had never liked Colonel Igor Sharpinsky, but close to the moment of parting he had a grudging admiration for the KGB colonel. The bastard has guts, he was thinking. With the rolled-up signal concealed inside the partially hol-lowed-out cigar he was smoking, Bühler left the compartment as the express was slowing down, coming into Karlsruhe. The German dog-handler who had returned to the corridor saw nothing strange in a passenger disembarking.

Only a handful of passengers got off the train at that hour of the morning as Rudi Bühler left the station, walked a few hundred yards, and slipped into the rear seat of a waiting BMW, which immediately drove off. He stubbed out his cigar containing the signal. A minute later the radio detector vehicle disguised as a refrigerated truck followed the BMW – a little behind schedule because the driver had trouble starting his engine. Wander had surrounded Karlsruhe Hauptbahnhof with a variety of BND transport and every single passenger leaving the express was followed.

Reaching an apartment block, Bühler hurried inside and up to the sixth-floor where his radio operator was waiting with the transmitter. As he had commented to Sharpinsky, the signal was extended and two radio detector vehicles located its source just as the transmission to Amsterdam was completed. Bühler had destroyed the encoded signal when German police burst into the apartment. The GRU sabotage chief was inside a bedroom when he heard the outer door crashing open and he moved instantly and with great speed. Throwing up the bedroom window, he stepped out onto the fire escape, turned and fired his Walther five times at policemen coming into the room. Then he started to run down the fire-escape steps. But he overlooked one thing: the iron steps were coated with ice. Slipping, slithering, he tried to save himself as he pivoted over the low rail. He let out one long scream that only ended when he hit the concrete pavement five flights below.

At 3 a.m. in the old Amsterdam house overlooking the canal Rolf Geiger read the decoded signal from Karlsruhe. Looking up at Erika Kern, who was waiting with an expectant expression on her long-jawed face, he nodded.

'The operation is on?' Erika asked.

'Indeed it is,' Geiger replied suavely. He was relieved, already looking forward to completion of the job, to the moment when he could return to Paris and its fleshpots, resuming his Argentinian identity of Leo Sanchez while he directed the group's operations in Holland by remote control. 'Send the signal to Willich,' he ordered. 'And tell them to move fast – very fast . . .'

At Willich, Jacek Wojna, the activist leader of the terrorists, reacted instantly on receiving Geiger's signal over the transmitter inside the split-level house where he had waited so impatiently. Within ten minutes he was driving his Mercedes 450 SEL out of the garage and eastward from Willich. Gaten, the Norwegian expert on sabotaging oil rigs, was by his side; crammed inside the rear were four other men.

Heading down the autobahn leading to Düsseldorf,

Wojna soon turned off the autobahn on to a side road, and then swung the car down a track leading to a large old barn. Inside, an ambulance stood alongside a large gasoline truck. Wojna, Gaten, and another terrorist changed into ambulance attendants' clothes and scrambled inside the ambulance. As Wojna drove the vehicle away one of the three men he had left behind took the Mercedes under cover into the barn alongside the patrol truck.

With the siren screaming, Wojna drove at speed through the snow-storm that had started toward a point north of Düsseldorf where a deserted stretch of the main railroad track from Basel to Amsterdam crossed a long embankment. Gaten was terrified by the speed at which the Pole was travelling and once they skidded, but the Pole, an expert driver, brought the vehicle back under control.

'For Christ's sake watch it,' Gaten snapped. 'You're going to kill us all.'

'Shit!' Wojna sneered. 'Left your guts behind you in Willich?'

Wojna, born and brought up in the Paris slums of the Goutte d'Or district where he had led street gangs when he was twelve years old, despised the educated Norwegian anarchist and took every opportunity to put him down. 'We're nearly there,' he said after a few minutes, peering through the windshield.

It took them five minutes to place the explosive charges they brought from the back of the ambulance at several carefully selected points, to wire them for time-fuse detonation. Then, their uniforms covered in snow, they left the isolated section of embankment and drove a short distance toward Holland, stopped, and waited.

The detonation was enormous. There was a brilliant flash, a great burst of snow as whole sections of railroad track were hurled into the air. And one hundred metres of embankment slid like a wave onto the nearby highway. The main line north from Düsseldorf to Amsterdam had been severed.

'Now for the next move – to cross the border,' Wojna told Gaten.

The ambulance started moving at speed again toward Holland, its siren screeching nonstop, and in a few minutes it passed a police car moving in the opposite direction. Gaten's hand clenched with tension but Wojna maintained his speed. The police driver never gave the ambulance a second thought as he remarked to his colleague, 'Some poor bastard in trouble . . .'

Arriving back at the barn, Wojna pulled up with a jerk that caused a slight skid, left the engine running, and jumped out of the vehicle. 'Get the lead out of your feet,' he snapped. 'In five minutes we're away and I'll smash the face in of anyone who isn't ready.'

Inside the barn the three men left behind had already removed the circular plate that had been skilfully cut out of the rear of the gasoline truck forming a concealed entrance through which they could crawl inside. The interior of the huge truck was stacked with the large quantity of explosives, timer devices, and distant electrical detonation systems Wojna was carrying into Holland. Hidden ventilation ducts had been cut in the roof of the wagon, enabling men to travel inside the cylindrical space for long distances.

'Hurry it up, for God's sake,' Wojna ordered as he tore off the ambulance driver's uniform and put on the boiler suit and cap of a gasoline truck driver. Gaten dressed himself in a similar outfit; he would travel alongside Wojna.

The other four terrorists climbed through the circular entrance into the bowels of the truck and Gaten then fixed the plate, sealing them inside. While the Norwegian went outside to get behind the wheel of the ambulance, Wojna examined the closed plate, scooped dirt off the floor of the barn, and rubbed it around the circumference of the plate. Not that he expected any trouble with the Dutch Customs officials at the crossing point – not in this weather when they would be only too anxious to get back to the warmth of their hut. Satisfied, Wojna climbed behind the wheel of the truck and drove it out, then waited.

Gaten drove the ambulance inside the barn alongside the Mercedes, hurried outside, closed the barn doors, and climbed up inside the cab of the truck beside Wojna. He hardly had time to close the door before the Pole was moving down the track and turning into the road.

They crossed the border into Holland without

trouble; the Dutch officials hardly glanced at the papers Geiger had prepared in advance. Long-distance gas trucks were constantly crossing the frontier from Germany. Once inside Holland, Wojna kept his speed down well within the limits – despite the lack of snow. The Pole felt pleased with himself; once again he had successfully completed another operation. And now they were heading for the new base Geiger had established for them, at Dordrecht, which happened to be close to the great railroad bridge over the Maas – the line the Atlantic Express would have to be diverted to.

At 4.20 a.m. the Atlantic Express had left Mainz and was on its way to Cologne when Captain Franz Wander woke everyone up in the rear Wagon-Lit and assembled them in Marenkov's apartment. Julian Haller, heavy-eyed from lack of sleep, was awake, but Wargrave and Elsa had slept for a while when they received the German security chief's summons.

'I thought you should know,' Wander informed them crisply, 'that the express is going to have to be diverted at Cologne to go via Aachen and Brussels to Amsterdam.'

'Why?' snapped Wargrave.

'A portion of the rail track north of Düsseldorf has been blown up, so the train cannot proceed by its normal route direct to Amsterdam. We suspect more fun and games by the Geiger Group,' he added, in his excellent English.

'I smell a rat,' Wargrave commented, 'a lot of rats . . .'

'I don't see any connection with Marenkov's being on the train,' Wander replied. 'Would it have destroyed the whole train if we had been passing over that section at the time? I'm sure it wouldn't – some cars would have had a bad time but a lot of the express would have survived.'

'Exactly,' the Englishman replied. 'They couldn't have been sure enough of getting Marenkov.' He stood up. 'I think I'd like to have a chat with Scholten on the radio telephone.'

Going inside the communications compartment, Wargrave asked Peter Neckermann if he could use the phone by himself. Alone in the compartment, he called the Dutch counter-espionage general in The Hague.

'Harry Wargrave here, Max. We're somewhere between Mainz and Cologne.'

'I know that,' Scholten replied instantly. 'Wander sends me frequent reports about your progress. Our co-operation is total.'

'What you probably haven't heard is that a section of track has been blown up north of Düsseldorf. I don't like this development one little bit.'

'I know that, too. Which means you will be diverted via Brussels and Roosendaal. Not a coincidence, in my opinion. Also – and this is strictly between the two of us – I know the Geiger Group, who probably blew up the line, have now moved into Holland.'

'So that's the next obstacle we face?'

'I'm sure of it. And a most formidable obstacle, Harry – but possibly also a golden, once-in-a-lifetime opportunity. If we are prepared to act with the utmost ruthlessness,' he added. 'You know that the Soviet freighter *Maxim Gorky* is at this moment lying at the mouth of the Rhine estuary, that she is taking aboard a great number of top GRU and KGB agents from France, Belgium, and Germany – especially Germany?'

'Wander did mention this, yes,' Wargrave replied cautiously. 'How far are you prepared to go? And surely your torpedo-boat patrols can intercept them?'

'In the prevailing storm conditions – and at night – that is not so easy as it sounds,' Scholten replied casually. 'Also, I have suggested to my good friend Commander De Vos that he does not exert himself too much in that direction.'

'You're suggesting . . .'

'I think I can locate the Geiger Group – it will be a race against time – but if I do I propose we go all the way.' Scholten detailed his plan and the Englishman suggested certain modifications.

They spoke together for no less than twenty minutes, then Wargrave left the compartment and went along the train to see Nicos Leonides. Closing the door, he began speaking rapidly. '. . . so, be ready for me,' were his last words to the Greek as he left and went into the next compartment to have the same conversation with Anna Markos. When he left her his expression was grim. In the end he was going to have to rely on his secret Greek cell to do the job.

Ten minutes before Harry Wargrave made his long phone call to General Max Scholten, a local call came through for the Dutch security chief. His deputy, Major Sailer, answered the phone, and then spoke to Scholten.

'There's someone called Panhuys on the line.'

'I'll take it,' Scholten said quickly. He listened for only a brief time, saying yes and no at intervals, then replaced the receiver and walked over to the wall map. 'The explosion on the line north of Düsseldorf will bring the Atlantic Express here via Aachen and Brussels,' he remarked. 'We know that already,' Sailer replied. 'We heard the news fifteen minutes ago.'

Taking out a pencil, Scholten ringed a portion of the map with a decisive sweep. The circle he had described covered the general area of the Rhine delta. 'Somewhere inside this ring the climax will take place,' he predicted. 'Alert the Venlo Team,' he added casually. 'For imminent action.'

The instruction startled Sailer. The Venlo Team was

a picked group of Dutch sharpshooters personally selected by Scholten for their marksmanship, a highly secret anti-terrorist section controlled by the Dutch security chief himself.

'Where do we place them?' Sailer inquired.

'At the secret base in Dordrecht.'

Without realizing it, Scholten was sending his men to the same town where the Geiger Group was assembling, but this was not entirely a coincidence. Scholten proceeded to explain his line of reasoning.

'We know the Atlantic Express is being diverted through Brussels to Roosendaal and Amsterdam, Sailer. How would you destroy an entire train – to make sure you killed the one passenger aboard you wished to kill?'

'Blow up the railroad track – as they have done north of Düsseldorf.'

'But then only a portion of the train would be wiped out. Marenkov might well survive. Think again.'

'I've run out of ideas,' Sailer confessed.

'I would blow up a whole bridge while the express was on it – say, the long Maas bridge. The whole express would then fall into the river.'

'Oh, my God . . .' Sailer stopped speaking as the phone rang. He took the call and then handed the receiver to his chief. 'Harry Wargrave wants to speak to you direct from the Atlantic Express.'

'Leave me alone while I talk to him.' Scholten spoke for twenty minutes with the Englishman over the radio telephone link-up, replaced the receiver, and then called back Sailer on the intercom. His deputy returned to the office in some excitement. 'We are getting reports that a lot of powerboats have been observed moving at speed toward the *Maxim Gorky*. Most of them made it but two overturned in the heavy seas before they reached the freighter. There were no survivors.'

'And all of them top Soviet agents clearing out. I like it when vermin eliminates itself,' Scholten commented. 'And now I have to ask you to enter into a conspiracy between the two of us . . .' Scholten watched his deputy carefully. 'Are you willing?'

'I have always fancied myself as a conspirator,' Sailer replied with a dry smile.

'Then go and steal from two different sports goods shops four sets of Geiger Group outfits – black ski masks, black windcheaters, and black ski pants. You can use skeleton keys to avoid the appearance of a break-in and for God's sake don't let the police catch you at it. Two different shops, I said – the loss may not noticed for months.'

'Any particular sizes?'

'Yes, I was coming to that. Two outfits for tall men, two for men of medium size. We are going to try and strike a very heavy blow at the Soviets, Sailer. Oh, and two more things. Get hold of De Vos, the torpedo-boat commander – tell him not to try too hard to intercept any of those powerboats. Risky work in this weather,' he added casually. 'After that I want a quiet word with my friend De Vos myself . . .'

About half an hour earlier, just after Scholten had taken the call from the man who had given the name of Panhuys, in Amsterdam Erika Kern had crept downstairs to the first floor with a Luger pistol in her hand. Opening the back door, which led on to a cobbled alley, she had come face-to-face with Joop Kist, also holding a Luger in his hand.

'What the hell are you doing out here?' she demanded in German.

'I heard a prowler – there's been an attempted break-in.' Kist showed her where there were jemmy marks on the outside of the door. 'I think they did the place next door and then tried here. I must have scared them off.'

Still suspicious, Erika looked at the window of the neighbouring house where the glass had been smashed. She peered inside and could see nothing. Joop Kist thanked God she had not brought a torch – otherwise she might have seen the phone he had used to call Scholten, even the jemmy he had left on the floor to fake the attempt to break into Geiger's house.

'Let's get back upstairs,' Erika snapped. 'And make sure you bolt this door.'

Left by himself, Kist sighed with relief as he bolted the door. It had been a stroke of luck for Scholten that he had managed to plant a man inside the Geiger

Group. The trouble was Kist had not been able to tell him much in the quick phone call – only that Geiger was planning a major operation, which was imminent, and that he had ordered Erika Kern to have the car ready to drive him south toward the Belgian border. In other words, as Scholten had immediately seen, in the general direction of Dordrecht and the Maas bridge.

At Schiphol Airport, the only airfield in Western Europe still open to flights to and from the United States, Dutch troops were guarding the Boeing 707 waiting inside a remote hangar. Jeeps carrying machine guns circled the hangar constantly; inside, more armed soldiers stamped their feet in the cold as they watched over the plane. It was already fully fuelled and the air crew slept in a building close by.

The *Maxim Gorky*, heaving to at the mouth of the Rhine, was now taking aboard very heavy seas. Despite her size, the 17,000-ton freighter was taking cruel punishment and her captain, Josef Morov, was becoming increasingly outraged as he discussed the situation with Commissar Rykin in the privacy of his cabin.

'By forcing me to stay here you are endangering the ship and all my crew,' he roared.

'My orders remain unchanged,' Rykin replied coldly.

'You talk like a trained parrot!' Ignoring Rykin's bleak expression, he thundered on. 'I have already lost one of my crew trying to take on board these crazy fools coming out to us in launches and powerboats.'

'Those crazy fools are some of the Soviet Union's most important citizens. We have already rescued over a hundred men – key agents it has taken years to train, the élite of our European underground apparatus.'

'And how long do you think it takes to train the crewmen of my ship?' Morov demanded. 'We are heaving to in one of the worst seas I have ever encountered.'

'I thought you were a skilled ship's master,' Rykin sneered. 'Surely you can cope in an emergency.'

'It is not your responsibility,' Morov rapped back furiously. 'You just sit on your backside and then claim all the glory if we ever get back to Leningrad. Not that I give a shit for the glory,' he went on. 'And do not look too complacent – ships have been known to capsize.'

'You are exaggerating,' Rykin replied, but there was a hint of nervousness in his tone now.

'Look out of the porthole,' Morov ordered him.

Clutching to furniture to keep his balance, Rykin went to the porthole and drew back the curtain. At that moment a gigantic green, foam-crested comber was sweeping toward the porthole. Rykin flinched as the monster struck the ship, blotted out the porthole, and hurled him clear across the cabin. He was still lying on the floor when Morov stood over him and said something that terrified Rykin.

'You seem to have forgotten that our original destination was Angola, and what this ship is carrying.'

It was the reference to the cargo that frightened Rykin. The *Maxim Gorky* was carrying in her holds arms and ammunition for guerrilla forces in southern Africa, including two thousand tons of gelignite and amytol. As Rykin picked himself up off the the floor he knew he was standing on a floating platform of high explosives.

Chapter Twenty-five

Maxim Gorky

At 6.15 a.m. the Atlantic Express left Cologne and turned west toward Aachen along the diverted route that would take it through Belgium on its way to Amsterdam. In the rear Wagon-Lit Elsa Lang sat with Marenkov and Julian Haller while she experimented with different sketch versions of Sharpinsky. Working from the original picture built up from Marenkov's description of the KGB colonel, she produced fresh pictures of Sharpinsky with a beard, then with a moustache, then again clean-shaven and with rimless spectacles.

'What's the point of all these scribbles?' asked Haller irritably. He had refused to sleep all night and was close to a state of exhaustion.

'The general says Sharpinsky is an expert at disguise,' Elsa replied, continuing her sketching. 'We are all pretty sure Sharpinsky came aboard at Zürich. One of these sketches may match someone on the train.'

'You've got a hope,' Haller told her.

'I've got obstinacy, Turtle,' she said, using her pet name for Haller. 'You stick your neck out – I'm sticking mine out now that sooner or later I'll spot him.'

She was still making fresh sketches when they arrived at the frontier town of Aachen, where Captain Franz Wander handed over to Belgian security. 'A safe journey to Schiphol,' the German said to Harry Wargrave as they shook hands. 'I'm sure you will make it now.'

'Thanks for getting us through Germany in one piece,' Wargrave replied. 'Probably largely due to your friends.' He indicated the file of German shepherds streaming off the train with their handlers. 'It was a damned clever idea.'

Between Aachen and Brussels Nord the dining car was opened for breakfast. One of the first arrivals in the dining car was Waldo Hackmann, still wearing his checked sports jacket and horn-rimmed glasses. He chose a corner seat at the far end of the dining car from the kitchen where he could observe all the other diners. In his American accent he ordered a large breakfast of bacon and eggs, lit a cigar, and opened a copy of *Time* magazine.

In the rear Wagon-Lit Wargrave had just suggested to Elsa that they should get some breakfast in the dining car. Julian Haller said he only wanted coffee and would they have it sent along with the meals they had ordered for Marenkov, Matt Lcroy, and Peter Neckermann. A Belgian security officer would supervise the preparation of the food in the galley to avoid any risk of poison being introduced into the food.

Entering the dining car, Wargrave and Elsa chose the corner table nearest the kitchen. A few tables away Nicos Leonides sat facing Anna Markos, ignoring her as though they were strangers. 'My God, what a feeling of freedom to be sitting eating breakfast,' Elsa murmured as she broke a roll. 'Sitting with everyday passengers and watching the countryside go by.'

'Not much of a view,' Wargrave observed.

As they passed through the fringes of the Ardennes Forest, it was still snowing heavily and the trees were crusted white with snow. While she ate her breakfast Elsa studied the other passengers, looking for Sharpinsky. At the far end of the dining car Waldo Hackmann had observed Harry Wargrave and it gave him immense satisfaction to see the Englishman sitting there. He glanced at his watch: 8.15 a.m. Within two hours the Englishman would be at the bottom of the Maas, drowned, his corpse carried out to sea by the swift-flowing Rhine. At the thought he savoured his next cup of coffee.

He was still sitting there when Wargrave and Elsa walked past him on their way back to the Wagon-Lit. It amused Sharpinsky that the Englishman never gave a second glance to Waldo Hackmann, the American picture dealer from Boston, Massachusetts.

At 7.45 a.m. – while Wargrave and Elsa were breakfasting in the dining car – Rolf Geiger left his Amsterdam headquarters to drive south to the Maas. He sat alone in the back of his Mercedes 450 automatic, smartly dressed in a fur-lined overcoat, reading a copy of *Le Monde*, with an executive case on the seat beside him. Behind the wheel, equally smart in her dark blue chauffeuse's uniform, Erika Kern drove with verve and skill through the early morning traffic. By her side, silent and morose, sat Joop Kist.

It was an impressive performance Rolf Geiger put on; in the past he had noticed that police patrol cars never gave him a second glance when they had the attractive Erika behind the wheel to distract their attention. Within fifteen minutes they had left Amsterdam behind and were speeding south as Erika stepped on the gas. They passed a signpost and Geiger glanced up. The signpost read *To Schiphol Airport*.

Less than an hour later they were south of Dordrecht and close to the great Maas bridge. As in most of Holland there was hardly any snow – only a few thinning streaks among the birch woods they were passing on a lonely stretch of the road. It was at this moment that Joop Kist spoke for the first time.

'Stop the car. I've got to have a pee.'

'For Christ's sake,' Erika snapped, 'we're nearly there.'

'I've got to pee,' Kist persisted. 'Now!'

In the back Geiger sighed. 'Stop and let him get on with it,' he said. 'And be damned quick about it,' he told Kist.

The Dutchman got out and hurried behind a copse of trees. Undoing the buckle of his belt, he took out

COLIN FORBES

the electronic signal capsule from behind it and laid it beside a rock. On top of the rock he scrawled a crude arrow pointing south. As he returned to the car he was adjusting his fly. Kist had no intention of risking a body search by the suspicious Erika when they reached their destination – and he had had no chance of attaching the device to the Mercedes. With an impatient snort, Erika drove on again.

Behind them the Venlo Team Scholten had stationed in Dordrecht had picked up the signal from the electronic device as soon as the Mercedes passed through the town. Keeping at least two kilometres behind the Mercedes, a plain van carrying six of the Dutch sharpshooters was now following the signal as Geiger proceeded south.

A short distance from where they had stopped to permit Kist to relieve himself Erika suddenly swung off the main highway along a track leading through a copse of trees to where an old barn stood well concealed from the road. Behind the barn stood the large gasoline truck that had been the transport used by the main Geiger Group to reach its destination. Installed with a special ventilation system – and with a concealed door cut in the rear of the vehicle – the terrorists had travelled inside the storage space until they arrived at the barn.

Geiger got straight out of the car and walked inside the barn. It was a strange scene. Neither the setting – the barn with its straw-strewn floor and stench of animal droppings – nor the six men clad in black ski masks, windcheaters, and ski pants really fitted in with the dapper Armenian.

'Everything is ready to blow up the Maas bridge?' he asked.

It was the leader of the action group, Jacek Wojna, who answered. 'The bombs are ready. I was going to use timer devices but they could misfire – it will be done by electric detonation from a distance.'

'And the guards on the bridge?' Geiger queried sharply.

'Only two.' Wojna gripped the automatic weapon he was holding. 'They will be easy meat. And the escape boat is ready.'

'You must wait until the express is in the exact centre of the bridge,' Geiger insisted.

'That also is clearly understood,' Wojna replied stolidly. 'We shall be leaving here shortly in the truck.'

He froze and a feeling of tension suddenly filled the barn. The men in ski masks gripped their automatic weapons tightly and looked to Wojna for guidance. In the distance, coming closer, sounding terribly loud in the hush that descended in the barn, was the sound of an approaching helicopter. Geiger turned to Erika. 'We must leave immediately – to pick up our friend off the Atlantic Express.'

A stream of reports continued to flow into Scholten's headquarters: reports of cars crossing the frontier into Holland illegally, which was so easy along the straggling border; reports from the torpedo command in the estuary of more powerboats heading for the *Maxim Gorky*. But one particular report attracted the security chief's attention.

'This message from a helicopter pilot, Sailer. It mentions seeing a gasoline truck and a Mercedes parked in the wilderness south of Dordrecht.'

'Probably the driver just taking a rest, sir.'

'The drivers, you mean – there are two vehicles. Taking a rest, you said? In this weather? In a benighted spot like that?'

'Does seem a bit peculiar . . .'

'And it's close to the Maas,' Scholten went on as he looked at the wall map. 'More than that – it's close to where they have just found Joop Kist's abandoned electronic device.' He stood up. 'In any case, we have to leave for our rendezvous – and I think we've found the Geiger Group, thank God. When we get into the car, drive like hell.'

'I have remembered where I saw Sharpinsky.'

The Atlantic Express, well north of Brussels, had passed Roosendaal and was approaching the great Maas bridge when Elsa said the words. She had just returned to the original sketch and drawn a pair of horn-rimmed glasses on the image. Haller looked dubious but Wargrave reacted instantly.

'Where? When?'

'At breakfast at the end of the dining car. But

earlier than that – in the middle of the night. He's in Compartment 19. The next car but one.'

'We'll go there now,' Wargrave snapped.

'Take a couple of Belgian security men with you,' Haller warned.

Outside in the corridor Wargrave shook his head. 'No Belgian security men. Just indicate the compartment to me – then we pick up a couple of other people first.' Elsa followed Wargrave as Leroy let them out of the coach. Close behind him she grasped hold of the Smith and Wesson inside her handbag. As they passed Compartment 19 she pointed to the door and Wargrave nodded without slackening pace. Once he glanced at his watch, then looked out of the window where the landscape of Holland was flying past. They were within twenty kilometres of the Maas bridge.

Reaching Anna Markos' compartment, he gestured to her to follow him and then entered the next compartment where Nicos Leonides sat smoking his pipe. He introduced Elsa briefly. '. . . and this is Anna Markos, and Nicos Leonides – they're working with me.'

'My pleasure.' Leonides stood up and bowed. Anna Markos and Elsa stared at each other, one woman sizing up the other with a certain wariness. Then Elsa held out her hand and was startled by the Greek woman's firm grip. Impatiently, Wargrave went on speaking.

'Elsa has located Sharpinsky – we're going to get him now. And we have damn-all time to do the job.'

Wargrave was still speaking when the express shuddered, gave a violent lurch, lost speed far too rapidly, and jerked to a sudden halt. They were thrown all over the compartment by the impact of the express braking so precipitately. Wargrave picked himself up as Leonides helped both Elsa and Anna to their feet. All through the express there was chaos as bags toppled from racks, as passengers were thrown bodily across compartments.

'A signal was supposed to stop us,' Wargrave snapped.

'That was no signal,' Elsa warned. 'Somebody pulled the alarm – Sharpinsky . . .'

'He's getting off the train,' Leonides guessed. 'I saw a parked car on the highway flashing its lights a few seconds back – on the east side.'

Wargrave led the way, running down the corridor, throwing open the car door on the east side, and dropping to the track. In the distance he saw the silhouette of a man running through leafless trees toward the nearby highway. 'He's over there . . .' They began running through a small wood toward the highway they couldn't see. As Wargrave burst out from the screen of trees a Mercedes flashed past, heading north. He was astonished to see a girl behind the wheel, a girl dressed in a chauffeuse's uniform. Two men in the back.

'Christ!' Leonides exploded behind him. 'Two seconds earlier and I could have killed him.'

Wargrave was standing in the road as a BMW

travelling in the same direction came toward them at a more sedate speed. He flagged down the car. As the vehicle stopped he opened the door next to the driver, who was alone, a sober-looking man in a business suit. Waving a card at him, noting the French registration plates, Wargrave spoke to him in that language.

'Security . . . we have to borrow your car. There are terrorists in that car just ahead of you.'

'I wait here – in the middle of nowhere?'

'For God's sake get out! There's a train just through those woods. Go to the rear Wagon-Lit and ask for a man called Haller. Tell him we're following the man we've been looking for.'

Wargrave slipped behind the wheel as Leonides sat beside him while Anna and Elsa climbed into the rear seats. He was relieved to see the bewildered owner of the car plunging back through the wood toward the train as he moved off. The road ahead was deserted; he pressed his foot down. The driver of the Mercedes had made good use of her head start. From the back of the seat Elsa asked a question.

'You said something about a signal when the express pulled up.'

'All arranged with General Scholten of Dutch security – to stop the train before we reached the Maas bridge.'

'The Maas bridge?'

Leonides gestured toward the railroad track on their left, which they had moved closer to. 'Is that your signal?' Above the line loomed a red signal facing the southern approach. Suddenly Wargrave began to lose speed. Ahead of them two vehicles were parked just off the highway: a Citroën car and a canvas-sided, military-looking truck. Standing beside the car in a heavy leather raincoat was the short, portly figure of General Max Scholten.

'No Mercedes has passed this way,' Scholten said after Wargrave told him what had happened. 'Obviously it must have turned down a track leading to the Maas – no doubt to some landing stage where a boat is waiting to pick up Sharpinsky and take him out to the *Gorky*. Everything is ready for you.' He looked at Elsa and Anna Markos, who were still in the rear of the BMW. 'Are they really the other two?' he inquired doubtfully.

'They're as good as men,' Wargrave snapped. 'In the past twelve hours one of them knifed to death a Communist agent.'

'Point taken,' Scholten replied. 'And I know what the loyalty of women can be. Now we'd better get moving.'

Behind the wheel of the BMW Wargrave drove off after the Dutchman, who was driving the Citroën. Behind them followed the canvas-covered truck. Wargrave could drive very fast but the pace set by Scholten was terrifying. Beside Wargrave in the BMW passenger seat Leonides blinked as Scholten drove like a madman, spinning around curves almost on two wheels, holding the road by luck as much as by skill. Then he swung off the highway to the right along a track twisting through trees and stopped in front of a barn. They all got out and six men with rifles met them.

'This is the Venlo Team,' Scholten told Wargrave. 'They have wiped out the Geiger Group.' He turned to one of the men. 'Jan, did you manage to save Joop Kist?'

'I am afraid not, sir.' Jan led the way inside the barn and pointed to a figure lying on the ground. 'It was the big bastard who killed him at the last moment. He must have guessed he was one of us.'

'What happened to the bastard?'

'He's over there.' Jan pointed to Wojna's crumpled form lying in a corner of the barn. 'I gave him a full burst from my magazine.'

'Good.' Scholten walked over to where Joop Kist lay and gently spread a handkerchief over his face. The security chief could not keep a hint of emotion out of his voice as he looked down at Kist. 'He was that old-fashioned animal, a patriot. Well, Joop, we will repay the debt one hundred times over.' His voice stiffened as he looked around the barn where the bodies of six men clad in ski masks and ski pants lay dead, riddled with bullets from the automatic weapons of the Venlo Team. 'You know what to do – we need four bodies put inside the truck. I shall drive, Jan. And our friends' – he indicated Wargrave with a brief gesture – 'will use the Citroën, which was, I regret to say, stolen from a garage in The Hague this morning.'

'That leaves two bodies, including the giant,' Jan pointed out.

'Throw them into the Maas,' Scholten said brutally.

He turned to Wargrave as the Englishman moved close to him and spoke in a low voice. 'Can you trust these men to keep quiet? And what about your minister? I don't want your head on the block, Max.'

'The Venlo Team is devoted to me,' Scholten replied. 'You see, officially, they never left their base at Dordrecht today. As for the minister, he will swallow the story because it will suit him. Like cabinet ministers all over the world, his main concern is his career. Also, I have tipped off a news agency that the Geiger Group are planning something big in Holland. Now, Harry, we must move . . .'

Aboard the Soviet freighter *Maxim Gorky* the radio operator had just run into Commissar Rykin's cabin in an agitated state. 'That signal you asked me to send to Moscow – I can't send it.'

'Why the hell not?' Rykin demanded. 'It's vital we report the present situation.'

'There is massive interference, Comrade. I can't send any signals at all.'

On Scholten's orders radio-jamming devices along the Dutch coast were now operating full blast to neutralize the Soviet transmitters. The *Maxim Gorky* was now sealed off from all communication with the outside world.

The four figures clad in black ski masks, windcheaters, and ski pants moved cautiously down toward the landing stage below where the Dutch torpedo boat rode at anchor under the lee of a small headland on the Maas. The torpedo boat had been held in reserve by Commander De Vos at the suggestion of Scholten; quite why he didn't know, but he was a close personal friend of the Dutch security chief and had agreed without question. The two Dutchmen guarding it sat playing cards inside the cabin.

One tall figure slipped down alone through the reeds and slipped aboard with a practised ease of a trained commando. Reaching the cabin door, he turned the handle carefully and then rushed inside. The first Dutchman had his back to the intruder as he coshed him not too hard – but hard enough to knock him out. The Dutchman opposite was half out of his seat when he, too, was struck with the truncheon and fell unconscious.

'Tie them up,' Wargrave ordered from behind his ski mask as the other three figures followed him into the cabin, 'and leave them in the landing-stage shed.'

Elsa Lang and Anna Markos dealt with the prisoners while Wargrave led Leonides to the controls. 'No problem here,' he told the Greek, 'I once drove one of these while I was in naval intelligence. British and French ones, too. I just hope you can take the helm at the critical moment – I shall be otherwise occupied . . .'

'I am a Greek,' Leonides reminded him, 'who once spent half his time at sea in the Aegean with motorized caïques and other craft. Just show me . . .'

Five minutes later the torpedo boat was moving out into the Maas with Leonides at the helm. He opened the throttle to get the feel of the boat and then nodded to Wargrave, who was watching him. The Greek was handling the craft as though he had driven it for years – with a certain panache as he felt the power building up, as the bows cut through the heavy swell. Going out on deck, Wargrave found Anna Markos taking off the canvas cover from the swivel-mounted machine gun.

'Show me how it works,' she demanded.

'This wasn't part of the plan.'

'Show me how it works,' she ordered him.

Shrugging, Wargrave quickly explained the mechanism. It was, after all, possible they might need to use it when he wouldn't be available to operate the weapon. Inside the cabin Elsa Lang had picked up a pair of night glasses from the chart table and was scanning the opposite bank of the Maas. With shoulders hunched, elbows pressed hard against the ledge, she went on sweeping the glasses across the distant shore. When Wargrave re-entered the cabin there was excitement in her voice.

'A big powerboat is taking off from the far side.

I'm damned sure I saw Sharpinsky aboard – with another smaller man. I focused full on them while they were on deck.'

'Are you sure?' Wargrave asked.

'Say that just once more and I'll hit you . . .'

'Then they must have waited for the weather to slacken.'

And the weather was improving as the gale blew itself out. Already the heavy swell inside the sheltered Maas was smoothing out as Wargrave watched the large powerboat gathering speed, heading out to sea, toward the *Maxim Gorky*. 'Do we try and head him off?' Elsa suggested.

'Too late, but he could take us just where we want to go.'

Wargrave went back to the helm, where Leonides was enjoying himself as he grew more familiar with the craft, as he built up even more power and exhilarated in the engine throb. They were now well out into the Maas, midway between the two banks with open sea ahead of them.

'Keep behind that powerboat,' Wargrave ordered. 'It will home us straight in on to the *Gorky*.'

Inside the cab of the canvas-sided truck General Scholten himself was behind the wheel, with Major Sailer in the passenger seat, as he drove it down the twisting, lonely track leading to a point at the mouth of the Maas River. In the back of the truck lay their grisly cargo – the four bodies of the dead Geiger Group men still dressed in their hideous 'uniform.' On the cab seat between Scholten and Sailer lay a large signalling lamp.

As they drove on, it was more like night than day; overhead the sky was dense with low, dark, scudding clouds and Scholten was driving with sidelights only, not wishing to risk the glare of headlights, which might be spotted from a distance.

'You think we'll get away with it?' Sailer asked.

'We have a good chance. One thing I didn't tell you: by now my wife will have phoned a further anonymous tip to the news agency that it's rumoured the Geiger Group have seized one of our torpedo boats. The whole outcome could be tremendously ironic.'

'Ironic?' Sailer queried.

'The GRU control the Geiger Group – although we have never been able to prove it. Moscow is in for a very nasty surprise.'

The powerboat carrying Colonel Igor Sharpinsky and Rolf Geiger toward the *Maxim Gorky* was moving at high speed as the storm died away, moving south toward the English Channel, throwing out a great wake as it bounced over the waves. Ahead, the twin-funnelled freighter with its masts laden with electronic gear was pouring out smoke as it prepared for its northern dash to the Kattegat, the Baltic, and

Leningrad. It was only waiting for the powerboat's arrival before Captain Morov gave the order 'Full steam ahead.'

Behind the powerboat followed Wargrave's torpedo boat, moving at top speed with Leonides at the helm while Anna Markos, her ski outfit soaked with spray, crouched behind the machine gun, her powerful legs splayed to hold her balance. It was Elsa, with her glasses trained on the Soviet vessel, who first noticed the mounted machine gun on the *Gorky's* deck, which Rykin had ordered to be divested of its canvas cover. At one point on the deck laden with cargo another canvas cover had come loose and was flapping in the wind.

'They have a gun on deck,' she warned Wargrave, who stood beside her. 'And I think I can see a tank . . .'

'Probably an armoured car.'

'Goodies for the starving Africans,' Elsa commented tartly.

Wargrave left her to direct Leonides to steer the torpedo boat into the required position. His glance fell on the two torpedo tubes, the ship's main armament, and he was trying to recall precisely the instructions a Dutch torpedo-boat commander had once given him during a dummy run. He would have only one chance to get it right. He looked at the two buttons, one for each torpedo. He was none too sure he was capable of pulling it off even in these calmer seas.

Through her glasses Elsa could now see the ladder leading down from the freighter's deck to a landing station below, a platform that was frequently sub-merged with water as the sea rolled over it. Above the ladder, men in oilskins were waiting to help Sharpinsky, Rolf Geiger, and Erika Kern on board once the powerboat reached them. Estimating distances, Wargrave gave an order and Leonides swung the wheel over. At that moment Rykin's machine gun opened fire.

The range was still too great and a spatter of bullets spurted tiny water spouts that danced across the sea – but the torpedo boat was moving closer into point-blank range every second. Behind her own machine gun Anna held her fire, her face frozen in a grim expression and showing not a trace of fear. Elsa was scared stiff – for Anna – and Wargrave was now staring fixedly through the target scanner with the fingers of his right hand close to the release buttons.

Sharpinsky's powerboat had now slowed down, was close to the platform, and through her glasses Elsa could see him clearly as he prepared to jump onto the heaving platform. Then Rykin's machine gun opened up again at much shorter range and a hail of bullets thudded across the deck of the torpedo boat. Two of them struck Anna Markos in the shoulder and she slumped over her own gun. Elsa ran out on deck, hanging onto the rail until she reached Anna.

'Hold me up!' the Greek woman spat out. 'I'm going to get the bastards . . .'

Elsa hoisted her by the armpits, holding her own balance by hanging onto the wounded woman. Anna's gun began to chatter as she moved the weapon in a slow arc, and suddenly Rykin's machine gun stopped firing as the Soviet gunner collapsed. Geiger, lighter-footed and smaller, had jumped onto the platform and was running up the ladder when Anna swivelled her gun again, firing nonstop. A fusillade of bullets struck Geiger as he reached the top of the ladder and he seemed to leap backward from the ship and down into the sea. Below him, Sharpinsky and Erika Kern waited a moment on the platform, soaked to the thighs in sea.

Staring through the target scanner, Wargrave was hardly aware of any of this, of the fact that Elsa was now dragging Anna away from the gun toward the entrance to the cabin. His face tense with concentration, his cheekbones hard and prominent, Wargrave pressed one button, then the other.

'Number one gone. Number two . . .'

He had a brief glimpse of the two acoustic homing torpedoes hurtling into the sea – acoustic so they would head for the nearest engine vibrations as the *Maxim Gorky* prepared to leave for Leningrad – and then they vanished. Leonides spun the wheel, taking the torpedo boat in a wide semicircle before he straightened up and headed for the winking lamp on the shore where Scholten waited.

One torpedo struck the *Gorky* near the stern, ripping away a huge portion of the superstructure. The second struck as Sharpinsky reached the top of the ladder – but it was this torpedo that struck amidships and penetrated the main hold where two thousand tons of high explosive were stored. There was a massive roar. The centre of the huge freighter lifted off – literally elevated into the sky – shattering the twin funnels, disintegrating into a thunderstorm of debris as a great mushroom of smoke rose to meet and mingle with the lowering clouds until it was impossible to distinguish one from the other. The bows of the freighter floated alone briefly, then upended and went down like the smashed fin of some misshapen shark. The echo of the boom was still in Leonides' ears as he reduced speed and beached the torpedo boat close to where the lamp continued to flash. There were no survivors from the *Maxim Gorky*.

It took General Scholten and Major Sailer – with the help of the others – only minutes to carry aboard the beached torpedo boat the four dead bodies of the Geiger Group men from inside the truck. They left them lying about inside the cabin. In the distance Scholten heard the engine of another torpedo boat approaching. 'Get inside the back of the truck and keep quiet,' he ordered Wargrave and his three companions. 'And this may help the woman; we'll get her to a hospital as soon as we can.' He handed a first-aid kit to Wargrave, who hurried inside the truck where Elsa and Leonides had carried Anna Markos.

The torpedo boat approaching appeared around a headland as Scholten and Sailer opened fire on the

beached torpedo boat with automatic weapons, rid-
dling the vessel from end to end, shattering every
window. They had just emptied their magazines when
the incoming torpedo boat stopped close in and Commander De Vos waded ashore in gumboots.

'They made a mistake,' Scholten informed the tall,
cynical-faced commander. 'They came in too close and
beached . . . I think you'll find they're all dead.'

'I'm sure I will,' De Vos replied with a blank
expression. He glanced toward the truck and then
away again. 'And I saw it all happen, so' – he smiled
dryly – 'if there is an inquiry I will be your best
witness. Congratulations, General – the Geiger Group
just made its last run . . .'

Chapter Twenty-six

Aftermath

One hour later a Boeing 707 took off from Schiphol Airport bound for Washington with General Sergei Marenkov, Julian Haller, and Matt Leroy aboard. Marenkov played a little joke on Haller, which the American, dog-tired from lack of sleep, did not fully appreciate. The Russian insisted on being shown that the altimeter registered thirty thousand feet before he consented to commence debriefing – to provide out of his phenomenal memory a list of all KGB agents in the Western Hemisphere.

One week later Harry Wargrave, Elsa Lang, and Nicos Leonides again visited Anna Markos in the Amsterdam hospital and found her sitting up in bed and being very rude to the doctor. 'He keeps me here so he can stare at my figure,' she complained in front of them.

'A very fine figure,' the doctor commented. 'So fine I regret to say I may feel compelled to discharge you as completely fit within a couple of weeks . . .'

Anna's dark eyes flashed. 'Meantime he will continue to fool around with his stethoscope, pretending he is being a doctor.'

Outside in the corridor, when Nicos Leonides had gone, Wargrave took Elsa by the arm as they walked toward his parked car. 'That's my last job,' he told her. 'I was keelhauled into it, anyway, by Julian Haller. So now why don't we go back to Canada, maybe British Columbia – I've always had a hankering to explore Puget Sound.'

'We?' Elsa inquired. 'Is that a proposition or a proposal?'

'Both.'

'Then I shall enjoy the first and insist on the second.'

On the tenth floor of the Baton Rouge Building in Montreal Julian Haller had called to say good-bye to William Riverton, the Canadian industrialist who had provided the funds and the accommodation for the Sparta Ring at the request of President Joseph Moynihan. And for the first time since the operation had started over a year before, Riverton stood inside the office suite they had used.

It was bare and empty now. All the equipment and furniture had been removed and their voices echoed hollowly as they spoke. 'I see,' Riverton remarked, staring straight ahead, 'that Marshal Prachko has been removed from the Politburo along with his cohorts – that for a while, at any rate, the moderates are in control in the Kremlin. I read it in the newspaper this morning.'

'Some kind of victory, I suppose,' Haller replied.

'I'm going to miss you all,' Riverton remarked, 'but there it is. And as in the past – and as it will be in the future, the West will be saved by only a handful of men and women.' His voice changed as he held out his hand. Even though no longer young, his tone was firm and decisive.

'In the end we'll beat the Soviets . . .'